JAMES ISLINGTON

THE WILL
OF
THE MANY

SAGA PRESS

LONDON SYDNEY **NEW YORK** TORONTO NEW DELHI

SAGA PRESS

AN IMPRINT OF SIMON & SCHUSTER, INC.

1230 AVENUE OF THE AMERICAS, NEW YORK, NEW YORK 10020

First Saga Press hardcover edition May 2023

SAGA PRESS and colophon are trademarks of Simon & Schuster, Inc.

For information about special discounts for bulk purchases, please contact Simon & Schuster Special Sales at 1-866-506-1949 or business@simonandschuster.com

The Simon & Schuster Speakers Bureau can bring authors to your live event. For more information or to book an event, contact the Simon & Schuster Speakers Bureau at 1-866-248-3049 or visit our website at www.simonspeakers.com.

Interior design by Kathryn A. Kenney-Peterson

Manufactured in the United States of America

1   3   5   7   9   10   8   6   4   2

Library of Congress Cataloging-in-Publication Data has been applied for.

ISBN 978-1-9821-4117-2
ISBN 978-1-9821-4119-6 (ebook)

For friends, lost.

CATENAN RANKINGS

RANK	RECEIVES WILL FROM:
1. PRINCEPS	40,320 PEOPLE
2. DIMIDIUS	20,160 PEOPLE
3. TERTIUS	6,720 PEOPLE
4. QUARTUS	1,680 PEOPLE
5. QUINTUS	336 PEOPLE
6. SEXTUS	56 PEOPLE
7. SEPTIMUS	8 PEOPLE
8. OCTAVUS	NONE

IMPERIUM SINE FINE

PART I

I

I AM DANGLING, AND IT IS ONLY MY FATHER'S BLOOD-SLICKED grip around my wrist that stops me from falling.

He is on his stomach, stretched out over the rocky ledge. His muscles are corded. Sticky red covers his face, his arms, his clothes, everything I can see. Yet I know he can pull me up. I do everything I can not to struggle. I trust him to save me.

He looks over my shoulder. Into the inky black. Into the darkness that is to come.

"Courage," he whispers. He pours heartbreak and hope into the word.

He lets go.

※ ※ ※

"I KNOW I'M ALWAYS TELLING YOU TO THINK BEFORE YOU ACT," says the craggy-faced man slouching across the board from me, "but for the game to progress, Vis, you do actually have to move a gods-damned stone."

I rip my preoccupied gaze from the cold silver that's streaming through the sole barred window in the guardroom. Give my opponent my best irritated glare to cover the sickly swell of memory, then force my focus again to the polished white and red triangles between us. The pieces glint dully in the light of the low-burning lantern that sits on the shelf, barely illuminating our contest better than the early evening's glow from outside.

"You alright?"

"Fine." I see Hrolf's bushy grey eyebrows twitch in the corner of my vision. "I'm *fine*, old man. Just thinking. Sappers haven't got me yet." No heat to the words. I know the way his faded brown eyes crinkle with concern is genuine. And I know he has to ask.

I've been working here almost a year longer than him, so he's wondering again whether my mind is losing its edge. Like his has been for a while, now.

I ignore his worry and assess the Foundation board, calculating what the new red formation on the far side means. A feint, I realise immediately. I ignore it. Shift three of my white pieces in quick succession and ensure the win. Hrolf likes to boast about how he once defeated a Magnus Quartus, but against me, it's never a fair match. Even before the Hierarchy—or the Catenan Republic, as I still have to remind myself to call them out loud—ruled the world, Foundation was widely considered the perfect tool for teaching abstract strategic thinking. My father ensured I was exposed to it young, often, and against the very best players.

Hrolf glowers at the board, then me, then at the board again.

"Lost concentration. You took too long. Basically cheating," he mutters, disgusted as he concedes the game. "You know I beat a Magnus Quartus once?"

My reply is interrupted by a hammering at the thick stone entrance. Hrolf and I stand, game forgotten. Our shift isn't meant to change for hours yet.

"Identify yourself," calls Hrolf sharply as I step across to the window. The man visible through the bars is well-dressed, tall and with broad shoulders. In his late twenties, I think. Moonlight shines off the dark skin of his close-shaven scalp.

"Sextus Hospius," comes the muffled reply. "I have an access seal." Hospius looks at the window, spotting my observation of him. His beard is black, trimmed short, and he has serious, dark brown eyes that lend him a handsome intensity. He leans over and presses what appear to be official Hierarchy documents against the glass.

"We weren't told to expect you," says Hrolf.

"I wouldn't have known to expect me until about thirty minutes ago. It's urgent."

"Not how it works."

"It is tonight, Septimus." No change in expression, but the impatient emphasis on Hrolf's lower status is unmistakeable.

Hrolf squints at the door, then walks over to the thin slot set in the wall beside it, tapping his stone Will key to it with an irritated, sharp click. The hole on our side seals shut. Outside, Hospius notes the corresponding new opening in front of him, depositing his documentation. I watch closely to ensure he adds nothing else.

Hrolf waits for my nod, then opens our end again to pull out Hospius's pages, rifling through them. His mouth twists as he hands them to me. "Proconsul's seal" is all he says.

I examine the writing carefully; Hrolf knows his work, but here among the Sappers it pays to check things twice. Sure enough, though, there's full authorization for entry from Proconsul Manius himself, signed and stamped. Hospius is a man of some importance, apparently, even beyond his rank: he's a specialised agent, assigned directly by the Senate to investigate an irregularity in last year's census. Cooperation between the senatorial pyramids of Governance—Hospius's employers, who oversee the Census—and Military, who are in charge of prisons across the Republic, is allowing Hospius access to one of the prisoners here for questioning.

"Looks valid," I agree, understanding Hrolf's displeasure. This paperwork allows our visitor access to the lowest level. It's cruel to wake the men and women down there mid-sentence.

Hrolf takes the page with Manius's seal on it back from me and slides it into the outer door's thin release slot. The proconsul's Will-imbued seal breaks the security circuit just as effectively as Hrolf's key, and the stone door grinds smoothly into the wall, a gust of Letens's bitter night air slithering through the opening to herald Hospius's imposing form. Inside, the man sheds his fine blue cloak and tosses it casually over the back of a nearby chair, flashing what he probably imagines is a charming smile at the two of us. Hrolf sees a man taking liberties with his space, and curbs a scowl as he snaps Hospius's seal with more vigour than is strictly necessary, releasing its Will and letting the door glide shut again.

I see a man trying too hard to look at ease, and do everything I can not to react.

Probably nothing. As much as I try to convince myself, after three years, I'm adept at recognising other actors.

Our visitor is nervous about something.

"Thank you, Septimus." Hospius's gaze sweeps over me, registering my youth and dismissing my presence, focusing instead on Hrolf. "I know this is irregular, but I need information from someone. A man named Nateo."

Hrolf pulls the jail ledger from atop the shelf in the corner, flipping it open. There are a few seconds of him tracing down the paper with his finger. "Nateo, Nateo . . . here he is. Deep cells, east forty-one. Vis, you wait here."

He grabs a key off the hook and takes three steps toward the jail's inner door— just a regular lock on this one—but on his fourth, he stumbles. And when he rights himself, he peers around at me and Hospius with lost uncertainty. The expression's gone in an instant, but I know what it means.

"My apologies, Septimus. I forgot about your bad knee," I lie quickly, striding over and snatching the key from his hand before he can protest. "It will be faster if I escort the Sextus. Deep cells, east forty-one, you said?"

Hrolf glares at me, but I see his gratitude in the look. He knows what's happened, but probably doesn't even remember who Hospius is.

"My knee could use the rest," he plays along. "If the Sextus has no objections."

"None." Hospius waves me on impatiently. I don't think he's seen anything amiss.

We enter the jail proper and I lock the door again behind us, hiding a vaguely dismayed-looking Hrolf from view. A lantern holding a candle, lit at the beginning of our shift and now closer to a stub, burns on the wall. I unhook it and hold it high, illuminating the narrow stairwell down. Clean-cut stone glistens wetly.

"Watch your step," I warn Hospius. "It gets slippery down here."

I walk ahead of the Sextus, too-dim light pooling around us as we descend. My back itches with it facing him. I can't get his initial moment of affectation out of my mind. But his document—or at least, the seal affixed to it—was imbued by Proconsul Manius, impossible to fake. And I know better than to press. So I simply have to hope that his nerves, and his attempt to hide them, are not from anything untoward.

More importantly, I have to hope that whatever his purpose here, it will draw no attention to me.

"How long has your Septimus been like that?"

Vek. Still inclined to curse in my ancestral tongue, even if I can only risk it in my head. I paste on a puzzled expression and cast a glance back. "What do you mean?"

"He's been working here too long." Hospius's intense brown eyes search mine until I turn forward again, focusing on the steps. "You don't have to worry. I won't say anything."

I force a chuckle. "I'm not sure what you think you saw, but you're wrong." If Proconsul Manius finds out, Hrolf will lose his position here. He's old enough that he'd be placed in a retirement pyramid, and with a suspect mind as well, he'd almost certainly be demoted to Octavus. Forced to live with constant exhaustion as he's slowly used up, the Hierarchy stealing years and quality from his life just as surely as they do the men and women here in the deep cells.

And, of course, I would have to navigate another new Septimus. Of the three who have managed Letens Prison since I started, Hrolf has been by far the easiest to deal with.

Hospius just grunts in response. He doesn't sound persuaded, but nor does he press.

We reach the end of the stairs, my lantern revealing smooth walls slick with damp stretching both left and right. A low hum touches my ears, almost imperceptible. Even after more than a year here, I find it unsettling.

There's a half cough, half gag from behind me. "What is that smell?"

"The prisoners." I barely notice the stink of sweat mingling with urine anymore. It's really not that bad, on this level.

"Why don't you keep them clean?" Hospius is incensed.

"We do. We wash them twice a day, as best we can. But they can't control their bowels in the Sappers." I smooth the anger from my own voice, but can't help adding, "Catenan regulations are to wash them twice a week."

Hospius says nothing to that.

We turn several corners and start down another flight of stairs, leaving the upper floor in darkness. These lead to the deepest level, where the long-term prisoners are kept. Sentences of more than two years: murderers and purported Anguis collaborators, for the most part. It feels like we've been sending more and more people down here, recently.

"You know your way around." Hospius's deep voice booms off the austere walls, despite his attempt to match his voice to the hushed surrounds.

I don't want to make conversation, but it's riskier by far to be rude. "I have to come down here every couple of nights."

"So you and the Septimus alternate looking after these prisoners?"

"That's right."

"Despite his bad knee."

Vek. I shrug to cover my concern at Hospius's persistence. "It's sore, not crippling. And he takes his responsibilities very seriously."

"I'm sure he does." Hospius is walking alongside me now, the stairs wider than before. He's taller than me by a head. I see him glance down at me, his interest apparently piqued. The opposite of what I was trying to achieve. "What's your name?"

"Vis."

"And how long have you been helping the Septimus here, Vis?"

"A few months." Not a lie, even if it's not what Hospius is really asking. I'm not about to let on how long I've really been exposed to the Sappers.

"You're young, for this work."

"Vis Solum." I expand on my name by way of explanation.

"Ah." The pieces click into place in Hospius's head. I'm an orphan. Clearly one who's had difficulty finding a home, given my age. So Religion—the third senatorial pyramid, who run the orphanages in the Hierarchy—and Military have found a use for me here instead.

We've reached the end of the stairwell; two pitch-black passageways branch out at right angles away from us, and another goes straight ahead. I move left, into the eastern one. "We're almost there," I say, more to head off any more questions than to fill the silence.

The stench becomes worse, thicker, and Hospius holds a kerchief to his nose and mouth as we walk. I don't blame him. I retched the first few times I came down here. Accustomed to it as I am now, my eyes still water as my lantern casts its light into the first of the numbered cells.

Hospius comes to a dead halt, hands falling to his sides, smell temporarily forgotten.

"Never seen a Sapper before?" It takes all I have not to show satisfaction at the towering man's horror.

The cells in Letens Prison are demarcated by stone walls, but there are no doors, no front sections to them whatsoever, making their contents easily visible. Only six feet wide and not much deeper, each unlit alcove contains only two things.

A prisoner. And the Sapper to which they are strapped.

The man in east cell one is around Hospius's age, but the similarities end there. Fair skin is deathly pale in his nakedness, almost grey. Body thin and frail, cheeks hollow, blond hair long and matted. A wheezing rasp to his breathing. Steel manacles encircle his wrists and ankles, joined by dangling chains to a winch fixed above him. His blue eyes are open but filmy, unfocused as he lies atop the mirror-polished white slab, which is near horizontal but angles just barely down toward us. Toward the thin gutter that runs along the front of all the cells, where the worst of the prisoners' waste can be easily washed away.

The truth of the Hierarchy is laid bare down here, as far as I am concerned.

"No." Hospius's answer to my question is soft. "I . . . no. How long has he been in here?"

Eight months. "I'd have to look at the ledger." I remember strapping him in.

"What did he do?"

Does it matter? "I'd have to look at the ledger." I keep my tone bored. Neutral. Try to make him understand that this is every day down here. "We should keep moving, Sextus."

Hospius nods, though his eyes don't leave the prisoner's spindly form until the departing of our lantern returns him to the darkness.

We walk, and to our left and right, our small circle of light reflects copies of the first cell as we pass. Men and women, manacled and feeble and naked, all lying against cold white. Their emaciation is a result of the devices to which they are bound, I think, rather than lack of sustenance. I feed them far more at mealtimes than I would ever eat, and they get no exercise.

Hospius is silent next to me, no indication whether he is affected by the wretchedness of our surrounds. I want to watch him more closely—something still feels not quite right about him, his presence here, this entire night—but my desire to avoid notice is stronger. Regardless of whether he is all he claims to be, if he spots my suspicion, it will only draw attention.

"East forty-one," I say as our flickering light reveals the number engraved large into the back wall of the stone recess. The man here, Nateo, has been with us for less than a month: I remember him coming in because unlike most prisoners, he'd evidently been transferred from another Sapper facility. He's as gaunt as everyone else, cheeks hollow, combining with a hooked nose to give him a distinctly hawk-like visage. His stringy black hair splays against the white, down past his shoulders. It's hard to tell prisoners' ages, but I don't think this one is older than thirty.

There is no response to my announcement. I glance across at Hospius to find that he's peering at Nateo, a small, inscrutable frown touching his lips. The man on the Sapper gazes back glassily. No recognition, no reaction to the light or our presence.

"I need to talk to him." Hospius steps forward.

"*Stop.*" I snap out the word in panic, then hold up a contrite hand immediately as Hospius freezes. "My apologies, Sextus, no disrespect intended. It's just dangerous to get too close. It takes days to prepare a prisoner for a Sapper. Touching it could kill you. *And* everyone ceding to you."

"Ah." Hospius heeds the warning, doesn't venture closer. "But you can shut it off? Temporarily?"

"I can winch him up. Break the connection." Nausea threatens as I consider what is about to happen. "It will not be pleasant, though. Especially for him."

Hospius rubs the dark surface of his shaven pate. It's a moment of doubt—I'm sure I see it in the motion—but when he looks across at me, his face is hard. "I came here for answers. Do what you have to."

I start edging around the white slab, deeper into cell forty-one. I've been unaffected by the Sappers, so far—mere proximity affects most people within months, and I've been working here for almost fifteen—but still I move with care, fastidiously avoiding brushing against anything. Immune or not, these things are designed to instantly drain Will on contact. Not just the portion the Hierarchy usually takes from the millions of Octavii who form its foundation, either. *All* of your drive, your focus, your mental and physical energy, is funnelled away by these pale stone beds to be received by some distant, particularly favoured Septimus.

In my eyes, death would be a preferable fate.

And the worst part is that I know many of the men and women in here would agree.

I reach the farthest section of the cell and crouch, moving the lantern along until I find the spiked wheel. I begin turning it, muscles working. There's a jangling and grinding above as chains shake and then pull taut. The man on the Sapper sags at the waist as he's drawn in ungainly fashion upward, peeling from the white stone, swaying. A couple of more rotations until he's a few inches clear, then I lock the wheel in place.

I straighten, eyes fixed on the flaccid, bony man suspended above the slab in front of me. I've only seen prisoners being released a few times; the managing Septimus is always in charge of end-of-sentence procedures, and other reasons for waking a captive are rare.

I rejoin Hospius at the mouth of the alcove as he fiddles uncomfortably with his tunic. Governance uniform, a dark blue pyramid sewn over the heart. It's crisp, perfectly clean, folded in all the right places. Unfaded.

Immaculate, in fact. Like it's never been worn before.

"Why isn't he waking up?" Hospius hasn't noticed my examination, his complete attention on the man in front of us.

"It takes a minute." Even as I say it, something changes. A break in the steady, gasping rhythm of the prisoner's breath. A less desperate sigh escapes his lips. His chains twitch, then his eyelids flutter and cognizance seeps back into his gaze as, for the first time, he is at least partly here with us.

Hospius glances at me, and I can see him debating whether to try sending me away. I won't go, though; even at the risk of angering him, I would be breaking too many rules to leave him alone down here.

Evidently reaching a similar conclusion, he says nothing and moves closer to the Sapper, into the prisoner's line of sight. He crouches alongside, so their faces are at the same level.

"Nateo. Can you hear me? My name is Sextus Hospius. *Nonagere.*"

He says it all carefully, enunciating, but it takes me a second to place the last word. It's Vetusian.

Don't react.

Hospius looks up at me again and I do everything I can to apply the warning he's giving Nateo. I'm not supposed to know what the word means. Why would I? Vetusian is a dead language. An academic oddity. Aside from the odd word already integrated into Common, it was excised by the Hierarchy more than a hundred years ago. Its only real purpose is to allow for the reading of original texts from an era long past.

But my father was passionate in his belief in the importance of a history uncoloured by Hierarchy translators. My mother was a scholar, fluent in three languages herself. And I was groomed by both them and my tutors for fourteen years to be a diplomat, to support my sister in her eventual rule by travelling to other nations.

Nateo's head lolls as he gazes blearily at Hospius. He runs his tongue over his lips. Then he slowly, painfully nods.

He understands. These two men know each other.

Blood pounds in my ears. Is Hospius here to break Nateo out? I can't allow that; the kind of scrutiny it would bring would be the end of me. But I cannot act pre-emptively, either. He's done nothing wrong so far. His documentation looked genuine. *Was* genuine.

I say nothing, do nothing. I have to wait.

"You talk?" Again in Vetusian. The way Hospius speaks is stilted, like he's dragging the words from some long-past schooling of his own. Neither man is looking at me, but I feign perplexed indifference, just in case.

"I can. A little." Nateo's voice is like nails scraped weakly across stone. He uses the dead language too, though with far more comfort than the man here to see him. "How long?" His gaze roves, as if seeking the answer somewhere other than Hospius.

"Five years."

A flicker in Nateo's eyes, and he focuses again on Hospius. Sharper this time. "Here to release me?"

"I hope. Information first." Hospius sees the rising panic in the imprisoned man and reaches out, grasping his shoulder, steadying him as the chains begin to rattle from his trembling. "I know . . . you innocent. Need to understand . . . why you in here. Veridius?" The name is a question, asked with quiet intensity.

"Could have been." Nateo calms, but there's doubt in the response.

I pretend to stifle a yawn as I leave the lantern on the ground and wander away, out of sight, as if I am inspecting the nearby cells while I wait. Hospius will know I'm not far, but it's easier to focus on translating if they can't see my reactions.

"Need you . . . think. About Caeror. Anything he said before . . ." He trails off, and though I can't see his face, this time I don't think it's because he's struggling with the language.

"Long time ago." A bitter, choking laugh from Nateo.

"He sent a message, before it happened. Names I do not know. Obiteum. Luceum. Talked about a . . . gate. Strange power from before Cataclysm. Do you know what . . . mean?"

Silence. A faint clinking. Then, "I need to be out first. No more."

I close my eyes, mouth a curse into the darkness before forcing boredom into my stance, scuffing my boots along the ground and strolling back into view as if nothing important were happening. Reminding Hospius that I'm there. I don't think he was planning an escape, anymore. But I don't want him to change his mind.

Hospius looks up at the motion of my arrival, meets my questioning gaze. His nod says he doesn't expect to be much longer. I conceal my relief. Nateo notes the exchange, his breath quickening. The chains begin to shake again, Nateo's fear chattering at the darkness.

"I will do all I can. Oath." Hospius draws Nateo's attention away from me. "But you . . . his friend. Please. If you know . . ."

Nateo stares back stonily. This is his only card.

Hospius wears his disappointment as he straightens and steps back.

"Please." Nateo speaks in Common, this time, not Vetusian. Begging. "*Please*. No more. Don't put me back. You don't know what it's like." The words are pure misery. His head twitches around, enough to include me in his gaze. "You. You're nicer than the others. Gentler. I know. I know, because being on this slab isn't like sleeping. It's worse. You're *almost* asleep. *All the time*. But awake enough to recognise that things are happening. You know your mind should move faster. You know the world is passing you by." There are tears, now. Desperation. He's blubbering. "Five years. Five *years*. Look at me! I didn't even—"

"Nateo." Hospius, trying to calm the man. Concerned. No doubt worried his secrets are at risk. He takes a half step closer.

Then Nateo is twisting, far faster than a man in his state should be able. He bucks, roars, wrenches around, animalistic desperation lending strength to his spindly limbs. Metal clatters deafeningly. He uses the momentum of his swinging form to twist and lunge and grab Hospius's too-new tunic.

"*Rotting gods.*" I'm cursing and moving before I have a chance to properly assess. Sliding around the white stone, slamming hard into Nateo's arm, jamming myself between the two men before the Sextus can be dragged onto the device. Nateo's grip breaks. His hand scrapes along my shoulder. I'm already off-balance.

I fall backward, tangled in chain, the slick surface of the Sapper ice against my hands.

A slinking, sick tingle creeps over my palms. Acidic, cold and burning, sharp and wet. Terror rolls through me. I launch myself away, flinging myself free of the mess of metal links and kicking desperately at the lever locking the winch. The rimless, spoked wheel spins madly as I scramble back, away from where Nateo might be able to grab me again.

The jangling sound of unspooling chain, and then just heavy breathing.

"Gods' graves," mutters a shaken-looking Hospius from where he's slumped against the cell wall. He watches Nateo's metal-draped figure as if he expects the man to leap up and attack again. But the tangle of limbs and links is sprawled flush against the Sapper. Nateo's eyes are empty as they stare into mine. I still feel their accusation.

"Are you alright?" I stand, unsteady. Heart thumping. The old scars across my back are taut and aching with tension. I touched the Sapper. Skin to stone. I risk a glance at my hands. From what I can see, they're fine. Still tingling, but fine.

"Yes." Hospius fingers his tunic where Nateo clawed at it. His gaze lingers on the man, nakedly melancholic before he remembers himself. "Thanks to you."

He straightens, focusing on me again. There's a query in the look.

"No harm done." I reply to the question I hope he's asking. If he actually saw what happened, I'm in trouble. "Lucky, though. Almost fell on the gods-damned Sapper." The tremor in my voice isn't faked. I'm still waiting for something terrible to happen to me.

"But you didn't?"

I push out a laugh. "You think we would be having this conversation, otherwise?"

Hospius steps forward and thumps me on the shoulder. "True enough. Fine work, Vis Solum. Fine work. I was fortunate you were here." It's high praise, from a Sextus. Another man would probably be flattered.

I set about resetting the winch, then somewhat tentatively adjust Nateo's positioning on the Sapper using the almost-taut chains, ensuring he's lying as comfortably as possible again. I don't blame him for his actions.

That's reserved, as always, for those who put him in here.

The candle in the lantern burns low as we make the return trip. At the base of the second flight of stairs, I light another from the nearby shelf and hand it to Hospius. "I should fetch some things from the storeroom while I'm down here." It's true, but more importantly I need some time alone, to properly inspect my hands, to let out the terrible tension that's threatening to break free with every breath. "The guardroom is up ahead. Just knock. Septimus Hrolf will let you through." Hardly protocol, but Hrolf won't care.

Hospius pauses as he starts up the stairs, turning back. "Vis. It may be best not to mention what just happened." His voice is abrupt against the quiet. "I wouldn't want you getting in trouble with the Septimus, or the proconsul."

"Of course, Sextus. Thank you." A threat? I can't tell. It's true enough that I'd be blamed for the incident, no matter what was said. But it seems neither of us want the attention. That suits me.

Those penetrating eyes of his study me. Then he digs into a pocket and flips me something that glitters; I catch it neatly, surprised to find a silver, triangular coin in my hand. It's worth more than I'm going to earn from my shift tonight.

"For your trouble. And your discretion."

He resumes his climb. The light of his candle drifts away.

Only when the echo of his boots has completely faded do I drop the coin into a pocket and let my hands tremble.

Setting my lantern on the shelf, I splay my fingers out, palms up, peering through the dim light at every line, every pore. The skin's a little red from where I've been rubbing my fingers nervously, but I don't see any damage. I roll up my sleeves, just to be sure, but there's nothing wrong with my arms, either. And the discomforting sensation in them is completely gone.

I'm alright.

I exhale shakily and slump to the floor, back against the wall, giving myself a minute to let the fear leave me. I've often wondered if I might be able to survive contact with a Sapper. I've never ceded before—never once allowed my Will to be taken at one of the Aurora Columnae scattered around the Republic. Almost all children are brought to one of the ancient pillars when they turn twelve, after which they're able to cede to anyone, any time, without needing the presence of the massive pre-Cataclysm artefacts. My best theory is that my refusal to go through the ritual is why I've managed to stay unaffected all this time, working here.

But it was always just conjecture, a semi-educated guess. I never meant to put it to the test.

My candle is threatening to gutter out and Hospius took the only spare, so I hurry to the storeroom, sweep up the food and cleaning supplies needed for the next shift, and haul them back upstairs. To my surprise, voices seep under the guardroom door.

". . . it up for me anyway. I'd like to know." Hospius is still here. I curse myself as I remember why I took the man down to the cells in the first place, then mouth furiously at the door for Hrolf to keep his stupid mouth shut. I've no love for the old man—no one in the Hierarchy has earned that from me—but nor do I think he deserves the fate in store if Hospius decides he's no longer capable of performing his duties.

There's a rustling of paper. "Three years and seven months left," says Hrolf. "Is there anything else, Sextus?" Not rude, but a clear indication that Hospius is welcome to leave.

There's silence, and I wish I could see Hospius's expression.

"Your young assistant seems to know his work." Casual. Conversational. My heart still clenches.

"Should do. He's been here longer than me."

"How much longer?"

"Months," says Hrolf vaguely. I can almost hear his shrug.

"You know him well?"

"He's quiet. A bit aloof, really. Doesn't like to talk about himself. Why?" There's no suspicion, just curiosity.

"He impressed me. I'm wondering whether he's being wasted down here."

Hrolf chuckles. "Oh, no doubt about that. The boy plays Foundation like a demon. And he's smarter than he lets on. Quoted gods-damned *Fulguris* at me the other day, even if he pretended he hadn't read it afterward."

I berate myself again for that lazy conceit, then debate interrupting before Hrolf makes more of a mess—he thinks he's helping me by embellishing my merit to the Sextus, never imagining that the attention could get me killed—but if Hospius is after information, my presence isn't going to change anything. Better to wait and find out what, if anything, he's fishing for.

"Hm." Hospius, fortunately, doesn't sound as impressed as Hrolf seems to think he should be. "Well, if a more appropriate position for someone his age should come up in Letens, I'll mention him." There's a vague, dispassionate note that signals it's a conclusion to the conversation. I puff out my cheeks in silent relief.

A scuffing of boots, then the door in front of me rattles as the outer one admits a blast of air.

"Thank you, Septimus. Stronger together," says Hospius, his voice more muffled now.

"Stronger together, Sextus," replies Hrolf formally. The wind-induced quivering of the door in front of me stops.

I wait two minutes before knocking, using the time to decide what to tell Hrolf. He'll be curious about what transpired.

"So what was that all about?" is his greeting as I admit myself back into the guardroom.

"Not sure. They were talking in some other language." I deposit the fetched supplies onto their shelf, then flop into my seat.

Hrolf emits an intrigued grunt, but realises there are no further conclusions to be drawn from the information. "Any trouble?"

"Just what you'd expect. Prisoner wasn't exactly happy when he realised his time wasn't up. Bit of kicking and screaming." There's the burn of bile in the back of my throat as I think of Nateo's terror, his begging. His fight. But I don't let it show.

Hrolf claps me on the back in manly sympathy anyway, knowing I'm understating, if not by how much.

"Thanks," he adds.

We spend the next quarter hour talking of nothing, whiling the time until I normally depart. Hrolf will stay all night—alone, from when I leave until dawn—though with the prisoners already fed and washed for the day, his responsibilities during that time are nominal. He'll sleep for most of it.

Somewhere outside in Letens, the city's common clock faintly shivers a single note. The end of evening, and the beginning of true night. It won't sound again until dawn. I stand.

"Offer's still there, Vis," says Hrolf, watching me. His eyes are suddenly sad, though he tries to hide it. "I don't mind changing our terms if you want to stay, help awhile longer."

"You don't need me here." I collect my threadbare cloak, shrug it on.

"The proconsul doesn't know that. Your matron doesn't know that. And it's not as if the coin isn't already paid."

"Thanks, but no. It's yours." Better his than the matron's, anyway. I assess the Septimus, looking for any sign that he's thinking of backing out of our deal. That's not what this is about, though. The worried crinkle around Hrolf's eyes gives him away.

"Less bruises if you stay here," he observes, confirming it.

"Better conversation, too." I hold out my hand, palm up.

Hrolf sighs, but there's no surprise on his weathered face as he retrieves my pay from the Will-secured box on the far wall. Copper triangles, each one etched with eight parallel lines. I get six for my work today. The other nine that Hrolf tucks away were meant to pay for my time tonight, but instead go toward his tolerance of my absence.

The metal jingles, a comforting weight in my pocket, as I move to the heavy stone door. I don't offer any words of thanks for his concern. Part of me wants to.

But then I remember that if he knew my real name, this seemingly humane grey-haired man would see me dead just as quickly as anyone else.

"See you tomorrow," says Hrolf as he inserts his key into its slot. The door grinds open.

"See you tomorrow." I walk out into the blustery cold of Letens, and head for the Theatre.

II

LETENS IS A STRANGE CITY.

Here at the southern edge of civilisation, more than fifteen years after joining the Hierarchy, Catenan influence still mixes uneasily with the old world. The lamplit streets are twisting, muddy, and narrow, ill-suited to the Will-powered carts and carriages that occasionally squeeze along them. Buildings veer sharply from barely functional wooden boxes to citizens' towering, walled mansions of stone. The many-arched Temple of Jovan soars above it all in the distance, crowning the Tensian Forum. It's surrounded by the last of the sacred druidic grove that once formed the heart of the city. There are no druids, anymore.

While Letens Prison is not exactly on the outskirts, the city is vast, and I'm still heading toward its centre after more than ten minutes. This late, there are more red-cloaked soldiers about than anyone else, though a few others do still brave the icy wind sweeping in from the south. Octavii, mostly. You can tell from the way they trudge, avoiding eye contact as they murmur wearily to one another in their native Tensian. A few of the women wear stolas with their children's names sewn into the cloth above the left breast, proud proclamation of their contributions to the Hierarchy. Their clothes are threadbare and stained, otherwise.

Even so, there's less of the Hierarchy this far south than almost anywhere else in the world. I sometimes tell myself that's why I stopped running.

Of course, if I'm honest, the hunger and loneliness contributed.

At least the hunger's no longer a problem.

The quiet streets finally lead me into the unlit deep of an alley that's almost invisible beside the ugly curvature of the long, sloping building next to it. Mud squelches beneath my boots. Side streets like this would have been dangerous once; crime in Letens does still exist, but now it caters far more to the thrill of the forbidden than the violence of need. The Catenans are nothing if not serious about Birthright, their set of laws ostensibly meant to safeguard human life. Anyone desperate enough to challenge it inevitably finds themselves in a Sapper.

Just as the light from the main road behind threatens to become too dim, there's a short set of stairs that descend to a door sunken below the street, all but hidden from view. I push it open without announcing myself. Inside, three men and a woman break from their conversation at the table in the corner of the small, stuffy room, the hint of tension dissipating as I'm recognised.

"Vis, my boy!" Septimus Ellanher rises as she utters the words in her rich, aristocratic voice, a hawkish smile splitting her angular face. She's powerfully built, a head taller than me, with a mass of wavy raven-black tresses that fall freely to her waist. Her arms are bare, glistening in the candlelight from the sweat of some exertion or other, highlighting both muscle and scars. "Just who I was hoping to see!"

I carefully close the door behind me and stop dead, giving her a flat stare. The welcome's too warm for Ellanher by far.

She rolls her amber-flecked brown eyes, joviality only slightly diminished by my response. "Come, now. Can't a lady be enthusiastic about the arrival of her favourite fighter?"

"I'm sure a lady could." I nod politely to the three men at the table. All are bigger than even Ellanher in height and brawn, if not in presence. Two, Caren and Othmar, I recognise from previous nights. Their eyes glitter resentfully as they nod back. "What do you want?"

Ellanher chuckles throatily, unfazed. She knows I'm partly joking, and the other part she takes as a compliment anyway. "You are a rascal. But I suppose I do have a special bout for you, tonight."

I don't like the way the three men are watching me as she speaks. Anticipating . . . something. Like most people they're Octavii, normally ceding half their Will to a Septimus's command. My skin crawls to think of it.

Tonight's different, of course. Usually Will is ceded in perpetuity; the Hierarchy organises and tracks all such arrangements with fastidious care, and only whoever controls someone's Will can return it. But these men's Septimii have seen fit to do exactly that for the evening—presumably in exchange for a share of any earnings. Illegal, of course. But the sort of thing that would incur only a small fine if discovered.

Any of the three could break my back with an embrace. But ceding day in and day out has slowed their wits, their reaction times, whole again though they temporarily are. Something has been taken from them. They're broken in ways they don't understand, and it makes them fodder in a fight.

They've never liked that I, smaller and younger than they, am not.

"A special bout," I repeat, my attention returning to Ellanher.

"Yes, dear boy! I was approached a few days ago by an older gentleman. I shan't tell you his name, but he's rather well-known up in northern Tensia. A knight, if you'd believe it. He had heard of our little shows here, from an acquaintance who has enjoyed our hospitality from time to time. This man had a very interesting proposition. His son has accrued some unfortunate debts, and—" She sees me yawning exaggeratedly and scowls. "He's a Sextus," she finishes somewhat tetchily, disappointed I've ruined her build up. "You'll be fighting a Sextus tonight."

I don't think I've heard her correctly at first, but the smug expressions on the Octavii's faces tell me otherwise. I'm to be meat for the grinder. It feels as though the air has been sucked from the room.

"What are the rules?" I'm relieved to find my voice is level, neither fury nor fear showing through. Ellanher's had this arranged for days. She's sprung it on me because she knows I'm not going to pull out, not when the fight's set and the crowd is waiting. I'd never be allowed to see the inside of this place again.

"No weapons. No killing."

"I'll do my best," I mutter, though the bravado rings false in my own ears. I stare at the ground, coming to grips with what's about to happen, then straighten. Look her in the eye. "Triple pay."

"Double."

"Quadruple."

"You're supposed to meet in the middle when you haggle, darling."

I say nothing, but I don't break the gaze.

There's silence, and then Ellanher gives a small, acceding laugh. Delicate and refined, still so strange to hear emerging from that powerful physique of hers. "Triple, then. But no extra for a healer, even if that handsome face of yours needs it."

And it probably will, but this is the best deal I'm going to get. I gesture toward the narrow hallway leading farther inside, somewhat curtly, indicating both my acceptance and that she should lead the way. Ellanher smiles serenely, murmuring a farewell to her companions. The three men are glowering again as we depart. They'd hoped to get a better reaction from me.

Inwardly, I'm still reeling.

We make the short journey to Ellanher's "office"—her dressing room, during the day and early evening—without talking. Once inside, I'm struck again by the incongruity of the space. A well-lit mirror, a dresser with vials of makeup. Feathered hats and soft fur cloaks and a rack full of wildly different dresses. It's surreal to imagine Ellanher readying herself to sing and dance and boldly act out her lines on the same stage where she's about to send me to get my head caved in.

The Septimus strides over to the safe on the wall, taking the Will key from around her neck and inserting it into its slot. The granite latch clicks aside, revealing rows of carefully stacked coins. Will-locked vaults, even small ones like this, are a hundred times more secure than anything mechanical. Priced accordingly, too. Ellanher's late-night side business is paying handsomely.

She counts out my compensation—six silver triangles, worth sixty coppers—and presses them into my palm.

"I admit to being curious, Vis," she says as she locks the vault again, some of her grandiose act faded away now we're alone. She knows it doesn't impress me the way it does the others. "What you earn here . . . it's hardly riches, but it is a lot for an orphan. And you're willing to go through so much pain to get more. So what is it all for? Debts? A woman? Some vice that you cannot bring yourself to give up?" Her tone's light, as it always is with me, but she's far from joking. It bothers her that she doesn't know.

"This Sextus I'm to fight. I assume he'll be ceding?"

"Of course." If Ellanher's fazed by my pointedly ignoring the question, she doesn't show it. "I don't want you dead, my boy."

"Just badly beaten."

She sizes me up, coming to a decision. "Yes." There's neither apology nor regret. "A little fight from the underdog can be fun, Vis, but too much becomes a statement. The sort of statement that gets Catenan attention."

I close my fist around the coins in my hand, the sharp points digging into my skin until they threaten to do injury. I've been testing my Septimus opponents more and more during the months I've been fighting here. Won more than I've lost, over the past few. To think, I was actually feeling good about that. I should have realised it would be noticed. Commented on. Disapproved of, in certain quarters.

"I'll see you onstage," I growl, wheeling and leaving before I say something to make my situation worse.

The dimly lit passageways here seem tighter than ever. The bowels of Letens's largest auditorium are a warren of private rooms and preparation areas, most of which have been shut off since the last of the actors left more than two hours ago. I don't pause at any of the many branching paths, though, heading almost inattentively for the stairs leading up to the very top of the seating area. I've been here three times a week for more than six months. I know my way around.

I'm accompanied only by my apprehension at what's to come until I'm almost at the very top of the stairs, when the murmur of voices bleeds into my consciousness. The first arrivals of the night have trickled in. In about thirty minutes, that murmur will become a rumbling, expectant buzz as seats fill. Then a primal roar as the first fight gets underway.

I emerge onto the top row of the semi-circular white stone amphitheatre, my entrance unremarked by the smattering of people already present. The stage below is distant; this place can hold several hundred spectators at capacity. Once open to the air, a vaguely foreboding, sound-deadening dome now sits overhead. Three layers thick, it's a special design by Catenan architects, who were commissioned several years ago by some of the wealthier citizens migrating from Caten itself. Apparently, the disturbance rowdy Tensian plays caused to their evenings was becoming simply unbearable.

The curved mass of stone was not exactly popular with the Tensians—it's hardly aesthetically pleasing, and the crass nickname the locals have given it very much reflects that—but it *is* effective. Even the most raucous of noise from in here won't escape.

I scan the crowd nearby and spot the man I'm looking for quickly enough, familiar black notebook clutched in his hand as he talks animatedly to someone. Gaufrid's energetic for an Octavii, even if the effects of more than a decade of ceding have him looking closer to fifty than his late thirties. What he likes to refer to as his receding hairline is well into the realm of balding, though at least he keeps the remaining sandy-coloured strands neat and close-cropped. He's dressed entirely in an off-putting shade of green tonight, for some reason.

I loiter near the exit, mostly out of sight from the gathering crowd, waiting patiently until I catch his eye. When he notices me, he excuses himself and hurries over.

"Vis!"

"Gaufrid." I eye his attire. "Lose a bet?"

"Ha. Ha. My wife's choice, if you must know."

"One way to make sure you're faithful, I suppose."

"You're an ass." Gaufrid's grin shows he doesn't think much of the outfit either. He grabs my arm, draws me conspiratorially into the shadows. "Your admirer's back."

I follow his nod to the sparse crowd, spotting the girl soon enough. A thick dark cloak still swathes her, despite the relative warmth indoors. My age, at a guess, maybe a few years older. Dark skin and long, curly brown hair. There's something unsettling about the way she leans forward in her seat, ignoring those around her, gaze fixed on the empty stage below. Though as we watch, her concentration breaks and she frowns around before abruptly drawing her hood up, concealing her face. As if she can somehow sense our examination.

"Lucky me." I've never spoken to her, but she's been here for every fight over the past two weeks. Quietly asking around about me. Gaufrid thinks it's romantic. I'm concerned she's recognised something about me. "Still not interested."

"And good friend that I am, I continue to tell her that you are as enigmatic as you are handsome." As usual, though, Gaufrid looks vaguely disappointed. "So. Come to make an early wager?"

I feel the weight of the coins in my pocket. Calculate. Gaufrid is the unofficial bookkeeper for these evenings: if you want to make a wager that will actually pay out when you win, you go to him. "Last fight of the night."

"Octavus or Septimus?"

I grimace. "Special circumstances. This one's against a Sextus."

A frown of confusion, then the blood drains from Gaufrid's face. He grabs my arm and pulls me deeper into the passageway, completely out of sight of any spectators.

"Are you *mad?*"

"I didn't find out until five minutes ago. Not much I can do."

I see Gaufrid's mind working, see the moment where he understands that this is a punishment being meted out.

"Go to Ellanher. Tell her that you'll lose to every Septimus you're put up against for the next month. She'll accept the compromise." Gaufrid looks genuinely troubled. "One wrong hit from a Sextus could cave your skull in, Vis. It probably wouldn't even be deliberate. Even if he—he?" I nod. "Even if he is ceding, he'll have the strength of ten people behind every punch! You understand that, right?"

"Nine and a quarter people, actually," I correct him in irritation. "And he can't be particularly skilled with Will if he has to earn his money here. With weak Septimii ceding to him as well, he might only be self-imbuing worth three or four." Something similar to Gaufrid's suggestion had already crossed my mind. Call it pride, call it stubbornness, but I'm not going to do it. I've worked too hard, suffered through too many injuries and too much mockery to return to constant defeat.

Besides, I'm not here for the coin alone. I gave up on dreams of exacting revenge on the Republic long ago, but that doesn't mean I'll never have to defy them.

This is practice.

Gaufrid growls something under his breath. I'm not sure whether it's concern for me, or concern that he's about to lose the benefits of this mutually beneficial deal we have. I can't guarantee wins and I won't guarantee losses, but most of the Septimii fighting here are regulars: those I haven't already faced, I've studied. Which means I know my chances, more often than not. And, importantly, can usually drag out a match to any length of my choosing, even if the result doesn't go my way.

So I bet largely on how long I think I'll last, and Gaufrid uses that information to . . . *adjust* the odds he offers everyone else.

"What will you give me on three minutes?" It sounds ludicrous even as I ask it, but I'm here now. In this mess. I may as well try and use it to profit.

Gaufrid chokes a disbelieving laugh. "Vis, when this is announced, I won't be able to sell odds on you lasting more than three seconds." When I don't back down, he sighs. "Twenty to one."

"For *three minutes?*"

"Those are the best numbers I'm going to give you," he assures me. "For all I know, you could have an agreement in place with this Sextus to split the winnings."

"I wouldn't do that to you," I say, offended.

"I believe you. Doesn't change the risk."

"What about for two minutes?"

"Same odds." Gaufrid fixes me with a serious look. "Same again for one minute."

I scowl, but I know Gaufrid well enough to know he's not going to budge. He thinks he's helping me, forcing me to shorten the fight rather than aim for a big windfall. I draw four silver triangles from my pocket, holding them out. "Longer than one minute, then. Less than one and a half."

Gaufrid whistles between his teeth as he takes them. "Stupid *and* rich today. Alright." He slips the coins into a pouch at his waist. There's no entry into his small black notebook, no receipt listing the amount or the odds he's given me, but that's normal. The man has a remarkable memory, and I know he's good for it. If for no other reason than Ellanher's aware of our arrangement, and though she takes her cut, she'd tear him limb from limb—perhaps literally—if she ever thought he was cheating one of her fighters.

I turn to go, business complete, but Gaufrid grabs my shoulder.

"No shame in calling it at first blood." He looks frustrated, almost angry, that he's issuing this advice. Given how people are likely to bet, that's unsurprising. "I know it's not in your nature, but Vis—if you're ever going to swallow your pride, tonight's the night."

He releases his grip and strides back into the amphitheatre, still looking faintly ridiculous clad in green.

Gaufrid's warning echoes uncomfortably as I descend the stairs again, heading this time for the waiting area just offstage. He might be right. Once there's blood, either fighter can concede the bout—and there will almost certainly be blood before the end of the first minute, no matter how fast I move.

But it's one minute. One minute for *eight gold*. That's almost double what I've managed to save since I started here.

It's not just the amount of coin on offer, either. I've been feeling the inexorable press of time on my shoulders lately. I'm seventeen years old in truth, as of two months ago, even if the Hierarchy's records for Vis Solum say that milestone isn't for another ten weeks. Part of me regrets not stretching the lie further when I first came to the orphanage, but the risk of the claim drawing notice was too great.

Regardless of whether it was a mistake, it means I have little more than a year before the law demands my Will. Either ceded after a trip to the Aurora Columnae, or taken by a Sapper.

And all the ways I can think to try and avoid that involve *significant* expense.

I navigate the back hallways and arrive at the room the Octavii are given to prepare, still deep in thought as I enter. It's to the right of the main stage, an austere stone box that's large enough to comfortably accommodate the dozen men within. A small, temporary shrine to Mira is, as usual, erected by the door. I ignore it. The room already stinks of stale sweat and animal fat as men grease their arms and run on the spot, or jump repeatedly, or do whatever they can to expel the stiff cold from their muscles.

None stop their exercises, but eyes surreptitiously fix on me as I find an open space to warm up. They've heard, then.

Like Othmar and Caren earlier, none of the gazes are especially sympathetic. I've always been an oddity here, I suppose, even before I started winning. The youngest by at least two years, and easily the least physically imposing. Not that I'm weak—the Theatre, not to mention my time prior competing in the gladiatorial competition of Victorum, has made me leaner and stronger than I'd once thought possible—but these men were singled out for their physiques. They're mountains of brawn, without exception.

And now I'm to fight a Sextus. It will be an insult to some; they'll see it as an acknowledgment by Ellanher of my successes, rather than the castigation it is. Others will just be delighted that I likely won't be around for a while.

Time passes at an interminable crawl as I suffer their constant sideways glances, each one only adding to my concern. The buzz of excited murmuring from the amphitheatre builds steadily, muffled though it is in here, until finally it's cut short by Ellanher's voice. Warming up the crowd. There's laughter, cheers. She's beloved out there.

Ten minutes go by, allowing enough time for bets on the first fight after its announcement. Then the stage door is opening and Idonia—Ellanher's younger cousin, supposedly, though with her short-cropped blond hair and bright blue eyes, they bear no physical similarities whatsoever—peers through. "Pabul." A giant with long reddish-brown hair and a front tooth missing slips through the door after her.

It's a parade of names called and men departing after that. They don't come back the same way; we never know how any single bout has gone until the end of the night. Though you can usually guess. There's a certain feel to the crowd noise when a match is close. Or when an injury is particularly nasty.

I block it all out tonight, formulating a strategy. I've thought about this plenty of times before, albeit in the most abstract terms. No weapons is a good start. Still, most Sextii can imbue things—a simple touch and he could make my shirt start to strangle me, or if he doesn't want to look like he's cheating, just pull me off-balance at the wrong moment. Unpleasant though it is, there's only one way to avoid that.

He'll be strong, of course. I briefly consider the tactic of *letting* him imbue something; Will is a finite resource, and however much he infused elsewhere would leave him with that much less to bolster himself. But I immediately dismiss the idea. An errant punch to the head might only maim rather than kill, in that scenario. Not much of an advantage.

Then there's the question of his speed. That's harder to predict, and the one area which gives me hope. The Will being ceded to him improves his reaction times, but it's a marginal enhancement over a Septimus. Training and experience play more of a role, there. And if this Sextus is only fighting tonight because he thinks it's an easy way to make coin, then it's possible he may not have the discipline of others I've already faced.

As I assess and reassess my logic, around me, the room gradually empties. Quietens. The heavy stench lingers. The roars of the spectators out front ebb and flow.

Finally, suddenly, I'm the only one left.

I strip, carefully and methodically. Cloak, tunic, underclothes. Folded neatly and put in a pile. I have to believe that I'm going to need them again. Then I use the pot of animal fat to grease my entire body. It's disgusting, but if the Sextus gets a good grip on me, he'll be able to snap or crush bone. And the substance won't keep its form, so it can't be imbued.

The door opens just as I finish.

"Vis, you're . . ." Idonia sputters as she sees me. Gapes, then glances away. She's more shy than her cousin. "You're up. I mean, you're ready. It's your turn. To fight." She's red. Almost flees back toward the stage.

I chuckle to myself as I pad after her, though mostly to avoid thinking about my own discomfort. Living on the run meant that propriety and advantage were rarely companions, that first year and a half, and any reservations I may have once had were beaten out of me long ago. Still, there's something inherently unsettling about being naked. Some part of me that can't help the embarrassment, feel exposed in more than just the physical, regardless of whether it's the smart thing to do.

It's a short walk down the corridor to the stage. Ellanher's making the big announcement about the Sextus. There's a renewed thrill in the air, gasps and excited chattering. Ahead I can see Idonia has dashed onstage, cheeks still flushed, whispering in Ellanher's ear.

The burly woman's dark hair swings as her gaze snaps to me. Those brown eyes of hers are fathomless as she watches me stride onto stage, expression not changing as the first of the crowd notices my lack of attire and starts to whistle and laugh. I walk past her toward the onlookers seated in the dim beyond the stage, a broad grin on my burning face, raising my arms as if they're cheering me. The laughs increase, but they're mostly approving, not mocking. Confidence, real or perceived, has a peculiar power over people.

I look back over my shoulder at Ellanher. Her eyes are fixed on me, but something's changed. They're puzzled. A hint of shock. I realise she's seeing my back for the first time. The terrible mass of scars upon scars upon scars. It doesn't matter. I doubt she knows what they mean, and I have no intention of sharing.

My breath shortens as I catch movement from the other side of the stage.

The Sextus is . . . imposing. Perhaps a decade older than me. Tall. Athletic—not built of muscle like the Octavii but with more of a graceful power to him, a litheness as he saunters out onto the stage, giving an easy smile and waving at a crowd who are now cheering in earnest. He's handsome into the bargain, brown hair cut fashionably short, square jaw covered in dark stubble. An automatic favourite.

He removes his tinted spectacles—proof positive that he's a Sextus; no one of lesser rank is allowed to wear those—and hands them to Ellanher. His self-assuredness falters when he spots me, only for a second. Then his smile returns. It's harder this time, though. He's not pleased.

I smile back.

Idonia's already darted away. Ellanher glides to the front of the stage, raising her hands and gazing up into the back rows of the amphitheatre as if she can see every single person sitting in the shadows. She holds that pose. The whispers stop, the murmuring fades. It's as if the entire building is holding its breath. Everyone is focused on her.

Blood thunders in my ears as I turn and face the Sextus, moving to the balls of my feet, readying myself. There will be no introductions, no names. Not here.

Finally, satisfied that the tension is at its peak, Ellanher drops her arms again. Steps lightly off the stage as her voice rings out, a dagger into the eager silence.

"Begin."

III

THE RELEASED BELLOWING OF THE CROWD IS A WAVE HITTING the stage, crashing down from the surrounding darkness.

Exhilaration courses through me at the sound. They're unique, these eternal moments before a match truly begins. Blood pounding. Fighting to keep my breathing steady. Not sure whether it's excitement or fear that's heightening every sense, making my skin tingle and hands twitch in anticipation. Every second seems to draw out, every minor detail of the stage and my opponent seems to be brighter, *clearer*. There are the spindly cracks in the faded white stone underfoot, several spaces coated in fresh splashes of red. The warm heaviness of the air from a night of bodies packed together. The way the Sextus's lip almost imperceptibly curls as he stalks forward, green eyes bleeding to black and glittering in the light of the torches arrayed around the stage.

Ellanher asked me what it's all for. I tell myself that it's for the coin, for the practice. For survival. And none of that's a lie, but as the shackles on my mind fall away, I acknowledge that there's another truth beneath it all.

This is the only place in the world where I don't have to pretend to be friendly. Or dull. Or servile. Or weary.

This is the one place where I don't have to hold back.

I start my mental clock. *Five seconds.*

The stage is large, a semi-circle perhaps fifty feet in radius. The bounds for the contest are set by the surrounding torches; if one of us steps past those, the fight ends. Of course, doing that too early doesn't just destroy a career here. Ellanher made it clear before even my first bout that whatever injuries a fighter might avoid in doing so, would be revisited double upon them by the end of the night.

I head across to the centre of the stage, at an oblique angle to the Sextus's path. He's moving determinedly, but not hurrying. It occurs to me that he's probably intensely conscious of making this look effortless; anything else would be embarrassing for him. That's good. Means he's more likely to act bored, rather than work to chase me down within this vital first minute.

I slide back as he nears and begin circling, staying out of range. He follows, still at the same deliberate pace. *Fifteen seconds.*

The first mocking call drifts from the crowd, quickly taken up by others. Baiting me. Baiting him. The Sextus's pace subtly increases. I match it, drawing more scorn. I don't care. I'll throw punches and risk hits only when it's smart, regardless of how I look.

Twenty-five seconds. Plenty of bawdy jokes about the Sextus enjoying the chase too much. Laughter. There's something dark about the other man's expression now, beyond the night in his eyes. They're getting to him. Normally I'd enjoy that, but more anger means less mercy. I feint forward, as if to attack. It gives the athletic man pause. I resume my circling. *Thirty seconds.* I can barely believe my luck so far. No actual fighting.

The Sextus has remained at an exasperated stop at the centre of the stage. I slide to a halt as well, never taking my eyes from him.

"Octavus!" His voice booms, rich and louder than it should be, cutting easily through the jeers. I'm not technically an Octavus, having never ceded before, but neither he nor anyone else here knows that. "Are we really doing this? In front of everyone?" Trying to put the onus to engage back on my pride. Clever, and yet a complete misunderstanding of his opponent.

I don't respond. Don't move. *Thirty-five seconds.*

He steps forward, and I step back. He scowls openly this time. "I'd have thought twice about coming out here if I'd realised my opponent was such a coward!"

"Says the big brave Sextus fighting the Octavus," I call back, to scattered approving laughs from the darkness.

I bite my tongue as soon as the words are out of my mouth. Stung to a reply. Perhaps not a *complete* misunderstanding by the Sextus, after all.

And he sees that.

"Ellanher told me about you." His voice is still raised, but quieter than before, and I doubt his words carry beyond the stage. "She said that you're an orphan." There's an ugliness to the way the words fall, and something deep in my chest shifts, tightens in response. Preparation for a different kind of assault.

He advances, I retreat. *Forty-five seconds.*

"But you're old, for an orphan, aren't you? So for some reason, no one wants you." Advance, retreat. He shows me perfect teeth. His eyes are dead and cold. "Starting with your parents, I imagine. Did you even know them? Do you remember when they abandoned you, Solum, or have you always wondered about why they did it?" Advance, retreat. "Were they the ones who whipped you? Or did they just leave you to the ones who did?"

I try to block out his words but it's hard to both focus on him and ignore them. He's wrong, of course. Wildly off target in his guesses. But my breathing's too shallow, for some reason. More of a growl. And I've lost track of the count. Is it a minute yet? There's heat against my back. A torch. I'm too close to the edge. Hemmed in.

"I bet they were worthless anyway," the Sextus crows as he closes in.

Everything goes cold. Sharp. Not here. Not out here, the one place I don't have to think about them.

I advance.

Distant, the crowd roars.

The Sextus is smug as we meet. He throws the first punch, but it's an obvious one and I let it sail over my left shoulder, closing in and delivering a swift strike to his ribs before darting away again. I'm not running anymore, but even through rage's red veil, I know not to get close enough to be grappled.

It was a hard hit—I'm nowhere near as heavy as the Octavii who fight here, but I *am* fast—and the Sextus takes a step backward, smirk replaced by a grimace. It's brief, though. Surprised rather than pained. I might have cracked a rib if I'd taken a blow like that. A Septimus would at least have a bruise. But the Sextus? His Will probably makes it feel more like I gave him a sharp push.

"A little sensitive, Solum?" he sneers, coming at me again.

I snarl and swing first this time, but he's ready for it, dodges faster and more smoothly than I could possibly anticipate. Not as unskilled as I'd hoped. I overextend, try to twist away from the elbow I see coming in the corner of my vision.

It's a glancing blow, in the end, more arm than elbow. Barely making contact with my left shoulder.

My face burns as it skids along cold stone. I'm blind. Winded, hacking. Cheers muffled and twisted in my ears. I gasp, vision and awareness returning enough to roll away from the Sextus, who towers over me. Not even looking at me, I realise. His back to me. Waving almost disinterestedly to the adulation of the darkness.

He grazed me. It feels like the building fell on my head.

My left shoulder's in agony, so I put my right hand to my cheek. It comes away sticky, bright red. I steady and haul myself to my feet, bitterly grateful for the Sextus's arrogance as my head clears. It has to have been more than a minute. My reward, not to mention survival, awaits. I just need to step off the stage before he turns.

But something still seethes, and it's calculating my odds.

I know, both academically and from fighting Septimii, that even a hit that appears to do nothing is still a hit. For a Septimii, a blow needs to land in the same place at least twice before it starts to take full effect. For a Sextus, that's likely to translate to at least seven or eight times.

So, terrible odds. But the idiot's back is to me.

A voice from the corner of my mind is shrieking at me to be smart. It's so distant, though.

I launch forward.

Perhaps the Sextus thinks I'm down. Done. Or he thinks I'll fight honourably, wait for him to face me again before attacking. Or, perhaps, it's just inexperience. Whatever the reason, he doesn't respond quickly enough to the rising warning of the crowd.

I scream as I pour all my fury and momentum into the hooking, running punch at the side of his jaw, aiming for the point I know would knock out any regular person. He realises something's wrong at the very last second, but I still make almost perfect contact.

There's a shiver down my arm at the impact, and the Sextus groans as he staggers.

The enthusiastic shouts from the audience cut off, replaced by the sound of a hundred people gasping in unison. I don't pay it any attention. Even at a fraction of its real strength, the positioning and power of that hit has made a difference. The Sextus is dazed. Stumbling.

I'm on him, right fist crashing again, missing the same spot on his jaw but connecting with his cheek. No time to think. I swing again, barely blocked this time. He's reeling. Recovers enough to swat furiously at me; heat sears down my injured shoulder but it's a panicked shot, no venom behind it, and I'm braced this time. I'm too far gone to care about the pain anyway.

It's a cold, disconnected fury that drives me now, one that clears my head, slows time, and focuses. I feint and get in a hard strike to the Sextus's collarbone, then another. I feel it give way on the third. He's wheezing. Eyes black and wide. Struggling to comprehend. I surprise him by getting in close and delivering a savage knee to the groin—an effective strategy no matter how much Will is cushioning the blow, I've found—and then step back and follow with a thundering uppercut to his jaw as he doubles over.

He goes down.

I don't stop, don't give him a chance. I kick aside his warding arm and fall at him, bringing my fist down on his face. There's blood, and it's not mine. "You want to know about my parents, Sextus?" I'm snarling. I barely know what I'm saying. I straddle him and strike again, same place. "You want to know about my family?" Again. "You want to know why I have these gods-damned scars on my back?" The words come out ragged. A stranger's voice.

He's not answering. He's not fighting back anymore.

There are strong hands looping under my armpits, pulling me off him. I thrash until I realise it's useless to resist; then the rage is abruptly draining away, leaving me with nothing but ache and weariness. My vision's blurred. The blow to my head? Tears? Blood? I don't know. The Sextus is motionless on the ground. The stone near his head is splashed crimson.

Ellanher's saying something, but the words are just a strange buzz. Now my wrath's died, I think the Sextus's hits are taking their toll. There's a cloak being draped over my shoulders. Ellanher's tone is worry overlaid with calm. She's speaking slowly, as one would to a child. I still can't understand her.

I let her half carry me off the stage. There's no applause, no cheering. Just stunned muttering from the surrounding darkness.

As we shuffle away, I let out a bitter, tired laugh as I realise something. I won the fight. Which means I just lost my bet.

I'm barely going to earn anything from tonight at all.

IV

CHAIN YOUR ANGER IN THE DARK, MY MOTHER USED TO TELL me, and it will only thrive.

I never really understood what she meant, growing up. Why would I? I was a prince of Suus. I had comfort, safety, tutors and servants and family. I was loved. My ire was over being forced to attend dull lessons, over imagined slights and the unfairnesses of entirely fair parental restrictions. A petty wrath, gone almost as soon as it was expressed.

When the Hierarchy came, though. When they took all of that. When I had to learn to hide among them every day. When I had to smile and nod and engage in conversation with people whose weakness allowed the Catenans to be powerful. When I had to swallow rage in every reply and pretend to agree with their excuses for their slavery, *my* slavery, just to survive.

Then I understood.

Though until tonight, I did think that my chains were strong enough for it not to matter.

I hate it, but I can't help but wonder what my mother would think of me right now.

The boos coalesce, rain down as I stand alone back in the centre of the blood-spattered stage. I keep my eyes on the ground, not letting anyone see my defiance. Ellanher has just finished telling them all that I cheated. That I've admitted to buying the Will of a Totius Septimus, a Septimus who doesn't cede to someone else, for the evening. She played the hurriedly crafted lie to perfection, mortification heartfelt as she addressed her patrons. Even gave a traditional Threefold Apology, by Catenan custom preventing retribution if accepted. The crowd was sullen at her first appeal for forgiveness. By the third impassioned plea, she'd won them over.

Of course, the subsequent announcement of my banishment has helped. As has that any successful bets on my fight tonight will be honoured, and all others will be repaid in full.

Even through my boiling frustration, I cannot help but think of how much Gaufrid will *hate* that last part.

My fists clench against the ire of the crowd. Teeth grinding. Breath coming short. I've complied with this charade only because Ellanher has assured me that far worse than an aching shoulder and bruised ego awaits me, otherwise. This way we can part, as she puts it, "amicably." If there's been no upending of the natural order here, then there won't be any extra scrutiny from the Hierarchy. And we both know I can't exactly go to the authorities about any of this.

The heckling peters out soon enough. Grumbling turning to mollified chatter. Everyone here got to see a Sextus beaten, even if it was through cheating. A scandal to talk about for weeks to come, and no money lost from it. They've had a good night, all told.

"That will do, my boy." Ellanher's at the edge of the stage, waiting for me to start walking. We leave the already-gossiping rumblings of the departing crowd behind us.

The journey back to her office seems too long. Our footsteps echo.

"About your back—"

"No." I growl the word. I've expected the question since the fight, saw Ellanher's glances as she bandaged my shoulder before we went back out there.

Ellanher knows she doesn't have much left to bargain with. "Of course, darling," she says softly.

Another silence as we trudge through the empty corridors. She eventually sighs. More regret than anger in her. "There's always a return to Victorum. I hear they miss you down there."

I snort. Letens's Victorum league is where Ellanher found me, first approached me to participate in these nights. It's the less-consequential cousin of Caten's great gladiatorial bouts: voluntary and, more importantly, without the shadow of being consigned to a Sapper if you reach three losses.

It's still dangerous work, despite the blunted steel we used—and worse, comparatively pointless. It's a Hierarchy-sponsored activity. The matron would have to officially approve my involvement again, meaning I wouldn't even get to keep the coin I earned.

"You were good, my boy," presses Ellanher as we reach her office. She does seem genuinely disappointed that I'm leaving. Sincerely trying to encourage me. Though she is also a fine actor. "And you may be less tempted to try and kill your opponents there."

"I wasn't trying to kill him." I haven't seen the Sextus, whose injuries are undoubtedly being treated somewhere nearby, since the fight. A bloodied and broken nose. Bruises. A headache. Despite my rage, it won't be anything worse than that. He'll hear secondhand what was said out there and tell himself that it's why he lost. That it's the *only* way he could have lost.

She opens the door. "You can wait in here until the . . . less pleased of our customers are gone. If you wish."

I'm tempted to refuse, but I'm in no condition to handle being confronted by disgruntled spectators. I step inside, ease myself into one of the chairs.

Ellanher stays in the hall, hand on the door. "And Vis? I was right there. I saw your face when you were hitting him, darling."

She smiles sadly, and leaves me alone.

I sit for a while, wrestling my heavy-hearted frustrations under control. My shoulder throbs beneath its strapping. It's been a mess of a night.

It's perhaps forty minutes later when there's a short knock. I hold my silence, assuming that whoever it is will be looking for Ellanher.

"Vis? I know you're in there."

It's Gaufrid. I stare at the door, trying to decide whether the man would be angry enough at me to have brought muscle.

Probably not?

I unlock it, easing it open. Gaufrid hears and turns from where he had already started walking away, green suit even more garish surrounded by the drab hallway. He looks tired rather than irate. He's alone.

"Come in." I open the way a little wider. "But I'm leaving soon."

"I know. This won't take long." Gaufrid joins me in Ellanher's office but stands awkwardly by the door, not shutting it, shaking his head when I motion to a chair. Instead, he digs into a pocket and abruptly leans forward, grabbing my wrist with one hand and then pressing something cold and sharp into my palm with the other.

Four silver triangles.

"Just refunding your wager," he says gruffly. As I inspect the metal in my hand, puzzled, he moves to depart.

"Why?" I'm confused. Grateful, but can't help but be suspicious at the same time. Gaufrid has to know that he's never going to see me again. And I'm responsible for him losing a *lot* of money tonight.

The balding man pauses. "Two minutes and thirty-seven seconds."

I look at him quizzically.

"That's how long your fight lasted. And then you *won*. Seeing an Octavus beating a Sextus? That was a damned fine thing. A *damned* fine thing." He keeps his voice low. Afraid of being overheard, but emphatic, determined to say the words anyway. "And I don't care what Ellanher says. You didn't cheat."

He leaves, shuts the door again. No goodbye. Not even a nod.

But I'm standing a little straighter. Smiling, despite myself, as I let the four coins jingle in my hand and then join their siblings in my pocket.

Another half hour passes before I deem it safe to leave. No one accosts me as I slip out into the early morning darkness of Letens. The wind has died down, but the chill is more than enough to stir me from the threat of sleep.

I stand there for a long second, melancholic despite myself. These past six months have given me a strange kind of stability. The last of that is almost over, now.

There's just one more thing I need to do tonight.

※ ※ ※

I RETURN TO THE ORPHANAGE A FEW HOURS LATER, JUST AS the cloudless sky starts to reveal sharp blue.

I'm feeling better as I approach, albeit still sore. My detour to Letens's Bibliotheca was a success, the travelogue I stole strapped to my back beneath repurposed bandages. It's filled with maps and descriptions of the archipelago of uninhabited islands about three weeks' voyage to the east. A bad option, a desperate option. But after tonight, I may not have the chance to find better.

I use my key to unlock the door, slipping inside. I've already re-tightened the concealing bandages and tucked the remainder of what I earned from the Theatre tonight into my boots, so when movement greets me before I can even start toward the stairs to my room, I'm ready.

"Vis." Matron Atrox rises smoothly from her chair. The Septimus in charge of the orphanage is a slim woman, her blond hair shoulder-length and features petite. In her forties, from what I gather, though she could pass for younger. Probably quite attractive, if you don't have the disadvantage of knowing her.

I make a show of reluctance as I dig the single silver and five copper triangles from my pocket, offering them to her. "For all your hard work, Matron."

The matron's smile withers to something cold and hard, and far more familiar to me. "Careful. Your work at the prison is at my discretion. There are always . . . *other* ways I could task a boy like you with earning his way." From the lascivious way she says it, there's no doubting her meaning.

I ignore the threat; it's long since lost its sting from repeated use. The hateful woman frowns at my lack of response, then scrapes the metal from my hand. "I need your help as soon as mid-morning bell rings today," she tells me as she checks the amount. She signed the contract for my work at Letens Prison. Knows down to the coin how much I'm supposed to be paid.

I try not to show how much pain her simple statement brings me. Mid-morning's only a few hours away, and my throbbing shoulder exacerbates my need for rest tenfold. "Why?"

"A messenger came not long before you. There's a potential adopter coming at noon today. The children will be excited, and I need your help getting them ready."

"That's short notice. And a strange time to be notified." I'm getting an odd sense of enthusiasm from Matron Atrox. She usually considers adoptions as chores to suffer through.

"The recommendation came from Proconsul Manius himself. And the adopter is a Quintus." She waits, nods as she sees my reaction. Important men in the Hierarchy, far more so than we would usually be entertaining. In fact, I've been here for a year and a half, and we *once* had a Sextus adopt someone. "It's vital that everything go smoothly today, Vis."

It's a statement and a threat. A statement because if a Quintus adopts someone in her charge, that raises Matron Atrox's stock considerably. It could lead to increased funding from Religion, maybe even a promotion to Sextus for her down the track.

And a threat, because my presence would reflect poorly on her. A near seventeen-year-old who still refuses to visit the Aurora Columnae?

The deep, layered scars on my back reflect exactly how much of an embarrassment that is to her.

"I'll stay clear." I haven't been interviewed for months, anyway—not since the matron gave up on getting rid of me or farming me out for my Will, and decided to put me to work in other ways. Which involves doing the majority of her job, during the day.

Now she's seen past the frustration of not being able to break me, I think she rather likes the new arrangement.

"Good boy." The matron smooths her white skirt as she stands. I'm not sure what time she rises in the morning, but she's always impeccably dressed and made up. Never a hair out of place. "I'll send Vermes to wake you."

She sweeps away toward the kitchen, not giving me another glance.

I wait until she's gone before I move. As expected, the fresh abrasion on my face hasn't elicited comment—she assumes, and I've often implied, that I'm treated poorly at the prison—but if she notices my shoulder, then she'll want to make sure I'm fit for work. And at present, an examination would lead to the discovery of the travelogue.

Once I'm certain she's disappeared, every muscle groans as I climb the stairs and follow the long hallway to my room. It's at the far end. Tiny. Space for a single mattress on the floor, and not much else.

It's all mine though. The twenty or so other children here have more space, but bunk two or three to a room. I was moved here when I started working outside the orphanage, so as not to disturb anyone with my unusual schedule.

It's suited me. There's a panel in the wall that I managed to pry loose early on without any visible damage, with a cavity behind it that's large enough to secret away the extra coins I've been earning. I deposit the few leftover from tonight, then slowly, stiffly unwind my bandage and add the book. It's a tight fit, given the nook isn't especially large, but after some careful manoeuvring, I get it in and move the panel convincingly back in place.

Despite my exhaustion, I take the time to rebandage my shoulder as best I can. It's a clumsy process. Painful. Certainly not as effective as Ellanher's work. I won't be able to hide the injury, come morning, so instead I'll have to convince Matron Atrox to do a better job of it when I figure out how to excuse its existence.

For now, though, I just need to sleep.

V

"WAKE UP, REX, YOU LAZY ASS."

Pain ricochets through my shoulder as I'm prodded roughly. I growl as I open my eyes, glaring at the smug-looking fifteen-year-old looming over my mattress.

"Vermes." I say his name like a wearily uttered curse, which is exactly how I mean it. "I'm up."

"Doesn't look like it." The blond-haired boy nudges me again with his boot, dancing back with a smirk as my temper flares and I sit up. His thick bulk is mostly muscle, and he's tall for his age. Still smaller than me, but he knows my position here is too tenuous for me to react with violence. "Matron says there's an adoption happening today, and you need to get everyone ready."

I close my eyes. Let my irritation settle as the early morning conversation with Matron Atrox comes back to me. The curtains in the north-facing window have already been drawn back, and the sun's angling through enough to touch my feet. "Time?"

"Bell went ten minutes ago."

I massage my shoulder. It's stiffened overnight, but the ache's less. "I'm up," I repeat, more firmly this time. Far from a good amount of sleep, but enough to function. "Tell her I'll be right down."

"Tell her yourself. I want to get ready." Vermes leaves before I can respond.

I drag myself up and to the washroom, splashing my face with water and using the mirror there to smooth my steadily lengthening brown hair. Until the orphanage, I was shaving it in the Aquirian style—doing everything I could to change my appearance in line with my story—but the only razor allowed here is Matron Atrox's. And I'm not going to let that woman touch my hair.

It likely doesn't matter. Even with the thick, wavy strands growing back, I barely recognise the hard and hollow face beneath them anymore.

I head downstairs, stopping first by the kitchen to sneak some leftovers. There's exhilarated chatter from some of the girls in the next room as I tear away chunks of bread from a half-eaten loaf. A potential adoption always generates excitement—letters of recommendation are hard to come by for most people—but today, I can almost taste the anticipation in the air. A Quintus. If someone here is fortunate enough to be chosen, they'll be departing to a lifetime of comfort.

I take a few moments to eat and then venture out to the main hall. It's the largest room in the house, and most of the younger children will be playing in there already.

Some of the older ones spot my passage and trail behind, knowing why I'm there. I tell them to pass word that it's time to get ready; they obey, even as they call me Rex in response. "King," it means. A curse in the Republic and a mockery of my refusal to attend the Aurora Columnae, not to mention my flimsy façade of authority here.

I ignore the name. Uncomfortably close to the mark, but they're children, and reacting only ever makes it worse. Neither friendliness nor reason travel far with them, either. So most days, I do my best to just view it as an honorific. A reminder that I've held out, when so few do.

It doesn't always work.

Before long, everyone is assembled in the main hall. Its unadorned stone walls are sterile and characterless. Most of the children have taken seats at the long dining tables in its centre. As always, it's easy to spot the ones whose turn it currently is to cede to Matron Atrox. They're quiet, less obviously enthusiastic. Skin slightly wan. Distant stares and slow blinks as they wait, especially from the younger ones. At least they'll get a brief reprieve today, when the matron temporarily returns their Will to them so that they can cede in their interview instead.

Of the room's twenty-odd occupants, more than half are between seven and ten years old. Aside from myself, Vermes is oldest at fifteen, followed by Brixia and Jejun at fourteen, and a close-knit group of five who are all around twelve. The presence of the older ones typically means plenty of sneers, jokes, and back-chat aimed at me, but today that's kept to a minimum. Everyone's focused on getting ready.

"I don't know why you're bothering." Vermes smirks as I line the children up and start neatening hair and straightening clothes. "A Quintus will want whoever can cede the most here, and that's me."

"Let's just hope they don't care about personality," I mutter, not stopping.

There's a tittering from some of the others, but Vermes's glare around the room silences any mirth. "Not like you need to worry about what they want, *Rex*." I'm fairly sure he bullies a lot of them when I'm not around. I wish they'd confirm it for me so that something could be done, but I'm too much a pariah to have their confidence.

Any response I might have made is quelled by the appearance of Matron Atrox, who sweeps into the room and favours the children with a beatific smile. Almost all of them reflect it back, even Vermes. They adore the matron. And why wouldn't they? She treats them with patience and respect. She feeds them and clothes them, gives them hope for a family. And all they have to do is regularly cede to her, and then occasionally to strangers for a day or two.

I've thought about telling them the truth. That most of those strangers aren't potential adopters but rather Octavii, so desperate to gain a temporary edge for one thing or another that they pay Matron Atrox handsomely for the extra Will. That if a child ever refused to cede, she would beat them within an inch of their lives. But I don't. Even if I could convince them, I'm not sure what good it would achieve.

"My girls and boys! You all look wonderful." Matron Atrox beams, her very slight acknowledgment to me indicating that I've done an adequate job. "Are you excited?"

There's a chorus of loud, muddled responses, all variations of an enthusiastic yes.

"Well, you won't have to wait too much longer. Our guest has just arrived!" Her eyes go to me again.

I take the cue, and leave.

My chores for today are mostly yard work, but interviews can take all afternoon, so I exit the hall via the kitchen. The massive walk-in pantry is always well stocked, and I spend a minute picking through what's on offer.

The muffled sound of eager young voices raised in greeting soon filters through from the hall. Cradling an apple and a couple of pastries, I pause. I'm not awed like the others, but I've also never seen a Quintus up close.

I put my food on the bench and crack open the door to the hall again.

Everyone is facing away from me, circled around the newcomer so that I can't get a good look at him. I shift, standing on my toes.

Freeze.

It's only a glimpse—the impression of a face—but I'm certain.

It's the man from the prison last night. Hospius.

I pull the door closed as gently as I can and flee for the yard, food forgotten. Why is he here? It cannot be coincidence. He *did* see me touch the Sapper. That has to be it.

I feel able to breathe again only once there's sunlight on my face and I'm hidden by the greenery of the orphanage's expansive gardens, my flight unseen. I'm anxious, but I know how to keep outright panic at bay. Too many years of lying, of close calls. This is no different. Stay calm. Think through the problem. Rashness could easily make a bad situation worse.

I run back our conversation from the previous night, the timeline of events. I told him that I was an orphan, but there are a dozen orphanages in Letens. Could he have sent messengers to them all, and this was simply his first, or maybe second, stop? That seems likely. He's trying to be subtle about finding me, else he would have simply walked in and asked for me by name. And Matron Atrox knew he would be coming before I got back to the orphanage. He didn't follow me here.

The Matron won't mention my existence. I doubt any of the children will.

If I stay here, stay quiet, he'll just move on.

I set to work trimming and weeding, twitching at every faint sound from the direction of the house. Meditative labour though it is, I don't get much done. The more I consider, the stranger the situation becomes. He had papers indicating he was a Sextus last night. Is he here accompanying the Quintus, or is he impersonating one? Or was last night the impersonation? And if he did see me touch the Sapper, then why not apprehend me, then and there? Why leave, then search for me later?

Something's not right, but I can't see what. And it makes me nervous.

The crackling of twigs underfoot, only a half hour later, exacerbates the feeling.

"You're needed, Rex." It's Brixia, glaring and out of breath from her search.

"For what?"

"Don't know." She looks at me with glinting eyes too small for her pudgy face. "But Matron didn't look happy."

I consider. If I run, right now—if I can subdue Brixia quickly and quietly, gather my hidden stash from my room, and flee before anyone else comes looking—then all the reasons I didn't do so long ago come into play. I'm recorded under the Hierarchy's census; it's the price I paid for stumbling half-starved into the orphanage a year and a half ago. They have my age, name, description. Even if two of those things are made up, it's the listing itself that is the issue.

Because as soon as I try to flee from what's seen as my place in the system, I'll be proscribed. Publicly made a prize for anyone who can capture and turn me in. The Hierarchy circulates those lists with terrifying efficiency. Within a day, there won't be an inhabited place that isn't dangerous for me.

And if Matron Atrox, her greed no longer a motivator, reveals my refusal to cede Will as well? Or worse, Hospius mentions what he saw? My bounty gets raised, and if I'm caught, there's a good chance I'll be confined until I turn eighteen. Destined for a Sapper unless I give up my resistance to the Aurora Columnae.

I clench my hand into a fist, then let my fingers loosen again. I'm not ready. I don't have enough coin, a solid plan, a direction.

"Coming."

We walk back to the house, Brixia looking sullen. There's a low, bemused chatter that drops away as we enter the hall, replaced by angry stares in my direction. They all think I'm sabotaging them somehow.

Matron Atrox straightens from her consoling of one of the younger boys, Lacrimo, whose interview plainly didn't go so well. Her eyes fix on me.

"Vis." She walks over. Leans close, so only I can hear. "I don't know how you managed to get his ear, but I swear to you—if you foul this up for the children, or for me, there will be consequences."

I almost laugh. Just like the others, she thinks that this is what I want.

She leads me through a gauntlet of glares to the door to the library, clearing her throat and knocking. "I've found him, Quintus. He appears to have recovered." She shoots me a meaningful glance. Illness, evidently, was offered as an excuse for my absence.

"Send him in."

With a final glower, Matron Atrox opens the door and all but shoves me inside.

The orphanage's library is not much bigger than a large room. Worn couches sit beneath two long windows, though the view through them is only of the grey stone of the building next door. Shelves filled with Hierarchy-supplied books are everywhere.

Hospius—or whatever his name actually is—reclines in a chair on the opposite side of the table that dominates the middle of the room. He indicates the seat across from him.

"Vis."

"Sextus." I sit. Resist the urge to say more, to risk filling the silence with things he may not yet know.

"Quintus, actually. Quintus Ulciscor Telimus. I . . . apologise for yesterday evening. It was a necessary deception, and one fully sanctioned by Military." Ulciscor—for now, I'll assume the name isn't another fake—fiddles with the sleeve of his shirt. "You're not surprised to see me."

"I saw you come in." I consider what he's just told me. If Military really did send him to the prison, it would explain the quality of his false credentials.

And mean that I have absolutely no hold over him.

"Hm." Even seated, the man opposite is imposing as he scrutinises me, rubbing the dark stubble on his chin. I get the impression this wasn't how he expected his introduction to go. "And you didn't think to mention to the matron that you'd already met me? That I used a different name?"

"There didn't seem to be much point."

"Because you wouldn't be believed?"

"Because you wouldn't have come here, if you didn't think you could pass a closer inspection."

Ulciscor, to my surprise, nods in an almost pleased manner. He waits for me to ask why he's here. When I don't, he lets his gaze rove to the books surrounding us. "How many of these have you read?"

I pause at the change in direction. "A few." A large portion of this library has been irrelevant to me since the day I arrived—the material is aimed at younger children, or those with less tutelage-heavy backgrounds. The rest, I'd all but memorised from lack of alternatives within my first few months here.

"Not as good a range as the Bibliotheca, I imagine."

The words cut through me. Delivered so casually, but those deep brown eyes across the table are stalking my every nervous twitch.

"Not even close. Matron Atrox used to send me there sometimes, when she realised I was too old for a lot of what's here." Not a perfect recovery, but it's not bad.

"Used to?"

"When I got older, she decided my time was better spent elsewhere." As soon as she realised there was no chance of my getting adopted, in fact. It's why, after every fight, I've been using a portion of my winnings to bribe the Bibliotheca's night guard for entry instead. Studying any and every subject I can in those last spare hours before returning here. At first, it was to find a way to avoid ceding—some distant Catenan province where it wasn't a requirement, maybe. Or a little-known legal loophole. An historical precedent. *Anything.* And after I uncovered only bad options like the archipelago from the travelogue, I kept going there anyway because knowledge is always useful, and I was learning more about Will and how Catenan society works than I could ever have through mere observation. More knowledge meant more ways to hide. More avenues to survival.

But it was also simply because the time there, lost in those books . . . it reminded me of Suus. My lessons, once something I hated. Once something I shirked.

It felt like, just for a few hours, I got to live a sliver of my old life again.

Of course, without a way to earn any extra coin, that's all over now.

I'm growing increasingly tense—which, I think, is the point. Ulciscor's prodding, poking. Trying to unsettle me. He somehow knows, or at least suspects, where I was last night.

I let my shoulders slump, a quaver enter my voice.

"And . . . I've been sneaking back there, some nights. You obviously know. I'm sorry. I just . . . I don't have any other way to see her anymore."

Ulciscor, for the first time, is visibly thrown. "Who?"

"I'm not going to tell you her name." I let some defiance seep into my voice. A boy in love, not wanting to get his lover into trouble. It's a contingency meant for Matron Atrox, but it will do just fine here. "And if you need to punish me, I understand. But I'm *not* going to give her up."

It's a decent story. It fits the recklessness of what I've been doing, provides motivation for most of my actions. I could even work in my refusal to cede Will, if it came down to it.

Ulciscor adjusts his sleeves again; it seems to be a habit of his when he's thinking. I stare down at the table, trying to look a mix of determined and vulnerable. I was a terrible actor when I left Suus. I'm much, much better now.

After an interminably long silence, there's a disappointed sigh.

"You're not in trouble, Vis."

I plaster hope on my face and look up again. Ulciscor waves at me tiredly. "It seems I've made a mistake. You can go."

I still want to know how he knew about the Bibliotheca, but I'm not about to ask. I thank him with the sort of nervous profuseness he'd probably expect for such a reprieve, and hurry for the door.

"Another step, I kill you." He says it in clear, quiet Vetusian.

I like to believe that I'm quick on my feet, but when someone issues a death threat in a language you're not supposed to know, your mind and body fight themselves.

I flinch. Stumble. Stop.

I know I've given myself away, but try to rescue it regardless. "Is that the language you were speaking last night?" I'm still facing the door.

"Sit back down, Vis." It's not a suggestion this time.

I'm frozen. There's no running, not from a Quintus. No way to fight him, either. I force air back into my lungs. "I have coin."

"Not interested."

Unsurprising. The panic subsides enough for my body to come back under my control, and I turn to see Ulciscor watching me. Not angry, not wary, not stern. Just thoughtful.

But there is a black tint that's fading from his eyes.

I return to my seat, trying not to shake.

"That was a good try." Ulciscor sounds reluctantly impressed. "Impossible to prove, but plausible. Relatable enough that anyone with a romantic bone in their body wouldn't come down too hard on you. Take away your understanding my conversation last night, and I might have believed it."

I'm not inclined to enjoy the praise. "How did you know?"

"A man's face is different when he's hearing and when he's listening. Something about the eyes." Ulciscor shrugs. "If it's any comfort, I almost missed it."

It's not.

There's silence as I struggle with the situation. Maybe all of this is just about what I overheard.

"I didn't really catch much of what you said to the prisoner. And I barely understood what I did."

"Any of it is too much." There's implied menace in Ulciscor's gentle smile. "But I think there may be a way we can work this out, to both our benefits. So let's start again. Without the lies, this time."

"Alright," I lie.

"Good. Now. Let's start with the Sapper. I saw you touch it last night. Don't deny it," warns Ulciscor, stilling any protest I might have made. "Do you know why you weren't affected?"

There's too much confidence across the table for repudiations. "No."

Ulciscor nods, approving my lack of dissembling. "I have a theory, but first I need you to cede some Will to me. Just a little."

There's a sudden, familiar heaviness in my chest. This is traditionally the first question that's asked in an adoption interview, given it's the easiest way to assess someone's strength of Will. It's also where the interview traditionally ends, for me. Usually accompanied by outrage. Shouting. Punishment.

"No."

Ulciscor doesn't even twitch. "It will only take a minute. But I need you to do this if we are to work out this little problem between us."

"Still no." I say it firmly. I used to prevaricate, apologise and make excuses, as if I was in the wrong for refusing. It only ever made things worse.

Ulciscor leans forward. "Vis, let me prove my theory and I will forget about last night. I will give you as much money as you need. I will get you out of this orphanage, ensure you are in line for whatever position you'd like. A word from me, and you'll start life after here as a Sextus, no matter the career you choose. I'll guarantee you all of this in writing if I need to. Sealed with my Will. All you have to do is cede for a minute."

It's the most I've been offered, ever, by a long way. Unfortunately for Ulciscor, I'm just as comfortable rejecting the carrot as taking the stick. "Thank you, Quintus—that's very generous—but my answer hasn't changed. It *won't* change."

I make sure not to even hint at the molten anger that sits, hard and heavy, somewhere in the pit of my stomach. This is the dividing line: me on one side, the people who killed my family on the other. The idea of crossing it revolts me. I'm not even tempted.

The corners of Ulciscor's mouth quirk upward.

My grimly certain strength falters as I frown back at him, too confused to do anything else. Wondering if I'm somehow misinterpreting the expression. He looks *pleased*.

"You haven't been through the Aurora Columnae rituals," the man opposite concludes with satisfaction.

My blank look lingers, and then I exhale as I understand. Of course. I'm so used to being defensive, so thrown by this surreal conversation, that I missed it. "You think that's why the Sapper didn't work on me." That's my theory, too—there's only one obvious distinction between me and everyone else in the Hierarchy—but it feels like Ulciscor's conclusion is more than just a guess.

"It's something I heard years ago. Just idle speculation from . . ." He trails off. A flash of melancholy. "I'd forgotten about it until last night."

"So you're here to make sure I keep quiet, then." I don't hide my bitterness. A potential immunity from, or even just resistance to, the Sappers is something that the Hierarchy wouldn't want getting out.

"Partly." Ulciscor looks at me like a puzzle he needs to solve. "Why don't you want to cede?"

"So I can walk around exhausted all day like those children outside? Eventually become an Octavii and lose, what—ten, fifteen years off my life?"

He ignores that last part, even though the Hierarchy doesn't officially admit it. "I'm not talking about refusing to cede to your matron out there, or refusing to be slotted into some dead-end pyramid. That, I understand. But not submitting to an Aurora Columnae at all? I assume you've at least been taken to one before." I give a dour confirmation. "Surely that would be worth it, even if it's just to have the ability in adoption interviews."

"They can't force me."

"I imagine they tried." His gaze flickers unconsciously to my shoulder. He knows about my scars, has guessed their origin. Which means he was at the fight, too, or has at least heard a report on it. I assumed as much—it would be strange if he knew about the Bibliotheca and not that—but it still makes me cornered prey.

"Not hard enough." I let him know I saw the glance and understand what it means. "Why do you care?"

"Because it means that what I have to offer will be of particular interest to you. I can guarantee you won't be asked to cede Will again for at least another year. And after that, you may even be able to earn the chance to go somewhere that won't require you to cede at all."

"No such place."

Ulciscor pulls a book from somewhere under the table. It takes me a moment to recognise the travelogue. The one I took last night, that's supposed to be safely hidden in my room.

"How . . ."

"I ducked upstairs after I used the facilities earlier. Don't worry, nobody saw. The rest of your little stockpile is still there."

I scowl. "How did you *find* it?"

"I'll give you until the end of our conversation to figure that out." He waves a finger. "But we're getting distracted. I'm in a position to help you. You *might* be in a position to help me. That's what matters."

I stare at the book. Verbalised or not, Ulciscor's uncovered enough that the warning is there among the promises. That's how the Hierarchy operates, after all: the potential of reward ahead, the menace of punishment chasing behind. Even if only one of them is usually real.

"Alright. I'm listening." I exhale the words a little fatalistically. The decision's made. Whatever else may be happening here, we're still talking, which means that I have something Ulciscor wants. I can work with that.

And gods know—if he's telling even half the truth, I can't afford to pass up this opportunity.

Ulciscor beams.

The questions start.

It's slow, at the beginning. Boring, if the discussion were in another context. Ulciscor is prodding around the basics of my education, the sorts of things well covered in the books around us. My understanding of the Hierarchy, its structure, its laws and traditions. Geography, which areas are considered provinces, and which are simply "friends of Caten." Caten's own history, which I dutifully recite according to their accounts. Aside from the specifics of the latter, I knew the answers to all these questions before I left Suus.

But then the tone changes. We start to cover economic considerations of the spread of the Hierarchy into other systems of government. Philosophical takes on the morality of Will, its exponential growth and application. The mathematics of its distribution and how that's carefully balanced against the need for oversight and control. Even the debate over whether it could have contributed to, or even caused, the Cataclysm three hundred years ago. I'm taken aback at first. Some questions require the dredging of my memory for obscure books I read years ago. Some I outright don't know. A lot, I'm only able to answer thanks to my time at the Bibliotheca. And almost all require genuine extrapolation from me, actual thought rather than just recitation of facts.

Occasionally, Ulciscor will argue a point I've made or look disappointed in one of my answers. But I warm to the task, and more often than not, he appears satisfied when we move on. It starts to feel like the sparring conversations I used to have with Iniguez, my favourite tutor. The weathered old man with the straggly grey hair was the only one who never spoke down to me or deferred to me, never treated me as either child or prince. The only one who ever seemed interested in whether I was filling my own potential, rather than exceeding that of others.

Ulciscor and I talk for two hours, in the end. Matron Atrox checks on us five times in the guise of offering refreshments. Ulciscor accepts on her fourth interruption. When she opens the door the last time, she finds me wetting my throat with the drink she prepared for the Quintus. She doesn't look pleased.

For my part, I try to remember the situation and not enjoy the conversation too much. Ulciscor is an intelligent, well-educated man—the kind I haven't spoken with in years—but his motives, even his personality, remain inscrutable. There are flashes of passion when we talk about certain topics, or when he strongly objects to something I've said. And he's certainly interested in what I have to say. But he lets nothing significant slip.

When the questions stop, my mug is empty and throat sore. This is the most I've talked in one sitting for a long time.

"I think that will do," says Ulciscor. He sounds contemplative. "You've put your time at the Bibliotheca to good use. There are gaps, but nothing we can't fix."

I study his expression. "You have other concerns." I make sure I sound analytical rather than anxious. Ulciscor may not have made up his mind, but I have.

I want to see where this opportunity leads.

"Yes." He tugs absently at a sleeve as he locks his gaze with mine, searching. "Your temperament, for one."

Of course. The fight last night. A topic as yet untouched. "I can keep my temper under control."

"Easy to say, but it's in the way you bear yourself, Vis. The way you talk. I think you're so used to resisting, you don't know how not to."

I feel some irritation at the words, but now is fairly obviously not the time to display it. "I'm not sure there's a way for me to convince you, when it comes to that."

"Hm." Dissatisfied. "Tell me. Why did you fight naked, last night?"

"I was worried the Sextus would imbue my clothes. Stop me from getting away."

"He wouldn't have been able to. Refined, flexible materials and limited time, at his level . . . impossible. But I suppose you wouldn't have known that," Ulciscor allows. "Was that the only reason?"

"Why else would I do it?"

"I thought it might have been to embarrass him."

"I wanted to put him off, I suppose. But I didn't go out there hoping to humiliate him, if that's what you're asking."

"Alright." Ulciscor believes me. "You did show composure under pressure, earlier. The ability to think on your feet like that is useful. Your disposition, the other rough edges . . . we can likely smooth them out." He's only half talking to me. As if he's trying to picture me in a particular situation.

He's still wavering, though.

"The coin you gave me. You imbued it with Will."

Ulciscor blinks, focuses back on me. "Why do you say that?"

"You followed me to the fight and to the Bibliotheca, through all but empty streets, without me noticing—and you're working alone, otherwise why come here yourself and risk the trouble that false identity could cause you?" The first half of the interview, when I barely had to think about the questions, let me chew over the problem. This is the only explanation I could come up with. "Plus, you must have sent messengers to all the orphanages last night, but you knew I was here this morning. And I doubt you asked the matron for directions to my room, let alone had the time to search it for that loose panel in the wall."

A coin's supposed to be all but impossible to imbue, given that it's forged, but he *is* a Quintus.

Ulciscor reaches into his pocket. Displays a silver triangle. The tightness in my chest eases as he nods his decision.

"Alright," he says quietly. "Let's tell the matron the good news."

VI

THE HALL STILLS AS WE EMERGE FROM THE LIBRARY. Matron Atrox breaks from her conversation with Vermes and strides toward us, sparing me a glare as she does so. All the children are still here. Restless, understandably, after so long.

"Quintus! I hope Vis has not been making a nuisance of himself." She gives me another dark look. She's already implied several times to Ulciscor that I'm not to be trusted. Trying to mitigate the things she's imagining I'm saying about her, no doubt.

"Not at all. We've had a delightful conversation." Ulciscor talks so that everyone in the room can hear. "In fact—I've made my decision, Matron. If you could please fetch the paperwork, I would like to formalise the adoption."

Matron Atrox looks at him blankly. The expression, I note with some amusement, is mirrored behind her.

"For *Rex*?" It's Vermes, speaking into the shocked hush. He suddenly laughs, the concept so impossible to him that he thinks it's a joke. It still manages to come out as mostly a sneer. "Quintus, who did you really pick?"

A few other titters echo from Vermes's simpering coterie. They cut off quickly enough when Ulciscor's expression hardens. Matron Atrox opens her mouth but, seeing Ulciscor's face, instead pales and scurries off to collect the necessary documents.

"You're really taking *him*. Above any of *us*." Vermes has always been terrible at reading situations. Doesn't have the self-control or sense to know when to back down, either. "You know he wouldn't even cede when they dragged him to the Columnae, right? He's useless to anyone. He's a joke." He spits the words. There's a low mutter of agreement from some of the other older children, though they stay in the background. Smarter than Vermes by a hair, at least.

"Vermes, wasn't it?" Ulciscor gazes at the large boy. "Do you want to know why you haven't been adopted?"

Vermes blinks. Looks lost at the question.

"It's because you're a deeply unpleasant child," continues Ulciscor calmly. "Immature. Spiteful. And honestly, not very bright. So it doesn't matter how strong your Will is. Nobody wants to have someone like you living with them. You need to change, Vermes. Better yourself, or you'll be a Solum for the rest of your life."

His gaze sweeps the rest of the room. The other children cringe beneath it. Vermes's lip curls. He's bright red.

He turns and stalks away.

I watch him go, oddly tempted to call after him. Offer him some measure of comfort to balance the acid in Ulciscor's lecture. I've despised the boy for a long time, but I can't help but pity him, too.

"A little harsh, don't you think?" I murmur as the other children begin to drift from the hall, seeing that Ulciscor's decision has been made. They're bitterly disappointed. A few of the younger ones look on the verge of tears.

"Maybe if I had more time with him, I'd show him the compassion he needs. But kind words from me in passing aren't going to have any effect. Sometimes bullies are better off with the truth, no matter how unpleasant." He eyes me. "You disagree?"

"No."

Matron Atrox reappears, papers in hand. She begins laying them out on the table.

"Quintus," she says carefully, not looking at either of us as she fastidiously arranges the documents. "Before you finalise this decision, would we be able to have a word in private?"

"Certainly." Ulciscor doesn't blink at the request. "Vis, perhaps it's time to collect your belongings from your room."

"That's not necessary. Vis doesn't have—"

"Here." Ulciscor cuts her off as he unslings a satchel from around his shoulder. "Will this be big enough?"

I take the bag, glancing inside. There's only the travelogue in there. More than enough room for the coins I have hidden away.

"Thanks." I glance past him at Matron Atrox, who is giving me a look that promises violence, and then at Ulciscor. His back still to the matron, he gives me a near-imperceptible nod.

It only takes a few minutes for me to hurry upstairs, shift my stash from the hole in the wall to the satchel, and then return. I pass a few of the children in the passageways. They glare at me jealously. None say anything.

When I step back into the hall, Matron Atrox is seated at the table as Ulciscor signs documents. She's white. Trembling.

Ulciscor pauses his writing to glance up at her. She leaps to her feet.

"Vis." Her voice is tight, but it's not with anger anymore. She's *meek*, as she holds out a small leather bag. "These are your wages from Victorum and the prison. That

I've been . . . keeping, for you." She stumbles over the words. Her hand shakes as she proffers the purse.

I take it with a frown, surprised at the weight. When I glance inside, gold glitters back at me. No way to tell if it's the amount I've earned, but it looks about right.

Before I can respond, Ulciscor signs the last page with a flourish and straightens, clapping me on the back. "Ready?"

"I suppose so." It's all happened so fast. No one here I particularly want to bid farewell to, and no one who will care if I don't. As surreal as it is, there's nothing stopping me from leaving.

We start toward the door, but something makes me stop. I walk back to the matron. She looks old, smaller and more tired than I can ever remember seeing her. It doesn't matter, when I think about the scars on my back.

I lean forward so that my whisper carries to her ear. "I'm going to come back one day." There's no trace of anger in my voice.

Just promise.

Any façade she was maintaining falls away, and I see cringing terror in her green eyes. I stare at her a moment longer, locking her gaze to mine. Making sure she understands.

Then I'm walking away, out the door.

Ulciscor takes the lead once we're outside, and I'm content to follow, still acclimating to my life's seismic shift. It's colder than I expected. The sun from this morning has vanished, and heavy clouds to the west threaten rain.

"What did you say to her?" I ask eventually.

"Nothing that didn't need to be said." Nonchalant, but there's an edge somewhere underneath the words. "You?"

"Same."

It's mid-afternoon, and the streets of Letens are busy, though not as crowded as I know they will be in the market district. Ulciscor observes all the activity—Will-powered carts, clumps of pallid Octavii labouring for their Septimii, a group of younger Tensian children playing Victorum with wooden swords—with mild, albeit unimpressed curiosity. He clearly hasn't been here for long.

"So. I believe you owe me some more information." It's finally dawned on me that Ulciscor's taking me *somewhere*, but I know nothing beyond that. We're heading toward the city outskirts. Probably leaving Letens altogether.

"I'll explain everything on the way."

"To where?"

"Deditia."

Somewhere behind us, there's a scream of triumph from one of the children as she knocks her larger opponent to the ground, straddling him. I flinch. Not entirely at the sound. Before Caten was the capital of the world, it was the capital of Deditia.

But it's been three years, and the official story is that I'm dead. No one is looking for me anymore, if they ever were. Whether I'm here or in the country cocooning the beating heart of the Republic, it probably doesn't matter.

Besides. There's no going back, now.

※ ※ ※

TWENTY MINUTES OF WALKING—LARGELY IN SILENCE, AS IT appears Ulciscor does not wish to discuss anything further while we're among crowds— brings us to the edge of Letens.

I haven't been this way since I first arrived in the city eighteen months ago. It's changed. The squat, ramshackle wooden buildings that housed Octavii and their families have vanished, replaced by either towering façades of stone or the half-fleshed skeletons of them. Streets have been widened. Straightened. Paved. Octavii still roam them, but they're hard at work, using what remains of their strength to haul masonry or lumber. It's a hive of construction, Septimii barking orders and even what must be a Sextus, eyes clouded as she raises a massive slab up three full stories, allowing several struggling Octavii to secure the levitating stone.

Ulciscor has noticed the Sextus too. "Inefficient," he mutters disapprovingly.

It's enough of a conversational opening for me to take it. "They're building warehouses?" It's the only thing I can come up with. This is a strange part of Letens to be improving, otherwise. And I don't think most of these buildings are meant to be residences. The doors are too tall and wide, and there aren't enough windows.

"Part of Tensia's treaty with us was a split of any resources we harvested from their land. Grain and stone, mostly. They were never able to extract it efficiently themselves. Things only properly got underway six months ago, though."

"So this is all for storing it?"

"This is for storing the Tensian share. Though eventually, they'll realise they can't put it to good use and ask for our help in deploying it. Or this will all fill up, and they'll start selling it to us at cost." He talks absently, neither boasting nor sad at the prospect. Just assessing how events will play out.

"Then what happens to the Catenan cut?"

"It gets sent to Caten."

I scoff. "It can't have been much of a split, then." We're almost three thousand miles from the capital, and that's with the Sea of Quus in between. The logistics would be a nightmare.

Ulciscor just smiles.

Soon enough we're leaving the rising buildings and worn workers behind, moving past the line where a great stone wall once guarded the city—dismantled under the Hierarchy's treaty with Tensia, ensuring their reliance on Will alone for protection—and out onto a long, grassy plain. It's not hard to guess what we're angling toward. The white monolith, three-sided and impossibly tall, has marred the skyline since not long after we left the orphanage. I've wondered at its purpose since spotting it, but thought it best to follow Ulciscor's example and remain mute.

We're close enough to see it properly now. It's granite, I think, the white speckled with streaks of black. Perhaps thirty feet wide on each side. At least two hundred high. Taller? A single building also blights the plain, directly behind the column. It's huge as well, even comparatively, an unusually elongated mass of wood and steel and stone and even glass that dominates the landscape. Workers march, ant-like, along a paved road that skirts the monolith and scythes through the grass, connecting the structure to the city. Will-driven carts clatter along it.

And underneath the building, at points.

I stumble, not quite processing that last part. There are no supports visible, and yet it's suddenly clear, even from here, that the whole thing is just . . . *hovering*.

"What in the gods' names?" It comes out in a whisper, involuntary. I squint, but we're still too far away for me to make sense of it. If it's distance that's the problem, of course.

"It's a Transvect." The corners of Ulciscor's lips quirk upward as he takes in my reaction. "Never seen one?"

I shake my head, unable to rip my gaze from the sight.

"The anchoring point was completed six months ago." It's subtle, but there's a note of pride. "It's loaded and ready to depart. Just waiting on us, actually. We'll be in Deditia by morning."

"By morning," I repeat faintly. I've heard of Transvects before, of course—briefly studied the concept, in fact, all those years ago in Suus. Will-powered behemoths that move at several times the speed of the fastest horse, carrying massive loads of troops or supplies to the farthest corners of the world. Or in this case, I suppose, to its centre. It's not that I ever doubted their existence, exactly, but they always seemed too much like propaganda. An exaggeration of the Hierarchy's making, a story they circulated to vaunt their power. So I never really tried to envisage what a Transvect might actually look like. Certainly never imagined the sheer *size* of the thing.

Even staring at its reality, I can't bring myself to imagine this colossal, hovering creation moving fast. Or at all.

A gust of chill wind carries the first flecks of rain, and I draw my cloak tighter, shivering.

The walk to the Transvect is interminable; just when I think I've come to grips with the enormity of it, we get closer. It's mostly wood, but with what looks like enormous granite strips forming a core running along its belly. There are windows here and there. Massive doors for loading. The edge nearest the city tapers sharply for a few feet, a stone nose in the shape of a squat, sideways pyramid.

I can't remember the last time I felt so small.

We're hailed as we pass into the Transvect's shadow and near the stairs rising to a hundred-foot-long platform ahead, our path blocked by an officious-looking woman.

"Workers only," she calls out as soon as we're in earshot. It's a warning.

"And passengers," Ulciscor corrects her. He produces signed documents—he seems to excel at obtaining those—and proffers them with a cheerful flourish.

The woman—a Septimus; her movements are too energetic by far for an Octavus—snatches the papers disbelievingly. Scans them. Stops. Starts reading again, her face paling.

Her hand quivers as she returns them.

"Magnus Quintus Telimus. Welcome. Welcome. I was not told . . ." She's flustered.

I wait for Ulciscor to correct her on her misuse of his title, but he doesn't. More false credentials? "It's fine. May we proceed?"

"Of course. Of course you may." She looks at me. Reddens. "There was nothing about—"

"This is Vis Telimus. I trust that a family member accompanying me won't be a problem?" He starts digging under his cloak in exasperation. "I can provide those papers too, if I—"

"No. No. Not necessary. Of course, please proceed, Magnus. Master Telimus." I swear she almost bows.

Vis Telimus. Of course. I try not to let the new name bother me. It barely occurred to me, among everything else, that I was no longer a Solum. It shouldn't make a difference; Vis isn't my real name, and the nomenclature of an orphan was never a badge of honour.

And yet, Solum always felt more apart. Fitted with my relationship to the Hierarchy. This step is closer in symbol only, and yet part of me can't help but be uncomfortable with how personal it feels.

There's no time to linger on the thought. We climb past the woman, up onto the elevated stone platform. The Transvect fills my vision. We're about fifty feet from the very end, and I can see another stubby pyramid-shaped nose jutting from its front.

I've unconsciously paused at the top of the stairs, but Ulciscor nudges me forward. "We're in that one."

I head reluctantly toward where a sole door conspicuously gapes. There's a richly carpeted room within. Several comfortable chairs fixed to the walls. A cupboard at the back, and small tables with food on them. There's no one inside.

The Transvect is motionless as it hangs mid-air, not even a tremor to indicate that Will alone holds it aloft. I still hesitate.

Ulciscor moves past me and inside. He turns around, arms outstretched, then jumps up and down a couple of times to prove his point.

I glower at him, and step on.

Nothing gives as my weight leaves the safety of the platform. It's as solid as if I were walking on the ground.

Ulciscor watches my trepidatious first step with amusement, then shuts the door behind me and throws himself into a chair, looking entirely at home.

"It's just us?" This section isn't especially large, but I'm still surprised. None of the other ones I could see looked suitable for carrying people.

"No other passengers and completely unmanned. We have the whole thing to ourselves for the next fifteen hours." Ulciscor relaxes into his seat. "Hopefully enough time to answer your questions."

"Hopefully." Fifteen hours. Fifteen hours to travel near three thousand miles. I stand there, gazing around, a little awed. Daunted, in fact. Hate the Hierarchy though I do, some of the things they've achieved are truly incredible. It's been easy to forget, here on the edge of the continent, where only the most modest of their advancements are ever in evidence. "How much Will does this thing use?" Hardly my most pressing concern, but I'm still off-balance, need some time to gather myself.

Ulciscor waves me into the seat opposite him. "How much do you think?"

I can see in his eyes that it's another test, albeit an impromptu one. I take my time settling into a chair that's plush, more comfortable than anything I've sat on in years, and let my wonderment fade to assessment.

The basics of Will usage—*peliphagy*, the Catenans call it, though the term rarely enters common parlance—are relatively well-known. Any of the children back at the orphanage could have explained that a Septimus has eight Octavii ceding half their Will to them, a Sextus has seven Septimii ceding half of their *collected* Will, and so on up the pyramid through Quintus, Quartus, Tertius, Dimidius, and finally, Princeps. Each level higher becoming increasingly powerful. And the older children could do the resulting mathematics, too. A Septimus wields the equivalent of five people's Will: four from their combined Octavii, plus their own. That halves when they're ceding to a Sextus. A Sextus, therefore, starts with the Will of more than eighteen people. And so on.

But the nice, theoretical simplicity of the calculations end there: they're useful for understanding someone's *physical* strength, but that's only the most basic use of Will. Imbuing *objects*—controlling them through mental effort—is where the true power of the Hierarchy lies, exponentially increasing the efficacy of that strength for anyone who can do it. I can still only guess at how much, though. My studies at Suus only ever referenced estimates based on rumour and observation. And the Hierarchy doesn't exactly shout the secrets of high-level Will usage to the masses. I've eked out an understanding of some of the methods they use, over the years, but the exact costs and efficiencies surrounding it all remain murky to me at best.

Ulciscor knows this better than I do, of course; his questions have already exposed my lack in this area today. Which means he doesn't expect me to come up with an exact answer. Still, after hours of doing everything I can to impress him, I'm finding it difficult to resist the urge to show off a little.

"I think a single Quintus could probably power it," I say, repressing a shiver as I come to the realisation. The strength of fifty-five men, but worth so much more if properly applied.

"Really?" There's humour in Ulciscor's eyes, but also a spark of surprise. "You think I could run it by myself?"

"If you're not ceding." So he really is a Quintus. Probably. "Those separated stone strips underneath must be imbued, so I assume they're locked together with Will. Which means you wouldn't have to lift the entire thing, just the heaviest section." A method I read about in the Bibliotheca. I stare at the floor as I speak, brow furrowed. There were a half dozen of the weight-bearing stone slabs, at least. "You'd still need power to provide lift. But once that was done, you could use more imbuing to push or pull the whole thing fairly easily. I imagine that's what that giant stone column out there is for. The anchoring point, you called it?" I gesture back the way we came, my voice warming as I engage with the puzzle. "So, yes. You couldn't be on board yourself—I know self-propulsion isn't possible with Will—and you'd need the infrastructure, but otherwise I think you could move the entire thing."

I look up, concealing an onset of queasiness as I remember who I'm talking to. Ulciscor's watching me. The rain is starting to pick up outside, rattling the glass.

"Harmonic and Reactive," he murmurs eventually. "When objects are locked together, it's a Harmonic relationship. When they push or pull, it's a Reactive one." He leans back and smiles abruptly, waving his hand to indicate the information isn't important right now. "Most people assume it would take at least a Quartus to move one of these."

"Most people are stupid." It's an absent response, out of my mouth before I can stop it.

Thankfully it only prompts a guffaw from Ulciscor. "You're not wrong." Despite his amusement, he looks impressed by my analysis. "And it's not a bad guess, either. A strong Totius Quintus *could*, theoretically, power all the mechanisms that drive a Transvect. Of course, if something happened to them, the whole thing would come crashing down, so . . ."

"So you need to distribute the imbuing between multiple people for safety, if nothing else."

"Exactly."

There's movement outside the window, a worker checking something or other farther down the platform, half shielding herself from the inclement weather with a raised cloak. She steps back, waving a signal toward the ground.

There's the tiniest of jolts, and we start to rise.

I find myself gripping the sides of my chair as the platform recedes, though the motion itself is smooth, quite gentle. I'm not sure I'd even have noticed it if not for the windows. "Why are we going *higher?*" I peer down at the platform through streaks of water, an anxious strain to my voice. We're thirty feet above it, still climbing. Fifty off the ground.

"Easiest way to avoid obstructions. Rockfalls, landslides. Ships. People. That sort of thing."

"Ah." Our steady rise finally stops, and I clutch tighter to my seat. Seventy feet off the ground.

"Afraid of heights?"

I'm not—the cliffs of Suus were taller than this, and I climbed those all the time—but I'm not going to tell him that. My eyes are still glued to the increasingly distant illusion of safety. I can all but hear Ulciscor's grin.

The Transvect starts to move again. Forward, this time.

I'm mesmerised as the platform far below begins to slide from view. We move slowly at first but steadily build momentum; I press my face against the glass to try and see farther, marvelling at the vista both outward across the rolling plains and vast forests of Tensia, and back over the increasingly distant, sullen structures of her capital.

"Quite a sight, isn't it." There's no teasing to Ulciscor's voice this time.

I don't respond. Already our speed's increased enough that I can barely see the platform anymore. There's only one person still visible on it, absurdly tiny from this vantage. The woman who stopped us, I think.

"She called you Magnus Quintus." My queasiness has returned. I'd been hoping Ulciscor would bring this up on his own, but I have to mention it. I have to know, before anything else.

"It's my full title."

I continue to gaze out the window. Afraid that he'll see my dismay if I look at him. "Why didn't you tell me? Or the matron?" There's no way she knew.

"Her, because I didn't need her thinking she could use your adoption to some political advantage. It's why the proconsul agreed to leave it off the paperwork. Fairly standard stuff, when we have dealings in the provinces." I can hear the shrug in his voice. "And you, because it hadn't come up yet. Is it relevant?"

I almost laugh.

"Quintus"—*fifth*—is an enormously powerful position within the Hierarchy; there are twenty-four million people in the Republic, but most pyramids still peak at Sextus. The mayor of Letens, an important and well-respected man, is a Sextus—albeit a Totius Sextus, the very top of his pyramid. Proconsul Manius, the current governor of all Tensia and thus in charge of an entire Catenan province, is a Totius Quintus.

There are only three pyramids that stretch higher than Quartus, though: the three senatorial pyramids, which everyone refers to simply as Military, Governance, and Religion. Only the strongest, the most skilled, are recruited for those. Quintii from standard pyramids vie to become a Septimus in a senatorial one.

And only those in the senatorial pyramids are allowed to use the title "Magnus." Which makes Ulciscor one of the most powerful men in all the Hierarchy.

"Well, it's certainly a surprise." The Transvect is still picking up speed. Hurtling along, judging by how fast Letens is disappearing behind us. "You're a senator?"

"I am. The Senate will need to ratify your adoption, actually—it won't be official until that happens," Ulciscor adds absently. "You'll need to present yourself to them in Caten, at some point."

"Is that necessary?"

"It's just a formality." The distracted reproach in his tone means yes, it is necessary. "The name Telimus may not be universally beloved like a Valerius or a Tulius, but its history is still proud. The Senate will want to make sure I'm not opening a door for someone who doesn't deserve it."

I nod, not knowing how else to react, focusing on the streaks of water sliding sideways across the glass outside. There's the sudden, sinking dismay of being trapped. Wondering if I've acted rashly.

Nothing to be done about it now, though. I steel myself, tear my gaze from the window. We're high enough that I can't really see the ground anyway, unless I lean. "So. Why am I here, Father?"

Ulciscor allows a smirk at that. "Good question, Son. Have you heard of the Catenan Academy?"

"Of course." Everyone in the Hierarchy knows about the Academy. The children of senators and knights are usually privately tutored, but some very few get to spend the last eighteen months of their childhood at Caten's most prestigious institute. Being groomed for leadership, politics, the Senate. Catenan dignity and glory.

Ulciscor stares at me steadily, waiting.

"Oh. *Oh.* Me?" I snort a laugh. The concept is so absurd, I'm sure he's joking. "You need me to become a Magnus, too?"

"Not exactly." Ulciscor is smiling back, but none of my humour is reflected in his eyes.

My own smile withers into something more sickly. "You said I wouldn't have to cede."

"You won't. The Academy is the one place in all the Republic where ceding Will, or receiving it, is forbidden. They want it to be a level field for every student. 'A ladder should not be climbed from the shoulders of others,' and all that." The last is clearly a quote, though I don't recognise it. "We're on our way there now, in fact—I arranged for the Transvect to be realigned. We'll need to present you in person to make your application official."

I'm silent, trying vainly to grasp the enormity of it. I do remember hearing somewhere that Will usage was banned in the Academy. That doesn't mean I'm convinced. "There will always be something, though. Some emergency. Some test you don't know about that ends with them asking me to cede."

"I was a student there myself. They *expel* anyone who's found breaking that rule, even if it's during trimester breaks away from the school. There are no exceptions. Never have been." Ulciscor's dark brown eyes are earnest. Excited. He thinks he has a winning argument.

"You said this was an opportunity." There's plainly a reason Ulciscor wants me at the Academy, but before we address that, I want to fathom why he thinks *I* want to be there. I feel like I'm missing something. "I don't want to appear ungrateful, but . . . all that would really do is make my life easier for a while. Once I leave, I'm no better off."

"No one graduating from the Academy has ever been assigned a position lower than Sextus. And the better you do there, the more choice you'll have. Finish high enough, and you could be a Totius. Never have to cede Will at all."

I curse inwardly at his misplaced enthusiasm as I understand. Ulciscor's made the assumption—a reasonable one, given what I've said thus far—that I'm only intent on avoiding *ceding* any Will. He hasn't even considered the possibility that my distaste extends to being part of the system at all.

"What if I don't want to receive Will, either?" I could let it slide, but Ulciscor's about to tell me why I'm really here—which he doesn't want widely known, given his secretive visit to Nateo. I'm past the point of backing out, but my options will be even more limited once he's entrusted me with that information.

Ulciscor blinks. Thrown.

"There are some positions like that," he says slowly. "The Keepers of the Eternal Flame in Caten. Special auditors under the Censor, who need to operate without even a hint of undue influence. Of course, you'd need to be a virgin woman for the first, and a retired senator for the second. Those might be out of your reach." He thinks. Reluctant. "You *could* ask to be assigned to the ambassador in Jatiere, I suppose. Our treaty with them says that no one from the embassy is allowed to use Will. But it's far from prestigious. And very unusual. You would have to finish in Class Three—that's the top-ranked class—for the Senate to even consider letting you choose a post like that. And the only way you could be certain of it is if you finished Domitor of the entire Academy." There's doubt in his voice. As impressed as he's been with me, he doesn't think I'm on that level.

He pauses. Studies me. "Very few people's Will comes from the Sappers. And there are ways of making sure that none of yours would," he adds, sympathetic.

I show him a quietly grateful expression. Let him think my reluctance stems only from what I saw in Letens Prison.

Secretly, though, there's a thrill at what he's just revealed. I've no desire to remain in *any* official position within the Hierarchy, long-term, but this sounds like an option I can live with for a while. A chance to survive, to keep searching for a real way out, without having to utterly betray myself in the process.

I could buy *years*, if I needed to.

"Alright." I'm pleased with how composed I sound. No need to let Ulciscor know how badly I want this. "So why am I going to the Academy?"

"Because we—Military—need eyes and ears in there."

"You need a spy." I smirk, despite myself. "In a school."

"A school that hosts children from the most prestigious families in the Republic, where student rankings can determine the future leadership of Caten." Ulciscor doesn't share my mirth. "Religion's security is as good as any fortress. Better, in fact. They provide the Praeceptors, the guards, even the Octavii who cook and clean. It's a stronghold, Vis. A little nation unto itself."

"Even to the rest of the Senate?"

"Especially to the rest of the Senate." The certainty in Ulciscor's tone wipes away any doubts. "Religion's mandate clearly encompasses education, and the Academy is their crown jewel. Military demanding access would be like Religion demanding control of the Seventh Legion. It's simply not done."

I nod understanding. "Not without proof of some sort of wrongdoing." Of course. Military, Religion, and Governance each have their own areas of authority in the Republic; while I've heard those are a source of constant tension and bickering between the three senatorial pyramids, responsibility for the Academy seems clear-cut. Challenging that boundary—making any move on another pyramid's authority within the Senate—would be an ugly precedent.

I say no more, turning my last statement into a question.

"Yes. Well. That's the *interesting* part, I suppose." Ulciscor is wry, almost embarrassed. "We're not exactly sure what they're hiding in there. We're confident it's something important, but we don't have enough information to speculate as to what it might be yet."

"Oh. Good. So . . . you want me looking for proof of . . . *something*." I motion expansively, emphasizing all which that encompasses as I deadpan the vagueness of the task. "Easy."

"If it was easy, we wouldn't need you."

I grunt an accession to that. "Any suggestions as to what I should be looking for at least?"

Ulciscor tugs at a sleeve. "Our best guess, so far, is that it's to do with Solivagus itself—the island where the Academy is located. Religion has exclusive use of the entire place." He hesitates. "There are a lot of old ruins there."

"How old?" From the way he said it, and his conversation with Nateo earlier, I already know the answer.

"Pre-Cataclysm."

"So you think they're searching for some piece of lost technology?" Those are rare finds, these days.

"Or a weapon."

I shift uneasily. No one knows what caused the Cataclysm, the world-spanning disaster three centuries ago that left less than five people in every hundred alive. Most of the survivors were mere children, too; records to emerge out of the chaotic decades that followed were few, and the ones that did recalled towns filled with the dead. Cities burning. Whole nations erased in a moment.

But almost nothing of any of the times before that.

It seems clear, from what has since been uncovered, that pre-Cataclysm civilisation used Will in ways the Hierarchy is still struggling to understand. The purpose of the Aurora Columnae, which are the only reason Will can be ceded at all, was only realised by the Catenan Republic a century and a half ago. The Sappers, too, were discoveries rather than inventions. And many of the Hierarchy's other advancements have come from deconstructing devices excavated from old ruins, rather than any particular Catenan ingenuity.

Which means that an actual weapon from back then has the potential to be very, very dangerous.

"Why would Religion be looking for something like that?" I let puzzlement inflect the words, though there's an obvious conclusion. "And keeping it secret from Military?"

There's more than a suggestion of irritation in the look Ulciscor gives me. He's not buying the nonplussed act. "We can discuss that later. Maybe. For the moment, all you need to know is that it's a possibility."

Interesting. Matias, one of my tutors at Suus, used to theorise that the dynamics of power between the senatorial pyramids would change drastically once there was no one left to conquer. Perhaps even become antagonistic. I always dismissed it as wishful thinking.

"Alright." I tuck the information away without further comment, for now. "I assume there are particular people you think might be doing the looking, at least?"

"The Principalis of the Academy. Quintus Veridius Julii." It's subtle, but there's something about the way that Ulciscor shifts when he says the name. An almost imperceptible hardening around the eyes. He doesn't like the man.

"Veridius. I heard you use that name at the prison."

"I think he put Nateo in there. Organised for him to be Sapped. I was hoping to figure out why." Ulciscor's admission is grim. "Nateo graduated from the same class as Veridius six years ago. Veridius was Domitor of that year, and every tie he had—everything he'd said, every action he'd taken up until the moment he won the Iudicium—indicated that he was going to join us. Join Military, like the rest of the Julii. But instead, he asked for a position at the Academy. Under Religion."

"And that was . . . strange," I infer.

"Very. Controversial, too. Not the switching of loyalties, so much, but asking for a role that commanded so little prestige. We all thought he'd been blackmailed, pressured into the decision somehow. And the way he won the Academy's final test, the Iudicium . . . well. Two other students were killed. Accidents, supposedly." There's an edge to Ulciscor's voice at that, and he pauses before pressing on.

"The outrage around it all eventually faded, but we've been keeping an eye on him ever since, trying to figure out what really happened. He was Principalis of the Academy within a year, when his predecessor died. Natural causes, as far as we could tell." Thick doubt in the statement. "But as soon as Veridius was in charge, he started changing things. The Academy's main campus used to be in Caten, but Veridius's class was moved to Solivagus due to the grain riots of 297, and Veridius insisted that it be housed there permanently once he took over. He said it was because there was rampant cheating, that the island was the only way to properly isolate the students. Religion backed him. And ever since then, others from his year—like Nateo—have been quietly disappearing. More "accidents," or imprisonments, or sudden assignments to the far corners of the Republic. Nothing categorical. Nothing actionable. But there's a pattern." He leans forward. Intense. "So. You see why we're suspicious?"

I contemplatively acknowledge that I do; Ulciscor lapses into silence, and I don't say anything for a while, thinking. It's still mid-afternoon outside, but clouds have turned the sky a threatening black, rain assailing the Transvect loudly and constantly. There's forest below us, the nearer treetops blurring along the bottom of my view out the water-streaked window. Given how fast we must be moving, the interior of the carriage feels little different to when we started. I'm surprised at how rapidly I've become, if not exactly *comfortable*, then at least accustomed to this mode of travel.

"Why not just get another Military student to spy for you? Someone who's already meant to be attending?" I have a lot more questions, but I'll start with the obvious.

"Veridius won't have evidence just lying around, which means you're going to have go looking in places that could get you expelled if you're caught. Maybe worse, depending on what you find. Not many parents or students are willing to risk that. Not when just attending means so much to them." He sounds vaguely bitter. "Besides, we can't trust them. Half of them would go straight to Veridius, try to leverage what they know into a better ranking as soon as they got there. The other half just wouldn't bother making the effort."

I grunt, following the logic. "But you can trust *me*, because if I don't find something before I graduate, you'll . . . what? Force me to use the Aurora Columnae, then sell my Will? Give me to Military so they can experiment with the Sappers?" Both legally feasible options for Ulciscor, now he's adopted me.

"Something like that." There's not a whisper of either humour or apology from the man. It's just the way it is.

"What if I can't find anything? Or I get caught?"

"Look harder, and don't." His matter-of-factness eases into something approaching empathy. "But let's hope it doesn't come to that."

"Let's." I hadn't expected better, but it's discomforting to hear so plainly. He's not worried about me turning on him—the scars on my back have told him how much his threat means to me. And even if I was willing to risk it, who would give me a better deal? I have the knowledge of Military's suspicions, of which Religion will doubtless already be aware. Some limited utility as a double agent, perhaps. Nothing that would make me particularly valuable to Religion. Nothing that would protect me from the fate I'm trying to avoid. "Isn't it going to be obvious why you're sending me there?"

"Not if you distinguish yourself. It's not uncommon for senators to adopt someone they're confident will do well. Someone they can see themselves guiding into a position of influence one day." He taps a finger against his chair. "On the other hand, Veridius himself will *absolutely* know why you're there. He's too smart and too mistrustful not to. He won't expel you without cause—that would only risk triggering an investigation—but you're going to have to be careful around him."

"So we'll each know the other's up to something, but be pretending not to. Wonderful." I rub the back of my neck, trying to ease the tension there. "You're placing a lot of faith in the abilities of someone you've just met."

"Well. From all appearances you're bright enough, given how you've managed to educate yourself." A tinge of wryness to that. Like everyone else since Suus, I've told Ulciscor that I'm from a middle-class Aquirian family, that my parents were killed in an accident not long before that country signed the Hierarchy's treaty, and that all our property was claimed by the nobility upon their death. The timeline matches closely with the invasion of Suus, and our language and culture were somewhat similar. It's also a common enough story from a region that was infamous for its lack of documentation. Which makes it completely unverifiable.

Ulciscor is suspicious—I've spent half of today showing him the fruits of a royal education that spanned the first fourteen years of my life, after all—but for the moment, he seems content enough to leave the matter alone.

"That can't be the only reason you chose me," I press, my words punctuated by a distant peal of thunder. It's starting to storm properly outside. "You're a Magnus

Quintus; it would be *nothing* for you to find some prodigy from among the Octavii to use, or even the Septimii. Any of them would leap at the chance to become a Telimus and attend the Academy. And *they* would all be willing to cede." I make a point of that last part. It has to have been a factor in all this, though I can't see why.

"Which would mean I had no hold over them." Ulciscor gives me a vexed look, but eventually nods. "And fine. Yes. A few of the other students won't have been to the Aurora Columnae yet, either. Since Veridius took over, he seems to have preferred applicants who have never ceded before. Not openly, of course, but the pattern is there to see for anyone who's looking. That's a *very* rare quality in someone your age." He pauses, deep brown eyes never wavering as they meet mine. "I have a question of my own, actually."

"Alright."

"You say you haven't ceded at the Aurora Columnae because you don't want to be an Octavii. Which I understand, but . . . I saw your scars. I saw how many there were." He's quiet, but there's an intensity to the statement. As if he's furious on my behalf.

"That's not really a question." When he keeps looking at me, I sigh. "I held out because I'm convinced the alternative would be worse. It's that simple."

"No, it's not. Conviction is admirable, but it can only take a man so far." He leans forward. "So what I want to know, Vis, is what are you punishing yourself for?"

I stare at him, a jolt of sick, uncomfortable emotion low in my chest, lost for how to respond.

The Transvect shudders.

I grasp the arms of my chair, almost relieved at the distraction, then tighten my grip as I see Ulciscor doing the same. "Is it supposed to—"

"No." Ulciscor's peering out the window, his question forgotten. We're still moving fast but there's a real judder to the Transvect now, a thick, unsteady vibration that rattles my teeth.

And it looks as if the forest below is creeping closer.

"Emergency stop, I think. There must be some damage. We might be delayed a while." Ulciscor stands, steadying himself against the top of his chair before staggering over to the window on the other side and squinting out toward the front of the slowing behemoth. Unlike me, he's not overly concerned.

That changes when the section in front of ours explodes.

VII

ULCISCOR UTTERS A CURSE AND STUMBLES BACK AS THE RAIN-streaked glass in front of him shatters. Blazing, orange heat roars inside. I'm flinching to my feet, unsteady against our shuddering descent, though I'm not sure what I can do. The Transvect is still moving fast enough that the flames look like they're pouring off the timber, flattened by the momentum. Flowing toward us.

"Maybe more than a while!" shouts Ulciscor over the thundering hiss of rain and shrieking of wind as it pounds through the carriage. His eyes have gone completely black as he moves, much more smoothly this time, away from the flames and over to a large window farther along. He peers through, down at the storm-shrouded forest rushing past.

"Are we under attack?" I raise my voice as well, an arm up to shield against the heat and light as I reel my way over to him. That was an explosion. No suggestion of a simple fault now.

The Transvect has slowed enough that the trees below are passing at a less dizzying rate, though still considerably faster than I'd like. The tallest ones are edging closer. Shadows from the blaze in front of us create deranged, flickering orange-and-black motion in the nearest foliage as we hurtle past.

I'm on the edge of panic, but I've been there a lot over the past few years. I know how to control myself through it.

"Does it matter?" Ulciscor is disconcertingly unaffected by either the cacophony or the roasting heat creeping toward us. He strides—impossibly balanced, compared to my desperate clinging to the seat next to me—to the very back of our section, then crouches, peeling back one of the thick rugs.

"What are you doing?"

"A friend of mine used to imbue Transvects. Every section should have . . . *ah!*" He's triumphant as he grips something beneath the rug and twists. The grinding's audible even above the assault of the shrieking wind, and suddenly there's a square about three feet in diameter missing in the floor.

"Access hatch," explains Ulciscor calmly as he straightens.

"To *where?*"

Ulciscor replies by taking two long steps across and grabbing me by my bad shoulder, spinning me roughly. I don't have time to react to the pain before the window to my left shatters and glittering, orange-flecked splinters arrow past as Ulciscor shields me with his body. Fresh, icy wind whips us, a counterpoint to the encroaching inferno.

Ulciscor doesn't seem to be injured, holding me in place as effortlessly as he would an infant. "There's a platform underneath. Stone above and below. We can shelter there without you being burned alive." His midnight eyes reflect my terrified visage back at me.

I feel my teeth bare in resistance to the concept, but the heat pressing at my back is too compelling an argument. Ulciscor goes first, dropping through the opening as easily and lightly as if he did it all the time, landing so that his head is still visible above the floor. He motions for me to follow, then ducks down and out of sight.

I lurch to the edge of the hatch, the icy air shrieking through it threatening my balance almost as much as the quivering of the Transvect itself.

I'm not enthused by what I see when I look downward. Ulciscor, it turns out, exaggerated when he described the section below. It's a stone pillar about two feet wide, and from my position, I can see flame-lit treetops on either side of it. It's not a platform.

"This is not a platform!" I yell, unable to contain a slightly hysterical note.

There's no response, and the crash of more glass behind me gives me little choice. I perch on the edge before awkwardly sliding through, injured shoulder creaking, stone scraping against skin through my tunic. There's a surge of panic when my feet dangle what feels like too far down, but then Ulciscor's steadying me with that impossibly iron grip, lifting me the rest of the way as if I weighed nothing. I'm shorter than he is, barely able to see back into the cabin. What I can make out is already bathed in fire.

"Duck."

I obey the command; a moment later the stone hatch is sliding back into place, sealing away the inferno. Ulciscor's still holding me with one hand, but I clutch a rain-slicked beam with manic determination anyway. The treetops are less than twenty feet below us now, flickering past, still disappearing into the darkness far too fast. The wind howls, rips at me, trying to tear me from my perch. Stray droplets of rain sneak their way underneath the Transvect somehow, stinging at exposed skin. Above us, the conflagration continues to thunder around the cracking of wood.

It hasn't been thirty seconds since the explosion.

Ulciscor tightens his grip on my arm, dragging my attention to him. "When the Transvect is about to hit the trees," he yells calmly, "we jump."

"*What?*" I try unsuccessfully to shy back, stopped by his vise-like hand.

Ulciscor's attention has returned to the blurred treetops below, which whip in the storm. This is an old forest; those trees are a hundred and fifty feet tall, maybe more. "Get ready."

"No. I don't think so. Not a chance." It comes out as a mutter. I still can't extricate myself from the Quintus's grasp.

If Ulciscor hears, he doesn't bother to respond. Instead, he turns and wraps me in an embrace that I'm powerless to resist. Lifts me off my feet.

"Here we go," he yells in my ear.

He leaps and twists, facing his back in the direction we're hurtling.

My stomach lurches. I think I shout, or try to, but there's a screeching from behind us, a rending that fills the night and covers any sound I might make. I have the impression of the flaming Transvect plunging on without us, a pyre against the thunderclouds. Then branches rushing up, snapping and tearing. There's a sickening lurch as we glance to the side off a tree trunk. Ulciscor's grasp never wavers.

We hit the ground.

Air explodes from my lungs as we bounce and roll and skid to a stop in the damp; I gasp, cough, flail weakly against Ulciscor's grip. It's instinct, panic. I know he's taken the brunt of the impact. Saved my life. Somewhere ahead of us there's a blast of sound, a thundering reverberation that crashes over us and through the trees beyond. Ulciscor's embrace finally slackens and I roll away, just in time to see a hellish glow vanishing behind thick foliage and sleet.

"Ulciscor." I'm still on the ground as I turn back to him. Fear the worst when I realise he hasn't made a sound yet.

Sudden movement and a pained growl make me start. I crawl over, putting a hand on the prone man's shoulder. "Are you alright?"

"What do you think?" Ulciscor groans and rolls over, glaring up at me. His eyes are still flooded with darkness. Despite his grumbling, he doesn't seem to be favouring any particular injuries.

I stagger to my feet. Badly bruised, shaken, still winded. But able to move everything. The wind and rain are not as bad down here, the leafy canopy providing some protection. I offer Ulciscor my right hand, and he pulls himself up with another groan, which I echo at the strain. "What was that?"

"Will shell, I think. Easy to make. Must have been hidden in the section ahead of us." He massages a leg, wincing.

I recall the term. The Catenan legions used them decades ago, before Birthright was extended to foreign combatants. "What do we do now?"

The big man tests each limb gingerly. "We get back to the Transvect."

"Is there any point?"

"If the core lift and propulsion mechanisms are undamaged, then there are some simple override levers in the front cabin. I can use those to get us moving again."

"And if they're damaged?"

"Then we're walking a little farther."

I grunt. Easy for the Quintus to say. We have no food or water. And we've been travelling into Tensia's vast northern wildlands for at least a half hour, moving incredibly fast. It won't be a short hike back to civilisation.

Ulciscor ignores my lack of enthusiasm, gripping my shoulder. Half to steady me, half for himself. He's hurting more than he lets on, I think. "Come on. And keep quiet. That explosion only did enough to bring the Transvect down, not destroy it."

"You think someone wanted it intact?" I'm dubious.

"Well. Not *intact*, I suppose. But we've been close to starving out the Anguis down here, and there was certainly plenty of grain on board. On the other hand, it could have been sabotage from Tensian dissidents, who didn't know how to use the Will shell effectively. Hope for the latter but plan for the former, I suppose." He bends down, rooting around in the grass and pocketing something, then gestures cheerfully in the direction the Transvect disappeared.

I watch the ease with which he's moving again, then glance back in the direction we fell, squinting and shielding my eyes from the heavy droplets that are making it through the canopy above. The brooding clouds aren't enough to hide the devastation our path down carved, describing an almost perfect tunnel of destruction through the foliage. Several heavy branches are hanging like broken limbs; one tree in particular has snapped at the trunk, its upper half almost at right angles as it rests awkwardly against its neighbour.

It's not a *small* tree, either.

I shiver, then hurry to catch up.

We push our way through dense walls of damp, raking bracken for a time. Ulciscor's clearing of the way ahead, and the sullen chittering of the forest, are the only sounds competing with wind and rain. I'm sodden within minutes, tunic clinging, my torn cloak doing little to fend off the chill. We eventually spot smoke billowing above the treetops ahead, and alter our trajectory.

I'm not sure for how long we trudge on after that. Ten minutes? Twenty? Neither of us speak, all our energy spent on pressing forward. We move slowly. Everything aches. Despite initial appearances, I can tell Ulciscor is tired too. His eyes are still bathed in black. He's using Will just to keep going.

We eventually stumble upon the Transvect's path, recognisable both by the massive, obliterated corridor of forest, and the flaming debris that still burns in its wake. The hiss and crackle of the smouldering Transvect fills the air for more than a minute before we reach it.

The wood and stone behemoth is a dying animal in the mud. Some sections still burn fiercely, some are no more than glowing embers. Others still are missing entire pieces, chunks torn away on impact. The rain seems to have prevented most of the surrounding forest from catching. Only a few nearby trees roar their violent, brilliant death throes.

Ulciscor stops a good hundred feet away, his cautioning hand on my arm urging me to do the same. "We'll circle around," he murmurs, peering through the rain at the seething wreckage.

There's no one in sight and I'm exhausted, bruised and thoroughly drenched, but I follow his lead. We cut around the Transvect and begin creeping through the still-standing brush along its sides, toward the front.

"*There.*" I mutter the word urgently, stooping lower and gesturing. Figures are picking their way along a section near the very front. Four of them, little more than silhouettes against hungry flames.

Ulciscor doesn't follow suit, watching for a moment, then digging into his pocket and tossing something a distance off to the side. Small, whatever it is. "Stay here." Taut. Tense. *Angry.* He grimaces as if he's trying to shake off the physical shock of everything he's done tonight, but it's not working. He sways before managing to steady himself against the thick, gnarled trunk of an old tree, then steps out into cleared space.

I do as he suggests, and stay low.

"What are you doing here?" As weary as I know he is, Ulciscor shows none of it as he calls the question imperiously.

The people ahead flinch and stumble to a halt.

"Ah. We were on board when the Transvect crashed. My name is Sacro." I can see them more clearly now. All men. Startled by Ulciscor's appearance. The one who's talking has dirt and blood smeared across his thin nose and lips. His dirty-blond hair is dishevelled.

"Doing what?"

"Maintenance work. A couple of the Will pylons were coming out of alignment. We figured we'd fix it during the—"

There's a wet, thudding sound.

Sacro's head explodes.

It takes a second for anyone to react. Everyone's frozen. Uncomprehending. Sacro's body has slumped to the ground by the time the other three men shout and stagger back, half ducking, looking around wildly for whatever has dispatched their friend. There's violent red viscera painting the Transvect's façade. I flatten myself hard against the wet ground, every muscle screaming at me to run.

Ulciscor just watches. I understand his calmness only just before the others.

"You killed him." Dismay, from the pudgy, olive-skinned man on the right. Shock. Not dissimilar to how I'm feeling. I've been through some terrible things these past few years, but Birthright means I haven't seen a dead body for a long time. Not since . . .

I push the thought away.

"He lied to me. And I'm *not* in a good mood." Ulciscor takes a step forward. The other men respond with a scrambling step back. "Let's start again. Who are . . ."

There's a faint zipping, buzzing sound, barely audible above the crackling Transvect and whipping wind. Ulciscor trails off. Lurches. An arrow's sprouted from the back of his left leg. He half turns, looking down at it, puzzled.

Then he crumples, face-forward, into the churned-up mud.

I wait for him to move, to rise and retaliate despite the shaft sticking out of him. Ulciscor's a Magnus Quintus. Weakened though he is, an injury like that, no matter how painful, shouldn't be the only one necessary to fell him.

The remaining three men have scrambled away and taken cover behind various pieces of debris from the crash, gazes flicking from Ulciscor's prone form to the surrounding forest, seemingly as startled as I.

Finally, the one with the black braided hair breaks the frozen tableau. "Who's there?"

Only pelting rain and the constant rustling of leaves greets his yell. I peer intently in the direction from which the arrow came, but no one's visible.

There's a tense hush, the men hunkering down behind their cover, unmoving. I stare at Ulciscor's motionless form, willing him to get up. If I try to help him, I'll be exposing myself not only to these strangers, but to whoever shot him.

"We should get out of here." It's the portly man finally breaking the silence, calling out to his companions from where he's cowering behind a fallen tree trunk. He's wide-eyed, still twitching at every sound from the surrounding brush.

His wiry, red-bearded companion, who's hunkering about ten feet away, issues a fervent agreement, but the final one's hard gaze doesn't leave Ulciscor. "Not yet. He killed Sacro." His hand strays to his side, and I spot a sheathe on his belt.

"Don't, Helmfrid. He's at least a Sextus. They'll hunt us to the ends of the earth."

Helmfrid ignores the warning. He stands, releases a held breath as no arrows fly. There's a pause, then the other two reluctantly scramble to their feet as well. Still nothing.

Helmfrid takes a step toward Ulciscor, steel glinting in his hand now.

Ah, *vek*.

VIII

I'M MOVING, SPRINTING HARD THROUGH MUD AND BURSTING from the brush in an explosion of leaves and snapping twigs, waiting for an arrow to bury itself in my back. I only have to cover about fifty feet but all three men are alert, their attention on me immediately, the short sword in Helmfrid's hand snapping in my direction. He doesn't hold it with confidence, though, nor adopt any particular stance as he takes in my charge. He doesn't know how to use the weapon.

I still have to deal with him first.

It probably takes less than five seconds to cover the distance to Helmfrid. It feels an eternity. It *should* be an eternity, as far as the black-braided man preparing himself is concerned. And yet he's strangely passive, sluggish; I expect to have to dodge, but he's still on his backswing when I'm barrelling into him, fist aimed at his jaw.

I miss.

It's the mud, more than anything else, heavily agitated from the Transvect's rough landing and too slick for proper footing. Instead of connecting cleanly, my good shoulder catches Helmfrid in the chest and we go down in a tangle of limbs, both of us thrashing wildly. There's pain in my right side, sharp and hot and terrifying, but I jerk away from it, snarling and twisting. I have a second to see Helmfrid's panic up close before my forehead finds his nose with an audible crunch. His eyes flutter into the back of his head.

I put one hand to the blazing, sticky wet of my side but don't stop to check the injury, staggering to my feet and rushing grimly at the stocky man next, who's flailing backward and slipping in the churned-up muck as he realises his armed comrade is down. This time my punch lands; teeth buckle, and he gives a gargling scream before I follow up with a second strike to the jaw. He drops.

The red-bearded man hasn't moved yet. Shocked. Then his expression turns resolute and he charges, I think from desperation more than confidence. His fist sails well wide of anything he could possibly be aiming for; I'm almost bemused as I watch it pass. Then I close, clumsily thanks to my throbbing side, but still far too fast for him. I deliver a glancing blow to his shoulder, then use my momentum to grapple him around and slam him down against a thick, fallen log. The branches still attached rustle and quiver.

"Who are you?" I snarl, my face inches from his as I pin him, forearm against throat.

The man's face is mostly in shadow. Stringy red hair falls over his eyes. "Anguis." He chokes it out, struggling to breathe. "We just want food."

I must ease up at the claim, or perhaps he senses hesitation. He twists, trying to deliver a hard punch to my wound.

I don't give him the chance, elbowing him in the temple.

"What a surprise," I mutter as I let his limp form slide against the sodden tree, though it's more from frustration than any real disgust. Anguis. The only ones, as far as I'm aware, who are still fighting the Republic. Years ago, in those terrible months after Suus, I would have given a limb to have made contact with these people.

That was before I saw the results of their resistance firsthand, of course. I once heard my father describe the Anguis as children throwing a tantrum, but I never believed it until I witnessed the aftermath of one of their attacks on a small northern Tensian village. Octavii crippled and unable to work, a dead Septimus with a weeping family. Homes burned, valuables looted, and stores for the winter stolen.

No one there had any love of their conquerors, and yet the lips of every villager I passed cursed the Anguis, not the Hierarchy. And rightly so.

I shudder as the thrill of the fight leaves me, pulling into focus the pain just above my hip. Still on my knees, I carefully bring my left hand across to the wound. It comes away red. My tunic and cloak are both slashed, and blood is seeping from the gap. I press my hand back firmly. Not a scratch, but not fatal either. I think.

"Well. At least we know you can beat up untrained Octavii if you need to."

I whirl at the woman's voice. My eyes take a second to adjust as I turn from the flaming wreckage; the first thing I see is the nocked arrow pointing right at my heart, not twenty feet away. As I raise my free hand, the face behind the drawn bow resolves. Blank confusion overpowers everything else as I try to place her. Brown eyes, dark skin. Curly brown hair plastered to her cheeks. Maybe a few years older than me.

"You." I find the match, finally. She's from the Theatre. The one who kept asking Gaufrid for an introduction.

"Me." The bow doesn't move an inch. "Nice to finally meet you, Diago."

There's a mental dissonance when the name I haven't heard for three years registers. A full eternity-like second where I move inexorably from convinced I've misheard, to terrified numbness. The danger from the crash, the shock of Ulciscor's actions, my injury—they're all distant compared to how naked I feel. How utterly exposed.

I'm too unbalanced to hide my reaction, at least fully, and I silently curse when I see a glint of satisfaction in her eyes at the confirmation.

My gaze flicks toward the naked steel that's lying next to Helmfrid, only a few feet away.

"Uh-uh." She ushers me in the other direction with her bow. A relaxed motion, but one I can tell she means. I obey, standing and moving a few stiff steps to the right. "Better."

"Who are you?" I monitor Ulciscor's prone form from the corner of my eye, arrow shaft jutting from his leg. He's breathing, at least, but there's no sign he's going to wake up and help.

"My name is . . . Sedotia." The deliberate way she says it is to let me know it's not her real one. "And I just want to talk."

"I can see that." I try not to let pain seep into my voice as I indicate the arrow still pointed at me. I'm starting to feel light-headed.

"You dealt with these three rather quickly. I thought it might be best to prevent any misunderstandings, on your behalf." Sedotia watches my face, then unhurriedly lowers her bow. The arrow remains nocked, though. "And we don't have much time before more of them arrive."

"Them?"

"Us," she corrects herself, somewhat tetchily. "Anguis. There are about twenty men on their way, expecting to be liberating sacks upon sacks of grain soon. We need to be gone before they arrive."

"I'm not going anywhere with you." I try to make sense of what's happening, glancing at the three unconscious men, then at Sacro. He's lying on his face. There's a pulpy red hole the size of my fist in the back of his head. "If you're all Anguis, why aren't you working together?"

"Rotting fools weren't supposed to be here yet. I suspect they were trying to take a little extra for themselves." She follows my gaze. "Choices and consequences, Diago. As for why I'm not with the others who are coming, there are currently only three people in the Anguis who know who you really are. I'd like to keep it that way, and I imagine you would too."

I grit my teeth. "So this raid just *happened* to take place today?"

"This raid was meant to happen in another month, on a Transvect carrying a far more valuable cargo. I spent most of last night bringing the plan forward." The last statement is prickly with impatience.

"How did you know I'd be on board?"

"As soon as I realised he was at the Theatre last night"—she jerks her head at Ulciscor—"I knew you'd be on board for Solivagus today."

"Which is when you decided to make us crash?"

"Not my first choice." Sedotia gives me a reproving look. "There would have been a lot less fire and violence and death and so on if you'd just spoken to me on any of the . . ." She ticks off fingers. "Four? Four different times I tried to contact you, at the Theatre. And I thought I still had weeks, but *someone*"—she casts a glance at Ulciscor that seems mostly peeved—"got to Letens Prison *much* faster than I expected."

She pauses, looking at me expectantly, and my breath catches as I understand.

"You planned for the Quintus to meet me."

"We planned for him to hear about a particular prisoner's transfer in about a month, and then for you to get his attention when he arrived. Deliberately, following instructions we gave you." She shakes her head. "He's been wanting someone in the Academy for years, but still. We were lucky he noticed you."

She leaves the last part as something of a question. I ignore it. I'm having trouble concentrating. I can't let this go on much longer. "The Anguis want me in the Academy, then. Fine. Surely that means I should be saving Ulciscor and getting this thing back in the air, not leaving with you."

"You're not ready." The unflinching certainty in her voice is chilling. "You're not ready for the Academy and you're not ready to deal with the Magnus Quintus. He is . . . formidable. He will already have realised that something's off about your background, your education. He'll have agents looking into every aspect of your past within hours of your arriving in Deditia. Every conversation you have with him, with his friends, with his servants—they will all be tests, traps. Every. Single. One." She softens, a touch of desperation as she glances at the still-silent forest. "Look, you're clearly wounded. You need help. Give us three weeks to prepare you—a month at most. He won't be sending you to the Academy before second trimester begins anyway."

The rain's easing, I note absently. Behind me, the popping and snapping of burning wood is dying down. There's an eery hush.

"And how would I get back to Ulciscor?" I feel like my words are starting to slur, but Sedotia doesn't appear to notice.

"Easy. We ransom you. Or we *try* to ransom you, but you heroically free yourself before the Quintus makes payment. The Senate does love a good story." She looks around again. Nervous.

"Assuming your other men don't kill him today, of course."

"They're not that stupid. He'll be fine."

I pretend to consider as I give myself a few seconds to steady. "The answer is no."

"*No?*" Sedotia's tone is dangerous. Her bow twitches upward a touch.

"I don't know what the Anguis want of me, but I can guess." Do well at the Academy. Graduate to a powerful position of their choosing somewhere in the Hierarchy, where they can make best use of me. Somewhere I'd have to cede. "I'm not interested. And Ulciscor is already intending to train me before I leave for Solivagus."

"Ulciscor wants you to fit in enough to find out what he wants to know. *We* want you to be Domitor. Believe me, there's a difference." There's frustration in Sedotia's every line. "Gods' graves. They killed your family. Stole your home. Don't you want to *do* something about it?"

Even through my physical pain the reminder's a dagger, made keener by accusation.

"Of course I do," I say softly. Witheringly. "But it's *not possible*. I made my choice three years ago. I ran." I say it with neither pride nor shame. It's not entirely an act, but nor do I add that I have my own plans, or that I consider the Anguis to be little more than ineffectual thugs. "This is my best chance at finding something approaching a normal life."

I can hear Sedotia's teeth grinding. "If you knew the risks I've . . ." She trails off and her bow comes back up, drawn and pointing squarely at me again. "It doesn't matter. You only have this chance because of me, and you seem to be under the mistaken impression that this is some kind of offer. So let's go, before I have to carry you."

My heart thuds. I can still feel blood leaking between my fingers. "You don't gain anything from shooting me."

Sedotia sights down the arrow. "I'll feel better."

I keep my hand raised and breathe out, then take a sidling step toward Ulciscor. "I'm going to pick him up. Then we're getting back on board and leaving."

There's a distant shout, barely audible through the trees, back toward the rear of the Transvect. Sedotia hears it too and curses. "You're making a mistake."

"Maybe." I take another step.

Sedotia closes her eyes, shoulders slumping as she lowers her bow. "Brat. Fool. Ungrateful little . . ." she mutters, loud enough that I'm plainly meant to hear it. Then, louder, as I hurry over to Ulciscor, "I'll give you a month to reconsider. There's a naumachia being held in Caten during the Festival of Jovan. Be there."

I sling Ulciscor's arm around my neck, straining to lift him. Fire blazes across my side, and my injured shoulder screams at me to stop. "Or what?"

"Or everyone finds out who you are. The Senate executes you. Maybe you're a martyr. Maybe having an enemy infiltrate so deep causes political chaos, new suspicions that we can take advantage of." Sedotia's voice is laced with promise. "We've made an investment in getting you here. We'll take our due, one way or another."

The shouts are louder. I'm already stumbling toward the front of the Transvect, half dragging Ulciscor along with me. I believe her. "How am I supposed to get there?" I gasp.

"That's not my problem." She glances along the length of the Transvect, then strides toward me. My hesitation at her approach is just long enough for her to reach down and rip the arrow from Ulciscor's thigh.

I recoil, expecting blood to bubble from the wound, but there's oddly little. Maybe something to do with his self-imbuing? Sedotia flicks crimson from what appears to be a stone arrowhead, then spins and stalks into the forest.

"One month, Diago," she calls as she disappears.

I redouble my efforts, cursing at the pain in my side, growling insults at the unconscious man about his eating habits, and coercing my body to keep plodding through the thick mud. Only mounting apprehension overcomes my aching, woozy exhaustion; the shouts have drawn close enough to pick out individual voices, almost to hear the words themselves.

I finally reach the front cabin, throwing open the door in the Transvect's pointed nose and dragging Ulciscor inside. It's small, barely more than six feet high, and less than twice that in length. There's a single, narrow window in the door. A bench sits opposite a stone panel that's clearly the focus of the space.

I abandon Ulciscor to the seat and inspect the panel, but it's an effort just to move now, and the dizziness that's been tugging at me for the past few minutes is getting worse. There are four levers, colour-coded. No writing.

Wonderful.

Urgent calls come from outside as someone spots the bodies on the ground. I shut the door as quietly as I can and then frown at the controls, doing my best to peer through the fog of my fatigue to any logic behind their arrangement. Three are up, and one—the red lever, right-most in the group—is down. That could be the emergency stop, I suppose.

I shrug to myself. Throw the red lever.

There's an alarming shudder and I stumble, sagging back against the cold stone wall. The shouting outside has turned furious and panicked.

The Transvect begins to rise.

I sway to my feet again. Go from feeling inordinately pleased with myself to anxious as the ground falls away, realising that I truly have no idea what I'm doing. But the Transvect would have been built with limitations on how much damage a single person could do from in here. Wouldn't it?

I run my hands over the other three levers. Blue, yellow, white.

I throw the blue lever, mainly because it's next to the red one.

There's nothing but a strange clunk, and I wonder if anything's happened at all. Then a horrendous crashing sound draws me to the sole window; I stare downward in bewilderment before realising I'm watching most of the Transvect rolling, crashing, and crumpling its way through the forest far below.

"Not the right one," I mutter hazily, shaking my head admonishingly to myself. Then I brighten as I remember it was the Hierarchy's. "Not the wrong one, either." My words are coming out slurred. Hopefully I didn't kill anyone down there. I snicker to myself as I realise how strange I'd look to anyone watching. Some part of my mind is wittering at me, warning me that I'm losing to the wound and the shock of everything's that happened. That I need to get us moving forward.

Two levers left. Yellow's next.

We stop rising and start moving forward.

I crumple to the stone floor; there's nowhere else to sit. Ulciscor is splayed on the only seat. Still unconscious, still breathing. I glare at him.

"You had better appreciate this," I mutter drowsily.

The Transvect's picking up speed. I'm not sure whether the final lever should be used to limit it, or whether throwing it will drop us from the sky. I'm too tired to figure it out. Blood, I note absently, is still pulsing from underneath my tunic. Dragging Ulciscor in here did nothing to improve my injury.

Perhaps, I tell myself fuzzily, sleep will help.

IX

THE RISE AND FALL OF WAVES CRASHING, MUTED BY WALLS
but distinct and so, so familiar. For the haziest, most wonderful moment, it's years ago
and I'm back in Suus. In my own room. Safe.

Reality reasserts itself, ugly and sharp.

I'm lying on a bed. There's a dull, throbbing pain in my side. People are talking in
hushed tones. It takes me a few breaths to process it all, to remember that last I knew,
I was on the floor of the Transvect's control cabin as we ploughed through the murk
of the receding storm.

With an effort I stay still, eyes closed. Focus on the voices. There's an annoying
tickle in my throat, but I suppress it.

"We're going to get in trouble." Male. Whispered. More annoyed than worried.

"Better than being bored." A feminine voice, this time. Soft as well, but cheerfully
wheedling. "Aren't you curious? That Transvect turned up from Tensia looking like it
was more ash than stone. Most of it was missing! And the only people who know what
happened are the Quintus, and *him*." From the way she says it, she's pointing at me.
"Come on. We can be subtle about it."

"Of course I'm curious. I just don't—"

The feather in my throat becomes too much and I cough, as lightly as I can,
but the way the conversation cuts off indicates they know I'm conscious now. I feign
waking—not that they've revealed anything particularly illuminating—and then crack
an eyelid.

"Hail?" I rasp the word at the ceiling.

"He's awake." A scuffling of movement, a mutter of protest from the male. Then
there's a cup being pressed into my hand and the face of a girl about my age comes
into view, peering down at me. She has smooth, light olive skin and bright green eyes.
Straight brown hair cascades forward over her face as she grins sunnily at me through
the strands. "Welcome."

I grasp the cup and then prop myself up on one elbow, my body immediately
regretting the motion. I've been tended to, bandaged and bathed, but I still ache everywhere, my side especially. With the driving terror of the crash and ensuing fight no
longer pulsing through me, I'm beginning to realise just how badly bruised I truly am.

"Who are you?" I gulp the water gratefully after asking the question, using the time to take stock. A boy—again, my age—stands a little back from my bed, looking disgruntled. He's the very image of handsome Catenan stock, with thick, fashionably tousled black hair and a jutting jawline. Intelligent brown eyes examine me curiously, but he doesn't respond.

Beyond him, the room we're in is a long one. I'm in one of five separate single beds. The others are empty. Thick, seamless stone makes up the walls, upon which hang a variety of tasteful paintings, mostly peaceful landscapes interspersed with an occasional portrait. I don't recognise any of the people depicted.

Along the shorter wall, though, opposite the sole entrance, a massive symbol is etched into the stone: three separate lines stretching upward to a common goal, forming a pyramid. The words STRONGER TOGETHER are written underneath.

Just in case anyone forgot who was in charge, I suppose.

"My name's Emissa. The scowl-y one is Indol. Don't drown yourself," Emissa adds, eyeing a dribble from my steadily emptying cup.

Behind her, Indol scowls. "I'm not . . ." He seems to realise he's proving Emissa's point and shakes his head, breaking out into what appears to be a genuine, if rueful, smile.

"Where am I?" Their ages, and the Transvect's original destination, means I'm already fairly confident of the answer. Better to know, though.

"The Catenan Academy. The Catenan Academy's infirmary, to be specific. You arrived last night on a Transvect. Well. A part-Transvect. A *well-cooked* part-Transvect." Emissa leaves no doubt that this is something that requires explanation.

Behind her back, Indol rolls his eyes apologetically at me. "Maybe let's ask him his name first?"

I test each of my limbs, relieved to find them all working adequately. "Vis." My torn and bloodied tunic has been replaced by a simple, well-fitting white one, but I have no shoes or cloak. "What happened to the Quintus who was with me?" There's nothing to suggest I'm in trouble here—no hint of a guard, and I'm not bound—but I feel trapped all the same. The sooner I find Ulciscor, the better.

"Talking with some of the Praeceptors." Emissa makes a dismissive motion. "He's a Quintus. He's fine."

"And I'm sure he'll be by soon," adds Indol, addressing me but clearly meaning it for Emissa.

"How long have I been here?"

"Half the night. It's just past dawn." Emissa studies me. Intense and curious. "What happened to you?"

"Subtlety incarnate," mutters Indol, not quite under his breath, behind her.

"Our Transvect was attacked." I'm thinking as furiously as my fresh-from-unconsciousness mind will allow. How much did Ulciscor see before he was knocked out? What should I tell him?

"By who?"

"I didn't get names. On account of all the fire and the crashing and the running," I clarify.

"Excuses." The corners of Emissa's mouth are turned upward. "So the Quintus saved you?"

"Something like that."

"Strange. Because Belli—she's in our class—overheard him and Praeceptor Nequias talking not long after you turned up, and she *swears* that it sounded like you're the one who . . ."

She trails off at the sound of the door opening. All three of us turn to see a girl leaning anxiously through, breathing hard. Her skin's pale beneath a mass of curly auburn hair that hangs almost to her waist.

"Someone's coming," she hisses, beckoning urgently, acknowledging my presence with her eyes but directing the gesture at the other two.

"Rotting gods. Told you." Indol scampers toward the door.

Emissa makes a face at me that's somehow amused and panicked and apologetic all at once. "Feel better. And, if you don't mind, if anyone asks . . ."

"You were never here."

She flashes another smile, then flees after Indol.

I lie back on the bed once they're gone. So Ulciscor's already discussed the attack with others here. He'd remember confronting the Anguis—but not necessarily *know* that they were Anguis—and then nothing, presumably, until whenever he woke up. Probably on the Transvect sometime between the Tensian wildlands and here.

I should avoid mentioning that he killed a man. I'm not sure the consequences for a Magnus Quintus would necessarily be severe, Birthright or no—but he'd surely see it as disloyal.

I'm interrupted after not more than a minute of thought by the door opening again. The sole man who slips through brightens as he sees me.

"You're awake." He's in his mid-twenties. Handsome, with short, ruffled dirty-blond hair and thoughtful blue eyes. The white cloak of a physician is draped across his shoulders. "How are you feeling?"

Despite the situation, my tension eases a little at his genuinely concerned tone.

"Fine." I'm betrayed by a wince as I shift, sharp pain tugging at my side. "Where am I?" He's likely only here to check on my health, but no need to let him know I've spoken to anyone else.

"The Academy. You're safe. As is Magnus Quintus Telimus, I'm told," he adds with brisk efficiency as he checks my dressing. "And you're not 'fine,' I'm afraid. The Quintus bandaged you up as best he could, but even with salves and rest, that wound is going to take a week or two to heal."

"Could have been worse." My teeth clench as he begins grasping each limb in turn and pressing, pulling, rotating, and generally probing them systematically. Every touch seems to find a fresh bruise. "Is that necessary?"

"Have to check nothing's broken." He shakes his head in vague dismay as he gets to my bad shoulder, noting its resistance and the pain on my face. "What happened here?"

"It took a hit when we jumped out of the Transvect." He looks at me, puzzled. "While it was still in the air," I elaborate.

The physician pauses, just enough to show nonplussed amusement. "Ah. Well. That would do it," he allows with exaggerated mildness. "I think the medical advice would be to *not* disembark that way next time."

We share a grin.

"There was an explosion not long after we left Letens, and our section was burning. Plus it looked like the whole thing was going to crash. Which it did." I twitch beneath his ministrations, relatively gentle though they are. "Magnus Telimus took the brunt of the fall." I'm not sure if I should refer to him as my father yet, given the need for senatorial ratification, so I don't.

"That cut in your side wasn't from a fall, though."

"No. We were attacked. I caught a sword." No way to deny it.

The physician moves on from my shoulder. "Even with the Quintus there?"

"He got knocked out. I'm not sure how." I'm still a little groggy, finding it hard to focus. This is probably ground I should be steering the conversation away from.

There's respect in the man's appraising glance this time. "So you fought them by yourself? How many were there?"

Definitely dangerous territory, but it will look strange if I become reticent. "Three left, when Magnus Telimus got hit. I was still hiding at that point. I managed to take them by surprise, and only one of them was armed. It's all a bit of a blur, to be honest. I was lucky." I think that covers everything Ulciscor might have seen.

"Sounds like a nasty business."

"It was."

The physician makes a sympathetic sound, moving on to carefully unwrap the bandage around my wound. It's smeared with some sort of thick green unguent, and dark red fluid still seeps from the stitched-up slash, but it's not as bad as I expected.

"You said only one of them was armed," the blond-haired man says absently as he works, dabbing the gash clean with a damp cloth and then applying more salve. "How did the Quintus end up with an arrow wound?"

Vek.

"It came from somewhere else in the forest. I never saw who shot him." I'm proud of how smoothly I recover, no hesitation to the answer. "I expected to be shot too, but . . ." I shrug, immediately regretting the motion as pain washes through my torso.

"Strange." It's not delivered with even a trace of suspicion, thankfully. More of a distracted observation. "Was there anything unusual about the arrow?"

"I don't know. It hurt Magnus Telimus more than I expected. Nothing specific, though," I hedge. Feeling my unease build, even through the patina of haze coating my mind. Too many questions.

"Not even when you took it out of his leg?"

I'm saved from another scrambling lie by a commotion outside, voices raised. The argument's muffled, but I recognise Ulciscor's commanding tone even so.

The door opens and another man sticks his head in. He's swarthy and slim, wearing horn-rimmed spectacles with clear glass in them. I can't help but notice the dark bags around his eyes as he gives the man tending my injuries an enquiring look.

The physician sighs, more resigned than irritated. "Let him in, Marcus. He's Vis's father now, after all."

The head at the door vanishes, and a moment later Ulciscor is striding through. His black cloak is gone, replaced by a pristine white tunic and toga with a single purple stripe, indicating his senatorial status. He has clearly bathed, but otherwise looks just as he did yesterday. No obvious bandaging on his leg. He doesn't even look like he's favouring it.

His eyes—a shade darker than usual—don't leave me as he walks over. There's a bleak quiet to him. He stops just short of my bed, then turns to the physician.

"Hail, Veridius."

X

"ULCISCOR." THE MAN IN THE WHITE CLOAK STRIDES OVER and wraps Ulciscor in a fierce embrace. "It's been a while."

"Too long." Ulciscor's pensive demeanour melts away as he pounds Veridius on the back a couple of times before breaking away again. He jerks his head toward the door. "The guard was a bit much."

"Sorry. My assistant. He's been rather security-oriented, recently. Nothing to do with Vis here, or you." His cheer slips to something more apologetic. "A long story."

I watch the exchange. Genuinely confused. *Veridius*. The man I'm supposed to be spying on. The man in charge here.

"You two know each other?" I ask a question with an obvious answer, mostly to cover my surprise. Trying to look curious rather than terrified as I replay what I've just revealed. I *was* being careful. Not nearly as careful as I might have been, though.

"We do. Veridius here is actually head of the Academy," Ulciscor tells me, a small smile on his lips. Acting as if he's revealing a remarkable truth.

"What?" I play the part, looking at Veridius in shock. "I'm so sorry, Principalis. I thought you were . . ." I indicate his cloak, giving a nervous and contrite half laugh.

Veridius chuckles genially. "No apology necessary, Vis. I should have introduced myself, but I know my presence for prospective students can cause more stress than comfort sometimes. Given the circumstances, I thought it might be better that we simply focus on your injury. Which I *am* trained to tend," he assures me. "Ulnius usually heads up the infirmary here, but I step in when needs be. He asked me to look in on you while he attended someone else."

"That makes sense. I appreciate it." My mind's still racing. Veridius says it all so smoothly, amiable and warm and effortless. He radiates affable charm. And yet as I replay our conversation, there's no doubt he was poking for information.

Doing it well, too. Another minute, and I may well have dug myself too deep a hole.

Ulciscor vacillates, then glances at me. "You mentioned that you were applying, then?"

I'm blank, then inwardly curse as I realise. "No." Another mistake. I'm off-balance.

"We had the manifest transcribed over from Letens. I just assumed, when I saw you'd adopted him," supplies Veridius to Ulciscor. He claps me gently on the back. "I know Ulciscor wouldn't choose just anyone—not with all the history his family has here. The application was always just a formality, and I'm glad to accept it. If your mettle after that attack is anything to go by, I'm looking forward to seeing how you fare."

"Thank you, Principalis." I don't know what else to say.

"There will be some paperwork for Ulciscor to fill out, so if you're well enough, perhaps you would like a tour of the facilities while he—"

"I wish we could stay, Veridius, but we need to get to Caten," Ulciscor interrupts. "Quartus Redivius and the others will have already heard about what happened, and . . . well. You can imagine. Thank you for admitting him. I'll send the forms along as soon as I can." He's brisk, acting as if it's important we get moving. "Can he travel?"

Veridius hesitates, so briefly that I'm not sure it isn't my imagination. "He'll be fine." He turns to me. "Just make sure you rest as much as you can, and see a physician regularly over the next week or so to get the bandages changed." That same gentle, genuinely concerned demeanour. If it's an act, it's near perfect.

"I will."

Ulciscor steps forward before Veridius can say more. "Then we should go."

"You'll need this at the gate." Veridius hands Ulciscor a thin, triangular stone tile, not much larger than a Foundation piece.

Ulciscor accepts it and then the two men embrace again, for all the world looking as though they're old friends. "It was good to see you, even if it's been brief."

"If Vis is coming here, I have no doubt our paths will cross again soon."

"I hope so." Ulciscor says it cordially, then heads for the exit. I bid my farewell to Veridius and trail after the Magnus Quintus.

"Ulciscor."

We stop just short of the door, and Ulciscor turns. Completely casual, but I swear his eyes go a shade darker.

"Is this the first time you've been back?"

"Yes." Quiet. That darkness in his eyes isn't my imagination. We're away from the window, though, so I don't think Veridius will be able to see it in the dim.

"His memorial is over past the quadrum, just to the west. Facing the sunset." Veridius's smile has vanished, replaced by unaffected sadness. "If you were interested."

Ulciscor stares, and for just a second it looks like the mask is going to slip. His throat tightens. Breath shortens. He responds with a stiff nod, then whirls and walks away.

Not before I see the darkness completely flooding his eyes, though.

※ ※ ※

OUR FOOTSTEPS ECHO AGAINST THE HEWN GRANITE WALLS OF the empty hallway. Morning light spills through tall archways onto the stone. The corridor we're walking is set into the side of a cliff; the view is of a vast, forested island to the north, and swelling water everywhere else.

I stumble at the sight of the latter, heart wrenching. The peaks of waves glitter. Sparkle. I can smell the salt. A series of massive white stone monoliths jutting from the blue, perhaps a mile from the shore, mars the view. But otherwise, it's all light and clean colours and open horizons down there.

I haven't seen the sea in almost two years.

"We'll talk once we're away." Ulciscor's eyes have cleared again, returned to their thoughtful deep brown. As if that repressed, low-burning fury was never there.

It takes only a couple of turns before we're climbing spiralling stairs and emerging into a massive hall, grand marble columns supporting a curving roof above. Floor-to-ceiling arches on one side reveal that we're at the very top of the cliff. Several doorways opposite branch out into separate rooms, and a smattering of students mill and chatter just outside them, congregating in small groups.

Ulciscor doesn't pause, angling for the main entrance. We catch several stares as we pass, particularly me with my stiff gait. A trail of hushed, curious murmurs forms our wake.

"So this is the Academy?" I ask the question mostly to distract myself from the pressure of everyone's eyes.

"This is the Curia Doctrina. The main assembly hall." We exit the building and Ulciscor motions back behind us, up at the yawning archway we've just walked through.

I turn to see friezes carved with lavish intricacy across it. Etrius with his famed wingblade; the capture of the fortress Orun Tel; the forming of the first Triumvirate. Other instantly recognisable glories from Catenan history.

It takes me a moment, but I realise that the pictures all flow into one another, combining with remarkable artistry to spell out words. *STRONGER TOGETHER*.

"*Mawraur, bacpidyn*," I murmur to myself, without really thinking.

Ulciscor gives me an appraising look. "Cymrian?"

I nod, surprised by his recognition of the language: it's not just rare, but officially considered dead by the Hierarchy. The only reason I know it is that my mother's father was from the icy Cymrian wastelands, and despite the nation's fall more than twenty years before Suus's, she insisted I be tutored in it. The man she chose for the job,

Cullen, used to delight in teaching a young prince the most foul phrases his native tongue had to offer. Not that I was ever an unwilling student.

"What does it mean?"

I cough. "It's, ah . . . something about using extravagance as . . . compensation for other deficiencies."

"Ah." Ulciscor eyes the frieze. "Yes. *Mawraur, bacpidyn,*" he concedes with a smirk.

There are more students out the front of the Curia Doctrina, though fewer of them take note of us as we descend the sweeping white stairs. We're entering an enormous open square, easily more than three hundred feet in both length and width. Buildings rise on each edge—temples, a gymnasium for training, a Bibliotheca, even what looks like a set of baths—and people come and go from almost all of them. Despite the sun being barely above the horizon, the space is brimming with activity.

"Hm." Ulciscor cocks his head to the side. "I've heard you use *vek*. An Aquirian curse?"

"That's right." Suus and Aquiria mostly shared a tongue; the dialects were different, but only native speakers would know the difference.

"What about *guiro thanat?*"

My brow furrows. I must have said that in front of him at some point. "Sytrecian. It's more of an insult. The rough translation is someone who could 'brighten a room with their absence, or dazzle it with their corpse.'" I smile slightly. I've always liked that one.

"All that in two words?"

"Apparently so."

"I've studied a little Sytrecian and Cymrian, and never heard either of those phrases."

"I guess you didn't study hard enough." I wave off his penetrating look. "I had a Cymrian tutor, back in Aquiria. He was the one who taught me a little Vetusian, too—he always said I had a knack for languages. And I picked up Sytrecian from the crew of the ship that got me to Tensia, after . . ."

I trail off. Deliberately, carefully let memories of my real family flood my mind. Let the grief in, just briefly.

Ulciscor watches me, then nods and lets the matter drop. He steers us off to the left, away from the bright white of the square and down a narrow, garden-lined path. A chill breeze whips in off the ocean. I breathe in salty air and aching nostalgia.

"Alright." Ulciscor glances behind us. "I came as soon as I heard you were awake. How much did Veridius get out of you?" An uneasy edge still to his tone, even if he thinks we're safe to talk.

I relate what's happened since I regained consciousness, recounting what I said as

accurately as possible. Ulciscor listens intently as we emerge from the ring of buildings and strike out along a path that traces the line of the clifftop, a short stone wall
providing safety without obscuring the view. The entire Academy's built atop this high
plateau, apparently.

My eyes stray to the vista beyond as I talk. The island is vast, from what I can see
of it from here. It's blanketed by verdant forest; much is also mountainous, steep cliffs
vanishing into puffs of low-hanging clouds in the distance. Deep ravines form in between. I think I can see the winding glint of a river through the foliage in one of them.

To the west the sea roils, white-tipped waves smashing against bluffs that appear to
form the entirety of the island's beachless shoreline. Past my initial emotional reaction,
I can see now that this place has none of the golden beauty of Suus. It's austere. Bleak.
The waves crash rather than lap; the sky is grey; the air bites where it touches skin in a
way that it almost never does in the lands farther north.

"He was focusing on the attack, then. Not you specifically." Ulciscor's relieved as I
conclude my explanation. "Probably wanted to figure out how I managed to get myself
injured. Not to mention lose most of a Transvect along a route that very few people
should have known we were taking."

We're approaching a much taller section of the stone wall, this part made of
twenty-foot-long slabs of granite and spiked at the top, a clear warning against entry.
Or exit, I suppose. It curves away from the cliff's edge, dividing the Academy from the
wilderness of the island. "He was certainly interested in how you got knocked out."

"He's not alone there." Ulciscor half stoops to rub the back of his leg. "What *did*
happen? I remember the men who were pretending they crashed with the Transvect.
And then . . . nothing."

I lick my lips, the Anguis fighter's exploding head an indelible image.

"There was a woman hiding in the forest with a bow—she shot you, and you went
down like it hit you in the head. She came out once you were unconscious, pulled her
arrow out of your leg, said something to the men, and left. After that, it was pretty
much what I told Veridius. They looked like they were going to kill you, so I took a
chance." I shrug uncomfortably. "Caught them by surprise, and I think they were only
Octavii. Compared to the Theatre, it wasn't hard."

Ahead in the wall I spot an arched, covered passageway about thirty feet long and
half as wide jutting from the stone. There are tall double doors set into its end, manned
and closed. The Academy's entrance, I assume.

Ulciscor eyes me. "Why not tell all that to Veridius?"

"I'm assuming there was something special about that arrow. I've never heard of a

Quintus going down like that—maybe you have, but either way, it didn't seem like the sort of thing you'd want me telling just anyone."

Hardly a work of art, but given how little time I've had to come up with the answer, it's not bad. Sure enough, Ulciscor nods his approval. "I'm going to have to ask around. Quietly. Hearing about a weapon like that is going to make a lot of people nervous. You're sure they didn't give any clue as to who they were?"

"None."

Ulciscor looks like he wants to say more, but stays silent as we reach the gate.

There are guards standing to either side of the vaulted passageway, women wearing ankle-length tunics and stolas in sharp Catenan red. The older one with short-cropped black hair moves to block our path, albeit affably enough.

"Names?"

"Magnus Quintus Ulciscor Telimus. And Vis Telimus." Ulciscor hands her the tile he got from Veridius.

The sun-browned woman slots the triangular stone into a thin slot in the wall. The granite doors grind aside, the sound echoing down the passageway and crashing against a matching rumble from the other end, where I can see a slit of daylight growing as an identical set opens to the forest beyond.

She signals to the other guard, who makes a note on a wax tablet. "Very good, Magnus Quintus. We've had word that a Transvect is on the way. It should be here soon." She doesn't return the stone tile.

We walk into the brief tunnel. I roll my shoulders as we enter; there's something different about this space. An inscrutable oppressiveness. I quicken my step.

"Will cage," Ulciscor explains, noting my discomfort. His words reverberate against the stone.

"Which is?"

"A way of ensuring nothing imbued gets into the Academy. When the doors are closed, the passage is completely encompassed by Will—a perfect seal. It cuts off any external Will connections to an object. What you're feeling is someone else's Will, all around you." He looks resentfully at the surrounding granite, lowering his voice so that the guards can't overhear. "It's excessive. Gods-damned expensive to make and maintain."

I try to keep the way my skin crawls from my expression. We're soon exiting again, and I exhale, relishing the emergence. Behind us, the doors to the Academy rasp shut, a permanence in the boom of their sealing.

We're greeted immediately by thick forest, the sole path through sloping violently downward directly ahead. Otherwise, the encroaching woodland forms walls to both sides and a thick roof above, creating the sense that we're descending into another tunnel.

"The Transvect's this way," Ulciscor says, somewhat unnecessarily.

Before I can respond, I'm hit by another wave of light-headedness—something I've felt a couple of times since I woke—and stagger. Ulciscor notices. Steadies me with a hand on my arm and then stops, stooping to peer into my eyes.

"Did Veridius give you anything? Medicine?"

"Just the salve on my wound."

"Too risky; he knows our own physician will be looking at it soon. Anything else? Something to eat or drink?"

"No." I gather his meaning. "Surely he wouldn't."

"Nothing strong. Nothing provable. But a pinch of blackroot, maybe some ground-up wolfshem, would be enough to keep you off-balance. Would encourage mistakes in a conversation, without you necessarily noticing the effect."

I think back uneasily. "I did have a glass of water. I think it was left by my bed. That was when the students were there, though, not Veridius."

"You didn't mention any students."

I'd forgotten about them, to be honest. "There were three of them. They snuck in to find out what happened to the Transvect, but I didn't tell them anything. I think they were just bored. We barely got a chance to speak, anyway."

Ulciscor tugs at his sleeve. "Do you remember names?"

I wrack my brain. "Emissa, Indol, and Belli."

"Hm. Indol would be Quiscil's boy. Magnus Dimidius Quiscil. He's Military," Ulciscor extrapolates for my benefit. "I can't imagine he did anything to you. And the other two names are familiar; I think they're from Military families as well. Who gave you the water?"

"Emissa."

"I'll look into her." He sees my expression. "Veridius is the Principalis, Vis. He'll have a lot of sway with the students." He makes sure I'm steady on my feet again, then releases his grip. "I'm not saying the ones you met did anything; this is probably just your body trying to catch up. The point is, you can't discount it. You have to think of them in that light. Everyone you meet."

"There's something to look forward to." Just the fact that the possibility occurred to Ulciscor is unsettling.

The big man frowns at the steep incline ahead. "Are you going to be able to manage?"

"Easier if you carried me."

Ulciscor hesitates, then snorts. "Come on. If we miss this Transvect, it will be hours before we can schedule another."

Despite my gentle mocking of Ulciscor's concern, my side aches as we traverse the downward path. The surrounding brush remains green and thick, brambles and out-of-season wildberry cut back. A couple of other trails branch off into the darkness along the way. I'm too focused on my footing to wonder where they lead.

Soon enough the ground levels out, and we're emerging onto an entirely empty platform that juts from the side of a cliff. There's no way off it except the way we've just come, with a fifty-foot drop revealing itself on the three sides that aren't hemmed by trees.

I perch beside the Magnus Quintus on one of the benches that line the two-hundred-foot-long stretch of stone. Even having spent the last minute descending, we can see almost the entire breadth of the island from here; it has to be at least twenty miles wide, maybe double that in length. Parts are still obscured, but I can't spot anywhere that looks like a point of ingress. It reminds me of Suus's south-eastern shore: no beaches, no gentle slopes leading onto the island itself. Nothing but cliffs and bluffs.

"Religion made it this way." Ulciscor's following my gaze and reading my thoughts. "It was mostly inaccessible to begin with, but three years ago they removed the remaining beaches. Activated the Seawall, too."

"The Seawall?"

"Did you see that group of anchoring points from the Curia Doctrina? They're part of a security measure that surrounds the island. It only allows Transvects through, and only at one specific access point." He shakes his head. "It's pre-Cataclysm, we think. Adapted by Veridius, somehow. But Religion isn't exactly interested in letting us know the details."

"Rotting gods." I can't even imagine how much Will that would take to work. Or *how* it would work. "Just for the Academy?"

"So they say." Ulciscor gazes out at the horizon.

Neither of us speak for a while. Birdsong warbles at us. Distant, there's the crashing of waves against cliffs.

"My little brother died out there."

Ulciscor says the words so softly, I'm not sure I hear them correctly. I keep my eyes on the vista, then look at him questioningly.

He doesn't turn from the deep forests of Solivagus. "His name was Caeror. He was in the same class as Veridius. We think he was killed to cover up whatever they're hiding." He draws in a precarious breath, then finally meets my gaze. Sad and grave. His expression brooks no follow-up. "This is a bad place, Vis. Dangerous. You can still back out, but this is your last chance to do it. Is this opportunity worth it? Is it worth your life?"

I study him as he hunches forward and looks over the jagged island again. A light sheen of sweat covers his dark pate, glinting in the sun. A few more things about the man click into place.

"I need to hear you say it," he adds quietly.

This, or running forever at best. "Yes. It's worth it."

He gives a vaguely sorrowful smile, still gazing out into the distance. "They say that young men know they will die, but only old men believe it. For some reason, I don't think that's true of you, Vis. I hope it's not." He sighs. "Alright. There are two sites you're going to need to look into when you're here, locations we believe are important from years of investigation. The first is about a mile east of the Academy. Ruins that Religion are actively working on, but we don't know any more than that."

"Why can't we just go and look at it now?"

"Don't for a second think that because we're alone out here, they're not watching us. Besides, there will be alarms if it's not actively guarded. *And* I don't know its exact location."

I feel a prickle along the nape of my neck at the suggestion of eyes on us, and nod.

Ulciscor subtly motions north and slightly westward. "See the large natural arch over there? Coming off the side of the cliff."

I spot what he's talking about, at least halfway across the island.

"There are significant ruins, about a mile farther, around the other side of the mountain. That's the second site. For the past three Iudicia, that entire section of Solivagus has been kept off-limits. Religion's hiding something out there."

The rocky outcropping is miles away, across terrain that looks all but impossible to traverse. I'm perfectly capable of surviving in the wilderness—I've had the requisite training and plenty of experience in the forests of Suus—but a trip there and back would take a couple of days, minimum. "You want me to actually go to these places."

"Unless you think you can investigate some other way."

I consider what I've already seen of the Academy. The security Ulciscor's already described. "How, though?"

Ulciscor shrugs. "You're here for your ability to solve problems, Vis."

The sea of treetops stretching out below ripples in gusts that streak across the island, an undulating green ocean between us and the arch.

"I'll see what I can do," I say eventually.

Ulciscor accepts the statement as if it's exactly the response he was expecting. Perhaps it was.

Silence falls between us again, comfortable at first, but then weighed with a sense of anticipation from Ulciscor. He's waiting for me to speak. To broach something else with him.

I stare out across the carpet of forests. I don't think he wants to talk about his brother; there was too much pain in the revelation, a distinct effort to move the conversation on. I have concerns about it—Ulciscor's stake is far more personal than it first seemed—but this isn't the time to raise them.

There's really only one other thing that's looming over us.

"You killed him." I say it quietly, but there's only the sounds of nature around us. No doubt that Ulciscor can hear.

Ulciscor's thoughtful gaze out over the vista doesn't waver for a few seconds. Then he sighs. Regret in the act, though no remorse that I can see. "I did."

"What about Birthright?"

He finally looks at me. Curious. "Do you think I did the wrong thing?"

I resist the urge to be honest. To tell him that Birthright has always existed not for any moral reason, but as a means of maximising the Hierarchy's power. To be applied only at their convenience. There's a heartbeat where I see my father's bloodied form as I fall, my sister's ghostly hair in the water. The old rage stirs.

"I suppose you didn't necessarily break the law." It's what he wants to hear, if not exactly an answer. "You could argue that killing a man intent on destruction is a net gain for life. That letting him live could easily have resulted in more deaths." The loophole. My lungs are tight just thinking about it.

"I could. I would." It's that simple to him. "Is that a problem?"

"If it was, I would have mentioned it to Veridius."

Ulciscor pauses, then grunts an acknowledgment. My point's been made. I won't press the issue, but I don't for a second believe it would be ignored if others knew.

And I'm not alright with him just killing people.

There's silence again, and I stew, though I'm careful not to show it. Birthright. The protection of every human life. Not the Hierarchy's only hypocrisy, but one of their greatest. And Ulciscor treats it as blithely as any of his countrymen.

I wonder again whether I should have listened to Sedotia. Whether I'm in over my head here.

Too late now.

I examine the rocky curvature of that distant arch, and wait for the Transvect to take me into the heart of Deditia.

XI

As a boy, I heard a thousand different tales of Caten. The great harbour capital of Deditia. The shining bastion of innovation and art and beauty. The beating heart of the world.

I'm still unprepared for my first sight of it.

We've been travelling for almost two hours across the Sea of Quus, the Transvect speeding hundreds of feet above even the tallest swells. The sun emerged an hour ago and water has been glittering as far as the eye can see, but now a thin, hazy line of land darkens the horizon. I lean up against the window as a jutting peninsula begins to take shape ahead.

Within minutes the Transvect is slicing across the mouth of a bay that has to be at least ten miles wide. Ships dot the sparkling surface below: fishing vessels, schooners, even what looks like a trireme in the distance. Farther still, there's a mass of stone wharfs, bustling with activity.

And beyond, Caten.

The sunlight shimmers off an ocean of polished stone that screams the supremacy of Will. Sprawling mansions, triumphal arches, temples replete with towers that stretch impossibly high, each one distinct, twisting and curving and angled in ways that no standard construction method could ever achieve. Some of those have walkways between them, passageways with long arches that gaze imperiously down onto the streets beneath.

Between and surrounding all of that is . . . more. Smaller wooden structures, ten times the number of the stone ones. There are paved roads. Bustling squares. Expansive baths. Statues. Even from here, I can see that everything's in constant motion throughout it all—not just people but larger objects, stalking or rolling along the streets. The great Will-driven machines I've heard so much about, presumably. Too distant to properly make out.

"Quite a sight, isn't it?" Ulciscor is watching me expectantly.

It's terrifying. *Terrifying.* This is my enemy. These are the people who want me dead. The Hierarchy's shadow lies over all, and I've never considered myself blind to their power, but this is something else. I can't calculate the city's size; I can't see its end. Buildings both lavish and shabby coat the shores of the bay and then sprawl back up the gently rising ground beyond, until they fill the horizon in every direction. There's no way to grasp its enormity, no mental comparison by which I can diminish the horrified awe it inspires.

Sometimes I believe my resistance means something. Sometimes my anger keeps me warm as I tell myself that somehow, one day, I might figure out a way to repay the pain and loss I owe to Caten.

It's hard, when the lies that let you sleep are so cruelly laid bare.

"Not bad." I keep my tone light. Grin in Ulciscor's direction to show that, yes, I'm impressed. Tamp down the melancholy, burying it deep.

Ulciscor doesn't follow up the observation, seeing I'm distracted. There's been a lot of that, over the past two hours. He wants to talk—to start impressing upon me the countless things I no doubt need to learn before attending the Academy—but he's giving me time to settle. To finally process the events of the past two days.

I've needed that, if not for the reasons he thinks. I spent the first half of the trip combing through every moment of the attack on the Transvect, everything I said to Veridius and then Ulciscor. Trying to decide if I gave anything away, and then making sure I have reasonable explanations for inconsistencies, strange behaviour, anything at all that could be questioned later.

For the second half, my worry has been focused squarely on Sedotia.

In the whistling hush of the Transvect's cabin, I've been forced to acknowledge that she's a problem I can't ignore: the woman knows who I am and the more I replay her parting threat, the more I'm convinced she wasn't bluffing. I have no intention of becoming an Anguis spy, but nor can I simply walk away.

Which means that I'm going to have to find a reason to be at this naumachia, somehow. I've heard of such events before: gladiatorial combat, but exchanging chariots and sand for ships and water. A massive, staged naval battle, put on at extraordinary expense and effort for the pleasure of the Catenan populace.

Not the sort of thing that Ulciscor is going to just let me wander off to see.

"How many people live here?" I tinge my voice with awe, knowing it's what any Catenan expects from this experience.

"A little over a million, as of last census. More, if you count the outer districts."

"Gods' graves." I make it a murmur, almost speaking to myself. "The old gladiators who were overseeing Victorum used to talk about the great arenas here, how many people would come, but I never really believed them." I finally glance at Ulciscor. "Is it true that the Catenan Arena can hold more than fifty thousand people?" Understating the number, guessing how he'll react.

"More than a hundred thousand." Unmistakeable pride this time.

I scoff and shake my head, as if still not quite willing to accept it. Somewhere between impressed and disbelieving. "I can't imagine it."

"And yet," Ulciscor insists, the smallest hint of annoyance in his voice.

"You've seen it? Been there, when it's full?"

"Once or twice. The games are more entertainment for the mob than for senators, but it's necessary from time to time. And they are spectacular," he concedes, almost an afterthought. He smiles as he sees my fascination, how engaged I am at the thought. "Perhaps you'll get the chance to see them for yourself, one day."

I resume my observation of the city, content to leave it at that: Ulciscor will only find it suspicious if I press further, but the seed's been planted. When I do express a desire to see the games being held during the Festival of Jovan, he'll remember this conversation and think it's because he's piqued my interest.

"We won't see much of the city itself today," Ulciscor eventually says, apologetic. "The Transvect is stopping in the Praedium District. Warehouses, mostly. We'll be taking a carriage from there to Sarcinia."

That makes sense. This Transvect was redirected from the eastern provinces to pick us up; from what I saw, its cargo is largely grain. Even for a Magnus Quintus, I can't imagine anyone would have been willing to divert a whole supply shipment farther than necessary.

"That's where your estate is?"

He nods. "It's about an hour's ride."

We're bound for Ulciscor's family estate, where I'm to spend the next two months. The Academy's current year-and-a-half course started four months ago; the month-long break over the Festival of Jovan is only a few weeks away, so the Quintus has decided I'm to be tutored until the holiday has finished. That it's better to "smooth out my rough edges," as he puts it, rather than throw me to the wolves straight away.

He's also warned me that he'll be departing for his residence in Caten in a couple of days, leaving me in the care of others for my tutelage. I'm still not sure what to make of that. On one hand, it makes sense: he has senatorial duties, and he's already made it clear that he wants to keep me far from the politicking of the capital while I train. On the other, though, it feels odd that he's so willing to leave me without personal oversight.

"Will . . ."—I try to remember the name—"Lanistia meet us there?" The Sextus who will be in charge of my lessons, apparently.

"She should already be there."

I squint at the insinuation of doubt into his voice. "Does she know we're coming?"

"She knows *I'm* coming." Ulciscor is vaguely sheepish. "I didn't want to say too much about you in a public communication. So you'll be a . . . surprise." The way he says it, I'm not sure I'm going to be the kind of surprise that Lanistia necessarily likes.

"Ah. She knows about Veridius, though? About what we're doing?" My gaze has drifted back to the city; we're travelling obliquely to it, about to move from harbour to land. A schooner crosses my vision, and I barely pay it any attention before I realise that its bow is rising and falling sharply as it skims across the swells, despite having no sails raised. It zips beneath us, out of sight.

"She does, and she's alone in that. Which means that when she speaks, she speaks with my voice—I expect you to show her the respect that demands, and do all that she asks, no matter how hard she drives you. And if there's something you need to tell me, you can tell her, too. I trust her completely."

The increasingly familiar shape of an anchoring point looms as the Transvect begins to slow. The wharves are below us now, a hive of industry in the midday sun, hundreds of ant-like figures loading and unloading enormous ships and what appear to be long, horseless carts. I spot some of the latter rolling smoothly away from the docks, ushered by sets of Octavii but clearly powered by Will. They're laden with sacks, heading in the same direction we are.

I tear my gaze from the window. Caten is vast and foreign; I knew that already. I can't get distracted.

It's five minutes until we're at a stop, coming to rest amid a sea of large, bland, similar-looking wooden warehouses. Across from me, Ulciscor dips into his pocket and slides on a pair of tinted glasses—the type reserved for Sextii and above, supposedly made using some special process in the faraway deserts of Nyripk—before standing. "Come on."

I'm not sure whether it's the Magnus Quintus's glasses, the purple stripe on his toga, or both, but the swarm of workers hurrying to unload the Transvect parts like a wave before him. I trail in his wake, feeling the press of a hundred curious eyes.

The air at street level is thick, rancid, dust mixed with sweat and fish and human excrement from where Octavii have relieved themselves in nearby alleys. I gag at my first unsuspecting lungful. There's a clamour, an assault of shouting across paved roads as workers compete to communicate with one another. It's chaotic. Unpleasant.

"Over here." Ulciscor beckons me to a carriage waiting on the other side of the street.

The driver alights from his seat as he spots us. "Sextus Tohrius sends his best regards, Magnus Quintus." The sandy-haired man with a pockmarked face offers a small bow as he opens the door.

"Good to see you again, Marius. Please tell him I'm grateful for his help, and that I will be in Caten again in two days."

"I shall." The driver waits for me to climb in stiffly behind Ulciscor, sparing me a respectful acknowledgment before closing the carriage and resuming his seat. We're rolling within moments, and I can hear Marius's gravelly voice competing with all the others to clear the way.

"Tohrius is a client of mine," Ulciscor explains as he pulls the curtain next to him, hiding us from view, "and Marius can be trusted to keep his mouth shut. Sarcinia's far enough from Caten that as long as no one is sure you're there, nobody will bother making the trip." He signals for me to draw the curtain on my side, too.

I do so. "You really think anyone's going to be that interested?"

"In an orphan who's suddenly become a Telimus, adopted into one of the oldest patrician families in Caten? Yes, Vis. They'll be interested." A dry understatement. He turns his attention to a pile of documents that are waiting on the seat next to him. "I have a few things to catch up on here. You should sleep, if you can. Try and recover a little more from that wound. It might be your last chance for a while." He licks a finger and begins flicking through the pages, focus fully on their contents.

I acknowledge him reluctantly, then settle back into my seat and close my eyes as the carriage begins to rattle across the cobblestones and out of Caten.

※　※　※

"WE'RE HERE."

Ulciscor's words stir me from a sun-induced torpor. I blink blearily, stretch muscles stiff from bracing against the constant juddering of the carriage. I'm not sure when I fell asleep, but at some point Ulciscor opened the curtains again. It's mid-afternoon.

I crane my neck to look ahead. We've just crested a rise, and I can see for miles. Everything is a lush green. The occasionally cloud-diffused sun beats down on fields of olives, carefully planted orchards, and the distant gold of wheat. Octavii—I assume— dot the landscape, working the soil with Will-powered machines, or picking, or in some cases tending livestock. There are hundreds of them.

"Our Sarcinian estates." Ulciscor says it without any prideful inflection, despite the beauty on display. He indicates the mansion just up ahead, which the tree-lined gravel road is curling around toward. "Your home for the next two months."

"Looks like it'll do."

He glances at me, then chuckles. "Don't let Kadmos hear you say anything like that." He starts gathering up the papers next to him.

Before I can ask who that is, the carriage is pulling to a stop and Marius is leaping down from his position at the front, opening the door for Ulciscor with practiced smoothness. "I apologise for the rough ride, Magnus."

"Not your fault, Marius. The roads out here need maintenance, but we've had problems with brigands lately." Ulciscor alights, and I follow. "You should be careful on the return journey."

"I will, Magnus."

"You're welcome to rest and eat before you go."

"I'm grateful, but Sextus Tohrius needs me back in Caten before nightfall." The pockmarked man gives a deferential bow and then, seeing Ulciscor's recognition, swings himself back up onto the driver's bench. I watch as he deftly adjusts a stone dial, then uses the spoked wooden wheel to steer the carriage as it rolls forward.

"Ulciscor."

The flat female voice turns both the Quintus and I. A young woman stands, arms crossed, on the portico to the villa. Wavy black hair falls around her face, and she's wearing the reflective dark glasses of a Will user.

None of it covers her scowl. It's clearly not directed at me, but that doesn't stop me from taking a step back.

"Lanistia!" Ulciscor runs a hand over his shaven pate, face splitting into something that's half genuine pleasure, half sheepishness. He shuffles in front of me, as if to block Lanistia's view. "I thought you'd be—"

"Who's this?"

"This is Vis. Vis . . . Telimus," he adds with a cough.

Lanistia's eyes are hidden beneath those glasses, and the rest of her face doesn't move. She doesn't say anything. Her disapproval still radiates like a physical heat.

I decide to stay silent.

"Sorry I'm late. The Transvect from Tensia was attacked," Ulciscor continues after an awkward pause.

"I heard. Are you alright?" Reluctant care to the last part. She wants to be angry with him, I think, but she's too concerned not to ask.

"Thanks to Vis here." Ulciscor gives her the slightest of nods. A reassurance that he's genuinely well.

Something in Lanistia's face softens. "Good." She strides forward. There's a natural athleticism to her movements, reminiscent of the more talented Octavii I fought in the Theatre. Now she's closer, I decide she can't be more than five or six years older than me. "I'm Lanistia," she says to me.

"Vis."

Introductions apparently done, she turns back to Ulciscor. "The house isn't set up."

"Kadmos will manage." He grins at her. The first time I've seen him smile with his eyes.

She growls, but the corners of her mouth quirk upward back at him. Not as austere as she first appeared, then. "Fine. Come on." She heads back toward the mansion.

Ulciscor gives me a wry look, then motions for me to follow.

"Welcome to Villa Telimus," he murmurs.

XII

THERE'S SOMETHING ABOUT THE BODY LANGUAGE OF TWO people who are desperate to discuss something privately. A latent tension, an unconscious stiffness in their interactions. I remember seeing it often between my parents over those last few months, but being too young and too naïve to wonder why.

And I can see it now in the way Ulciscor and Lanistia talk, no matter how well they try to hide it.

I trail after the pair. Gravel crunches beneath our feet, loud in the hush of the country. The house is three stories high and made of mottled sandstone, looking like it belongs to an era from before Will was used in construction.

"So you brought back a son." Lanistia glances over her shoulder at me; I smile but she doesn't return it. "That's sudden."

"I know how bored you've been. Now you have something to do for the next two months."

Lanistia's unamused.

We pass through three tall archways, Lanistia leading us inside. The villa is richly appointed, large rooms divided into subsections by thick curtains and decorative latticework, everything very much in the style I know is popular with the Catenan elite. The rooms are airy, natural light filtering through windows set high above. Mosaics cover several dividing walls. Off to one side, I spot what appears to be the entrance to a large set of private baths.

"What did Relucia say?"

"Nothing, yet."

Lanistia stops dead. "You didn't tell her?"

Ulciscor just winces.

I cough. "Who's Relucia?"

"Rotting *gods*. You didn't tell *him*?" Lanistia's disapproval bristles from behind her dark glasses.

Ulciscor sighs, turning to me. "Relucia is Sextus Relucia Telimus. My wife. Who likely won't return from Sytrece until the Academy's second trimester has already begun," he adds emphatically, clearly for Lanistia's benefit.

I feel my eyebrows rise. The woman is legally my mother, then. That *does* seem like something he should have mentioned. "Will she be alright, with all this?"

"She knows I've been hoping to find someone to put through the Academy." Not the reasons why, though, from the careful way he words it. A flick of his eyes to the surrounding walls indicates that I shouldn't say anything about it here. "She even suggested we adopt, not long ago. It will be fine. She's been chosen to help the Censor for the next year—she's often abroad—she'll understand. You may not even have a chance to meet her until after graduating."

I suppose I shouldn't be surprised. Ulciscor is well past twenty-three, when taxation for the unmarried becomes burdensomely high. And there are plenty of monetary and social bonuses for having children in the Republic; if nothing else, Relucia will probably consider my adoption a prudent financial move. Assuming they don't already have any children of their own, of course.

"You'll still send word before tonight." Lanistia's firm. The way she speaks to him, the way they naturally fell into step as soon as we arrived, shouts familiarity. A comfort that only comes with friendship, regardless of her brusque attitude.

"So I don't have any brothers or sisters that you haven't mentioned?" It feels strange to ask, but it seems I have to.

"No." Ulciscor takes a breath as if to say more, then changes his mind. "No."

"Dominus!"

All three of us halt as a man in his fifties, clean-shaven and jowly, detaches himself energetically from a passageway to the left. He's sporting a severely receding hairline, and it looks like he's grown out the rest of his still-black hair to compensate. The stringy mass dangling limply to his shoulders does nothing to improve his looks. Still, his smile is excited, wide, and welcoming. Seems genuine.

"Kadmos." Ulciscor grips him by the shoulder in greeting, smiling as well. "Good to see you. Everything's well?"

"The reaper in the eastern fields needs replacing. Some more of the olive crops got hit by that strange rot. And Incusi has been muttering to her friends about how much work they have to do, even though they're properly paid for it. So, as well as it usually is, Dominus." The news is delivered in a jovial way. They're not pressing concerns.

His smile fades a little at the end as he finally registers my presence. He's not displeased, exactly. More confused.

Ulciscor chuckles. "We'll get to all of it soon. I promise." He's seen Kadmos's glance, turns to include me in the conversation. "But in the meantime, meet Vis. I've adopted him, and he will be attending the Academy at the beginning of the second trimester. Vis, this is Dispensator Kadmos. Anything you need around the villa, he can help you with."

I nod politely. The introduction suggests that the house steward isn't trusted to the same extent as Lanistia, and that assumption's backed up by Kadmos's bemused, vaguely dismayed expression as he looks between me and Ulciscor. This is definitely a surprise to him.

"Kadmos, if you could please take Vis by the kitchen to get something to eat, and then show him to his rooms? The guest quarters, I think. We can arrange for something more permanent tomorrow."

"Of course, Dominus. Master Vis, if you'll please follow me?"

"Get settled in," Ulciscor adds reassuringly to me. "Rest some more. Lanistia will come and find you soon enough."

I acquiesce, but take careful note of the direction in which Lanistia and Ulciscor start walking as I follow Kadmos. I don't think the Magnus Quintus has been lying to me, necessarily, but there's more going on than he's admitted.

"Welcome to Villa Telimus, Master Vis." Kadmos has a light Sytrecian accent, reinforcing my impression of his origins. His voice has lost all threads of joviality. In no way rude, but certainly nothing beyond polite as he guides me deeper into the mansion. "Do you have any belongings I should arrange to have taken up to your rooms?"

"No."

He eyes my clothes. They're the ones from the Academy. Clean, but ragged where Ulciscor carefully cut them with a blade after we left Solivagus—just enough to destroy any imbuing that Veridius might have used to trace me. I can already see Kadmos mentally compiling a list of things he needs to buy, even as he tries to puzzle out my origin. "You'll be needing a wardrobe, then."

"Yes. Thank you."

He signals for me to stop, and slips over to a young Octavii sweeping the floor, murmuring an instruction. The rotund, freckled girl bobs deferentially to Kadmos, giving me a wide-eyed assessment as she hurries off.

We arrive at the kitchen, which is even larger and better-stocked than the one at the orphanage. There are no cooks in sight, so I scoop up what I want from the laden benches onto two separate plates. I've barely eaten since the previous day, and the food on array—cured meats, olives, and freshly baked wheat bread with honey—is better than anything I've had in a long time.

Kadmos gives my larger-than-strictly-necessary haul a disapproving look, but says nothing as he guides me and my precariously balanced load up to the second-floor guest wing of the mansion. He stops at the entrance, handing me a folded tunic that was waiting on a nearby seat before gesturing me inside. "This should fit well enough for today." The Octavii did her work quickly. "If you need anything else, Master Vis, just ring the bell by the door and someone will come."

The room's spacious, ten times the size of the one I had at the orphanage. The bed in the centre is enormous as well, with what looks to be a feather mattress below the bronze-decorated headboard. My body aches longingly at the sight.

"Thank you, Kadmos." I turn back to the steward in time to see him touching a stone tile to a matching one set into the door. "What are you doing?"

"Disabling the security. The Magnus Quintus doesn't always trust those we accommodate here." He tucks the tile back in his pocket.

I hide my vexation behind feigned disinterest. The steward wanted me to see him. He knows there's no way for me to tell if he's lying, and that the door could easily be attached to an indicator somewhere else in the house—meaning that as soon as I open it, someone will know. I can't risk sneaking out through it now.

I set down my two plates of food on a sideboard, not having to fake the yawn that accompanies the motion. "I suspect it will be a few hours before I want to go anywhere, anyway."

"I'll let you rest, then. Enjoy your meal, Master Vis." He gives a small, politely deferential bow, and is gone with the door shut behind him before I can reply.

I snatch a slice of bread from one of the plates and wolf it down, vaguely irritated, though I suppose I can't blame the man for being cautious. I'm an evidently not-well-to-do stranger who is suddenly heir to the patrician family he's probably served his whole life. Utterly insane though I would have to be to try anything nefarious against a Magnus Quintus, it's hard to begrudge the man some reservations.

I deliberate as I discard my shredded clothes—shoulder protesting and bandaged side pulling uncomfortably—and change into my new ones, which I'm pleased to find are much finer than I'm accustomed to and, as promised, fit almost perfectly. Once my tunic is properly cinched, I scoff some more food and then cross to the large, east-facing window, pushing the shutters wide. The view is all green rolling hills, the tallest ones tipped by the last of the setting sun. I can see for miles.

I don't tarry to take it in; it's pretty enough, but I've always preferred the sparkle and clear horizons of the ocean. The important thing is that the dimming fields are motionless. The Octavii have either returned to their homes, or are busy inside the villa.

There are no stone tiles set into the sill, I'm relieved to see. The sandstone bricks beyond have distinct clefts between, where the mortar has worn away. Not ideal hand-holds, but enough for my fingers to find purchase.

I hesitate, then perch on the ledge. This is going to look bad if I'm caught, but I need to know if something is being kept from me. And I've managed more difficult climbs at much higher heights along the cliffs of Suus. Even with my aching shoulder and side, I'm confident I can safely descend a single storey and get back inside without being noticed.

I'm barely out the window when I fall.

I'm not sure whether it's the unexpectedly severe twinge in my shoulder or just the rust of years that causes me to twitch at the wrong moment. Either way, I'm suddenly flailing backward, heart in throat, unable to resecure a handhold. It's not more than fifteen feet to the ground, and I manage to twist in the air so that I'm landing on my uninjured side. It still hurts.

I lie there on the grass, gasping to reclaim the air that's been knocked from my lungs while trying desperately to be quiet about it. It's probably ten seconds before I get my breathing under control, and as long again before I've recovered enough to test my limbs. Nothing broken, I think. There's the muted chatter of voices from inside the villa, but no shouts, no indication that anyone saw or heard anything.

"*Idiot,*" I whisper to myself as I struggle to my feet, brushing myself off and checking I haven't immediately stained my new white clothing. I'm not sure whether I'm more annoyed at the mistake, or my confidence that I wouldn't make one.

It's dusk now, the shape of the world still visible, but the colour all but gone. Sheathed torches crackle over the villa entrance; I can't see anyone around, but I skirt them anyway, heading for the section of the building into which Ulciscor and Lanistia disappeared. Most of the windows are dark, but a couple have outlines of light around closed shutters.

It's not long before I recognise the deep tones drifting from one. Muted by the wood, but definitely Ulciscor. I sidle closer to the window. It's in the open, unfortu-nately, no nearby cover to duck behind should someone happen along the path. I check my surrounds for any sign of movement, then position my head carefully next to the opening.

Ulciscor's in the midst of relating the attack on the Transvect—muffled, but the hush from outside allows me to hear the words. He's eschewing drama for dry fact, done within a couple of minutes, interrupted only a couple of times by soft ques-tions from Lanistia. He doesn't shy away from his killing of Sacro, nor how he was knocked out.

He finishes with his waking up on the moving Transvect, halfway to the Academy and with me bleeding on the floor next to him. There's a brief silence once he's done.

"Anguis, then. You think Melior was involved?" Lanistia's higher voice is easier to make out through the dampening wood. It doesn't take me long to place the name. Melior is the leader of the Anguis. A well-known name thanks to his proscription, and the size of the reward for his capture.

"They were too well-informed for some local faction. I only asked for the Transvect to be realigned a few hours before we left." Ulciscor's bothered by the fact. "And it can't be a coincidence they were able to take me down so easily. You don't bring a weapon like that on a whim."

"Any idea what it could have been?"

"None. Wasn't pleasant, though. I was vomiting for hours after I woke up."

"At least you woke up." There's the creaking of furniture as one of them shifts. "They found more bodies in Masen. Heads smashed in, just like the others."

"Gods' graves. Who? When?"

"A couple of Sextii. Regional leaders, but neither of them with names you'd recognise. Two days ago."

"How did Quiscil and the others react?"

"In the Senate? They condemned the murders as nothing more than cowardly desecrations. But word is, it's upset them. There's something about these attacks that has them worried, beyond just the Anguis becoming bolder."

"Perhaps it's who they're targeting."

"There's no connection between these two and the others, as far as I've been able to tell. But I'll keep looking."

"Do. I believe them when they say they're close to catching Melior. I'd like to know what's going on before that happens."

I grimace. There's a good chance the head of the Anguis will be one of those who knows who I am.

A faint clink—a glass being set down on a table, I think—and then a sigh. "What about the Correctors? Have they been administering more of their tests?"

"They drew blood from Magnus Quintus Cerrus last week. He's the only new one I heard about. But they said he wasn't infected."

A grunt from Ulciscor. "Shame." There's a low chuckle from Lanistia.

There's silence, and I begin to wonder whether one or both of them has left the room. There's still no movement outside the villa.

"So your son seems nice." There's an acerbic edge to Lanistia's abrupt observation.

"Look, Lanistia—"

"What were you *thinking?*" Low but intense. "How could you be so rash?"

"You weren't there. If I believed in the gods, I would say they led me to him. He was *made* for this."

"You do know what that implies, right?"

"I've gone over every aspect of how we crossed paths, and there was too much chance involved. He's nobody's spy." He says it with absolute confidence, and I feel something loosen in my chest at the words.

"Despite your being the target of an Anguis ambush within a day of meeting him."

"From which he *saved* me. If he was with them, the only point of the whole attack would have been to gain him a little more trust. Not even the Anguis are that wasteful with their resources."

"But you don't *know* him. I know you haven't had time to look into his background." Lanistia's caught between frustration and pleading. "What if he slips up? Or breaks? Or turns?"

"That's why you're getting the next two months with him. If you say he's not ready at the end, or that he can't be trusted, then I'll call off the whole thing." Ulciscor sighs. "There *is* something off about him. He's better educated than a war orphan has any right to be. Boy took multiple floggings rather than submit at the Aurora Columnae, too. He's burdened, and stubborn, and angry, and definitely hiding things. But whatever's driving him, it's something we can use."

"And if Veridius just decides to kill him?"

"Then we gain our legal foothold. Another Telimus dying on Solivagus would force the Senate's hand, this time."

"Ulciscor." Lanistia's soft, heavy disapproval does nothing to alleviate the chill that runs through me.

The pause is a touch too long before Ulciscor adds, "Veridius knows that as well as I do, anyway. So he won't."

"You're guessing."

"It doesn't matter. We're running out of time, Lanistia."

"There's no proof of that."

"You know it's true." He's chiding. "I wouldn't have involved him otherwise."

If there's a response, I don't hear it; the sound of a nearby door creaking makes me straighten, leap back onto the path. There's nowhere to hide, so I aim myself away from the doorway, hands clasped behind my back. Force the rigidity from my shoulders and amble. As if I'm just out enjoying the night air.

"Master Vis."

I flinch at the words, turning to find Kadmos standing behind me, arms crossed. I smile genially at him. "Caught me." When his frown twists into something more questioning, I gesture in mild embarrassment toward the starlit hills. "I changed my mind. I haven't been in the country in *years*. I'd forgotten how peaceful it is."

"Oh." He sweeps a limp strand of hair from his face as his gaze flicks to the shuttered window, not five paces from where I am. He's off guard, but not an idiot. "How did you get out here?"

"What do you mean?" I feign mild confusion.

"I . . ." He trails off. Annoyed, though he's trying to hide it. "I didn't see you leave your room." He doesn't want to confirm that he expected an alert from my opening the door. He probably isn't sure whether I deliberately avoided it, or it simply didn't work for some reason.

I indicate my own bafflement. "Is it a problem? I won't be long. You said you were disabling the security, so I assumed I didn't have to confine myself." I add the hint of a question to my tone.

"No, it's fine," says Kadmos, though it plainly isn't. The portly man glances again at the shuttered window. "But I should have specified: the Magnus Quintus is a very private man, and I suspect there will be some areas which he would prefer remained off-limits. So I'd feel much more comfortable if you stayed indoors this evening. Just until I can speak further with him, and then give you a formal tour tomorrow."

"Of course." I'm not realistically going to get another chance to listen in tonight anyway.

Kadmos indicates I should follow him. Evidently not willing to let me find my own way back.

I frown at the Dispensator's back as we enter the villa again. It's odd, that he would be the one to stumble upon me, rather than one of the several Octavii still bustling about the house. And so soon, too. Not more than ten minutes after I left my room.

Kadmos is talking, but it's idle chatter now, not something I need to pay attention to. Could moving the shutters on my window have triggered something, too? Unlikely; it would be a waste to monitor actions as innocuous as letting in some air. Besides, as I so ably proved, descending the outside wall isn't the easiest of tasks.

That leaves some sort of tracking on my person. It fits—would allow Kadmos to locate me, but would also require him to actively check on my whereabouts, explaining why there was a minutes-long gap before he came to find me.

I flick at my new tunic irritably.

We reach my rooms and Kadmos lets me in again, frowning at the open window, though there's no indication I used it to leave. I keep my cheerful expression until the door's closed and then collapse onto the bed. I've been pushing myself all day to focus, to pay attention to everything that's been said and everything that's been happening. The things I overheard have only served to swell my concerns. My side hurts. My shoulder hurts. My head hurts.

I'm ready to get some rest.

XIII

THE SUN'S NOT YET EVEN LIGHTENING THE HORIZON WHEN there's a crisp knock. Before I can properly wake and without my invitation, lamplight from the hall is spilling through the doorway, interrupted only by Lanistia's silhouette.

"I hope you got some sleep." She's still wearing those reflective dark glasses of hers, despite the pre-dawn dim outside. "Time to get started."

"Now?" I prop myself up on an elbow and give my pillow a bleary, longing glance.

"Now." She leaves, clearly expecting me to follow.

I groan, but—remembering how Ulciscor emphasised her authority over me here, and then that he left assessing my suitability for the Academy entirely in her hands—enjoin my aching body to roll out of bed, drag some clothes on, and trudge after her.

All's quiet in the villa. I'm not sure how early it is, but everyone appears to still, sensibly, be fast asleep. We head downstairs and across an open courtyard to the eastern wing of the house, the short walk in the cool morning air enough to clear my head. Soon enough, we're settling into a private office, shelves of books lining the wall. Lanistia sits in a chair facing me. Her hands are clasped and she leans forward, features thrown into sharp relief by the lamp burning between us.

"Ulciscor says you're quite well-educated, given your background." She manages to make the first part doubtful and the second mistrustful. "He also says you're lacking in some areas. We need to determine which ones."

I resist a mild surge of annoyance. Remind myself again that based on what I overheard last night, I need to impress this woman. "Alright."

Lanistia pushes back some stray strands of long dark hair that are brushing her cheeks. Takes a breath.

Starts.

The next three hours are a blur. Where Ulciscor probed, Lanistia bludgeons. I'm guessing at the mechanics of a Will-powered vehicle, then explaining my understanding of the historical legal areas of control between the three senatorial pyramids, then interpreting the philosophical musings of Arinus against current Catenan provincial policies—all within the space of minutes. Answers she likes earn a grunt and a quick change of topic. Those she doesn't—which are uncomfortably many—get assaulted, abused, dissected. If I present a flawed argument it's not just refuted, it's bloodied meat thrown to rabid wolves. Any trace of sleepiness has vanished after the first ten minutes. I'm dizzy after an hour. Barely able to think at all, by the end.

But end it does, eventually, just as the sun's crept far enough above the horizon to pour clean light through the east-facing window. I finish answering a question, and Lanistia stands.

"Are we . . . done?" I ask cautiously.

She inspects me from behind those glasses. I'm beginning to suspect she never takes them off. "Yes."

"So." I shift in my chair. "What do you think?"

"What do I think?" Lanistia extinguishes the low-burning lamp. "I think Ulciscor has been hasty in adopting you. I think he has severely overestimated your abilities. Perhaps he's seen something in you that I do not, but you are not ready for the Academy. Not even close. And I am not sure that I can make you so within the next two months."

My jaw clenches as I fight the instinct to react. The words cut. My tutors at Suus tended to be effusive about my ability to learn, but I've always wondered how much of that enthusiasm came from my status, rather than my results.

"But what do you *really* think? Be honest, now."

Lanistia's expression doesn't even twitch. "Quips aren't going to help you." She's stepping over to the bookshelf as she says it, running a finger along spines until she finds the title she's looking for. She repeats the process twice, then dumps the collected tomes in my lap. "These will. They cover your weakest areas. Read them. *Thoroughly.* We'll revisit these topics tomorrow and see whether you're actually capable of learning."

"You want me to get through these today?" I try not to sound aghast. I'm already exhausted, and none of the books look like light work.

"Problem?"

"No." A defiant lie. "But I was hoping to talk to Ulciscor today."

"He's not here."

"Where is he?"

"At the moment? Attending to some concerns of the clients he received this morning. But after that, he will be returning to Caten." She shrugs in response to my consternation. "He *is* a member of the Senate. He still has to submit his report about the attack on the Transvect, and officially announce his adoption of you, among other things."

It's a deflection. Ulciscor wasn't expecting to leave so soon.

"When will he be back?" I growl the words. He told me that I could trust Lanistia, but I don't know her. And perhaps more tellingly, if I'm being honest, I don't like her much.

"When he's done." Matter of fact rather than dismissive, though it's hard not to take it that way.

I say nothing. Lanistia doesn't seem the type to give ground if I dispute her claim.

She takes my silence as submission. "Kadmos will come to check your bandages later. And there's food in the kitchen if you're hungry."

She leaves without anything further.

I glower after her, but the reminder that I haven't yet eaten drags me into action. The kitchen is bustling this time, but no one stops me from piling a plate with wheat pancakes topped with dates and honey. I cart food and books back to my room. There's no point trying to poke around the villa anymore while it's light.

Outside my window, the sun is a warm, sleepy gold as it presses higher over the rolling green hills. Octavii are already toiling, though they seem happy enough; the sound of laughter echoes up to me as a group nearby chats amiably while they work.

I glare out over it all, chewing grimly. Ulciscor's absence is a problem. I was counting on at least one more conversation with the Quintus before he left, hoping to negotiate some freedoms for the month ahead. Nothing major—a small stipend, the ability to stretch my legs as far as the nearest village on occasion—but things that would establish me as a real Telimus, not a prisoner in all but name. The sort of manifest trust I could commute into a trip to Caten for the Festival of Jovan, and thus the naumachia.

Lanistia, I can already tell, is not going to agree to anything like that. But it seems that I'm stuck with her now.

I sigh, and start reading.

The books are well-chosen, I admit begrudgingly after a while, covering a breadth of knowledge that I've not previously had access to. My weariness fades. The Letens Bibliotheca was a wealth of information, but my time there was still self-directed—still by necessity building on existing competencies, not creating new ones. These tomes are revealing entirely different areas of education. Things I could never have even known to investigate.

Kadmos announces himself around mid-morning, checking my wound and applying a cream. A brownish one, this time, which tingles where it touches the gash.

"This salve will itch, but it will speed the healing process faster than anything else," he explains as he works. "Even so—you're going to feel some discomfort for at least a week or two, and Sextus Lanistia says that you need full mobility straight away. So starting tomorrow morning, I'll have a tea brewed for you to drink twice a day. You'll have to be careful while you train, but it will numb the pain, keep you focused. Just be aware that it will take a toll once it wears off at night."

"What's in the tea?"

"Some lionweed. Sana extract. A very small amount of voluptasia. Other things." Kadmos starts rebandaging me, then pauses as I shift uneasily. Softens, just slightly. "I do know what I'm about, Master Vis—I've been the Telimus physician for near thirty years. It won't do any harm, as long it's not for an extended period."

I reluctantly accept the statement. I have a vague recollection of voluptasia being dangerous in high dosages, but if I know the name, then it must have medicinal properties too. I don't recognise the other ingredients. Still, the pain in my side and shoulder has already been distracting me today, and that's just while I've been sitting. If there's something that can help me push through, I'll take it.

Kadmos soon leaves, and I resume my reading. Outside the window, the sun crests and then begins its descent; by the time I register its progress, the lengthening shadows suggest it's well into the afternoon. I consider, and then discard, the idea of taking a break. I'm making good progress through the texts, but not quickly enough to relax.

And besides—as strange as it is to admit, I'm enjoying myself.

It's not that the subject matter is easy—far from it—but a whole day of just this? Fed and warm and engaged, rather than working my fingers to the bone for Matron Atrox? It's like my stolen hours at the Bibliotheca, but better. The closest I've come to reliving my old life in a long, long time.

Kadmos briefly intrudes to deliver a dinner tray just as I'm lighting the lamps, dusk fading to a clear, starry night outside. The evening's tranquil, breeze still holding hints of warmth as it rustles the curtains before whispering through the empty vineyards and fields below. A sliver of moon has made its way into the sky by the time I close the last of the three books. My vision's started to blur—from extended concentration, as much as physical weariness—but I think I understand the basics of what I've read, now. At least enough to pass whatever test Lanistia has planned for me in the morning.

I blow out the lamps and collapse onto the bed. Unconsciousness greets me eagerly.

It can't be more than minutes later when I wake. Alert.

Something changes, I think, when another person enters the room. There's a new pressure in the air, a weight that's subtly different from when you're alone. I never noticed it at Suus, never thought anything of it as a child. But years of running have honed my perception of it. Heightened it into something instantly recognisable.

I fling myself desperately to the side as something heavy and violent thumps against the mattress. The room is dim, lit only by silver seeping past the still-open curtains, but I can see the outline of my attacker. I lash out with my leg as I lurch off the bed, weight and momentum behind the strike. There's a soft grunt and the looming form staggers back a step, but my bare foot feels as though it's hit brick.

A Will user, then. Not good.

I scramble backward, trying to regain my feet. My injured side burns at the unwelcome movement. The dark shape recovers and launches at me. I roll away again, snatching up a sandal from the floor as I tumble and flinging it behind me, hoping to cause the intruder at least a moment's distraction. I can't win this fight. I need to get out.

The figure's in between me and the door. I sprint for the window. Too slow. Air explodes from my lungs as an iron grip takes me, slams me back to the floor. Then my assailant is straddling me. Hand around my throat. I can't move. Can barely breathe.

"What are the three types of refined Conditional relationships of Will?"

I'm frozen. Uncomprehending. "Lanistia?" It comes out as a disbelieving croak.

The grip on my throat tightens. "Answer." It's her voice. A growl, but her voice.

"Sub-harmonic, managed, and . . . causal," I wheeze, not knowing what else to do. I should be relieved, but I'm not feeling that way. Ulciscor's confidante isn't going to kill me.

Right?

There's no reaction to my response, at least none that I can see. Lanistia's face is shrouded by darkness.

"What is Caten's most important area of innovation in the past hundred years?"

"Agriculture."

"Why?"

"Can you just—"

"*Answer.*" The grip on my throat tightens enough that I'm not sure I'll be able to.

"Because it's key to population." I give a rasping cough. "The agricultural advancements of the two-twenties allowed for a massive increase in food production, which in turn allowed for the population explosion created by government incentives."

The questions continue. Rapid-fire, no indication of whether I'm answering correctly. Like this morning's exhausting session with the woman, but infinitely more stressful. My injuries ache with no respite. Every time I struggle, or refuse to respond, or try to question what's happening, I'm pressed down. Slapped, once, hard enough that everything spins afterward. It's humiliating. Infuriating. Terrifying.

After a minute, though, it's easy enough to see the pattern. A few unrelated questions sprinkled in, but concentrated around the books I read today. Once I can focus in on that detail, things become more manageable. This is a test, albeit one that's making me by turns rattled and furious.

I answer a final question. There's a heartbeat, that hold on my throat unrelenting. Then it loosens. The weight on my chest vanishes.

I roll onto my side, rasping and hacking my relief. There's motion off in the darkness, and then the gentle light of a lamp.

I slowly sit up straight, feeling at my side to check the wound there hasn't torn open and glaring balefully. Lanistia is standing in the doorway, arms crossed. Expressionless. Still wearing those gods-damned dark glasses.

"What in all hells?" I snarl the words, though their effectiveness is dampened by the hoarseness of my voice. "*Why?*" My hands ball into fists. I haven't felt this helpless in years.

I hate her for reminding me of what it's like.

"I needed to test your recall under pressure."

"You needed to attack me to do that? While I'm rotting *injured?*"

"Your physical state is irrelevant." She's gallingly composed about it. "Ulciscor had doubts about your temperament; I can help prepare you intellectually for the Academy, but not emotionally. And if you're not ready for the latter, then I'm wasting my time on the former. So I had to see."

"It's a gods-damned *school*," I spit. "Check my back. There's nothing more they can do to me."

Lanistia reaches a hand to her face. Removes her glasses.

I falter.

Where her eyes should be are two white-scarred and empty sockets. I look away on polite instinct, then force my gaze back. She doesn't have any trouble making her way around, doesn't seem crippled by her lack. How?

"This is a small part of what the Academy took from me." She replaces her glasses, and I notice her hand trembles almost imperceptibly as she does so. "There is always something more to lose, Vis."

I bite my lip. I have so many more questions now, but I'm tired, and sore, and still disoriented, and partly just grateful that Lanistia's assault on me appears to be over. I give a single, sharp nod of acquiescence.

Lanistia seems able to see it. "Good. Sleep. We'll begin your lessons at dawn." She turns for the door.

"Did I get the questions right?" I want to know that much, at least.

"If you hadn't, I would have kept squeezing."

She leaves.

XIV

"YOU HAVE GOOD REACTIONS. GOOD INSTINCTS IN A FIGHT."

Today's hot, sun baking down from directly above. Lanistia and I are taking lunch, our table shaded by the painstakingly manicured hedge that forms an airy, light-speckled green tunnel almost the entire length of the courtyard. There's a fountain tinkling pleasantly in the background.

It takes me a second to realise Lanistia's talking to me, alone though we are. I think it's the first time she's paid me anything close to a compliment.

"Thanks," I say cautiously around my mouthful of bread, wondering what the follow-up punch will be. And whether it will be only metaphorical. While Kadmos has been true to his word and my body feels fine—almost good, in fact—after dosing myself with his tea, I'm still emotionally sore from her assault last night.

"Ulciscor mentioned that you fought. Against Septimii. Even a Sextus."

"I did." The switch in conversation has thrown me. Lanistia's every breath since I woke has been directed toward either figuring out if I know something, or making certain that I learn it.

"Why?"

"It was good money."

She scoffs. "*Why?*"

"How are you able to see?" It's a blunt quid pro quo, but the question's been eating at me. If her interrogation is going to turn personal, there's no point letting it be one-sided.

"How do you think?" No hesitation. No trace of offense. She's probably been expecting the enquiry for a while.

I compose my thoughts. "You're using Will, somehow." That much has become obvious. The woman moves as if she has full use of her eyes. Better than full, a lot of the time. I wouldn't want to try and sneak up on her. "If I had to guess, I'd say you were imbuing the air around you, somehow. Getting feedback from it. But to do that, you'd have to be constantly re-imbuing to account for the changing receptacle . . ." I chuckle, shaking my head. My best guess, but it's ridiculous.

"Two hundred times per second."

I feel the smirk slide from my face. "What?"

"That's our estimate of my imbuing speed." Lanistia doesn't smile. "Now. Why did you fight?"

I take a heartbeat to recover. Tempted to believe it a lie, though I can tell it's not. The sheer concentration, the intensity and focus needed to keep that up? Just to be able to *see*? I can't imagine.

Lanistia's waiting. I meet her reflective-tint gaze.

"Because I liked it."

I expect a follow-up. There isn't one. Lanistia studies me, then stands.

"Then I expect this afternoon will be to your liking, too."

%% %% %%

A CLOUD OF DUST ERUPTS FROM BENEATH ME AS MY BODY skids backward along the paved stone. I slide to a groaning, ungainly standstill, holding up a hand for clemency as I struggle back to my feet, holding my side.

"Just . . . a moment," I gasp, feeling at the bandaged area nervously, despite the pain there being no worse than anywhere else.

My opponent—Totius Octavus Conlis, a frankly huge man and most definitely larger than anyone I ever faced in Letens—either doesn't hear me or, more likely, doesn't care to grant the request. He lumbers forward, teeth bared in a grin that splits his broad face, sharp grey eyes fixed on me. Like some kind of giant bear about to crack open a beehive.

"Try and actually hit him this time!" calls Lanistia sternly from the stone bench where she's watching. I fire a scowl in her direction before staggering back another few paces, giving myself room to manoeuvre. Like the Octavii from the Theatre, Conlis's size makes him ponderous compared to me, but I was overconfident. Too eager to show off after Lanistia's apathy at my academic prowess. I deserved the barrelling hit, but I won't let him get in another.

Conlis comes at me again, still smiling, buoyed by his initial success. I wipe the expression from his face after I slide around his wild second swing and drive my fist hard into his side, eliciting a surprised grunt. I'm used to punching men who are imbuing. Conlis may be all muscle, but I know exactly where to make him feel it.

I don't let up, don't let him retreat, and within ten seconds I know I will win. There's a flow to this. A dream-like joy when you realise your opponent cannot hope to match you. You start to see their punches coming from so far off that it's tempting to let them get closer than they should. You choose where to hit, when to hit. You think about the fight in an almost abstracted way. Strike there. Disable that. You can see the realisation creeping over their face. You can see when they've recognised the loss, long before they actually go down. You become the tide. Inexorable.

"Enough!"

I falter as Conlis staggers back, the effort to stop almost as physical as the act of fighting. He's relieved at Lanistia's call. I'm annoyed, though I quickly stuff down the emotion. This isn't Letens, isn't a bout for money. I've proven my point.

The big man watches me warily, perhaps seeing the fire still in my stance, and then rubs his side gingerly.

"Good fight," he mutters begrudgingly. He sticks out his hand.

I stare at it in surprise, then grasp it. "Thanks."

"Well done, Conlis." Lanistia spares a rare smile for the hulking man, though it clearly also serves as a dismissal. He bows before taking his leave. The athletic woman watches until he's disappeared, leaving the two of us alone again.

"How are your injuries?"

"I can feel them, but they're not affecting me."

"Then you'll need to improve."

I glower at her before I can help myself. "I won."

"You won with a minimum of strategy and technique. Efficient enough for a fist-fight against an untrained Octavus, but if you're tested at the Academy, that's not a measure they'll be impressed by."

"Why would they put me in a fight?" I can't help but feel insulted, and—secretly—a little deflated.

"Did you read those books yesterday or not?"

I stop short, then grumble in recognition. "The need for physical control over Will." I try not to sound sullen. "Manipulating it at higher ranks requires more than just focus, and more than just brute strength. It takes precision. Speed. Endurance."

Lanistia jerks her head in acknowledgment. As positive a gesture as she's likely to make. "Which is why physical skills are prized in the Academy too. A student who's simply academic can rise, certainly. But only so far."

"I'd like to think I'm already more than just academic."

"Well. Let's get you into one category before we try for a second." Lanistia delivers the words with her customary dryness.

I've been trying not to let her dismissive manner get under my skin, but it's hard to ignore. "You're exaggerating," I say flatly. "I know I need to improve, to learn more, but there's no way I'm as deficient as you're pretending."

Lanistia's mouth twists. "Ulciscor said your pride might be a problem." She stands, shrugging her cloak from her shoulders. The tunic beneath is relatively short, more in a fighting man's style. Her arms are bare. Not muscular like Ellanher's, but definitely toned. "If you're so sure, let's see how you do against someone who's actually been to the Academy."

"You're a Sextus." I'm uneasy, and not just because of that fact. Her self-assurance holds menace.

She leans over. Places her hand against the stone bench she was just sitting on. "There. I'm holding no more Will than Conlis, now. Everything else is going to my vision."

"How do I—"

The bench hovers briefly before settling back to the ground. I snap my mouth shut. It's granite, thick, nearly six foot long. If she's rapidly imbued enough Will to lift something like that, then I'm going to have to take her word for it.

Lanistia wanders over to a nearby hedge, rooting around before snapping off a long twig and denuding it. It's perhaps twenty inches. Willowy. She swishes it back and forth in front of her, letting it whistle.

"If you can touch me, I'll stop. And I'll never imply that you're *deficient* again."

"So I just have to touch you?"

"A hit. A brush. A finger. You make contact, you win." Lanistia whispers her newly formed switch through the air again. "Of course, you're injured. And I do have a weapon."

I don't need further clarification. I charge.

It should be simple. I'm athletic, muscular but without the burden of a truly bulky physique. I have quick reactions, a long reach, and a high tolerance for pain. My injuries aren't bothering me, either. All I have to do is crash through whatever defence Lanistia thinks that twig gives her, and the rest won't matter. By her rules, it will be over.

It's not that easy, of course.

Her wrist flicks out and somehow, just before I reach her, there's a shocking, slashing fire below my left eye, sharp even through the numbing effects of Kadmos's tea. I growl and flinch away; when I turn back, Lanistia has moved back and to the side. Far enough to be out of reach. Not so far that it could be taken as a retreat.

The sting on my cheek isn't close to enough to deter me; I press more quickly this time, arms up to protect against another lash. It doesn't work. She leans and reaches and then there's more searing pain, almost in the same spot. It's impossible not to baulk. She slips away again.

I stop this time, studying her, breathing a little more heavily than I'd like. Lanistia is motionless. Not smiling. Not amused or enjoying herself. If anything, she looks bored.

"Are you sure your injuries aren't slowing you down, Vis?"

I'm sizing her up, planning my next attack, when she takes two dance-like steps forward. A whistling, biting slash for a third time on my left cheek, then again on my right as I twist away, snarling in frustration. The pain blinds me for an instant, makes me panic. I stumble.

When my vision clears, Lanistia's back where she started. In exactly the same stance. As if she'd never moved.

"That's not fair." I touch the burning welts on my cheek.

"I have no eyes and a twig for a weapon. All *you* have to do is touch me." Somehow as she's finishing the flatly delivered sentence she's coming forward again. I try to react, go on the offensive. She slips past anyway. Another smarting strike to my right cheek, delivered with infuriating indifference. My face must look a mess.

I'm angry now. Angry at the taunts—no matter how stoically they're delivered, I know that's what they are. Angry that one of the things I've prided myself on over the past six months is being so comprehensively proven inadequate.

Angry at the idea of her being right about me.

I snatch up a stone from the ground and hurl it at her, trying to come in behind the attack while she's off-balance. It doesn't come close to working. Lanistia's pivoting smoothly, sliding effortlessly to let the rock smash against the cobblestone behind her. There's yet another sting on my right cheek, and then a punch delivered to my gut. Not hard, but with pinpoint accuracy. My breath detonates. I double over.

She's circled behind me, grabbed my arms, and shoved me to the ground before I can recover. My face scrapes against gravel. I buck, but her grip is a vise.

"Concede?"

I jerk backward in an attempt to headbutt her, but she's too savvy to get that close. It just hurts my neck, and then my bad shoulder as Lanistia wrenches warningly on my arm in response.

I grit my teeth, and let my body go limp.

"Good." The pressure on my back vanishes, and I see Lanistia's shadow step away.

I lie there, trying to let go of my embarrassment. It doesn't work. Eventually I roll into a seated position, unwilling to meet her gaze, brushing dust from my tunic and then rubbing my burning cheeks.

"So you're faster than me." My voice grates on the words.

"I'm better trained than you. More disciplined." Lanistia says it with her usual dispassionate bluntness. "Go and clean yourself up, and then we can talk about how to try and change that."

I give her a black look, but lever myself to my feet and shuffle across to the nearby fountain. The pool is hexagonal in shape, a sculpted column in its centre gushing a steady, sparkling flow of clear liquid.

I look into the gently rippling water, pausing as I catch my reflection. Frown. Peer closer.

My cheeks display near-matching raised welts. Six thin lines, striped almost evenly.

"Gods *damn* it." I erase the image in the water as I splash my face, then turn back to Lanistia.

"Tell me what I have to do."

XV

THE TRAINING AREA IN FRONT OF ME—IF THAT'S ACTUALLY what it is—is like nothing I have ever seen.

We've descended through several Will-locked doors into some sort of basement beneath the eastern wing of the villa. Lanistia is lighting torches on the near wall; every time she does, dozens more immediately sputter to life farther away, revealing more of the cavernous room. It's at least two hundred feet wide, maybe five times as long. Most of it, though, is comprised of an enormous pit. Only a fifteen-foot-wide stone platform—on which we're standing—hugs the wall at our height, encircling the deep sub-level.

It's the area below that commands my attention, though. The flickering orange light reveals hundreds of rough-cut stone walls criss-crossing the vast space. My eyes try to trace a path through the twisting passageways formed. They can't.

"What is this?" My voice echoes.

"Something that will help." Lanistia keeps lighting torches.

There's a shelf cut into the wall, on which sits a laden leather bag and what looks like a long, heavily studded bracer. Strange. I wander closer to examine it.

"Don't touch anything."

I scowl. Almost all the torches are burning, but her back's turned. Can she see me, despite that? I reach for the bracer.

"I mean it."

I pull my hand back, satisfied at the tiny victory. Good to know.

Lanistia finishes her task. The torches around the edges of the room are bright and evenly spaced, their smoke filtering out through some sort of ventilation in the ceiling. A bewildering sea of shadowed stone now glowers below.

"It's called the Labyrinth. It's a replica of a training device at the Academy." Lanistia comes to stand at my shoulder.

"Why do you have one here?"

"For training."

I draw a breath, then just exhale again, turning to stare at her balefully.

"Your arrival was a surprise, Vis, but not the fact that we were going to have to prepare *someone*." Her gaze is focused out over the torch-lit pit, hands clasped behind her back. "And this is considered the most effective test for deciding how well some-one will be able to handle Will. You can be the smartest and strongest student in that school, but if you can't show a high level of competence at the Labyrinth, you won't progress far enough to be useful."

I frown down at the ocean of walls. "How does it work?"

Lanistia beckons me over to the shelf, picking up the bracer and displaying it to me.

If it *is* a bracer, it's unlike any I've seen before. A leather base is surrounded by three pieces of thin grey stone; arrayed across those are perfectly cut circles of what appear to be onyx, each one smaller than a fingernail. There have to be close to twenty of the strange studs on each strip. It's unwieldly looking, to say the least.

Lanistia straps it to her arm, then points to a section of the Labyrinth below, about fifty feet away. "Watch."

She touches one of the onyx studs, and slides it a mere fraction to the left.

It happens so fast that it takes me a second to understand. There's a grinding sound; a section of wall in the direction Lanistia indicated abruptly moves, slamming to the side and instantly opening a new pathway, even as it blocks another.

I survey the section of Labyrinth that just changed, then glance back at the dark-haired woman's left arm.

"So these stones are Will-locked to sections down there, somehow. To pieces of the wall," I posit, trying to puzzle it out. "You can rearrange the layout as you want?"

"There are limitations, but yes. Each control stone is locked to a specific panel. The symbol here shows which one." She lifts the bracer toward me, and I lean closer to see three horizontal slashes on the stone she just used. Sure enough, the same symbol is etched large on the section that just moved down below. "You can also reorient panels, like this." She carefully twists the black circle, and the six-foot-wide slab below snaps violently into a perpendicular position, neatly cutting off the corridor it had previously helped form.

I frown down at the maze. There are at least fifty onyx stones on Lanistia's bracer, and presumably a matching number of the myriad different symbols that I can see carved into sections of wall. "How does it work?" I know my understanding of Will is still limited, but most of the Hierarchy's inventions are at least somewhat compre-hensible. Like the Transvect—the implementation's far from simple, but I can see how it *could* function.

This . . . this seems like something far more complex.

"The mechanics are too difficult to explain, at your level of education. All you need to know is that it does."

I bite back a snide retort. There's nothing personal in her tone. And given that I genuinely can't guess at the systems in play here, she may well be right.

"So what's its purpose?"

"In the Academy, it's a contest. Whoever wears this has to make it from one end of the Labyrinth to the other, while other students team up to try and stop them—some run the maze, others act as spotters around the sides." Lanistia unbuckles the bracer and offers it to me. "But even if we had the bodies, you're not ready for that yet. Here and now, we're just going to concentrate on you learning how to manipulate the walls properly—and even that is probably going to take a while. So put this on and wait for me to talk you through it."

I fumble it even with the expected weight, and then cinch it onto my left arm, grimacing at the faint pull on my shoulder. It feels like . . . well. It feels like my forearm's encased in stone, I suppose. With an effort, I bring the bracer up for a better look at the onyx pieces on it. Every circle has a symbol scored into its surface, abstract but easily identifiable. I find the stone with the three horizontal lines that Lanistia used. "Doesn't seem too complicated."

"Don't—"

I nudge the stone to the left.

There's a screeching sound as the panel below shivers, trembles. The stone I'm pressing against suddenly burns; there's a scorching flash against my skin and then the onyx shatters, my forefinger sliding across a newly jagged edge. I yell in surprised pain, snatching back my hand and shaking it furiously. Bright red droplets arc through the air as the broken stone detaches from the bracer, clattering to the ground.

"Idiot." Lanistia grabs my hand, holding it steady as she examines the cut. "*Idiot.*"

I grimace, but take both the examination and reproof in silence. I'm already inwardly muttering far worse curses at myself.

"It's deep." Lanistia takes a wad of cloth from her pocket—I'm not sure what its original purpose was—and jams it, none too gently, against my finger. "You need to listen to me."

"Maybe I would, if you weren't so gods-damned condescending all the time." I snap the words. Angry again. I was too hasty, but it doesn't mean I have to take her constant disdain.

"Because I'm realistic about your abilities? I'm not going to coddle you."

I take over the application of the cloth from her, trying not to make it a petulant act. "I don't want to be coddled, and I don't want you to lie. I'll listen, I'll work hard. I'll take Kadmos's rotting tea to push through these injuries. I accept that I need to improve." The words are ash in my mouth, but I've seen my father win arguments too many times to give in to touchiness. "When you remind me of it every few sentences, though, it just makes me want to prove you wrong. So maybe judge me when I do something that needs to be judged?"

"Like just now?"

I hold her gaze, then can't help but give a soft snort and look away as I shake my head, my anger dissipating beneath the beginnings of an unwilling smile. "Like just now." I wrap the cloth tighter around my seeping finger, ignoring the burn that follows. "Sorry."

"Happens to everyone, eventually." Lanistia's gruff, but in a mollified sort of way. "Come on. We need to stitch that up."

We head back to the stairwell. She doesn't say anything else, but it feels like some of the tension, the unconscious aggression that I thought was just part of her character, has eased from her posture.

I squeeze my wounded finger. Could be my imagination, too.

Time will tell.

※ ※ ※

I'VE HAD STITCHES PLENTY OF TIMES OVER THE YEARS. LANIS-tia doesn't have the touch of a royal surgeon, but she's deft and surprisingly gentle as she slides the needle in and out of my flesh.

"You've done this before."

"Younger brothers." It's said absently, her focus on my wound.

I brighten, seizing on the scrap of personal information. "How many do you have?"

There's a sting and I flinch away as the needle stabs too deep, Lanistia faltering. Or maybe jabbing me. "Enough." Something in her tone tells me not to pursue it.

I glance down at my injury. It's a bad gash, deep, running from the tip of my forefinger down to the second knuckle. There's copious amounts of blood. I'm lucky Kadmos's tea is still at work. I reluctantly offer my hand back to her, then focus on her face rather than the wound. Her black glasses mirror the light streaming through the window.

"You must be able to see fairly well, to do this," I observe cautiously.

Lanistia doesn't respond for a second, and I think she's going to ignore me again.

"When I focus, I can." It's partly an irritated rebuke to the question, but she takes a breath and continues. "If I use Will to concentrate on something in particular, I can see it perfectly. Every detail, and from every angle. Far better than someone with regular eyesight could."

"But?" There's clearly a "but."

"But when I do that, I can't see anything else. Or I can, but it all moves in flashes." She hesitates, needle hovering above my forefinger as she searches for the words. "Imagine that you have to keep your eyes closed, but you can open them for a moment every second or so. Like a very slow, constant blink. That's how everything looks to me right now, except for the area around your hand." She's matter of fact about it, but there's discomfort beneath the statement. She's not used to talking about this.

"Sounds like it would be distracting."

"You get used to it." Closing off the topic. She resumes her needlework, neatly adding the last couple of stitches and tying the thread. "There. You'll have to be careful of it for the next week or so, but it will heal."

"Thanks."

She nods curtly. "Listen to me next time."

I accept the reprimand, and at a silent agreement we start back toward the east wing of the villa. It's mid-afternoon, the hallways shady and cool and quiet. I glimpse a couple of Octavii hurrying about some task or other in the distance, but no one else.

"So the control stones can shatter if you try to move a wall into a position it's not meant to go," Lanistia says abruptly, breaking the hush between us.

"Sounds like something I should be careful of."

"Mm-hm." There's a pause, and then, "Using the bracer requires absolute precision. Even if you'd moved that stone in the right direction, they're easy to push too far. Or not far enough. Or at a slightly wrong angle. Any of those things can cause a transference into the control stone. That won't usually break it—you *really* need to push it in the wrong place for that to happen—but it will make it fall off, stop it from operating until a reset. Which is as good as an automatic loss at the Academy," she adds.

I think about the difficulty of sprinting through the Labyrinth, trying to accurately manipulate the bracer as I try to both make my own path and evade pursuers. "So these contests. They're really that important?"

"You need memory, logic, speed, precision, and physical strength to win one. Not to mention the ability to split your focus between multiple problems at once. For higher-ranked Will use, those qualities are all key. And the Academy puts a lot of stock in the results." We start crossing the courtyard. "So, yes. They're that important."

"But surely there are better ways to test those things."

"Individually? Maybe. But together . . ." She splays her hands. "I was sceptical too, at first, but competing in the Labyrinth does feel *exactly* like using Will. I tell Ulciscor the same thing all the time. It's just hard to explain."

"Ulciscor doesn't know from experience?"

"The Labyrinth wasn't around when he was at the Academy. He's old." There's the ghost of affection in her tone, though it vanishes immediately. "It only came in when . . ."

She trails off as a figure appears in the doorway ahead of us.

"Injured yourself again, young master?" Kadmos puffs the words as he approaches, the stout man carrying a crate of something evidently heavy. He stops just ahead of us, giving a groan of effort as he sets the unwieldy box on the ground, then wiping a rivulet of sweat from his nose.

"Sparring accident. Cut himself on a rock. Nothing serious," says Lanistia, chiming in before I can speak.

"Not the best start."

"No," Lanistia agrees. "I'm glad we ran into you, Kadmos. Did the Magnus Quintus speak to you about Vis's education?"

"He did, Sextus."

"I'd like you to start tomorrow morning."

Kadmos gives an acknowledging bow to the two of us. "Where might I be able to find you, Master Vis, in the meantime? I was hoping to take a measure for your new clothing earlier, but no one knew your whereabouts."

Lanistia replies again before I can open my mouth. "We were at the Magnus Quintus's training ground. We'll come and find you when we're done." Distinctly a dismissal.

"Ah." Kadmos bows again, a few stringy strands of hair falling over his eyes. His gaze flicks between us, then he bends and lifts his cargo again with a grunt. "I look forward to it. Until then, young master. Sextus." He trundles off, breathing heavily at his renewed exertion.

We continue on into the eastern wing. I glance across at Lanistia once we're out of earshot. "Training ground?"

"I should have said earlier. The Labyrinth isn't *exactly* something we're supposed to have, here. Ulciscor had several people break a writ of Silencium to get the plans. Kadmos, the rest of the staff—they don't know about it. No one does except you, me, and Ulciscor."

I process the statement. "So it's meant to be exclusive to the Academy," I conclude. "We're cheating?"

"The other students already have several months' head start on you. This is giving you a chance to catch up." She sees my look, shrugs. "Yes. We're cheating. You need the advantage."

I acknowledge the assertion, barely feeling more than a flicker of irritation at it this time. "How in the gods' names did you build it without anyone knowing?"

"Slowly. We had to source the stone without raising questions, so we bought it from different suppliers, different regions. Had it shipped on roundabout routes. Took months." She unlocks the outer door to the Labyrinth, and we start down the stairs.

I almost laugh. I was talking about the manpower to construct this massive cellar—but of course, the Magnus Quintus would be more than capable of doing that by himself. "Seems like a lot of effort."

"It was. Don't waste it."

We emerge onto the platform overlooking the enormous maze. The torches are all still lit, the bracer sitting on the ground where I left it. I take care not to bump any of the stones as I pick it up, inspecting the gap where the one I pushed broke. "How do we fix this?"

Lanistia moves over to the shelf it was originally on, dipping into the leather bag there and pulling out a circular piece of onyx. Then she joins me again. Holds the stone between thumb and forefinger, and positions it over the empty space on the bracer.

She doesn't move, but the onyx is suddenly sucked from her grip, snapping into place. I flinch. There's a scratching, grinding sound, and the smell of burning drifts to my nostrils as the surface of the stone begins to change, three horizontal slashes gradually etching themselves into its surface.

"Gods' graves. How . . ."

"I told you. Beyond your level of education."

I tear my gaze from the newly engraved stone. "How much Will does all of this take to run?"

"A lot." Lanistia stares implacably at me and when I stare back, she grunts. "I'll make you a deal. As soon as you've mastered the Labyrinth, I'll fill your head with all the irrelevant details of how it works. Sound good?"

"Do I have a choice?"

"Not really." She smiles tightly. "Let's get to work."

※ ※ ※

AFTER TWO HOURS OF PRACTICING, I'M BEGINNING TO UNDERstand why Lanistia was so comfortable offering me her compromise.

Hazy torchlight shifts and flickers against the stone panels, many of which now show ugly scores along their faces. It's cool down here, isolated as we are from the baking sun, but my palms are damp. Tension cramps my hands. My cut finger, and side, and shoulder, all pulse with a dull ache. I think Kadmos's tea is wearing off.

"Try using the double triangle to shut off the left passage." Lanistia has her arms crossed, focusing expectantly down over the Labyrinth. Doesn't even look toward me.

My eyes and hand rove uncertainly over the bracer for a full three seconds before finding the stone with the corresponding symbol. Every muscle is taut. I slow my breathing. Assess where the corresponding panel is below, where it needs to go. Check my orientation. Allow myself a hopeful heartbeat.

Then I shift the onyx about a quarter-inch to the left. A quick, decisive movement. The only way it will work.

Juddering resistance. An awful, shivering shriek. Sparks fly below as stone scrapes madly along stone. The sound echoes away almost as immediately as it began, the panel motionless again the moment I jerk my hand away. A fine cloud of dust rises from that section of the Labyrinth, reddish in the torchlight. Only the skittering sound of the stone falling from my bracer breaks the abrupt hush.

"*Rotting damned gods.*" I step back. I've contained my frustration to this point, but the dam is breaking. "This is impossible."

It's too exacting. That tiny movement needs to be angled perfectly—no tremor, not a breath to one side or the other throughout the entire motion. Otherwise, the mistake is magnified a hundredfold down below. The panel being manipulated smashes into one wall or another. Things break.

And this is while I'm standing still. Concentrating with everything I have.

"It's your first day." Lanistia hasn't moved, though she is frowning at the dissipating cloud below. It's reflected in her glasses.

"So most students are this bad to start with?" I'm somewhere between bitter and hopeful with the question.

"No." Lanistia finally glances my way. "But precision is key to manipulating Will, so most students have already trained for years to hone these sorts of skills. You're no prodigy, but your progress so far isn't cause for despair, either."

I study her. There's no warmth to her tone or sympathy in her posture. No attempt to pacify me that I can see.

I exhale. Bring my arm up again.

"Good. Diamond and square to open the fourth row." Lanistia's already gazing back out over the maze. "Don't overthink it."

I quickly assess the relative position of the panel to its destination, then locate the stone. *Push.*

The panel with the diamond and square engraved on it slides along its corridor. There's a squealing grind until it stops in place. As intended.

The onyx still falls from the bracer, but I suppress a smile this time.

"Better." Lanistia is watching the puff of dust rising from the right-hand side of the passageway. She sounds more alert than before. Surprised. "Still not good enough, obviously, but . . . better. Now, open up a route to the centre."

I take a breath longer to enjoy my small victory, then comply. The attempt ends like almost all the ones previous. The screeching and crashing from below doesn't set my teeth on edge quite as badly, though.

I just need to keep practicing.

XVI

I ALWAYS THOUGHT MY EDUCATION ON SUUS WAS INTENSIVE.
Two weeks into my stay at Ulciscor's villa, and I'm more than beginning to reassess my younger self's impression.

Here I rise in darkness each day—or more accurately, am risen by a dangerously-close-to-happy Lanistia bearing my first dose of Kadmos's foul-smelling tea. It's the only time she seems cheerful, as if the pain of my waking is some sort of salve.

We start with an hour of physical training in the dim pre-dawn, on the immaculately kempt lawn a little away from the main house, so as to not disturb anyone. There's always dew on the grass, and the chill never quite leaves the air. The focus is on my speed. I've always considered my reactions to be fast, but Lanistia continues to prove me wrong, and isn't shy about reinforcing the lesson. She never hits my injured side or shoulder, yet I still usually have bruises on top of bruises by the time the sun peers over the horizon.

If I'm being honest, back at Suus, I would have had her replaced as a tutor within the first week. Her attitude's never softened, never warmed: she doesn't like me, and I don't like her.

But as painful as it is—both literally and emotionally—she's smart. Effective. Probably what I need, right now.

I'm allowed a half hour to use the villa's heated baths to recover, and then breakfast, full and delicious though it always is, is taken as I begin my studies. Lanistia disappears at this point, and Kadmos takes her place. Each day there's a different topic, different texts to read between bites of fresh-baked bread dipped in honey. The information I'm presented with is always supplemented by Kadmos himself, and despite my initial scepticism, it's soon apparent that the Dispensator is a more than adequate tutor. He imparts wisdom on everything from geopolitical treatises to mechanical dispersion rates to the Echelon Philosophies with confident, brusque authority.

Kadmos's lessons, while instructive, are no more enjoyable than the ones prior. His is a different kind of cold. Where Lanistia is disdainful, he's suspicious. Where she's harsh, he's aloof. He corrects without bile when I need correction, acknowledges when I succeed. Is unfailingly polite. But there's always the sense that he's there more to watch me than to see me learn. He still considers me an intruder.

It's not until the fourth day that Lanistia mentions that he was the youngest-ever head of the Azriat—the most respected learning institution in Sytrece—before he was proscribed, his possessions and property confiscated, and then taken to Caten as an Octavus several decades ago. I try to bring it up with him, but he dismisses the conversation as quickly as I can raise it. While I cannot imagine having your name on one of the Hierarchy's proscription lists could be something you ever truly surmount, I don't think it's a sore point for him anymore. He simply doesn't want to discuss personal matters with me.

Once breakfast's over, we move into the shade and privacy of the inner courtyard, where Lanistia joins us again as an observer while Kadmos shifts to questions about a previous day's topic. He's not interested in my memory, for the most part. Never asks me to recite facts and figures. Instead, he pushes for explanations. Wants me to infer, to reason out conclusions. To prove that I've been absorbing the information rather than learning by rote.

I'm mostly successful, here. Lanistia never compliments, but there's also rarely criticism as she watches. I've come to recognise that as an equivalent, from her.

After that—with me already exhausted from the day's efforts—Kadmos resumes his duties elsewhere and Lanistia and I have lunch, a light meal taken with a heavy side of lecturing on the political landscape of Caten. There's a *lot* to digest; the Senate is comprised of four hundred and fifty-nine senators, and at least half of those are considered important in one way or another. So we go over their responsibilities. Areas of governance. Ancestry. Alliances. Grudges, old and new. Some I need to know because their children will be attending the Academy, and—as Lanistia keeps insisting—I'll need to choose my friends there wisely. Others, she says, are simply too significant for me to remain ignorant of them and not look a complete boor.

Though I hate to admit it, and am tempted to blame weariness, I'm less adept at these lessons. There are dozens upon dozens of faceless names, and the details of too many slip away before the next time Lanistia mentions them. It's partly instinctive disinterest, I think: I've always hated the gossipy, ugly web of relationships that invariably form around power. But I believe Lanistia when she says it's important, too. So I try, and she persists.

After my second dose of tea, the routine continues in the afternoon, which we spend almost exclusively down in the relative cool of the Labyrinth. I'm getting better at manipulating the maze, sliding and twisting the control stones with quick, precise movements. It's satisfying, even fun to respond at speed to Lanistia's instructions, snapping the panels below into position with steadily increasing confidence. Only one out of every four or five attempts results in a piece of onyx detaching from the bracer. Even if I am, as Lanistia takes great pains to remind me, doing it all from a vantage point while standing perfectly still.

Those hours in the Labyrinth are draining, far more so than the academic learning and physical training of the rest of the day. I have to focus so intently and so consistently that I'm ready to sleep by the time we emerge. Not that I get the chance. Dinner and the hours after involve more lessons with Lanistia, more study, more probing quizzes.

And then finally, blessedly—if all too briefly—I'm released to my rooms.

As I lie my head on the feather-stuffed pillow each day, I can't help but fuzzily catalogue my worries. My progress, which feels significant but is hard to gauge against Lanistia's and Kadmos's lacklustre feedback. My impending presentation to the Senate, which Ulciscor has scheduled for straight after the Festival of Jovan.

And before that, of course, there's the looming puzzle of how to get to the naumachia.

Ulciscor's continued absence has made negotiating my way there a task I'm not sure is even possible. The Magnus Quintus might have been swayed enough to let me go, I think, over time. Lanistia's a different story. She sees the Festival of Jovan as frivolous at best; the one time I've mentioned it, she was so scathingly dismissive that I haven't risked raising it again, fearing I'll only call attention to my interest.

Which leaves sneaking away my only option. Getting there in the first place isn't an easy prospect: all my clothing has been supplied by Kadmos, and if I'm being tracked, there's no way I'll be able to make it all the way to Caten without being caught. And even if I do, the journey's too long for my absence to not be noticed. The very best outcome would be that I return with a good enough excuse to continue to the Academy, but destroy any slim trust I've managed to build here in the process.

Still. I've reached the heavy acceptance that I can't risk not going; the threat the Anguis are holding over me is simply too great to ignore. There has to be a way to get there without ruining everything. There has to be a solution I'm missing. I just need time to think.

But no matter my determination, just as he said it would, Kadmos's concoction takes a toll as soon as it starts to wear off. My eyes never stay open long enough to figure it out.

%% %% %%

IT'S SIXTEEN DAYS AFTER MY ARRIVAL AT VILLA TELIMUS WHEN my body wakes in anticipation of Lanistia's firm, insistent prodding, rather than as a result of it.

I lie there in the dark, wondering whether I've somehow, horrifyingly, woken early. There's no sound from outside or deeper in the house that could have disturbed me, as far as I can tell. And outside the window, the first tinges of pre-dawn light are turning the inky black a deep purple in the east. Lanistia's usually in here by now.

I rise. Splash my face in a basin of lukewarm water. Watch the closed door, expecting it to open. Still nothing.

I glance back toward the bed. If she's not coming, or even just delayed . . .

But I need to train. Lanistia's not forceful in her lessons from some kind of pent-up spite: there's a genuine urgency to what she's doing, a resolve that comes from more than her temperament alone. When she says I'm not ready for the Academy, it's not just because she's trying to motivate me.

With a sigh, I tear my longing gaze away, trudge to the door, and open it.

"Master Vis."

I flinch, sleep-dulled senses not having registered the figure in the hallway. There's a low-burning lamp at the end of the corridor, but it's barely enough to see by.

"Kadmos?" I squint. Drowsy, but mildly unsettled by the idea of the steward lurking in the dark outside my room.

"My apologies. I didn't mean to startle you." The man steps forward, allowing the lantern to better illuminate his face. His jowly features are emphasised by dark bags beneath his eyes. He looks about as pleased to be up at this hour as I am. "Sextus Scipio requested that I direct you to the baths, once you were awake."

"Lanistia wants me at the baths?" I repeat obtusely.

"The baths." He twitches his shoulders into a weary shrug, indicating he's as mystified as I. Then he hesitates. "No headaches this morning?"

I consider whether my fuzziness is anything out of the ordinary for the hour. He's been weaning me off the tea for the past few days, ever since my side stopped needing bandages. Yesterday was the first day I had none at all. "No."

"And your injuries?"

I roll my left shoulder. "This is fully healed, I think. Side's not much more than itchy."

"Good."

I don't have the energy for polite acknowledgment yet. I rub my eyes, then shuffle away down the hall without a word.

We didn't have baths back in Suus: they were always a distinctly Catenan thing, part of their culture and not ours. I remember my father's advisors suggesting that we build one, once—a way to make visiting dignitaries feel more "at ease," as they put it.

Everyone knew why we really needed one, though. Baths have been a symbol of civili-sation to the Catenans for over a century. They're where the true business of the realm is conducted, where power flows and deals are made in the Hierarchy. Our lack of even a single one was a source of poorly concealed derision from abroad.

My father was a stubborn man, though, and I honestly think he liked the idea of making our Catenan visitors uncomfortable. Or hated the idea of adopting anything that was so distinctly Hierarchy. Or both. Either way, his response to his advisors was . . . strongly dismissive. Enough so that the matter, to the best of my knowledge, was never raised again.

His disdain for the practice has stuck with me; I've reluctantly used the heated pool as a means of recovery after training, but haven't been near that section of the villa otherwise. It feels especially strange to be going there at this hour, but I'm too asleep to reason out what's going on. The only sound is my feet slapping against cobbled stone as I cross the dim courtyard, the bite of the night air doing its best to clear my head. A few stars still glimmer above. The entrance to the baths, between two ornate columns guarding the expansive northern wing of the villa, is lit by a single flickering torch.

Lanistia is waiting beneath it, slouching against the wall. Her hand taps a steady rhythm against stone. Across from her and a little distance away stand two men.

"What's going on?" I eye the strangers.

"You have a visitor."

"What?" My brow furrows as sleepy bemusement wrestles with the statement. "Who?"

"Magnus Quartus Advenius Claudius. He's inside, waiting." She says it through gritted teeth.

"I see." Making it clear that I don't. Claudius is an important man; I recognise the name from my daily lessons, though the specifics of who he is are hazy. He's from Governance. The senator in charge of . . . something economic. To do with the knights, I think?

"He has estates nearby, which he is visiting, and thought he might stop by and welcome the newest member of the Telimus family." The official reason, not the one she believes. "I imagine he would also like to meet a prospective Academy student, given that his daughter Aequa is there currently."

"But why come so early? Why . . . ?" I gesture behind her at the baths. Still confused.

"Why do you think?"

I suck in a lungful of the chilly air and close my eyes. Lanistia's question is pointed. Definitely not rhetorical.

The hour suggests that Advenius doesn't want anyone to know he's here—if he had arrived later, when all the Octavii are working, word would have spread. And the baths indicate he wants privacy: he must know Ulciscor's in Caten, and it would beyond stretch propriety for Lanistia to try and bathe with us.

Of course, the man could just as easily have demanded a private audience with me—he's a Quartus, after all—but that's not the Catenan way. They'd see such a direct approach as clumsy. Oafish. A wasteful use of power.

Lanistia sees my realisations, but is evidently mindful of not saying too much in front of Advenius's men. "And I am sure he is curious to find out why you're worthy of the Telimus name."

Of course. If I show weakness here, Advenius will undoubtedly present that information to the Senate. Undermine the ratification of my adoption before I ever get a chance to defend myself. "I look forward to showing him." I say it so that the two men across the way can hear.

"Good. Particularly given the disagreements he and your father have had over the years." Her back is to the men as she issues me a meaningful look. So there's some personal squabble between Ulciscor and Advenius, then. Even better.

I scrub my forehead with the palm of my hand, and head between the sandstone pillars.

The baths are a modest affair compared to some of the others I've seen over the years, but that's not to say they're unimpressive. There's a differently heated room and pool for each stage of the bathing ritual, and even a courtyard to the side for exercise. Striking mosaics decorate the walls.

I find Magnus Claudius submerged in the most pleasantly warm of the four pools, reclining with half-lidded eyes. He's a large, olive-skinned man with an almost entirely bald pate, though a few damp hairs still cling desperately to its sides. He stirs as he registers my presence, and fat jiggles around his chest and stomach. There's heavy muscle lurking beneath that outer layer, though, something about the way he stretches indicating a strength that belies his initial appearance. Not a soft man, by any means.

He watches me. Warmth radiates from the floor as I pad over. The only sounds are the gentle gushing of water flowing from a slit in the wall down into the bath, and the echoing slap of my bare feet.

"Vis Telimus." Advenius's voice almost elicits a snigger; it's squeaky, far too high-pitched for his heavyset form. "A pleasure to meet you, young man."

The Quartus's tone is lazy, dismissive, despite the friendly words. I try not to bristle. "And you, Magnus Quartus. It's an honour." I try to hit somewhere between polite-but-false sincerity and sarcasm. I'll be civil, but I'm not going to pretend to fawn over the man. "What can I do for you?"

"You can sit. Sit," he insists with that incongruous voice, gesturing to the sunken concrete seat opposite. "I've been so looking forward to meeting you, ever since I heard Ulciscor had adopted."

"Losing sleep over it, I take it." I yawn to emphasise the point as I step into the warm water.

Advenius chuckles. More of a titter, really. "I do apologise for the hour. I thought I had another three weeks out here in the country to drop by, but the Senate informed me otherwise just last night. My carriage to Caten leaves not long after dawn." He spreads his hands. "A slave to the vagaries of their schedule, I'm afraid. This remained my only chance to introduce myself before the Academy's next trimester."

He talks indolently, as if not really paying attention to the words coming out of his mouth. In another man, I might have believed he was bored or distracted, or even that what he was saying might be true. I slide onto the step opposite Advenius, submersing myself up to my chest, careful not to show him my back as I do so. Too many questions if he sees the scars.

"I didn't think anyone knew I was here."

"Yet here I am." The most explanation I'm going to get.

"And I'm flattered." Still carefully neither sarcastic nor sincere. Polite, but by no means impressed. "Not sure I'm worth the notice, though."

"No?" Advenius arches an eyebrow as I settle into the pool. "Plucked from obscurity by one of the most private men in the Senate. Being sent to the Academy, despite it meaning you'll start a full trimester behind everyone else. Then not just surviving an Anguis attack, but single-handedly saving a Magnus Quintus from it." He watches me with languid curiosity. "You may not be hearing it here in Ulciscor's walled garden, my boy, but expectations are high. People are *talking*."

"Sounds like they're getting ahead of themselves." I can't help but try and brush it aside, play down the Quartus's statement. I know this is probably what Ulciscor wants; it will be hard to advance in the Academy if I don't stand out. It doesn't make me any less queasy. I can handle whatever extra pressure the attention may bring—I grew up with far worse, after all. But the scrutiny itself, after working so hard and so long to be invisible, is a difficult thing to embrace.

"Modest as well?" The large man shifts, slow ripples gliding away from his torso. Despite his relaxed posture, there's something sharp in his brown eyes. "How refreshing. A hard quality to find among your contemporaries. Though I imagine their up-bringing must have differed from yours."

"You'd like to hear the specifics, I take it." A bit too blunt and tired to be considered well-mannered, this time. It's early, and I'm not going to feign interest in being subtle.

There's a flash of irritation from Advenius. Catenans—*cultured* Catenans—always make an effort to participate in these careful conversational dances. Still, he recovers with barely a pause. "I suppose I am curious."

So I tell him, calmly and succinctly. The more recent parts which he might be able to verify, I'm entirely honest about. Everything else is a practiced lie. Words so comfortable and familiar that it would feel far stranger to be talking about things that actually happened, the life I've actually led. I smile absently as I relate my privileged childhood in Aquiria. Gather myself as I speak of the fluke riverboat accident that took both my loving parents from me. Grit my teeth in quiet rage, almost choke up as I explain how our local lord gave me the terrible news on the same day he came to evict me.

Finally I grow sober, contemplative, as I talk about what followed. The aftermath of Aquiria's signing of their treaty with Caten, and how it affected a boy drifting alone and penniless through the country. Then my time at the orphanage in Letens and, in the story Ulciscor and I agreed upon, the Quintus's entirely fortuitous discovery of me there. I brighten as I explain how I managed to impress him in my interview. Hint at pleasure as I relay the moment he informed Matron Atrox that he would be adopting me.

That last is mostly unfeigned, actually. I do enjoy recalling that part.

When I'm done, Advenius exhales as if it's the first breath he's released since I started. He's been watching me with an unblinking gaze. Drinking in every word, from all appearances. I'm sure it's at least partly an act. People tend to be more pliable, more forthcoming, when they feel like you're fascinated by them.

"Remarkable." The pudgy man shakes his head, that high-pitched squeak of his still discordant. "And now here you are. Training in the home of one of the most powerful men in the Republic." A languid examination of me. "That's going well?"

"Well enough." As noncommittal as I can make it.

"It must be hard with so little prior education, preparing for something like the Academy."

"My parents saw to it that I had some of the best tutors in Cartiz." I try to relay facts rather than be defensive. It's by far the weakest point in my story; adoption's not uncommon among senators, but it usually happens years in advance of a child attending the Academy. The idea that someone my age, without a deep formal education, would be expected to compete there is . . . far-fetched. Even to me.

"What were their names?"

"My parents?"

"Your tutors." Still talking as if he's about to fall asleep, but there's no dodging the question. "I try to keep abreast of all the best educators in the Hierarchy. Perhaps I've heard of them."

I nod as if I believe him. "Falcona De Guez and Servanda Arales."

"Both women?" Surprised.

"Yes." They're Aquirian names—the same as I gave to Ulciscor, the same as I've given to everyone who's heard this story—but not real people. It won't matter. Aquiria's infamous record-keeping, combined with their complicated and disorganised union with the Hierarchy, means that there will never be a way for anyone to determine that those two women *didn't* exist. Which is all that matters. "No Birthright in Aquiria, back then." There's no law against women holding positions of power and education in the Hierarchy, but Birthright's complex system of taxation and legal obligation around marriage and children makes them more rare.

Advenius accedes the point with a musing sigh. He finally looks down, away from me, gazing into the gentle swells of the glassy pool.

"Tell me, Vis," he says eventually. "Have you studied Magelicus?" Nothing in his tone has changed but there's nonetheless a subtle shift, the sense of an uptick in importance to the conversation. We're finally getting to the point.

"Of course. Will strengthens Will. No man can truly learn, grow, or become wise within himself." Magelicus's philosophies are more than a hundred years old, from a time when Will users were little more than a small, suspiciously viewed sect in Catenan society. I don't think much of the man's teachings, but he's revered in the Hierarchy, seen as a founder of the nation. I'm not about to scorn him to the senator.

"I've always thought it to be true for peers, particularly. None of us can reach our potential without them." Advenius's eyes flick up from his introspection, meeting mine again. "My daughter, Aequa, is also attending the Academy this cycle. She's in Class Five, and she has an exceptional mind, if I may be so boastful. But she'll be out this way without much to do once the end of the first trimester comes, now I'm heading to Caten."

He leaves it there. Waiting.

"A shame. If Lanistia wasn't focusing on helping me in such specific areas, I would have liked a training partner."

"I'm sure Aequa could help. If you're covering ground she's already familiar with, she'd undoubtedly be an asset. And either way, she would still benefit more from listening to Lanistia than if she simply sequesters herself away for weeks on end." He issues an affable smile. "She would be able to give you some valuable insight into the Academy, too. It's been years since Lanistia and Ulciscor attended, after all." Despite the casual delivery, it's no idle request, not something he's simply decided to ask on a whim while he's here. I'm not sure why, yet, but Advenius wants this.

"Still. I'm not sure how either of them would feel about it."

Advenius gives another odd, soft, tittering laugh to that. His way of suggesting that we both know exactly how they would feel about it. "I am asking you; if you agree, the rest is simply detail. And while I have nothing but the utmost respect for Ulciscor and Lanistia, I worry that their opposition may stem less from concern for your success, and more from their past with the Academy."

Advenius's gaze never wavers as he finishes. The silence hangs.

He's right about the first part, at least: as a Telimus, if I give my word, it won't be a small thing to go back on. Lanistia will be unable to gainsay the decision, and by the time he hears of it, I doubt Ulciscor would invite an argument with a Quartus over it.

It's the latter statement that's caught my attention, though. It's subtle, but the way he says it, the way he's looking at me, suggests that he knows I'm in the dark about whatever he's referring to. Or at least, he strongly suspects so.

"You're talking about Ulciscor's brother?" He might be referring to Lanistia's past, too—her history with the Academy is evidently a bleak one—but this is my best guess.

"Young Caeror. His tragic suicide. Yes, yes, that's part of it, but . . ." He looks appropriately, demurely uncomfortable as he registers my surprise, hard though I try to hide it. "Oh. Perhaps I've already said too much. I thought you would have been told. I apologise for bringing it up."

I recover, shaking my head. So the official story is that he committed suicide. That doesn't necessarily clash with what Ulciscor told me, but it's strange that Advenius has made a point of it. I haven't pressed Lanistia or Kadmos on the subject of Caeror's death: I assumed there was no more to glean, and if nothing else, there simply hasn't been time. It sounds like I need to rectify that. "Not at all. In fact, if I understood more, it might make my decision about Aequa easier."

"Even so. It's not my place." An apologetic finality to it. "And I'm sure it goes without saying, but if you do agree to spend time with Aequa, please don't pester her about it. She's a wonderful girl, but can be less than circumspect about these sorts of things."

So it's something he thinks I should find important. Or, equally likely, he's attempting to sow discord.

Advenius leans forward suddenly, wrinkles in the water slithering away from his corpulent chest. "Tell me, Vis. When the Anguis attacked your Transvect. How did the Magnus Quintus react?"

I frown at the abrupt change of topic. "What do you mean?"

"Was he panicked, or calm?"

"Calm. At least compared to me."

"Would you say he was surprised?"

"Of course. But he recovered quickly."

"Hm." Advenius looks thoughtful. "What about when he confronted the attackers, after the crash? Do you remember him showing any signs of . . . recognition?"

"No." The implication's clear, now, and I let hard anger insinuate my voice. As would be expected from me.

"Ah." Advenius makes a placating gesture. "I only ask, as there have been . . . rumours, which I have been asked to look into. And this was such a strange attack, after all. So coincidental. It would be a terrible thing if you were caught in the middle of something you had no part in. Truly terrible. Good to have an unbiased observer to confirm you weren't involved, if it comes to that."

So he's here to investigate the Transvect attack, and he thinks Ulciscor might be in league with the Anguis somehow? The idea's ludicrous—but, I suppose, only because I know the truth.

I don't for a second believe that Advenius wants his daughter here as an "unbiased observer," of course. This is a manoeuvre for position, an attempt to further his own agenda somehow. Probably something to do with whatever bad blood there is between him and Ulciscor.

But, I realise with a jolt, I can use that.

There's just the gentle lap of water against the square-cut stone edges of the pool as I think.

"If Aequa and I were to train together," I say, making it sound reluctant, "I would prefer to get to know her first, away from all this. The schedule here has been hard. It's not the best setting for introductions."

"I'm sure something could be arranged. A dinner, perhaps, or—"

"I was thinking I would like to visit Caten for the Festival of Jovan. See the sights. Take in some of the games." I look hopefully at him. Letting him see an orphan now, an unsophisticated member of the mob who's been dragged up to his level of society. "I've never been."

"Of course. Of course! If you've never been, you simply *must* go. A tragedy that you have been deprived for so long. I will *insist* to your father that he allow you the day to accompany Aequa." The only clue to Advenius's satisfaction is the smooth alacrity with which he responds. His high-pitched proclamation bounces around the room.

"Then I would be delighted to have a training partner." I try not to sound like I'm forcing the words through my rictus smile. Lanistia's going to be . . . displeased, with the inconvenience of having to hide the Labyrinth from Aequa. Ulciscor, too, when he hears about it. They're going to wonder about this conversation, wonder what exactly Advenius offered me, no matter how truthfully I relate it to them afterward.

"Wonderful. Yes. Wonderful." The Quartus beams and stands, water pouring off him. I keep my gaze fixed determinedly on his face. "I would very much like to talk further with you, my boy, but unfortunately time has gotten away from us. Not even a chance to sweat a little in the next bath, I'm afraid. I'll make the necessary arrangements with Aequa, and send word. I trust I can leave you to sort out the details with young Lanistia?" Inferring, of course, that I'll make sure any opposition she has comes to nothing. He doesn't really wait for an acknowledgment, climbing out of the water and shrugging on the robe draped across a nearby bench.

"I can do that."

"Good. Good. A pleasure to meet you, my boy." Advenius dabs the black strands of hair clinging to the side of his scalp with his sleeve. His squeaky voice echoes off the stone walls. "I have no doubt that we will be seeing much more of each other in the coming years."

"I'm sure we will."

If Advenius is annoyed that I didn't reciprocate the pleasantries, he doesn't show it. "Stronger together, Vis." His movements as he heads to the exit are as languorous as his speech, but there's a visible power to them. A coiled energy in each motion, impossible not to notice as he departs.

It's a sense of physicality that's hard to marry to the overweight, middle-aged man, but I know it has to be because he's a Quartus. A pyramid of more than fifteen hundred people ceding to him. It's a frightening thought. Ulciscor gives off a faintly similar sense of undefinable strength, to be fair, but a Quintus only has a few hundred beneath him by comparison. This is something very different.

If Advenius is aware of my observation, he doesn't show it. He disappears without a backward glance.

I sit in the warmth of the pool for a while longer, contemplating its placid undulating. Then I sigh. Hoist myself from the water.

Time to face Lanistia.

XVII

STRONGER TOGETHER.

It's the great lie of the Hierarchy, proclaimed generation after generation by an ever-growing mob in thrall to the concept. Part of me understands why. There's a power to the phrase, an allure. It promises inclusion. Protection. Comradery. Common purpose. *Belonging.*

But you never have to look far to see its hypocrisy laid bare.

"She's a spy." Lanistia pivots away from my strike, the motion effortless. Her unique vision allows her to see my muscles tensing before I even begin my attack. I'm faster and smarter than I used to be, but still rarely manage to make contact.

"Obviously." The air is cool against my still damp skin as we spar beside the lush, empty, barely lit fields of Ulciscor's estate. Gravel crunches underfoot in the pre-dawn hush. Wind whispers through fields of grain, producing shadowy ripples at every touch. Stars still shine bright overhead in the west, even as those in the east fade from sight.

Lanistia's glasses reflect the slash of the horizon behind me as she circles to my left. "So what did he offer you?"

"Protection against prosecution. He's investigating the Transvect attack. He thinks that Ulciscor is in league with the Anguis, somehow. Or wants him to be."

"Advenius has been trying to prove that link forever."

"Why?"

Lanistia feints forward, but drawing no reaction from me, continues to sidestep. "Advenius and Ulciscor have always had something of a rivalry. A few years ago, someone in the Anguis uncovered an affair involving Advenius's sister. Advenius was on track to become Censor, but as soon as the details were made public, Governance dropped him from consideration. It was all rather ugly." She feints again. "If Advenius had been Censor, he would never have approved Military's nomination of Ulciscor for the Senate. So naturally, Advenius thinks Ulciscor had a hand in it somehow."

"Did he?"

"No. If he had, he would never have used the Anguis."

"Good." I have to let her think Advenius placed at least a shadow of doubt in my mind.

"I hope that wasn't the only reason you agreed to have the Claudius girl here. It's going to be a nightmare, keeping her away from the Labyrinth."

I tense the muscles in my right arm, just a fraction. When Lanistia hesitates, I launch in with my left. The attack comes close. She still dodges.

"I know, but the Quartus wasn't wrong about one thing: his daughter's been at the Academy far more recently than you or Ulciscor. She could tell me things that you two can't." I'm feeling the exertion now, breath misting in front of my face. "And I think it will help, training with another student. At the moment I have no gauge for my progress. No comparison."

Lanistia's suddenly flashing forward and I'm ducking to the side. She sweeps my leg from under me as I move. My back hits the ground hard.

She stands over me, silhouetted against the dawn. "I'm the gauge, Vis. You made a mistake, inviting her here."

"We'll see." The statement's undercut somewhat by my wheezing gasp.

"Surely you see the benefits don't outweigh the risks, though."

I think back to Suus. A pang as Ysabel bowed over a book, the image faded so terribly by the years, drifts across my mind. "They do for me."

Lanistia seems to hear something in my voice. She leans down. Offers her hand.

I grasp it and let her pull me to my feet.

"Anything else you need to tell me?"

"The Quartus made a point of saying that Caeror's death was a suicide."

She hasn't let go yet and there's a tightening of her grip. "It wasn't."

"I assumed, given what Ulciscor's already said. But what happened, exactly?" It's intimidating, being this close to her, but I keep my gaze steady. She doesn't move to release me.

Her lips thin. "Veridius killed him and lied about it. The details don't matter."

"Advenius seems to think they do."

"Advenius is a snake."

"That doesn't make him wrong. How do you actually *know* Veridius killed him?" When there's no response, I start to feel uneasy. "Look—Ulciscor has made it clear that I'm headed for a Sapper unless I find out what's going on at the Academy. But I know some of his suspicions are because of what happened to his brother. If Caeror really did—"

"*He. Didn't.*"

The words are low and sudden. More emotion, more conviction and sadness and rage, than I've ever heard from her.

I choke off, whatever I was going to say next forgotten.

She seems to come to herself, releases my hand and steps away. My fingers are white where she's squeezed the blood from them.

"He didn't," she repeats, firmly and in her normal, brusque tone. "And we're certain."

I massage the feeling back into my hand. "You knew him." I don't make it a question. I've wondered if that were the case, given my guess at Lanistia's age puts her and Caeror in the Academy at the same time. But she's never brought it up. Never been willing to talk about her past there at all, in fact, pointedly deflecting the few enquiries I've made.

She looks angry, but I think it's at herself more than me. "If you want to know about Ulciscor's brother, then you need to talk to *him*." No doubting the finality of her tone. This isn't open to negotiation.

"Easy to say," I grate, "when he's not actually here to do the talking."

"Patience. I got word last night: your presentation to the Senate is confirmed for directly after the Festival of Jovan. So you can go and meet the Claudius girl for the festival, then stay with Ulciscor until the Senate convenes. You'll have plenty of time to speak with him then." She's more gruff than furious now as she watches me dust my clothes. "And as far as your decision-making goes . . . what's done is done. We'll just have to schedule your transport to Caten soon. That can be hard to arrange once the festival gets closer."

She doesn't give me time to react or press further, dropping into her stance. I copy her from habit. We resume our bout as the first rays of dawn pierce the sky.

And that, it appears, is the end of the matter.

※ ※ ※

THE CIRCUMSTANCES SURROUNDING CAEROR'S DEATH CONtinue to scratch at the back of my mind over the next three weeks. Advenius mentioned suicide deliberately, of that I have no doubt. It could have been to sow discord, I suppose, an attempt to unsettle things here as I train.

It could also have had a more dire meaning. If it's widely known that Ulciscor thinks Caeror was killed—but no one believes him—then his motivations for adopting me, for sending me to the Academy, may be even more transparent than he or Lanistia have admitted. And *that* could be a problem.

I'll have to wait until my introduction to Aequa to find out.

I reveal none of these concerns to Lanistia, and following Advenius's visit, things quickly fall back into the same exhausting rhythm. Train. Learn. Test. Eat. Sleep. My wound fully heals. I begin to see the effects of good food and daily, strenuous activity in the mirror, filling out my physique, hardening it far beyond what my circumstances in Letens would ever have allowed. I had a rough, pugilistic strength from the Theatre, but this is turning it into sleek athleticism, the variety of exercise providing a far more complete mastery over my body.

That's beginning to show in my control of the Labyrinth, too. My reactions are becoming honed, instant, precise; I rarely lose stones from the bracer now, even through gruelling afternoons of Lanistia snapping out section after section for me to manipulate. The dark-haired woman never loses her severity, but even she acknowledges my improvement. On the day before the Festival of Jovan begins, she tells me I'll be ready to try the challenge of running the Labyrinth, changing sections as I move, after I return from Caten.

The weight of that impending trip—first trying to meet Sedotia, and then being presented to the entire Catenan Senate—has seemed distant. Most days, I don't have time to feel it.

But weeks spent in routine disappear, and then one morning I'm dressing for my journey to the naumachia.

XVIII

LATE AFTERNOON IS PAINTING THE TREETOPS AS MY CAR-
riage rattles its way along the road, the clattering of hooves accompanying it echoing
off the surrounding hills. I gaze out the window, fiddling with my toga. It's pristine
white, no stripe to indicate status, as appropriate for the festival.

I'm alone in the carriage, and have been since we left Villa Telimus almost a half
hour ago. It's a horse-drawn one today, and I'm also flanked by a half dozen riders. All
Septimii. All here to ensure that brigands don't cause me any trouble as I travel first to
Villa Claudius, and then to Caten itself.

I've never felt so uncomfortably like a true citizen.

"We're here, Master Vis." Torvus, the rough-looking head of my protective entourage, sees me peering ahead. I've already spotted the mansion towering amid the
surrounding fields. Newer and more ostentatious than Villa Telimus, it sprawls around
a long pool at the front. Columns upon columns of Will-cut white stone line the
portico, while the flowering gardens are ringed by hedges and poplar, immaculately
kept and perfectly symmetrical. Candles adorn the balconies, ready to light at dusk in
keeping with the holiday.

The only person in view is a young woman, seated on a low wall as she watches our
approach. She's wearing a fashionable blue silk tunic with a many-layered white mantle
draped across her shoulders; raven-black hair cascades over it, wisps catching rays of
the dipping sun behind her. The driver swings down as the carriage stops, opening the
door for her. She appraises him, then stands smoothly and allows him to assist her in.

"You must be Vis." Demure, though there's no hesitation in the introduction. "I'm
Aequa Claudius." She offers her hand, palm down, and I clasp it briefly to complete the
formal greeting as she seats herself opposite.

"A pleasure." The door's already shut and we're pulling away again. "Thank you for
agreeing to accompany me this evening."

There's more than a hint of wry humour to her expression. "Of course."

"Are you looking forward to the fighting?"

"The naumachia?" She looks as if she's just tasted something bitter. "No. Not . . .
not particularly." Just enough of an apology in the words to not be impolite. It's as
expected. Like most patricians, she feels that attending this sort of event is beneath her.

"Ah." I pretend to be disappointed, then lean forward, letting eagerness creep into my tone. The common-birth orphan, talking about an event I could never have dreamed of seeing a few months ago. "I've just . . . never been to the Catenan Arena. I'm interested in the chariots and gladiators too, of course, but when I heard this was on, I knew I had to get there somehow. But if you would prefer to find your own entertainment once we reach Caten, I'll understand."

She examines me, and though she makes some attempt to conceal it, she's bored by what she sees. That's good. I need her to underestimate me today, to not care about my whereabouts when the time comes.

"No," she says eventually, reluctantly. "My father would be displeased, if he heard."

We're already leaving Villa Claudius behind, our pace increasing as the Will-built road south straightens and widens. There are traces of Advenius's features in Aequa, though surprisingly few that mar her looks. I accept her response affably. It was worth trying.

The rhythmic clopping of hooves against stone and the creaking of the carriage are the only sounds for a few seconds.

"So. Tell me about the Academy," I say before the silence grows awkward. "Your father said you were in Class Five?"

"Four," Aequa corrects me. "I broke my arm riding about a week before the entrance exam, so they started me in Six. But I've worked my way up."

"Was that hard to do?"

She almost chokes. "Two promotions in six months? Nobody else has done it."

I can't help myself. "But is it *hard*?"

She frowns this time. Sees that I'm wheedling, but not charmed by it in the slightest. "Yes."

I grin cheerfully at her, determined to maintain the genial, relaxed demeanour for the duration of the trip. Partly because I can tell it bothers her, and I'm under no illusion as to why she's really here. And partly because she seems the type to underestimate anyone who's outwardly friendly. "Very impressive, then."

Her exasperated look almost makes me laugh.

"I imagine they'll start you in Seven, so you'll get to experience it for yourself soon enough." The thought seems to make her feel a little better. She relaxes as she considers me. "How long has Magnus Telimus been preparing you for the Academy?"

"About a month?"

She smiles dubiously. "How long, really?" An eye roll as I look at her blankly. "It's a nice story—a gifted war orphan, discovered by chance, taken in by a Magnus and elevated straight to the Catenan Academy. But my father said he could tell that Magnus Telimus has been preparing you for a while."

I cough a surprised chuckle. "I'm flattered. But I met Ulciscor for the first time a month ago."

She sighs, not surprised and not believing me. "Well. In any case, this trip is a good opportunity for us to learn each other's capabilities, given that we'll be training together for the next few weeks." Aequa makes no attempt to hide her hesitancy at the prospect. Her unblinking eyes are a startling shade of blue as they meet mine. Almost violet. "Any objections?"

"Not at all." She's not one for pleasantries, that much is evident.

"Then I'll start."

The next hour consists largely of Aequa throwing problems at me, and my occasional and half-hearted returning of the favour, as the countryside rolls swiftly by. I don't object. None of her questions are particularly taxing; in fact, they're almost laughable after having endured Lanistia's near-abusive interrogations. I make sure to answer correctly—I'm not trying to drive Aequa away—but I don't try to impress her with any sense of ease or alacrity, either. No benefit to her seeing me as a potential rival.

It's an easy enough ruse, with my mind largely on what's ahead now. How will Sedotia even find me, once we arrive? I have no way of contacting her, no way to signal to her where I am. And there will be a hundred thousand people in the Catenan Arena watching the naumachia. A *hundred thousand*.

I've already been chewing over the problem for weeks, and the extra hour doesn't help. At least, despite my distracted state, I notice the superciliousness of Aequa's interrogation is starting to abate. I'm better educated than she anticipated.

The road has become crowded over the past twenty minutes, one long caravan of pilgrims. The late afternoon light outside is just giving way to a true gold when we crest a rise, and the immense, imposing breadth of Caten appears up ahead.

I trail off mid-answer as I catch the sight. My first impression of the city, brief though it was, has lingered, and I've since wondered whether my memory had been exaggerating its ugly, intimidating grandeur. Hoped, really. We're approaching from the north-east. The horizon has resolved into an ocean of buildings and roads and towers and people scurrying everywhere, all silhouetted against the fading orange burn of sunset.

My recollection of Caten is entirely accurate.

"You haven't been here before?" Aequa's following my gaze. There are coloured lights flickering to life around the outside of some of the taller structures, special lanterns that stain the façades in dramatic, festive hues. As the carriage starts its descent along the road, I catch a glimpse of the bay beyond, reflecting the gentle glow of dusk. It's dotted with ships, some larger ones lit up as gaudily as the buildings.

"Only briefly."

"It's the greatest city ever built." There's no irony to Aequa's voice, no sense that she's anything but genuine in her assessment.

"What about Tolverium? Or Sena Corlisis?" I should let it go, but a part of me is on the defensive at the mere sight of this place.

"You mean their ruins?"

"But in their day," I press. Stubborn. "Tolverium was twice Caten's size. And even fifty years on, we're still finding new innovations in Sena Corlisis."

"You can't compare cities from before the Cataclysm to now. We don't know anywhere near enough about them." Aequa's put out that I'm not just agreeing with her, as most everyone else here would. Describing Caten as "the greatest city" is supposed to be small talk. Not even rhetoric. Like describing the clear sky as blue.

"I agree."

Aequa glowers, but gestures to show she can't be bothered pursuing the matter.

The carriage rolls on, and I return my inspection to the world outside. We've left the open fields, moving downhill and looking out over wooden buildings that are built low enough to the ground that we can see over their flat-topped roofs. This outer district of Caten is brightly lit, candles in every doorway, but away from the main road we're travelling, I can see ramshackle structures as high as three stories that look dangerously close to toppling. Everything's jammed together here, dirty, and the smell that wafts in the window is an assault.

It doesn't seem to bother the revellers, though. The streets are packed; I can hear Septimus Torvus yelling at the people ahead to clear the way.

"This is Esquilae District. Octavii, mostly." Aequa's over her pique, drawing my attention to an enormous statue ahead. "There's not much here, apart from Sere."

I recognise the Catenan goddess of spring and fertility easily enough. A naked woman with a wistful expression, hand outstretched as she gazes into the distance. The statue's twenty feet tall, marble and beautifully crafted, incongruous to its surroundings. Created using Will, no doubt. Religious symbols are required to be by law.

We're past in a few minutes, leaving the dilapidated residences behind us and nearing the sprawling central section of Caten. Roads widen. Houses becomes grander, interspersed with temples and statues and friezes. Coloured lanterns are everywhere, some carefully coordinated to give buildings their own distinct hues. A tapering, artistically twisting tower lit up in cool blue. An angled, polished stone monstrosity coated red. Another green, another yellow, another some deep shade of purple.

And below it all—crowding every brilliantly lit street—are people.

So many people.

Our carriage presses into the multitudes. All of Caten slopes toward the harbour, and we have an excellent vantage through the buildings. There's motion for as far as the eye can see. Individuals, couples, families. I see stalls lining the streets, merchants red-faced in the heat as they shout their wares at anyone foolish enough to make eye contact. I see people crowding around makeshift rings that contain men circling each other, occasional fists raised in excitement as one or the other lands a blow. I see children and adults trying their hand at games of skill or chance. Food being given out. Contests of strength. Of speed. Of Will. It's dizzying to watch, a throbbing mass of faces and bodies and movement.

There has to be ten thousand people here. More.

It's minutes later when I tear my eyes from the window. I've still been answering Aequa's questions, but absently, and it's only now I catch a glimpse of her smug expression as she watches me be overwhelmed. I pretend not to notice.

I shouldn't be surprised by the tumult, I suppose. The Festival of Jovan is one of the biggest celebrations in the Hierarchy; every major city holds parties in the streets, games, and produces countless lavish Will-powered displays to celebrate. I even attended once in Letens, prior to joining the orphanage. Some places give away food and drink to the crowds, all paid for by the Triumvirate—the three Princeps atop the senatorial pyramids. An expression of their generosity, of the wealth and security and greatness of Caten.

I liked taking their alms almost as little as I liked the idea of ceding, but hunger can have a tendency to trump principles, sometimes.

"Master Vis." It's Torvus, riding closer and leaning toward the window. "I think this is about as close as we can get."

The carriage, which has been inching along, comes to a complete stop as it's hemmed in by packed bodies.

"I know the way from here." Aequa's opening the door and disembarking before I realise what's happening.

"Oh . . ." Torvus looks at me questioningly.

I give him a nonplussed look as I follow her. "Thank you, Septimus. I'll be sure to let my father know you discharged your duties properly."

Torvus is relieved. "If you need us, we've rooms reserved at the inn in Alta Semita."

He glances across at Aequa, who nods her recognition of the location. "We'll be there until morning."

Aequa slides away from the carriage, and I follow her into the heart of Caten. It's claustrophobic as the structures around us loom, criss-crossing stone walkways high above covering sections of the still-fading sky. Everyone around us seems to be talking, laughing, calling out to someone in the distance. Music plays at every corner, notes discordant as they clash. It combines into a low, unsettling thunder.

I hate it. I've been in cities before, even during festivals, but I've never had to navigate a crush of bodies like this. The jostling, the heat, the smell, the noise: it's all unpleasant, all an experience I immediately wish to be over. How can people come here, knowing it will be like this? How can they *enjoy* this?

I scan each face we pass, not expecting to see Sedotia or anyone else I recognise, but alert nonetheless. They all belong to strangers.

"I understand you want to know about Caeror Telimus's suicide."

Aequa's words are all but shouted over the hubbub, as abrupt as the topic is unexpected. I almost choke. "I . . . ah." I lean in close to make my voice as low as possible, given the circumstances. "Yes."

"He died during the Academy Iudicium six years ago. Threw himself off a cliff. Apparently he had been acting erratically for weeks before the Iudicium started. Nearly got kicked out of Class Three because of it." Aequa calls it as she concentrates on our path forward. Simply a recollection of well-known facts, not something she considers private. "Quintus Veridius, who's the Principalis at the Academy now, saw it happen. They were friends. There was a terrible accident, and Caeror thought he'd killed another student who was competing. He didn't want to face the Sappers, so . . ." She takes an exaggerated, hopping step forward, miming the act.

This is news. "So he killed someone?"

"*Thought* he'd killed them," corrects Aequa, brushing a long strand of black hair back from her face and turning sideways so she can avoid touching a large, sweaty-looking man carrying a sack. "The Principalis thought they were dead too, but when it turned out they'd survived, he carried them back on his own. It took him almost a day. The Principalis doesn't like to talk about it, but the story's something of a legend at the Academy."

The public nature of this conversation is frustrating, but no one is giving us a second glance. I suppose in many ways, Aequa's not relating anything that's not already widely known. "And what did the injured student say?"

"No idea. I assume they didn't accuse the Principalis of murder, though, because he was given a Crown of the Preserver by Princeps Exesius himself. I've seen it. It's on display in his office."

I chew my lip. She's right: an honour like that means the rescue was never under any real cloud. "Why did your father think it was worth mentioning?" Aequa doesn't seem inclined to play the games that Advenius did. It's worth asking directly.

"Because your father"—there's a half breath of hesitation on the word—"spent months after trying to convince anyone who would listen that the Principalis was lying. In the end, the rest of your family had to step in and insist that he stop." She's still speaking loudly to be heard above the surrounding racket. "From what my father says, he just couldn't accept what had happened. But it was very public, very bitter. Nobody's forgotten."

I sigh. Exactly what I'd feared, in essence. "So everyone's going to think I'm at the Academy to get revenge on the Principalis, somehow."

"Aren't you?"

"Obviously not. I didn't know about any of this." Ulciscor must have been planning to tell me at least some of it before I left—he'd have to realise that I'd find out, once I was at the Academy. Perhaps there's more to the story, and he just hasn't had time to explain everything yet.

Or, perhaps, he was holding off for as long as possible, knowing what I'd deduce from the information. If I'm going to be under this much suspicion from the moment I walk into the school, then Ulciscor being the senator to adopt me seems a very poor choice indeed.

Which means he probably doesn't have the backing of Military at all.

I feel sick, but it makes sense. This whole thing is personal for him. A crusade sparked by his brother's death. For all I know, Military might be actively *against* my attending the Academy, not wanting to risk sparking an incident with Religion.

And worse—much worse, for me—is the possibility that Ulciscor is reaching for excuses. That there's nothing going on behind the scenes there at all, that Caeror really did commit suicide. If that's the case, then there will be nothing for me to find. Ulciscor will blame me no matter how hard I try. I'll end up in a Sapper.

My gloomy rumination is interrupted by a blast of air that thunders down the street, and I flinch to a dead stop as a massive dark shape flits overhead. I'm the only one who reacts.

"It's not going to kill you."

I tear my gaze away from the disappearing Transvect to see Aequa watching me with amusement, then grunt, vaguely embarrassed. "That hasn't been my experience with them, thus far."

"What? Oh." She shakes her head, admonishing herself as we start forward again. "Of course. Some kind of attack, wasn't it? I heard about it at the Academy." Unsurprising; I doubt the Praeceptors would have been able to keep gossip like that from spreading. "Do they know who did it?"

"No."

"Word was, you saved your father from them."

I snort at that. "You do know he's a Quintus, right?"

"It's what everyone was saying." I don't have time to react to the statement as Aequa points ahead. "We're here."

I falter, raising my eyes beyond the immediate press of bodies for the first time in a while. I've been so busy scanning the crowds for any sign of Sedotia that I hadn't registered the horizon gradually disappearing. Hadn't noticed the crush of people around us becoming a stream, all flowing inexorably in the same direction, the towering structure ahead an irresistible vortex. Arches and frescoes and grand pillars fill my vision against the dying light, stretching three hundred feet up and continuing along for at least ten times that, curving gently along its entire length. The throng splits into distinct rivulets as it approaches, each one pouring eagerly into the Catenan Arena's belly through a dozen manned entrances.

We've arrived at the naumachia.

XIX

I HATE THIS. THIS SENSE OF OVERWHELMING HELPLESSNESS. The feeling of being awed and dismayed, all at once.

If the outside of the Catenan Arena was impressive, the inside is nothing short of magisterial. We emerge from the great, arched, echoing tunnel into stands that stretch and stretch and *stretch*, stone benches curving around in a great oval that heaves with white motion and noise. In the middle of it all is an enormous lake, murky water sloshing and slurping at its containing barriers, the smell of salt mingling with a thousand other, less-pleasant aromas.

Ships moored to temporary docks tower nearby, blocking some of the view. Biremes surround a massive trireme, bobbing as they're swarmed by men and women making preparations. I can see a similar fleet on the far side of the Arena; at first glance I think it's smaller, but a more intent inspection suggests it's simply the distance. They're a mile away across the water, at least. I have to squint to make out the individuals on their decks.

Though the sun has sunk low enough that the walls now hide it from view, everything is brilliantly lit. There are lanterns on long poles at regular intervals in the stands, and countless candles are already held by eager spectators ready to celebrate the God of Light. High above the water, thousands of dark points hang suspended in mid-air, littering the fading sky. More lanterns, I realise. Suspended by Will, as yet unlit.

I'm buffeted by the crowd as Aequa grabs my arm and pulls, clearly not as shocked by the enormity of it all. I stumble on behind her, trying to calculate. How much Will was used to create all this? How much time and effort and engineering would it have taken to funnel this much water from the harbour? To build these ships? Even just to hold those lanterns aloft?

All for a spectacle. A frivolity meant purely to entertain.

Or, as my father would have insisted, to distract.

Aequa and I let ourselves be pushed along for a while; only the eastern entrances are open today—the others all sealed off to help contain the water, presumably—and our seats are on the opposite side. It's long minutes before we're descending toward the very front benches. Red-uniformed Praetorians patrol this area, eyeing newcomers from behind their reflective dark glasses. There's no mistaking the vicious slivers of glimmering, jagged obsidian hanging at their sides. The Razors are carved by their own hands and imbued with Will. There are more efficient weapons in the Hierarchy, but none as terrifying.

We receive a long glance from the guard nearest us, but Aequa's attire seems enough to convince him of our right to be here. He passes without stopping, and the clenching of my stomach eases a little.

We settle on a cushioned bench next to a middle-aged couple, who ignore us and continue arguing about whether holding the naumachia is worth shutting down the local baths in order to redirect water here. We're later than many, and a lot of the seats in the stadium are already filled. The ages of the crowd range from at least ten years my junior, to men and women too elderly to find their seats unassisted. It's as if the entire city has come.

"Will there be anyone else from the Academy here?"

"I can't imagine so. Most of us got tired of these things when we were children."

"Including you, I take it?" It's a fairly plain jab from Aequa, but I continue the amiable façade.

"Yes."

"Did your parents bring you?"

"Tisiphone did, a few times." She shifts at my questioning look. "One of our Octavii. My mother's a Sextus, and she was away a lot, so . . ."

I feel a flicker of sympathy. Not an uncommon practice, as I understand it, for high-ranking Catenans to leave raising their children to an educated Octavii.

"Siblings?"

"None we officially recognise." Her tone's too careless to be unaffected.

"Ah." A lonely life, then. One probably plagued by worry about the illegitimate children her father has produced, especially if they're male.

Silence falls between us, and I take the opportunity to scan the crowd. No one appears to be paying me any particular attention. I clench a frustrated fist by my side. We're too exposed, here at the front. Far too prominent for Sedotia to make an approach, even if she knows where I am.

The eager chatter is steadily swelling to a dull, smothering roar; everyone's animated, enthusiastic, anticipating. I hear words like glory and victory and hero. Bets being taken on who will win, who will fall, and who will take the prize for most "kills."

"So how does this work?" I already know, for the most part, from my lessons at Suus, but an orphan from Letens wouldn't have as clear an idea. I indicate the lines of armoured men boarding the ships nearby. "Those weapons look like proper steel. How do they uphold Birthright out there?"

"Their armour's Conditionally imbued. Too much damage in the wrong areas, and it drags them out of the fight."

"But there are *thousands* of them." It's not an exaggeration, if the same number of fighters are embarking on the opposite side of the Arena. "What if one gets stabbed in the face? Or falls overboard, or—"

"Obviously some will see a shameful end," Aequa interjects impatiently, making it sound like she's describing the weather. "That's what makes it so tense to watch, after all. And there will be a lot of injuries. But most who fall will survive for the Sappers." She must see something in my expression, because she makes a conciliatory motion. "They *are* mostly convicted criminals, Vis. Birthright doesn't technically even apply to them."

I repress a surge of revulsion and nod, as if her explanation's perfectly acceptable. Aequa likely has no idea what the Sappers are really like, given my impression that few in the Hierarchy do, but it's a cold assessment. For a time, Ulciscor's villa isolated me from this world. These people. With only Lanistia and Kadmos for company, and those two focused only on my training, it's been easy to forget their ugly realities.

"How will they find the Sappers for so many at once?" I know she won't know the answer—the source of the Hierarchy's supply has always been a mystery, its limits known only to a few in the Senate—but I'm curious to see what she thinks.

"No idea."

When it's clear she's not interested in expounding, I stand. "I'd like to walk around a little, before it all begins. Stretch my legs. Take it all in." I have to at least give the Anguis an opportunity to reach out to me.

Aequa moves as if to rise as well. "Alright."

I cough. "And . . . I need to locate a toilet."

She rolls her eyes and sinks back into her seat, the need to relieve oneself apparently beneath her. "You have about twenty minutes."

I leave, making careful note of where our seats are, then move out of sight and start to wander. Every face is a stranger's, and there are *so* many.

A minute passes. Two. This was a mistake. I could have bartered for anything. Forced Advenius to guarantee my safety after the Academy, somehow. Or refused to train with Aequa at all. But here I am. Roaming the Will-cast paths of the Hierarchy's greatest monument, just another member of the Catenan mob.

I'm so lost in my frustrations, I don't notice the pressure on my shoulder at first.

It takes me a moment to recognise Sedotia. In the light of the burning Transvect she was fierce and cold. Here she's well-dressed, prim and half-hidden behind a veil. Married, then, or pretending to be for anonymity. She looks smaller. Wan, even, beneath the rosy glow of the lantern-light.

"Come with me."

"How did you find me?"

"*Come with me.*" She sees my hesitation, and though she doesn't raise her voice, there's no doubting the seriousness of what she's saying. "Now."

I don't argue. We move through the crowd without talking. I can't help but cast an anxious glance over my shoulder, back toward where I know Aequa is sitting, but I needn't have worried. Our seats are well out of sight.

"I can't be long."

"I know." Her stare is withering. "It would have been better if you'd come alone."

"Oh. I should have thought of that." I slap myself lightly in the forehead. "Why didn't I think of that?"

Sedotia's not amused. "You'll be back in your seat before everything starts."

We're heading through a passageway into the covered outer ring of the Arena and then down a set of stairs, travelling against the flow of the majority. At first I think Sedotia plans to leave entirely, but before I can voice my concern, we're turning aside and descending another staircase, this one cleverly hidden from the public concourse and barely wide enough to allow a single person. Nobody else is coming or going, but we aren't spared a passing glance by anyone hurrying by. They're all rushing to be in their seats in time.

"Where are we going?" My voice echoes off stone. Ahead, I can hear trickling. My nostrils flare and I cough at the fetid smell.

"To meet someone." We've reached the bottom of the stairs, which end abruptly in a four-foot-high hole that opens into a long, low, arched tunnel. Water—or some kind of liquid—sloshes along inside it.

Sedotia leans down and reaches into an inconspicuous cavity in the wall, emerging with a hand full of cloth. She tosses the threadbare tunic to me. "Before we go any farther, you need to change clothes."

"What? Why would I . . . oh."

She nods. "Anything Ulciscor's given you, you need to leave here. It's for the best anyway. Whatever you wear isn't going to come out smelling particularly pleasant."

I don't bother to argue; I wouldn't put it past Lanistia to track me. I pull my tunic over my head.

"Your side's healed well."

I concur absently. "The staples came out a couple of weeks ago."

"Lucky." When I glance askance at her, she adds, "We would have had to remove them, too."

I stiffen as the implication settles, then continue dressing. I hadn't considered that. Veridius was the one who applied them.

"Leave your sandals here as well—they'll just get the smell in them."

I do as I'm told, grimacing as I follow the young woman into the sewer. It's cold and slimy beneath my bare feet, sludge seeping between my toes. I try not to think about what it consists of. The stench that worried my nostrils earlier attacks now, an assault that threatens to leave me hacking and heaving at every unwilling breath. The walls glisten, sweating in the dim and dank. I do my best not to brush against them. I'm not entirely convinced that's just water, either.

"Stay quiet. These ways will be flooded in a few hours, but there might still be workers around." Sedotia wades ahead of me. Careful amid the muck. Most of the women I've known would be gagging and forcing every step, if they'd even made it down this far.

"Flooded?"

"When the naumachia finishes."

There's an itch of unease as I understand. Once the spectacle above is done, the Hierarchy will waste no time in draining the artificial lake. And these are the sewers they'll use to flush all that water back into the harbour.

We press on through calf-deep streams, each step cautious on the sludge-slick stone. It's hard to see more than a few paces ahead, most of the time, the illumination of the streets above—we're out past the walls of the Arena, by this point—barely reflecting down through small grates at the end of long, narrow pipes. Talking and singing and laughter echoes, bouncing around the low-arching tunnel system, surrounding us. The only sounds we make are small, lapping splashes.

It's a maze down here, but we're only walking for a minute when Sedotia pulls up short, gesturing to a side opening. Past her, I can see there's orange light shimmering against the greasy stone wall, brighter than anything cast by the festivities above.

I bend almost double to slide under the low archway. A torch dribbles dying embers from where it's affixed to the wall, revealing another stairwell that disappears upward about thirty feet away. This area's slightly raised and the sewage is only ankle-deep here, though the smell is no better.

Sitting casually one step above the sludge is a man, features half-hidden in shadow.

Plainly dressed and apparently comfortable, despite our surroundings. The way he's lounging indicates a kind of bored confidence.

He uncoils as Sedotia ducks under the opening to join me. He's probably my height, but the extra step means he's peering down at us. I still can't see his face properly.

"Diago." His voice is smooth and deep. It resonates in the cramped space.

I won't risk admitting it, not out loud. Not even down here in the dark among Caten's putrescence. "My name is Vis."

"Of course." There's humour in the words. A clear indication that we both know I'm lying, but he's happy to let me pretend. "And I am Melior."

He steps forward. Down off his perch, into the muck with us, revealing his features. He's perhaps forty, a dusting of grey in both his close-cropped hair and light beard. Lantern-jawed, sun-browned skin a dark gold in the light.

And I recognise him. Not who he is, straight away, but there's an immediate sense of familiarity, confusion as my mind tries to separate face from surroundings. I say nothing for several seconds, the man waiting patiently.

Then, finally, it hits.

"*Estevan?*" He's older, more grizzled and worse-dressed, and the beard is new. But it's Estevan. A man I never had a lot to do with, but he's from Suus—one of my father's most trusted advisors, and as fiercely against the Hierarchy as any of them. Someone I assumed would be either dead or in a Sapper, after the invasion.

"May I call you Diago now?"

"Vek. Rotting gods. I . . . *vek.*" I'm grinning. Laughing. I step forward to embrace him, but he wards me off.

"Sorry. Hard to explain, but don't come any closer." He smiles at me. "It is good to see you, though, my prince."

There's a hard lump in my throat at the title. "You too, Estevan. Vek. You too." There are a thousand questions spinning in my head, my absence from the naumachia suddenly a secondary concern. "How did you get out? Are there any others with you? How did you find me?" I squint at him. "Are you really Melior?" Sedotia knowing my identity suddenly makes a lot more sense.

"I am. I needed safe harbour, after Suus, and the Anguis needed the information and connections I could provide. It's been a good match." He glances at Sedotia, who has been watching the exchange with interest. The young woman shakes her head. Estevan sighs. "As for the rest, Highness, it will need to wait until we have more time. There are more urgent things to discuss."

"Such as?"

"Your helping us."

We watch each other, some of my giddy joy fading as I remember why I'm here. Ripples slosh up against the stone.

"What do you want me to do?"

"*Now* he's willing to listen," mutters Sedotia from behind me.

"We need you to be Domitor at the Academy, or as close as you can get. Then when you graduate, pick any position you like that places you in Caten, but with either Religion or Governance. Not Military."

"That's all?"

"That's obviously not *all*. But for now, it's what we need you to do."

I consider, and the silence stretches. I know my answer almost immediately, though.

"I'm sorry, Estevan." I truly am.

My father's old friend frowns. "Don't you want to fight?"

"Not the way I know you want me to." Half explanation, half weary remonstrance. I don't want to anger the Anguis, but Estevan's presence has disarmed me, compels me to be candid. In fact, this might be the most honest thing I've said in months.

"I told you. A broken blade," murmurs Sedotia.

Estevan ignores her, keeps his eyes on me. Curious rather than indignant. "Why not?"

I consider my answer. I desperately want him to understand.

"About six months after Suus, I was travelling through Tensia. There was this little village on a hillside. Aiobhinn. A hundred people, maybe—mostly farmers, only four Septimii. I had no money, no food. No identification. They had to know what Catenan law demanded, but instead they fed me, let me sleep under a roof, and turned a blind eye when I pocketed some coin they'd left lying around. It wasn't much, but it kept me going when I was ready to give up. I managed to stay out of Catenan orphanages for more than another year because of that one experience."

I hesitate. Not sure if this level of honesty is a good idea, but I plough on anyway. "I came back, about half a year later. It was almost harvest, and I thought that they might have some work. When I got there, the Anguis had just raided them. Half of the village was burned to the ground. The children and wife of the man who had taken me in were busy burying him. And everyone was lining up to talk to the proconsul. To give him the descriptions of the men who had attacked them, and *beg* him for Caten's protection." I've been staring at the water around my ankles as I talk, but now I look up, meeting Estevan's gaze. "So I left, because I knew what would happen this time. The Anguis aren't winning hearts, Estevan—you're hardening them. I'm not sure what the answer is, what the alternative is, but . . . your way doesn't work. And I want no part of it."

I fall silent. Done. He wanted to know, and now he knows.

"They were Hierarchy. They were our enemies long before they were attacked," says Sedotia quietly.

"They were innocent."

"Innocent?" Estevan has just been listening thoughtfully but he stirs at that, offended. "Were they not Octavii and Septimii, ceding their Will to Caten, for Caten's purposes?"

"Yes, but—"

"Then they were participants and by definition, shared guilt."

"They didn't have a choice."

"Did you? Did she, or I?" There's an unmoveable force behind Estevan's words, his voice stone grinding against stone. "Or should we not hold others to the standards to which we hold ourselves? Anyone who does not resist them, Diago, is lending them their strength. Is complicit in all that they do. The Octavii are not just guilty—they hoist the entire Hierarchy on their shoulders. I would think that you, above all others, would have reason to hate them for that."

"And I do." The admission snaps out rawer than I intend, almost a snarl. I bring myself back. Calm. "But I can hate without it coming to violence."

"Hate is its own violence, my prince. Your only choice is whether to let it hurt them, or you." The older man considers. Sighs. "Very well. I'm not going to threaten you. But I'm not going to give up on you, either." He turns and steps back up onto the ledge, out of the water. "Have you ever wondered why the Republic attacked, that day?"

"Of course. All the time." I frown. "But we were the last ones to hold out. I assume someone in Military got impatient, and—"

"No." Estevan's face is covered in shadow again, but I can hear the conviction. "For an extra ten thousand pieces to prop up their pyramids, when they already had twenty million? No. All Caten had to do was sit back and let their propaganda take effect. You were there—you know it's true. Sooner or later, your father would have had to sign *something*, or face revolution. Maybe not right away. Maybe not for another five, ten years. But eventually." He crosses his arms. "So why do it? Why risk resistance, potentially having to kill the very people they wanted as Octavii? And then why kill your family?"

Because they fear what we know. One of the last things my father said to me as we fled that night through the palace's secret tunnels, after I asked him much the same thing. Something I've tried not to dwell on these past three years. He could have meant anything. And he never got to explain further.

"I don't know."

"I do." Estevan takes a breath. "It won't be long before you do as well, Diago. And I hope that will change your mind enough to join us." He glances at Sedotia, who signals to him. "Our time is up. Keep in mind what I've said. Victims can still be enemies." He moves to depart through the way behind him.

"Estevan? Be careful. I overheard Magnus Telimus talking about you. About Melior. It sounds like the Senate are confident they're going to catch you soon."

He lingers at the base of the stairs. Doesn't turn, but a soft chuckle echoes off the walls ahead of him. "Thank you, Highness."

He leaves.

The meeting over, I turn to Sedotia, who jerks her head toward the low archway. "Let's get you back. It will be starting soon." Her voice is taut. She's displeased with the outcome of my conversation.

I follow her, wading once more into the flowing murk. We just walk for a minute, tense. My eyes have adjusted enough to see the deliberateness with which she places her feet, this time. The occasional slip that she's almost a half-step too slow to recover from. The way she has to pause afterward, her eyes struggling to track, wobbling as she balances.

"How did you knock out Ulciscor, back at the Transvect?"

"You heard Melior. If you want answers, you know what you have to do."

"Worth a try."

We reach the base of the way up. Sedotia rummages inside the hidden cavity and this time emerges with a full waterskin and rough chunk of soap. I strip my half-sodden tunic and sit on a stair, hurriedly scrubbing my legs and feet, then using the dry upper part of the tunic to start towelling the moisture from my legs and feet. "You're ceding." I'm certain now, her wan skin obvious in the light. "To Estevan?"

She doesn't respond, but I can see the answer in the set of her shoulders.

"I thought the Anguis were better than that." I don't bother to hide my bitterness. No wonder the Senate's been intent on finding Melior.

"That's not . . ." She shakes her head. "Fine. Think what you will. But you were right—this is a war we cannot win, not the way we've been fighting it. And if it's the choice between using the enemy's weapon against them, or giving up, I know which I'll choose every time." She holds up a hand as I move to put my good, dry tunic back on. "Wait."

Every passing second feels heavier, my absence above surely growing more and more suspicious. "What?"

"I need to draw blood with this." She pulls a stone stylus from the same cavity where the soap had been stored. It's about ten inches long, similar to the steel and bronze ones I've seen some men wearing at their hips. Weapons aren't allowed within the city limits, and so long stylii—which are in theory for writing on wax tablets, but make perfectly good substitutes for blades, in a fight—are quite fashionable.

"From . . . me?" I'm confused.

"Yes."

I shift. "No thank you."

She rolls her eyes and moves before I can react, whipping the slender grey spike at my bare chest. The tip's sharp and scores along it, blood welling immediately along the line. I snarl at the sting and step back, ready to defend myself, but Sedotia isn't threatening. She holds up the stylus so I can see it.

Right at the point, where crimson glistens and beads, it's starting to steam.

"We need a little more on it, to be safe." She's stepping forward; I retreat, bemused as much as angry, but suddenly my bare back is against cold stone. This time, she simply presses the edge of the stylus against my bleeding wound. There's an audible *hiss*.

"What are you *doing*?" I shove her away, incensed. "What is that?"

"Protection." She issues an infuriating smile at my blank expression. "Now put on your clothes. You're out of time." I glare at her, but the knowledge of how long I've been gone is too great a pressure. She waits until I've furiously tugged my attire back into place, then holds out the stylus to me. "Don't lose it. Under any circumstances."

I waver, then take the weapon. My skin tingles where it touches the stone. I can't see a drop of my blood remaining on its surface.

"I don't understand." I reluctantly thread the stylus into a fold in my toga. The hole will be apparent once I take it off, but no one will see it in the meantime.

"You will. Now go."

I'm torn between confusion, anger, and stubbornness. But it's been twenty minutes since I left Aequa. Probably more.

I bite my tongue, and storm up the stairs.

※ ※ ※

"WELL, YOU FOUND THE TOILET, THEN," AEQUA OBSERVES AS I sit down, wrinkling her nose.

I wince. Clearly not thorough enough with my scrubbing. "Eventually. This place is . . ." I gesture, indicating I can't put into words the enormity of it.

"I suppose it would be, to you." She's put out by my extended absence, I think, but not suspicious. "It doesn't matter. You're just in time."

The crowd is beginning to quiet, the crashing of conversation around us dulling to a low hum as an announcer—one of hundreds around the stadium, from what I can tell—bellows the details of the battle that is about to be re-created. The line along my chest burns, and I can feel the hard resistance of the hidden stylus along my body whenever I move. To the west, the last of the sunlight seeps from the sky, leaving only the brilliant illumination of the thousands of lanterns ringing the arena. Men and women stand tautly at the ready on decks, fully armoured, blades out as they peer toward the opposite side of the artificial lake.

The announcer finishes, and across the Arena, his colleagues fall silent one by one. Then, from all around us, horns ring out. Clear. Challenging.

Below, the naumachia begins.

XX

I'VE SEEN THE GREAT WHALING SHIPS OF SUUS TRAIN OFF-shore, manned and navigated by some of the most talented sailors in the world. I've seen men perform acts of daring and courage on small fishing boats in storms, riding waves twice the height of their vessels, that would defy the imagination. I can't count how many times I've watched from my clifftop window and seen wild manoeuvres succeed that should have been impossible in the most ideal circumstances, let alone in the gales in which they were attempted.

The naumachia has none of that.

There's no seamanship on show here. No waves, no wind. Vessels burst smoothly from their docks, led by the two giant triremes, water rippling soullessly away from prows, powered and steered by Will rather than oar and rudder. Every hull is fitted with a wicked ram in order to create spectacles of splintering wood and chaotic platforms of mock-death when they meet. It's all choreographed, gaudy decoration for the screams and blood and desperation that will follow.

That's never more evident than in the burst of hellish light that abruptly illuminates the lake, eliciting gasps of appreciation amid the thunder of voices that accompanies the starting signal. I flinch, squinting up at the thousands of mid-air lanterns. They've all sprung to life simultaneously, some Will-triggered mechanism lighting them. Unlike the warm gold of the lanterns in the stands, though, these all burn a deep, ugly crimson, staining ships and water alike.

There's no need to guess at what the light symbolises.

As I watch, the hovering lanterns start to move. Sluggishly at first, barely notice-able, but as the ships begin to pick up speed so do the lights, each one tracing its own circuit around the centre of the arena. The vessels draw closer and closer and the lights move faster and faster. They're quick, then urgent, then a swirling, wild maelstrom of red as the ships come within shouting distance of one another. Armoured naumachiarii stand in file on the decks, glittering darkly as they brace themselves. The crowd around me is screaming, cheering, voices already hoarse.

Their hunger can't drown out the splintering crack of wood against wood, rams rending and tearing at hulls, men and women on the decks thrown into the air, losing their grips on whatever they thought would secure them. Many of them smash into masts or rigging, limbs suddenly protruding at awkward angles, or tumble over the side, splashing once or twice before being dragged down by their armour, vanishing quickly beneath the frothing chop.

The crowd roars louder.

Then the first bodies are flying up into the air, some of them flailing, others limp as their armour carries them up to vanish into the blinding crimson dervish. Signifying their shameful withdrawal from life, their erasure from history. Saved from drowning so that they can be fed to the Sappers. I don't think I'm imagining the futility in every line of those helpless, struggling forms, even if I'm too far away to hear their screams.

The mob behind us are mostly standing, though at least these front seats—those filled with patricians and knights—have the decorum to remain seated as they cheer. The shouting is less deafening now, more sporadic as clumps of spectators spot one particularly impressive fight or another and renew their enthusiasm.

I glance across at Aequa. She's watching the proceedings with interest, but there's none of the savage joy others around us are displaying. If anything, she looks as though she finds the entire thing almost as distasteful as I do.

"How many people are out there, do you think?" I asked the question through the cheers, even as I try to make the estimate myself. Thirty or so ships all up. Biremes and the two triremes that have already smashed into one another.

Aequa continues to gaze at the carnage. "Two thousand, maybe?"

It's close to what I would have guessed. Two thousand men and women. Some will be volunteers, I know: Totius Octavii, even Septimii looking to make a name for themselves. But the vast majority in the fight will be imprisoned Octavii.

The naumachiarii on the triremes have almost recovered from the impact, but more ships are streaming toward their position. They're going to get hit again, and again, and again. It's easy to make out which sides are which; one has the traditional red uniform of the Republic, while the other wears the brown and gold of . . . Butaria? I think that's what the announcer said. A re-enactment of the Battle of Callage, from around fifty years ago.

I can see smears appearing on faces, glistening, too thick and dark to be water. They start to paint armour and blades, too. I see a monster of a man swinging feverishly, screaming as he scythes his way onto an enemy deck, crushing skulls in the process. Each strike jettisons another crippled fighter into the raging red vortex above. People in the crowd are pointing at him, cheering him on. They're chanting his name. Vulferam?

Everywhere, the crowd bays for blood. I try not to show how sick I feel. The combatants are mostly fodder down there, prisoners gasping and terrified and swinging weapons for which they have only the most rudimentary training. Afraid of the Sappers, and desperate for a pardon. Some few, maybe one or two in every thousand, will even impress enough to achieve the latter. But like everything else, the Hierarchy dangles it. Always a way up, even for the condemned. Always a way out from under the misery they've heaped on you, if you work hard enough. Fight hard enough. Take your chances.

People start settling back into their seats as the last of the smaller vessels begin their journey into the chaos. Somehow that makes what we're watching even worse. Men are still screaming and dying, still fighting valiantly or manically, still breathless and blood-slicked and doing all they can to survive. Yet they don't do it to rapturous applause anymore. People shout encouragement, or gasp when something horrific happens, but it all combines to a low, muted rumble now. Something more mundane. The initial rush has worn off, and everyone is just enjoying themselves.

They're not that way for long. It might be because I'm looking for it, but I think I'm among the first to notice that something's wrong.

It's a frothing in the water, initially. Ugly, red, bubbling lines from the edge of the arena to the very centre, where the triremes are. Five or six of them around the lake, evenly spaced, like spokes on a wheel. No one reacts, no one seems to think anything of it.

Then stone bursts from the water, sending a haze of fine dark liquid high into the air, huge swells rolling away from its emergence. Newly formed, jagged paths glisten in the lurid light as spray settles on them. People everywhere stand and exclaim and point as one of the triremes is tilted sideways, its keel lifted within view, naumachiarii screaming as they tumble from its sharply slanted deck. Other, smaller ships crash hard into the rocky peninsulas, the shrieking of tearing wood audible from here as wounds are ripped in their hulls.

Conversation buzzes at the development. Everyone's assuming this is part of the entertainment, some unexpected wrinkle. A new, dramatic feature of the Arena on which the combatants can do battle.

After my conversation with Estevan, I'm not so sure.

Then something thunders. Faintly, as if distant, but deep and somehow encompassing, too. The air quivers.

"What was that?" Aequa echoes the question being asked all around us.

Another shuddering peal. This one closer. Louder. Rolling over the increasingly agitated mutterings of the crowd. I see fighters on the remaining trireme falter as the sound penetrates the haze of battle. Some of their opponents ignore it and take merciless advantage.

The lanterns floating above the water fall.

It's a surreal, almost beautiful sight as the crowd hushes again, crimson lights raining silently down, reflections off the lake becoming brighter and brighter until most are abruptly extinguished. The remainder smash; some shatter and spread puddles of flaming oil across the long paths to the centre of the Arena, while others break apart on masts and decks, causing panic. The biremes are slowing, I realise. Still moving forward, but drifting through the water rather than ploughing.

"PEOPLE OF CATEN."

The words roar around the Arena, spin and crash and echo as if one of the gods has taken it upon himself to speak. A shocked sigh escapes thousands of mouths. The combatants on the trireme freeze and then warily, at some unspoken agreement, disengage and back away from one another.

I spot him, my eyes drawn to him as others around me point excitedly. Striding toward the centre of the lake along one of the newly formed paths of stone, flame-tinted water still unsettled on either side of him.

He's a good distance away—perhaps five hundred feet—but there's no mistaking Estevan.

"MY NAME IS ARTURUS MELIOR LEOS. I AM THE LEADER OF THE GROUP YOU KNOW AS THE ANGUIS, WHO FIGHT FOR A BETTER WORLD THAN THE ONE YOU HAVE CREATED." He pauses about halfway to the centre of the lake as he turns, taking in the crowd. **"AND LET THERE BE NO MISTAKE: IT IS YOU—ALL OF YOU—WHO ARE RESPONSIBLE FOR CREATING IT. NOT THOSE IN POWER. NOT THE ONES WHO WIELD WHAT YOU GIVE THEM, BECAUSE *YOU GIVE IT TO THEM. YOU* LET THEM STAND ON YOUR SHOULDERS, ALL FOR THE DREAM OF ONE DAY BEING ABLE TO STAND ATOP OTHERS'. EVEN WHEN YOU KNOW, DEEP DOWN, THAT IT IS AN ILLUSION. AS UNATTAINABLE FOR MOST OF YOU AS IT IS SELFISH."**

Estevan's voice splits the air like nothing I have ever heard, overpowering. I'm not alone in pressing my hands against my ears, fearful the painful noise is doing permanent injury.

"A PYRAMID'S STRENGTH IS IN ITS FOUNDATION, NOT ITS PEAK. SO I HAVE COME HERE TODAY TO JUDGE. I HAVE COME TO BRING A RECKONING FOR YOUR DECISIONS. YOUR WEAKNESS. YOUR BLINDNESS AND COWARDICE AND COMPLICITY."

The crowd is rapidly swinging from thrilled to fearful to enraged. There's shouting, more and more as Estevan's lecture rumbles on. Obscenities rain down upon my father's former adviser, curses rolling off thousands of tongues as onlookers scream and point and surge forward, as if to collectively leap the barrier and rush at him.

I don't know what to do other than watch in horror. Is he mad? Most of these people are Octavii or Septimii, but there will be plenty of higher-ranked Will users. Not to mention the hundreds of Praetorians here. Assuming they recognise his name—and he's infamous enough, here in Caten—he'll be dead from a swarm of Razors within the next ten seconds.

"No one can use Will."

Aequa's leaning forward in her seat, eyes wide as she studies the Arena, her dismayed mutter barely audible over the tumult. I return my gaze to the lake, seeing what she's seeing. The fallen lanterns. The ships drifting gently to a stop against the raised stone paths.

The absolute lack of an attack upon one of the most wanted men in the Republic.

"Rotting gods," I breathe.

It shouldn't be possible, and yet, Aequa's right. I can see a red-uniformed Praetorian standing only twenty feet away. His expression is stricken. Utterly panicked.

Down in the middle, Estevan has turned toward the centre of the Arena, lit starkly against a still-flaming puddle of oil. He's facing the ships, the majority of which have now grounded themselves against the spoke-like paths. Facing the fighters who have begun to cautiously disembark.

"HAIL, NAUMACHIARII. HONOUR AND GLORY. I AM SORRY THAT YOU HAVE BEEN SACRIFICED UPON THE ALTAR OF DISTRACTION. I AM SORRY THAT YOUR FELLOW MAN HAS FAILED YOU SO DEEPLY. TODAY, I OFFER YOU RELEASE FROM THIS DEGRADATION. I OFFER YOU A WAY OUT. BUT WHEN YOU GO, DO NOT FORGET HOW YOU GOT HERE, OR WHO IS RESPONSIBLE FOR IT. SEEK US, ONCE YOU ARE FREE. JOIN THE ANGUIS."

A raucous cheer registers as the last words scream off the water and roll away. At first I think it's in response, but then I turn at motion somewhere to my left, watching with heart in throat as a dozen Praetorians leap the barrier onto Estevan's stony peninsula. Several men wielding stylii follow, no doubt eager to share in the glory of killing the Anguis's leader. Hundreds in the crowd who have spotted their incursion are boisterously urging them on.

In the centre of the lake, where the ships have run aground, the naumachiarii are in disarray. Some few have resumed their fighting, as if unable to even conceive of anything else, steel flashing dark orange against the burning of decks and sails. Many are streaming along the far rocky paths toward the edge of the stadium, clearly intent on the freedom Estevan has just promised them. I can already see spectators fleeing from where they're headed.

The rest of the naumachiarii are sprinting toward Estevan. Their blades are out and from the way they're charging, they're aiming for him rather than the Praetorians. Hoping to deal the killing blow. A reward, a pardon, would surely await whoever managed it.

Estevan has finished his speech, and he must see both them and the Praetorians converging on him. Still he just stands there, head bowed, as his attackers draw closer. A hundred feet. Fifty. Twenty.

A deep, discordant *thrum* screeches through the Arena.

There's a flicker in the darkness around Estevan, like the afterimage of a lightning strike, and the men and women rushing toward him seem to just . . . evaporate.

A moment later, across the lake, the rear section of the eastern stand explodes.

It's impossible to comprehend, in those first terrifying seconds. No one's running or screaming or panicking. Just still. Mute. Stunned. Around the distant thundering of disintegrating stone, there's . . . silence. A dark, roiling cloud of grit is rising; though the still-standing part of the stadium mostly prevents it from flowing down onto the lake, I can only imagine what it must be like in the city. Distant figures scramble to flee whatever's just happened. The lanterns over there are winking out in rapid succession as they're enveloped by dust. Darkness chases after.

Another *thrum*. A rippling in the air, closer this time, above the stand about five hundred feet to my left. There's a *compression*. I feel my ears pop.

And every person in that section—four, maybe five thousand people—explodes as one into a sickening, violent haze of crimson mist.

Another second. Nothing but pounding heartbeat. I can feel fear building to a crescendo around me, thick and sharp.

Then there's running and screaming and panicking.

Everything's chaos. A blur. Aisles clogged, people falling down and others trampling them to flee. Bodies flail, scramble over seats. I'm shoved and elbowed from all sides as people force their way blindly past me. They're stampeding toward the exit in the eastern stand, the only way out, though I'm almost certain that's what has just been obliterated.

Aequa and I are both standing; she's pale, breathing heavily, looking like she's about to run too as she stares wide-eyed at the glistening, viscera-coated benches where people used to be. To her credit, she also seems to be assessing. Her refusal to give in to the panic helps, and I forcefully resist the pure, animalistic fear that's crawling beneath my skin, begging for me to follow the crowd. The seats around us are already empty.

"What do we do?" Aequa's voice quivers. Her attention's turned to the cloud of debris on the far side of the lake. That's why she hasn't moved. She's realised that the only way out is gone.

My gaze is on Estevan again, head still too full, too taut and overwhelmed to answer. The man is sitting now, cross-legged. Head bowed again. I can't imagine how he's doing any of this, but I don't believe for a second that he's finished here. Even in his passive position, even from this distance, there's a palpable aura of menace radiating from him. A heavy, hostile layer that billows, drapes the entire stadium in dread.

The clarity's sudden and sharp. I grab Aequa's arm, pulling her against the flow of the fleeing mob. "Follow me."

Aequa resists. Appraises where we're heading—directly toward the stand where Estevan has just murdered thousands—and then me. "Are you insane?"

"However he's doing it, he's trying to kill as many people as possible. He's not going to target an empty stand." I can't believe how calm my voice is. Even if it does sound as though it's coming from far away. Someone else's. "I think I know a way out."

I turn to look at the frenzied masses still spilling past. The entire stadium is filled with screaming, shouting, cries of pain and confusion and utter, manic fear. There's no way I'll be heard over this noise.

"Don't!" It's Aequa, the shout in my ear somewhere between plea and command. She puts her head close to mine. "They're not going to listen to you. And if they do, there will be a stampede, and none of us will get away."

I clench my teeth. Nod.

We force our way westward, toward the last of the light in the sky. It's not difficult; the seats ahead have all but emptied and only stragglers shove their way past, eyes glazed and faces set in rictuses of trauma. Dotted around the stands are those who haven't yet moved, either. People just sitting or standing, staring blankly.

There's another dark *thrum*, vibrating through stone and into my chest. I stumble, turn to watch despite the dread the sound carries with it.

Estevan is looking toward the north-eastern section of the Arena, which heaves with a crush of desperate bodies pushing vainly against one another. His right hand is outstretched, palm out.

He clenches it into a fist.

Again that flicker against the dark, a ripping of the air, this time streaking out from Estevan across the water. There's something in it, I think. A distortion. An *image*, though it's so fast it's impossible to tell of what.

None of that matters amid what comes after. Bile burns the back of my throat as I take it in. I don't even know how many people die this time. Ten thousand? Fifteen? Impossible to tell at this distance, but an entire wing of the stadium glistens a wet, dark red. Murdered. Massacred in a heartbeat.

Estevan was waiting for them to flee. To bunch together, exactly as they did.

The panic in the screaming, if possible, becomes harsher, more fraying. The press of bodies that had been flowing toward that stand ripples in hesitation. I see people start to leap into the water. Higher, I can see shadows scaling the back wall of the stadium. Vanishing as they fling themselves off toward Caten. The drop is hundreds of feet onto the street.

I shudder and press on, Aequa by my side. We're approaching the edge of the stand which suffered the first attack, and despite the urgency, neither of us can help but falter. A faint steam rises from the scene ahead, bringing with it a salty, damp stench that hints of rot. There's nothing to identify as bodies beneath it, nothing which could resemble human remains. It's all just shredded flesh and blood. Mangled bones protruding through raw lumps of muscle and cartilage, draped across benches and ground, scattered randomly. An unendingly grotesque paste of death.

"Come on." I make it an apology as well as an appeal, pulling Aequa with me into the red damp. I suspect only the chorus of terror behind us pushes Aequa enough to come with me.

Both of us choke and hack as the full extent of the hot reek hits our nostrils, creeps into our mouths. We pick our way carefully over rent flesh, me guiding Aequa to the stairwell. Our feet slap in the wet. Aequa's not making a sound, but her eyes are red, tears on her cheeks.

It's an eternity until we reach the welcoming tunnel down to the outer ring of the Arena. I risk a glance back after ushering Aequa ahead of me. Estevan is still seated, looking at the ground again. Recovering from his strike, bracing himself for the next one. More people have leapt the barriers and are charging toward him. It's probably what I would do, in their position.

I don't wait to see the result. I already know what it will be.

Another soul-shaking *thrum* chases me down into the passageway.

The stairs aren't as coated in viscera as the seating above, though there's still plenty of evidence of death. The same goes for the inner ring of the Arena. Stone is no shield against whatever Estevan is doing.

The area around the sewer stairwell is deserted. It's quiet, the distant screams all but muted by the thick stone, though another juddering, dissonant chord soon growls its way through. Aequa and I both flinch. Who knows how many more Estevan just killed.

"Where does this go?" Aequa's breath is coming in shallow, short gasps. I'm not much different, to be fair. She's holding herself together remarkably well.

"Sewers." I don't see the need to elaborate, the faint smell from the opening—sickening and yet better than what we experienced above by far—backing up my statement. Aequa pauses for a half step; I can almost see the questions forming on her lips. Then she sets her jaw and forges downward.

The sound of rushing water greets us a full twenty seconds before we reach the bottom. The first two steps are underwater now, the flow not quite knee-deep. It's fast, too, I quickly discover as I step into the current. Not pulling me off my feet, but strong enough to be worried about my balance.

"Careful." I let Aequa grab my arm as we hurriedly wade. It makes it harder to stay upright and I nearly slip a couple of times, but she's lighter than me, needs the extra support. It's almost completely dark down here. I can hear her heavy breathing over the torrent rushing by. Another *thrum* vibrates the stone around us, eliciting a squeak from Aequa, though she never stops moving.

My heart pounds out of my chest, and I try not to imagine the water level rising. Estevan tore up the base of the Arena to create his paths across the lake; there's no telling what damage that caused, what weaknesses it's created in the Arena's basin. This stream could become a deadly torrent at any moment. There's nowhere to take refuge if it does.

Though it feels slow, it's probably only a minute until we reach the narrow archway where I met Estevan. It's almost too low to the water to duck under, but we manage; the torch within has gone out but there's light filtering down the shaft where the stairs end. We splash our way over and I help Aequa up onto the first step. She sobs with relief as her feet touch dry ground again.

"These should lead out. Get clear of here. There's no telling how far that *thing* he's doing reaches."

She stops. Shakes her head, unable to process the words. "What?"

I hesitate. The current's not strong in this side room, just deep. I'm going to have to fight against it going the other way. In the dark. By myself.

I know I should leave with Aequa, and my every instinct is pleading with me to do just that. Not only from fear. If I walk away, I can actually think. Assess what the

Anguis having this terrible power means. Understand the consequences, come to grips with Estevan's intimation that *this* is why the Hierarchy invaded Suus.

And . . . for all I'm appalled by Estevan's actions, his words resonate. These people *are* my enemies. The Octavii here *did* choose their side. That they didn't expect there to be consequences is their failure, not anyone else's.

But.

My father's voice, like so often in my life, echoes in my head. *The power to protect is the highest of responsibilities, Diago. When a man is given it, his duty is not only to the people he thinks are worthy.*

He was talking about leadership then, but I know what he would say to me now. Know what he would want me to do. Know what he would do.

And if I had to guess, based on what Sedotia said, the stylus still tucked hard against my chest means I may be the only person here who can get close enough to Estevan to stop him.

"Luck, Aequa."

I squeeze her arm in a vain attempt at comfort, then turn and plunge back into the icy water.

XXI

THE WATER'S RISING FASTER THAN I'D ANTICIPATED. I STRUGgle against it. I can't let myself lose my balance—I haven't swum in years. Not since Suus. But it's up to my knees. Stronger, faster, more violent as it batters me. Everything it touches is numb. It's up to my thighs. My waist. I slip. Somehow catch myself against the slick stone of the sewer wall. Press on.

Then I'm out, dragging myself up the stairs, gasping and hacking as water splashes high enough to inhale. Behind me, there's a gurgling crash as a torrent floods past, frothing so high it's almost submersing the entrance. Somewhere, the path between the lake and these tunnels has cracked opened.

There's no getting out this way until the Arena is dry, now.

I take precious seconds to catch my breath and rip off my sodden toga, rescuing the stylus from its folds. The stone sliver feels warm against my hand. Then I'm hauling myself up the narrow stairs, back into the mausoleum of the Arena's outer ring. Dashing around raw flesh and trickling blood as I climb into the main stadium again.

The screams are ominously fewer. More grieved than horrified, hopeless rather than panicked. Fainter and sporadic. I stop short as I emerge into the red-coated stands, hit by that hot, thick, cloying smell. The lake has started to drain; the jagged pathways Estevan created jut from the water, decorated by the dark wreckage of ships draped with the dead. Flames still burn everywhere, though lower now, a darker orange. But it's enough to illuminate the sole man out in the centre, cross-legged, looking as calm as when I left.

My gaze switches to the stands, and something breaks in my chest. There are fewer people than there were before. *Significantly* fewer. The remainder are cowering, hiding behind one another, bunched around where the exits should be like frightened animals. Whole swathes of the stadium are empty. Impossible to tell from this distance and in this light, but it's not hard to conjure images of the same hideous, slick carnage that's all around me.

I start for where Estevan's jetty meets the seats. It's not far. It feels like miles. I keep one eye on Estevan, but either he doesn't notice me or he's ignoring me.

I reach the intersection where smooth, Will-cut stone meets the haphazard path stretching across the Arena. It's only a few feet wide, slick with water overlayed with sporadic red where Estevan detonated his attackers. The stylus in my hand is getting warmer.

"Idiot," I mutter to myself as I clamber over the barrier and step out onto the narrow bridge. "Vek. Idiot. *Vek.*"

The water's draining fast, and I'm elevated here. Precarious. I won't die if I slip and fall into the dark swells below, but there won't be an easy way to climb out, either. My sandals are well-made and give me a decent footing, at least. I press forward, step after gradual step, clutching the stylus like a totem against Estevan's power.

I'm about fifty feet away when I start to see the distortion in the air.

It's almost invisible, at first. A tremor, a trembling vibration that I attribute to some mixture of encroaching darkness and fear. But every step brings it into sharper relief against the background of the far stands. A jagged visual warping with Estevan firmly in its centre. My father's former adviser is little more than a silhouette, still sitting, head bowed. The blurring agitation in the air makes him look like he's phasing in and out of existence a hundred times a second.

The stylus in my hand is hot now. Close to burning my skin and buzzing against my terrified grip, trying to worm its way free. I don't let it.

Estevan still has his back to me; I'm tempted to call out, to plead with him to stop, but the images of the men who approached him before, their fates, are etched on my mind. I'm numb, and not only because my tunic still clings cold and sodden to my skin. What am I doing? The air feels thicker here, hotter and hard against my face. Dread flows through my veins. I step forward. Again. *Again.* If I stop moving, I won't be able to start again.

I take a clumsy, desperate run at the last few feet, skidding to my knees and breathlessly grabbing Estevan, the sharp tip of my stylus at his neck.

As soon as I touch him, everything *flickers.*

For a moment—not even a second—we're not in the Arena anymore. I'm still on jagged stone, the spoke-like pattern jutting from the earth. But the water is gone. The surrounding walls, the stands beyond, are gone.

Caten is gone.

It's too brief for more than an impression. The purple-and-orange bruise of smoky, lightning-cracked sky. Some sort of impossibly vast pyramid, surface smooth and black and mirrored, its base stretching for miles. The harbour with a vast, lit bridge dividing it, lined by statues that must stand a hundred feet high. Waves, monstrous curling whitecaps, towering over them. Exploding against them.

Pain accompanies the sight. Rippling through my body, a burning from the inside out. I'm screaming. Blind. My blood boiling, my flesh peeling, every muscle and joint drawn inexorably, mercilessly apart.

Then I'm back, breath coming in ragged sobs, barely aware enough to keep my grip on the stylus. Estevan is still in front of me. We're still kneeling in the semi-darkness against slick, torn rock, surrounded by dark stone and death. Only the memory of that place, and the agony that accompanied it, remains.

"So you came." It's Estevan. He sounds unsurprised. He hasn't moved, though he must feel the point against his neck. His voice is cracked and sombre.

"Stop whatever you're doing, Estevan." He's calm enough, but I'm in no state to be the same. I push the stylus harder against his throat, dizzy from the echoes of what just happened. The air is heavy and charged, buzzing. The stone in my hand almost too hot to grip. "*Please.* Don't make me do this."

"I'm not. You can still walk away." The pulsating vibration around us beats faster, harder. Building.

"No, I can't." I grit my teeth. "Come *on*, Estevan. We're on the same side. We're not monsters."

Estevan tilts his head up and to the side, enough so that I can see his face. His eyes are red. Tears leak from them. "We are what they make us, Diago."

"We don't have to be."

He laughs, a hollow sound against the ethereal moans of terror still echoing to us over the water. "That's the power of the Hierarchy—we do, because there is no standing apart. You fight the tyranny of the many, or you are one of them." He hangs his head again. Tired. "Silence is a statement, Diago. Inaction picks a side. And when those lead to personal benefit, they are complicity."

It's a strangely melancholic statement, delivered without malice. I still feel its accusation.

Energy continues to build around us, vibrating against my skin. I can feel Estevan's muscles begin to tense beneath my grip. "Maybe you're right, but there has to be a better way. If we do this, then what do *we* deserve?" My voice is shaking. The stylus has broken his skin, a thin line of blood wending its way down his neck. "I'll help you, if that's what it takes. I'll help the Anguis if you just *stop*."

"No, you won't. Sedotia was right about you." Estevan sighs. Still staring at the ground, he slowly, gently, reaches up, clasping my hand where it's holding the stylus. A comforting gesture. "But a broken blade can still cut, Diago."

His grip abruptly tightens.

Then in one savage, sharp motion, he's twisting and thrusting the stylus upward, through his neck and deep into his brain.

XXII

I HAVE NEVER KILLED A MAN, THOUGH MY TRAINING HAS taught me how. Come close a few times, since Suus. Always believed I could if I needed to.

As Estevan's body sags against my chest, hot blood dribbling down the embedded stylus and over my hands, I'm aghast. Bewildered. Sick.

And, for a single, shameful moment, relieved that the decision has been taken from me.

I cradle my former countryman as the terrible build-up of energy around us vanishes, allowing an eerie hush to slither into its place. Waves lap the path, gentler now, motion driven by the steady escape of water somewhere far below. Occasional cries still echo through near-darkness, wails that speak of shock and grief, but most of those who remain in the stands are mute.

I bow my head over the body resting against me, just breathing. Mind clouded by shock and an exhaustion that's hitting me too hard, even for what I just went through. People will be watching; I can't look like I'm mourning a man who just killed tens of thousands. And I can't have this strange stylus tied to me.

So, unspeakably queasy though it makes me, I use the smallest movement possible to pull the stone spike free. Warm, sticky liquid spills over my fingers and onto Estevan's tunic. Then I stand, letting his corpse slide off me. It slouches to the edge of the narrow peninsula. Teeters.

With an effort, I use my foot to kick Estevan's body off the side.

His form tumbles into the dark; there's a splash and then he's bobbing, floating face-down, barely visible. I toss the stylus the opposite way, toward the protruding mast of a bireme, trying to make it a wrathful act of disrespect. I don't think many people will be able to see what I'm doing—the scant illumination created by the broken lanterns has all but vanished by this point—but I need it to look disdainful, not suspicious.

The stylus makes the smallest splash and sinks from sight. Even if it's found, noticed amid the ruin of what's happened here, plenty of other people carried stylii today. There will be no reason to think it's the one I used. No reason to examine it for anything unusual.

The deed done and the driving terror that's been keeping me going finally leaking away, I find myself staring down at my hands. Crimson drips from them as they shake.

It's a few seconds before I register the cheers floating across the inky water.

I look up. In the distance, people are moving. Standing. Emerging from their huddles up against the blocked exits, shifting cautiously for a better view of the lake. Of me.

My whole body's trembling from fear, from stress, from pain. The applause is just one more assault. I try to take stock, to figure out whether I'm missing anything that could give me away. Where is Sedotia in all of this? Has she already escaped? Will she be looking for revenge, given what I just did? There are too many people still in the destroyed stadium and my vision's starting to blur; if she's nearby, I can't see her.

My knees give way and I slump to the ground. There's blood where I'm lying, but I'm too tired to care. It's not a natural exhaustion. My face hits sticky, cold stone.

I close my eyes and drift as ovation echoes around me.

%. %. %.

WHEN I WAKE, I'M IN A BED. WARM AND COMFORTABLE, ALBEIT stiff. There's a lot of light and it hurts to open my eyes; I spend several seconds adjusting, the glaring white pain fading into images.

I'm back in my room at Ulciscor's villa. It's late morning, judging from the angle the sunlight is pounding through the window. For an instant I think I've overslept, and my body tenses and tries to rise on instinct. An abrupt ache keeps me down, and I'm suddenly reliving flashes of my last waking moments before now.

Oh.

I test my limbs more cautiously this time; I'm sore, but nothing seems injured. How long has it been since the naumachia? At least the night and some of the morning. Probably longer, if I'm back here.

Nobody's around, and the door is shut, so I allow some time to steel myself. Sitting up still makes the room spin. There's a tray of bread and water on the sideboard, and after a few steadying breaths I'm acutely aware of how hungry I am. I tear into the loaf.

I'm still wolfing down chunks of torn-off bread when the door opens.

"Master Vis!" It's Kadmos and, to my bemusement, he both sounds and looks pleased to see me. "How are you feeling?"

I swallow awkwardly, partially chewed mouthful forcing its way down my throat. "Sore."

"From everything I hear, that's understandable. Very understandable." He's still smiling. Beaming, in fact, to the point where I wonder whether there's some terrible news he's eager to share with me. "The Magnus Quintus will be delighted you're awake."

"Ulciscor's here?"

"He is." He doesn't even flinch at my familiar use of the name.

I rub at my eyes. "How long have I been asleep?"

"The better part of a week, young master." The sombre way he says it, I can tell there was some debate as to my chances of waking up. "Which means I should fetch the Magnus Quintus immediately." He moves to leave and then hesitates. Nods to me, genuinely respectful. "I am glad to see you well, Master Telimus."

The portly man leaves, fast enough that I don't think he sees my jaw hanging.

I haven't had enough time to digest Kadmos's words or his deference before there's motion again in the hall.

Ulciscor smiles as he fills the doorway, relief easing the lines of worry around his brown eyes. He's composed but his close-cut black beard looks a touch scruffy, as though he's neglected trimming it for the past few mornings.

"Well. About time," he says, walking over to the bed and gripping my forearm in glad greeting. "How are you feeling?"

"Sore. Confused. A little worried that Kadmos just told me it's been a week since the naumachia." I look to Ulciscor for confirmation, squeeze my eyes closed in frustration when he gives it morosely. *Vek.* A week of training lost, then. Just like that. "Was I injured?"

"We don't know. We couldn't find anything physical, but after what Melior did . . ." Ulciscor peers at me. "You truly only feel a little sore? Don't hide it if it's worse. You've been accepting food and water, when prompted, and relieving yourself—but otherwise, you may as well have been dead."

I shift uncomfortably at the thought and then gingerly stretch, testing everything. "Honestly, if I've been lying here for a whole week, this is probably just stiffness."

"Good. That's good. Let someone know straight away if something's wrong, though." He's genuinely relieved. "A lot of people are going to be pleased to hear you're alright."

"Even Kadmos, apparently."

"*Especially* Kadmos. Rotting gods, the man's been hounding me to arrange a Vitae-rium for you, of all things." He waves a hand at my blank look. "They're a little like Sappers, but for keeping people alive. *Very* expensive. Still something I might have tried, if I'd thought it would work on you."

I'm glad he didn't try. I haven't heard of them before, but the thought makes my skin crawl. "I didn't think he liked me much."

"You were right. But with the credit you just did to the Telimus name, that won't be the case anymore."

I digest the comment in silence. I'm not under any suspicion, then.

"Melior?" I ask eventually.

"Very much dead." There's satisfaction in Ulciscor's voice. He must see something in my expression because he holds my gaze, serious. "Feel no shame in the act, Vis. He was a monster and in taking his life, you saved thousands of others. *Thousands*." He gives the last word real weight, trying to drive home its importance. "They say more than half of the people in the Arena survived, thanks to you."

I nod hollowly. Collected enough now to quell any sign of sadness or regret. No matter what Estevan was doing, he was a subject of Suus. And he was fighting for people like me.

"What about Aequa?"

"She's well. She's asked to come by to check on you more than once." He seems caught somewhere between amused and irritated by that. "Your . . . illness has given us a reason to forego your training with her, at least." His tone indicates that's a separate conversation. One he'll be having with me sooner rather than later.

I chew my lip. Not wanting to ask, but knowing that I have to find out, eventually. "What happened after I . . ." I trail off, gesturing to my head.

Ulciscor takes a seat opposite, then briskly starts running through events since Estevan killed himself.

The hours immediately following the attack were chaos, naturally enough. More than a third of the people inside the stadium died, by all estimates; the resulting, massive weaknesses in some Will pyramids caused a ripple of infrastructure problems that the Hierarchy is still scrambling to resolve. Small issues such as city lanterns not lighting, to things like a Transvect carrying more than three hundred soldiers crashing somewhere north of Sytrece.

It seems the Anguis expected this and planned accordingly, coordinating more attacks elsewhere in the capital. Three senators were killed on their way to oversee celebrations in the Forum. A dozen Sextii died in an assault on the Praedium District. Other raids, though, were turned back, the Anguis fighters annihilated when they discovered their targets weren't as debilitated as expected.

Neither result makes me feel any better.

I don't say much as the Magnus Quintus talks. Occasionally ask for a clarification here and there, or acknowledge something he's said. I'm listening, but I'm also using the time to furiously catch up. Retracing my steps at the naumachia. Figuring out who might have seen something that could give me away.

"The gathering of large crowds in Caten has been temporarily prohibited, as a precaution. The public have been asked to submit the names of any suspected Anguis members for proscription, which will continue for another week. The Senate's suspended until that ends." Ulciscor's moving on to the more recent consequences, now. "There were a lot of Magnus Octavii and Magnus Septimii among the casualties at the Arena, though. There's been disagreement about how to fill so many key roles. Some squabbling over how to divide the strongest candidates, even within Military." He sounds disgusted at that.

"Were you affected?" I'm suddenly curious.

Ulciscor's confirmation is bleak. "I was walking through the Forum and next thing I knew, I was on the ground. It wasn't painful. Just . . . shocking, to be diminished like that. To feel so much weaker. Like I'd suddenly been bound and blindfolded." His voice is quiet. He rubs at his dark pate. "I only had seventeen deaths in my pyramid, and most of them were only Octavii. Some of the others had hundreds."

I study Ulciscor. He's sincere, I think. Far more open than he was the last time we spoke. The attack truly shook him.

"I'm sorry."

He snorts softly. "You, of all people, don't need to be. I cannot imagine how much worse it would have been without you. It will take us months to recover, but if you hadn't done what you did, that might have been years." The Quintus forces a smile. "At least national heroes have a much better chance of advancing through the Academy."

I chuckle, but my humour withers as I realise Ulciscor's serious. "Lanistia has been telling me it's best not to draw attention. Do my impressing of people at the Academy, rather than build up expectations."

"Gods' graves, Vis! You just killed the leader of the Anguis and single-handedly stopped the most deadly attack on Caten in its history. The Senate has just hailed you Vis Telimus Catenicus! It's far, far too late to arrive quietly." My dismay must leak onto my face, because he laughs at my apparent modesty. "This is *good*, lad. Be proud! We Catenans do love our heroes. You couldn't have asked for a more perfect introduction."

Vek. He means it to be motivating. I feel like I need to bathe.

"What about the Anguis who are still out there?" I ask eventually. Sedotia doesn't strike me as the type to forgive what I've done. In fact, I'm surprised she hasn't already exposed me. The weight of that—the realisation of what is surely a looming threat—settles deep.

"Only a few people know you're here, but we've arranged for extra protection around the villa anyway. And the Academy has pledged to increase their security as well." Ulciscor's apologetic about the latter. Knows it will make my job harder, once I'm there. "They've given you special dispensation to arrive on the first day of classes, too, rather than the usual three days beforehand. To give you as much time as possible to recover."

"Kind of them," I mutter, doing a quick calculation. A full two weeks left to train, then. Still not much.

Ulciscor eyes me, and I can see he's finally going to ask what he's been itching to since he arrived.

"Can you tell me . . . what exactly happened? From what I hear, many others died trying to do what you did."

I supply my own version of the naumachia in as much detail as I dare. Fortuitously noticing the sewer entrance before the attack, guessing its purpose, and then realising that it might be a way out for Aequa. Chancing upon a dropped stylus on the way back. Noticing the way Melior seemed to build up to his attacks, and waiting until he was in the process, distracted, before I struck. Then succumbing to the strange energy around him.

I still have no idea what Aequa's said, but when I'm done, Ulciscor, to my relief, seems satisfied.

"It's possible that you were resistant to whatever he was doing because you've never ceded," he muses, nodding agreement to an implication I've already made. "That's tricky. It's important we find a way to counter whatever power the man was using, but your circumstances aren't something we want to make public. Too many questions." He leans forward and gazes at the floor, deep in thought.

"Will I need to worry about that when you present me to the Senate?"

"What?" Ulciscor looks at me blankly, then, "Oh! Good news on that front, too. Your adoption was unanimously ratified before things were suspended. It seems that saving sixty thousand or so Catenan lives earns you some credit, even with senators." He grins. "You should have seen Advenius's face when he stood with the rest of them."

I allow some amusement, then cough. "About that."

"Advenius made it seem like I was a bad bet, and you panicked." Ulciscor sighs. "Lanistia told me everything. I wasn't pleased when I heard the news. But it's water past the mill. Done and all for the better, as it turns out. We don't need to speak of it anymore."

A moment, and he sighs again—heavily, this time—as he sees my expression. "Or perhaps we do?"

"Advenius . . . Advenius said that your brother committed suicide. And Aequa told me that everyone believes that, except you. That your opinion about Veridius being responsible is common knowledge." I'm still catching up, mentally, but I have to know, and I can't summon a more tactful way to raise it. "I asked Lanistia, and she only said that you were sure Veridius killed him. She didn't want to go into the details." I shift uncomfortably. "It's just . . . given our deal . . . that worries me."

"You think I'm grasping at straws. Trying to restore my brother's honour, rather than following evidence." His expression doesn't reveal what he thinks of that. "You think there might be nothing at the Academy for you to find."

"No. I just want to understand why I *shouldn't* think that."

Ulciscor observes me impassively for a few more seconds, then leans back. There's weary acceptance in the motion.

"As I've said, Caeror was in the group who first trained at Solivagus. For a while we thought the entire Academy cycle would be cancelled because of the grain riots, and he was devastated. Then *so* excited when they announced the move. We all knew before he even left that he was going to be in Class Three. My parents were so proud of him. So was I." He's talking deliberately now, a tautness to his voice. Like he's trying to focus on the words and avoid the memories.

"The first trimester, everything seemed to be going well. He came home for the Festival of Jovan and was so happy about everything. His progress, what he was learning. His new friends. Including Veridius." Acid enters Ulciscor's tone at that. "And then two months later, he missed the Festival of the Ancestors."

"That was unusual?"

"Very. And when I tried to go and see him, I got stopped. Blocked. Religion had told us there were new rules around visiting, but I didn't think they'd enforce it." He plucks absently at his sleeve. "But I didn't think too much of it, either. Religion's always been protective of the Academy. And you have to understand what being there is like. The outside world feels so distant. I just assumed Caeror had gotten caught up in the life."

I nod, not saying anything. Not wanting to interrupt.

"We weren't supposed to be in communication with each other, but security on Solivagus was still basic back then. No Will cage at the entrance, so after the festival, I managed to sneak him in a stylus that was sub-harmonically locked to one on my end. Too risky to use often, but he'd send me messages from time to time. Mostly jokes.

Stupid things." He cracks a wistful smile at that. "He seemed fine. Content, even. Just before the end of second trimester, he sent me a note to say he wouldn't be coming to stay with me in Caten like we'd planned. He and two of his friends were going to spend the winter on Solivagus, to get ready for the Iudicium. I thought it was a little strange, but I was excited for him, too. Sad that I wouldn't get to spend time with him, but he was seventeen, and it seemed pretty clear that he was with a girl, there. I wasn't going to be the one to drag him away."

His smile fades. "I'd just made Quintus back then, anyway. I was working day and night. My parents asked me a couple of times to use my influence to check on him, but I kept telling them it would be inappropriate. That he was alright." He swallows. "The messages started drying up in that third trimester, but I assumed he was just studying hard. Then he sent me one about a week before the Iudicium. A long one. He really wanted to meet, but I thought he was just nervous, and . . . it would have been against the rules. He could have been expelled, and my position could have been affected. So I ignored it."

There's so much regret in that last sentence.

"Two weeks later, we got word that something terrible had happened during the Iudicium. There was an accident, and the girl Caeror was with had been terribly, permanently injured—was probably going to die. Caeror had blamed himself. Veridius, who was the only other one there, said that he was inconsolable. Couldn't face the idea of going to a Sapper with the guilt. Went mad and threw himself off a cliff in a fit of grief, despite Veridius's best efforts." He finishes softly. The words are raw.

I'm silent, digesting for the first time how hard that would have been for Ulciscor. For his family. Not just the loss, but the manner of it. Suicide in the Hierarchy is the most fundamentally dishonourable act, the ultimate shame. The circumstances of Caeror's death would be a stain against the Telimus name, even today.

None of that does anything to explain why Ulciscor is so convinced it's a lie, though.

"I'm sorry," I say. Hesitate.

Ulciscor sees my indecision, saves me the indelicate question. "I knew him, Vis. I *knew* him. I cannot imagine a soul less inclined to despair, no matter what had happened." He holds up a hand as I open my mouth to respond. "But I hadn't seen him in almost a year, so that alone wouldn't have been enough."

He reaches into a pocket, pulls out two neatly folded sheets of paper. He opens one on the table between us, the way he carefully smooths the creases almost loving. "This came two days before Caeror died. I almost threw it out without looking at it again. Didn't want to torture myself." He pushes it across to me. It's old, the ink faded. "Tell me what you see."

I scan the letter. It describes being nervous about the Iudicium. The writing's messy and it's stilted in places, rambling. But that's all.

I shake my head. "I don't see anything."

"Caeror and I, when we were children, used to pretend we were spies in the Catenan army and pass coded messages to each other. Our favourite cipher was the rule of three—first letter of every third word after 'brother.'" Ulciscor indicates the paper. "Look again."

I do, taking my time.

"The first word is 'translation.'" He's right. There's something hidden here.

Ulciscor pushes across the second sheet of paper. More writing, much shorter and in a different, neater hand.

"'*Translation right. Obiteum lost. Luceum unknown.*'" I read the first part aloud, brow furrowed. "I remember hearing you mention this to Nateo, in the prison. But 'Obiteum' and 'Luceum' . . . they don't mean anything in any language I know." I move on, silent again as I check the words on the second sheet against Caeror's letter. *Scintres Exunus worked. Gate still open. More strange pre-Cataclysm power. Only Veridius knows.* It all matches.

I examine them a moment longer, then hand the sheets back. "You're right, it's a message. But it doesn't make much sense."

"There were dozens, before that one. I remember some of them seemed strangely worded, but I didn't pay enough attention. The whole point of giving him the stylus was that he could write to me privately—I have no idea why he needed to use code. It never occurred to me to look for something like that. And I had no reason to keep the letters."

"You think they would have provided context."

"I do."

I watch as he meticulously folds the pages again. "I agree that this is strange, but . . ."

"It's not proof of anything," agrees Ulciscor. "And I could have forged this letter myself, which is why I never showed it to anyone. But it was enough for me to find the girl Caeror had been spending so much time with. The one who got injured. She survived, but she was the daughter of a Sextus who couldn't afford the ongoing treatment necessary. Veridius was trying to step in and take care of her, but I convinced my parents that we should intercede. That it would go some way toward . . . improving our image." The words still leave a bitter taste in his mouth. "She couldn't talk for months, but eventually, everything healed. Everything but her memory, and her eyes."

He looks at me expectantly. My suspicions have been building as he's talked, but even with the last part, I'm still certain I've somehow reached the wrong conclusion. "*Lanistia?*"

"Yes."

I have a hundred new questions. "So she and Caeror . . ."

"Yes."

Attractive or not, it's hard to picture the woman romantically involved with anyone. "Gods' graves. That's . . ." I shake my head. Still bewildered, but a few more things are making sense now. "And you said her memory never recovered?"

"The Iudicium and the months before it are gone, for her. Whole other swathes of her life are missing too. The physicians said they might come back over time. They never did." Ulciscor says it all in a flat monotone, but I can hear the strain beneath. "Veridius was the one who supposedly saved her. Carried her out of the forest, half-dead, and told the Praeceptors his story. By the time they got to Caeror, the alupi had done their work. No way to tell what had really happened."

No wonder Lanistia didn't want to explain it. "So she doesn't remember *anything?*"

"She remembers Caeror. She remembers enough to know that he and Veridius found something out there. Something they were keeping secret. Those ruins in the woods near the Academy I told you about, and then the ones out to the west." The man opposite rubs his shaven scalp. Voice quiet. Looking more tired, more vulnerable, than I have ever seen him. "She says that Caeror thought of Veridius as a friend. As a *brother*. At least, as far as her most recent memories go."

He doesn't bother to disguise his acrimony.

"But why would Veridius say he committed suicide?" Ulciscor's right: put it all together, and it *does* seem like something is off. But that doesn't make it any less puzzling. "Why not just say it was an accident? And if he was willing to kill Caeror, why save Lanistia? He couldn't have known about her memory."

"An argument Veridius himself made." Ulciscor's grim. "And neither I nor Lanistia have the answers. Maybe she didn't see anything, or maybe he thought she was going to die anyway. But as far as claiming suicide? That was probably part of his deal with Religion—which he clearly *did* have, given that he defected to them immediately upon becoming Domitor. Suicide protected the Academy from any recriminations or investigations. Even my parents wanted it all put to rest as quietly as possible." He rolls his shoulders, quick to glaze over that last detail.

I watch him, hiding a genuine wave of sympathy for the man that I know he would see as pity. "You should have told me all of this from the beginning."

"It would have complicated your training. For you, because you would have questioned every demand Lanistia made of you. And for Lanistia, because I think she would have seen it and wondered if you were right to do so. But I was always going to tell you before you left."

I move to protest, then subside. He might be right. I can only imagine how much Lanistia must hate Veridius, must be desperate to find out what happened to Caeror. To her. Enduring her relentless pushing, her endlessly aggressive lessons, with that knowledge in the back of my mind—it would have been hard not to wonder at the necessity of it all. To think that, just maybe, she wasn't approaching my instruction as objectively as she should be.

"You're telling me now," I point out eventually. "I still have two weeks of training left."

"I'm hoping you know each other well enough by this point to deal with it." He eyes me. "And that you're smart enough to see that Lanistia's methods are working. Even after a week in bed, you look bigger than you did a month ago. Stronger."

I concede his point with a grunt. The constant training and full diet has continued to bear fruit.

"She says you're improving academically, too. Filling in the gaps. Even after losing a week, she thinks you'll be ready."

"Rotting gods. She actually *said* that?"

"Don't let on that I told you."

We share a grin, some of the weight of the conversation lifting.

We talk for a while longer, but the consequential matters have been dealt with. Ulciscor's soon noting my drooping eyelids and suggesting that he instruct Kadmos to check in on me, and for Lanistia to give me the rest of the day before we resume training. I don't argue either proposal. We say our farewells.

"I should mention, lad. I've already been back and forth between here and Caten too often these past few days—and I'm needed there. So this is the last time we'll speak before you leave for the Academy. Probably the last time until the Festival of the Ancestors." Ulciscor's standing. Clapping me on the shoulder. An awkward, almost affectionate act. "Life and luck, Vis. Be careful."

"I will."

He leaves.

XXIII

IT'S JUST PAST DAWN WHEN I WAKE TO A ROUGH SHAKING. I groan and open my eyes to see Lanistia's dark-glassed visage glowering down at me.

"You overslept."

"Gods' graves, Lanistia. Nice to see you too." I bat away her hand and sit up, scrubbing the blurriness from my eyes. No dizziness this time. The aches of the previous day seem to have eased considerably after the extra rest. "I thought I might have earned a later start."

"I thought a week's sleep would be enough."

"You would," I grumble as I swing out of bed. I splash my face using the bowl of water on the table, rake my fingers through my hair, straighten my tunic. She watches impatiently.

"How are you feeling?"

"Good enough." It's mostly true. There's still stiffness in every movement, but as I stretch, I can feel the muscles loosening. And though I'm tired, I don't have the weariness that plagued every breath yesterday.

"Then let's get moving."

It's a strange morning. On one hand, there's a comforting sense of familiarity as we spar above Ulciscor's verdant fields, gravel crunching, clouds of breath dissipating into the young light. A few of the Octavii toiling below cast glances in our direction—in my direction, I suspect—but otherwise, it feels as though I could have been simply imagining the naumachia. As though it never really happened.

But I'm all too aware of the passage of time, too. Of how dramatically things have changed since the last time I did this. When I got aboard the carriage a week ago, it felt as though I still had an eon to prime myself. I felt in control, as far as that was possible.

Now I'm underprepared, relative to my time left. Behind.

At first Lanistia doesn't seem to be treating me any differently than usual; we train hard, and I begin gathering bruises at a steady rate. But as the session drags on I start to notice that her blows don't sting the way they usually do. That I'm getting away with mistakes.

After the third time she doesn't take an obvious opening in my defence, I step back. "You're going easy."

"Perhaps." Lanistia straightens. "You were unconscious for a week. Better to ease back into this."

"We don't have time for that." I growl the words. Annoyed that I'm the one having to say them.

"We also don't have time for you to relapse. Just because Kadmos hasn't been able to find anything wrong with you, doesn't mean we can ignore what happened."

My lip twitches in frustration. "I know you want to push. So push."

Lanistia moves to take her stance again, then hesitates, instead brushing some imaginary dirt from her tunic. "Ulciscor said he told you about Caeror."

"He did."

"And there's nothing you want to ask me?"

"Is there anything you think I need to know?"

"Not particularly."

"If there's something you should be telling me, I assume you will." I *am* curious about no small number of things, but it's not fair to sate my curiosity at the expense of her pain.

Lanistia studies me a moment longer. "Alright." There's the slightest relaxing of her shoulders. An almost imperceptible nod of what is very nearly gratitude.

We resume, and I quickly discover the bite to Lanistia's attacks has returned. I'm surprised to find myself . . . if not *pleased*, exactly, then content. I feel like Lanistia and I understand each other a little better than before.

Our sparring continues in relative silence for several minutes, until the young woman opposite me abruptly stops, holding up her hand to indicate I should do the same. She swivels toward the road leading to the villa.

There's the faint, persistent crunching of wheels against gravel, and a carriage trundles into view. Lanistia and I frown at it together in the hazy half-light of the cloudy dawn.

"Expecting someone?"

She shakes her head, wiping a thin sheen of sweat from her brow.

It's early for an unannounced visitor. The carriage has stopped outside the villa's entrance; Lanistia and I walk over together as the driver opens the door. The man who emerges is Ulciscor's age, I think. Short and rakishly thin, almost bony, with hollowed cheeks and wavy dark hair. He moves with lithe confidence as he dismounts, turning to observe our approach.

"Welcome to Villa Telimus." I take the lead, as would be expected now my adoption has been ratified. "I'm Vis Telimus."

"Ah! Young Catenicus himself." The stranger scrutinises me, looking more fascinated than impressed. "I was told you were still unconscious."

"Sorry to disappoint. And you are?"

"Sextus Gaius Valerius. I'm here to examine you."

"You're a physician?"

"Something like that." The man turns, pulls a bag from the carriage and starts rooting around in it. "I just need a few samples. And some answers, as you're in a position to give them. Nothing that will take much of your time."

"Our Dispensator is an excellent physician, and he's already cleared Vis of any lingering illness." It's Lanistia, curt and impatient. "Under whose authority—"

"The Senate's." Gaius is calm as he interrupts, producing a stone tile from his bag and presenting it to me. "The authorisation from Magnus Tertius Servius."

I take the tile. It's blank on both sides. I frown over it, then, assuming it means what Gaius is saying, but not sure how, show it to Lanistia. She examines it with her customary lack of expression.

"Ulciscor isn't here," she says eventually.

"I'm sure you can find something to verify it against, Sextus Scipio."

Lanistia grunts—irritated that the man knows who she is, I think—but then with an obvious effort, modifies her tone to be more accommodating. "Of course. Please come inside. We do have to check, you understand, given recent events."

"Naturally."

Gaius trails after us into the villa, and Lanistia instructs him to wait in the atrium before ushering me toward Ulciscor's office. As soon as we're out of earshot, I glance across at her. "What's going on?"

"I'm not sure." A crease in her forehead. "Ulciscor is in Servius's pyramid, so this should . . ." She's putting the tile up against the entrance to the office as she talks; there's a click, and the door swings open.

"It's genuine, I take it?"

"It's genuine. And this is an old form of authorization. It's unusual. Direct and discreet. Even if Ulciscor was here, he'd be expected to comply without asking questions. And then forget Gaius was ever here." She pulls the office door shut again, adjusting her glasses distractedly.

"So he's not a physician?"

"I have no idea. But I can't imagine he's been sent here like this just to make sure you're well."

"What do I do?"

"Whatever he says. Take note of everything he asks, everything he does. I'll get word to Ulciscor later."

We return to the atrium, where Gaius is crouching, examining the intricate mosaic floor. "This is beautiful craftsmanship," he observes as we enter, not looking up. When neither of us respond, he sighs, standing and stretching. "I trust everything is in order?"

"It is." Lanistia hands back the tile.

Gaius nods in unsurprised fashion, then gazes at Lanistia steadily. There's a good five seconds of tension before Lanistia grimaces and walks out, shutting the door behind her.

"Well then." Gaius motions me into a chair, then begins extracting things from his bag. Several small, coloured stone vials, which make a clinking noise as he places them on the table. A series of unpleasant-looking bladed tools. "Tell me, Vis. When exactly did you wake up?"

He speaks easily, assuredly, with none of the hesitation that comes with deference. That's strange; the man's not obviously anyone of importance, and I've learned enough of Catenan society to know that a plebian Sextus would normally be more cautious around a patrician's son.

"Yesterday."

"Not long, then. Good. Good." Gaius talks distractedly, unstoppering a vial that appears made of topaz and peering inside, then swishing the contents and giving it a brief sniff before putting it back. "Can you relate exactly what happened at the naumachia? Everything you saw Melior do, every interaction you had with him. In as much detail as possible, please."

I start my story, which quickly turns into a halting one as Gaius interrupts again and again, requesting explanations or clarifications or more details about almost everything I mention. He works as he does so. He takes samples of my hair, my nails, my spit. Scrapes flakes of skin off one arm, then makes a cut on the other and, to my concern, starts draining a small amount of my blood into an obsidian vial.

"Rotting gods, what is that for?" I break off what I'm saying as globules of red begin disappearing into the container. I didn't raise an objection when the scalpel broke my skin, but this is too much.

"Testing."

"For what?"

Gaius doesn't reply. He's watching the vial intently, holding it up to the light. I'm not sure what he's looking for. It's definitely obsidian. Completely opaque.

"What are you testing for?" I repeat the question. Harshly, this time.

Gaius frowns at the vial for an infuriating second longer, then grunts, as if surprised. "Anything strange. The power Melior used is new to us. There's no telling what effect coming into contact with it might have on a person's body. We need to be thorough." He starts tending to my cut, staunching the trickle down my arm.

It's a deflection, albeit a well-delivered one. I don't press. Whatever the real answer is, Gaius isn't about to give it up.

The physician's questions resume, and I continue to play the compliant, somewhat bemused boy who simply wants to forget about a traumatic experience. I repeat a lot of the same excuses when he asks for specifics. It all happened so suddenly. It was so violent. I was panicked, did what I thought was right at the time without much critical thought involved. I was lucky.

In the end, much to the man's evident irritation, I give him nothing beyond what I've already supplied to Ulciscor. Just as when I talked to the Magnus Quintus, part of me wonders if I should be saying more. Helping prevent another such attack from ever taking place. The carnage Estevan's weapon caused is something I would never want to see repeated. A memory that will haunt me forever.

And yet . . . it *is* a weapon. One the Hierarchy doesn't have. One they may actually fear.

Gaius eventually concedes defeat, packing away his samples carefully. He lingers before closing his bag, though, then draws a sheaf of creased papers from it.

"One last question," he says, his tone a mix of exasperation and resignation as he unfolds the sheets, splaying them out disinterestedly on the table in front of me. "I don't suppose these mean anything to you?"

There are four pages, each bearing images sketched with extraordinary artistry. A night sky, the silhouettes of what look like people eerily hovering in front of a full moon. A desolate alien landscape, dunes half covering a city's worth of broken buildings, shattered glass pillars rising from the sand between them like jagged knives. A massive hall with an equally enormous triangular opening at its end, writing in a language I don't recognise inscribed on the walls all around.

But it's the fourth that captures my gaze. A giant black pyramid set against towering waves.

It's not exactly what I saw, in that uncanny second before I reached Estevan. But it's close enough.

Against my will, my gaze loiters on that last image too long. I do everything I can to recover and tear it away, but Gaius's casual tone, the way he seemed to be signalling the interrogation was over, disarmed me. A deliberate ploy, judging from the way his eyes gleam, sharp and appraising, when I look up again.

"They're very strange." I squint back at them, more to collect myself than to take in more detail. "What are they from?"

It's a reasonable attempt at salvaging the situation, but even without looking at him, I can feel the heat of Gaius's scepticism. There's a breath, and then, "You recognised this one." The physician leans over, jabbing the black pyramid pointedly.

"I *did* think it looked familiar," I admit, trying to sound both sheepish and dismissive. "Would I have seen it in a book, perhaps?" I look up, letting the question hang.

We stare at each other for a full couple of seconds before the spindly man sighs, looking down and collecting the papers again. "No. It wouldn't have been from a book." He's perfectly nonchalant, but he doesn't believe me. He returns the pages to his bag, then taps the table with a finger twice. A leaving signal of irritation, I think. "If you do . . . remember . . . anything, send word to Tertius Servius. I'll come. Any information you have will be well rewarded."

"I will."

Gaius gives me a brief, almost curt nod, then leaves. He's replaced by Lanistia, who promptly shuts the door behind her. "Well?"

It doesn't take long to relate the encounter, Lanistia's usual inscrutable expression firmly in place. She's worryingly silent after I finish.

"You should talk to Kadmos about this," she says eventually. "You're due to have your lesson with him after the morning meal anyway."

"Kadmos? Why?"

"I don't know. I thought maybe his extensive medical background. His decades of study. The fact he was the youngest ever head of the Azriat. His—"

"Alright."

"Good. If he has any new insight, let me know. I'll send word to Ulciscor now." She balances on the balls of her feet, as if about to leave, then plants them again. "Why did you do it?"

"Do what?" I'm genuinely puzzled.

"Go back. At the naumachia." She's intent. Her glasses are divided into the green and blue of the horizon outside the window. "Aequa told us you could have escaped with her. Why didn't you?"

"It seemed like the right thing to do."

"You can do better than that."

"You think I'm lying?"

"I think it should have been suicide. And we both know those scars on your back mean you have no real love for Caten." Her voice is low. Certain. "You're brighter than most, Vis—but bright doesn't mean brave, or caring, or heroic. More often it means the opposite. Ulciscor may not see it, but don't think I'm as blind." She taps her glasses with a small, ironic smile.

I chew over the words.

"No. *No.*" When I do eventually speak, I don't conceal my anger. My indignation. It's real enough. "It was the *right thing to do.* Just because I don't want to be one of the Octavii, doesn't mean I'd leave them all to die."

"I didn't say that. I said it's strange that you were willing to sacrifice your life for them."

"Maybe I'm a better person than you," I snap.

Something about the remark hits home; Lanistia doesn't outwardly react, but it definitely gives her pause. Her silence allows me a chance to consider. I doubt I would have gone back without Sedotia's stylus. Even as it was, I hesitated.

But I don't regret it.

"Maybe you are." Lanistia says the words quietly. "But that's not necessarily what we need from you, Vis. It's a quality that won't serve you well in the Academy."

She pivots and is striding from the room before I can respond, leaving me to worry about the peculiar happenings of the morning alone.

XXIV

"HAIL, MASTER VIS."

It's turned into a preternaturally muggy summer morning, the air heavy and my tunic still clinging to me after training, despite the respite of Gaius's examination. My head's bowed over a tome detailing a very Catenan perspective on pre-Cataclysm society; I'm chewing bread absently, don't register the words for a second.

"Kadmos." I push the book aside and greet the Dispensator affably as he takes a seat opposite, brushes his stringy black hair back over his shoulders, then wipes away the sweat that's already beading on his extremely high forehead.

The portly man returns my cheerful expression once he's settled, startling me. Nothing's regressed since yesterday, then. "You're well enough to resume our lessons, I trust?"

"I feel fine. Good, in fact, after the extra rest I got yesterday," I assure him. "I have to thank you, too. I didn't realise that you were the one tending to me while I was unconscious. Lanistia tells me you lost a lot of sleep, making sure I got through those first few days safely."

"It was nothing, young master."

"Not to me." I mean it. The way Lanistia described it, the man all but attacked anyone who tried to take over for him. I make sure he sees that I'm being genuine, then lean forward. "Speaking of which, there was a man here this morning. Another physician, sent by Tertius Servius."

"They sent someone else to attend to you?" Kadmos is offended by the concept. "Ulciscor and I have been updating the Senate on your well-being, right up to and including this morning."

"This was something else." I tell him about Gaius's taking of samples, though I leave out his questions and the drawings. "Do you know any reason why he would do that?"

Kadmos's consternation has grown as I've explained what was done to me, until his eyes are bulging with indignation. "There is *no* reason that would be of assistance," he sputters, dragging the back of his hand across his creased, glistening brow. "Some of the old cults might have burned what this man took from you—Tarchanism, was probably the last surviving one. But even that would have been in some misguided attempt to heal you. There is nothing anyone can glean from dead skin and a little dried blood."

I shift. "And there's nothing they could *do* with it?"

He's stares at me blankly, then chuckles. "No! Gods' graves, no."

Lanistia said the same thing, but it's a relief to hear it confirmed. I hadn't been able to think of any nefarious purpose, myself, but I'm also keenly aware that my knowledge of higher-level Will use is still limited. "Good. Thank you."

He hears the dissatisfaction in my voice, I think, though it's not aimed at him. "I could investigate further, if you wish? I still have contacts in Sytrece who might be willing to look through some of the libraries there."

"No, thank you, Kadmos. That's very kind, but the Tertius clearly meant this to be done quietly. I wouldn't want there to be any trouble."

"Of course, young master."

I eye him. I've known from the beginning he was a learned man; the proof has been in every lesson we've had together. But his surliness always meant the source of that knowledge was never a topic of conversation, and his mention of Sytrecian contacts has reminded me of it. "You were really in charge of the entire Azriat Institute?"

Kadmos shifts, chair creaking beneath his weight. "It wasn't for very long. I got the position about six months before the proscriptions began."

"Oh. That . . . must have been awful."

"Such were the times," he says with no trace of bitterness, splaying his hands. "I was young, even to be a professor, and my position was one that garnered no small amount of jealousy. When the pretender Erimides made his claims, very few in Deopolis thought it was wise to risk the friendship of Caten—myself included—and sure enough, when Dimidius Carthius inevitably crushed the revolt, he wanted to make examples. I still don't know who named me, but they took me from my bed one night, and . . . here I am."

"But you weren't guilty of conspiring?"

He chortles. "I would not be much of a conspirator, young master. I was never exactly the dashing, secrets-in-the-night type."

I don't know what to say. It seems so obviously, outrageously wrong.

Kadmos sees me struggling and smiles again, only the barest trace of sadness in the expression. "A man will always wonder what might have been, but a wise one recognises fortune when it comes. For all I left behind, life has not been unkind to me."

"How could you just *accept* it though? How could you not resent them for what they took from you?" The words are out of my mouth before I consider them; I reach out my hand as if to snare them back and then let it fall, wincing.

He ponders me. Still glistening with a sheen of sweat, but dignified. Then he rises and turns, uncinching his tunic and raising it so that I can see his back.

"We all have them, young master," he says quietly. "Or did you think you were the only one to ever refuse the Aurora Columnae?"

I survey the pink and milky-white stripes layered across his skin, speechless. They're old, faded—but there's no mistaking them.

"There comes a point in every man's life where he can rail against the unfairness of the world until he loses, or he can do his best in it. Remain a victim, or become a survivor." Kadmos lets the cloth fall to cover the scars again. "Submitting was a burden, but never one I would trade for the alternative. I have thirty years more of memories, many of them fond. I live well, surrounded by luxury and with the trust and respect of a family I love. And yet I had colleagues who went to the Sappers, or who got sold to knights and were sent to work in the mines. Learned men all. Long dead."

He holds my gaze. He thinks he's helping me, I realise. Thinks that by doing what I did at the naumachia, I've made my choice. That I'm him thirty years ago, giving in to the enemy and joining them.

I try to look as though I'm not sick at the idea of living out my life like Kadmos. I empathise with him more, certainly.

But his approach to the Hierarchy is the opposite of who I want to be.

We move on to study for a while, Kadmos deciding to use my illness as a practical lesson, cheerfully explaining the various tests he put me through while I was unconscious. Despite the bleak subject matter, I enjoy the work. Kadmos is more free with his praise now, remarking several times how far I've come in the past month, even as he still corrects the occasional mistake. I'm surprised by how much I find myself glowing beneath his approval. It's feels like a long time since I've been given any sort of acclaim for my efforts.

We're interrupted a few times—the Dispensator still has charge of the estate, even as he teaches me—and just as the sun is reaching its zenith, an Octavii approaches, carrying a letter.

"Hm," the rotund man says, poring over the missive with a frown. "Lady Telimus writes. She's heard about the naumachia and asks after your well-being." He raises an eyebrow as he reads. "There's an implication she might be coming back to Caten sooner than expected too."

I'd almost forgotten about the woman. "Do you think she'll be a problem?"

"Not that you'll have to worry about. I doubt you'll meet her until after the Academy, even if she returns early."

"What's she like?"

"She's lovely." It's not sarcasm, but it's not said with the warmth required for it to sound honest, either. "Often away, though."

There's plenty of implication in the second part, even if Kadmos again delivers it as simple, uncoloured fact. Women in the Hierarchy—particularly young wives such as Ulciscor's—are generally expected to focus on family, no matter their skills wielding Will. The fact that Relucia is abroad working, when she and Ulciscor have no children, speaks volumes.

I'm tempted to ask more, but I doubt Kadmos will stretch propriety so much as to tell me anything I can't already glean.

I let the matter drop, and we resume our race to prepare me for the Academy.

%% %% %%

THE NEXT TWO WEEKS PASS IN A ROUGH BLUR OF TRAINING, learning, and practice in the Labyrinth.

My anxiety over a potential Anguis response to the naumachia remains unfounded: there's no hint of retribution, no concerns from any of the guards posted around the Telimus estate. No statement from the Anguis at all, in fact. Lanistia guesses the organisation is in disarray, scrambling to recover now their leader is dead and their major attack largely foiled.

That doesn't mean I rest easy. There's some part of me that was forged into steel after Suus, I think—some part of me that knows exactly how to wall off memories that would otherwise tear me apart. And I could feel it hard at work over those first couple of days after waking, when I was asked to relive the naumachia again and again. But the nights are a different beast. I close my eyes and see a lake of blood. I clamber over slick, steaming entrails and bones. I wake sweating, or shivering, or sometimes crying out into the darkness.

It fades, as all things do. And the relentlessness of my days means that even when I do start awake, exhaustion forces me back to slumber within minutes.

But my sleep is never the same.

Dawn is bright and clear the morning of the day I leave for the Academy. Lanistia and I have just finished our final sparring session; I'm bathed in a light sweat, breath misting as we walk back to the villa. Around us in the fields, Octavii are starting their labour, distant chatter ringing across the hills. Lanistia's uncharacteristically mute; usually this is where she berates me on all the mistakes I've just made, and then berates me about all the mistakes I'm about to make in studying. And then berates me for being behind.

I'm not sure what it says about me that I find the silence uncomfortable.

"Ulciscor sent word yesterday," Lanistia says suddenly. "He's arranged for you to travel to the Necropolis for the Festival of the Ancestors—that will be the next time you're allowed out of the Academy. And he looked into the students you met after the Transvect attack."

"Oh?" With everything else that's happened since, I'd almost forgotten his suggestion that I might have been drugged.

"Indol Quiscil is the Dimidius's son, as he thought. Belli Volenis and Emissa Corenius were the other two. Belli is the daughter of Quintus Volenis, the governor of Sytrece. Emissa is the daughter of Magnus Quintus Corenius."

I recognise the names from my studies. Important families. Important students.

"They're in Class Three, so they're among the elite in the Academy. And they're all from Military families. Ulciscor says that makes them unlikely targets for Veridius— much easier to co-opt students he could offer advancement to. So they *probably* didn't do anything to you."

"One more thing to *probably* not worry about, then."

Lanistia grunts. "You won't have much to do with them for a while, anyway— remember, you'll be starting in Seven, and classes at the Academy are meant to mimic pyramid rankings in the real world. Unless you reach Class Three, the most they'll interact with you is to give you orders."

I nod. Silence again. *Unless you reach Class Three.* I don't want to ask. It feels too much like conceding defeat, admitting I actually care what she thinks.

"You'll do well." She volunteers the statement as begrudgingly as anything she's ever said. She's facing straight ahead, though for all I know she could be focused on my expression. "If you keep working, there's a chance you can do what you need to do."

"Find what you and Ulciscor are looking for?"

"Get into Class Three."

I swallow. Tension drains out of my shoulders as I acknowledge the statement.

Then I allow myself a grin. "You think I'm pretty good."

She snorts. "I definitely didn't say that. Or imply it."

My grin widens. "No, no. I can see it now. You secretly like me. You think I'm—"

I'm staring up at the sky, rasping, air vanished from my lungs. From the corner of my eye I can see Lanistia walking away, her gait as calm as it was just a moment ago.

I groan, roll to my feet. Smile. Jog to catch up to Lanistia for the last walk back to the villa we'll ever take.

※ ※ ※

IT FEELS STRANGE, LEAVING. THIS ISN'T A HOME, NOT BY ANY measure of the word as I understand it. There's no love here, from or for me. Not truly, anyway, regardless of how the others feel. There can be no love without honesty.

But I still feel an emptiness as the door to the carriage closes. A sense of loss as I peer out the window and watch Lanistia's and Kadmos's forms slide from view. It's been a sanctuary, of sorts. A place where I've found a renewed sense of purpose.

Eventually the green hills vanish on the horizon and I sit, alone with my thoughts, as landscapes roll by. It's a short trip from here to the Transvect platform. Any sense of nostalgia is quickly swept away by anxiety, no matter what I pretended to Lanistia.

In a few hours, I'll be at the Academy.

DEUS NOLENS EXITUUS

PART II

XXV

I STILL REMEMBER THE TIME I HAD TO GIVE MY FIRST OFFICIAL speech at Suus. A small thing, a few words of introduction to a feast. I was all bravado until the afternoon before. Then something snapped. My heart wouldn't slow down. My hands shook. I threw up.

"I don't want to do it," I eventually told my father. Voice small. Head bowed.

He sat me down. Put his arm around me. Said nothing for a while.

"You should be glad you're nervous," he told me finally.

I remember laughing bitterly, sure he was joking.

"It's true." He was always so gentle. "Nervousness means there's a fear to be faced ahead, Diago. The man who is never nervous, never does anything hard. The man who is never nervous, never grows." He stroked my hair. "Do all you can to think of it as an opportunity. A blessing. No matter how it makes you feel in here." His hand pressed lightly against my chest, covering it.

I place my own hand to my chest now, imagining it's his touch. Feel my heartbeat. Hold tight to his words as the Transvect skims the chop of the Sea of Quus.

Though I've been to Solivagus before, I have no memory of actually arriving, and today I'm the only person on board. So I soon find myself pressed up against the window, watching with unabashed curiosity as the island looms on the horizon.

The sun's well past its zenith as the Transvect first flits along the sparkling water and then eases to a crawl, sliding low past one of several white monoliths jutting from the depths. It did the same thing on the way out, last time. It's the only way across the Seawall, according to Ulciscor: anything else that attempts to cross the submerged stone barrier that rings the island—ships, even just people swimming—is sucked down by some unseen force. Dragged to the bottom of the ocean floor and held there.

From the bleak way he said it, it wasn't a theoretical knowledge.

The wood and stone around me gives the shudder of a waking animal and starts to build speed again. I try to estimate how far we are from the shore. A mile, perhaps? The Transvect skims the waves for a few more seconds before prying itself upward. The sheer bluffs that guard the shoreline gradually begin to drop on the approaching horizon.

I move to the other side, trying to catch a glimpse of the ruins Ulciscor told me about when we were here. We're too low, though, and Solivagus is an obscuring green mass of steep hills and deep canyons.

I've been jittery all trip, but it's only now, as the Transvect finally crosses the threshold of the island, that the first real pangs of anxiety start to hit. All of the chaos and stress of these past months has been about this. Preparing for *this*.

There's no more room for mistakes.

"Vis Telimus?" A white-cloaked man is waiting alone on the platform as I step out of the Transvect. A crooked, blunt nose dominates his craggy face.

"That's me." I present the stone identification tile Ulciscor gave me with what I hope is a winning smile.

The stranger smiles back, revealing a missing tooth. He doesn't look much past forty. "I'm Septimus Filo. But call me Ulnius." He accepts my tile and then eyes the satchel slung over my shoulder. "Is that everything?"

"It is."

He holds out his hand and beckons for me to give it to him. The motion's economical more than demanding. "I'll have it taken to your quarters."

Which means it will be searched first, of course. But there's nothing to find. I hand it over.

"Follow me. And keep close." Ulnius starts walking. There's a slight limp to his gait. "We've had some reports of alupi around here, these past couple of weeks."

"Wolves?" Ulciscor mentioned them.

"Big wolves." The way he says it, he's understating. "They usually know better than to come near the Academy, though. I doubt there's anything to worry about."

I'm not exactly reassured, but it's not as if I have a lot of choice. I trail after the man.

"Did you recover well from your injuries? After the last time you were here," he adds, seeing my confusion at the question.

"Oh." The white cloak registers, and then more vaguely, the name. "You're the Academy physician?"

"I tended you when you and the Magnus Quintus first arrived," he confirms. We start up the steepest part of the path. Ulnius seems to have no trouble with it.

"Everything's healed well. Barely a scar." I hesitate. "Thank you."

"Please. I get to boast that I sewed up young Catenicus himself. I should be thanking you."

I give an awkward chuckle in return. As little as I'm pleased by the name, I'm going to have to get used to it.

We walk for a minute, just the leaves rustling to accompany us. The trail branching off to the east—the one Ulciscor thought might lead to the nearby ruins—soon appears, but I don't let my gaze linger. Whatever lies out there is going to have to wait for a while yet.

Ulnius looks several times like he wants to say more. Eventually, he does, faltering to a stop.

"Before we go any farther, I . . . need to say something. The Principalis is probably about to tell you how that name of yours doesn't mean anything in here. That you still have to earn your way. And as far as your lessons go, he's right. But . . . look. One of my sisters was at the naumachia. And she survived, praise Arventis."

He falls silent. Searching for the words. I let him.

"I talked to her, about a week ago. I'd heard the stories already, but watching her actually remembering it . . ." He exhales. Meets my gaze. "Whatever you need, Catenicus. While you're here. After graduation. Whenever. Just let me know."

He dips his head earnestly, then turns and presses on up the steep path.

※ ※ ※

IT'S NOT LONG UNTIL WE'RE ADMITTED THROUGH THE DIS-comforting Will cage of the Academy entrance, Ulnius pointing out the various buildings he thinks will be of interest as we walk the manicured path down to the quadrum. The massive stone square is eerily quiet compared to the last time I was here, only the tinkling of its central fountain audible. That's to be expected, though. The sun's dipping low. Everyone is surely taking dinner by now.

Ulnius guides me into the Praetorium, then up a winding staircase. Knocks confidently on the door at the top.

A moment later, Veridius's youthful visage is smiling out at me.

"Vis! Welcome. Please, come in." His expression is warm, genuinely pleased. He turns his smile on Ulnius. "Day's almost done. Did we make it?"

The physician smirks. "Estellia from Five came in with a cut on her hand about an hour ago."

"Bah." Veridius laughs ruefully, managing to infuse even that simple word with unaffected charm.

"So I'll let you know when you can take my shift?" Ulnius looks pleased with himself as Veridius gestures in amused defeat. "Vis. Principalis." With a nod to both of us, he disappears back down the stairs.

I enter Veridius's office, which is the only room on the first floor, judging by the lack of doors leading elsewhere. It's well-appointed but not grandiose: a desk in the centre with a couple of seats opposite, a couch in the corner, one wall lined with full bookshelves. On one shelf, displayed without ostentation, is a circlet of golden leaves that must be Veridius's Crown of the Preserver. Windows face both north and south. In one direction I can see the breadth of the quadrum. The other provides a spectacular view over the treetops of Solivagus and beyond, the ocean.

And, peeking out from behind one of the mountainous rises, what I think could be the ruins Ulciscor told me about. They're barely visible on the horizon, little more than a glimmer of stone among the trees.

"I've worked with worse views." Veridius is following my gaze. His thoughtful blue eyes turn back to me, and I shuffle my feet, unable to help feeling as though he knows what I was focusing on. "How's the side?"

"It's healed well, thank you."

"Good. Walk with me? I have other duties to attend, but I wanted to at least be the one to show you to your quarters."

I trail after him downstairs and into the quadrum.

"So. Magnus Quintus Telimus thinks very highly of you. His letter of submission was glowing."

"I'm pleased to hear that, Principalis."

"How did you meet him?"

"Good fortune. Our paths crossed in Letens, and . . ." I shrug modestly. "He's been searching for someone to take in, to support. Someone who might be able to do well here. I was a little older than what he had in mind, but I'm grateful to be given the chance to prove myself." It's what Ulciscor and I agreed upon—uncomplicated, and with relatively uncontroversial implications. Most people will see a childless senator spotting a talented orphan and assume we struck a bargain: me gaining access to the Telimus name, and Ulciscor gaining a powerful, beholden family member if I do well here. An unusual move, but not without precedent. Not outside of decorum.

"Good fortune indeed," murmurs Veridius. There's no sarcasm to it, no insinuation. We've left the quadrum, heading away from the clifftop. Painted statues of the gods line the path here, and traditional pyramidal shapes infuse much of the decorative work in the gardens. A few cork oaks dot the green expanse; in the distance I can see a couple of students reclining in the shade of one, books in hands. A shallow stream cuts through the grounds. Everything is quiet and perfectly kempt. An oasis against the wilds beyond the wall.

Veridius pulls me to a stop. Delays as he examines me, then sighs.

"I can only assume that Ulciscor has told you of the past I share with his family." He's placid as he says the words, neither blame nor concern to them. "And thus, of the things he believes I did to his brother. To Lanistia. Am I correct?"

I'm caught off guard at the directness of the question. "Yes."

"Which means I can safely assume that he has asked you to do *something*, while you're here." He waves a hand at my expression. "I won't insult you by asking for the details. But I do hope you realise that Ulciscor's accusations are those of a man who loved his brother, not of a man with cause. Caeror and Lanistia were my friends. My *good* friends." His voice has gone quiet, and there's heartache in it. Genuine sorrow. If it's a performance, it's a good one. "He acts on his pain as best he can, and I find it hard to blame him for that—so I swear to you, you will get no disadvantage from me because of it. But nor will I look the other way if you break the rules in service of his misguided revenge." He holds my gaze as he says it. It's a simple statement of fact, delivered firmly and gently. He just wants me to have fair warning.

"I understand." I'm thrown by the man's candour. I should be strenuously denying any hint of Ulciscor having ulterior motives, but doing so right now would feel childish.

The Principalis clasps his hands behind his back as he starts walking again, and I take a couple of jogging strides to catch up. "So. Do you prefer Vis, or Catenicus?"

"Vis."

"You don't like the honour?"

"It's not that," I lie quickly. "I just prefer not to think about it."

Veridius is sympathetic. "Of course. Of course. And along those lines, I have asked Aequa and I will ask you as well: please don't go into the details of what happened. Most of the other students only have rumours that they dismiss as exaggerations, currently. And those few who are aware of the truth don't need to be reminded of it. Better all-around if we just keep the focus on what we do here."

"Alright."

"Thank you. I read the reports, by the way. This weapon the Anguis used is monstrous. You are a true hero, Vis." Heartfelt. Completely sincere.

Despite myself, I can't help but feel a brief flush of pride. Followed by immediate irritation at my own reaction. Rotting gods, but the man is charming.

We keep walking. A brisk sea breeze sweeps in, dulling the last bite of the sun and whipping the Principalis's toga dramatically behind him. I can see him wanting to ask more about the naumachia, but instead he moves on. "So what are your goals here, Vis?"

"To rise to the highest class I can." An obvious one, and something Ulciscor assured me there was no point being shy about. If I let the Praeceptors know my intent to advance, they'll pay more attention to me.

"And how high do you think that is?"

"Hard to say, when I haven't had a class yet."

Veridius chuckles. "Truth." He steers us to the right, along a new branch of the path, returning the friendly waves of a couple of passing students in the distance. "There's been some talk of placing you in a higher class, thanks to your . . . new profile. What do you think of the idea?"

I vacillate. He's actually asking, or at least seems to be.

"I think I should start in Class Seven."

He runs a hand through his tousled, dirty-blond hair, looking vaguely surprised. "You want to?"

"Of course not." I'll probably regret this—if I push the idea, Veridius might allow the head start—but it's what feels right in the moment. "I'd be displacing someone without proving myself. I need to work my way up, the same as everyone else."

Veridius thinks and then nods, again in that approving way that makes me feel as though I've done exactly the right thing.

For the next few minutes, he probes more. About my past, my education. But it comes across as curious rather than suspicious. Rote, to an extent, but friendly—questions he asks every student. He's getting to know me. When I shy away from giving specifics, he doesn't press. It's not an interrogation.

I don't know what I expected from him, but this is different. Disarming. Exactly what I would have wanted from an introductory conversation, in fact. He tells me a little about life here. Reiterates how the classes work—the bulk of the students are in Class Seven, and then a steadily decreasing, set number as the groups are considered more advanced. Forty-eight in Class Six, twenty-four in Class Five, twelve in Class Four. There are only six in Class Three, and those compete at the end of the year in the Iudicium for the final, elite placings.

I already know it all, of course, but listen patiently, more than happy to be doing that rather than answering questions.

We arrive at a tall, tapering cuneate building that I'd noticed from a distance several minutes ago. It's intimidating up close, a couple of hundred feet wide at the base and almost a hundred to the jagged tip, decorative edging on each floor painted bright red.

"This is where you'll be living for the next year," says Veridius as he pushes the double doors wide. "The Sevenths all share a communal space, I'm afraid. You only get a bed and a desk."

"I've had less."

Veridius surprises me with a chuckle. "That's nice to hear. Sometimes the reactions are not so understanding."

"Really?"

"Most students are accustomed to the lifestyles of their parents." He's still smiling. "They all adapt. They just complain while they do it."

We enter the cool interior of the boys' dormitory. The entire ground floor is one enormous connected space, though it's sliced into thirds by a series of short, dividing walls. A large Will dial on the wall shows that it's almost seventh hour past noon. From the hush and lack of motion, we're the only ones here. Cots and desks alternate along the walls, carefully positioned to give each set its own space, which is also denoted by a number carved into the stone. The orderliness of the arrangement is offset by the mess of crumpled, shoved-aside sheets on a lot of the beds and the paraphernalia strewn across most desks. And the floor, in many cases.

Veridius runs a displeased eye over the scene before beckoning me farther in. "There are some unused beds in here somewhere. I imagine they won't be hard to spot," he adds dryly.

We've been walking for about ten seconds when I catch movement from the corner of my eye.

"Callidus?" Veridius has spotted the figure too, sitting at a desk with head bowed in concentration. The boy starts at his name. He's lithe and dark, with a thick mop of curly black hair and sharp features. My age, but small by comparison.

"Principalis!" Callidus is abashed as he scrambles to his feet.

"Why aren't you at dinner?"

The young man's brown eyes dart to the side. "I wanted to figure out something from class this afternoon. Get ahead early."

"Hm." Veridius sounds about as convinced as I feel. "Well, as you're here, this is Vis. He needs someone from Seven to show him around. Starting with a meal."

Callidus doesn't hide his grimace. "Principalis, I have to—"

"Not a request."

Callidus studies me. He looks more uncomfortable than anything else. "Of course."

Veridius begins amiably quizzing Callidus about his study habits over the break as I wander a little way off to find a vacant cot. It's easy enough to spot one, thanks to neatly tucked sheets and an accompanying desk completely absent of detritus. I half listen to the conversation in the background, but it all seems innocuous enough, even if Callidus continues to sound awkward in his answers.

"Bed number thirty-three," I announce to Veridius. I can't help but think of the numbering system in Letens Prison as I do so.

"Not superstitious, I take it?" the Principalis asks with mild amusement. I snort and shake my head. "Thirty-three, then. Your things will be waiting for you when you get back. Callidus will take you to the mess hall now, but if you have any concerns—if you need to talk to me about anything at all—don't hesitate. You know where to find me." He watches me to make sure I understand, to make sure I see that it's a genuine offer, before ushering us back toward the entrance.

Veridius bids us farewell; Callidus eyes his retreating figure and then angles us along the path back toward the quadrum, significantly more reluctant now that Veridius isn't watching.

"Sorry we interrupted you. If you'd prefer to just tell me where the mess is—"

"Thanks, but he'll check I went with you."

"Really?"

"Definitely. He noticed that I wasn't at the midday meal, too." Callidus isn't resentful, just certain. "It doesn't matter. I was getting hungry anyway."

Still, as we enter the quadrum, I can't help but notice the worried cast to Callidus's features, the way he scans ahead. The square's still all but empty.

"Vis, wasn't it?" Callidus asks the question absently. "I'm guessing the Principalis wasn't impressed that you arrived so late."

"He knew about it in advance. Extenuating circumstances."

Callidus glances at me, interest piqued. "Really?" Then he slows for a step. "Wait. Vis *Telimus?*"

I try not to wince. "Yes."

"Huh." Callidus guides me up the stairs of the Curia Doctrina, under the lavishly carved STRONGER TOGETHER and inside.

"You were at the naumachia." Callidus's curiosity has clearly overtaken his restraint. "You're the one who killed Melior. You're Catenicus."

I nod, not really sure how else to respond.

"Rotting gods." Callidus rubs the back of his neck as he processes.

Thankfully he doesn't have time to say more; we're passing between painted marble columns and descending a wide set of stairs, plunging into the muted roar of a hundred and fifty students talking among themselves.

The hall down here is massive, its entire eastern wall a series of archways cut from the cliff itself, allowing a spectacular view down over the glimmering ocean. We've emerged onto the lowest of five distinct levels, each one set about three feet higher than the next. The tiers looking down over us have fewer students sitting at their tables. At the uppermost level, it appears there's just a single table with a few couches sprawled around it.

Nobody pays us much attention as we enter, but I can see Callidus casting a concerned eye over the room. "We sit down here." He indicates the tables near where we're standing. It's the most crowded level by far, at least fifty students crammed in. "Sixths get the level up, Fifths the next, and so on."

I continue to scan the crowd. Aequa's up on the second-highest tier of the hall, her back to me. Above Aequa, reclining on the couches, are Emissa, Indol, and Belli—the three who snuck in to see me after the Transvect attack. In Class Three, just as Ulciscor said. Emissa and Indol are laughing about something, and Belli is focused on what looks to be a Foundation board. None of them have spotted me. There don't seem to be any Praeceptors in the room.

"Where do we get our meals?"

"Upper level." Callidus indicates a servery opposite the archways on the top tier. His gaze slides to the side, lingering on the half dozen students on the couches up there.

We head for the servery, Callidus with conspicuous reluctance. A few of the Class Seven students—Sevenths, as they're apparently known—have noticed us now, but aside from my catching a few curious glances, nobody says anything. They don't hail Callidus.

We're only one level up when one of the Sixths spots us and freezes. Stops eating and rises. And *rises*. The pale young man is enormous; his auburn hair is cropped short, though there's also light red stubble along his jawline. That and his burly physique made him look older than I assume he must be.

He's sitting apart from the other students in Class Six, not in any of their conversations, but the heavy menace in the way he stands draws their notice.

"Ericius." The boy growls the name, sharp blue eyes on Callidus. "Finally."

Callidus has stopped in his tracks. "Of course they chose him," he mutters, low enough that only I can hear it. He takes a breath and straightens, facing the other boy's approach. "We don't have to do this, Eidhin." He rubs his neck. "I know it must be Prav, or Ianix, or maybe even Dultatis who asked you. But I'd *really* prefer we didn't do this."

"And yet we must." Eidhin's speech is slow, careful. Not comfortable with speaking Common. "Your father has made mistakes."

"Well that makes two of us," Callidus retorts.

It's a flippant, nervous reply, not particularly directed. Yet something moves in Eidhin at the words. His face darkens to something ugly. "Say that again." He's only ten feet away. Advancing. The rest of the hall has started to quieten, most of the upper levels now having noticed the confrontation. Nobody's moving to intervene.

I sigh, then step forward next to Callidus. Just far enough to be a cautioning presence.

Eidhin pulls up short at the motion, looking at me for the first time. "You are?" His tone is dismissive.

"Vis." I paste on a friendly smile and take another step forward, between Eidhin and Callidus this time, sticking out my hand. "I'm new."

"Yes." Eidhin slaps my hand aside and moves to push past me. I know I should let him. He's in Class Six, a rank above me.

But I'm moving back into his path anyway. Eidhin is much larger than me. Muscular. Callidus wouldn't stand a chance in a physical confrontation, and doesn't seem inclined to run despite that fact.

"Sixth." I glance over Eidhin's shoulder. It's Emissa, calling out from the level above. The Thirds have descended a couple of levels to watch. All except Belli and the boy opposite her, anyway, who are still poring over the Foundation board in the background. "Don't."

She's a Third, speaking with unmistakeable authority. Eidhin's lip curls anyway and he moves to shove me aside this time, but I'm accustomed to dealing with men much bigger than him, and simply move so that he stumbles. I'm not trying to embarrass him, but a ripple of laughter runs through the onlookers. Which appears to be just about everyone, now.

"We're only here to get some food," I say quickly, holding out my hands palms-outward to show I have no ill intent. Already cursing myself for this decision.

Callidus says something from behind me, and I half turn instinctively.

Which means I don't see Eidhin's left hook coming until just before it connects with my ear.

⁂ ⁂ ⁂

I WORK HARD TO CONTROL MY ANGER.

My nature has always been to be quick with a sharp defence, either verbal or physical—even before the Hierarchy took my family, my country, and everything else

I've ever cared about. But that's been an unaffordable luxury, these past few years. A bane to anonymity. So I'm always reminding myself not to be reactive. Not to draw attention. Step aside, stuff my fury deep down, and always keep to the background.

On the other hand, the Theatre was my release from all that. Fighting on that stage was one of the only ways I felt I could still stand up for myself.

So when Eidhin—this bullying stranger—actually lands a hit, I gods-damned well answer.

The blow's a stinging one but I know how to take a punch and recover quickly; the larger boy's eyes widen in shock and pain as I pivot in response and swing low, striking him hard in the stomach. A familiar, wheezing gasp as air rushes from his lungs. I step back. Let him double over and then coldly, furiously uppercut.

There's a sickening crunch as I connect with his nose. Blood. Eidhin drops as if dead.

I stand there, red painting the knuckles of my right hand, and for a horrible second have to study the body on the floor to make sure Eidhin's chest is still rising and falling. I'm used to fighting Septimii, used to pouring every inch of power I can find into every hit.

Probably shouldn't have done that with Eidhin, even if he is bigger than me.

The whole hall's gone silent, the weight of eyes on me crushing. Callidus is gaping at me, a half-awed, half-dismayed expression frozen on his face. I move before anyone else can, dropping to my knees by Eidhin and removing my toga, tucking it gently behind his head and then staunching the flow of blood with its hem. There will be consequences for this, but at least if I show contrition, it might not be as disastrous as it feels.

"You shouldn't have done that." The voice is angry; I look up again to see another Sixth rising from the table nearby. He's athletic, strands of black hair falling over high cheekbones and a dark, brooding expression. Piercing green eyes glare at me, then at a hand on his arm. The girl beside him pulls the young man forcibly back into his seat. He goes reluctantly.

A breath later, Emissa, Indol, and two other Class Three members I don't recognise are joining me, though they've seen what I'm doing and are moving to help, rather than showing aggression. Interesting. They're in charge here, at least while there are no Praeceptors around. Their lack of outrage is encouraging.

"Idiot," mutters Emissa with a shake of her head as she kneels opposite me, pushing her hair from her face and pulling a cloth from her pocket, dabbing some of the dribbling blood off Eidhin's cheek.

"Me, or him?"

"Me. Your new friend's father isn't exactly popular at the moment; I should have known someone would want to send a message." She glances up at me. "Though it does also apply to you, a bit. And him. Especially him. Let's just call it all-inclusive," she concedes, tone light as she quirks a quick smile, dimples forming.

I find myself grinning back. Her eyes are very green. I almost forget the situation.

There's a loud cough from Indol, who's hovering over us. "Nequias."

"Rotting gods. Don't argue with him; you'll only make things worse. Good luck," murmurs Emissa with a wry shake of her head, standing quickly. I do the same, following her and Indol's gazes to the older man stomping his way over to us. He's middle-aged and angular to the point of being gaunt, though toned beneath his fine tunic and red-hemmed toga. A sharp nose holds up a pair of tinted glasses, not dissimilar to Lanistia's.

"What happened here?" He glances from Eidhin to me, looking like he's already come to a conclusion. "Who are you?"

"Vis Telimus, Praeceptor." I keep my voice respectful. Nequias is the Praeceptor for Class Three, the highest position in the Academy behind Veridius. "I only arrived today."

"An exceptionally short stay, then. We don't take kindly to Sevenths attacking their betters here."

My heart drops. He's not joking about the short stay.

"It wasn't him, Praeceptor." It's Indol speaking up, to my surprise. I turn to see him meeting Nequias's gaze. "Eidhin started the fight."

"Not that it was much of a fight," murmurs one of the other students, a girl with bright blue eyes whose name I don't know. Beside her, Emissa hides what I suspect is mirth with her hand.

Nequias ignores the by-play, focusing on Indol. "Why would he do that?"

"He was targeting Ericius there. You can probably guess why. The new boy wasn't standing for it."

Nequias scowls, looking more rather than less angry at the explanation. "So Eidhin *might* have been going to start a fight with *someone else*, is what you're saying. But our Seventh here actually did."

"Eidhin swung first."

"Swinging first in a fight isn't the same thing as starting it."

Indol's jaw clenches, but he says nothing.

"Telimus. Telimus." Nequias switches his attention back to me, rolling the name along his tongue as if suddenly discovering it. "Of course. Ulciscor's boy. *Catenicus*. Don't for a moment think your reputation will keep you from the consequences of something like this."

Murmurs ripple down the hall as those closest to us catch what Nequias is saying. There's no visible movement, but the sense of those farther away straining to listen becomes almost palpable.

"Of course, Praeceptor." This is unfair, but I'm used to that. And it's not that I trust Emissa—Ulciscor's initial suspicion about her still plays on my mind, no matter his eventual conclusion—but her warning makes sense. Angering Nequias further is a bad idea.

Callidus is standing behind the Praeceptor, and I can see the lithe young man starting forward, mouth open to protest. I give him the slightest shake of my head. He's a Seventh, too; I doubt he can say anything that will deflect the blame from me, but there's a good chance he could get himself in trouble as well.

At the moment, he owes me. It's not a lot, but I can use it.

"Indol, Ianix, get Eidhin to the infirmary and let Septimus Filo know what's happened." Indol moves to comply, as does the dark-haired Sixth who looked like he was going to defend Eidhin earlier.

Nequias glares at me. "And you? Follow. Now."

He storms off toward the main staircase and I trail after him pensively, trying to ignore the weight of the eyes of what appears to be every student in the Academy.

XXVI

THERE'S AN UNCOMFORTABLE, HEAVY NERVOUSNESS THAT'S unique to waiting on a punishment that *means* something. I remember it well from my days at Suus, sitting outside the Great Hall until my father finished his business. Aware he was about to hear of whatever I'd done wrong and then pronounce judgment on me, the same way he had to on so many of his people.

The lead-up was always the worst part. Anticipation and uncertainty. Knowing I'd made the mistake, but not yet having met its consequences.

I never once felt like that in the orphanage. There was fear, yes, when I knew the lashings were coming. Rage and frustration. But never this biting, gnawing unease that worries at me as I sit in the side room not far from the mess hall, gazing out the eastward window at the dusk-lit ocean.

"Vis?" The feminine voice makes me start; I didn't hear anyone enter, buried too deep in my worries. I turn to find a woman settling into a seat opposite. Middle-aged, judging from the streaks of grey dusting her hair. She fixes me with a sharp, hazel-eyed gaze, though the lines around her eyes make her appear amiable rather than stern.

"That's me." I smile to indicate I wish it weren't the case right now.

"I'm Praeceptor Taedia. I teach Class Five." She returns the expression as she says it. An encouraging sign. "I've been speaking to some of the students who saw what happened. I've heard enough to know that Eidhin brought this upon himself, but . . . needless to say, this is not an auspicious start to your time here."

"I know."

"Do you?" Her smile fades a little. Worried. "You're a Seventh, and you just struck a Sixth. *Publicly*. If Eidhin decides to pursue the matter, he could have you expelled."

I'd wondered, but a cold fist still squeezes my heart at the confirmation. Lanistia warned me many times that the class rankings here were born from the Academy's origins as a Military institution. What I just did is the equivalent of a conscript punching an officer in the face.

"How do I avoid that?" It's an open plea. Taedia seems kindly, concerned. She's more likely to respond to vulnerability than bravado.

"Swallow your pride."

"Vis." Veridius's voice pierces the room from behind me. I jump to my feet, turning to see the Principalis enter, followed closely by Nequias and another boy I vaguely recognise. He was sitting with Emissa, I think. A Third. Veridius's expression is sombre. Nequias just looks smug.

"Principalis." I resist the urge to launch into a defence of my actions. I'm frustrated but if I show that, if I seem like I'm hot-headed, it will only weaken my case.

"Praeceptor Nequias has been keeping me informed." Veridius doesn't sit, arms crossed. The sound of his disappointment cuts. "And Iro here has verified that you were the aggressor. Solely at fault."

I gape at the Third. He's tall and muscular, with a prominent, hooked nose. Very Catenan. I don't know him.

He stares back at me, and though his expression doesn't change, I swear there's the glint of satisfaction in his eyes.

"However," continues Veridius, "before passing any kind of judgment, I would like to hear your side of the story."

"I apologise for what happened." I sound as contrite as I can be. "But the other boy, Eidhin, was about to attack Callidus—"

"You don't know that," interjects Nequias.

"Let him speak." Veridius's tone is sharp as he admonishes the older man. Nequias glowers but subsides.

I continue, relating events as accurately as I can. There's no need to lie, no benefit to it. Iro looks dubious the entire time, as if I'm making the whole thing up. Nequias tries to interrupt me again at one point, but Veridius quashes him with another sharp reproof. I can see from the way Nequias stands apart from him, the way they interact, that there's no love lost between the two men. Given how quickly Nequias seems to have taken a disliking to me, that's surely to my advantage.

Veridius contemplates me for a good few seconds after I finish. "Bring him in." He directs the command to Nequias, who disappears through the door before returning with a grim-looking Eidhin in tow. The boy's nose is taped, and ugly bruises are forming under both eyes. He doesn't hesitate to meet my gaze, though. There's barely checked anger there.

"I'm sorry, Eidhin." I address him calmly and directly, putting every ounce of sincerity I can into my voice. I have to take control of the situation, give them what they want to hear. "I honestly thought you were going to attack the boy who was showing me around, and . . . I reacted poorly. I was part of an orphanage until a few months ago, and I'm used to having to deal with things through violence. That doesn't make it justified, though. You have my word that it will not happen again." I step forward, extending my hand.

There's a surprised silence, Eidhin coming to a standstill, clearly not knowing how to react. He was expecting more aggression, probably. Denials.

"It is . . . not excuse." He says it roughly, voice nasal. He doesn't make any move to take my hand.

"Of course," I say quickly. Obsequiously. "Please understand, though, that my actions were through ignorance as well. I simply didn't know who you were. So again, I apologise." I keep my hand outstretched. It almost physically hurts to scrape like this, but I'm trusting it will be worth it.

"It changes nothing." Eidhin just looks awkward at my insistence. That's good. Behind him, I can see Veridius suddenly lean forward, intent. He sees what I'm doing. I will him not to open his mouth. Eidhin isn't Catenan. He might not know.

I thrust my hand closer to Eidhin. My arm's beginning to ache. "Please. Eidhin. Whatever consequences may come from my actions, I just need you to know that I am truly sorry for what I did."

Eidhin's bemused. "Fine. Yes. You are sorry," he says in disgust, limply grasping my hand—barely more than a slap—before dropping it again.

There's an exhalation from Veridius, and from the corner of my eye, I can see Taedia shift as she understands what's happened. "The boy knows how to apologise," she murmurs approvingly, loud enough for me to hear.

For Nequias, Iro, and Eidhin, too. Eidhin glances askance at Nequias; the older man's face is turning red as he catches up. Iro's expression is black.

"That was not a Threefold Apology," Nequias says quickly.

"The form was observed, Nequias. Messy, but observed." Veridius looks amused. "I will still set a penance, but Eidhin here has forfeited any right to pursue the matter."

"*What?*" It's Iro rounding on Veridius. Incensed.

Veridius locks eyes with him, his calm gaze turning cool. He says nothing. Iro scowls and looks away, while Eidhin continues to look baffled.

"Praeceptor Nequias, perhaps you can escort Eidhin and Iro back to the dormitory. And then I'm sure you have plenty to do to prepare for tomorrow's class." Veridius's voice remains mild as he stands and moves to the door, opening it and stepping politely aside.

Nequias, unmistakeably fuming, grabs Eidhin by the arm and almost bodily hauls him out, a seething Iro trailing behind. The Praeceptor passes close as he leaves. "Learn to respect your betters, boy." He murmurs the words.

I meet his gaze and give him my widest, friendliest smile. "Thank you for the advice, Praeceptor."

Nequias's lip twitches and he looks like he wants to say more, but instead straightens haughtily and stalks out, shutting the door behind him with more force than is strictly necessary.

"Gods' graves, boy," says Taedia as soon as they're gone, jovial even as she's admonishing. "Maybe you're not the stupidest student on campus after all."

"Arventis blessed you today," adds Veridius, with a reproving look at Taedia.

"It's justice," counters Taedia irritably. "I talked to some of the students who saw what happened, and they all said the same thing before Iro started whispering in their ears. Breac started it, Telimus finished it."

Breac. I don't recognise the name, but it's certainly not Catenan, which means Eidhin's not an adoption like me. I haven't just made an enemy of a powerful senatorial family, at least.

"The details don't matter. At best, Vis here was careless. I need to set a penance." Veridius rubs his face. "Mucking out the stables every evening until the Festival of the Ancestors, I think should do it. During dinner. It won't hurt to keep you and Eidhin out of each other's way for a while."

"You have horses here?" I'm surprised. We had some on Suus, but I can't imagine they have much utility here.

"We keep a few. Mounted combat training, mostly." Veridius doesn't expand on that. "Praeceptor Taedia will point out where you need to go, but you can start tomorrow night. Septimus Ascenia looks after the animals; I'll make sure she's there to show you what to do."

I've never mucked out stables before, but I've seen it being done. Even worse than the general unpleasantness of the task, it's time consuming—and having to do it over dinner means I'll miss my one good chance during the day to socialise, to perhaps undo some of the damage I've done today. The Festival of the Ancestors is two months away, too. But I'm not going to push my luck by protesting.

"Well. I think we can all agree that this has been an *eventful* first day." Veridius sighs and stands. "You can go. Get yourself a meal. But Vis? That little trick with Eidhin won't work again. This is a second chance. It will be beyond anyone's power to give you a third."

I take the warning with as good grace as I can and trail Praeceptor Taedia out the door. We start along the hallway, the entire right-hand side a series of long arches overlooking the ocean. It's barely visible now, out there. Dark shapes shifting and swelling, white caps occasionally catching the last of the light.

"Between you and me," Taedia says quietly as we head back toward the mess hall, "seeing what you did to Eidhin wasn't the worst way to start the trimester."

I almost choke and eye the grey-haired woman, trying to decide whether she's testing me. "Really?"

"Boy barely knows the language. Does nothing but scowl and snap. He's not exactly a favourite around here."

I check again to make sure she's not baiting me. "There certainly didn't seem to be a lot of people rushing to help him."

"You've probably only upset whoever put him up to it, and a couple of the Praeceptors who think we should act like we're in Military. Though I'll feed you to the alupi if you tell anyone I said that." She's cheerful, relaxed. I decide I like her. "Just steer clear of Iro Decimus."

Decimus. Easy enough to place the name: Magnus Tertius Decimus, of Religion, must be his father. "Did I wrong him, somehow?"

"No." She takes a breath, as if wanting to say more, then shakes her head. "No. Not at all. Just stay away from him, and you'll be fine. As long as you don't do anything else stupid, of course."

"I'll keep my head down."

"Will you? From what I can tell, that's not a strength of yours." She opens a door, ushering me through and into the kitchen. Three people bustle around, moving between a bank of ovens, a preparation bench, and a larder. They barely look up when we enter before returning to their tasks. "Why did you even do it?"

"Stop Eidhin? He was angry, and a lot bigger than Callidus."

"What if Callidus deserved it?"

"Then there are more measured approaches to justice than punching."

Taedia chuckles at that, waving absently at one of the Octavii, who starts piling food onto a plate for me. "True. True. Well. Whatever the reason, thank you. This has been more entertainment in a single day than I got all of last trimester."

Once I've been provided with a seat and a meal, Taedia bids me farewell. I sit in the kitchen for a while, hunched over my food, ignoring the occasional glances of the Octavii and assessing how things have gone so far.

Badly, I decide. Quite badly.

I eventually push my plate aside, nod to the Octavii, and trudge my way back to the dormitory. It's all noise and activity as I enter. Boys congregate around desks or beds, while others play a game involving some sort of ball over in the corner. From the cheering and yelling of both participants and spectators, it's a regular thing.

Nobody notices my entrance at first, though I catch a few looks as I make my way over to my space. Then there's a ripple of quiet—not silence, but pauses in conversation as more and more of the Sevenths notice me. They're surprised, I realise. Shocked. They didn't expect me to be back.

I walk the gauntlet of sideways glances, at first heading to my bed, but changing my mind halfway and angling instead for where I first met Callidus. Sure enough, the lithe boy is at his desk, head bowed over a book and studiously ignoring the goings-on around him.

I stand to the side, then cough. "Callidus?" He turns, and I blanch. A dark bruise swells his left cheek, and a long, red scrape lines his temple. "Rotting gods."

Callidus's curly hair shadows his eyes, but it's not hard to see that the look he gives me isn't a welcoming one. "Eidhin didn't have you expelled?" When I shake my head, he grunts. "Well I'm glad this worked out for you, anyway."

I swallow an irritated reply. "He accidentally accepted my Threefold Apology."

Callidus stares at me, then laughs softly. "Of course he did. Idiot." He touches his bruised face, still chuckling bitterly.

"Eidhin did that?"

"No." Callidus shifts gingerly in his chair. His injuries extend to beneath his clothes, then. "Of course, if he'd just been allowed to push me around a little in front of everyone, the second messenger wouldn't have been needed."

My heart sinks. "I was trying to help."

"You were trying to make an impression." It's not an accusation, exactly. More of a weary observation, even if it's an incorrect one. "And congratulations to you, because it appears you did." He motions over my shoulder, and I crane my neck to see half the dormitory watching us.

When I look back, he's returned to his book.

"I'm sorry. Truly," I say to his back, trying not to make it sound as though it's coming from between gritted teeth. "I didn't mean to make things worse."

Not knowing what else to do, I leave him and return to my own desk, ignoring the curious eyes that follow. My satchel's waiting, and I start unpacking the bag's few contents. A couple of books Kadmos insisted were important but that had remained unread. A wax diptych and stylus. Some clothes. Nothing valuable, nothing particularly personal.

"Don't worry about him."

I turn to find a Seventh standing a few feet away. He's got chiselled features, blond hair and blue eyes suggesting southern heritage. He steps forward, extending his hand amiably. "Drusus Corani."

"Vis Telimus." Corani—a Military patrician family, from memory. Powerful. I clasp his hand, then cast a glance over at Callidus, who's still poring over his book. He's about thirty feet from us. "You're talking about Callidus?"

"He's not worth your time." Unlike me, Drusus doesn't bother to keep his voice down. "He still thinks he's better than us because his father bought him a starting position in Three. But as everyone can see, it was a waste of money." He wields the pronouncement with loud satisfaction.

Nearby, several other boys who are paying attention to the conversation nod their agreement. "It's true," adds one with a squashed nose and blocky face, vociferous too as he spares a disdainful glance for Callidus before shuffling closer. Keen to be part of the conversation, but still either wary of me, or intimidated. Maybe both.

"And don't think he's a way into the good graces of Magnus Ericius, either. His family have all but disowned him, after last trimester," a burly boy wearing the earrings of a Sytrecian chimes in. Loudly.

Magnus Ericius. I recall that one immediately: Governance's Censor, the one man who can veto appointments to the central pyramids and thus the Senate. A Tertius, but along with the two Consuls from Military and Religion, one of the three most powerful men in the Senate. One of the most powerful men in the Hierarchy, in fact.

"Not that you can blame them," adds Drusus with dark enjoyment, more confident now he has a chorus behind him. He glances across at Callidus, who's still hunched over his book at his desk and hasn't overtly reacted. There's a tense, defensive set to his shoulders, though.

I watch him for a second. Three. Not saying anything. I should just accept the opinion of Drusus and these others, endear myself to the group. It's clear Callidus isn't liked. It's an easy win.

But what he said to me before stung, untrue or not. And worse: my time in Letens echoes in these boys' ugly smiles, the way they're so eager to jump in with a spiteful quip, piling on top of one another's attacks in search of easy bonding. I've been on the other end of that mentality. I remember how helpless it made me feel—that once started, there was no way to make it stop. No one who wanted to stand against it.

"I'm surprised any of your families still admit to being related to you, to be fair."

The laughter dies, replaced by an air of scandalised confusion. Drusus's eyes narrow. "What?"

"Well. You're all Sevenths. Same as him." This is stupid. Social suicide. "From what I can tell, the only difference between you and him is that his father is more successful than yours." I should stop. "It just seems that if you're saying he's not worth my time, you're saying none of you are." I pronounce it calmly. Meet his gaze.

Gods, but I hate my temper sometimes.

There's a mutter from the half dozen boys listening, and Drusus's lip twitches. His composure is gone. "And you think you're better—why? Because you fought Melior?"

"Because I killed him."

Drusus pales. So do several of the others.

"Be that way, then," he mumbles, almost inaudibly. The small crowd quickly disperses, muttering among themselves and occasionally casting dark backward glances.

Callidus, I note, is still reading, acting as if he hasn't overheard. I sigh and turn back to my own desk. I don't know what I expected.

The conversations around the large hall are dying down as everyone begins preparing for bed. I follow suit. Unsurprisingly, neither boy on either side of my space seems interested in talking, so I douse my lamp and lie down.

A few minutes later, the majority of the hanging lamps are extinguished as one, plunging the room into near darkness. A Will-based mechanism, I assume. The dim is broken by occasional spots of shuttered light where some students haven't finished retiring, and there's still some chatter from a few corners of the room, but soon enough those wink out and fade away, respectively.

Then all's quiet. In the distance, I hear waves crashing against the shore somewhere far below.

I close my eyes, but Suus is there. It takes me a long time to sleep.

XXVII

THERE'S A DISORIENTATION TO WAKING UP SOMEWHERE FOR the first time. A brief disconnect between your memory and the present, as if your mind is refusing to acknowledge that you're in unfamiliar territory.

Years ago, I liked the feeling. That slow realisation usually meant I was on holiday with my family somewhere.

This morning, it brings a jolt that is very close to panic.

I sit upright, fully awake, terrified that I've overslept, that I've forgotten some important detail to do with my first day of classes. It's not yet light outside. The hanging lamps burn low. Everything's still. The sound of constant breathing fills the room, broken more often than not by sharp snorts and snores. Somewhere several beds away, I hear one of the Sevenths murmuring something in his sleep. There's the crisp sound of a page turning, and I twist to see Callidus alone is awake, at his desk again and reading by the light of a shuttered lantern.

I glance at the massive Will dial on the wall. Not out of routine; in another hour, it will be dawn. I'm just one of the first to wake.

I think about lying back down, but more than two months with Lanistia has trained my body not to listen to what I want. I'm sliding out of bed and padding over to my satchel, pulling cloak over tunic and fastening my sandals, before I can decide to do otherwise. Callidus's back is to me; he doesn't notice my waking, and I don't disturb him.

The communal latrine also provides basins of water for washing up, so I relieve myself, splash my face, and go through my usual preparations for the day as I try to decide what to do next. There's no point in studying, as I don't have anything to review yet. And I don't have anyone with whom I can train.

It seems like this might be a good time to familiarise myself with the grounds.

Outside the dormitory, the Academy is hushed, covered by a light, damp mist. The ocean hisses in the distance. Clouds diffuse the starlight, though in the east I can see a false dawn beginning to brighten the sky.

Off the path, in the heavier darkness beneath the trees lining it, a shadow stirs.

"Vis." A slim black shape detaches itself and stands a little way in front of me. "Can we talk?"

"Aequa?" Her skin is almost silver in the dim light, her long black hair shadowing most of her face, but it's definitely her. I stop short, nonplussed. "What are you doing out here?"

"Waiting for you. My father mentioned you rose early, during your training. I'm usually awake now, anyway, and thought you might be around." She sounds abashed. "Sorry. I know it's a bit strange."

"No. No, it's fine." I'm prepared for this conversation, though I didn't expect to be having it before dawn. I gesture toward the quadrum. "I don't suppose you'd care to show me around while we talk?"

"Of course." There's relief, the release of nervous energy as she snaps into motion, beckoning for me to follow her along the path.

We start walking. I'm tempted to broach the topic first, but if I do, it will feel obvious that I've been planning my response. Our breaths mist.

"Isn't anyone else awake?" I ask.

"Most of the Praeceptors will be. And there are plenty of us studying." She indicates behind us, back at the dormitory. The windows on the first two floors are dark, but light fills several farther up. "It's the same for the girls. They won't be down until breakfast, though. And the Sixths and Sevenths won't even bother getting up until then." There's a measure of disdain at that.

Silence falls between us again. Aequa fidgets as she walks, and I can see my patience won't be necessary for long.

"I . . . had a few questions," she says abruptly, her quiet voice cutting through the still of the early morning. "About what happened at the naumachia."

"Alright."

She smooths her tunic. Nervous. "We didn't pass the sewer entrance on the way in. And you'd never been there before."

"That's not really a question."

She eyes me.

"Sorry." I smile easily back at her. "I knew where it was because I noticed it on the way to the latrine. And I guessed what it was because that older couple next to us kept arguing over whether the whole thing was worth it, given that the aqueducts had been diverted from their baths." She'll remember that. It will help. "It got me thinking about how they were going to get rid of all that water once it was over, and I realised the stairs must have been a sewer access."

"It wasn't anywhere near the latrines."

Vek. She's looked into this fairly seriously, then. "It was the way I went—I wandered around for *ages* before I found them." I chuckle. "Or did you think I spent a full twenty minutes relieving myself?"

Aequa shows a hint of amusement, though there's also a twist to her mouth that suggests dissatisfaction. It's not a perfect story—I doubtless seemed too sure in guiding her through the sewers themselves—but that's the sort of thing that's difficult to gauge and easy to deny. "Of course." She bites the left side of her lower lip. "I just . . . I keep thinking back to it. When it all started. You were different from everyone else. More confident." When I try to look modest, she shakes her head. "No. I didn't mean it as a compliment. It was like . . . you knew you couldn't get hurt. You were upset about what was happening, but you didn't seem *afraid*."

We're at the quadrum now, as public a place in the Academy as there is. I wonder whether it's a conscious decision on her behalf, given what she could be implying.

"You know my past, don't you? I was in Aquiria when it collapsed—but before that my birth parents were killed, my lands stolen, and then my life threatened for months until the Catenans came. I never went to sleep without wondering whether I would wake." I focus on the Temple of Jovan ahead. Eye contact usually indicates sincerity, but for revealing what should be a difficult truth, awkwardness can come across as more genuine. "It's not that I wasn't afraid at the naumachia, Aequa. It's just that I'm more used to it than everyone else."

I say it with sadness, then look at her. Driving home the sincerity of the statement. My past, fictional though much of it is, is a powerful tool if I use it right.

"Oh." Aequa's quiet, and I can almost hear her probing at the assertion, wondering if there's some way she can dissect it, investigate it further. "So when you went back . . ."

"I was terrified." I shuffle my feet. "But it also seemed like an opportunity."

"*Oh.*" I can immediately tell that's a motivation she can understand. Catenans love their heroes, and making a name for myself won't have harmed my chances at the Academy.

"I'm sorry for leaving you like that."

"Given the outcome, I think it's alright." Aequa indicates it's the end of the matter, and I inwardly relax. I don't think she's entirely convinced, but she's not going to pursue it. Not for the moment, at least.

The conversation moves on to the promised tour of the Academy, and we spend a fairly pleasant half hour roaming the grounds as the east begins to brighten. Aequa points out buildings of interest both around the quadrum and beyond. The temples of

Jovan and Mira. The large gymnasium for physical training. The Curia Doctrina and Praetorium, which I already know, alongside baths that are apparently open to Fourths and above. She's a little awkward at first, as if unused to talking, but she warms to the task as we go.

"What's that?" I point to a long building set well away from the others, almost hidden behind a copse of trees.

"The Labyrinth." She glances at me, clearly curious to see if I know what she's talking about.

"Ah. My father told me about that. He said it's one of the more difficult tests here."

"It's not easy." Aequa's gaze lingers on the low-slung stone structure. "I imagine you'll be asked to run it, soon enough. Everyone else did as part of their entrance exam."

"How did you do?"

"Not well—mainly because of my arm. Only a few people were better than awful the first time, though. Most of us have improved a lot since."

There's a pause, and Aequa glances up at the sky, where the sun is threatening to peek over the horizon. "I should get back." She draws in a breath. "I owe you, for the naumachia. I know that. But the way things are here, with you in Seven . . ."

"It's alright. I understand." Even without Lanistia's many warnings, my experience with Eidhin has made it clear that differences in class rankings are taken seriously here. Aequa associating too much with me would be frowned upon by her peers, maybe the Praeceptors too. "We'll talk more when I'm a Fourth."

She chortles before she can stop herself, then waves a hand apologetically, still smiling. "When you're a Fourth. Of course. I look forward to it." It's delivered with amusement rather than malice, and I accept her incredulity with a grin before bidding her farewell.

She stops after a few paces, though. Turns back, all trace of humour gone.

"I still have nightmares."

I don't say anything for a long second, then nod. Just slightly.

It's all the confirmation she needs. She leaves.

A chime rings out as I'm walking back to the dormitory, a single, crystal, quavering note that invades every corner of the Academy's grounds. The bell for the morning meal. There are more students about now, and the majority seem headed for the Curia Doctrina.

I square my shoulders, and follow suit.

‰ ‰ ‰

I SPEND BREAKFAST, UNSURPRISINGLY, ALONE ON THE LOWEST level of the mess hall. Drusus and the other boys must have been busy relaying some version of our exchange last night, because I receive nothing but cold looks from the other Sevenths as they trickle in. Callidus sits apart, too; his face doesn't look as swollen as it did, but the bruises remain painfully obvious. Nobody seems inclined to ask him about them.

I'm not unaccustomed to solitude, but this doesn't feel like an auspicious start to my time here.

The repast—some wheat pancakes with dates and a drizzle of honey—is filling enough, if a little cold by the time I make it back to my seat. I eat unhurriedly amid the susurrus of voices, using the time to observe the levels above me. Everyone seems quieter this morning, more circumspect, the excitement of the first day back faded. I catch a few wondering glances from those higher up. Another series of dark looks from green-eyed Iro in Class Three, whom I seem to have wronged somehow. A friendly dip of the head from a red-headed Fifth, a scowl from a lean girl next to him. People I don't know, don't recognise. I see one of the Praeceptors present this morning—a ruggedly good-looking man of around forty, with a scruffy beard and black, shaggy hair— openly watching me. He doesn't bother to stop, even when I boldly meet his gaze.

It's an uncomfortable meal, all up.

When the next chime heralds that it's time to go to class, I trail after the other Sevenths into the heart of the Curia Doctrina, then to a side room off the main hall. Most of the students cluster around desks in small groups once we arrive, laughing and talking among themselves. Callidus is already seated, reading something. Alone.

I inhale, then stride over and sit next to him. He looks up at me but doesn't say anything, quickly returning to his book. I don't try to interrupt him.

The chatter wanes as a woman all but bounces in, cheerful as she surveys the group at large. She's plump but not unfit, her easy confidence marking her as the Praeceptor for Class Seven. She signals me up to the front of the room.

"I'm Praeceptor Ferrea," she informs me as I approach, pushing back shoulder-length red hair that is fading to dark auburn. If I had to guess, I'd say she was in her forties. "You must be Vis."

"I am."

"Welcome." Brisk but friendly. "We're still reviewing last trimester, so you should have a chance to catch up if you need to. And the rest of this week will be focused on lessons in rhetoric. If you have any questions as we go, just ask." It's a dismissal, introduction apparently done.

Once I'm back in my seat, Ferrea stands in front of the class, book in hand. "We're going to continue with the principles of Will today."

I squint, fairly sure I misheard. The principles of Will aren't exactly advanced—the opposite, in fact. I was never meant to wield Will, and I still learned them when I was at Suus.

But perhaps I'm misunderstanding. Perhaps there's more to it than I realise, some extra level of complexity that would have been too difficult to explain to me back then.

"Imbued Will can be applied in three ways. Can anyone tell me what those are?"

I smirk. But my amusement dies as no one calls out, no one raises their hand. Not one student out of the more than six dozen in the room.

I glance at Callidus beside me. He's not paying attention, curly black hair hanging over his face as he bows over a wax tablet, scribbling something on it.

"Direct, Relational, or Conditional." I call out the answer loudly and clearly.

Students twist in their seats, faces turning toward me as Ferrea—surprised that someone has spoken up—nods. "Exactly." She returns to her book.

"Although Kaspius says that Relational is too general these days, and should be split into two sub-categories."

I'm taking a chance. It's the bluntest method possible, aggressively showing off my knowledge like this. I don't like it, feel uncomfortable doing it. But Ulciscor and Lanistia both suggested it would be the quickest and most effective way to move on from Class Seven.

Ferrea pauses, cocks her head to the side before looking back up at me. "And why is that?"

"Because 'Relational' covers too much ground. Harmonic and Reactive relationships are being grouped together by the same term, but they're vastly different from one another. Given that we use this language to describe every single imbued object, he argues that the lack of specificity hurts development, hurts documentation, and thus hurts advancement."

Ferrea walks down the aisle between desks, closer to me. "You're paraphrasing." The rest of the class is watching. Silent.

"I can quote verbatim if you want."

"No." She waves away the offer. "Paraphrasing is good. It shows you understand the material. Anything else you want to add?"

"Not for the basics."

A small smile plays around Ferrea's lips as she acknowledges me. Good. She's impressed.

She turns and walks back to the front of the class. Callidus finally stops writing.

"You sure you want this?" He says it quietly, not looking up. It takes me a second to realise he's talking to me.

"What do you mean?"

"You're going to be put up a class if you keep doing that."

"Isn't that . . . good?"

Callidus hesitates. "If it's what you want." He resumes his scribblings, almost seeming annoyed at himself for speaking.

The lesson continues, and I make a point of answering every question Ferrea poses—adding more information where I can, making sure I show a deep understanding of the concepts involved. It's not hard; in fact, it's fair to say I'm a little bemused by how easy it is. I might be misremembering, but I feel I could have answered many of these questions almost as well when I left Suus three years ago.

As time passes, I can see her interest quickening. The questions become probing—not in the way Lanistia's were, or even Aequa's, but definitely increasing in difficulty. And she starts standing in the middle of the room, near my desk, looking at me directly half the time. As if I'm the only one she's really talking to.

The other students, thankfully, don't seem to care that they're being ignored. In fact, many of them seem blissfully happy that the Praeceptor's attention is elsewhere; when we began most of them were sitting at attention, but now there are plenty of heads leaned together in casual, albeit whispered conversation.

As the sun peaks outside, we break for lunch in the mess hall. I collect my food and sit at a table by myself. Ferrea seats herself with the group, a little apart, head bowed as she works on something while she eats. Still, I occasionally catch her throwing considering glances in my direction.

To my surprise, Callidus plants himself opposite me a minute later. The lithe boy gives me the slightest of nods, then pulls out his book and continues to read, ignoring me.

I chew my salted bread, surreptitiously eyeing the tome Callidus has been reading most of the morning, then frowning as I recognise one of the diagrams on the upside-down page.

"Some light reading?" The book is *Analysis of Pattern Recognition in Will-based Systems.* I tackled it at the Bibliotheca. For a month. I'm not sure I understand all of it, even now.

Callidus doesn't look up. "Something like that." I can't help but feel a little concerned. Perhaps I'm underestimating what it will take to move on from Class Seven after all.

"I struggled to understand the principles he talked about in the later chapters. When he gets into Conditional imbuing and the theories behind physical versus mental degradation of linkages . . ." I gesture, indicating bewilderment.

"You've read it?" Callidus, for the first time, looks genuinely taken aback.

"Read. Not necessarily understood."

Callidus chews his lip. Reassessing me. "I haven't made it that far yet." There's another moment, a held breath, and then something seems to go out of him. Tension slips from his shoulders, and he leans over the table, holding out his hand. "I'm sorry. About being upset last night. I know you were only trying to help."

"You do?"

"Either that, or you're even dumber than the Sevenths over there. Only a true idiot would think that punching a gods-damned Sixth was a wise way to introduce yourself."

I grasp his hand. "I promise I'll let you get beaten up next time."

Callidus snorts a laugh. "Fair." We sink back into our seats, both more relaxed. "So. Is it true?"

"Is what true?"

"What they're saying about you." Callidus sighs with exaggerated frustration when I look at him blankly. "You heroically stopped the attack at the naumachia. Swam through a lake of blood to kill the Anguis's leader while ships burned dramatically all around you. Saved the whole rotting city from some mysterious Will-weapon. You remember that, right?"

"Oh. *That.*" I smile, despite myself. "I'm not really supposed to talk about it."

"Why not?"

"The Principalis asked me not to."

He rolls his eyes. "Because the man's done you so many favours, thus far."

"What do you mean?"

"The Principalis had to know he was putting you in a difficult situation when he paired you with me." He shrugs. "He knew I was at the dormitory when he brought you in. And he definitely knew why I wasn't going to dinner."

"But he had no way of knowing what would happen."

"*Everyone* knew what was going to happen. My father vetoed a half dozen applications for the Senate over the trimester break, which is more than any Censor has in the past ten years combined. Plenty of people here are from families who had years of planning ruined." He shakes his head. "There were always going to be repercussions. Which means the Principalis put you squarely in the middle of a conflict. Or at least adjacent."

"I could have stayed out of it."

"You're Catenicus. I think that would have seemed unlikely." He peers at me. "Besides, the bad blood between him and your father isn't exactly a secret."

I shift in my chair. "Ah." Callidus might be right. Veridius couldn't simply refuse me entry, or even be the one to expel me—my reputation after the naumachia has seen to that. But no one could protest if another, higher-ranked student pressed a case. I'm a little unsettled I didn't see it myself.

"Ah," Callidus agrees glibly. He's intense when he actually talks. Quick and intelligent. "At least you're still here, I suppose. What I want to know is: how in the gods' graves did you get Eidhin to accept a Threefold Apology?"

I tell him. When I finish, his unaffected laughter rings across the mess, turning several heads. Including Eidhin's, who glares down at us through puffy, purple-and-black circles. I know I should care—the Sixth is doubtless assuming we're laughing at his expense—but I don't. Instead, I grin along with Callidus. A genuine expression.

"Rotting gods but I wish I'd seen that." Callidus is still chuckling. "It must have felt good."

"It certainly didn't feel bad." I raise my mug. "To our enemies, and the destructions they bring upon themselves."

He clinks his mug against mine. "Seriphius?"

I don't hide my surprise. Seriphius's philosophies are far from basic reading. In fact, those books were in the restricted section of the Bibliotheca in Letens. "You've read him?" When he indicates he has, I lean forward. His current book, casually recognising Seriphius—and yet he never raised his hand today. Never tried to answer any of the questions. "You don't really belong in Class Seven, do you?"

Callidus's eyes slide toward the rest of the Sevenths, a large group of whom have just erupted at a bawdy joke. "I could probably be higher."

He seems about to say more when the chime signalling the end of the meal sounds and Praeceptor Ferrea stands, commanding our attention. Within a minute we're heading back to class, the chance for any significant further conversation lost.

The afternoon progresses much as the morning, the sun creeping farther and farther inside the long archways and across our desks. The Will dial at the front of the class indicates we're about an hour away from dinner—or, in my case, mucking out the stables—when Ferrea finishes the lecture she's been giving on the finer points of oratory.

"Now. We're going to be testing for the remainder of today." There's a collective groan from around me, and she waves away the sound with a half smile. "I warned you. I need to reassess you all, figure out how many of you actually *did* anything during the break."

"I wonder what number that will turn out to be," murmurs Callidus, not looking up from his book.

Ferrea walks up, stops at my desk. "Vis, I need to get a baseline for your knowledge, so you can ignore the questions being asked to the class. Answer these ones instead."

I accept a sheaf of papers. It's what she was working on at lunchtime, I realise. Her handwriting is neat, precise.

I bow my head and start reading as the red-headed woman resumes her place up the front of the class, calling out questions at regular intervals. There's the heavy, urgent scratch of stylii on wax tablets in the silence between, and when I glance up, I can see everyone writing furiously. Interesting. The Sevenths aren't as apathetic as they first seemed, then.

I correct myself as I gaze around: everyone's answering the questions except the boy next to me. Callidus *is* writing—but only to take notes on *Analysis of Pattern Recognition*, which he's brazenly kept open in front of him.

The questions I hear being asked are very basic; the ones I'm reading are less so. They're still nothing compared to what Lanistia would grill me on, or even the reading I'd been doing in Letens's Bibliotheca before that. If anything, some of the most simple are the hardest, as they require dredging fundamental answers from my memory that I didn't expect to need to recite here.

But I finish within thirty minutes. As the other students answer the latest question, I wave and catch Ferrea's attention.

"Struggling with something?"

"Finished." I brandish the wad of papers at her to emphasise the point.

The Praeceptor looks dubious but beckons me forward, issuing another problem to the class as she does so. I hear a ripple of frustrated mutters. She's moving faster than a lot of the students would like. When I reach her desk, she takes the pages and flicks through appraisingly.

"Hm. I'll look at this later. You can go back to your seat. Answer the rest of the questions with everyone else."

Despite her words, once I'm seated again I can see her arranging the pages on the desk in front of her, glancing up only now and then as she delivers the next part of the test. Her face is expressionless as she reads.

A few students sigh in relief as the Will dial slides around to indicate the end of the lesson, Ferrea sending a couple of girls to collect everyone's answers. Callidus glances up, looking surprised that it's already time to leave, then starts packing his things away. I lean over.

"Didn't think the test was worth taking?"

"Did you?" He stretches, considering my answer a foregone conclusion. "Time for dinner."

I'm blocked several paces short of the door by Praeceptor Ferrea. "The stables are a little to the east of the quadrum, out toward the wall. You can't miss them. Septimus Ascenia will tell you what to do. She'll be waiting for you." From the way she says it, the Septimus probably won't be waiting patiently.

I carefully keep my face clear of any vexation, giving a polite acknowledgment. After she's gone, I sigh and glance at Callidus. "Until tomorrow, then."

He gives me an encouraging slap on the back and joins the flow of students heading to the mess, while I split off into the grand, columned main section of the Curia Doctrina.

I slow, appreciating the view. It's getting close to sunset and the island is tinted a ruddy, burning orange, though the water beyond still gleams blue. There's a Transvect approaching; I watch with interest as it skims the waves, moving at a crawl as it approaches one of the white anchoring points before shaking itself into motion again, surging forward and lifting off toward its destination.

I go to keep walking, then stop again. Consider. According to Lanistia, there will be a single Transvect commissioned to run between here and Agerus—where the Necropolis is located—during the Festival of the Ancestors. Going back and forth, returning to the island every couple of hours over the course of two days.

I've been wondering how I can possibly reach the ruins Ulciscor told me about. There might be something there I can exploit.

I'm deep in thought for the rest of the short walk to my punishment.

XXVIII

THE STABLES ARE APART FROM MOST OTHER STRUCTURES IN the Academy. The smell of horse dung flares my nostrils as I get closer, and I can hear the occasional clopping of hooves within. I find myself loitering before heading inside, though. Assessing. It's more isolated than I expected here, and I'm not more than a few hundred feet away from the eastern wall separating the grounds from the rest of Solivagus. Treetops beyond sway in the breeze.

I can't see anything else, but if my orientation is right—and Ulciscor was correct about their location—the ruins I need to investigate should be somewhere not too far beyond.

I gaze at the barrier. Fifteen feet high, stone spikes along the top tinted gold by the setting sun. Difficult, but not impossible. Certainly not compared to getting through the guarded Will cage at the entrance and back again. All I need is some way to scale the wall, and a period where my absence won't be noticed.

Night would be the best time to do it, of course. It's just all but unviable while I'm occupying the same room as more than fifty other boys.

Eventually, I make myself move on. I need to be patient. Spend these first few weeks simply settling in, not doing anything risky.

Septimus Ascenia, a raspy, brusque woman in her fifties, is waiting for me in the stables. She tersely explains how to muck out the stalls. Emphasises in no uncertain terms that I'm not to touch a hair on any of the animals if I value my life. Leaves me with a pitchfork and the promise that if the job's ever not done to its usual high standard, she'll be dragging me back at whatever hour she happens to notice.

The next ten minutes pass in monotony as I scrape piles of hay-riddled horse dung from the floor and carry it to the designated area outside. It's not difficult work, and it gives me a chance to settle. To review. I'm comfortable with how today went, I think, especially considering the preceding one. The work in Class Seven was dull, but I feel like I've made a good start in impressing Ferrea. And I'm confident she'll approve of my answers to her test.

"Anyone in here?"

The female voice echoes through the stables; I stop mid-scoop, then lay the pitchfork against the wall and stick my head out of the stall.

"Emissa?" It's the girl from Class Three. Her dark hair is bound back away from her face, and she's changed out of her finer clothes and into the more practical attire of a simple tunic bound at the waist.

"Evening, Vis." She gives me a sunny wave.

I step out of the stall, smiling back. "What are you doing here?"

"Penance."

"Ah." I raise an eyebrow as she walks over to the nook where the implements are kept and snatches up another pitchfork. "You know what you're doing, I take it?"

"It's a popular punishment around here." She struts into the stall I'm working on, spinning her tool in a showy twirl before stabbing it into the hay. "Though if yesterday's anything to go by, I imagine you're going to find that out for yourself soon enough." Bright green eyes betray her amusement.

"I'm already here for two months. That will be quite enough experience for me, thank you."

"Rotting gods. Two full months?" She shakes her head as she starts working. "Better than the alternative, I suppose." A definite question to the observation.

I tell her how I avoided expulsion as we scoop wet shavings into a bucket. Emissa listens with an entertained smile, her company making the work less onerous.

"Lucky," she says as I finish, giving a quiet laugh. "I might try and spread that around a little more, if I were you."

I frown. "Why?"

"Well, you hitting a Sixth and getting away with it isn't exactly a precedent anyone higher than Class Seven will like, around here. Even if it *was* justified. Half of them will think you're getting special treatment, and the rest will think it devalues their own position." She falters. "And . . . I'm fairly sure Iro has been telling the lower classes that's what they should be thinking. As well as suggesting that your reputation from the naumachia has been exaggerated for political purposes."

I restrain a curse. "Why would he do that?"

"No idea. He might believe it. Or maybe it's something he's been asked to do by his father. Either way, he seems to have taken a disliking to you. And I don't think the Fourths will take it too much to heart, but the Fifths and Sixths . . . well. Even if they don't believe Iro, they won't want *him* to see that." She winces as she sees my expression. "Sorry."

"Not your fault." My good mood sours. I'm already unpopular with the Sevenths, but I was hoping that if I could advance quickly into Class Six, it might not matter.

Worse, I'm stuck here during dinner for two whole months: the punishment seemed like a reprieve at the time, but more and more I'm wondering whether Veridius might actually have preferred this outcome. Isolating me, rather than expelling me and drawing attention as a result. Whatever the case, it's going to be hard to improve my reputation if I'm never around. And from watching the politics of my father's court, I know how swiftly even unfounded rumours can turn ruinous.

"I think you did the right thing, by the way." She doesn't look up as she sifts through another batch of hay for droppings. There's a modest flush to her cheeks as she says it.

"Hitting Eidhin?"

I get an eye roll of mock reproof. "Stopping him. Nobody else would have."

"Thanks." I scrape my shovel beneath a pile of dung. The fresh odour hits my nostrils with force, and I wrinkle my nose. "Though at the moment, I'd argue the others are the smart ones."

"Oh, they are," she agrees readily. "I only said you did the *right* thing."

I concede a chuckle at that.

"How were your first classes today?"

I hesitate. "Class Seven was . . . less demanding than I expected."

"That's diplomatic."

"Yes it is." I scrape some clean shavings to the side. "Any advice on how to move up a few classes?"

"Really?"

"Of course."

"Well." She leans on her pitchfork, pinching the bridge of her nose as she thinks. "It's about impressing the Praeceptors, I suppose, more than anything else. Ferrea is easy: be nice to her. If she likes you, and you show her you're smart enough, she'll force the issue straight away. From Class Six, though . . ." She screws up her face.

"What?"

"Dultatis." The way she says the name isn't exactly respectful. "It will be up to him to advance you, and he's . . ." She sighs. "He's friends with Praeceptor Nequias—think a shorter, fatter, more weaselly version. To me and any other 'true Catenans,' they're polite. Friendly, even. But anyone like you, born in . . ."

"Aquiria," I supply.

"Aquiria, or anywhere outside the heartland, they have a tendency to look down on. I'm not sure that any amount of impressing Dultatis is going to help with that."

"Oh." That sounds less than ideal. "Good to know."

"Sorry."

The conversation moves on to lighter things, and soon enough we've finished one stall and are onto the next. Horses stamp their feet as we pass, as if trying to get our attention. The sunlight has faded outside, but Will-triggered lanterns burst to life as soon as the light dimmed and now cast a rosy glow across the stables.

We chat the entire time, mostly about the Academy and what I can expect over the coming weeks. There's an easy, immediate connection with Emissa; she has an effort-less likeability about her, a vivaciousness that seems unaffected. It also doesn't hurt, I'll admit, that even in her work clothes she's undeniably pretty.

I have to be wary of that, too, though.

My parents would often warn me that attraction—the rush of flirtation, the ex-citement of seeing someone reciprocate your interest—can become compulsion, if left unchecked. A desire that encourages poor decisions. The king and queen of Suus, of course, were warning me of girls more interested in my position than me, but the prin-ciple remains the same. And I can already feel the tug in my chest when Emissa laughs at something I've said, my instinctive smile in response. Can sense my enjoyment of the conversation edging past being just appreciative of the company. It's not something I can afford to ignore.

"I have to admit," I say as we're loosening and spreading fresh shavings around the final stall, "after seeing what things are like around here, I didn't expect to be having a friendly conversation with a Third tonight." I leave the hint of a question in there. I don't really want to ask—don't want to threaten the pleasure I'm taking in the com-pany, I suppose—but it seems unusual, that she's so willing to ignore the rigid-seeming social barriers of the Academy. Coincidental that it's her here with me tonight, too. One of the few people in the entire school who I've already met.

I've been trying to ignore it, but Ulciscor's concern from after the Transvect attack still sits uneasily in the back of my mind.

"I'll do what the Praeceptors want while they're watching, but honestly? It's ridic-ulous that we can't socialise outside our classes. For me, that leaves *five other people* I'm allowed to talk to. And I don't like more than half of those." She grins. "Also, we're shovelling manure together. I feel like that tends to level things out a bit."

I chuckle, though I can't help but feel the tiniest flash of disappointment, too. This won't carry over beyond tonight, then. At least it probably absolves Emissa from any suspicion. She hasn't asked any prying questions. She's even only mentioned the naumachia in passing, though I know she must be as curious as anyone else about it. I'm grateful for her restraint. It feels like it's dominated every other conversation I've had since it happened.

Between the banter and the extra set of hands, we're replacing the water in the last stall before I realise it. Despite my sudden reluctance to finish, we're soon stowing our tools and walking back to the quadrum together.

"I should report back to Ferrea and get my dinner," I admit as we reach the vast cobblestone square. Torches flare and sputter in a stiff breeze. No one else is around. "Do you need to see her, too, or someone else?"

"Neither. I'm off to study."

"I thought you said you were doing penance?"

She's untying her hair, starting to angle away in the direction of the girls' dormitory. "I never said anyone *set* it. I just . . . felt bad. That I didn't do more to help, yesterday." She's still smiling at me. Her green eyes sparkle in the torchlight. "I'll see you around, Vis." She's turning with a cheerful wave and walking away before I can respond. Doesn't look back.

I stare after her for a full second before starting back into motion, vaguely annoyed to find a smile on my face.

I head into the Curia Doctrina and down into the mess, where Ferrea said she would be waiting. Sure enough, the woman's sitting alone at one of the long tables.

"Vis." She looks up in surprise as I approach. "You're finished?"

"I am."

"Ascenia will be dragging you out of bed in the early hours if you haven't done everything perfectly."

"I know." I consider mentioning Emissa's contribution, but it will only make it seem like I got away with doing less than my punishment required.

"Very well. Your food's waiting for you in the kitchen. After that, you'll need to go to the dormitory and collect your things."

Cold washes over me. "Why?" Surely Nequias and Eidhin haven't figured out some way to get me expelled after all.

"Because you need to move up a floor. There's a bed waiting for you in Room Nine." She stands, gifting me with an approving beam. "Congratulations. You'll be reporting to Praeceptor Dultatis in the morning."

XXIX

THERE'S LIGHT AS I WAKE, MORE THAN THERE SHOULD BE. I rub my eyes against the red sting through my eyelids, opening them to find one of the desks in the corner occupied, a lamp burning above it. Shuttered, but still bright in the enclosed space.

It sluggishly comes back to me where I am. Only three other boys share the same room as me now, though I haven't met any of them yet: it was late by the time I gathered my belongings and found my way up, and it didn't seem polite to introduce myself by waking them. The floor belonging to Class Six—marginally smaller than the one below, but housing almost half the number of students—is divided into several rooms, each one offering more space and significantly more privacy.

Just enough, I think, to sneak out one night soon without anyone noticing.

I lie motionless, observing the figure at the desk across the room. It's ominously large. Familiar. Close-cropped hair is auburn in the lamplight.

Vek.

Eidhin is shirtless, which I think is strange given the evident chill in the air. Though if he's a southerner, he's accustomed to much colder climates. He's bowed over a wax tablet, stylus in hand, jabbing at it with short, sharp motions and muttering something just low enough that I can't make out the words. There's no mistaking his vexation.

Darkness glowers through the window beyond but my body tells me it's time to get up, so I roll to my feet. I don't think I make a sound, but the murmuring from the corner cuts short, the broad-shouldered boy twisting in his seat to look at me. The whole of his chest is tattooed in complex patterns, black lines intersecting and overlapping in dizzying knots and whorls. His eyes are a startling blue as they bore into me.

We watch each other for a couple of wary seconds.

"Lentius is gone?" He enunciates each word in a careful growl.

"I . . ." I'm ruffled, not following, then, "Oh. The boy who was here before me? Yes. I'm his replacement." Lentius must be the name of the boy who was ranked last in Class Six. He'll be a Seventh, now.

"I liked Lentius. He said little." Eidhin examines me, then deliberately turns back to his desk, resuming whatever he was working on.

I stand there, debating whether to say anything else, then shake my head in irritated resignation and start getting dressed.

With no materials of my own to study, I splash my face with water using the bowl on the table, then head for the exit. I can at least get in a run before breakfast.

The red-headed boy at the desk doesn't stir from his frustrated attack on the wax tablet as I leave.

※ ※ ※

DESPITE THE BRUSQUE INTERACTION, I'M FEELING GOOD AS I jog down the lantern-lit external stairs of the dormitory, the dewy chill of dawn nipping at exposed skin. I'm two days into my time at the Academy, and already advancing. Getting into Class Three before the end of the year feels just a little more possible.

I spend some time exercising in the quiet of the parkland nearby, morning air starting to burn in my lungs by the time the chime for breakfast quavers across the grounds. I spot Callidus a little way ahead on my way to the Curia Doctrina and, after a second's hesitation, jog to catch up to him.

"So. I saw your things were gone this morning. Ferrea didn't waste any time," he greets me cheerfully as I fall into step with him.

"She recognises excellence, clearly."

He grins. "Well. She recognises participation. A lack of incompetence, maybe."

I make an amused, acceding gesture. "And as it turns out, that lack of incompetence has landed me in the same room as Eidhin."

"Ooh." Callidus cringes. "Tense?"

"He didn't seem pleased to see me."

"To be fair, I don't think Eidhin has ever been pleased to see anyone. But you're a Sixth too, now. If he didn't try to hit you again, you'll probably be fine. Probably."

I cough a laugh. "Thanks." My good mood improves at the easy way we've slid into the conversation. It's been a long time—a *long* time—since I've felt even the tenuous bonds of friendship, and I'm surprised to discover just how much I've missed it.

When we reach the mess, though, Callidus shakes his head emphatically as I move to the seat opposite him.

"Sit with the Sixths," he urges me seriously, his gaze assuring me that he neither means offense, nor will take any from my conceding. "You burned your boats with this lot"—he jerks his head toward the steadily filling tables nearby—"on my account. Don't make me feel guilty twice over."

I vacillate, but can see the wisdom in his advice. "Alright. But don't think this means I won't drag you out for some sparring tomorrow morning."

"Sparring?" He groans good-naturedly, but when I raise an eyebrow he waves me away with an agreeable nod. For all his complaining, I think he enjoys the company, too.

There are already a group of Sixths gathered with their morning meals, perhaps ten boys and half as many girls clumped around one of the long tables. Eidhin, I note, is seated there too but separate again. Not ostracized, but with just enough space between him and the others to indicate that he's not part of their conversation.

That conversation trails off at my approach, then stops altogether as I slide into a vacant seat with what I hope is sociable confidence. "Sorry to interrupt. I'm Vis. I've just come up from Class Seven."

There's a long, awkward silence.

"We know," one of the boys eventually says edgily. It's Ianix, the brooding Catenan who was angry at my defending myself against Eidhin. "We've heard all about you."

"Oh?" I ignore the implication, maintain my genial expression.

"What Ianix is trying to say, is that it might be better if you don't sit with us." The interjection from the dark-haired girl on the left is quiet but blunt. She pushes long curls away from her face, glancing around at her companions rather than me as she says it.

"Sorry," adds the girl who was speaking when I arrived. It's a soft apology, seems genuine. None of the remainder of the group will meet my gaze, though.

I let my friendly façade fade, trying to look offended more than angry. "Look. I know I didn't make the best first impression, but I promise you that—"

"Come on." Ianix pushes back his chair and stands, addressing his companions. "There are plenty of other tables."

I feel my jaw twitch as the other students follow suit. The way they move—hurriedly, anxiously, with none of the stalking offense that would indicate an actual dislike of me—indicates they're more afraid of appearances than anything else. A few of them even steal glances up toward Iro at the Class Three table as they go. The result remains the same, though. Within ten seconds, I'm left at the table with only Eidhin sitting a few spaces away.

The muscular, red-headed boy looks up from his food at me, as if sensing my intent to try talking to him. "No." He bows his head again, ignoring me. Resumes his meal.

I sigh. Briefly consider pushing my case, or trusting that some of the Sixths yet to arrive might be more receptive.

"No. Rot this," I mutter, feeling heat in my cheeks as I pick up my meal and head back down to Callidus's table. I pause before putting my plate down, though. "Do you mind?" Genuinely asking. I don't want to be responsible for Callidus getting in more trouble.

He gives me a sympathetic grimace, evidently having seen what just transpired. Unfortunately, I think just about everyone else present did, too. "No," he says, drawing out the word, his hesitation suggesting he considered answering otherwise. "But you do this, and it's as good as admitting you belong down here. It won't help your standing with anyone."

"I'm not sure that can get much worse, anyway."

"Alright." He shrugs and raises his mug jovially. "To the Pariah Table."

Despite Callidus's good cheer it's hard not to remain stiff as I start eating, but soon enough the other boy's laid-back demeanour rubs off, and there's only the occasional prickling at the back of my neck as I imagine scornful gazes settling on me from above. The conversation stays light, and by the time the chime sounds to signal the start of class, any embarrassment has faded. Replaced, if I'm being honest, mostly by hot annoyance.

If everyone in Class Six is going to try and ignore me, then I'll just have to make them pay attention.

XXX

THE NEXT SIX WEEKS ARE AMONG THE MOST FRUSTRATING I can remember.

It's clear from the outset that in some ways, Class Six isn't going to pose much of a challenge. While the Sixths are more willing to engage in work than the Sevenths, what they're being taught doesn't seem to be any more difficult; half the time, the lectures cover things I learned before fleeing Suus. And when we shift to tasks of a more physical nature—sparring in the gymnasium, mostly, interspersed with running the limits of the Academy grounds to test our endurance and speed—I consistently prove to be better conditioned than most of the rest of the class. Of the forty-seven others, in fact, only Eidhin, Ianix, and a girl called Leridia push me in either discipline.

None of that seems to matter to Dultatis.

Class Six's Praeceptor is large and round-faced, most of his hair having fled the crown of his head, the scant remainder a close-cropped black. Despite his paunch there's no doubt he must have once been a strong man, and the hardness hasn't left his demeanour: from the moment I join his class, it's clear he doesn't like me much. When I attempt to answer questions, he ignores me in favour of others; when no one else is willing to speak and he's forced to listen to my responses, he derides them, quibbling over wording or implying that I haven't given him anywhere near enough information. Even when he simply looks at me, his eyes are cold. *Angry*. It feels like there's a special enmity there, though aside from my not being Catenan—and there are others in the class who match that description just as well—I cannot fathom what I've done to earn it.

The remainder of Class Six seems to pick up on the Praeceptor's disdain. Combined with Iro's lingering influence, it means I rarely hear more than two words from them in my direction. Certainly none of my friendly overtures go anywhere.

I bite my tongue, though, every day. Accept the isolation, the disregard and pedantry, as gracefully as I can. Technically, I'm not being wronged, and there's no ignoring the fact that my introduction to the Academy was far from poised. I can't afford to be seen feuding with a Praeceptor, no matter the man's attitude toward me.

So instead, I try to focus on the small positives.

I fall into a comfortable routine of pre-dawn sparring and spending the two earlier meals of the day with Callidus, whose company I increasingly value. He's charming, quick-witted, and affable, and my conversations with him become a balm against the wounds of class. He's also far too smart to be a Seventh. I can tell there's more to the story of his fall from Class Three; more than once it seems Callidus is about to elucidate on his position, only for him to abruptly change the subject. As curious as I am, I don't press.

Emissa materialises several times more to help me while I muck out the stables, too, claiming a sense of obligation. I can't deny I enjoy the company. Those nights, when I go to sleep, I find myself replaying my banter with her and smiling. There's no harm in it. I need to find joy in this place somewhere.

But that warmth in my chest has always faded by morning, and I fast return to feeling like I'm stuck. Without options.

Which is why, halfway through my second month, I finally break.

% % %

"OVER THE NEXT TWO DAYS," ANNOUNCES PRAECEPTOR DUL-tatis once everyone has assembled, "we will be running the Labyrinth." His small, faded brown eyes glare around at the class, which has gathered at the base of the Curia Doctrina's stairs in the quadrum. I get the impression he's not angry, particularly. It's just the way he always looks.

I lean forward in anticipation. My abilities manipulating the Labyrinth at Villa Telimus had come a long way by the time my training with Lanistia came to an end. I've been quietly eager to measure myself against the other students here.

"This will be our only access for the trimester. So we need to make our time there count." His voice booms across the massive square, which is otherwise unoccupied. "Perhaps someone can remind me why this is such an important assessment?"

There's a heartbeat of silence, and then I call out. "Because it tests the same skills that are needed for using Will." I'll be expected to know all about the Labyrinth, by this point, even if I'm not supposed to have seen anything like it before.

Dultatis's eyes roam the crowd, as if searching for someone else to answer, before sliding unwillingly to me. "That's an overly simplified—"

"It tests memory, which is needed for any long-term imbuing; physical strength for capacity; speed and precision for efficiency; logic and split focus for Harmonics and Conditionals."

"Vis?" I nod. "Don't interrupt me again." There's a titter of amusement from a few of the students.

Dultatis is already moving on. "Your results will also contribute significantly to your standing in the class. So make sure you give your all." He's watching me while he says it. I tamp down my irritation, make sure I look nothing but polite and attentive. As usual.

The Praeceptor's speech apparently done, he strides off and the class trails after him, down a narrow path past the Curia Doctrina and out of the quadrum. There's excited chatter among the students, but nobody directs conversation toward me. In fact, I'm a somewhat notable island amid the crowd. I do my best to ignore the deliberate isolation. At least Eidhin, toward the front of the group, commands an equally apprehensive ring of space around him.

It's only a few minutes before our destination appears ahead: a long, sleek, flat-roofed building, almost temple-like in the way its entrance is adorned with a colonnade. It's a uniformly dark grey stone, though, without any of the friezes and artistic additions meant to flatter the gods. A dark, strangely hollow shrine if there ever was one.

I'm caught up in the general feeling of anticipation as we pass between the towering triangular-cut columns and start descending a torchlit staircase. Even if Dultatis hadn't already stated as much, this is obviously a rare event for Class Six. The lightly polished, charcoal-grey stone continues below, and the sound of our footsteps clatters off the walls, mixing with the enthusiastic babble.

I'm prepared to feign awe when we enter the main chamber—there's no telling who will be watching my reaction, after all—but I don't have to pretend.

While the layout of the Labyrinth is comfortably familiar as soon as we file onto the platform overlooking it, it's the only thing that feels the same. Where there were rough-hewn walls at Villa Telimus, here there are smooth dark panels, polished to a mirror-like sheen; where there were barely visible symbols carved into doorways, there's now artisanship on display, each representation large and inlaid with burnished bronze. The sparse torches of the Telimus Labyrinth are here replaced by a line of fire that rings the entire arena, unbroken flame dancing red and reflecting vividly against the dark mirror of its surroundings. The control bracer sits atop a triangular pedestal of polished black, silhouetted, the smaller gemstones studding its surface giving it a vicious aspect.

My surprise at the ostentation of it all causes me to stumble, and I look up to see Dultatis smirking, though he's not looking directly at me. Good. The more overawed I appear, the more effective my performance here is going to be.

"Praeceptor Dultatis." The call comes from off to the left, farther along the platform, and the press of bodies spreads out enough for me to see Veridius striding toward us. The excited conversation around me quietens to a surprised murmur as others register his presence, too.

"Principalis?" Dultatis looks as taken aback as his students. "I was told the Labyrinth would be ours today, but if I've been misinformed—"

"No, no." Veridius waves his hand in genial dismissal. "I simply discovered some extra time and thought I might watch this morning. If you have no objections?" He comes to a stop in front of Dultatis. He's a head shorter than the man, but Dultatis feels the smaller of the two; Veridius's presence is charming more than imposing, yet it commands the space in ways I suspect Dultatis can only dream of.

"Of course not, Principalis." Dultatis's answer is less than convincing.

Veridius amicably takes his response at face value. "Wonderful. I'm eager to see how your students have progressed since last trimester." The matter settled, he steps back, gesturing with a flourish to the Labyrinth. "Please! Pretend I'm not here."

Dultatis nods brusquely, turning to face us again. He doesn't bother to conceal his irritation once Veridius can't see, and his glare searches me out before moving on. He obviously considers me the source of the Principalis's intrusion, no matter what Veridius just told him.

"We'll proceed according to class standing. Top ten and bottom ten run today, everyone else tomorrow. If you're not running today, you'll be a hunter at some point," the balding Praeceptor announces. "You all know the rules. If you're responsible for injuring someone while using the control bracer, it's immediate expulsion from the Academy. There's no combat here, and no trying to just run past people, either. If the hunters corner you, you lose. That's all. Now: choose your partners."

The instruction's an anticipated one; students around me immediately begin gravitating toward one another, and within moments most are standing in pairs.

All, in fact, except myself and Eidhin.

I hesitate. I've successfully avoided interacting with the large southerner for almost the entire time I've been in Six. His nose has long since healed, and he's never threatened me. Even the one time Dultatis paired us in sparring—deliberately, I'm sure—Eidhin never tried to do more than the practice demanded.

That doesn't mean his glare doesn't burn whenever he glances my way, though.

I sigh, then walk over to the square-shouldered boy. "Looks like it's us."

He grunts, looking about as pleased as I feel.

We shuffle over to the edge of the balcony, joining the others overlooking the Labyrinth as the first pair is chosen. It's Ianix, who's ranked first in Class Six, along with Leridia, the girl with the curly dark hair and generally unpleasant attitude. Along with them, a half dozen other students are being directed to head to the other side of the Labyrinth. They leave at a brisk jog.

The Praeceptor takes the control bracer from its position atop the pillar. It looks smaller than the one at Villa Telimus. Lighter. He signals to Ianix and then, as the boy descends the gleaming stairs to the maze's entrance, starts affixing the bracer to Leridia's arm.

"They don't wear the control bracer while they run?" It's not how Lanistia described it to me.

I direct the question to Eidhin, but it's a girl off to my right who answers. "They only do that in Class Three." She opens her mouth as if to say more, then registers who she's talking to and snaps her mouth shut again, turning away.

Seeing it's the most response I'm likely to get, I watch curiously as Leridia positions herself on the balcony above Ianix, at the centre of our side. In the distance, four of the six students have reached the far end of the maze; one of them stands opposite Leridia while the other three descend from sight. The remaining two of the group are perching on the east and west balconies, respectively, closer to our side than the other.

Leridia will be controlling the maze while Ianix runs it, then. And the three around the sides must be the spotters Lanistia described to me, there to call out Ianix's position to their partners down below as they try to prevent him from getting to the other end.

When Dultatis is satisfied everyone is in position, he raises a hand until silence falls. Leridia, Ianix, and the three spotters all watch him. Unblinking. The fire lining the walls crackles. Leridia's hand hovers over the bracer.

Dultatis drops his hand dramatically. "Begin!"

Ianix is sprinting around the first corner and heading west before the Praeceptor's echoing bellow fades, Leridia manipulating a stone and a grinding below answering as the first panel rotates, clearing what was previously a dead end. I flinch at the sound; Leridia's control wasn't so graceless as to lose the stone from the bracer, but I can almost hear Lanistia's disapproval at the inelegance of it.

"My side!" The boy on the western balcony yells out, positioning himself level with Ianix and holding up his hand. There are flickers of movement on the far side of the maze as the three hunters start in. Leridia's walking westward, eyes roaming the way ahead of Ianix, looking for the next panel to move.

The rest of Class Six hang over the balcony, some whispering among themselves as they watch. Those are occasionally shushed by others, who follow with nervous looks over toward the Principalis. While Veridius doesn't appear to notice, absorbed as he is in the contest, it's evidently frowned upon to make too much noise here.

There's a breathless minute as Ianix progresses deeper into the maze, the spotter whose hand is raised keeping level with him and occasionally calling out the specifics of his movements to those below. Leridia stalks around the side and ahead of her partner, silhouetted by the fire, stopping twice to focus on her bracer. She gets a harsh grating from a panel and a flinch from me both times. She's calling out different numbers to Ianix whenever she alters something, but I can't see any relation between them and what she's doing. Some sort of pre-arranged code to avoid helping the hunters, I assume.

A sharp curse bounces around the vast space when Leridia attempts to use the bracer a third time, and I can tell the stone's fallen off. She immediately shouts out another number to Ianix, who skids and changes direction. Leridia's skill might be lacking, but the communication between her and her partner is impressive.

I join the crowd as everyone begins trailing around the edge of the maze, the group staying close while taking care not to interfere with Leridia or any of the spotters. I can feel interest around me sharpen when Ianix nears the centre and begins slowing to a cautious jog, increasingly hesitant at every intersection. We've still only been getting flashes of the hunters as they close in. They're keeping low, using the walls to conceal themselves from Leridia as much as possible.

I spare a glance for Veridius, who's still back toward the entrance. The Principalis is watching—to all appearances intently—but there's something absent about his expression. Something that suggests his mind is elsewhere.

"Eleven!" Leridia calls, almost a scream, as a blond girl suddenly sprints into sight only a couple of turns away from Ianix, and with no barriers between them. Ianix tears off to the right as the underground chamber explodes into urgently shouted commands from spotters and Leridia alike, the latter fumbling with her bracer, frantically trying to find the right symbols on it. A panel shudders into the blond girl's path, mere moments before she would have been past, blocking her way. She snarls and wheels, glancing up at the spotters for guidance.

The spotter on the far end of the maze has raised her hand as well, I notice. She can see Ianix, is keeping herself in line with him as he moves. Between her and the spotter on the side still doing the same, it should make it easy for the hunters to calculate where he is.

The two other hunters have broken cover too, now, converging from different directions, and I can see the frustration and panic on Leridia's face as she wrestles with the bracer. Ianix has seen the dark-haired girl's struggles and is responding by retreating, looking rattled himself, moving in increasingly random directions and sometimes ducking down to try and break line of sight from above.

None of it matters. A minute later, it's over, with Ianix trapped against a dead end by the blond girl. There's a sigh of disappointment, a smattering of applause from the class. Veridius claps as well, but it's clearly encouragement, not adulation.

"Do the runners normally get caught?" I ask Eidhin, not really expecting an answer.

He watches Ianix trudge dejectedly back toward the stairs. "Always." The way he says it, it's a stupid question.

I cough. "Should we work out some sort of code? Like Ianix and Leridia?"

He turns his back on me and starts toward the maze's entrance with the rest of the class.

"That's a no, then," I mutter to myself, joining the flow. Up ahead, Ianix emerges onto the balcony, exchanging a few terse words with Leridia along with the bracer. A similar changeover is happening between the spotters and the hunters, albeit a more congratulatory one.

Soon enough the contest begins again; though Leridia is a faster runner and Ianix better at manipulating the maze, the combination's still nowhere near strong enough for Leridia to evade capture. Another smattering of applause once she's caught. Apparently this is a good showing as far as the class is concerned, though Veridius continues to look more supportive than impressed. That doesn't surprise me. If Lanistia were here, she wouldn't be shy about showing her dismay at these performances.

"We're going to have our lowest rank run next." Dultatis makes the announcement with a distinct lack of enthusiasm. "Telimus. Get your partner and get into position."

I don't move for a breath. Surprised to be called so soon, and stung, perhaps naïvely, to be named worst-ranked in the class. It makes a sick sort of sense, though, I suppose. It's not as if Dultatis has given me the opportunity to prove anything yet.

Eidhin is already stalking toward the control bracer, so I still my anger and head for the entrance to the Labyrinth.

I glance over at Veridius as I walk. He's watching me thoughtfully. Gives me an infinitesimal nod as our eyes meet.

Once down the stairs into the maze, I have a minute to settle as the hunters and spotters take up their positions. I steady my breathing, calm my nerves. I spent most afternoons of my last month at Villa Telimus wandering the Labyrinth there: partly to practice my manipulation of it on the run, but also to translate my intimate knowledge of its top-down layout into an equally exhaustive confidence while inside it. And the Academy's Labyrinth is structured identically. *Identically.* Superficial differences aside, every corner of this place should feel familiar.

I scan the crowd above. Plenty of curiosity up there, but not much in the way of support. Eidhin is in position, bracer strapped to his arm, alternately studying it and the maze. Dultatis is by his side, staring down at me. He looks away when he realises I've seen his gaze, checking across the chamber before raising his arm and then letting it drop almost immediately. "Begin!"

And then I'm running.

The Labyrinth is more than a thousand feet long and has more than fifty panels that can be manipulated; if I sprint along the most direct route possible, I can get to the end in less than two minutes. Of course, the most direct route also has the fewest options, the highest number of choke points for the hunters. The only way to slip past all three of them is to choose a path with plenty of potential variability, and trust that Eidhin will make the right decisions for me.

So I angle off to the right, the side of the maze opposite to the one both Ianix and Leridia chose. I move at a good pace, but take care not to wind myself, reserving my energy for when I'll need it most. Ahead, there's the booming of panels sliding into place. No horrible, shivering grinding, though. That's a good sign.

My breath's hot in my lungs as I proceed, doing all I can to hug the concealing walls between myself and the spotter at the far end. The one on the right has already marked me, has her hand in the air as she keeps pace. I'm about a third of the way through the maze now, and I can feel tension causing my feet to drag, make me hesitate every time I approach a corner. Eidhin hasn't made a sound, hasn't communicated once. I use a precious second to glance behind me up at the balcony, where he's trailing. He's scanning the way ahead. Doesn't see my frustrated look.

Another minute passes as I jog, apprehension growing. I flinch when the passage-way ahead of me slams shut without warning, closing off the way I was intending to go; I falter and then dash down the newly formed corridor instead as the spotter on my right shouts furious, frustrated information to someone. The spotter at the back is yelling too, his hand raised. I'm sweating, heart pounding. There must have been another student just in front of me. I recalculate my route, try to envisage where they're likely to go next, especially if they know my exact position. There are only bad options ahead. I whirl and double back, taking a different path.

It's not panic, though. If there was a hunter that close, they've potentially locked themselves in to this route; with a little backtracking, I may just be able to get around them. I feel a flicker of excitement as the corridor rearranges itself again, giving me an opening to the left. More panels boom farther along. Eidhin, still silent, has had the same idea.

Time drags in a breathless, tense haze. A minute. Three. I've lasted longer than either Ianix or Leridia. Eidhin's manipulation of the maze directs me back again, but the third time, I can hear panels slamming *behind* me. The back of my mind registers a murmur from the rest of the class, quickly shushed. I take the cue and burst forward, lungs burning. I'm two-thirds of the way through.

I'm just beginning to feel a grin split my face when sandy-haired Stult steps out of a side passage. "Got you."

I skid to a stop. Spin. There's a slender girl—Tanila—about twenty feet behind me, hands on her knees, dripping sweat. She looks up, damp black hair slapping her face, and gives me something between a smile and a glare.

There's no way past either of them. The two paths leading out of this corridor finish at dead ends, with no panels to change that fact.

I've lost.

XXXI

"A LITTLE COMMUNICATION WOULD HAVE BEEN WELCOME." I snatch the control bracer from Eidhin. Frustrated. It hasn't helped that the first thing I spied after emerging from the Labyrinth was Praeceptor Dultatis's smug expression. "I almost made it."

The hulking red-headed boy's gaze as I slap the device on my arm is implacable. Not defensive, not reactionary, just . . . steady. I open my mouth to say more, then exhale instead.

"*We* almost made it." It's not an apology. I'm just correcting myself. "You're quite good with this." I waggle my arm, indicating the control bracer, which is significantly lighter than the one from Villa Telimus. I make it a half question.

Eidhin grunts. Shrugs. "You were . . ." Vexation flashes across his face. "*Gwyll cymlys*," he finishes, a mixture of exasperated and begrudging. Before I can respond, he's walking away.

I frown after Eidhin as he stomps down the stairs into the maze. *Gwyll cymlys*: "better than competent." A weak compliment, but that's not what has me taken aback. It's a phrase peculiar to the officially dead Cymrian language.

I study my partner's burly form below, playing back our rare, brief exchanges over the past weeks. He certainly has the look of a southerner, but that applies to the far south-west, too. His short responses have to be at least partly from surliness, but if—

"Begin!"

There's a savage satisfaction in the booming announcement; I suspect Dultatis has noticed my distraction. I scramble to orient myself as Eidhin sprints hard up the centre, and for an awful moment I think he's simply going to plunge into the series of corridors from which it's almost impossible to escape. But at the last second he dashes left, into a tight, twisting section that already branches into four quite disparate exits.

I can see his plan, I think, after another thirty seconds of chasing after him while he confidently twists and turns. He's got a set path in mind, but it's winding enough and he's moving so fast that it's difficult for the spotters to properly relay. They're desperately yelling instructions, and then corrections, and then corrections of *those* corrections as even the two with their hands raised have to jog to keep up. The hunters are already drawing closer but there's a hesitancy to their approach, an uncertainty bleeding over from how quickly their information is getting adjusted.

One thing's abundantly clear: my partner doesn't expect any help from me. I feel a flush of anger at the presumption. Eidhin's tactic isn't a terrible one, but he won't win with it alone.

I've got the pace of his movement now. And the paths I think the hunters will be taking, based on the flashes I've seen from them. I take a deep breath, glance down to check I've got the right stone, and *twist*.

The way ahead of Eidhin slams shut.

"Go right!" I yell as the red-headed boy stops and wheels, scanning the balcony until his murderous glare comes to rest on me. He gesticulates furiously at the blocked way ahead, but I shake my head with equal fervour. "*Go right!*"

There's a full second where he just stands there, frozen by frustrated indecision. Then he slaps the stone wall with his hand hard enough that it must surely hurt, and dashes off to the right.

"Alright," I murmur, letting out a long breath.

For the next two minutes, I change the Labyrinth constantly as Eidhin runs. I'm hesitant, at first. Nervous. It shows in my first couple of adjustments, the rending of stone screeching across the chamber. But once I settle, that odd out-of-body calm, almost meditative *flow*, washes over me. I'm completely focused and I *know* I'm completely focused, some small part of my mind watching my actions and thrilling at how precisely I'm working. I'm seeing three, four choices ahead for the hunters, blocking off their best options at every turn. Redirecting them away not from where Eidhin is, but from where Eidhin *will be*.

I stop being worried about the crowd, about Veridius or Dultatis. My only anxiety now is that I'll fall from this wonderful mind-state too early, falter, and lose confidence before I can finish.

Eidhin, for his part, has adapted well, responding to my opening or shutting panels exactly as I did for him. It's a crude method of communication, though, and while we've maintained a safe distance thus far, the hunters are closing in.

"They're trying to flank you! Take the second left and double back!" I shout the warning as I see it happening, knowing it's giving too much information to the hunters, but left with little alternative.

Eidhin stumbles as he hears my yell. Fades to a stop. There's uncertainty in his every line.

I remember our brief encounter earlier, and something clicks. *"Take the second left ahead and come back this way!"* I roar the command.

But this time, I do it in Cymrian.

There's a raised murmur from the watching class, and I can't help but enjoy the utterly startled look I elicit from Eidhin. He gawps in my direction, static.

Then, abruptly, he's running again.

He takes the second left.

I continue to shout out instructions in Cymrian, excitement mounting as Eidhin takes turn after turn as directed. I'm far from fluent, but my mother was, and she ensured I was learning her father's native tongue as soon as I could talk. These simple commands aren't difficult to dredge up.

It's almost easy, after that.

Between Eidhin going exactly where I need him and my increasingly confident adjustments to the maze, the hunters start to flail. The buzz from the class on the balcony grows louder and louder. Sixths crowd the railing, elbowing others aside and leaning over to get a better view.

I cannot remember a more satisfying moment than when I twist my last stone on the bracer, and then Eidhin is suddenly charging down the final corridor, hunters trapped in the passages on either side of him. He's clear.

There's no applause, only animated chatter from the rest of the class, but Eidhin still stabs the air in triumph as he jogs up the stairs on the far side. I laugh delightedly at the sight, then start unlacing the control bracer, hands shaking as the tension drains from my body. Ulciscor and Lanistia emphasised time and time again how important these tests were. I've done everything I can, today.

Dultatis and Veridius are both watching me when I look up. The Praeceptor's face is flushed in the light of the fire, looking the very opposite of pleased. Veridius seems more intrigued than impressed. When he sees my glance, though, he gives me a deep, approving nod.

Eidhin joins us after a minute, just ahead of the spotters and hunters, who cut dejected silhouettes against the flames. He's not smiling, but there's an energy to his step. As happy as I've ever seen him.

Dultatis eyes us both as Eidhin comes alongside me. The red-headed boy still doesn't crack a smile, but the way he stands is close to companionable.

"I enjoyed that," he murmurs in Cymrian, staring straight ahead.

I feel the corners of my mouth tick upward, though I try to keep a blank face too.

Dultatis's frown deepens, as if he suspects Eidhin just said something about him.

"You did well," he announces loudly, so the entire class can hear. "Unfortunately, you also broke the rules, so this won't be entered into any official records."

"What?" I blurt the word disbelievingly, and beside me, Eidhin tenses.

"You communicated in a foreign language. Code is allowed because it encourages planning, teamwork. Both of you knowing the same dead language is an advantage of coincidence, nothing more. It cannot be rewarded."

"It *was* in code," says Eidhin immediately.

"Pardon?"

"We. Spoke. In. Code," he says, emphasizing each word deliberately, as if Dultatis were a child. "You did not say the code had to be in Common."

"That's true," I agree calmly.

Dultatis's eye twitches as a few titters echo through the class watching on. "Code is also allowed because there is the possibility of it being broken by the hunters if it's not opaque enough. So while you are still to be congratulated"—he utters it through gritted teeth, the words undoubtedly for Veridius's benefit rather than ours—"you are nonetheless disqualified."

I stare at the Praeceptor silently. There's that special rancour in Dultatis's eyes again when he looks at me.

My gaze goes to Veridius, who's standing a few paces behind Dultatis, watching. He gives me the slightest shake of the head.

Resentment boils deep in my chest. I'm a heartbeat away from exploding.

I calm myself through sheer force of will, and bow my head in grim acquiescence.

From the corner of my eye, I can see Eidhin looking between me and Dultatis, expression darkening. He whirls in disgust and stalks off to his usual position at the back of the class, whatever joy he'd taken from our victory vanished. I inhale, then make my way back to the other Sixths, refusing to look any of them in the eye. Any of the emotions I might see there—amusement, pity, whatever—could too easily provoke me right now.

I take up a position apart from everyone else, at the balcony railing, gazing out over the maze without really seeing it. In the background, Dultatis is picking a new pair to run. I don't pay any attention to who. I don't really care.

I watch the proceedings below alone, disinterested and brooding, as pair after pair run and fail over the next hour. I don't bother to follow the class as they move along the sides, trying to keep view of the proceedings: Ianix and Leridia, it turns out, were by far the most skilled of the group. Nobody comes close to breaking through.

"What do you think?"

I start; I've been so lost in my frustration that I didn't even notice Veridius sidling up to me. He's watching this latest run with absent curiosity, not looking at me, but there's no one else around he could be addressing. "Of?"

"Them." He indicates the flurry of motion below and around the sides of the chamber. "These runs."

I follow the current runner as he weaves pointlessly through passageways that are all but static, his partner up on the balcony already having lost three stones from his bracer. "It's basically just one person trying to sprint their way through, hoping the hunters and spotters will be dumb enough to make mistakes. A *lot* of mistakes. And whoever has the control bracer seems to be there more to yell coded instructions than to actually adjust the maze." It's a blunt assessment, I know, but I'm in no mood for tact. "They're terrible."

I expect a rebuke, but instead Veridius just shakes his head. "They're average," he corrects me. "Just because you are good at something does not make others bad at it." He winces as the boy below careens into a dead-end passageway, easily cut off by the single hunter in pursuit. "Well. Some of them are average."

I feel a grin pull at the corners of my mouth, but it quickly slips again. "Praeceptor Dultatis doesn't seem to share your opinion. That I'm good, I mean." I fail to keep my tone light. "At anything."

"Well. I fear that may be less about your performance, and more your name."

I frown, finally glancing across at him. "What?"

Veridius looks as though he's debating whether to expand on his statement. "Praeceptor Nequias and Praeceptor Dultatis were among those in charge here when I was a student," he says eventually. "Praeceptor Nequias was all but guaranteed to be the next Principalis, and he would have picked the Praeceptor over there to be his second in command. Then your uncle . . ." He exhales. "Well. His death had ramifications."

"So they were demoted." My voice goes flat as I understand what he's saying. "And they blame me?"

"They blame me. But they have no love for the name Telimus."

My brow crinkles in frustration. While I'm not inclined to take Veridius's word, what he's saying makes some sense: the Hierarchy would be keen to punish anyone who oversaw the death of a prized student, no matter the circumstances. And it would have been an internal disciplinary matter for Religion. Ulciscor wouldn't necessarily have known to warn me about a petty, long-held grudge like that.

"You can't do anything about it?" I'm only half asking. I know the answer.

"It's his class. His assessment." Veridius shakes his head. "But even if I could, the Academy is meant to reflect the challenges we face in life, not protect students from their realities. Most pyramids out there are full of Dultatises. And Iros," he adds meaningfully. "Whether the obstacles to our advancement arise from our ties or our actions, we need to learn to overcome them ourselves. It's not fair, but nor is the world." His expression is earnest, warm. Meant to encourage. "I imagine you already know something of that."

"I do." Veridius's gentle, understanding manner makes it tempting to keep talking. To unburden myself. But the more I say to him, the more chances I'm giving myself to slip up.

Veridius sees I'm not going to expound, and straightens, turning back toward the rest of the class. "This place is often empty, early in the mornings." He says it distractedly, talking more to the air than me. "And it's never locked. An enterprising student might find it a good time to practice."

He walks off, smiling and waving to another student he's spotted. I watch for a while. He's stopping and chatting with everyone. And everyone seems to welcome the conversation, is eager to bask in the Principalis's brief attention.

I resume my ruminating glower over the Labyrinth, turning Veridius's words over in my head. I can't see any trap to them.

But even that realisation is an aggravation. I'm pinned down here. Stymied. Helpless. I can train all I want, and never progress past Class Six. I can physically feel the frustration building. A shortening of breath, a tightening in my chest.

As I watch another student fail below, I come to a decision. I need to do something. I need to *act*.

Tonight, I'm going to take a look at the ruins beyond the Academy's wall.

XXXII

"YOU LOOK DISPLEASED," SAYS CALLIDUS AS HE SLIDES INTO the chair opposite me.

Our table in the mess is, as usual, vacant other than the two of us. The chatter of over a hundred and fifty students fills the large, graduated hall, though I deliberately have my back to the raised sections today, not wishing to endure more of the speculative looks I've been getting from the Sixths all morning. It's sunny outside and the view out over the ocean is spectacular, shining swells undulating far below, a vivid blue against the green of Solivagus's forests.

I sigh, pushing my plate away even as Callidus dips his bread in oil and begins enthusiastically devouring it. "You could say that." I tell him about my morning. Guiding Eidhin through the Labyrinth, only to be disqualified. Veridius's subsequent admission about Dultatis.

"Gods' graves. I'm sorry." He shakes his head in dismay. "No wonder half the Sixths keep peeking down this way. You really got Eidhin through the Labyrinth? On your first try?"

I allow some pride at Callidus's impressed tone. "Only because I happen to know Cymrian."

"Now you're just showing off." Callidus chews and swallows, his gaze moving over my shoulder. "Cymrian, you say."

"That's right." I twist, following the direction of his contemplation. Eidhin is sitting on the level up, with the rest of Class Six, and yet as usual, also apart. He doesn't notice our observation.

"Huh."

"Does that mean something to you?"

"Not really. Someone told me last trimester it's what he speaks, but the rest of what she said was so far-fetched, I didn't believe a word of it."

I cock my head to the side. "Such as?"

"He's meant to be from the mountains, somewhere. One of those small pockets past Cymr itself that never got properly civilised." He looks reluctant. "I *heard* that when the Fifth Legion came for them, his whole family—or his whole tribe, one of those—committed suicide rather than surrender. That he *helped* them. And then killed a dozen Praetorians before they caught him." He says it all in a low, uneasy voice. "But we both know not to put faith in rumours. He wouldn't be here if it were true."

"He'd be in a Sapper," I scoff in agreement. "Who told you that?"

"One of the Thirds. Just about everyone had heard it, though, after the first few weeks. It got around fast."

"Lies tend to do that."

He chuckles. "Truth."

"Did you ever talk to him? Not counting the time he tried to punch you, obviously."

Callidus smiles wryly. "No. I was in his class for all of a week." He says it with the tiniest twitch of the shoulders, as if it's of no consequence.

"Ah." I push at the food on my plate. "I get the impression he should be higher than Six."

Callidus chuckles again.

"That's funny?"

"It's funny that you're surprised."

I take a bite of my food, speaking around the mouthful. "What do you mean?"

Callidus shrugs. "The structure of this place is meant to mimic the Hierarchy. So how hard you work and how smart you are is . . . not irrelevant, obviously. But they're only factors in a much larger equation." He sees my sharpening curiosity and mistakes it for confusion. "You keep thinking of it as a fair system. Be good enough, and you'll be justly rewarded. The best rise to the top. All that rotting nonsense."

"You don't believe it?" I find it hard to strain the incredulity from my voice.

Callidus stares out through the massive archways to the left, over the glistening ocean. Considering his words.

"Do you think it's any different, out there?" He gestures to the west when he does eventually speak, in the direction of Caten. "Do you think that every single Septimus stuck in their position is less talented than every single Sextus? Or even less talented than the Sextus they're ceding to? A fair system only works if there's an unbiased means of assessing merit. When there is no pride or selfishness involved." He gives a soft snort, shaking his head. "Which means that fair systems cannot exist where people are involved."

He doesn't meet my gaze. He has to know how unpopular this line of conversation would be with most of the students here.

He's not wrong—I know this because I studied the Hierarchy for years and, moreover, did so from the outside, under people who were neither indoctrinated nor seduced by it. But it's a dangerous topic.

"You've read Thavius, I take it," I say noncommittally.

"Yes! The Academy's a perfect example of what he talks about: we're meant to be the brightest of the Republic, but almost all of us here are the children of senators and knights. We've been trained, educated, since we could walk. Of course we're going to be 'better' than some fifth son of an Octavus who's been ceding half his life, just so his family can get by. Especially at tests which are devised by the same people who trained us. Who decide what merit *is*." He eyes me. Apologetic. "And then when there are exceptions like yourself, who come from nothing, teach yourself, save half the rotting city—there's still the detritus like Dultatis to make sure that nothing changes."

I'm silent. Not sure if I should feel shame at the deception. My upbringing was as advantageous as anyone else's here. More so, maybe; my father had his pick of Sytrecian defectors as tutors, and my formal education began years before a Catenan's would. It's a necessary lie, of course, but one that feels oddly dirty here and now.

Callidus mistakes my discomfort. "I know this isn't what you want to hear. We can just leave it alone." He's awkward. As unsure as he is passionate. He believes what he's saying, but undoubtedly hasn't received a warm reception to these sorts of opinions in the past.

"No." I can't make myself dismiss the topic. Hearing someone else talk about it feels like fresh air. "Do you really think that?"

Callidus relaxes a little. "You saw what the Sevenths are like—they make no effort at all. Do you know why?"

"I assumed laziness."

"Well. Yes. Obviously." He makes a conceding motion. "But also because they know at the end of it all, they're guaranteed to be given the rank of at least Sextus." He scoots around the table to sit beside me, taking out a wax tablet and erasing what was on it, showing me as he starts to write. "You know who my father is?"

It's a rhetorical question. Callidus's father is Magnus Tertius Ericius. The Censor, responsible for the management of the Hierarchy's most important resource. The man charged with structuring and monitoring their pyramids.

"So the thing he has access to, which almost no one else does, is census data. All of it," Callidus continues. He begins scribbling numbers. "Based on a standard pyramid, how many people out of every hundred would you expect to be Octavii?"

"A little under ninety?"

He pauses, stylus hovering. "Yes." A touch of surprise in the word.

"I can do the math."

"Most people can't. Or don't bother. Or don't want to." He makes a face, then keeps going. "About ten should be Septimii, a couple of Sextii. Quintii and above don't even factor into it at those numbers, but you get the idea. Given that, with twenty-four million people in the Hierarchy, how many would you expect to be Octavii?"

"About . . . twenty-one million?"

"A little less. Then two and a half million Septimii. About half a million Sextii." He jots the numbers, then glances up at me to check that I'm following.

"So?" The ratios do sound a little off to me—I'd say that Sextii were more rare than that—but then, I've hardly shared the same space as senators and the like over the past few years.

He draws the symbol of the Hierarchy beside his numbers. Three lines meeting at an apex, forming a pyramid. Then he starts a new batch of figures.

"Regionally, most communities are arranged so that Sextus is the highest position; everyone else of importance out there is a Septimus. Census data from last year said that there are only sixty thousand Sextii, eight thousand Quintii, and about two hundred Quartii in the Republic. Not in Caten, or in Deditia. In the *entire* Republic." He looks at me significantly.

I frown, doing the calculations in my head. "That's . . ." I shake my head. "That doesn't change the Octavii and Septimii numbers much, but it means that one person in every *thousand* is a Sextii. Not one in every hundred."

"Exactly." Callidus draws a second, distorted pyramid beside the new numbers. The sides of this one curve sharply inward and then upward, leaving a thick base and a long, thin, barely tapering pillar to the top. "And it gets better. One of the other things my father and the Consuls manage is the Academy intake. How many students they're allowed to accept. It varies from year to year. Do you know why?"

"Enlighten me."

"It's based on a calculation of how many high-level openings will become available over the following eighteen months. Expected retirements, deaths, pyramid expansions due to population growth—anything that might become free that they can foresee leading to a position of influence." He's written a figure as he speaks; now he underlines it with vehemence. "This was the number, when we started first trimester."

"One hundred and seventy-four," I read. I do a quick sum in my head, but I'm not sure of the exact size of Class Seven. "The number of students here?"

"One more. Two students dropped out, first trimester. And you arrived." Callidus looks pleased I'm not arguing. "This is why position confirmations are on an eighteen-month cycle. They want to make sure that when we graduate, they can shift people around to more regional pyramids if needed. Make sure that there are enough *good* positions for all of us."

"Not quite the 'anyone can be a senator with enough hard work' story they tell the Octavii."

"You need Arventis more than Vorcian," agrees Callidus, invoking the gods of luck and effort, respectively. "And I know that it's just part of life—no different to being born smart, or strong, or handsome. But if you want to succeed here, Vis, you need to see things as they are. You can't expect to be promoted just because you should be. The Republic rewards people who take, not who deserve." Quoting Thavius again.

"A system built on promise, and therefore on greed," I murmur, supplying my own quote from the book. He's right. I've been training so hard, been so intent on being better than the others in Six, that I've lost sight of the fact that it won't necessarily help me. I'm going to need to find another way past Dultatis.

My resolve to get to the ruins tonight strengthens. If I can discover something important for Ulciscor, perhaps I can press him for help when we meet at the Festival of the Ancestors. Get him to exert influence over Dultatis, somehow.

I study the boy sitting beside me for a long moment.

"Can I ask you a question?"

Callidus screws up his face. He knows what I'm about to say. "Alright."

"How in the gods' graves did you end up in Seven?"

Callidus moves back over to his original position opposite me. Grabs his bread, takes a bite, chews. Waits to respond until he's swallowed. "What makes you think I don't belong there?"

I give him a stern look.

He smiles, despite himself. "Fine, fine." His gaze flicks around the room, as if concerned someone will be listening. He opens his mouth to say more, but instead the crystalline chime to end the meal shimmers through the room, sparking a flurry of movement as everyone stands. Callidus exhales. "A story for another time."

"I'll hold you to that."

"Sure. And Vis?" Callidus is talking quietly, so much so that I can barely hear him above the hubbub of sandals stamping their way to class. "Those numbers that I just told you? Don't repeat them to anyone. I'm not really supposed to talk about it."

I feel my brow crinkle, but he's serious. I nod.

We depart into our separate classes, me joining the flow of Sixths marching out of the Curia Doctrina and toward the Labyrinth. My mood's improved. I can't trust Callidus simply because he sees the rot beneath the Hierarchy's veneer—if he found out who I was, I doubt it would matter—but I still feel an affinity with the other boy. Genuine affection, even if it can't be accompanied by honesty.

It's the closest I've come to actual friendship in a long, long while.

The afternoon passes much as the morning did, deep in the bowels of the Labyrinth as I half watch run after unsuccessful run lit by the dramatic framing fire. Veridius doesn't return. I occasionally find myself scrutinising a brooding Eidhin from the corner of my eye, wondering at what Callidus told me about him. For Eidhin's part, he appears not to notice my examination, the muscular boy taking in the proceedings below as dourly as I. Neither of us is called upon to participate again, even as spotters or hunters.

Mostly, though, I use the time to mentally prepare myself for what I'm considering this evening. Once I've mucked out the stables, I just need to store the equipment I need, go to the dormitory as usual, and then wait for Eidhin and the other two boys in my room to fall asleep. There are stirrups in the stables; no one will notice if I take a pair, and they're strong enough to act as rope for the wall. A section of cataphract armour—an armoured saddle, basically—from the stable can cover the spikes on the top, too. I've already picked out a spot on the Academy boundary past the horse paddock that the lights don't touch. It's well away from any buildings.

Once I'm over, though . . . well. I try not to think about how little information I have about the ruins. How well they might be guarded, or worse, warded using Will. Or how long I can safely be gone before someone wakes and notices my absence.

The time to dwell makes me waver but every time I do, I glance across at Dultatis's smug face and firm my resolve. Callidus is right—there's not a lot I can do here. But I can't sulk, just sit on my hands and hope for the best. It's only two weeks until the Festival of the Ancestors, and if I want to advance, I need to give Ulciscor a reason to help.

It's time to find out what Religion is up to out there.

XXXIII

WHEN I WAS YOUNGER, YSA AND I WOULD OFTEN MAKE A game of escaping our studies through the twisting palace hallways, dodging servants and tutors alike who would be guaranteed to either order us back, or inform one of our parents. I was always better at it than she. There's a feeling in the air, when someone's about. An oncoming presence that I've always been able to sense in enough time to duck into the shelter of a doorway, or double back around the corner before they come into view.

A skill for darker times, these past few years.

The other three boys in my room have all settled into regular breathing patterns within an hour of the lantern winking out. I wait another few minutes just to be sure, then slide out of my cot, pull on my sandals, snatch up my empty leather satchel, and pad to the door. No one stirs.

I keep a sharp ear for anyone else awake as I slip through the corridors of the Sixths' dormitory, but everything's quiet. Soon enough I'm at the door to the external staircase, and out into the biting night air. There's a sliver of moon tonight, though it's diffused by a thin layer of cloud. I pause at the top of the stairs, letting my eyes adjust. Everything's coated in dulled silver, the bright reds, whites, and golds of the buildings all muted into shades. Nothing stirs below.

This is my last chance to turn around. To wait for a safer opportunity. There's a tacit curfew in the Academy, and if one of my roommates wakes and notices I'm gone, I doubt they'll hesitate to inform someone. Being caught roaming the Academy grounds this late will come with hard questions. Being caught past the wall will mean expulsion.

But if I can't advance, can't get a room to myself, a safer opportunity will never come. And the Festival of the Ancestors is looming. Even if Ulciscor can't get me past Dultatis, I at least need something to make sure he doesn't lose faith in me. Doesn't decide I'm a failed experiment, and send me to the Sappers.

I descend and start for the far side of the compound.

The violent illumination of the quadrum is something I give a wide berth, opting instead to keep to the trees that line the boundaries of the Academy. I spot occasional figures—Praeceptors or Octavii, I assume—but they're all in the distance, travelling well-lit paths and never once turning in my direction.

It's not long before I'm at the stables. I listen and then duck inside, risking the light to snatch up the sturdy set of leather stirrups, small lantern, and strip of armour I tucked away earlier. I'm gone again in moments, no alarm raised.

The wall is an imposing proposition from up close. Fifteen feet high and smooth, shadowed, Will-cut stone—no handholds. A forest of thin, vicious spikes at the top, painted grey by the dim moon. I consider them for several grim seconds before giving a last, cautious glance around, then unslinging my equipment.

It takes me a dozen attempts at leaping and flicking the stirrups upward, heart in mouth the entire time at the noise I'm making, before they finally settle over one of the spikes with a scratching clang. I give the leather a guarded tug, then test my full weight against it. Nothing budges.

I exhale. No cries of discovery so far. There are no moving parts atop the wall, so there can't be any simple Will-based alarms. I'm confident that there won't be any Conditional ones set, either; those would surely be far too expensive to add to every inch of the Academy's boundary, even for the security-conscious Veridius. Surely.

I hook the cataphract armour over one wrist, and start to climb.

My muscles cord as I pull myself up, the leather of the stirrups creaking, metal scraping against the spike it's caught on, the armour on my wrist clanking as it drags fiercely. It's loud against the surrounding hush but I forge on, reaching up and finding purchase on the edge of the wall with my fingers, arms trembling as I haul myself level. With a final heave, I sling the saddle up. It clatters over the top of the jagged array.

I have just enough anxious strength left to heave myself into an awkward, precarious sprawl atop the scaled armour. My side grazes one of the still-exposed spikes. It's keenly edged, sharp all the way along.

I hold my breath. Crane my neck around, gazing back into the shadows of the Academy. Despite the noise, there's no movement. Torches burn low at the entrance and in the quadrum, but the only other light is the soft silver filtering through the clouds.

I don't waste time staying exposed at the top of the wall, inching across the cataphract-covered spikes. Sweating as I twist and slither and try not to envisage what would happen were one to find its way through a gap in the plating. I stop only to carefully disengage the stirrup from its spike and secure it to another on the other side, letting it dangle. There won't be patrols outside the grounds, and I can do without the noise of attempting to hook it back on again when I return.

Finally I slide around until I can grab the stirrup with both hands and lower myself. Hold my breath once I hit the ground, eyes closed. Still no sound from the other side.

I'm out.

I turn to face a forest that's dense, dark, and immediate. The gloom is deeper here, cut only by the occasional beam that finds its way past a canopy of constantly shifting leaves. Rustling alone breaks the hush.

I unsling my small satchel and retrieve the lantern from it, quickly checking it survived the climb before shuttering it and striking it to light. The way ahead is far too dark, the terrain too treacherous, to depend on the moonlight.

I orient myself, and strike out eastward.

My tension doesn't abate as I press through a wall of bracken and then into the trees. I've been told by multiple people that alupi—the enormous, intelligent wolves indigenous to Solivagus—don't come close to the Academy, but I know that's a generalisation rather than a rule. Every shifting shadow beyond the lamplight makes me twitch.

It's fifteen minutes before I hit anything that looks like a path. Not much more than a well-worn animal trail, really, but I can see the vegetation's been cut away in places, and the hint of a heelprint or two in the dirt. It's probably the track that joins the main way between the Academy and the Transvect platform.

I follow it, ducking under stray branches that whip in the wind, skin itching at the worry of being stumbled upon at every turn. There's no one, though. The trail meanders but always keeps to the same general direction. I endure another ten minutes, at least, of picking my way anxiously forward.

And then up ahead, a hazy nimbus over the trees.

I slow. Extinguish my lantern, stow it, and depart the trail in favour of thick brush, ignoring the way the dry twigs dig at my skin. My ears strain, but there's only the scratching of branch against branch in the breeze, the skittering of fallen leaves.

I finally come to a stop, crouching, as the source of the light emerges from behind the last screen of shrubbery.

The ruins of an ancient structure—or structures—stretch out before me, cracked and moss-coated rubble covering a clearing that must be five hundred feet wide. Most of the broken grey stone is no higher than my waist, but in the middle of it all stands a tall domed building, several holes in its curved roof the only immediate sign of damage. It's ringed by a dozen bright lanterns, the gently swaying lights casting shifting blacks through the scattered stone nearby.

I watch for a minute. Five. Nothing moves. In the shadows, I spot a door waiting at the end of the short colonnade leading into the structure. The door's intact. Closed.

I circle the edge of the clearing, concerned about those lanterns. They could have been lit via Will from anywhere—be for precaution or convenience, rather than indicating someone's presence. But if Religion is willing to waste Will and oil doing that, then there will be security measures, too.

I don't see anything unusual in my tortuous circuit. Walls guarded these ruins once, but no longer: only a line of rubble remains as a barrier to the space beyond. The outer sections appear to be the remnants of a vast complex. Away from the lanterns, diffuse moonlight paints jagged stone. A chill breeze off the ocean unsettlingly rustles the long grass that grows between the boulders.

Most concerningly, there are no other obvious entrances into the central building. Doors are one of the easiest things to secure with Will: they can be harmonically linked either with an alarm on the other end, or simply with something so heavy they're impossible to open.

But there's nothing else out here to investigate. No other option, unless I turn back.

I creep from cover, and start picking my way across to the domed building.

Moving anything here could trigger a Will-linked alarm, so I take care where I step, ensuring I tread only on grass. Twice I take the time to clamber over stone where a more obvious path would require shifting rubble aside. There are still no sounds other than those whispered by the wind. I twitch and duck at every imagined movement, feeling far too exposed as I traverse the pool of light cast by the lanterns and then pass into the murk of the colonnade.

Once I'm at the door I stop, peering back out into the woods before inspecting the entrance. Up close, the building is in worse repair than I realised. The stone has crumbled away around the edges of most of the bricks, and there's more green than grey visible. It's not Hierarchy-era, that's for sure. It's been here for hundreds of years. More, maybe.

It could even be pre-Cataclysm, just as Ulciscor claimed. From the era of the Aurora Columnae, made before recorded history.

Now my eyes have adjusted, I can see the door's not stone as I first thought, but rather solid steel, cool to the touch. That's good: steel is much, much harder to imbue. Strange symbols are inscribed on its surface. Another language, I think. I don't recognise it.

I stand there, calculating. The door could be locked, in which case my evening is at an end. If it's not, there's still a good chance that opening it will trigger some kind of alarm back at the Academy. A self-imbued Veridius taking the trail at a run could probably be here in twenty minutes. Call it fifteen, to be safe.

Not much time to see what's inside.

I start a mental count and, blood pulsing in my ears, push.

The door swings open at a touch. Silent. Faint light spills out and I take a nervous half step back. There are no shouts though, no movement or sound. I slip inside, trying to mix the need for haste with prudence. There's only a single, large chamber. A circle of marble columns rings its centre, perhaps twenty feet in diameter. Leaning against the columns are tools—pickaxes, shovels. Rope.

I squint. The light's off, a dull green tint to it. As I creep farther in, I can see its source: a gaping hole at the centre of the circle. A rope tied to one of the columns vanishes down into the area of missing floor, which looks as though it has been smashed away.

Fourteen minutes.

I force myself to ignore the natural drag of caution and hurry forward into the green light. The hole leads to a tunnel not too far below, and the rope dangles to its floor. I grab it, test it, and swing myself down, palms burning from the speed of the descent. My sandals meet stone with an echoing thud.

I shake out my legs to lessen the smarting impact of the landing as I look around, though its sting is quickly forgotten as I take in the long passageway.

Everything's lit down here, but not by lanterns or flame.

Writing carves its way through the stone on both walls, and each and every letter glows a sickly green. Thousands upon thousands of words. Not carefully etched, though. Not done by an artisan's hands. These are scrawled. Uneven. Rushed.

Thirteen minutes.

"What in all hells?" I whisper it as I edge closer, though there's no one down here to hear me. I've never heard of anything that can illuminate stone like this. And the writing . . . it seems deep, engraved, and yet the way it flows speaks of someone hurriedly scribbling. Farther down, I can see words giving way to diagrams, complex drawings with more glowing notes scratched around them.

It's not a language I've come across before, I conclude after another minute of assessment. There's nothing familiar, no spark of recognition at the forms. I move my mouth silently to sound out the words, but some of the letters are completely foreign to me, rendering many of them even phonetically mysterious.

The passage stretches out in both directions, but I jog toward where the writing is broken by the series of small diagrams. These again have the appearance of being hurriedly sketched, yet are incredibly detailed—schematics of some kind, I think, dozens of lines and arrows criss-crossing a sea of notations. Strange symbols repeat on every single one. Numbers, perhaps? A sequence of instructions to create . . . something. The various stages of construction aren't clear enough for me to divine exactly what.

Eleven minutes.

I rock on my heels, the fingers of my self-imposed time limit resting light around my neck. Torn between studying the images for a better understanding of them, and pressing on to see what else this place might contain. This won't help Ulciscor, so the latter wins out. I tear my gaze from the strange glowing schemata and set out at a cautious trot, moving as fast as I dare while staying wary for any signs of company. The tunnel, and the writing, stretches unbroken for as far as I can see. I start to regret my decision. Every second I move away from the entrance is one I'm going to have to spend getting back.

I keep going for another two minutes, each step increasingly anxious. How far does this shaft go? It runs straight and narrow; smaller passageways occasionally split off but those are cloaked in darkness, unappealing even if I had time to spare. There are more diagrams amid the pulsing green scrawl that light my way: some are small, while others consume several feet of wall. I don't give any of them more than a cursory look as I pass. Whatever they're depicting, it's alien to me.

Until, that is, I spot a series of familiar symbols.

I stop. Frown. Take a few seconds to place them, but once I do, the surrounding pictures begin to take shape.

The symbols are the same as the ones in the Labyrinth.

And the diagram, I think, shows how to make the bracer that controls it.

My hand itches for something to copy this down. Instead I study it fiercely, trying to etch every line into memory. I don't know what this means, exactly, but it must mean *something*. Ulciscor will want to know about it in as much detail as I can give him.

I've almost resolved to turn back when I realise the tunnel ahead widens into an opening. I break into a jog.

Eight minutes.

The end of the passage is an archway that segues into a much larger space beyond. There's something written across it in that same glowing green scrawl, but the language is different. This one's recognisable. Not Common, but an old form of Vetusian. Native to this area, once.

In trying to become God, they created Him. I think that's the translation, anyway.

I creep the last few feet and peer through the arch. The hall beyond is enormous, more than fifty feet high and at least three hundred long. No writing in here but still lit entirely in green, thanks to the rows of dimly illuminated cavities cut into both walls. Maybe ten feet high and wide, and equally far apart. There are tens of them. Hundreds.

It's their contents that captures my attention, though. Makes my breath catch and blood freeze.

In each one, skewered by a long black blade through the chest, is a single, naked corpse.

I'm motionless, wide-eyed, for five seconds. Ten. My hands tremble as I prop myself up against the edge of the entrance. The green light is coming from the slabs of stone against which the men and women lie, making it seem as though they're in some sort of garish display. Little more than silhouettes, and yet there's no mistaking what I'm seeing.

They're not skeletal, either, I realise faintly. Not shrivelled from dusty centuries of waiting in this tomb. From what I can make out of their faces and bodies, these people look as though they could have been killed yesterday.

Seven minutes.

"Rotting *gods*," I whisper, mostly to steady myself. Whatever Religion are doing down here, I don't want any part of it. But Ulciscor's going to want to know more. Will value detail.

I take an unwilling step into the hall. Two. My footfalls echo. The imagined eyes of the dead bore into me. I ignore my crawling skin and break into a hurried stride, moving to the closest of the open coffins.

Features resolve as I near. The man was square-jawed, athletic. Black hair is combed back neatly from his face. His skin is smooth, unblemished save for where the darkly glinting sword pierces the skin above his heart. His eyes are closed. There's no blood.

I stop six feet away. The blade is entirely obsidian, I think. Worth a small fortune.

Six minutes.

I mutter a low, frustrated curse. I need more time. At a dead run, it's not more than a couple of minutes back to the rope, then another two to be up and out into the safety of the forest. I tear my gaze from the corpse and take another look around.

Now I'm farther in, I realise that the bodies don't take up the entirety of the room: there's a slender section in the centre of the far end which is dark, solid. Part of the wall there looks different. Shimmers.

I hurry across the vast expanse of the hall. The errant space between the macabre green-lit coffins is about twenty feet wide, and there's a plate set into its centre, roughly a man's height and width, which appears to be metal rather than stone. Not steel, though. Bronze? More strange words like on the walls outside are inscribed into it, though the writing's different. Fastidiously neat, etched with a steady, meticulous hand.

I stand close to the wall, squinting in the dim as I try to make out anything familiar. The metal's tarnished. I impatiently reach forward and brush my fingers against the cool surface, trying to make some of the symbols clearer.

There's a tingling shock where my skin makes contact. I snatch my hand back.

A low, resounding *thrum* shakes the room.

I retreat a step and then spin as new light blooms behind me. The stone floor in the centre of the hall undulates with white light. Glistens and ripples, as though water has formed and somehow ignited. Those swells are quickly coalescing, drawing themselves into three large, separate pools. Outcroppings of light start to rise within them. Firm into shapes.

Through the shock, I recognise the contours in the left-most one.

It's Solivagus.

The likeness to the island becomes more obvious as sections of the liquid light pull upward, hardening into peaks and troughs to create impossibly detailed mountain ranges, valleys. Lakes and rivers and headlands. Individual trees. A topology I'm partly familiar with from looking out the window of the Curia Doctrina.

The other two pools are forming land masses, too. The one on the right seems identical, but as I look closer, I can see that the contours differ. There are sloping beaches to the north, rather than sheer bluffs. A mountain missing in the west. An entire section of forest cleared in the shadow of a cliff, a small town nestled there.

The centre-most image differs significantly from the other two. There are no trees, though there are similarities to the land's shape in the east. To the west, though, there's nothing but a crater, barren except for an unsettling, hovering sphere in its centre. To scale, it's the size of a small mountain.

I study it in bewilderment, then let my eyes trace the shoreline to the south. It matches the two maps on either side.

That's Solivagus, too, then. But utterly destroyed.

Even as the realisation comes, a rasping voice starts drifting through the hall. Speaking Vetusian, I recognise after a startled moment. The words just slow and precise enough for me to translate.

"Obiteum is lost. Do not open the gate. Synchronous is death. Obiteum is lost. Do not open the gate. Synchronous is death."

And on. And on.

I whirl, skin crawling, looking for the source. There is none. Soon another voice joins it, perfectly in unison. Soft and harsh and sad. And then another. The sound fills the hall. I flee, skirting the brilliant map, fearful of what may happen if I touch it. The illumination from it overwhelms the dim green, casting the corpses to the sides in sharp relief. I catch a glimpse of a man to my right.

His eyelids flutter open. There's nothing but bloodied sockets beneath.

Cold fear claws at my chest. I stare at the body, frozen. It stares back. Unmoving. Ebony blade jutting through its chest.

"Obiteum is lost. Do not open the gate. Synchronous is death. Obiteum is lost. Do not open the gate. Synchronous is death . . ."

Its lips are moving.

I stumble back, almost fall. My gaze goes to the body in the next cavity. It's watching me with an eyeless gaze, too. And the next. And the next. All whispering.

"Obiteum is lost. Do not open the gate. Synchronous is death. Obiteum is lost. Do not open the gate. Synchronous is death. Obiteum is lost. Do not open the gate. Synchronous is death. Obiteum is lost. Do not open the gate. Synchronous is death. Obiteum is lost. Do not open the gate. Synchronous is death. Obiteum is lost. Do not open the gate. . . ."

I run.

Back through the tunnel of pulsing scrawls, lungs burning, not looking back. I've left the whispers behind but I don't stop; I reach the rope, leap at it, and haul myself up with manic energy, swinging wildly, panicked breathing loud in my own ears. The skin on my hands hasn't recovered from the slide down and it hurts but I ignore it, wrenching myself upward again and again until my feet are scrabbling for purchase on the floor above.

It's only when I'm through the hole and into the perceived safety of the upper building that I calm enough to bring myself back under control. I collapse with my back against the cold stone, gasping, letting my stinging hands shake. Just for a few seconds. Just until I can find the strength to roll and lurch to my feet again. I've lost track of the count, but I need to get out of here. Now.

I flee into the crisp night air, pausing only to yank the steel door closed again, the warm, natural light of the lanterns ringing the building feeling like home after the nightmares inside. I'm quickly past their illumination and into the silver-coated ruins.

I'm halfway to the forest when I hear the faint, sporadic gasps of breathless conversation coming closer.

I skid down behind one of the broken walls, hunkering deep into shadow as another muted exchange filters into the clearing, this one louder, though the words remain indistinguishable. Two men, I think. The rapid crunching of footsteps echoes. They're approaching at a sprint.

Then the footsteps slow. Break into the clearing and falter to silence as fresh light creeps over the rubble.

"See anything?" It's Veridius, exertion straining his voice. I risk a peek around the corner of my boulder. A torch is hovering aloft in front of Veridius and his companion, ten feet up, lighting the area. Veridius himself is scanning the ruins grimly. His eyes are black. Three obsidian daggers hang at his waist.

"Maybe . . . just let me . . . breathe first." The other man is swarthy and thin, around Veridius's age. Unlike the Principalis though, he's doubled over, hands on his knees. Uncoloured horn-rimmed glasses perch on his bird-like nose, reflecting the burning light.

Veridius responds by sending his torch higher still, letting it swirl above the ruins. My shadows melt briefly away, but I'm concealed from the two men by stone, and I hold my nerve. After thirty seconds of fruitless observation, the Principalis scowls. "I'm going inside. Stay back in the trees and keep watch. If I'm not out in ten minutes, or someone comes in after me, go back and contact Xan. He'll know what to do." Before the still-winded man can protest, Veridius moves past him into the lantern-light, stretching out his hand. The floating torch glides toward him; the Principalis takes it from the air without breaking stride, then pushes open the steel door and vanishes inside.

The next few minutes stretch interminably. The man keeping watch—he's vaguely familiar, but not a Praeceptor or staff as far as I know—does as he's told, disappearing into the nearby shadows of the trees. I have no way of seeing where he's looking, can't tell if it's safe to move. All I can do is wait, and breathe, and let my still-trembling hands come back under control. I don't think about what I saw in there. Can't dwell on it. Not yet.

Veridius reappears soon enough, his frown turned from forbidding to thoughtful. He waves vaguely toward the forest, a signal to his companion. "They're all there, Marcus."

"You're sure?" The other man, Marcus, emerges from the trees, brushing bits of leaves from his tunic. He joins Veridius, nodding in apologetic acknowledgment to the Principalis's reproachful look. "Alright. Rotting gods, that's a relief. But then what set off the alarm?"

"Who. *Who* set off the alarm." Veridius is talking absently, still thinking. "Someone was here, not ten minutes ago. Everything's still lit up." His gaze sharpens and sweeps the ruins. I jerk back, though there's no way he can see me in the darkness.

"You think the island's been breached again?" The tension in Marcus's voice is obvious.

"Perhaps." There's a long pause. "Go back to the Academy, as fast as you can. Taedia will be on her way here; get her to turn around and check that none of the Thirds or Fourths are missing from the girls' dormitory—if she asks why, tell her to talk to me *after* she's done it. You go and check on the boys. Thirds and Fourths. And Sixths," he adds, almost an afterthought. "I'm going to look around inside some more."

"Be careful."

I calculate furiously as the crunch of Marcus's hurrying footsteps fades away. He was already tired from running here, has to relay a message to Praeceptor Taedia on top of that. I can still beat him back. Maybe.

Veridius, true to his word, is heading back into the ruins. I wait until the steel door has shut behind him.

Then I run.

I try to vary my progress along the path between bursts of sprinting and brisk walking, all too aware that I'm trailing Marcus. It's unlikely that I'll catch the man, but I have to countenance the possibility of him stopping to rest, or at least pausing while he talks to Praeceptor Taedia.

It's five minutes before I reach the point I carefully noted when I first found the path, and another ten of me crashing heedlessly through brush and over uneven ground, risking a turned ankle in the heavily dappled moonlight, before I miraculously reach the Academy wall with only myriad scratches and shredded clothes to show for my recklessness. My chest heaves as I drink in the sight of it. Everything considered, I've made good time.

My makeshift rope, barely visible in shadow, dangles not a hundred feet from where I emerge; I rush over to it, focusing more on speed than stealth, all too aware that seconds could make the difference between safety and discovery. Even if he stopped somewhere along the way, Marcus is probably back at the Academy entrance by now. I just have to hope he decides to check the upper floors of the dormitory first.

I leap and snatch the stirrup at an angle, allowing my momentum to swing me up. It works, but when I reach for the edge of the wall I'm already higher than I realise, and tired, and I brush my urgently grasping hand against a spike instead. Pain flares, hot and sharp, along my palm. I bite back a curse and almost lose my grip, almost fall. Somehow, desperation overcoming pain, I haul myself up using fingertips alone.

I'm bleeding copiously as I unhook the stirrup from the spike, then lift the scaled armour, flinging them into nearby bushes below with an uncomfortably loud clatter. I'll be able to duck out and collect them tomorrow night when I'm at the stables again. A dark smear on the top of the wall glints even in the dim light, but there's no time to clean it.

I jump for the grass of the Academy, rolling to lessen the impact before scrambling to my feet and sprinting for the dormitory, wary for any signs of light or movement, half nursing my hand. Dark droplets shake loose as I run.

It takes me another three minutes at a lung-burning sprint to get back to the dormitory, only once having to deviate from a straight line when I spot some distant figure hurrying through the quadrum. There's nobody in sight, but there are lights burning in the windows of the top floor. Too many.

I finally slow my mad dash, pausing in the shadows of the parkland outside the tall building, tearing a limp strip of tunic off to wrap my smarting hand. I'm a mess: dirty, sweaty, bleeding, arms scratched, and clothes torn. But I can fix the worst of that by quickly rinsing myself in the fountain at the entrance; the scratches I can cover, and I have spare clothes. My hand's a problem—the cut's deep, throbbing—but I'll just have to hope Marcus is not doing more than a cursory inspection.

Lights begin to wink out on the top floor, and the upper door to the external staircase opens. I shrink back as a slim figure hurries down to the next level, disappearing inside. This is going to be close.

I scrub myself madly in the fountain, pulling off my tunic and using it to towel myself dry, anxiety a shield against the sharp chill of the night. Then I'm taking the stairs two at a time, quietly as I can. There are voices drifting from the floor housing the Fourths. Lamplight fills their windows.

I'm up the stairs to the first floor. Inside, padding down the hallway to my room. Nerves start to mix with disbelieving jubilation. I'm going to make it.

I slip into my room, pull the door shut behind me, and turn to find Eidhin twisting at his desk and staring at me.

Neither of us say anything, frozen. Eidhin's shuttered lamp is bright enough to show me naked to the waist, carrying the very obviously bloodied tunic that I used to clean myself. His gaze goes from me, to the tunic, and then back to me again.

"Strange dream," he says eventually in Cymrian. Softly enough that the other two boys don't wake, but firmly. Meaningfully.

Then he turns to his desk and bows his head over the book he's reading.

I stare at his back for a half-second longer, then scurry across to my bed, pulling a fresh tunic from my satchel and hiding the soiled and torn one in its place. I have clean clothing on and am beneath the blankets, eyes forced closed, within half a minute.

It's not two minutes after that when our door creaks open again, and bright lamplight swings into the room. I can hear one of the sleeping boys mutter and turn restlessly at the intrusion.

"Ah. Eidhin." I recognise Marcus's voice. "I didn't expect anyone to be awake."

A chair scrapes. "Sextus Carcius?" Eidhin evidently recognises the man. "Why are you here?" It's said in halting Common. Almost as many words as I've heard from the burly boy all at once.

"Have you seen or heard anything out of the ordinary tonight?" I can feel Marcus's gaze sweeping over the beds. I focus on deep, steady breathing. The slash across my bound palm aches. "There's been a small disturbance off-campus. Nothing to be concerned about, but I need to make sure no students were involved."

"I woke only . . . hour ago. Nothing since."

"You're sure?" An awkward cough. "I don't have to remind you of the consequences to your people of lying. Or the benefits of cooperating."

"You do not. I am sure." There's more than an intimation of anger in the deliberate, cold response.

"As you say." A long pause, Marcus evidently considering. "No need to wake the others, then. But do let me or the Principalis know if you hear anything." The lamplight begins to retreat, then lingers in the doorway, casting half the room into deep shadow. "And get some rest, son. Even the Aedhu need more sleep than this."

The door shuts. Footsteps pad away down the hall to the next room.

I don't move, even after I'm confident Marcus has gone, half expecting Eidhin to demand an explanation. There's no sound from the other boy, though. Just the occasional scratching of a page being turned.

After a minute, my pounding heart eases enough for me to breathe and take stock. The scratches on my arms are light enough that they should be barely visible by morning, and I can wear clothing over them. I'll need to dispose of my torn and bloodied tunic, but I have plenty of time alone at the stables during dinner. I can burn it then without anyone being the wiser.

The wound on my left hand is another problem entirely. The cut is deep, is going to hamper me. And I'm fairly sure it's still bleeding. I'm probably going to have to go to Ulnius and have it tended in the morning. He's going to ask how it happened.

I don't think I left much blood on the spike atop the Academy wall, but if anyone notices it, the timing of my injury is going to look more than suspicious. I can't risk that. Not with what I saw out there tonight.

Whatever it actually was.

I repress a trembling shudder as my mind unwillingly returns to the crypt beneath the ruins. I didn't imagine those bodies opening their eyes. Did I? Their faces were shadowed before that strange map appeared. I was flustered, panicked.

Any momentary doubt is quickly stilled by the memory of their message, though. That *whispering*. My fear didn't conjure that. Another reference to Obiteum that I don't understand, the same word as in Caeror's hidden message to Ulciscor. And a clear warning.

I'm quite certain their eyes had been removed, too. Strange and unsettling, but also familiar. I can't help but wonder whether Lanistia's accident during her Iudicium is somehow tied to all this.

There's so much to sort through. My mind races, battling with exhaustion.

I don't get much sleep.

XXXIV

NECESSITY HAS MADE ME INTO A CONVINCING ACTOR, OVER the past few years.

The trick, I've decided, is to make myself believe what I'm saying is true. Not just tell a lie, but envisage the circumstances in my head. Imagine how I'd feel, what I would have done. Erase the truth of my past and replace it with a false one, not simply layer it over the top.

So when I trip going down a stair while carrying my breakfast, slamming into the student in front of me, I make sure not to brace for the impact. My chin hits the floor. Pottery smashes. And when my left hand folds awkwardly underneath my body, still holding the knife I was carrying all too casually, I don't stop it from digging into the raw, still-seeping wound I've been hiding since rising this morning.

I don't have to fake my agonised roar.

I curl around my hand in the messy aftermath, writhing, food and shattered plates all around me. Conversation in the mess has all but stopped. Blood wells, any scabbing formed from the previous night vanished.

Several Fourths—I'm on their level, currently—peer at me, murmuring among themselves as they spot the blood trickling down my wrist. I hear a snigger from somewhere lower. One of the Sixths, probably.

"Idiot." The student who I collided with picks herself up and brushes crumbs from her top. She's a Fifth. Short and wiry. I don't know her name. She glances disinterestedly at the blood dripping from my closed fist. "Watch where you're going, Sixth. And learn how to carry utensils." That brings a low chuckle from some of the Fourths.

She shakes her head in disgust and walks off back toward the kitchen, presumably to replace her ruined meal. Praeceptor Ferrea's shadow takes her place. "Is it bad?"

I show her my palm. She recoils, then waves me toward the door. "The infirmary, then. Ulnius will see to it."

I gain my feet awkwardly and hurry off as one of the Octavii from the kitchen approaches with mop in hand. The chattering conversation of the room has returned to its usual dull thunder, though I do see a few people still watching me. Callidus down at our table, looking genuinely concerned. Aequa giving me sideways glances from over in the corner. Eidhin observing my departure with an inscrutable expression as I pass him and the other Sixths.

I reach the door to the infirmary and use the small bell on the wall, which is Will-locked to another one out back. A minute later, Ulnius hurries into view.

"Vis Telimus." The white-cloaked man's cheer fades and his brow furrows as he takes in the way I'm cradling my hand, immediately limping forward and grasping my wrist gently. "Show me."

I unfurl my fingers, wincing as blood pulses from the newly reopened wound.

Ulnius guides me over to a nearby seat, then grabs a cloth, dips it in a bowl of water, and starts dabbing away the blood. "How did this happen?"

"I tripped on the stairs at breakfast. Cut myself on my knife."

His daubing falters for a heartbeat, and I can tell there's something he doesn't like about my explanation. "Sharp knife," he observes after a moment.

"I fell right on it. I was holding it by the blade," I admit sheepishly.

He doesn't stop what he's doing, doesn't look up at me. "Lucky, then. An inch lower, and you could have slit your wrist. Higher, and you might have lost the use of your fingers." He grabs his tools, eyes darkening as he starts to suture with a steady hand, quick and neat. "Funny coincidence. The Principalis was asking if I'd seen any unusual injuries only an hour ago."

"Unusual? Like what?" I grunt through gritted teeth.

"He didn't say."

I force a grin through the pain. "I'm assuming self-inflicted wounds due to idiocy don't count."

"They do not." He crouches in front of me. Fixes me with a look. "But you need to be more careful."

I lose my smile. Nod into the meaningful silence that follows.

Satisfied, Ulnius straightens, adjusting his white cloak. "This won't heal quickly—you won't be able to use it normally for a couple of weeks." He begins dressing it. "Come back every second evening to get the bandages changed. Don't use it unless you have to."

"What about mucking out the stables?"

"If that's something you're meant to be doing, then it falls into the category of 'you have to.' Just find me straight away if the stitches come loose."

I expected as much. "Understood."

"Then we're done." He finishes the dressing with a cheerful flourish. "Stronger together, Vis. I hope not to see you for a couple of days."

I chuckle. "The same to you."

Alone once I'm out in the hallway, I lean against the stone wall and exhale, letting myself stop and just gaze out over the grey, crashing ocean far below. My hand's aching. I'm exhausted. I still feel a juddering chill every time I dare think about what happened last night. And I'm about to face a full day of watching the other Sixths run the Labyrinth, while I'm given no further chance to prove myself.

Life is far from good. But for now, at least, it seems my position here is safe.

※ ※ ※

"MADE IT ALL THE WAY DOWN HERE WITHOUT SLICING YOUR-self open," observes Callidus through a mouthful of fish as I slide into the seat opposite him at our regular table. "Well done."

I glower at him. "I suppose I earned that."

"Rotting gods you did. If I've seen a more spectacular failure of basic human movement before, I don't remember it." Callidus's humour slips to at least a hint of sympathy as he motions to my bandaged hand. "How bad is it?"

"Bad enough to hurt. Not bad enough to get me out of stable duty."

"Ah. The worst amount of bad," Callidus commiserates. He leans back, stretching lazily. "Other than that, I assume this morning went about as well as usual?"

"I was late because of the accident, so at least I didn't have to sit through *everyone* failing." The more I see of my classmates' clumsy attempts to run the Labyrinth, the more frustrated I become at being stuck in Six. "Honestly, I probably came out ahead."

Callidus chuckles and looks about to say something more when he gets a strange look on his face, attention suddenly locked onto something over my shoulder. I twist to see the Thirds coming down the stairs. Iro peers down his aquiline nose at me as he spots my inspection. Indol gives me a slight acknowledgment.

My eyes, somewhat instinctively, go to Emissa. Her long brown hair is bound up tightly today; the Thirds are probably about to do some sparring or other physical work. She's deep in conversation with Belli, but as they reach our level, she murmurs something and breaks off, veering over. Belli, looking surprised and mildly uncomfortable, trails after her.

"Catenicus." Emissa stops at the end of our table, bright green eyes focused squarely on me. She smiles as she says the name, dimples forming. "You got all the way to eating without serious injury this time, I see. Nicely done."

"Callidus already made that joke," I tell her with mock sourness, recovering from my surprise. Emissa's never gone out of her way to talk to me away from the stables before.

"Of course he did." She sighs, still smiling, glancing briefly at my friend. "How are you, Callidus?"

Callidus doesn't realise he's being addressed at first. His gaze, I realise, is fixed rather firmly on Belli, who's standing a pace farther back and is looking around disinterestedly, intent on showing she's not really part of the conversation. When Callidus does register Emissa's words he blinks, as if waking, then issues a half smile in her direction. "Afternoon, Emissa. Better than him, I suppose." He flicks his thumb in my direction.

Emissa agrees with an amused quirk of her eyebrows, then turns back to me. "I was hoping you might settle something for us. Rumour has it that you ran the Labyrinth yesterday with Eidhin over there"—she jerks her head toward the Sixths, not looking—"and won? On your first attempt?"

I break from giving Callidus a pointedly speculative look, which he's studiously ignoring, though the flush to his cheeks indicates he saw it. "That's right."

"But then you got disqualified for cheating?"

"We got disqualified because Dultatis is an ass." I say the words louder than I should, but fortunately, either no one hears or no one disagrees. "I just used Cymrian to call out instructions, rather than code. It should have been counted."

Emissa glances back at her red-headed companion. "See, Bel?"

Belli focuses her attention on Emissa, as if Callidus and I aren't part of the conversation at all. "If he got disqualified, it doesn't count. And we're still just taking his word for it."

"Except the part about Dultatis," I note.

"Except the part about Dultatis," agrees Emissa solemnly.

Belli fidgets, and I notice for the first time that her right hand is missing a finger. She registers my gaze and tucks the offending limb behind her, a familiar enough pose that I realise she must do it fairly often. Then she snorts, glancing between Emissa and I before ostentatiously rolling her eyes. "He was only up against Sixths, anyway." She stalks off, mass of waist-length red curls bouncing with the motion.

Emissa lowers her voice conspiratorially. "We were the fastest to clear the Labyrinth, during the entry exams—it's part of what got us into Class Three. We made it through on our fourth attempt." She glances ruefully at Belli's disappearing form. "Belli's not so bad. She can just be a little *competitive*, sometimes. Doesn't like to believe anyone can do a thing better than she can."

Callidus nods in absent agreement until he sees my glance and catches himself. Emissa doesn't seem to notice, attention back on me.

"I'm surprised you even heard about it." I'm pleased word has spread. If the other Praeceptors take note, it will help my case for advancement.

"People talk. Especially about you." Her bright green eyes dance. Amused by my genuinely surprised look. "They really don't know what to make of you, you know. Between the naumachia and what you did to Eidhin, running the Labyrinth one minute and stupidly injuring yourself the next . . . well. You're not *boring*."

I make a small, bemused motion. "Better than the alternative, I suppose."

"Emissa!" It's Belli, impatient as she waits at the bottom of the stairwell out of the mess.

Emissa sighs. Looks about to go, then pauses. "How bad was your hand? Really?"

"Just a cut. Won't stop me from doing anything."

"Good." She flashes another smile at me. "I'll be seeing you."

"Good to talk!" Callidus calls after her, not missing the fact that she didn't even glance in his direction upon departure. He laughs as Emissa makes a rude gesture without turning around, then focuses back on me. His glee is from ear to ear. "Someone's popular."

"Not interested," I lie firmly. He's been making similar intimations ever since I mentioned Emissa helping me in the stables.

"Liar."

I ignore him. "You know, I never noticed before that Belli is missing a finger. Did that happen recently?"

"No. She was bitten by a Yellowsnake when she was thirteen. They had to amputate to save the hand."

I feel a smirk pulling at the corner of my lips.

Callidus scowls as he spots it. "She gets chilblains from it in the winter. Everyone in the class knew," he mutters defensively, flushing.

There's a brief silence. He seems a strange mixture of eager to talk and genuinely uncomfortable, when it comes to Belli. "You never did get to tell me why you're a Seventh," I say eventually, overcoming my inclination to tease him. "You were obviously in Class Three long enough to be on friendly terms."

"A few weeks." Callidus takes another bite of his meal, chewing. He swallows. "Alright. You swear to keep this to yourself?" When I confirm I will, he leans forward, lowering his voice. "It's mostly because of my father."

I grunt. Unsurprised.

"How much do you know about the political situation in Caten at the moment?"

"Not a lot," I hedge. "Ulciscor mentioned there have been some conflicts in the Senate lately, but I got the impression it's not anything new."

"Yes and no. There's always been tension between the senatorial pyramids, but things have been getting worse over the past few years. Much worse. At least according to my father." Callidus keeps his voice low, though he's in no danger of being overheard amid the hubbub of the mess. "Military have always been the preeminent of the three, agreed?"

"Of course." A Military Sextus and a Governance Sextus are technically equals, but put them in the same room, and there's no question who would be considered superior.

"That's because the Republic is built on expansion." Callidus warms to the explanation. "Military either win a war or negotiate a treaty, and then Caten has a fresh influx of wealth for the next few years—gold, resources, Octavii. Their successes stocked the treasury, paid the armies. They were the reason we kept getting stronger, were able to constantly do *more*. They were the heart that kept our blood pumping."

"*Were*," I repeat, picking up on the past tense he's using. I think for a moment. "But now there's no one left to conquer?"

"Exactly." Callidus is pleased I'm following the logic. "Which means no more riches or glory. Less importance, fewer funds. Garrisons need to be reduced, standing armies disbanded—but that hasn't been happening. Not anywhere near as fast as the rest of the Senate wants, anyway."

"Oh?"

Callidus nods grimly. "It's tense. When the armies disappear, Military's power goes along with them, and Military have made it clear they have no interest in letting that happen. Governance and Religion could veto funds for the troops, of course, *if* they were willing to work together—but as things stand, that could be what Military are waiting for. Nothing would encourage an army to march on Caten like the threat of not being paid." He takes a breath. "So everyone's outwardly cooperating, but the whole thing's poised on a knife's edge."

"Rotting gods. I had no idea."

"Not many people do. A potential civil war isn't exactly something the Senate likes to shout from the rooftops."

I chew my lip. Civil war? My old tutor Matias would have been thrilled to see his theories were so accurate—and back then, I would have been delirious at the thought of the Catenan Republic tearing itself apart, too. But Suus is gone. The Hierarchy stretches across oceans. A civil war would be a world war, fought with Will on all sides. It would be bloody beyond imagining.

"That's terrifying, but I don't see how this relates to you being a Seventh," I admit.

"Well. As I see it, two things could happen. One: things keep escalating, and there's open conflict before the end of the year. We become hostages in all but name here—and you know who my father is. A son in Class Three is someone he has to worry about. A son in Class Seven isn't."

I study him. "But he's still your father. Surely that won't make a difference to him."

"He's already all but disowned me. He's not interested in mediocrity, and my sisters both have prospects just as good as mine were when I started. Religion know all that, so my value as a bargaining chip is negligible now. Which is how it should be." He rolls his shoulders and quickly moves on. "The other option is that this year passes without things spiralling out of control. Aside from whoever gets Domitor, everyone in Class Three or Four is going to get seconded to Military for their ten years of service, no matter what position they choose." He gives me a meaningful look. "Military. For ten years. With the possibility of civil war at any time. And my father will still be Censor for the first three of those."

"Whereas a Seventh could choose a low-level Governance position," I finish slowly. "What about option three? The civil war never happens?"

"Then I thank the gods, accept I miscalculated, and move on with my life." The way he says it leaves little doubt as to whether he thinks that's likely, though.

I take a bite of my fish, giving myself a chance to think. The political situation doesn't shock me; Ulciscor's suggestion that Religion are looking for a weapon here certainly hinted at something more than the usual internal tensions. And while Callidus's decision seems extreme, it does make some sense. Bloodlines are important in Caten, yet it's achievement and status that are seen as truly valuable. If there really is a war coming, Callidus removing himself from the equation could be vital for his father.

"You're a loyal son," I say eventually. I don't think Callidus has taken this upon himself due to fear, no matter what he says.

"I'm a son who doesn't want to end up in a Sapper," Callidus corrects with a chuckle. "It's not as if I can't advance after I graduate, anyway. The Ericius name opens many doors."

I'm curious to pursue the discussion, but the chime signalling the end of the meal interrupts anything more he might have said. We stand, the scraping of our chairs across the floor mimicked around the mess.

Callidus sighs. "Enjoy watching everyone else be incompetent."

"Enjoy pretending to be incompetent."

We grin at each other, a shared sympathy in the banter.

I begin the long trek back out to the Labyrinth.

XXXV

MY FATHER HATED LIES.

Not just the kind that were told to him—that, he once observed, was the opposite of a unique condition. But he hated falsehood itself, as a concept. Always told me that a hard truth was better than a comforting fiction. That there was no such thing as a harmless lie, and that the liar lost a part of himself in the act.

As I watch the flailing run below, I wonder what he'd think of me now. Sometimes I'm not sure there's anything of the real me left anymore.

"They are truly terrible."

I start at Eidhin's voice to my right; I didn't see him join me at the balcony. I refocus on the action down below, wincing as the screeching of stone squeals around the chamber, followed immediately by a cursing shout as the control stone breaks loose from the bracer. The run is over less than thirty seconds later. Eidhin snorts derisively.

I glance at him, then chuckle. Mainly to cover my unease. This is the first time Eidhin has come near me since last night.

There's silence for a minute as we watch the contestants trudge out of the maze. The rest of the class has moved along with the action, as has Dultatis. We're the only people within fifty feet.

"Did you kill someone?" It's asked in casual Cymrian. Like he's asking about the weather.

"What?" I straighten, for a heartbeat certain I've misheard. "No. No! Of course not." I keep my voice low and use Cymrian too. "It was my blood, last night. Mine. Entirely my blood."

"Ah." Eidhin looks vaguely disappointed.

Silence again, the two of us staring out over the Labyrinth. Me more uncomfortable than I was before.

"I cut myself climbing the wall." Eidhin already knows enough to turn me in. And though I have no reason to think he's trustworthy, the burden of what happened last night has been building up inside me. A great weight in my chest.

"Clumsy."

I stare at him, then cough a half-hearted laugh, no idea from his expression whether he is being serious. "I suppose so." I tap a finger on the balustrade nervously. "Thank you for covering for me."

"You were doing something they disapprove of. No thanks are needed."

I smile at that, though after a glance I'm again unsure whether Eidhin is joking. "You don't like the Praeceptors much, I take it."

"You are very observant." The muscular boy continues watching the proceedings down below, says nothing further. I reassess my inclination to tell him more. I expected him to be curious, to probe. Instead, he seems intent on finding out as little as possible.

"Not many people know the language of Cymr." Eidhin doesn't change position, but the tenor of his voice has changed with the abrupt observation. It's almost wistful. "You speak it well. Who taught you?"

"I had a Cymrian tutor, back in Aquiria. Before . . ." I trail off. Pretend to recover myself. "When I was younger. He used to call it the Beautiful Tongue. Said that he didn't care what the Hierarchy ordered—that if I was learning other languages, it would be a crime for me not to learn the speech of the gods. And music. And dance."

"And all things that delight the heart," murmurs Eidhin. The words sound strange, coming from the brusque, surly boy. Yet he softens, just for a second. The corners of his mouth turn upward. "What was his name?"

"Cullen." No need to lie. It's a common enough Cymrian name.

"Is he . . . never mind." The spark of pleasure I saw in Eidhin fades. "I am glad he taught you. It is nice to have someone in this forsaken place who speaks the Tongue. Aside from a few awkward words from the Principalis, yesterday was the first time I have heard it from another in a very long time."

"What about your family?"

From the way Eidhin's expression suddenly goes cold, I can tell I've said the wrong thing. "No." He ends the conversation with the word.

The next run on the Labyrinth is almost organised, and the flock of students is coming back toward us. I can't help but drift briefly back to last night, as I have several times already. Picture the diagrams on the wall. Wonder if Religion simply got the idea for this place from the ruins, or whether the connection is something more sinister.

Dultatis eyes us standing off to the side, but doesn't bother forcing us to join the rest of the class. Soon enough he's announcing the start of the run, and everyone is jogging away again.

"There's some sort of excavation site. East of the Academy, in the woods. Old ruins." There are only a few runs left, and the desire to talk about it is too much. "There was something strange out there, Eidhin."

Eidhin doesn't react at first. Then he cocks his head, turning his attention to me. "Strange?"

So I tell him. The glowing writing on the wall. The schematics for the Labyrinth's control bracer. The map. The eyeless bodies impaled on obsidian swords. I don't mention the way the latter seemed to stir, to talk; even now I can't bring myself to fully believe that wasn't more than my frazzled imagination, and I'm worried that if I say it aloud, Eidhin will dismiss the entire story.

It's an unburdening, but not without calculation. At the moment, Eidhin could still change his mind and tell someone about my absence. But once he knows what I saw, he's going to realise that Religion won't want him to have that information—making turning me in a much riskier proposition.

When I finish, Eidhin considers. "Why were you out there?"

"Military think Religion are searching for a weapon somewhere on the island. I was told to have a look."

"So you are working for them."

"I'm doing what I need to do to survive," I correct him. "They were not kind to my people, either."

There's a flash of something on Eidhin's face. Anger? Disgust? It disappears too quickly to identify. "Why tell me, then?"

"I had to tell someone." Trying to convey my sincerity.

The large boy growls, but accedes as he looks away. "You owe me a debt."

"I do," I agree cautiously.

"Then you can repay me by helping me learn this accursed language of yours."

I blink, surprised by the gruff statement. "I can do that." If that's the price for Eidhin's silence, it's an easy one to pay.

"Good." He pauses. "And tell no one."

"Alright."

The run we've been watching was a short one, comically so. We say nothing as the class returns. I gather from their conversation that it was the final attempt of the day. A few cast sideways glances at Eidhin and me standing together, this time, as if finally registering that we've been conversing. I suppose, given our respective reputations, it would be a sight of some curiosity.

Dultatis is soon brushing past us, coming to a stop only ten feet away. I glare at his back. "I'm sorry for our disqualification yesterday." I'm talking to Eidhin in Cymrian but speak loud enough for the man to hear, knowing he has no clue what I'm saying.

Eidhin follows my gaze. Grunts. "In that, you have no blame. He is a pig." He says it even louder.

I grin my agreement at that; unfortunately, Dultatis chooses that exact moment to glance over at us. He spots both Eidhin and I watching him, me showing clear amusement at what Eidhin has just said.

"You'll tell me what that was about. Immediately," he snaps at Eidhin.

Eidhin spreads his hands apologetically. "To . . . translate . . . is difficult," he says in painfully broken Common. Far more haltingly than I know he's capable of.

Dultatis reddens. Turns to me. "You speak the language."

"He said he wishes we hadn't cheated so flagrantly yesterday," I say solemnly.

"Tell him he looks like someone has taken all his Will and jammed it in places it should not go," adds Eidhin, looking directly at the Praeceptor.

Dultatis looks at Eidhin, then at me expectantly. I'm unconscionably proud of how straight I manage to keep my face.

"He's going to work harder. Be better," I say.

Eidhin nods earnestly to what I'm saying. "He is such an utter failure of a human being, I am often embarrassed to breathe the same air as him."

A small crowd has gathered—because the session has ended rather than with the intent of observing, but curious about the exchange nonetheless.

"And now he's telling me I should do the same," I say with mock exasperation, rolling my eyes. I turn to Eidhin. "Have you noticed he has a weird smell all the time? Like he bathes in perfume, but it's still not quite enough to cover his odour."

"Yes. Yes! It's awful, isn't it. Like a noblewoman who's been dead for a few days."

I feel the corners of my mouth twitch, choke down a laugh. Nod gravely and turn back to Dultatis, my mirth threatening to burst from me hysterically even as I paste a hurt frown on my face. "He's . . . not being very complimentary toward my effort."

Dultatis glowers at me, then at Eidhin as the burly boy launches into a cheerful string of invective, curses which would make even me blush flowing smoothly. I blithely translate them as questions about upcoming classes, which Dultatis answers through gritted teeth. He has to be aware, or at least suspect, that we're mocking him. But everyone else is looking on, and he has absolutely no way to prove it.

"What about his breathing?" I prompt Eidhin.

"It's loud, isn't it?"

"So loud."

"Sometimes I wonder whether he is dying. Or making love to himself."

The urge to giggle uncontrollably threatens again, but I swallow it manfully. "He apologises for how difficult it is to teach him. He wants you to know he's trying."

Dultatis watches us with narrowed eyes. "Try harder," he says to Eidhin, almost a snarl. Deciding that the conversation is over, he stalks off toward the exit, chased by the soft laughter of some of the other students who have guessed what we were doing.

Everyone else files out of the Labyrinth behind the Praeceptor, leaving Eidhin and I to trail after them. We start up the stairs.

"Today was not such a bad day," says Eidhin abruptly. He's still not smiling, but the expression on his face is different. More relaxed than I think I've seen him.

"Not such a bad day," I agree. I shield my eyes as we reach the top of the stairs and emerge into the golden afternoon sun. "When did you want to begin working on your Common? I have to work the stables in the evenings, but after that—"

"No." Eidhin looks at me speculatively, observing my bandaged hand, and shakes his head. "You have two weeks remaining of punishment?"

"A little less."

"Then conversation will suffice until then. I know what it is like to study tired," he adds gruffly.

I show him my appreciation. "Every night after the Festival of the Ancestors, then. No matter what. You have my word."

He acknowledges the statement with a grunt and increases his pace, ending the discussion. I feel a smile creep onto my face as I watch him stalk away.

Today was not such a bad day.

XXXVI

I T'S STORMING WHEN THE FIRST DAY OF THE FESTIVAL OF THE
Ancestors finally dawns.

The westerly sea breeze whips raindrops through the tall archways lining the
mess, distorting the dim, raging swells of the sea far below. The chatter in the long
hall is at a higher pitch than usual despite the weather, many students toting satchels
like the one I have tucked at my feet, ready for the Transvect that's due to arrive in less
than an hour.

I look up from my meal as Callidus's shadow falls over the table, my welcome
slipping to a puzzled frown as I take him in. "Where are your things?"

"I'm not going." Callidus sits heavily, sounding almost as surprised by the words
as I am.

"What? Why?"

"Word from my father. I'm to concentrate on my studies." He tries to force cheer
into his voice, but there's no hiding his downcast aspect.

"Oh." Callidus doesn't need to say more; Tertius Ericius's disillusionment with his
son is no secret. Still. The honouring of the ancestors is one of the most important traditions in Caten. It's the *essence* of family. To be excluded from attending . . . "I'm sorry."

"Thanks."

I hesitate. Study my food. "If you just told him—"

"No." Callidus isn't angry, but his tone forestalls any argument. "I've said it
before—he's reacting the way he needs to react. I'm sure he realises what I'm doing,
and is honouring the sacrifice by making sure it seems real. A year of being cut off is a
small price to pay for the safety it brings."

I accede, though I'm not convinced, and I don't think Callidus is either. "What
will you do, then, if you're stuck here?"

"What everyone else not going will do. Study. Train. Enjoy a couple of days without most of the Praeceptors around. It won't be so bad."

I can still see his disappointment, but it won't help to call attention to it. "At least
you don't have to go through the awkwardness of meeting your undoubtedly disen-
chanted mother for the first time."

A hint of Callidus's usual humour returns. "She's coming to the Necropolis?"

"Word arrived last night." It was ostensibly part of a longer message instructing me where to go if nobody met me at the platform, but I know Ulciscor sent it specifically to forewarn me. With his wife present, it will be much harder to debrief. "Relucia is taking a Transvect from Sytrece just to meet me, apparently. And I somehow doubt she's going to be impressed by a Sixth."

Callidus scoffs. "I know Iro and Dultatis haven't done wonders for your reputation in here, but you're still Catenicus out there. I think she'll give you a little leeway."

"Let's hope so."

I'm about to say more when a ripple of conversational pauses slides over the mess, and I twist to see Veridius coming down the stairs. The Principalis is a rare sight around the Academy, I'm discovering, usually eliciting immediate attention whenever he emerges from his office. I don't think I've ever actually seen him down here.

Veridius reaches our level, scanning until his gaze comes to rest on Callidus and I. He stops at the end of our table, indicating a spare seat amiably. "May I?"

"Of course," says Callidus as I nod my agreeance, careful not to show any discomfort. This is my first interaction with the Principalis since my expedition to the ruins two weeks ago. Not that it's ever fallen far from my mind. I still wrestle with what I saw—or thought I saw—when I close my eyes each night, no matter my exhaustion. Find myself fretting over how, or if, it connects to the Labyrinth. Between that and the ongoing red nightmares of the naumachia, my sleeping hours have been less than restful of late.

"Your injury is healing well, Vis?" Veridius eyes my left hand, which no longer needs bandages. It's said casually, cordially, with no trace of undertone. I still feel like he's making a point.

"It is." Ulnius did a good job, the scarring across the palm barely visible. I give Veridius a self-effacing smile. "Though the embarrassment of doing it so publicly may not go away quite as quickly."

Veridius chuckles, again as naturally as if he had absolutely no suspicion about the timing of the wound. He either doesn't—which I find hard to believe, no matter what Ulnius has told him—or he's again proving to be a remarkable actor. "I was pleased to hear it hasn't been preventing you from completing your penance at the stables. That's partly why I stopped by, actually. You are, officially, done. Once you're back from the Necropolis, you can start taking dinner with everyone else." He slaps the table lightly with one hand and beams, apparently enjoying delivering the good news.

Then his eyes stray to the pack at my feet, and his expression grows serious. "But mostly, I wanted to assure you that security will be tight for your trip. Praeceptor Scitus will accompany you on the way there, and we're issuing passes to every student to ensure that no one else will be allowed to board the Transvect coming back. The Transvect itself is scheduled to shuttle back and forth on a loop for the next two days, which means there is no way to know when you'll be on it. And in between, the Necropolis is always well guarded. You will have nothing to fear from the Anguis."

I shift uncomfortably. "Thank you." Locked away here in the Academy, it's been easy to forget that Sedotia and the Anguis probably want to kill me for what I did. Though, if they only wanted revenge, they could easily have revealed my true identity to the Hierarchy and watched me die. I'm not sure whether that makes their looming fury better or worse.

"I have to admit, I wasn't sure whether you would be attending the Festival."

"Well. I *am* a Telimus."

"Of course. Of course. It's just, Ulciscor is a very private man, and . . ." He looks uncharacteristically awkward, like he's struggling to word what he's trying to say. Then he sighs. "I'm sure there will be much talk of Caeror. Please pour out an offering from me, Vis. And remember what I told you about grief fading too easily to bitterness."

I look at him, and he returns my gaze steadily. Sadly. "Your father is a good man. Whatever he has said to you, I am not accusing him of lying," he adds softly. "I'm saying that sometimes we tell people what we have to believe. No matter how wrong it might be, or how much it might hurt them."

He claps me on the shoulder, and leaves.

We watch until he's out of earshot, and then Callidus frowns across at me. "I know what your father thinks, but the Principalis *really* doesn't seem the type." The historic tensions between Ulciscor and Veridius are well-known; I've already "admitted" Ulciscor's ongoing suspicions to Callidus, aware that most people assume I've been sent here to find out about Caeror's death anyway. Sure enough, he was unsurprised at the revelation.

"I am aware." I watch Veridius stop to speak with some Fifths, whispering something play-conspiratorially to the group that gets peals of laughter in response. Everyone loves the man.

"And even if he was, I can't imagine there's anything left to find. Not after six years."

"I am aware," I repeat in a growl, giving Callidus a reproachful look. "It's not going to stop me from looking into it, if I get the chance." At least if I need to do something suspicious down the track, it's a good excuse to enlist Callidus's help without explaining the real reason why.

Callidus drops the topic with a gesture of defeat, and we talk of small things until the chime quavers through the mess. I sling my pack over my shoulder, part ways with the wiry boy—who looks mildly forlorn as he watches me join the column of students heading toward the main gate—and then trudge into the driving rain, through the Will cage at the Academy's entrance and down to the Transvect platform, which the behemoth of stone and wood is already sitting alongside. I'm among the first to arrive, so I take a seat in one of the rear sections and settle next to a window. It's a little more than an hour to the Necropolis, I'm told. If I'm going to spend it alone, I may as well have a view.

Heavy droplets lash the glass, partially obscuring the view down to the churning grey waves far below. I think about what would happen if the Anguis managed to bring down the Transvect while we're over the sea. Then try not to.

"Hail, Vis."

I look up from my bleak inspection, surprised to see Aequa sliding into the seat opposite. She rakes water from her raven-black hair, then irritably brushes damp strands from her shoulders.

"Aequa." I'm too taken aback to say more than that. She hasn't spoken to me since our brief conversation on my first day here. And there are still plenty of other empty seats.

Before either of us can say more, there's motion to the side and then Emissa and Indol are taking the remaining two spots next to us, looking as though it's the most natural thing in the world. Emissa grins at me. "I wondered if you would be coming."

"You *hoped*. You *hoped*," corrects Indol. "You've been dying for a chance to ask him about the naumachia."

Emissa gives him a glare and leans across to punch him reprovingly on the arm. I watch, a little dazed by their abrupt appearance. Of course, Indol doesn't know we've already talked about the naumachia as much as I'm willing to—an easy reminder not to mention Emissa's visits to the stables. But it's been more than a week since her last one, and the Festival of the Ancestors was far enough away that it never came up.

"I'm . . . surprised you're allowed to," I admit, glancing around at the three of them. "You do all know I'm still in Six, right?"

Indol's dismissive. "We're not in the Academy right now. We're all equals out here."

"Says the son of the Dimidius," observes Emissa dryly.

Indol sighs. "Then we're all *potentially* equals out here. Academy ranks don't apply. Besides, everyone knows you should be in a higher class," he adds to me.

"Thanks." Emissa and Callidus have both said as much previously, but it's nice to hear it from someone else.

"Dultatis really does seem to hate you," adds Emissa helpfully.

"Thanks." I say it with a more sarcastic inflection this time. "I am *very* aware."

There's a pause as more students file past. I glance up to find Iro's disapproving sneer favouring our group. Both Emissa and Indol smile a greeting and readily meet his gaze. Iro's scowl deepens, but he eventually breaks off eye contact and stalks away farther down the carriage.

Emissa watches him go coolly, then glances at Indol. "No Belli?"

"She's not coming."

"Huh."

I stare after Iro. "He *really* doesn't like me very much, does he?"

There's a stiffening from Aequa, as if she wants to glance at the others but is restraining herself. "You don't know?"

"Evidently not."

"He lost his sister at the naumachia. She was nine." Aequa looks uncomfortable. "His family's unhappy you got named Catenicus, when so many people died."

I grimace. There's not much I can say to that. It explains a lot, though.

Emissa studies Aequa. "Are you sure? He's seemed more bad-tempered than usual since the trimester break, but I've never heard him even mention it."

"My father isn't exactly the biggest Telimus supporter. He tends to make sure I'm aware of these sorts of things." Aequa's cheeks redden at the admission, and she doesn't make eye contact with me.

There's an awkward silence, and then Indol chuckles. "Sounds like my father." He holds up a hand as I look at him. "No, no. Not against Telimus. But he's always telling me where people are weak. Always telling me where he thinks I should squeeze." He glances at Aequa. "Best thing to do is ignore them. We don't have to play their games."

Aequa gives him a small smile of gratitude.

"You should talk to Scitus," Indol says suddenly to me. "About Dultatis, I mean."

"It wouldn't do any good," Emissa counters before I can respond. "Dultatis has authority over his class; unless he does something against the rules, his judgment is all that matters." She pulls back a long lock of hair that's fallen over her face. "Of course, if you managed to prove the Praeceptor was doing something against the rules . . ."

"He'd need the entire class to back him up for that," interjects Aequa. "From what I've heard, I doubt that will happen. Sorry," she adds to me, almost as an afterthought.

The three of them launch into a spirited debate about how I can best work my way around Dultatis's grudge, which quickly devolves as increasingly impractical—and startlingly violent, in some cases—ideas are suggested and discarded, to everyone's amusement. Aequa remains a touch more aloof and reserved, but Emissa and Indol bicker and joke as if all four of us have been old friends forever. The confidence and security and ease of Catenan royalty on display, I suppose.

Soon enough we're descending to the Sea of Quus, easing to a crawl as we pass one of the white anchoring points jutting from the waves. It's a spectacular scene out the window; the late afternoon sun is struggling to break through clouds in the west, rays of light scything through and highlighting silvery-grey water that's being whipped into a frenzy by the buffeting wind. Even within the carriage there's a thundering whistle as the gusts hammer wood and glass and stone, and occasionally—somewhat concerningly, I have to admit—the carriage itself shakes, as if in danger of being pushed aside. I know the Will mechanisms will be more than strong enough to hold, though.

I pretend to gaze out over the water, but in fact I'm assessing. Really taking note of our speed. The Transvect's slow enough that I could dive off easily enough, if I was in a position to do so, but getting back on is an entirely different proposition. The thing hovers at least ten feet above the water at its lowest.

"What about you, Vis?"

I've lost the thread of the conversation; I turn back to the group, hiding my frustration at the interruption with an absent smile in Emissa's direction. "Sorry. What was the question?" We're already accelerating again. The rain lashing the windows hits harder as we gather speed.

"How many times have you been to Agerus?"

"Ah. This is my first."

"Lucky," says Indol, a little dolefully. "It can be quite spectacular, if you've never seen it before."

"You don't want to go?"

Indol makes a face. "No, it's fine. I almost told my parents it's a waste of time, but they'd be horrified to even imagine I wouldn't visit them once they're dead."

The next hour passes quickly. Aequa and I recount our experience at the naumachia for Indol and—supposedly—Emissa's benefit. I can still hear some of Aequa's lingering questions in the way she tells her side of the story. But she doesn't voice her doubts, is nothing but complimentary toward me.

After that, Emissa and Indol complain about Nequias, and I easily match their stories with ones of Dultatis. Aequa, for her part, seems to have only nice things to say about Scitus. I watch her as she talks, unable to help but wonder why she sat with me. The other two I can understand—Emissa because we're becoming friends, and Indol because he seems happy to play along. But there are other Fourths on the Transvect. It feels like Aequa's here to observe, more than converse.

Finally, just as the clouds are clearing to show a golden glow in the west, we enter Agerus.

It's immediately distinguishable from the surrounding countryside: vast fields stretch away into the distance, and all of them are lined with tombstones. Thousands upon thousands of them. Lantern-lit paths are cut between them, and bright flowers dot the ground everywhere. Clumps of people are already gathered around graves for as far as the eye can see.

The three Eternal Fires, burning strips that span at least a hundred feet each, separate the fields. Those are the flames into which most Catenan bodies go after the rites have been said.

Beyond, is the Necropolis.

The mountain range is immense, looming, concealing the horizon for miles to the left and right as we approach. The mountains themselves aren't incredibly high—they stretch hundreds of feet into the sky, not thousands—but they're steep.

And they're dotted with crypts.

I've read about the Necropolis, first years ago at Suus, then a little more over the past week as this trip approached. These aren't like the graves in the fields below, single tombstones which are tended once a year. These are entire mausoleums cut into the mountain, beautifully painted columns marking many entrances, statues of gods or flaming cauldrons outside of others. Steep sets of stairs wend their way among them. Whole generations are buried within, along with separate areas to privately celebrate the Festival of the Ancestors. Full rooms, where families can relax and eat in comfort as they honour their forebears.

In all, it's a strange and morbidly beautiful sight. The mountains hide the sun from us, casting the entire plain into deep shadow; entering Agerus feels like passing from life into the fabled underworld of the Catenans. From the corner of my eye, I can see Aequa almost imperceptibly shiver as the darkness drapes itself across the Transvect. Our conversation peters out as we take it in.

Indol suddenly frowns, leaning to the side and pressing his head against the window. "There are a lot of people down there."

I twist, and the others shift to the glass too as the Transvect begins its descent. Indol's right: the granite platform is crowded, far more so than families waiting for the forty or so arriving students would account for.

The Transvect slides to a halt. Praeceptor Scitus walks the length of the carriage, ensuring everyone disembarks in an orderly fashion, handing out the tiles that will allow us back on board for the return trip. He leaves us until last.

"You lot come with me," he says as Iro and a few others disappear out the door.

I rise uneasily, glancing out the window. A thick crowd still mills, despite half the students having already disappeared with their relatives. We leave the carriage. I note how Scitus stays close to my side.

As soon as we're on the platform, a ripple of excitement passes through the horde. I shuffle. Everyone seems to be looking at us. At me. The lingering disquiet of what the Anguis might want to do to me is suddenly, sharply in my lungs.

"It's *him*," murmurs someone nearby, whispering too loud to their companion.

Ahead of us, a large man all but shoves Iro aside, ignoring the boy's heated objection and coming to a stop in front of us. Scitus tenses. My heart reaches into my throat.

"Catenicus." He's looking at me. Growls the name into an abrupt hush.

Before Scitus can move to block him, he grabs my arm fiercely in the Catenan embrace of brotherhood.

XXXVII

IT'S AS IF THE ACT BREAKS THE DAM OF PEOPLE'S RESTRAINT; suddenly they're all crowding around me, talking at me, slapping my back so hard that I stumble, clasping my hands or forearms, kissing my cheeks. In moments I'm separated from Indol, Emissa, and Aequa as the other students are shoved aside, ignored, and almost trampled in the press.

"Clear a path!" Scitus's eyes are midnight as he starts pushing people away from me, without malice but firmly, his light touch enough to move even the largest of them. I'm too disoriented to do much more than watch. As anxious as I am overwhelmed. I know this isn't an Anguis attack, but if any were lurking on the platform, I would be the easiest of targets right now.

Having cleared us a little room—those closest to us recognising that Scitus isn't afraid to use force—the Praeceptor bows his head close to mine. "This Transvect will be travelling constantly between here and the Academy until sunset tomorrow. Doesn't matter when you get on. Just don't tell anyone else. And don't miss the last one," he adds as an afterthought. "You'll just be giving Praeceptor Dultatis an excuse to censor you."

I nod, spotting Emissa craning her neck to look back at me as she's whisked off the platform by a woman in her late thirties, the similarities between mother and daughter obvious even at a distance. I can't see Indol or Aequa, though I do spot Iro fighting his way through the mob, scowling and cursing and shoving as he's jostled from all sides. The sight cheers me a little.

"Vis!"

I turn to see Ulciscor forcing his way between close-packed bodies. He cuts an impressive figure, and most people who notice the purple stripe on his toga make sure to scamper aside.

I smile. Ulciscor's not a friend, but he's the closest thing I have to a confidante right now. "Father." We clasp forearms, then embrace warmly. It's part of the act we've agreed upon. Always believe someone's watching and taking note. Never show anything but goodwill toward one another in public.

"It's not safe here." He signals his thanks to Scitus, then heads off, assuming I'll follow.

We weave between groups of families too excited to catch up to leave the platform first; there's too much noise, too many bodies, to bother making conversation straight away. We head down a flower-lined path and deeper into the darkness cast by the mountains. The rain has stopped, but the air still smells damp. It's cooler here. I tug my cloak around my shoulders.

"You're popular," observes Ulciscor once it's quiet enough to hear him.

"How did they know I'd be on the Transvect?"

"Everyone knows you're at the Academy. Word must have spread once they saw me." Ulciscor sighs. "It's my fault. I should have known not to arrive early."

"I didn't think people would still be so . . . enthusiastic."

Ulciscor chuckles. "I suppose it's probably been different for you. Out here, all anyone knows is that you were adopted, heroically saved half the city, then vanished behind the walls of the Academy. So not only are you brave and mysterious, but you started as one of the people. One of them. Everyone who's not a patrician *dreams* about being you, Vis—and half the patricians do, too, I suspect. I get more questions about you than I do about the business of the state, most days." His dry tone indicates he doesn't think much of that particular situation.

"Ah. Sorry."

He snorts. "Don't be. It's doing wonders for the Telimus name. Which goes *some* way to making up for your lack of progress at the Academy. Though, I am hoping you have some news to help offset the rest, too."

"I do. In fact—"

"How was the trip?" Ulciscor's interruption is pointed. He doesn't think it's safe to say anything important just yet.

"Pleasant enough. I do have to make sure I'm back here by sunset tomorrow, though, else—"

"Else there will be consequences, and so on, and so on. I wouldn't worry about it. I've never heard of anyone getting punished too harshly for tardiness."

I cough. "I may not want to test that."

"Oh?" Ulciscor sees my expression. "Oh. Well. We'll keep that in mind, but I can't imagine it will be a problem."

"You're not worried about the Anguis?" I half expected to have a protective entourage.

"Military runs the Necropolis. There's nothing to fear from them here."

I glance at him. "Military do? Not Religion?"

He shrugs. "One of those strange assignments."

We keep going, past hundreds of groups huddled in the vast fields, a small fire burning for each one. Some of them pay attention when they spot Ulciscor, pointing and murmuring, but the excitement of the crowd on the platform isn't repeated. I can see flower garlands draped over many of the tombstones, and offerings of bowls of grain or wine-soaked bread are carefully perched atop graves everywhere. It's clear many families have come and gone already. Probably those who can't afford to travel by Transvect or carriage, who need to allow more time to get back to Caten.

It's twenty minutes before we reach the mountain; we work our way along the base for another ten before Ulciscor finally indicates a set of stairs leading upward, and we start the ascent.

It's a steep climb, though a beautiful one. There's soft, mournful music drifting from many of the tombs we pass, some just instrumental, some with a chorus of voices gently joining in. The valley below would be covered in darkness now, but the three Eternal Fires send slashes of dramatic red light through it, augmented by the smaller fires and lanterns.

"We're just up ahead," Ulciscor murmurs, not five minutes into the climb. He sees my surprise. "Telimus is an old family. Our name traces back to Catenans who saw the Cataclysm."

I believe him when I see the Telimus tomb. It's less than a quarter of the way up the mountain, sits by the stairs, and has an excellent outlook. A lower tomb indicates a more prestigiously old family name. Elsewhere, crypts are sometimes reclaimed as families get absorbed by others, their name withering and dying—but not here at the Necropolis. Here, burial is an eternal monument.

The entry is grand: not as grand as some of the more ostentatious displays we've already passed, but still a beautifully decorated, traditional pointed archway guarded by three massive marble dogs, life-like if not for the red paint that colours their features. The name Telimus is emblazoned proudly above the entrance, etched and gilded.

"Don't you have problems with thieves?" It's not the most respectful question, but I'm curious. This, I admit to myself, is more like what I expected from a Magnus Quintus. The gold used for decorating the name alone could probably feed a family of Octavii for several years.

"At the Necropolis?" Ulciscor looks offended at the mere suggestion. "No one would dare."

A torch-lined stone corridor leads us to a short set of stairs descending into a large room. Even having heard the stories, I'm taken aback by the luxury on display here.

Detailed red and gold tapestries drape the walls. The floor is overlaid marble, inset with triangular gold designs to honour both the gods and Caten. There's a large table covered in prepared food, comfortable seats, even a shallow, decorative pool in the centre with serene white flowers on its glass-like surface. A myriad of lanterns provide light, and there's some unseen source of warmth as well, because the chill of outside vanishes as soon as we enter.

It's the sarcophagus that demands my attention, though. It's built into the wall, a long stone cavity that's framed by glass so that it's possible to see the body within. And there is one: an older man, perhaps in his seventies, long and distinguished. Without his thick grey hair, it would have been easy to mistake him for an older copy of Ulciscor. He's lying on his back. Eyes closed. Hands folded over his chest.

"It's a Vitaerium."

I twitch at the feminine voice coming from my right, and turn to see a pair of flashing dark glasses observing me dispassionately.

"Lanistia!" Part of me is surprised. No matter her relationship to Caeror, the Festival of the Ancestors is meant to be about family—and hers, as far as I know, are still alive. "Hail." My attention returns to the body. "I thought those were for healing people?"

"Among other things." Ulciscor comes to join me in front of the sarcophagus, gazing at the form inside. "They also work to preserve from decay, trickling Will into something that was once alive. Many are actually used in Caten's storehouses, to keep grain and meat fresh—but each of the oldest families are allowed one, too."

I stare at the corpse, and almost don't manage to hide my disgust. The vanity of such a thing is astounding. "So this is . . . ?"

"My uncle," says Ulciscor quietly. "The Vitaerium is meant to be for either the most recently deceased, or the one who we wish to remember the most. But . . ."

He falls silent, blank as he focuses inward. I nod my understanding, though I'm not sure he sees it.

My gaze finally rips from the dead man back to the rest of the room. "So it's just us?"

"For now. My mother and father will arrive in a couple of hours. As will my wife." Ulciscor accompanies the statement with an unconscious frown of worry. "Before they get here, though, we should talk."

He motions to a seat.

"So you're still in Class Six," he says as I settle in opposite him. It's not an accusation. I can still feel his mixture of disapproval and disappointment.

"I shouldn't be. Dultatis—"

"You shouldn't be." Ulciscor repeats the words calmly, but with enough force to cut me off. "I did not pick you because you are educated, Vis—in that, there are a hundred students your better who aren't attending the Academy. I didn't even pick you because you've never ceded before. I picked you because you are *smart*."

"It doesn't help that the Praeceptor hates me because I'm a Telimus."

"So? I warned you from the start that the Telimus name is not universally beloved. And even if I had not, I *know* you understand that our world does not run on merit alone. I chose you because I expected there to be obstacles. That is what separates us, Vis. There are those who see what *should* be, and complain that they do not get their due. And then there are those who see what *is*, and figure out how to use it to their advantage. Or at the least, overcome it."

My face flushes as he speaks. Part of me knows Ulciscor is right. I'm here because he expects me to come up with solutions, not ask for help. But neither that nor the lecture changes the reality of my situation.

"Is there any way you can put pressure on Praeceptor Taedia to drop someone? Dultatis isn't going to budge, but if Taedia initiates the exchange, she'll have some input into who the replacement is." An observation from Indol on the journey here. I hope he's right.

"That sounds like you want me to fix your problem."

"You're a resource. This is me recognising what *is*, and figuring out how to overcome it." An unavoidable hint of snideness as I repeat his words back at him.

Lanistia coughs a laugh from the corner. Ulciscor looks annoyed. "Have you visited any of the ruins yet, at least?"

"I have."

"Oh." Ulciscor's taken aback. "Good. That's . . . that's good." His tone eases to something more conciliatory as he thinks. "Well. I doubt I can bring much pressure to bear on any of the Praeceptors at the Academy, but with the reputation you earned at the naumachia . . . perhaps. Perhaps. I'll see what I can do." He leans forward, eager. "Now. Start from the beginning—since we last spoke. Tell me everything that's happened."

We spend the next two hours in the unsettling surrounds of the Telimus tomb as I recount my time at the Academy. After the sedate pace of Class Six's lessons, I'd forgotten how intense Lanistia and Ulciscor's expectations can be. It doesn't take long to remind me. They're immediately stepping me through every aspect of my arrival as if it had happened yesterday rather than two months ago. Have me straining to recount the wording of vaguely remembered conversations with the Praeceptors. Are badgering me about the details of timing, of locations, whether students I've never interacted with are keeping the company of other students I've never interacted with.

We spend almost an hour on my excursion to the ruins, in the end, Ulciscor and Lanistia veering between impressed and horrified as I explain the risks I took to investigate. They stop interjecting, though, when I segue to the ruins themselves. The excavation. The glowing writing, the Labyrinth symbols, the maps, the bodies gruesomely pinned against the wall. Their hollow eyes.

I take a deep breath as I finish explaining the last part. I don't mention the way they seemed alive, or the fact I'm almost certain their eyes were closed when I first entered. And I don't mention the words they kept repeating. Ulciscor's trust has been strained by my lack of progress at the Academy. Having him wonder whether I'm cracking under the pressure isn't something I'm willing to chance.

When I'm done, there's a long silence. Eventually Ulciscor glances at Lanistia, then back to me.

"How many bodies were there?"

I try to picture the space. "A couple of hundred?"

"They all had obsidian sticking out of them?"

"I think so. Yes," I correct firmly when Ulciscor scowls at my prevarication. "Every single one I saw."

"It was definitely obsidian?" Lanistia, the first time she's spoken.

"I didn't touch it. But it looked that way."

"A lot of money there for Religion just to leave it," muses Ulciscor.

"And you're sure about their eyes?" There's more to the question from Lanistia, no matter how casually she tries to ask it.

"They looked like you," I confirm quietly.

"The dead skewered people looked like me," she repeats flatly.

I chuckle. "You know what I mean." We watch each other, and then I shift, smile fading as her expression doesn't change. "I just thought . . ."

"I know what you thought. Keep going."

The matter evidently not up for discussion, I press on. Every detail I can remember of the night is pored over, reviewed, and clarified.

When it's finally clear I have nothing new to say, Lanistia calmly stands. She exchanges glances with Ulciscor and then leaves.

"Did I say something wrong?"

"No." Ulciscor watches the doorway through which Lanistia has just disappeared. "You've done well. A huge risk, but better than I'd expected, given your lack of advancement."

"Really?" I squint at him. "Does any of it *mean* anything to you?"

"It's a piece of the puzzle. Proof that Religion are looking for something out there." Ulciscor's energised by thought. "It's almost certainly pre-Cataclysm, too. If it's a weapon . . . even some unknown advancement . . ."

I nod. More than enough to kill for.

"I'll need you to sketch out everything you remember," continues Ulciscor.

"I'm not the most talented artist." One of the few things that even my ever-optimistic mother, after viewing some of my paintings, had to concede I should no longer be pursuing.

"Do the best you can." He studies me. "You need to find out more, too. Get back there."

"That won't be easy." I hold up my hand, displaying the scar on the palm. "They have to suspect me. And I won't have the excuse of working in the stables next time."

"It will be easier once you've advanced a class or two. A lot more freedom, once you hit Class Four."

"So I've heard."

"You'll need to be in Three for the Iudicium, anyway." Ulciscor ignores my dry tone. "Because whatever *is* going on out there, at least some of the answers are in those ruins on the other side of Solivagus."

"About that. There *is* something I've been considering. I think I can make it work, but I need something from you. And it has to be tonight."

"What?"

"An imbued grapple. Two parts. Something with a strong enough attraction to reel me in, not just hold me in place." I outline my idea.

Ulciscor says nothing for a long few seconds after I finish.

"Rotting gods, lad. You really think you can pull that off?"

"Yes." The doubt in Ulciscor's eyes mirrors what I'm feeling, but I don't show him that. "How quickly can you make one?"

"An hour, maybe, by the time I find the right materials. Something that will hold together, but that you can break once you're done." Ulciscor's deep in thought now. "I'll have to do it straight after the ceremony. My parents won't be happy with me disappearing so soon."

"But you'll do it?"

"I'll do it." Ulciscor shakes his head, as if dazed at the idea of what I'm going to attempt. I don't blame him. "Understand, though, if you're caught, or if something goes wrong, you need to destroy it. No matter what. And if you get stranded, I won't be able to even suggest what's happened to you. Nobody will come looking for you."

He waits until he's sure I understand before continuing. "If you do succeed, I still won't be able to talk to you again until the trimester break. Whatever you find, you're going to need to make notes. You cannot trust your memory to hold details for that long."

All aspects I've already considered. "That's fine. But you're *sure* the hatch can be opened from the outside? Without Will?"

"It's a safety consideration. Easy if you know the trick." Ulciscor examines me a moment longer, then exhales a soft, admiring laugh and glances at the entrance. "The others will be here soon. You should go and find Lanistia."

I hesitate. "Will she want to see me?"

"She just needed some air." Ulciscor tugs absently at his sleeve. "She's the strongest person I know, Vis. She'll be fine."

I walk out of the tomb. Darkness has fallen properly now, but the valley below is ablaze with light. Faint strains of singing rise to my outlook, as well as drift from a couple of nearby, well-lit crypts. Others remain dark, their owners either celebrating the Festival of the Ancestors another night, or all permanent occupants.

Lanistia's nowhere to be seen, so I make my way along the narrow path, back toward the stairs. I wander for five minutes before eventually finding her sitting on a rock, legs dangling over a ten-foot drop, staring out over the fire-lit expanse of the valley. There's a torch perhaps twenty feet away, but it barely illuminates where she is. Her glasses mirror the distant orange flames.

"Lanistia."

She starts at her name; she must have been focusing her vision elsewhere. "Are you done?"

"We're done."

The young woman levers herself up smoothly, apparently unconcerned by the ledge only inches from her feet. We start walking.

There's a vast silence, broken only by the sounds drifting from far below. "I'm sorry if I offended you. It was a stupid thing to—"

"You didn't offend me." Lanistia is gruff. I think she's going to leave it there, but then she sighs, some of the stiffness receding from her shoulders. "I've lived for the past six years not knowing why I lost my sight. I honestly didn't think there were answers to find. Now it seems as though there might be, and I . . . cannot decide whether I want to open that wound again."

Another silence. A longer one this time.

"You need to do better, Vis." Lanistia's abrupt statement is soft, but loud among the emptiness of the tombs we're passing. She'd chosen a section of the mountain that had few visitors tonight, it seems. Most of it is dark. "You should be at least one class higher. This was meant to be the easy part."

"I know."

"I don't think you do." Lanistia doesn't look at me. "Ulciscor was making preparations last night, after he found out you were still in Six. If you hadn't made it to those ruins, you might not have been going back."

I feel the blood drain from my face. "It's only been two months."

"He's worried your reputation has made you complacent. That maybe you're starting to think you don't need to help him after all. And if that *were* the case, you would be more liability than asset." We reach the Telimus crypt. "So do better."

I swallow and nod, knowing that arguing is a pointless exercise, and trail after her. There are unfamiliar voices from within as we enter. I can't hear the exact words, but they sound relaxed. Light. We walk into the expansive inner room of the tomb, and the conversation peters out as our entrance is noted.

As well as Ulciscor, there are two newcomers. They're older—a man and a woman in their fifties, perhaps early sixties. The woman is tall and stately, traces of grey in her long black hair, olive-skinned Catenan through and through. Fashionable in a black silk stola slashed with a deep purple sash. The man is large in both height and girth, though from the way he slides gracefully to his feet at our entrance, it's clear there's still plenty of muscle within that bulk. His shaven scalp glistens in the lamplight, identical to Ulciscor's. Standing side-by-side, it's not hard to see the resemblance.

"Relucia!" Ulciscor calls the name toward the preparation area. "Come and meet our son!" He exchanges the slightest of grins with me.

I turn to the door, watching as a beaming young woman emerges. She's finely dressed, similarly to Ulciscor's mother, black silk stola crossed with a thin, light blue sash. Between the smile, the clothes, and the elaborate hairstyle, it takes me almost a full second to recognise her.

It's Sedotia. The woman who crashed the Transvect and shot Ulciscor. The woman who was helping Melior at the naumachia.

The woman from the Anguis.

XXXVIII

No matter how good an actor you are, no matter how much experience you have, it's hard to conceal any amount of surprise if you're not properly braced for the possibility. Fortunately, Sedotia—or Relucia, apparently, as it appears to be her real name—knows that all too well. She sweeps forward with a girlish squeal of delight, her over-the-top reaction taking the focus away from me. And then when she's wrapping me in a fierce embrace, my panicked expression can easily be mistaken for shock at the intensity of the greeting.

"Vis! I've been *so* looking forward to meeting you!" She kisses me on both cheeks and finally holds me back, clutching me by both shoulders as if to examine me properly. It prevents me from flinching away, tamps down my instinct to run just enough for me to hold my nerve. The way she's talking is nothing like in the conversations we've had before. It's exuberant, almost vacuous. "I'm Relucia. You must call me that, none of this formal nonsense. And my, Ulciscor didn't mention what a fine-looking young man you are." Her tone is uncomfortably approving. I flush, still dazed.

"Now, now," chortles Ulciscor, stepping forward and gently prying me from Relucia's grasp. "Try not to embarrass the poor boy as the *first* thing you do. Give him some room to breathe."

Relucia beams blithely in response, acknowledging the statement but not looking particularly bothered by it. "I'm sorry. I'm just excited. Ulciscor's been looking for someone he thinks might do our name justice at the Academy for so long. How are you progressing, by the way? Which class are you in? What do you think of the Praeceptors? I never went there myself, but I know some of them. Do you have any favourites so far?" It's a stream of questions that feels more like an assault than anything else; I can see Ulciscor's father beginning to smirk, and Ulciscor himself sighs and turns away with a similar expression, shaking his head.

Relucia continues to look at me, eyes wide. She's closer to me than the others, facing away from them. For the briefest of seconds, there's something in her gaze that sharpens. A warning.

I smile blandly back, finally recovering enough to internalise my shock. "Uh. Um. It's a pleasure to meet you, Relucia," I say, doing my best to look a mixture of taken aback and vaguely pleased at the whirlwind, overly affectionate introduction. "I . . ."

"Perhaps before we go further, I should introduce my parents, too." Ulciscor's wry observation saves me from having to mentally sort back through Relucia's questions. "Vis, these are your grandparents. My father, Lerius sese Quintus Telimus, and my mother, Milena sese Sextus Telimus."

Sese. Both in retirement pyramids, then—unsurprising, given their age and previous status. Still contributing Will to the Hierarchy, and seeing the benefits of wielding it, but tasked with less crucial jobs. The retirement pyramids are for those over the age of fifty: they manage small, non-critical infrastructure, but nothing like Transvects or anything that could compromise safety in the event of a failure. Nothing that could cause disaster due to a death in the chain, a sudden lessening or absence of Will.

"A pleasure to meet you both, as well." I try to focus, to not sound absent or disinterested, even as my mind races. I'm still reeling, finding it hard not to glance back over at Relucia. Ulciscor's wife. His *wife*.

"And you, Vis. And you! Catenicus. A most welcome addition to the family." Lerius has a deep, loud voice, the kind that seems like it would normally be telling a joke followed by booming laughter at his own humour. He repeats Relucia's greeting, kissing me on both cheeks. It's a far more restrained welcome, but not without warmth.

Milena doesn't move, studying me. "I hope you understand what an honour it is to be here, young man." An absolute contrast to Relucia. Not angry, exactly, but there's antipathy in the words.

"Mother," Ulciscor says sharply, at the same time as Lerius sighs and gives his wife a disapproving look.

"I do," I say quickly, forcing my concerns about Relucia temporarily to the side. She's not going to try and kill me here—not openly, anyway. I need to act naturally. Giving away that I know the woman will gain me nothing. "I promise I'll do everything I can to live up to that." I make my gaze earnest as I lock eyes with her.

"Hm." Milena doesn't look convinced, but there's the tiniest softening of her expression. "I suppose we'll see." She turns to Lanistia, who's been waiting just behind me. "Lanistia, dear. It's lovely to see you again. Would you come and help with the preparations?" She nods with cool politeness to me, then vanishes into the back room. Lanistia trails after her, and the sound of quiet conversation soon emanates from the doorway.

"Don't mind her." Lerius is apologetic as he leans in. "It's not you. She just doesn't like the idea of anyone else being here when we're remembering Caeror. She'll warm to you."

"Of course. Completely understandable," I assure him agreeably, doing my best not to focus on Ulciscor's wife. The young woman doesn't help as she merrily loops her arm around mine, guiding me over to the couches, where I'm forcefully made to sit. I try not to flinch at every touch. Lerius and Ulciscor follow and join us, both wearing amused expressions.

"Now," Relucia says, draping an arm around me in far too familiar a fashion. "I have *so* many things I want to know."

We talk for the next half hour—largely Relucia asking rapid-fire questions, and me sorting through the jumble and answering as best I can. Her enquiries are always either innocuous, or easily related to the past which Ulciscor and I have fabricated. Occasionally Lerius steps in to make a comment or joke, but for the most part he's content to just listen. He has an easy way about him, and appears more relaxed than his son. Far more at peace than anyone in the room except Relucia, in fact.

In the background are snippets of Lanistia and Milena's reunion. They seem to get along well, chatting and laughing, though it's never boisterous. Glad of each other's company but here to share their sadness, I think, not enjoy the time together.

For his part, Ulciscor seems pleased that his wife is taking to me so well, showing no sign of suspicion. My initial panic has waned, but I'm still reeling for most of the conversation as I reassess their relationship. Re-evaluate everything that's happened so far through the lens of this new information. She *shot* him. Relucia seems genuinely pleased to be here with Ulciscor, but is plainly also an exceptional liar. Even taking the political marriage and long stints apart into account, I can barely comprehend the lengths she must have gone to for this deceit.

"It's time," comes Lanistia's voice from the doorway behind us. Her tone's sombre.

We all stand, and Relucia touches my shoulder. "Tell me, Vis. Have you ever been to the Necropolis before?"

I shake my head.

"It's a beautiful sight after sunset. I must insist on showing you around once we are finished." She glances askance at Ulciscor, who wavers, then acquiesces. She smiles. "As a bonus, it will give us a chance to get to know each other better."

I smile back, and resolve not to stray anywhere she can easily try to kill me.

The ceremony is conducted by Lerius, who intones the sacred rites to the Telimus ancestors and offers sacrifices of wine-soaked bread and wheat on the tomb's altar. It's a brief affair, solemn. Melancholy radiates from the group.

As he talks, I feel the lump in my throat before I recognise the emotion starting to swell in me. I've deliberately ignored the Festival of the Ancestors since Suus, excepting when I stole offerings from gravesites in order to survive. But the sense of loss emanating from the others at the moment . . . it's too potent. Too familiar to ignore.

For the first time in too long, I find my thoughts drifting to my own family's fate. I've heard only the half whispered rumour that my mother, father, and sister were hanged before dawn, left there for hours so that the entire population of Suus could see them and know that their former rulers were truly gone. But even if that's true, there's no telling what might have happened to their bodies after that. Would they have been laid to rest in some unmarked grave? Burned? Tossed into the waters of the Aeternum to join Cari?

There's pain in my chest, pressure behind my eyes. I try not to think of them, most of the time, because I know deep down I haven't done enough to avenge their loss. Would they be proud of the decisions I've made? Would they approve of what I'm doing right now? I'm not sure. Part of me thinks they would be horrified that I'm pretending to be someone I'm not. The other part of me remembers my father's lessons about honour. About how it exists to provide a guideline for how to live, not how to die.

With an effort, I take a few discreet, measured breaths.

When Lerius is done, before we sit at the table, Lanistia steps forward and lays a flower garland on the altar, too. She says nothing, but Milena puts an arm around her. In that brief moment, Lanistia's stony façade crumbles. I pretend not to have seen.

I can't help but watch Relucia from the corner of my eye throughout. Ulciscor's wife seems genuinely sorrowful, albeit mourning the others' loss of Caeror rather than her own. She clasps Ulciscor's hand the entire time, and whispers something tenderly in his ear before we sit to eat.

Once the food is brought out, the conversation turns gently to memories—sometimes of other relatives, but mostly of Caeror. Much of the meal passes with Ulciscor and Lanistia laughingly reminiscing on his various irritating quirks, or Lerius recounting stories from twenty years ago that usually involve Caeror playing clever pranks on his older brother. He addresses many of those tales in my direction, I think understanding the awkwardness of being a newcomer, and doing his best to include me. And perhaps feeling that by sharing the memory, he is also sharing a small part of his son, too. I decide I like him.

Slowly, I get a picture of Caeror. Of the rarely serious young man who seemingly excelled at everything he did. Who, at least according to his family, was considered the very best chance for a Telimus to become Princeps of Military.

Unlike the others, Milena stays quiet and mostly watches the proceedings with a strange, sad smile. Occasionally her gaze drifts to the shrine, or the dead man in the Vitaerium, before she tears it away again, staring off into nothing. Lanistia sits next to her and every so often bows her head close, murmured exchanges between the two Milena's only conversation.

As the food reduces to scraps, Relucia stands, touching her husband's shoulder. "I can take Vis for that walk now."

"You don't have to," says Lerius.

Ulciscor glances at him, thinks, then nods to Relucia and puts his hand briefly atop hers.

"Come on." Relucia beckons, still playing her role to perfection. Light, but respectful to the mood. When I hesitate, she cocks her head to the side teasingly. "No need to be nervous."

Hoping she's telling the truth, I rise and follow her out of the tomb.

%. %. %.

I TRY TO SHAKE OFF RELUCIA'S OVERLY FAMILIAR ARM AS SOON as we're out of the crypt, but she holds tight, smiling all the while. "Don't. People could be watching." She waits until I stop resisting, then pulls me along the path running parallel to the Telimus mausoleum.

It's quiet up here, high above the red fires and soft dirges of the valley. Stars dot the sky. Our footsteps crunch against loose rock. There are a few other illuminated tombs nearby, but no motion from them. The high ledge we're walking along is only barely lit.

"So you're not planning to kill me, then." I'm proud of the calmness of my voice.

"Oh, dear boy. Don't tell me you haven't figured it out yet?" The cheerful, girlish demeanour from before is gone. This is the woman I remember.

We keep walking. Her tone indicates she thinks the idea of killing me is absurd. Which, now I'm able to clear the concern from my mind, leaves only one other option.

"You still want to use me."

We reach a set of stairs cut into the mountainside and Relucia begins to climb, forcing me to follow. "Keep going."

Another silence, then, "If you're still wanting to use me, after I killed Melior and stopped your attack . . ." I trail off, almost missing a foothold as it dawns on me. "*Vek.*"

"Good! Good. Slower than I expected, but you got there." Relucia takes a new path away from the stairs, settling onto a bench and patting the section next to her. It's almost completely dark here; anyone looking would be hard-pressed to spot us, but we can see the entire valley from our vantage.

I take the offered seat dazedly. "You cannot expect me to believe you *knew* what I would do. That you *intended* for me to . . ." Even as I say it, I can see Estevan driving the spike into his own brain. Sacrificing himself, when I couldn't make myself finish the deed. "You lost your leader. And hundreds of your people in failed attacks after, from what I understand. It was the biggest coordinated assault on Caten in a *century!*"

"We made them bleed. And had you not intervened, they would have been wounded far worse." Relucia's words barely reach my ears, despite the absolute lack of anyone else around. "But they will never die that way. Bleeding can be staunched, Vis. Wounds heal. The cut's only worth it if there's poison on the blade."

"But I already told you. I want nothing to do with you."

"What you want is irrelevant. I don't expect you to work for us. You will simply continue on your current path, and from time to time we will tell you what you need to do."

She doesn't have to explain what will happen if I refuse.

"If you expose me, I'll do the same to you."

"And that would be unfortunate." She smiles tightly. "Of course, I have reliable witnesses to my whereabouts for every instance you might say we've met. Even if anyone was willing to listen to the desperate reaching of a boy going to the gallows."

My lip curls. We stare out over the inky vista.

"You killed all those people," I eventually say softly.

"They were there to cheer on strangers to a worse fate. What happened gave me no pleasure, but nor did I weep for them."

The panicked screams and red-slicked stadium stand sharp in my mind. I let silence be my disgust.

"Caten is coming to a tipping point, Diago. The balance between Military, Religion, and Governance is shifting. Destabilising. The next decade will decide whether the Hierarchy survives, or is broken from within." Relucia is calm, confident of what she's saying. "Someone well placed, with enough influence, might be able to ensure the latter."

"And you think that someone is me."

"A champion of the system, beyond suspicion and reproach, raised up but not seduced by it? Yes, Diago. In time, I think it could be."

I stand. "I've heard enough."

"Sit down."

I glare at her, but sit.

Relucia examines me with exasperation, then sighs, some of the anger leaving her shoulders. "We do not have to be enemies. For now, all we want is what you want—for you to advance at the Academy."

"And after that? If I become Domitor, my goal is to join the embassy at Jatiere. Leave the whole rotting Republic behind. And if I *don't* make Domitor, I'm going to run. Either way, you won't see me anywhere near Caten after I graduate." I keep my voice low and hard. Lend emphasis to my point with a derisive gesture.

"Running isn't an option, Vis. I think you know that." Relucia's mild by comparison. Thoughtful. "Jatiere, though . . . that could work. Not as good as a position in Caten, but it's no worse than military service in some other dusty province. If you do your part and make Domitor, we can afford to give you a few years there."

I don't respond, taken aback. She seems genuine. The worst of the knot of tension in my stomach eases. I intend for my time in Jatiere to be longer than that, of course—and Relucia surely knows it—but it's a compromise, of sorts. Keeps us wanting the same thing for at least the short-term.

"What are your chances of reaching Class Three in time for the Iudicium, though? Your advancement thus far hasn't exactly been noteworthy."

"I know. Things have been . . . trickier than I expected." I explain briefly about Dultatis, something Ulciscor advised me against mentioning around his parents. Relucia follows up with some probing questions; I answer them, but avoid any mention of my trip to the ruins or Ulciscor's interest in them. It seems she doesn't know a great deal about what Caeror was involved in. I have no desire to give her more information than she already has.

"Well. I have no doubt an opportunity will arise for you to advance soon enough," says Relucia once I'm done, her dismissive, brisk tone indicating that I'm to figure it out. "Have they taken your blood, yet?"

"They did," I say slowly. "After the naumachia, though. I don't think it was anything to do with the Academy. Why?"

"We're still figuring that one out. Seems to happen to all the students eventually." She chews her lip as she says it, then stirs. "We shouldn't linger much longer, and I won't have an opportunity to talk with you again for a while. So if you have questions, now is the time."

I think. "How did Melior . . . do what he did?"

She snorts. "Questions within reason, Diago. You have made it perfectly clear that you're no friend to the Anguis. That is not information I am going to give you."

There's a tightening of need in my chest. This has been bothering me more than

I care to admit, even to myself. "Fine. But he said he knew why the Hierarchy attacked Suus. Was that power the reason?"

Relucia vacillates. "I think so. But I don't know for sure."

I exhale. Disappointed but unsurprised. "Alright. Let's start at the beginning, then. How long have you been watching me?"

"Getting reports on you? More than a year. You were spotted fighting in the Victorum league," she adds by way of explanation. "Melior gave some of our more trusted informants your description, though no one knew who you were—he'd been searching for you since before he joined us. And your sister." The last is half a question.

Dirges drift up to us from the valley, melding into a dark mess of melancholic chords.

"She died. In the escape." I hold her gaze as I say it, preferring her to see anger rather than pain.

She looks away. Nods. "I saw you, back there. When Lerius was going through the rites. I'm sorry." She sweeps back a strand of curly black hair, then continues. "I knew Ulciscor was looking for someone both desperate and educated enough to place in the Academy. And I knew he was watching for anyone else from Caeror's class to question. When I found out Nateo was in a Sapper, and you were working at Letens Prison . . . well. It was easy enough to pull some strings and have him transferred there. And then the transfer document was all it took for it to reach Ulciscor's ears."

I can't hide my dubiousness. "It was still pure chance that he talked to me."

"I told you back in the forest: I was *going* to make contact with you weeks beforehand. Prepare you to get his attention when he arrived." Relucia's annoyed at my doubt. "There was a miscommunication, and everything happened faster than it was meant to. Nateo got transferred two months early, and then Ulciscor's people were suddenly in Letens, watching the prison. While I was supposed to be a thousand miles away in a different country."

I grunt. That makes more sense. "You assumed I would be interested."

"I assumed your family's murder would be enough motivation, yes."

A cool breeze whips up out of the valley, causing the torches closest to us to flare and sputter. I let it cool the anger heating my cheeks. Bite down a response that would be too loud, isolated though we are.

"So why attack the Transvect, then?" I ask eventually. "Why not just visit me at Villa Telimus? It's not as if you didn't have an excuse to be there."

Relucia looks at me scornfully. "Because I'm not a fool. We'd never even spoken; for all I knew, you could have been a breath away from breaking and spilling your life's story to Ulciscor. I wanted to assess your state of mind before you found out who I was. Ideally, to train you well enough that I could actually be confident in sending you anywhere near him." Her mouth twists. "I wouldn't even be here, except Ulciscor insisted. I had no way of getting you a message beforehand. You did well to cover your reaction, though," she concedes.

Interesting. So there are no Anguis in the Academy. I mentally file away the information.

"Who else in the Anguis knows about me?" I do my best to mask my hesitancy. The thought of strangers out there knowing who I am, holding my life in their hands, is more than unsettling.

"One other person. So there's no point trying to kill me, even if you incorrectly thought you could succeed."

I choke off an instinctive chuckle as I realise she's not joking. "Who?"

"Someone reliable. Someone who will die before revealing your identity. Unless something happens to me." She smiles tightly. "Of course, that means everyone else believes just as the Catenans do. They blame you for Melior's death. For stopping the attacks."

Wonderful.

"We need to be getting back." Relucia stands, her features vague in the dim. "Make sure you go to Caten for the Festival of Pletuna. I'll contact you again there."

"Wait. I need to know. If this works. If . . . somehow in the future, the Hierarchy really does collapse in on itself." I stare down over the fires. "Are you going to destroy the Aurora Columnae?"

For the first time, Relucia looks surprised.

"I don't even know if that's possible," she says gently. Like a parent explaining a simple concept to a slow child. "And only the Princeps know where they all are. So . . . no. We'll wait for the right moment, wait until the Hierarchy is ready to crumble, and then strike. Remove our oppressors. Start again."

My fists clench. It's the answer I expected.

"That's the problem with people, though, isn't it? They always think that *other people* are the problem." Quiet. Angry. "You want to remove the Princeps? The senators? You'll just become them, sooner or later. If all you're trying to do is change who's in control, then you don't really want to change anything." I finish in a forceful, low growl. Letting her hear my disgust.

Relucia studies me.

"Maybe you're right," she says. "But you have to start somewhere."

Clearly considering the matter closed, she sets off down the stairs.

We descend largely in silence. Plenty of questions still burn in me—about the Anguis, about her, about what they actually expect me to do for them once my time at the Academy is over—but I know I won't get answers.

As we approach the lights of the Telimus mausoleum, Relucia slows. "If anyone asks about tonight, we talked about your past. Your time at the orphanage. That sort of thing." She straightens her stola. "I know more than enough of the story you and Ulciscor have been telling to make it work."

"How do you do it?" I frown at her. "I understand pretending, but this . . . you're *married* to him."

"Habit." Relucia's answer is brusque, but then she softens. "He's not the worst of them, you know. Not by a long way."

We're almost at the entrance. I stop, forcing Relucia to do so as well. It's not important—at least, it doesn't seem to be, to her—but I need her to know.

"Estevan killed himself. I couldn't do it. I had the spike at his throat, and he just . . ."

Relucia examines me. Nods sadly. "You cannot be free if you are afraid to die."

Without anything further, she pastes on a wide smile and strides into the light of the tomb.

XXXIX

Tense, raised voices echo down the short entrance to the Telimus tomb.

"I just don't understand why neither of you will *consider* it." It's Ulciscor's growl. "I'm not asking you to publicly denounce anyone. Just ask a favour of some old friends."

"Ulciscor, if it was for anything else, you know we would. But you cannot keep down this path. There was no *proof*." Lerius, joviality gone from his voice. Replaced by frustrated entreaty.

"There's no proof because nobody else is looking for any." Lanistia. Cold and sharp.

"We love you, Lani, but the two of you are dragging each other down with all this nonsense. And now you've involved someone else. A boy who doesn't know what he's getting into! Don't you dare tell me he has nothing to do with it," Lerius snaps, apparently pre-empting some perceived rebuttal.

"Stop it. All of you. Just stop it. It cannot bring him back." It's Milena. Her voice is cracking. "Please, Son. Lani. We loved him too, but none of this will bring him back." A soft sob punctuates the plea.

Relucia falters as she hears what I do. "This again," she mutters to me, barely loud enough to hear. Then she coughs noisily, pausing to ensure the occupants beyond have heard before striding into the main area with me in tow, smiling as if she'd overheard nothing at all.

There's definite friction, and Milena's eyes are red-rimmed, but both Relucia and I pretend not to notice. The tension recedes as Relucia begins obliviously enthusing about how delightful I am. Not disappears, not entirely, but fades into the background behind the conversation and laughter that follows. Only Milena doesn't seem inclined to pretend, watching the proceedings silently, scarcely acknowledging us when we sit.

The next two hours are long, albeit uneventful, with the awkwardness mostly managed by everyone focusing their attentions on me. Lerius and Relucia lead the charge, and after a while I realise Relucia's apparently blithe interruptions are often skilfully timed to head off potentially difficult lines of questioning. Lerius, for his part, seems more concerned for my well-being than suspicious. Given what we overheard of his argument with Ulciscor, I suspect he sees me as more victim than conspirator.

Ulciscor disappears not long into the conversation; I can see Relucia's curiosity as he excuses himself, but she makes no attempt to go after him. I'm mildly concerned when he returns not an hour later. The equipment I need him to make isn't something I want done in a rush.

I breathe an inward sigh of relief as, after another half hour, Ulciscor stands again and beckons me toward the door. "Vis cannot stay for the entire evening, I'm afraid."

"Oh?" Relucia pouts. "Why not?"

"Studies. I need every day I can get if I want to make it out of Class Six soon." There's approval from Lerius, who's already made it clear he doesn't think much of my lack of further advancement.

"Oh." Relucia doesn't hide her disappointment, flowing over to where I'm standing and flinging her arms around me. "Well, I am *so* pleased to have met you, dear boy. You're a delight. Again, welcome to the family." She kisses me enthusiastically on both cheeks. As she does so, there's an increase in pressure where she grips me. A gentle reminder.

Lerius and Milena follow in their farewells, the former still far warmer than the latter, though at least the stately woman remains polite as I leave. Lanistia sees Ulciscor and I to the entrance of the tomb, quickly checking no one else is around before speaking.

"Why so soon?" she asks pointedly, addressing Ulciscor more than me. "I thought half the point of this exercise was to ingratiate Vis to the family. Give him some stronger ties, some more vocal allies, should it come to that. Prove that we're not just using him to investigate Veridius."

"He has a way to get to the other side of Solivagus. But he has to go now."

Lanistia looks like she wants to know more, but a meaningful glance from Ulciscor and she just turns to me. "Be safe. And for the love of all the gods, don't get caught."

She's heading back inside before I can respond.

We start the descent. Some of the fires below are dimming to embers, though many still burn, and both conversation and song continue to echo up to us.

"You and Relucia seemed to get on well," Ulciscor observes. His tone's neutral, but there's the suggestion of laughter in it.

"She's . . . certainly talkative. Lovely, though." I feign the reaction I would have had, if Relucia's persona were real. "How long have you been married?"

"Four years." He eyes me. "And she *is* lovely, but be wary, too. She's a Sextus through merit. She's sharper than she lets on."

I refrain from commenting. "How did you meet?"

"Her family are the Cilaris. Knights—senators, but without much of a history."

He shrugs. "Her father approached my father, a year after Caeror. Our reputation had been dented, and our finances were not all they could have been. We were all but betrothed before we laid eyes on each other."

"How much does she know?"

"She knows what I think happened to Caeror. We don't discuss it, though. Her work means she's almost never around, anyway."

We reach the ground and begin walking along the carefully tended gravel path, lit by one of the three lines of fire that scar the length of the valley. Ulciscor glances around. "I need you to tell me something, Vis."

"Alright."

He slows to a halt, pulling me to a stop too. Serious. "Where are you from? Really?"

The question hangs in the air between us. I try not to look like my mind's racing. "I've already told you—"

"No, you haven't." Ulciscor's not angry—just certain. "I've brought you into my family today. Trusted you. And I know that no orphan from Aquiria could ever achieve the level of education you have. A lifetime of study and training isn't something you can hide." He sighs. "I don't care about your past, don't care what you're running from. But I do need to know what it is, in case it's going to be a problem. In case it's going to catch up with you."

I consider pushing my case, but Ulciscor's too sure.

"It . . . won't," I say eventually. It's an admission—which he needs—but also a promise that I'm not going to give him answers.

"How can you know?"

"Have you been able to find anything about me?"

"No." Ulciscor's clearly not satisfied. "But my resources are miniscule compared to others."

I take a long moment to deliberate. "I vow to you by all the gods and all I care about, I will do everything in my power to find out what happened to Caeror. And that my past will not interfere with that."

Ulciscor returns my steady gaze for what feels like an eternity.

Then he nods curtly and starts walking again.

"You remind me of him, you know."

"Of who?"

"Caeror." Ulciscor smiles at the darkness ahead, hands clasped behind his back, ambling more than marching. "I only realised it tonight, when we were talking. But you have a lot in common with him."

"Thank you," I say quietly. I mean it. I know Ulciscor's giving me one of the highest compliments he can.

We push on to the Transvect. As the platform comes in sight, Ulciscor reaches into his satchel and presses the spare tunic and cloak I asked for into my hands. Then he draws out two stone cuffs.

"When both are closed, the attraction will trigger. It's strong enough to lift you, so be careful," he warns, a little worriedly. "Open one, and it will stop again. Don't forget you're going to have to break one once you get back, too. If you're found with them . . ."

"I know." I take the cuffs, turning them over in my hands. Hewn stone, a simple Will-based hinge and clasp for each. The first closes with a snap, as if the separate pieces are being sucked together, and when I close the second one, the sections of the make-shift grapple wrench violently into each other. My fingers are almost caught in between.

"Told you."

I grunt, releasing the clasp on one again. Immediately the two cuffs separate. "You just made these?" It's more elaborate than I'd expected.

"Best I could do."

"I assumed I'd just be getting a couple of stones with an activation method. This is much better."

Ulciscor snorts. "You haven't thought through the forces at play, then. There's no way you could hang onto a stone at that speed. It would just slip out of your grasp and you'd be stranded."

"Oh."

"As it is, you're going to have to time it perfectly." Ulciscor's emphatic about this. "If the Transvect's too high, moving too fast, it will tear your hand off. And it'll hurt if you're not exactly in position; too far away, and you'll slam into the Transvect too fast. Probably break something."

"I'll manage." I try to sound confident, even if I'm not, now the reality of the endeavour is staring me in the face. "What about the locator?"

"A little easier." He presses two stones into my palm. One's small and circular. The other is thin, needle-like, with a chain attached to its end. Neither is bigger than my thumbnail, and they cling lightly to each other. "Constant attraction. Drop the round one when you jump. And needless to say . . . don't jump too early."

It's past midnight when we arrive. I've drawn my hood—it's cold enough to warrant it—and Ulciscor has covered his purple stripe. The platform is manned by a single dark-haired Praetorian who checks the stone tile Scitus gave me with bored efficiency before leaving us to our own devices.

After that, Ulciscor and I wait. We occasionally chat about inconsequential things, but mostly lounge in silence. I get the impression that he wants it that way; he spends most of the next twenty minutes gazing out over the Eternal Fires, deep in thought. I suspect he's thinking about his brother. I don't interrupt.

Finally the lamplit grey and brown of the Transvect resolves from the pitch-black, a disembodied form sliding downward into the torchlight. My hands are suddenly clammy. I stand, gripping the stone cuffs Ulciscor gave me tightly. I look around, but we're still alone.

"Here we go." There will only be a minute before the doors shut and the Transvect takes off again.

"Luck." Ulciscor watches as the behemoth settles. He clutches my arm in the traditional fashion, and I return the gesture.

The Transvect doors slide open, and I pause on the off chance that someone has caught it in to the Necropolis this late at night. There's no movement, though, only lamplit seats. The lamps themselves look like they're burning low. Probably haven't had anyone bother to check on them for a few hours.

I step inside the rearmost cabin and stride to the back, crouching. Then I snap closed one cuff and stuff it, as well as the clothing Ulciscor gave me, into a cranny between the seat and the rear wall. No one will see them there.

I peek out of the carriage again. Ulciscor is talking to the Praetorian, drawing his attention away. I jog the few paces to the very back of the Transvect. There's a short deck there beneath the jutting stone nose, just lower than the carriages themselves. Some sort of servicing platform, according to Ulciscor. I step onto it, then reach up and carefully extinguish the two lamps that are meant to delineate the end of the Transvect while it's in the air. In daylight, I couldn't get away with this; anyone looking up in passing would immediately spot me. But now, I'll be near invisible.

Once my surroundings are plunged into darkness, I feel around until my arms are linked through two long handles that appear made for the purpose. I'm facing away from the Transvect, gazing down into the fires that still illuminate the valley. I can't see how far down it is to the ground, but I can tell it's a long way.

I try to steady, body tensed and braced, heart feeling like it's beating out of my chest. I can't help but curse myself. This idea . . . this *really* wasn't a good one. I should probably—

The Transvect lurches into motion.

XL

I LET OUT A GASP AS MY BODY JERKS FORWARD, ARMS STRAIN-
ing before I pull myself back upright. The Transvect starts slow, thankfully, but we're
climbing and then building speed at a terrifying pace. The lit platform is already far
below, and I can see Ulciscor still talking to the Praetorian. He never looks up.

Soon enough Ulciscor, the platform, the fires in the valley, everything is lost to
view. The wind starts to screech and whip around me, though I know I'm sheltered
from the worst of it. Everything feels colder up here. The air knifes through my tunic.
I can't risk moving to tug my flapping cloak tighter.

Time slips. Begins to blur as the night screams around me, over me, through me.
Occasionally the great black is broken by the streetlamps of distant towns below, gone
again so quickly that I'm reminded only of how terrifyingly fast we're moving.

I cling on desperately, and regret my decision for what feels like forever.

Then, finally, the scything air somehow becomes even icier. A trace of salt to it.
I gasp my relief as a few lanterns on the ships from the fishing village reflect off the
rolling waves of the Sea of Quus. About twenty minutes away now.

Those lights are long faded from view when I feel the Transvect begin to slow.

It's easy enough to notice, even in the dark. There's the pressure against my back
as I'm impelled into the stone by the deceleration. The lurch in my stomach as we start
to drop.

The screeching wind quietens. My breath shortens.

If I jump off too soon, I'll be outside the Seawall's protective ring around
Solivagus—the one that, according to Ulciscor, will drag me to the ocean floor if I try
to swim across it. And if I leave it too late, the Transvect will be moving too fast, be
too high. I won't be able to control how I hit the water. A good chance I'll be knocked
unconscious from the impact and drown, in that scenario.

At least there's the faintest sheen of light from below, a smudge of illumination
off the swells appearing as the Transvect levels out. It's the reflection of the lanterns
underneath, I assume. Fortunate. The utter completeness of the darkness out here
wasn't something I'd anticipated.

My stiff, half-frozen arms almost slip as I finally risk loosening my grip in preparation for letting go. The glistening humps of water are close enough, without question.

But I have to wait until the anchoring point slides past. The window to jump will be a second or two. I won't have the luxury of hesitating.

The Transvect crawls forward for an eternity. I'm sure I've missed it. I resist the urge to look up and scan behind us, instead focusing on that tiny patch of illuminated water below. The stone will be most visible there.

I see it. A lighter, unmoving flash against the waves.

I jump.

There's a moment of displacement as my stomach sucks up into my chest; the darkness, the yawning depths at my feet, and I'm back at Suus. Falling, helpless and scared, my father's bloodied, pleading gaze on me as I vanish from his sight.

Then the water is smashing into me, cold and sharp as it covers my head. It's not nearly the fall I endured that night three years ago, and my eyes are open quickly enough to see the Transvect's lanterns through the water. I force back the memories and push desperately upward as those lights grow smaller. Break the surface with a gasp as they disappear entirely into the distance.

I got it right, at least. I'm between the anchoring point and the island. Inside the protective barrier.

I tread water to get my bearings, touching the buttoned-up pocket where the stone cuff is secured and exhaling in pure relief when I feel the lump. I can't wear it without activating it, but one of my worst fears was that it would come loose and sink when I jumped.

Wary of being swept too far out of position—or back into the Seawall—I dig into my pouch and fish out the locator stone, dropping it and letting it sink. There are too many identical-looking anchoring points out here, far enough from the shore that there's only the horizon to distinguish them against. I need to be certain I can find my way back to exactly which one the Transvect uses, when the time comes.

Everything's still pitch-black as I ride the waves, but I know I'm facing toward where the Transvect lights disappeared only seconds ago. After a minute, my eyes start to adjust; even in the cloudy night, away from the light of any lanterns whatsoever, there's enough to make out the shape of Solivagus up ahead.

I point myself roughly toward where I think the distant ruins lie, and start to swim.

% % %

THE DARK FORESTS OF SOLIVAGUS GLOWER AHEAD AS I FINALLY haul myself over the lip of the cliff and onto its windswept-smooth summit. My lungs burn. Arms ache. The last of my scrabbling sends loose stones skittering down the cliffside, their scrambling quickly lost against the lapping of waves. My cloak is still cold and heavy with damp as I collapse onto my back, gasping.

Eventually, still breathing hard, I force myself to roll and examine the stony shore far below. A couple of hundred feet, at least, to get back down.

"That . . . was easier . . . in my head," I wheeze to myself.

It's been more than two hours since the Transvect. A mile swimming would have been straightforward enough for me, once, but it's been years since I was in the water and my muscles stretched and strained at every unaccustomed motion. And then once I dragged myself up the rocky shore, gasping and shivering and already exhausted, everything was numb. It took longer than I'd have liked to scavenge what I needed for a fire and strike one to light with my knife and flint. Probably another hour hunched naked over it—huddled close to the flames both to absorb as much warmth as possible, and to hide them from any stray eyes out on the water—as my wrung-out clothes dried.

And after that, of course, there was the climb. Ascent tortuously careful as I methodically tested each handhold, much of the craggy cliff face cast into impenetrable black against the faint silver leaking from above. I slipped more than once. My hands are scraped and raw.

But I'm here now.

The easy part is done.

I take another couple of minutes to catch my breath. Orienting myself. I've arrived a little farther south than I would have liked, maybe another fifteen minutes away from the mountain Ulciscor originally pointed out, but thankfully still close enough to where I was aiming. I should allow another six or seven hours to navigate the forest to the ruins, and the same back. Or a little longer, actually, to safely descend the cliff again. And given I'm not as strong a swimmer as I once was, at least a half hour more—probably closer to three quarters of one—if I want to be in position again before the final Transvect run from the Necropolis.

That leaves only a few hours to explore the ruins.

I *really* need to get moving.

I drag myself to my feet. Spend a few minutes making a torch using tree resin—a risk, but it's not light enough to see my way otherwise—and, ignoring my protesting body, start walking.

The forest is still, though noisy enough thanks to the snapping twigs and heavy rustling of my passage. I push relentlessly forward, following trails made by animals where possible, although those are scarce. Several times I hit a dead end, gullies or gulches too wide or too overgrown to pass, and I have to double back around them. My arms start to show the effect of hundreds of small scratches, red lines etched along my skin. Crickets chirp ceaselessly. Wings flutter overhead. Occasionally the screeching of other nightlife pierces the gloom and I flinch, raising the torch high. Still concerned that someone out on the Transvect platform could notice my light—it might be visible from there, from time to time, through the trees—but that's a risk I have to take. With at least ten miles and deep canyons in between, there's no way they could reach where I am with any sort of alacrity, anyway.

Dawn is brightening the horizon when I first realise my locator needle has stopped working.

I come to a reluctant, apprehensive halt. Up until now, I've been using the dangling sliver of stone as a hedge against my sense of direction. But this time when I hold it out, there's nothing. No gentle tugging toward its counterpart at the bottom of the sea, even as I stand motionless.

I regard it grimly. It's not vital at the moment, but the swim back will be a different story. I spend a minute examining the needle for any defects or chips. Trying to decide what could possibly have gone wrong. Distance shouldn't affect its attraction.

In the end, dispiritingly, I realise there's not much I can do about it. I just have to press on. Hope that I can find my way back to the right anchoring point in the Seawall without assistance.

It's another hour and a half before the trees ahead begin to thin, and I see the first crumbling structures.

I slow. My breath comes hard, wisps of fog puffing out into the early morning sun, exertion and lack of sleep already weighing on me. There's a heaviness to the air. No sounds. Not even the crickets anymore.

The ruins here are in better shape than the site near the Academy. Far more extensive, too. I'm on a hillside looking down over a small town's worth of overgrown structures.

It's the enormous dome that draws my eye, though.

The clouds are now nothing more than a veneer of mist, and the morning light reflects sharply off a curved, apparently undamaged surface set into the mountainside itself. It's massive, far taller than anything else in the area, with a polished-smooth façade that time has coated with dirt streaked by rain. Beneath the grime, though, it's not the grey or light brown of stone. Hard to tell for sure, but it seems coloured a deep, blood red.

I stand there, assessing for a minute. No sign of movement. I start picking my way down.

Stones skitter and leaves crunch underfoot as I move, sharp in the silence. The back of my neck prickles. Down among the buildings the air's sullen, thick, feels like it's absorbing my footfalls. I still don't hear any of the soft calls of birds or scurrying motion of wildlife that accompanied me on my journey here. Some of the tangled growth around me is cleared, cut away to provide an easier path. I am not the only recent visitor.

I do a cursory tour of some of the smaller buildings, more as a formality than because I think I'll find anything important. They're dark and dusty, containing nothing but rubble and lichen. I'm unsurprised. Whatever Veridius wants with this place, it surely has something to do with that dome. The protrusion from the mountain must be five hundred feet across, at least as high.

I approach the crimson structure cautiously, dwarfed as I use the edge of my tunic to wipe a small section at its base clean. My haggard face peers back at me, tinged ruddy. Not as clear as a mirror, but not far off.

I tap the surface with a fingernail. It gives off a clinking sound, closer to glass than stone. Strange. I draw my knife and scratch the blade along the section I've cleaned. There's an unpleasant screeching sound.

When I take the steel away, there's no mark.

I scrutinise the spot uneasily, then step back. The entire thing appears to be one piece, the wall rising vertically for almost twenty feet before beginning its almost imperceptibly gentle curve inward toward the mountain. I can make out jagged, seemingly random lines caked in dirt farther up: not writing, but I don't think they're cracks, either. There are no balconies, no stairs, no windows.

No doors, either, that I can see. No indication as to its purpose.

I start along its curvature, apprehensive. This can't be it. I have . . . two hours, maybe, before I should head back? I glance at the sky. Maybe two and a half, given I'll be making the return journey in daylight.

"Rotting gods." I reach the edge where the dusty red glass vanishes into the cliff face, then spin back the other way, eyes straining for something to latch on to. "Vek, vek, *vek.*"

It's after a minute of travelling back in the opposite direction that I spy the symbol of the Hierarchy.

I hurry over. The emblem stands ten feet high, ending at the ground, but shows no sign of providing an entrance. There's writing above it. Letters I recognise. That same old form of Vetusian I saw in the other ruins.

LUCEUM. OBITEUM. RES.
REMEMBER, BUT DO NOT MOURN.

My heart beats faster. Obiteum and Luceum. Again, those unknown words from Caeror's mysterious communication to his brother.

I run my hand along the grooves of the symbol. The surface where it's etched is cool and hard, the corners sharp. No sign of wear. I push at it, boots slipping on the grass. Then try to find purchase in the deep furrows and pull. Nothing moves.

I make a quick circuit past, checking the remainder of the dome's base to ensure there aren't any other distinguishing features—there aren't—and then return. It makes no sense for this to be here, if there's no way inside. And this symbol is about the right size for a door.

I spend the next ten minutes clearing away dirt from around the pyramid image, running my hands along the smooth glass, looking for . . . something. More writing. Clues. Anything.

Eventually I return to the inscription above. Sit and endeavour to clear my mind from the weighing pressure of time. The sun's moving higher at my back.

I study the text. Repeat it to myself aloud, trying to decide whether it's imparting any clue, any meaning beyond simply what it's saying. Luceum and the other two are names. Places? People?

I close my eyes, trying to recall the rest of Caeror's message.

"Luceum," I mutter to myself. "Luceum and Obiteum and . . . Scintres Exunus?"

There's a grinding sound, a roar against the morning's hush that has me scrambling to my feet in panic. The reddish glass quavers as the pyramid symbol in it starts to split, each half gradually folding to the side. Light vanishes into the mouth of the opening as the groaning continues deep within the dome, the sound of hundreds of pieces of edifice rearranging.

It finishes with an echoing boom, leaving a triangular hole gaping into darkness.

The opening exudes nameless menace. I study it pensively. The timing cannot be coincidental, but I've never heard of any Will-based abilities that can activate on a specific phrase.

No time to be hesitant, though.

I retrieve my torch, light it again. Its illumination spills into the inky passageway. Stairs descend. My footsteps echo as I creep forward.

The way soon levels out, becoming a long, wide corridor where my flickering light barely touches the sides. I cannot see the roof. Dark rock seems hewn from the mountain, no trace of the red glass from outside. There's a sense of age to everything, as though I might be the first person to walk this path in decades.

I only take a few steps along before I come to a stumbling halt again, arm trembling as I raise the torch higher to look at the dark cavities along the wall.

It's just like in the ruins near the Academy. Men and women lining the corridor. Naked. Eyes closed and obsidian blades speared through their chests, pinning them to the stone behind.

None of them move. None of them open their eyes.

I shudder, and hurry past.

The end of the hall emerges before I've been walking ten seconds; there are maybe two dozen bodies in here, no more. The orange glow of my flame reveals a dead end, stone wall broken by a slim gap that allows the floor to protrude farther into a semi-circular platform. A waist-high railing suggests it's overlooking something. Beyond that, though, there's only darkness.

I approach, casting uneasy glances behind. Trying not to imagine movement back there in the void.

The balustrade catches the light as I near, glints red. There's only bottomless space past it, the platform itself barely wide enough for a single person to stand on. My shoulders brush the walls on either side as I step through the gap and onto it, eyes straining into the abyss.

A grinding and then I'm suddenly thrown, stumbling. Falling. My arm shivers as it smashes into the red railing. I can only watch in mute horror as my torch slips from my numb grasp. Tumbles over the edge, end over end.

It falls for a long, long time before it vanishes.

When I recover enough to scramble to my feet again, the platform has started to follow it down into the darkness.

XLI

I ALMOST ATTEMPT A WILD, ILL-ADVISED LEAP BACK UP TO-
ward the hallway before I realise my descent is smooth. Controlled, not falling. I've seen
Will-imbued transportation platforms move this way, though I've never been on one.

I cling to the crimson railing, breaths still ragged and flustered; as my skin makes
contact, the glass-like surface glows, bringing a startling respite from the utter darkness.
The light is tinted the same colour, though. Casts everything in a dark red. Preferable
to the terrifying unknown, but not by much.

I recover enough to take stock. The hallway above has already disappeared, and the
wall behind me is smooth. Unclimbable.

It seems I'm going wherever this is taking me.

I reluctantly stop craning my neck. My knuckles are white against the blushing of
the balustrade as the wall behind me is suddenly gone, replaced by inky darkness above
and below and around on all sides, as if I'm sinking into an unending abyss. The stone
platform's descent continues for anxious minutes.

My hands are beginning to cramp from their apprehensive grip when the red illumination from the railing winks out again. I hurtle through the void for several more
seconds in terrifying, silent darkness.

Then, finally, light flares below.

I flinch back, the abrupt restoration of my sight disorienting. Torches flicker to life
one by one away from me. The hall I'm descending into is hewn from the mountain itself,
hundreds of feet wide and long, probably a hundred feet high. Two rows of massive columns stretch from floor to vaulted ceiling, making the space appear almost cathedral-like.

And at the far end of the room there's an enormous Hierarchy symbol set into the
wall, glowering down over everything. Lines of bronze glitter against dark stone.

My platform slows as it nears the ground, then settles gently onto the floor. I don't
move. I have no idea where I am, but this place feels old. Off-limits. Dangerous.

Even so, there's no activity anywhere that I can see, no sound.

Fear tightens my muscles, but I'm still on a schedule—and whatever this place is,
it must have something to do with Caeror's time at the Academy. If I can find out what
happened to him, I can be free of at least one of the daggers poised at my back.

I force my fingers to uncurl from the railing, and disembark.

One step away. Two. My footsteps are swallowed by the enormity of the hall. I keep glancing behind me, but the platform remains grounded.

I steel myself, and start for the massive bronze symbol in the wall. It's the only point of interest in the whole place, as far as I can see. There are no doors, no exits that I've noticed. The columns are square and plain. For all its immensity, there's really not much here to see.

"What is this place?" I mutter the words absently, glaring at the massive symbol ahead.

"It is a test."

"*VEK!*" I whirl and stumble backward at the calm male voice coming from not far enough behind me. The man's only ten feet away, though I can't see from where he could possibly have emerged. He's dressed in rags. His feet are bare. Long, straggly black hair falls limply across his face.

It's not thick enough to hide that where his eyes should be, there are only gaping, red holes.

The stranger doesn't react to my fear. Just watches me. Motionless. Mute.

"Who . . . who in all the gods-damned hells are you?" I get the words out eventually. Still putting more distance between us, hand locked to the hilt of my dagger.

"I was known as Artemius Sel. I was a traitor to the commandment of isolation. I attempted to gain synchronism and remove the seal to Obiteum during the rebellion of the seventh era after the Rending. I have thus been lawfully condemned to servitude, guiding those who come after." He speaks listlessly, in monotone, though his words are also strangely slurred. I shiver. The raw sockets of his eyes are hard not to focus on.

"Alright." I'm as much confused as wary now. The man doesn't seem inclined to attack; even so, I circle around so that he's not between me and the platform I came in on. "What is this place, Artemius?"

The man rotates so that he's still facing me, but doesn't respond.

"Did you hear me? Do you . . . know where we are?"

No response.

"Alright," I say again slowly. "You said this was a test. For what?"

"Basic proficiency."

"In what? What does that mean?"

Silence.

I take a hesitant step forward. Wave my hand at him, peer into his face. There's no sign that he's observed my movement. "Why aren't you saying anything?" Still nothing.

I sigh, more bemused than anything else, even if an abundance of caution remains.

The man's only responding to certain questions, apparently. He's unsettling, certainly. *Very* unsettling. But doesn't seem immediately dangerous.

"What is the test, Artemius?"

"You must reach the entrance." He points.

I frown, following his finger to the massive symbol at the far end of the hall. There's nothing but an empty expanse of stone between me and it. "That doesn't seem . . ."

I trail off as I turn back to Artemius. The man had been clasping his hands behind his back but now he's unstrapping something from his left arm and offering it to me.

A bracer, studded with several dozen small stones. Each one with a unique symbol etched into it.

I don't move to take it, cold at the familiar sight. "I don't understand."

He doesn't say anything. Just continues to hold it out.

"Why do I need this?"

"You must wear it to reach the entrance."

I tentatively reach out. Accept the bracer. Artemius's arm drops back to his side. I squint at his empty stare, curiosity increasingly matching the creeping unease his presence brings. The way the man's responding is rote, as if reading from a script. Is he able to speak only when asked specific questions? Questions to which he knows the answers, or questions which he is *allowed* to answer? Whatever the case, and though I've only heard of such things in the most fanciful of fairy tales, he seems in thrall to some unseen force. Under the power of someone other than himself.

If I didn't know the bracer's purpose, I don't think I would have taken it. But after a long few seconds of hesitation, I'm slipping it onto my left arm and cinching it tight. It's absurdly light.

There's a crawling sensation as it settles against my skin.

And then the hall explodes into roaring, grinding activity.

I stumble back as stone bursts from the ground ahead. Austere black walls slam upward until they're towering, thirty feet high at least, partially blocking the massive Hierarchy symbol from view. A single, arched entrance to the newly formed structure lies straight ahead. Through it, I can see passageways branching off in multiple directions.

The walls are taller, and there's no way to view the layout from on high. But I know exactly what it is.

I pick a stone with two perpendicular crosses and give it a short, sharp twist. Sure enough, a soft grating echoes from the left-most corner section. Right where it should in the Labyrinth.

"What happens if I pass the test, Artemius?" I ask quietly.

"You will go through the gate to Obiteum and Luceum. But not be allowed to remain here. Synchronism is reserved for leadership alone."

"Obiteum and Luceum—they're places? Where are they?" No response. "What is synchronism?" No response.

I contemplate the daunting sight ahead for a little longer. Trying to understand. "If I go in there, will anything try and stop me from getting to the other side?"

"Remnants guard the way."

"What are Remnants?"

No response.

I massage my forehead. Sigh. Press on with my enquiries.

Artemius, for the most part, stares vacantly: he seems capable of answering questions related to this hall, this "test," but nothing else. When I ask for his history, he repeats his explanation about being a traitor. When I probe for more about the purpose of the Labyrinth, he tells me that I must wear the bracer to reach the entrance. That it is a test for basic proficiency. That passing will allow me to go through the gate to Obiteum and Luceum.

All my other questions are met with eyeless silence.

After perhaps fifteen minutes of fruitless investigation, I mutter a frustrated curse and start unhooking the control bracer from my arm. Whatever this test is, I don't know the risks. Don't understand the stakes. As soon as the device is free of my skin, there's the thundering grind of stone as the black walls start sinking back into the ground. Within seconds there's just smooth floor between me and the symbol on the far wall again.

I tetchily toss the bracer at Artemius's feet. "Why do I even need that? Why can't I just walk across there now?"

The eyeless man stoops. Takes it and impassively straps it to his arm. "Accord becomes too strong, so close to the gate. Remnants from Obiteum guard the way. Would you like me to demonstrate?"

I straighten. A new response.

"Alright," I say, drawing out the word to indicate my uncertainty. If the intonation has any effect on the man, he doesn't show it. He turns and begins walking toward the massive, three-pronged bronze pyramid.

"Wait." My brow furrows. Uneasy. Artemius doesn't stop.

There's an undulation as he crosses to where the Labyrinth was. A translucent blur that ripples through the air, as if the man has just stepped through an invisible wall of water.

And then, as the ripple reaches the Hierarchy symbol, something flickers into being.

I freeze. I'd swear there was nothing there a moment ago, but now there are three dark shapes. Waves of black, glittering in the dull light.

They rush toward Artemius.

I'm mute with horror. The surging swells are made up of thousands of shards of what look like dark glass, scraping and scratching and grinding as they sweep closer.

"Artemius! Get back!" I finally find my voice.

Artemius doesn't turn. Keeps walking.

"Run!" I scream the words this time.

The waves hit him.

They change shape as they strike. Sprout pointed lances that spear Artemius through the torso, gore-coated tips protruding from his back. I shout in helpless horror. I can hear the eyeless man's gasp from here. It's cut off as he's enveloped; there are flashes of skin being flayed away, red flecks through the black. He vanishes beneath a writhing mountain of shadowy glass.

The chaos clears quickly, the swells sliding away. Sated. All that's left on the floor is a glistening smudge.

I stumble back, double over, and retch. Everything seems distant, detached. As if this is happening to someone else.

When fear straightens me again, the dark masses have disappeared.

I spit and wipe my mouth with a trembling hand. Those must be the Remnants. Can they go farther than the boundaries of where the Labyrinth rose? Are they aware of my presence here?

I can't use the control bracer to raise the walls again, either. It was consumed along with Artemius.

When I finally tear my eyes from the red stain ahead and turn, there's a young woman standing silently about ten feet away. Hands clasped behind her back. Shoulder-length black hair matted. Her long tunic is torn. Her eyes are as sightless as Artemius's were.

I reel back. Let out a string of startled curses. She doesn't react.

"What in all . . . " I throw up my hands. Alarm fading to vexation. "Who are *you*?"

"I was known as Elia Veranius. I was a traitor to the commandment of isolation. I attempted to gain synchronism and remove the seal to Obiteum during the eleventh era after the Rending. I have thus been lawfully condemned to servitude, guiding those who come after." Her voice is high-pitched. Reedy.

My skin crawls. "Of course you were," I mutter. "Alright. Tell me everything you can about this test."

She brings her left arm forward, revealing a bracer. "It is a test for basic proficiency. The way is guarded by Remnants. I am able to demonstrate—"

"No. No. Gods, no." I wave my hands frantically to cut her off. "No demonstrating. Definitely no demonstrating."

I spend the next five minutes throwing every question I can think of at Elia. Probing. Experimenting. I learn little. And I'm acutely, acutely aware that my time here is running out.

"How do I leave, without taking the test?" I've already gleaned this from Artemius, but want to verify.

Elia indicates the platform on which I arrived. "That will return you to the entrance."

I exhale my relief at the confirmation and nod, though I don't think it matters whether I acknowledge her. "Can you leave?" No answer. "Can I get back in the same way?" No answer.

With a last, wary glance toward the bronze symbol on the wall—and the dark stain beneath it—I walk away. Elia makes no move to follow.

The return trip is bathed once again in red, the platform rising as soon as I step on and grip the railing. My mind races as I ascend. Was this what happened to Caeror? Did he try to run the Labyrinth and get killed by those . . . *things*? I don't even know what I'm reporting to Ulciscor. I understand that the maze is a test, now. A means of getting to a gate on the other side, which leads to Obiteum and Luceum. Beyond that, though . . . I don't even know where Obiteum and Luceum *are*. Or what synchronism is, or the Rending, or the commandment of isolation.

They're important, though, that much is clear.

The crimson light lingers once the platform seals to the end of the entry hallway, providing just enough illumination for me to stumble my way forward. The bodies to either side of me are cloaked in their recesses by deep shadow.

"Scintres Exunus," I yell once I reach the bottom of the stairs.

As the way above folds open and fresh air flows against my face, any relief is cut short by golden light. *Vek*. It's past noon. Much later than I realised. I clamber upward. No time to celebrate survival. Urgency lends vigour to my weary body.

This is going to be close.

XLII

BRANCHES TEAR AT MY TUNIC AS I PLOUGH HEADLONG through the forest, fatigued muscles straining, breath coming in ragged gasps. I'm able to risk greater speed than before thanks to the time of day, but not by much. The light's already fading. In fact, the cloud-obscured sun kissed the rise I'm currently slogging my way up more than twenty minutes ago.

I'm better than two-thirds of the way there, I think, but I'm exhausted. Stumbling more than running. My stomach sucks at my insides, my lungs burn, my throat can't remember what it felt like to be moist. Even with fretfulness coursing through me, my body can only take so much. I need to stop. Eat and drink. Rest, if only for a few minutes.

I push on until I reach one of the many streams my path crosses, then drop to my knees and drink before collapsing to the mossy ground, head on the grass. I don't close my eyes, tempting though it is. There's no chance I'll be back in time if I fall asleep.

The forest rustles around me, peaceful, and the water burbles cheerfully over the top. I'm not close enough to the sea to hear waves yet. I lie there, my panting fading to something more steady, taking stock. Trying to figure out how far I've come, how far there is to go. What my chances are from here.

I eventually sit up again. I'm light-headed, need to eat.

The stream is teeming with fish, and childhood practice makes it relatively easy to pull one. Its scales flash in the dying light as it flops and gasps on the shore. I use my flint to light a small fire; there's a decent breeze, and there shouldn't be enough smoke for it to be spotted. Soon the fish is cooking in the embers.

I take the locator needle from my pocket and dangle it again, straining for any sense that it's pulling one way or another. There's still nothing, though.

I'm so lost in my own thoughts, I almost miss the faint, pitiful keening coming from somewhere downstream.

I twist when it comes again, frowning in its direction. It's a pleading, pained sound. Not human.

I draw my knife. The fire's still going; a fish is one thing, but something larger would be better. And from the way I stagger as I rise, any extra time I have to spend cooking will be more than worth it.

I creep along the stream bed, knife out, crouching low. The sound gets louder. There's a persistence to it. An anguished whine, punctuated by yelps.

I round a bend, and see the alupi pup.

It's trapped, half-submerged, bucking and scrabbling to get out from underneath a heavy branch that's somehow fallen on top of it. The creature is only a foot or so long—it must be very young, given the size to which they are supposed to grow. There's blood pouring down the side of its face, mixing a bright red with the water before dissipating among the stones in the shallows. Its black fur is matted. Bright grey eyes spot me and flash with feral fury, teeth baring to a warning snarl.

I examine its surroundings, but there's nothing else moving. The cub's been abandoned by its pack, then. I've heard of this: unlike wolves, alupi young need to care for themselves. If one gets injured, it's excised like a gangrenous limb.

I stalk toward the cub, ignoring its raised hackles, knife held at the ready. Assessing. I can probably skin it, cook the meat in . . . half an hour? The creature growls again, its squeaky pitch far from terrifying. Then it yelps as it slides farther into the water, almost over its head, and struggles wildly to right itself. It slips around in ungainly fashion until it's finally far enough up the muddy bank to be safe.

It twists gamely to face me. Still showing its teeth. It emits another high-pitched warning, but then its spirit seems to break, and it trails off into a whimper as it starts to slide again.

I grit my teeth. I'll be doing it a mercy; it was going to die out here anyway. I slosh my way over to the shivering, snarling ball of hair. Steel myself. Raise the knife. It keeps looking at me, directly into my eyes. Afraid, but not cowering.

Cari had a pup, back on Suus. Got him . . . two months before the invasion? She called him Abrazo. Used to let him sleep in her bed. Against our parents' wishes, of course.

"Vek. *Vek.* Rotting *gods.*" I let my hand fall. "You gods-damned soft-hearted . . ."

I slide the knife back into its sheathe and crouch beside the alupi.

"I know exactly how you feel," I mutter to it, carefully holding out a hand to indicate that I don't wish it any harm. "Maybe I should call you Diago." I laugh bitterly to myself.

He bites me. Quick as lightning, far too fast for me to react. His small, razor-sharp teeth slice into my skin and I shout in pain, snatching my hand back and shaking it, flecks of red spattering into the stream. I almost decide that perhaps he would be better roasted after all. Then I stop, kick myself instead. It's not a dog. It's a wild animal in pain. Of course it was going to do that.

I rinse the wound in the stream before tearing a strip of my tunic to bind it. It's painful but not deep. Then I turn back toward my fire. The cub, seeing I'm leaving, whines piteously at me.

"Be patient," I growl over my shoulder. I retreat to where the fish is cooking—or rather, burned on one side and raw on the other by this point—and snatch it from the embers, half muttering curses to myself the entire time. Then I stomp back, too irritated to care about any noise I'm making.

"Here." I break off a piece of fish and offer it, very carefully, to the animal. The alupi regards me with deep suspicion, but as soon as the smell hits its nostrils, it's struggling forward, jaws snapping fruitlessly a couple of times before finally snagging the piece in its mouth. The animal gobbles it greedily.

It looks at me as soon as it's finished, anticipation in its eyes.

I scowl at it. "Oh for . . ." I shake my head, then toss the rest of the fish on the ground. It's gone almost as quickly as the first piece.

"Are you going to let me help now?" Too bad for the cub if it doesn't, because one more failed attempt and I'm going to do the right thing and put it out of its misery.

Fortunately, when I reach out—hand well protected by several layers of tunic this time—the cub's upper lip curls back, but it doesn't do anything more than that.

It takes a minute to untangle the animal; as soon as it's free it tries to limp away but immediately collapses, lying on its side, whimpering in between panting. I watch its heaving chest in dismay.

"You're fine," I whisper to it. Abandoned and alone, injured, struggling. Maybe I see more of myself here than I care to admit.

I tear yet another strip of cloth from my tunic and dip it in the water, carefully washing away the matted dirt and blood from the animal's long wound. The creature yelps and twitches, at one point twisting to snap unsuccessfully back at my hand, but I'm waiting for it and get clear in time. The gash is bad, but not fatal, and I don't think anything's broken.

I rinse the strip again and bind the wound. It's hardly an ideal solution—I imagine the animal will worry it off before long—but until then, it might be enough to let the blood congeal. I don't think regular movement will open the injury up again, either. The creature is trembling, so I take off my cloak and wrap it around the cub's body, drying it as best I can. I'm not sure when, but by the time I'm finished, the alupi has stopped shivering and is either asleep or passed out. Hopefully the former.

I watch it worriedly, then sigh. It's been almost fifteen minutes. I'm still hungry, but I'm rested. My head's clearer, too. I feel better than I suspect I would have had I killed the pup, but either way, I need to get moving.

I lay a hand gently on the alupi's head. Smooth its coarse hair back. It twitches, but its eyes don't open. I have no idea whether it will ever wake.

I leave it wrapped in my cloak. It can't be identified as mine, and I'm not going to wear it once I hit the water anyway.

I kick dirt over the last of my fire and start jogging again, my thoughts sharper, more ordered than they have been since I got out of the dome. I'm still weary, but the break has done me good. I press on for an hour and a half until the forest around me begins to thin, and the tang of salt touches the air.

Before long I'm at the cliff's edge: not exactly where I climbed up, but I don't think it's too far away. Difficult to orient myself against the unfamiliar shoreline or the string of identical anchoring points on the horizon, though. Peering over the edge, I can't see anything below that looks like the remains of my fire from the previous night.

The sun has already dipped below the cloud-clogged horizon, everything tinted in hues of pink and purple. The Transvect will already have left the Necropolis.

It's without much hope that I retrieve the locator needle again, but as soon as I dangle it from its chain, I can see the gentle, insistent pull at work. My heart leaps. A few more seconds of testing confirms it. Drifting to the west, right toward a distant white monolith amid the waves. I have no idea why it wasn't working farther away, but as long as it is presently, I don't care.

Relief lends me a burst of energy, and I don't waste any more time. The descent I pick out isn't the safest, exactly, but it is the fastest. There are spots where I can slide down to the next narrow ledge, the next outcropping, without too much fear of over-shooting my mark. It's painful—even with both palms wrapped, the rock and under-growth slices through my already shredded tunic, and before long there are splotches of red staining the white—but it's effective enough. I'm on the stony beach within ten minutes.

I remove my boots and tunic, burying them beneath some rocks. The light's fading. I have perhaps forty minutes before the Transvect returns. If I'm lucky.

I make sure my Will-imbued objects are secure, then plunge into the icy, choppy waters of the Sea of Quus.

My tiredness is washed away by that initial shock of cold; I gasp, forced to pause before gritting my teeth and pushing out against the waves. It's harder going in this direction, and my muscles are already spent. I haven't slept for almost two days. Every stroke feels like I'm dragging twice my weight through the water.

It's my years of swimming at Suus that saves me, I think. Instinctive technique keeps me going, minimises my exertion, ensures I don't drag in lungfuls of water even as my energy wanes. Whenever I start to flag—which is often—I look up. See how the darkness is truly starting to encroach upon the sky. Redouble my efforts.

Twice I tread water to check my position against a mixture of the shore, the anchoring point rising ahead, and the locator needle. The delay costs precious time, but I can't risk straying so far off course that I end up over the Seawall. But I only ever have to correct by a matter of degrees.

It's almost pitch-black now, clouds obscuring any stars overhead. I'm nearly there, but it must also nearly be time. My lungs burn and I almost weep with the effort of every stroke, desperation alone driving me on. I start pausing more and more, fearful of swimming too far out. The anchoring point towers over me.

I look up and see it on the horizon. Just a dot against the last kiss of dusk, but no mistaking it.

The Transvect's coming.

Hand shaking, I take out the locator once again. It barely sways, perhaps shifting very slightly to the left. I swim a couple of strokes, try again. No movement at all this time. Pulling straight down. This is as close as I'm going to get.

Everything shakes from tiredness and cold and anxiety as I snap the needle in half and let it go. Ulciscor's imbuing will be broken now. If he notices such a small amount of Will returning to him, he'll probably be relieved.

I fish in my pocket for the grapple. The Transvect's looming, descending. I'm too hasty, too twitchy and nervous, my fingers too numb. The stone cuff catches on cloth as I try to yank it free.

I drop it.

There's a moment of sheer, disbelieving, rattled horror. I flail through the inky water at where I think the bracelet might be, but my hands touch only liquid from several panicked attempts. From the corner of my eye I can see the Transvect growing, already impossibly large in my vision, sliding smoothly toward me.

I gasp a breath and dive.

It's hopeless, I know that already; the stone will sink far faster than I can push myself downward. I'm all but blind, barely enough light above to show me which way is up. I push down, down, as hard and fast as I can anyway, for what feels like far too long. It will be impossibly deep here. I'll never find it.

My hand hits stone.

Not the stone cuff, but something large and smooth and flat. It takes me a second to register what it is, though I should have known. The edge of the Seawall.

I repress a flash of fear and scrabble desperately, my lungs—already overworked to the point of exhaustion—barely able to hold. I'm light-headed. There's nothing but smooth stone beneath my hands.

Then my fingers brush something that shifts; I grasp greedily and almost lose precious air to a gasp of relief as my grip closes around the bracelet. I look up, and my joy's short-lived. The Transvect's directly above me.

No time to think, to consider the consequences.

I snap the cuff around my left wrist.

The rest of my air disappears in a bellow as my shoulder feels like it's being torn from its socket, stone gouging into the base of my hand as it tries to tear its way free of my wrist. I'm yanked like a doll through the water, faster than I could have believed. I inhale involuntarily. My lungs fill with salty liquid.

I half shout, half choke as I'm torn from the sea, frantically using my free hand to grasp the manacle, to lessen the intense pressure on my wrist. There's a surreal instant where I realise I'm flying, dark water below hurriedly falling away.

And then I'm slamming into the underside of the Transvect, so hard that I just hang there, too disoriented to do anything but moan. Wind whips me, cutting through what little clothing I'm still wearing. I dangle dazedly, precariously, as the Transvect continues to rise and pick up speed. My left wrist and shoulder ache terribly through the icy cold.

The haze in front of my eyes clears enough for me to try and steady myself against the bottom of the Transvect. I've been unimaginably lucky; it was past before I reached it, so I'm attached to the back end as planned. Any sooner, and the cuff inside might have shifted, leaving me hanging somewhere from which I couldn't recover.

The access platform is difficult to reach, but after swinging a couple of times and almost screaming at the pain in my arm, I manage to grip the edge with the tips of my fingers, then awkwardly wrap my legs around the post. As safe as I can be, I stretch across with my right hand and unclasp the stone manacle from my left wrist.

Immediately the fierce pressure on my shoulder eases. I let the manacle fall into the water far below—I only need the one inside—and then haul myself up. Following Ulciscor's instructions, I release the access hatch and shove aside the rug lying on top of it, peering through. No one was going to risk catching the last Transvect back, and Ulciscor was going to make sure this section was clear regardless, but I'm still relieved to see no one inside. At least one thing has gone my way tonight.

I scramble up into the blissful calm of the carriage and collapse on my back, fighting the temptation to stay there before dragging myself to my feet once again.

My bundle of clothing is still, thankfully, securely where I tucked it last night, along with the anchoring cuff that pulled me up here. There's no time to rest; we're already over the island itself. I shiver as I strip my sodden clothes, dry myself with the fresh cloak, then feverishly dress. We're almost there but I toss my ragged tunic and undergarments out the still-open hatch regardless, as well as the bandage for my hand. Even if someone somehow comes across those in the wilderness, there's no way to tie them to me.

The access hatch attempts to slide shut at a touch, successfully fracturing the stone cuff I jam in the way with a grinding crack. I toss the broken pieces. Let the hatch seal properly. Replace the rug. We're slowing again, and out the window I can see the Academy's platform. I rake fingers through my hair, scrub my face with my cloak again, conceal as many injuries as I can beneath clothing. Rub my hands together vigorously to try and stop shivering, then sit in the seat closest to the door and do my best to look bored.

Twenty seconds later, the Transvect slides to a stop. The doors open and I stand calmly. Fold my hands behind my back. Step outside.

"Vis? Cutting it close." It's Praeceptor Taedia, wisps of grey hair highlighted by the lamps behind her as she wanders over. She frowns around behind me at the Transvect, no sign of any suspicion. Barely paying any attention to me, in fact. "Is Feriun with you?"

I glance back, but there's no sign of movement. Feriun's a student in Class Four, I think. A tall, athletic boy, a bit reminiscent of Indol in many ways. Catenan through and through. "I didn't see him, but I was in a rush. He could have boarded after me, I suppose." It takes everything I can to keep the words smooth, rather than letting them out through chattering teeth.

"Hm." Taedia and I both stand and watch; after a good thirty seconds the doors close and the Transvect takes off again, back the way it came. Taedia scowls after it. "Foolish boy. Scitus will lower his ranking if he misses class."

I wait for her to say more, to notice my barely recovered breathlessness or wet hair, or even to ask about why I risked catching the very last Transvect back. She doesn't, though. Just pats me absently on the shoulder. "Come on, then."

I see her take her hand away immediately and glance at it; she's obviously felt the dampness there. She looks as if she's about to say something, then just glances at the cloud-covered sky and grunts.

The walk back is innocuous enough, Taedia disinterestedly asking about my experience at the Festival of the Ancestors. We're waved through at the Academy gates, my name checked off the list of returning students, and I'm sent on my way to the dormitory with barely a word of acknowledgment.

I hurry back along the well-lit paths, grateful not to encounter anyone else who might want conversation. The dormitory is quiet, no one in the halls. I slip into my room. Cyrus and Cato are asleep, but as is often the case, Eidhin is hunched over the desk in his corner, shuttered lamp burning.

He twists as I enter. Studies me. "You look awful."

It's not a question, as it would be coming from anyone else. He makes the observation and then turns without waiting for a response, resuming his studies.

I grin at his back, then shakily strip off my damp clothing and climb into bed. It takes some time for my jaw to unclench from not wanting to let my teeth chatter, but eventually my body's contained warmth does the trick. My breathing eases.

I still ache awfully, especially my shoulder. I have scratches from branches, the alupi bite on my hand, a vicious welt on my wrist. I'm pretty sure my entire left side is one massive bruise from the impact with the Transvect.

None of it stops me from embracing a deep, dreamless slumber almost immediately.

XLIII

I'VE BEEN BADLY INJURED BEFORE. FAIRLY OFTEN AT THE THE-atre in Letens, of course. After beatings and whippings at the orphanage. Even from the physical training I underwent as a prince, when my tutors were instructed never to hold back because of my youth or position.

I don't remember ever waking up in quite such *complete* pain before, though.

I sleep late; everyone's already at breakfast when I pry my eyes open. No one bothered to wake me, of course. I groan as I drag myself out of bed, every inch of me tender, every muscle feeling as though it's been stretched to breaking.

Remarkably, though, after a preliminary check, all the damage seems limited to the superficial. Bruising, strained muscles, sore joints: things I know I'll recover from in days, if not sooner. There's nothing broken. Nothing that inclines me to report to the infirmary for treatment.

I dress stiffly, then ignore my fiercely growling stomach and take the time to stretch out every single muscle I can before leaving for the mess. That, and the walk over, loosens me enough that by the time I'm making my way down the stairs—long-sleeved tunic on, cloak over the top—I don't think anyone would even be able to tell I'm sore.

There's a moroseness to the hall today, I notice as soon as I enter. Murmured conversation, fewer smiles, any laughs kept to a low, restrained chuckle. Half the students in Class Four are absent. I catch a strange look from Aequa as I enter, though she makes no move to talk to me as I pass. There's no line for food—one benefit to being late, I suppose—so I fetch my meal and then join an expectant-looking Callidus at the Class Seven table we usually frequent.

"Who died?" I ask lightly as I sit, cocking an eyebrow at the rest of the room.

"Feriun." Callidus nods sagely as he watches my reaction. "That's right. You're a terrible person."

I'm caught between dismay and a horrified chuckle at Callidus's jest. "Gods' graves. You're serious? Taedia was waiting for him last night, but . . ." I shake my head dazedly. "How?"

"The announcement wasn't exactly overflowing with details," Callidus observes, his flash of humour fading to something more serious. "But from what I've overheard, suicide's the popular conclusion."

I blanch. Caeror's supposed suicide still haunts his family more than six years on. The awfulness of even the suggestion is hard to shake. "Why?"

"He thought he'd be in Three by this stage, apparently. As did his family. The Necropolis must have been the final pressure." Callidus grimaces. "Expectations can be a terrible thing."

I never really interacted with Feriun, but I feel a kind of melancholy at the idea that anyone my age might sink that far. There's a brief, aching sadness that a face I can picture is gone from the world forever.

Callidus watches me sympathetically. "Not the way I would want to move up, either."

I hesitate, spoon halfway to my mouth. "What do you mean?"

"Well. Dultatis is going to have a hard time holding you in Class Six now." Callidus gestures to a girl with long black hair and sun-browned complexion a couple of levels above us. "Ava is ranked first in Five, so she'll be moving up. Which—and follow the complex logic closely, here—leaves a spot open for the top student in Six." He gives me a cheery, albeit somewhat forced, smile to indicate who he thinks that is.

"Dultatis will just choose someone else." The Praeceptor's rankings within the class are rarely confirmed, but there's no way he'll have me at the top.

"He can't. Everyone knows you should be higher. Taedia might not have been willing to risk the fallout of moving someone down to force the issue, but you can bet she won't accept anyone else coming up."

I say nothing to that, taking a mouthful of bread and chewing. Callidus is right. As awful as it is, this will mean I move on to Class Five. Realistically, it might have been the only way it could have happened.

Relucia would have known that, too.

"Don't feel bad about it," observes Callidus, my queasiness clearly showing. "You're not to blame."

I try not to bitterly laugh. It could still be a coincidence.

We lapse into silence, and then Callidus stretches. "How was the Necropolis, anyway? Strange, I assume, meeting most of your family for the first time?"

We make small talk about the past couple of days for the rest of the meal. Callidus delights in hearing about Milena's dislike of me, in particular, insisting on every awkward conversational detail. Thankfully the night's sleep and my careful clothing choices this morning have done enough to conceal my injuries, because he doesn't mention anything.

My meal is still mostly uneaten when the chime sounds, but I stand immediately, unwilling to risk being late to class this morning. I wouldn't put it past Dultatis to use tardiness as an excuse to try and pass me over for promotion. And while I desperately hope Relucia had nothing to do with Feriun's fate—the very thought makes me nauseous—it's not as if refusing advancement would change anything.

Callidus stands too. "Enjoy Class Five," he says, slapping me on the shoulder. He moves to leave, then his cheer fades a little. He looks awkward. "And, thanks."

"For what?"

He coughs. Flushes, keeps his voice low. "I've never been there, but . . . I can see what Feriun might have been thinking. Trapped. No way out. A disappointment." He shuffles. "But he didn't have any friends, really, either. It's just . . . it's the sort of thing that makes a difference." He screws up his face and shakes his head in embarrassment, then hurries off.

I stare after him, then smile and join the trail of students heading for Class Six.

⁊⁊ ⁊⁊ ⁊⁊

EIDHIN SLIDES INTO THE SEAT NEXT TO ME.

There's a lot of chatter today before class, low and restrained but with a thread of anticipation. Excitement at the prospect of a promotion, tamed by the manner in which it came about. I don't think anyone here really knew Feriun, though. The muted interest seems to be for good form rather than from any genuine sadness. There are a lot of sidelong glances being cast in my direction this morning, even more than usual.

"A good day for you," Eidhin says gruffly in Cymrian, gaze focused ahead.

I eye him. "Not so much for Feriun."

"Not so much for Feriun," he agrees. There's silence, and then, "Will your injuries mean you are unable to start tutoring me tonight?" There's a strange inflection to the question. I realise after a moment that he's really asking whether I'm going to bother fulfilling my end of the bargain, given I'm slated to move up a class.

"What injuries?"

Approval touches his face. "Tonight, then."

Dultatis soon arrives and launches immediately into a dry lecture on the mathematics behind basic harmonic imbuing, much to everyone's surprise. Despite trying to temper my expectations, I find myself with a sinking feeling. No mention of Feriun, no indication that anyone is about to be promoted. That's . . . worrying.

The day passes in an uncertain haze. It's hard to concentrate, and I can tell from the confused glances and muttered conversation within Class Six that I'm not the only one. When I eat lunch with Callidus, he hasn't heard anything. Even Eidhin, stoic as always, admits to puzzlement.

The sun's dipping low, class only minutes from over for the day, when the door opens. Taedia walks in, her abrupt, tense entrance drawing every eye.

"Praeceptor Dultatis." She waves a piece of paper at him. "We need to talk."

Dultatis frowns. "It's my decision, Taedia," he says mildly.

Taedia strides over and they engage in whispered, furious conversation; though everyone's supposed to be attending their own work, I can see most stylii have stopped moving as everyone listens intently for a hint of what's going on. Taedia's getting more and more annoyed, Dultatis getting more and more defensive, until suddenly the Class Five teacher straightens and turns. "Vis Telimus. Can you please come up here."

She sounds angry. I'm *fairly* certain it's not at me.

Everyone does stop what they're doing now, watching with open curiosity as I walk to the front of the room. "How can I help, Praeceptor?"

"Would you like to advance to Class Five?"

"Very much so."

Dultatis's face is red. "It doesn't matter. It's not his decision, and it's not yours. My assessment is the only one that matters."

Taedia's cheek twitches. She looks like she's having to deal with a small child. "Class Five is much harder than the nonsense you get to teach, Dultatis. Show me one student here who can perform one task better than Vis, and I'll take them instead." There's no doubting her exasperation, though her voice remains low enough to keep it from the rest of the class.

For a hopeful moment I think Dultatis is going to concede. Then his scowl deepens. "Alright. Ianix Carenius. His blade work is exceptional."

"Swords?" Taedia scoffs. "We're looking for future senators, not gladiators. Anyone in my class who ends up wielding a weapon will be forging a Razor first."

"It's still a measurement of aptitude. Of strength and skill. Of the ability to think on your feet."

Taedia looks about to argue, then throws up her hands and turns to me. "Is he better than you?"

"I doubt it," I say coolly, not taking my eyes from Dultatis. Ianix has never liked me—as far as I can tell, simply because he's jealous of his position as Dultatis's favourite in Class Six. I don't like him much, either. He reminds me a bit of Vermes from the orphanage in Letens.

I've never seen him fight with a blade before, but nor has Dultatis seen me. That makes me confident. Sword work was something I trained at every day—*literally* every day—for more than five years at Suus, and I was given the very best tutors. Men and women who actually fought for their lives with the weapon. Swordplay in the Hierarchy, by comparison, is more of a novelty. Considered a throwback to a less civilised time.

"He's certainly not at anything else. Seems like a terrible choice," I add.

Taedia covers her amusement, while Dultatis's red turns a shade of purple. Emissa mentioned that Taedia likes students with backbone, who aren't afraid to stand up to the Praeceptors when they feel it's right to do so.

Besides—I'm enjoying this. I glance across at Eidhin, who's seen Dultatis's reaction and is making no attempt to hide his delight. I repress a smirk.

"Then it's settled. A training duel between Ianix and Vis. The Academy will provide the equipment. The winner advances to Class Five." Taedia's attention flicks to me. "We'll hold it tomorrow, just before evening meal. That will give you both enough time to prepare, I hope?" There's a murmur from behind me; the Praeceptor has raised her voice so that the entire class is able to hear. Ianix included.

"It will." I respond confidently at the same volume; Ianix signals his agreement too.

"Excellent." She smiles at me, throws another half-disdainful, half-despairing look at Dultatis, then walks off before the man has a chance to say anything more.

To my surprise, Dultatis, though plainly frustrated at having been so publicly cornered, also seems happy with the outcome as he motions me back to my seat. "You're in this class until at least tomorrow," he sniffs. "And I imagine well beyond that. So you should get back to work."

I retake my seat, noting the wondering glances from those around me. Ianix, sitting a few seats over in the corner, is deep in conversation with one of his friends. He looks pleased about the situation too.

"Bold choice," murmurs Eidhin once Dultatis resumes his interminable explanation up front.

"Duelling Ianix?"

"Duelling the Catalan Games' most recent duelling champion. It's what got him promoted from Seven last trimester. He would *not* stop talking about it."

"Oh." Even with my body aching as it is, I didn't expect Ianix would be a threat. "I . . . assume that means he's quite good."

"He is better than everyone our age in the Republic."

"Better than everyone who entered the competition. Let's not build him up too much."

"Everyone who has an interest in duelling was *in* that competition."

"Well. There's nothing I can do about it now." I give him a cheerful, reassuring pat. "I'm touched by your concern, though."

"I am concerned that our Praeceptor may walk away without being embarrassed." He glares at me. "Do not *dare* to take that opportunity away from me."

I hold up my hands. "I'll do my best."

Dultatis chooses that instant to glance up from the text he's reading aloud to us, spotting our conversation. Looking for it, too; there are a half dozen others whispering idly at this point of the day, but he delights in singling me out.

"Vis! Not paying attention again, I see. For the third time today," he says, an ugly smile on his rotund face. "A simple scolding is not enough to cure you of this bad habit, it seems. I hear you are no longer on stable duty?"

"That's correct, Praeceptor." I say it with every scrap of politeness I can muster, but I already know where this is going. Beside me, Eidhin stiffens.

"Perhaps one more evening of it will remind you of your manners." As if to underline his words, the chime to end class sounds.

We stare at each other. My jaw clenches. He knows tonight will be my only opportunity to practice. He's not even trying to hide it.

"Thank you, Praeceptor," I manage to squeeze out, breathing until the haze of red passes. He's goading me. If I explode here, make a show of disrespect in front of the entire class, he'll have enough justification to call off tomorrow and promote Ianix against any objections. I've endured more than two months. I can restrain myself for one more day.

I stand with as much icy dignity as I can muster, unwilling to let myself say anything else. My motion breaks the tension in the air, everyone following my example. I join the line walking to the door, refusing to look at Dultatis, and head straight for the stables.

※ ※ ※

"I THOUGHT YOU WERE DONE WITH THIS."

I look up, smiling to see Emissa standing at the entrance to the stall, arms crossed as she regards me with good-natured exasperation. "So did I." I shovel another pile of manure into the barrow. The familiar physical work, while never exactly pleasant, has calmed me. It even seems to have helped loosen some of my aching muscles. Despite Dultatis's best efforts, as far as punishments go, this could have been a lot worse. "My esteemed Praeceptor had other ideas."

"The night before you're meant to duel Ianix Carenius. Convenient."

I pause, leaning on my pitchfork. "You heard about that?"

"Oh yes. Everyone's talking about it."

I make a face. "Of course they are."

"You do know he won the Catalan Games a few months ago?"

"So I've been told. After I accepted the challenge," I admit, a little ruefully. I resume my work. "It's fine. It's been a while since the Victorum, but I'll find a couple of swords early tomorrow morning, see if I can convince Callidus to help me shake off the rust." I see her expression. "No?"

"You'll need training armour, too."

"Why?"

"Because . . . that's what you'll be using tomorrow," Emissa says slowly. "You used training armour at the Letens Victorum, didn't you? You've worn it before?"

"Uh. I've *seen* armour being worn." I have worn armour, back during my training, but the past I've told everyone doesn't fit with that fact.

"I don't mean *armour*. I mean Will-imbued *training armour*. An Amotus. You *do* know what I'm talking about, don't you?"

"I don't think I do," I say uneasily.

Emissa studies me, then chews her lip and looks up at the stable roof. "Hmm."

"What is it?"

"I'm just trying to remember the last time I so vastly overestimated someone's intelligence."

I laugh despite myself. "Fine. I *may* have been hasty. What makes this training armour so special?"

"Easier to show you. There are sets in Class Three's storage in the gymnasium— you finish up here, and I'll go and find them. Meet me there. I'm not very good, but I'll be better than nothing. We can practice for a while once you're done."

I smile. She says it all matter-of-factly, but the fact she's willing to help speaks volumes. "Thanks," I say sincerely.

Then I hesitate. Remember Eidhin. I can almost hear my father's voice. *A man is nothing if he does not honour his debts.*

"I . . . may have another obligation tonight, though." The words slip reluctantly from my mouth, but I made the commitment. Eidhin has been nothing but patient. I'm not going to abuse that.

"More important than this?" Emissa's disbelieving.

"No. But I swore I would do it. I have to square it away before practicing."

"I'll wait for an hour. After that . . ."

"Understood."

Emissa assesses me, looking a little put out, then steps forward and jabs me in the chest. "You make sure you're there." She glares at me warningly and stalks off without another word, still shaking her head. I can't help but chuckle as I watch her go. She's been hearing from me about Dultatis's nonsense for weeks. Has been taking a lot of it personally, too. I suspect she may want me to win tomorrow even more than I do.

I finish up my tasks in the stables, amusement fading as I consider what Emissa said. Once I'm done, I head straight for the dormitory, relieved to find Eidhin at his desk as usual. None of our other roommates have retired yet.

The burly boy looks up as I enter, brow furrowing. "Why are you here?"

"I promised I would tutor—"

"Idiot. No. You need to practice." He stands, bustles me out the door before I know what's happening. "We are going to the gymnasium."

"Actually, I have someone already waiting for me there. She's getting some training armour?" I end it as a question, trying to indicate I still have no idea what that actually entails.

Eidhin smirks at me. Apparently focusing more on my mysterious female friend than my ignorance. "Even better. It has been a while since I have used an Amotus."

So he knows what it is, too. Of course he does.

Without anything further, he shoves me into motion, and we head for the gymnasium.

XLIV

EMISSA IS WAITING IN THE GYMNASIUM, A LONG, SPARSE SPACE with concrete walls and stone floors. Unsurprisingly given the lateness of the evening, she's alone. There are four sets of armour sitting beside her: two wooden and two steel. She leaps to her feet as I enter, though her smile falters a little as Eidhin strides in behind me.

"He insisted," I say by way of explanation. "Eidhin, Emissa. Emissa, Eidhin."

Eidhin stops. Eyes me, then Emissa, then me again. Grunts, as if something's just been made clear to him.

"You are skilled?" he asks Emissa in Common, pointing to the armour beside her.

"No. Nooo." Emissa draws it out the second time for emphasis. "You?"

"Some."

"Then please." Emissa steps back and gives a sweeping wave to the armour, indicating that Eidhin should be the one to wear it.

Eidhin doesn't argue, grabbing a set of wooden leg guards.

"The wooden ones are the control pieces," says Emissa, indicating I should do the same with the other set.

I furrow my brow but start donning the wooden armour. It's not much of a burden, clearly designed to be lightweight and sturdy. Only enough to protect against practice weapons, though. I doubt it would stop even a single blow from a real blade. "So what does this do, exactly?"

"It's Will-locked to the real armour and blade." She watches with amusement as I struggle to fasten my arm guard, then steps over to help. "You get all the experience of fighting with the real thing, with none of the danger."

Eidhin is already fully armoured. He walks to the opposite side of the room and turns to face me. "Stay clear." He inserts a triangular stone tile into a slot on his breastplate.

I flinch as the steel armour lying in a heap next to me bursts into unexpected motion, clattering and flying with alarming speed toward him. It freezes in mid-air perhaps fifteen feet in front of him, forming a perfect replica of Eidhin's outline. The hulking boy doesn't even blink. He stretches and uncannily, the hollow figure in front of him stretches as well, clanking. An identical movement. Completely synchronised.

"Ah." I mutter my understanding, more to myself than to Emissa.

"You've really never seen an Amotus before?"

"No." No point in lying. I continue strapping pieces to my body, though part of me recoils from touching the wooden plating, now. I can't avoid using Will-based devices, but attaching one to myself like this still makes my skin crawl. "How does it work?" I can deduce most of it already, but it doesn't hurt to have my suspicions confirmed.

"Will-locking?"

I pause in my fastening of the final bracer and give Emissa a stare.

The dark-haired girl responds with the slightest of crinkling around her eyes. "The link is in the crux on the back of each piece; it shouldn't warp even if it gets a direct hit. But if you can slip in behind anything on the limbs to where flesh would normally be, your sword"—Eidhin hefts his wooden blade on cue, his empty counterpart mimicking the motion with its steel one—"is imbued with counters, which switch on reactive repulsion for the corresponding piece on your opponent's body."

"Which will make it seem like it weighs fifty pounds. At least," I finish, nodding. It's smart. Get in a hit past a piece of floating armour, and it triggers an analogous reaction on your opponent's body, weighing it down to the point of disabling it. Stab their leg, and suddenly they're all but one-legged. Cut their arm, and they can't do anything except let it hang at their side. "And to win?"

"Anything to the head, neck, or chest will disable the harmonic connection completely."

"Makes sense." I stand, adjusting my right bracer a little and then slipping on the helmet. Unlike the corresponding helmet on the secondary armour, it's little more than a wooden hat. The one that Eidhin will have to target is much more traditional, with a guard at the back and a thin protrusion protecting the forehead. Only a clean stab into the hollow space where the face would be will net him a kill.

There are smaller circular shields rather than the heavier rectangular ones that the old Catenan legions used to favour, for which I'm grateful—my strength is largely recovered from last night, but I'm still loathe to place my shoulder under too much strain. And though I've trained with shields before, I've always preferred the free-flowing styles I was primarily taught. The more mobility I'm allowed, the better.

Once the wooden disc is fastened to my arm, I'm ready. Despite the lightness of the armour itself, movement feels awkward as I position myself thirty feet or so away from Eidhin, facing the final set of armour on the floor.

I slip the stone triangle into place on my chest.

There's a blur as the armour snaps into position in front of me; despite expecting it, I can't help but flinch back. Every piece of the wooden armour hanging off me immediately increases in weight. I stagger. "Rotting gods." When I adjust and straighten again, both Emissa and Eidhin are hiding smirks.

I ignore them, cautiously raising my arm and watching as the empty steel in front of me does the same. There's no delay to it, no visible difference in the timing. As I look closer, I can see other pieces of armour shifting minutely, the breastplate even rising and falling with my breath.

It's uncanny, dizzying to take in. I step forward, and the armour in front of me follows suit.

"How do you see what you're doing?" I answer my own question, turning a little to the side. My armour does the same; now I'm standing behind and perhaps two feet to the right of it. It's not perfect—there will always be a blind spot, no matter where I am—but it's much easier to imagine fighting from this position.

"It takes time to adapt." Eidhin reverts to Cymrian as he slashes the air with his blade, testing its weight. He, somewhat to my surprise, genuinely looks like he knows what he's doing.

I copy him, experimenting with my movement and the heft of my weapon and shield for a while. "Is it safe?" There's an initial disconnect between what I can see on my body and the heaviness of everything—once Will-locked, the wooden armour takes on the weight of the metal—but that quickly passes. "I don't want to hurt you."

"You don't want to . . ." Eidhin half scoffs, half glowers at me. "Very well, then. Ready?"

"Ready."

Emissa, evidently gathering the gist of our conversation, steps over to the side and sits, watching with undisguised interest. I grin across at her.

Then I barely bring up my shield in time to meet Eidhin's crashing first attack as he leaps forward, far faster than I could reasonably have expected. Steel rings on steel and the impact shivers up my arm. I reel away. I could see to make the block, but it was almost too late. Not an instinctive reaction at all, compared to if a sword were slashing at my real body. Eidhin was right. This is going to take some getting accustomed to.

Eidhin isn't interested in giving me time to adjust. He's stalking forward, shield up, blade licking out in quick, sharp jabs. I fend each one off awkwardly, then counter with a thrust of my own. It's disdainfully knocked away.

"I thought you said you were ready."

I glare across at him. Take a steadying breath. Set my stance, watching as my metal counterpart does the same. It's been years and I'm inevitably rusty, but you don't just forget the things drilled into you every morning for most of your childhood.

Balanced now, I flow forward.

I've heard people sneer about the impracticality of fighting styles that are likened to dancing, and in a pitched battle that's probably fair. A duel, though, is different. Fluidity—the ability to slide from one action to the next, to attack and then attack again without breaking—is vital. There's a mental game to it that's completely absent from the crunching, abrupt brutality of war. Smooth, mesmeric motions can intimidate as much as do damage. Cause an opponent to doubt. Be indecisive. Make mistakes.

I crash hard into Eidhin, leading with my shield—I don't have the physical advantage, but momentum makes a difference—and then deliver several flashing strikes as he's forced back. They're meant to distract rather than penetrate. A manifestation of my annoyance more than anything else. The wooden sword in my hand thuds to a stop in mid-air on every strike, impact shuddering along my arm. It's still surreal, still new, but I already feel a little more capable. A little more at ease.

I catch a glimpse of a scowl on Eidhin's face, have a moment of satisfaction before he's suddenly dropping, dodging around so that his proxy is positioned neatly behind my own. I try to jerk to the side to give myself a better view, but instead I'm lurching, my left leg all but stuck in place.

"Gods damn it," I snarl, mostly at myself, as I desperately retain my equilibrium. He's faster than I gave him credit for, must have somehow slipped a hit in behind the grieve. The one on my leg feels like it's anchored to the ground.

"Yield?"

"Convenient," I puff. "Just . . . as I was . . . getting a feel for it."

"So no?"

"No."

Eidhin shrugs, and starts to display exactly how much my newfound lack of mobility is a disadvantage. Within seconds he's moving nimbly—mockingly—around me, raining down quick blows that don't hurt, but are difficult to turn aside with either sword or shield. One strike slips under my left shoulder guard, and suddenly my shield arm is hanging useless by my side. I manage only a couple of more awkward blocks before he's thrusting forward, past my flailing defence and through the space where my neck would be.

The metal armour in front of me disintegrates into its individual pieces with an echoing clatter. The weight of the steel vanishes from my body and I stumble from the abrupt change, the anchoring of my leg and arm disappearing. The triangular stone that was attached to my breastplate drops to the floor.

I scowl at the pile of metal in front of me as I catch my breath. I only trained in armour once or twice, back at Suus. The extra weight definitely adds to the exercise.

"Not terrible," Emissa calls breezily from the side. "Given that it's your first time." Despite the light jab, she looks impressed.

I snort, trying not to look irritated. Unsure whether I'm more annoyed at losing, or that I didn't expect to. I make a face at her, then glance over at Eidhin. "Not yours, though, I take it."

"I was taught by the Bladesmiths of my tribe." From the way he says it, he takes great pride in this fact.

"Bladesmiths?" I'm hesitant to ask. Eidhin making mention of his past—or of anything personal, really—is beyond rare. I still haven't been able to glean who tasked him with attacking Callidus, or why he accepted. He never takes my invitation to sit with us at meals. Even when we speak in class, it's rarely for long. Despite the time we've spent together recently, I really know very little about him.

"Masters of the sword. They are among the finest in the world." There's a pause, an unusual hesitation from him. "They were."

It's said simply; he's not looking for sympathy. Still. "I'm sorry."

It's the wrong thing to say. Eidhin's face darkens. "They kept their honour."

I'm not sure how to respond to that. Emissa watches our conversation with interest, though we're speaking Cymrian.

"Could you beat Ianix?" I ask eventually, sensing I should change the subject.

"No." Simple honesty in the delivery.

"Alright. Again, then." I retrieve the fallen stone triangle and insert it into its slot. Sure enough, my armour instantly reassembles in front of me.

The next round is much closer, despite Eidhin striking harder this time, his anger at whatever insult I accidentally delivered bleeding through. Even so, I start to see how to use lines of sight to my advantage, how to position myself and my armour—my Amotus—in ways that are awkward for him. Emissa calls out suggestions this time, too, which help focus me on how I should react to various tactics. The fundamentals of duelling are the same, but the approach is different. There's no diving past and turning sharply; doing so would result in me facing away from the action. This is all about positioning. The footwork is about angles as much as balance. At the end, though I lose again, Eidhin is sweating and his jibes are a lot more forced.

The third time, I beat him.

I don't lose again for the rest of the evening.

※ ※ ※

"YOU ARE A CHEAT," GRUMBLES EIDHIN IN COMMON AS THE three of us depart the gymnasium, covered in a light sheen of sweat that immediately chills in the late-evening sea breeze. Torches flare and crackle around the quadrum. Otherwise, everything's quiet.

"He does seem the type," agrees Emissa, her face flushed from the exertion. She alternated with Eidhin after a while, showing far more skill than she initially let on. Still no match for a childhood of constant training, though. "Perhaps the armour we were using was faulty, somehow."

"Yes. Yes. It is the only explanation." Eidhin nods seriously to her.

I grin, enjoying their mock-griping, then hesitate and half turn back. "Ah. The armour. Do you need to put it back in storage?"

"I do. But if I happen to forget, and then you and Callidus wander in tomorrow morning . . ." Emissa spreads her hands, indicating her helplessness at the situation.

My smile broadens. "Thanks."

"Any time." Our eyes lock before she looks away, still smiling.

There's silence, and then Eidhin, who's been watching the two of us, sighs loudly. "She is very pretty. Why did you have me come along?"

I start to redden until I realise he's spoken in Cymrian, then cough to cover my reaction. "This was about practicing for tomorrow. And you didn't give me much choice."

"She likes you."

"And I like her."

"You know what I mean. The way you talk with each other is more than just friendliness." He gives me a leering grin.

"It's not like that." I try not to look in Emissa's direction, hoping she's not going to ask what we're talking about.

"It should be."

I glare at him. I've already had this conversation with Callidus, but it's still hard to explain. That I was raised never to pursue something that's guaranteed to fail. That my mother used to tell me that love is nothing without honesty. And that my father drilled into me, time and time again, that a prince of Suus cannot—*cannot*—have dalliances.

Those are not tenets of the Catenan Republic, certainly. And Suus is long gone. But it's who I am.

And I can never tell Emissa who I am.

"At least concede that she is beautiful."

"And smart, and funny, and unreasonably likeable. Of course she is. She's remarkable," I say with irritation. "Now leave it alone."

We walk on, Emissa thankfully not showing any overt interest in what we're saying. When it's clear we've finished, though, she suddenly shakes her head, as if just remembering something. "By the way. Did you say something to Aequa, at the Necropolis?"

I frown. "Aequa? No. I didn't see her after we all left the Transvect."

"She's been asking about you. Specifically, about when you got back. She was acting a bit strangely."

"Oh?" I furrow my brow and look as bemused as I think I should be, even as my heart sinks. Whatever Aequa's reasons, I don't want anyone looking too closely into when I left the Necropolis. "That's odd. I'll have to ask her about it."

We stop as we come to the point of divergence in our paths. Emissa holds my gaze, merriment in her green eyes. "Good luck tomorrow. I'll be cheering for you." She peels off toward the girls' dormitory, waving casually without looking back.

It takes me a moment to realise she said it in Cymrian.

I turn to Eidhin, who's staring after her, mouth as agape as mine. I don't think his face is flushing anywhere near as much, though. The large boy glances across at me. "Huh."

"Huh," I repeat, caught between mortification and amusement as I try to replay everything I've said to Eidhin tonight. The latter wins out, and I shake my head before gesturing in defeated humour.

"Come on, Eidhin. Let's get some sleep."

※ · ※ · ※

EVERYTHING'S QUIET IN THE MISTY EARLY MORNING FOLLOW-ing, dawn not even colouring the sky yet as Callidus and I trudge back from the gymnasium, where he's just helped me sneak in an extra hour of valuable practice. My friend is quiet as we walk. Thoughtful, I think, rather than sulking from the thrashing he's just received. He's an adequate opponent with the training armour, but not close to Eidhin or even Emissa in terms of skill.

I let the silence be, stretching out muscles as I go. The lingering stiffness I felt after waking seems to have been worked out by the exercise. I'm still bruised and sore from my brutal sojourn to the ruins two days ago, but with a day of classes ahead of me—no physical activity scheduled—I should be in reasonable condition for this evening's contest.

"Where did you train?" Callidus asks the question abruptly.

"Aquiria. My parents made me take lessons a few years back. My instructor always said I had something of a knack—"

He pulls up short, forcing me to as well.

"Enough." There's an unusual tension in his voice. "You don't have to tell me, but don't lie to my face."

I shove down a sudden discomfort, refusing to let a misplaced sense of guilt make me waver. "What do you mean?"

"You've read books that most of the Thirds wouldn't bother to try. Speak dead languages. Duel using styles I've never even heard of before." He glares at me, never once breaking eye contact. "You're about as middle-class Aquirian as I am."

Emotion battles with the need for a quick, convincing response. I make a light, dismissive motion. Paste on a puzzled look. "I don't know what to tell you."

"You don't . . ." Callidus trails off, shaking his head. Frustrated. "You know, I have access to my father's records. That's every single birth in the Hierarchy—even the ones our noble senators don't want made public. I could probably figure it out."

He thinks I'm the illegitimate child of someone powerful. Of course. It's the most logical conclusion. Someone brought up with every advantage but in secret, probably trained specifically for the purpose of succeeding at the Academy. Loyal to a senator without that connection being known.

"It's not Telimus, obviously. Too young. But I imagine someone in Military," Callidus continues, watching my face closely. "Someone powerful. A Quartus. Maybe even higher?" Probing.

I allow uncertainty to flit across my face. Permit him to see my desire to tell him the truth, and let him think he's on the right track. We stand for several long, awkward seconds, and then Callidus sighs.

"Alright." His disappointment is palpable. "That's how it is, then. But you should come up with a better answer for everyone else. Because after they see you fight today, there are going to be a lot more questions about your time in Aquiria. Trust me."

He walks off toward the Class Seven dormitory stiffly. I let him go.

I eat breakfast opposite Eidhin on Class Six's level, quietly discussing Amotus strategy with him. It's not in reaction to Callidus's questioning earlier—I mentioned

I was planning on doing so well before our discussion this morning—but it still feels awkward now. Like I'm avoiding my other friend. I mean to at least greet him when I leave the mess, but by the time I finish my meal, his table's empty.

I can't fault him for being hurt by what he sees as an obvious deception, earlier. And I hate that I've offended him. But I designed my past to be impossible to disprove. Admitting it's a sham to anyone at all is risking a crack in an otherwise perfect façade.

The lie was the right decision.

Class has a strange energy to it today, Dultatis smug whenever he addresses me, Ianix and his friends shooting me half-wary, half-confident glares every time I glance in their direction. More than once there's muffled laughter as one student or another discusses how badly I'm going to be beaten. I don't mind. Overconfidence, and the weight of expectation, is going to disadvantage Ianix far more than me.

Callidus, to my vague dismay, is entirely absent from the midday meal. Not unheard of, but I hope it's nothing to do with me. I sit with Eidhin again, and we watch as Dultatis draws Ianix aside and starts issuing advice, not even feigning impartiality. Not long after, Ianix himself—who's been conscientiously avoiding me up until this point—stops by our table, looming as I eat.

"You could concede, Vis." He's steady. Confident. "Know your limits. Concede, and maybe you have another chance to move up in a few months. Lose today, and you won't get another opportunity."

"No thanks."

Ianix waits, as if expecting me to say more, then glowers when I don't. "I tried." He stalks off. Eidhin nods approvingly.

The afternoon class drags; every time I glance at the Will dial, it's barely moved. Finally, though, the bell chimes. I stand. Dultatis smiles at me, but I don't flinch, don't look away as I walk to the door.

"See you tomorrow," the balding man murmurs as I pass.

I ignore him, and head for the quadrum.

XLV

AFTER DETOURING TO SCOFF A FEW NERVE-SETTLING BITES of dinner from the mess, I find the Curia Doctrina all but empty as I stalk through it. I don't understand why until I reach the great archway and emerge into the golden, late afternoon sun.

The immense crowd milling around the edges of the quadrum already contains what must be nearly every student in the Academy. I dither at the sight, almost freeze; I was assuming we'd draw onlookers, but this is beyond anything I'd imagined. The different classes are clumped together, with Seven taking up almost one side of the massive square. The Thirds stand apart with an entertained-looking Nequias on the opposite side. Emissa spots me and gives me a sympathetic grin. I force one in return.

I note Eidhin with the Sixths across the way, Aequa with the Fourths just ahead of me. The Sevenths are spread out, but I don't see Callidus. There's a distant, nagging worry that he's decided not to come. I hope our exchange this morning hasn't damaged our relationship that far.

There's nothing I can do about it right now, anyway. I push the concern to one side. Focus.

Ianix is already in the centre of the quadrum and outfitted in his Amotus, comfortable with both the equipment and all the attention as he swings his blade experimentally. Dultatis is standing a little way off, arms crossed, watching approvingly. Behind him is a displeased-looking Taedia, along with a gaggle of other Praeceptors. Veridius is with them.

I recover from the surprise of the crowd and start pushing through the throng. Conversation nearby eases as people recognise me. Aequa's one of them; she gives me a strange look as I pass, a mix of puzzlement and intense curiosity. I acknowledge her briefly before concentrating ahead again. Trying not to wonder whether her enquiries about me have turned up anything to worry about.

The onlookers quieten as I step out onto the white stone of the quadrum and start across the empty expanse toward Dultatis and Ianix.

"Thought you could use an audience, Catenicus." Dultatis has spotted me and waves lazily toward the second paired armour set lying off to the side, up against the fountain. He's enjoying this, enjoying the attention and spectacle. "Your Amotus is there. We'll begin as soon as you're ready. No point in dragging this out."

He likely thinks I'll be rattled by the crowd. He doesn't know about Letens. Doesn't know that I spent the first fourteen years of my life enduring constant scrutiny, being stared at wherever I went, always the focus of someone's attention. I hated it, but I know exactly how to endure it.

I ignore him, stride over to the wooden set of armour and methodically strap on the pieces. It's of a higher quality than the one I've been practising with. Once I'm comfortable, I slot the stone triangle into place, watching as the empty shell snaps into position fifteen feet in front of me. There's a swell in the murmuring of the crowd. Their anticipation is painfully thick.

I heft my sword and close my eyes, steadying my breathing as I've been taught. Everything else here is a distraction. These fights are won by whoever stays calm, whoever's most patient. I'm needled by Dultatis and his puerile antics, I can't deny that—but I have to ignore them. I have to be *better*.

Dultatis retreats to the sidelines. "This contest is for a position in Class Five," he announces, projecting his voice so that everyone in the rapidly hushing quadrum is able to hear him. "The usual rules apply: only a killing blow is a victory." He turns to us. "Ready?"

"Ready." Ianix's reply is clear and confident. He's enjoying himself, even gives a flashy, unnecessary twirl of his sword as he answers. I push down the flare of anger I feel at how happily he's gone along with Dultatis's plan. The boy's not even vaguely qualified to be in Five. If he had any sense of honour, he would have refused this challenge.

"Ready." No pretence at being relaxed. Guard up. Taut. I don't take my eyes from Ianix's Amotus when I say the word.

"Begin."

Ianix is still smiling in the background as he saunters forward and to the side, angling himself for a better view. He's strolling, glancing occasionally at the crowd and smirking to his friends. I mirror his position and orientation.

Then I sprint at him.

He's taken off guard, though he recovers well. My blade flashes down hard at his shoulder but he's twisting aside and bringing up his sword in an instant, meeting mine with a ringing of steel. The reverberation shudders down my arm as the sword in my own hand stops in mid-air. I back away. Ianix is focusing in on me now, smile faded.

Then he attacks.

It's a blur of steel, lightning-quick, strike after strike flowing at me in a flurry that is far stronger and more precise than anything Eidhin or Emissa were able to throw at me last night. I deflect desperately again and again while Ianix moves, circles, repositions himself and twists, trying to blind me by placing my Amotus between me and his blade.

I grit my teeth and respond, shuffling less than gracefully to the side, barely keeping up. The crowd cheers, a muted buzzing that I barely register. Eidhin wasn't exaggerating. Ianix is *good*.

And I don't get the impression he's even really trying yet.

Still, I haven't shown him anything to make him think I'm particularly skilled myself. That's my one advantage. Defend as though I'm only barely capable, wait for an opening, then hit him hard. Ianix finally breaks off his attack and backs away; I can see him still looking smug behind his Amotus but he's less so than before, vaguely annoyed. He thought I'd crumble under that first barrage. A quick glance across at Dultatis's irritated expression indicates the Praeceptor thought the same.

I attack this time, without too much nuance, just to keep Ianix busy while making sure I don't open myself to any counterattacks. I press, not successfully, but enough to occupy him for another ten seconds while varying sounds of appreciation and cajoling drift from the crowd. Some of them are a little surprised, a little more urgent than before. Ianix's friends and supporters, probably.

The delay of his supposedly inevitable victory is starting to annoy the other boy, I think. He's lost his amused look entirely, eyes cold as we circle again.

He slices forward but I'm ready for his speed this time. He *is* good, but I'm watching him as much as his Amotus, and I trained against better back in Suus. Men and women who would hit me before I even realised they were raising their sword. Ianix still has too much forecast to his moves; his muscles obviously tense, his mouth twitches well before he draws back for the strike. He's used to opponents trying to read his Amotus. It's the same problem Eidhin had last night.

And Ianix doesn't realise that yet, either. So when he prepares for his next hit, I'm ready. Moving. Flowing forward past his strike and going down on one knee, so close that he won't be able to see my blade coming.

I swipe, and cut him cleanly through the left leg.

I know the strike's true; I see the blade pierce the small gap at the knee. I immediately roll away again, avoiding Ianix's blind swipe and springing back to my feet, a thrill running through me. I've done it. He's crippled. All I have to do now is finish him.

I turn to find Ianix still standing.

My heart twists and I stop dead, confused for a long, ugly second. He's circling again. No indication of any encumberment.

"That was a hit." I hold up my sword, indicating I want the bout to stop, and call the words loud and clear toward the Praeceptors. "There's something wrong. That was a *hit*."

I refrain from using the word *cheat*, but the implication is strong enough.

Ianix pauses, then lowers his sword as well. There's a murmuring from the crowd. I glare over toward Dultatis, expecting to see him concerned; if this fight is fixed, then he's surely involved. But instead of worry, he's wearing an exaggerated expression of bemusement that's poorly concealing his real emotion.

He's pleased.

"Hold." Taedia's walking out. Though there are a few scattered boos coming from the students, I can see that I have an ally in her, at least. She saw what happened.

Dultatis trails after her. "The boy's just holding things up because he's losing," he says, loud enough to carry to the spectators. "Any excuse to catch his breath. It's poor form."

"It didn't look that way to me." Taedia signals to me. "Try again. Ianix, let him trigger the reaction in your knee."

I walk forward confidently and have my Amotus stab down, through the narrow gap in Ianix's armour.

Ianix grimaces and goes to one knee.

I frown across at him uneasily as the crowd starts to mutter and cat-call. He's faking, surely. Taedia has the same thought; she strides over and bends down, trying to lift his leg from the ground. After a futile struggle, she sighs.

"It's locked." She considers, then gives me an apologetic look. "It looked like a fair hit, but it must not have quite been enough to trigger the reaction."

It's wrong—I *know* it's wrong—but anything more that I say is only going to make me look worse. Dultatis is shaking his head in smug disapproval, making a joke to the other Praeceptors that I have no doubt is at my expense. Only Nequias laughs, but I see the students standing nearby smirking as well.

Others in the crowd jeer as it takes a minute to reset Ianix's armour. Every second of delay causes more voices to join the chorus. Frustration reddens my face beneath the calls. There are any number of ways Ianix's Amotus could still be rigged—some sort of Conditional imbuing, I assume, or perhaps Dultatis himself has imbued it—but there's no way to prove it. As the other boy inserts his stone wedge and his armour reassembles, I do allow myself a moment of doubt as to whether I was wrong. Whether I was imagining it.

I've been avoiding looking at the crowd, but now I do. Scan the faces watching us, watching me. Many are hostile. Some—few, admittedly—look more puzzled than annoyed. Emissa, Indol, even Iro are among the latter. Though Iro looks delighted as well, to be fair.

Behind the main cluster of Sevenths, I finally see Callidus. He's found a vantage atop the Temple of Jovan's stairs, leaning against one of the large columns that form its portico. He sees that I've spotted him. Hesitates.

Then he issues a single, sincere nod of encouragement.

I swallow, nod back, and refocus. Ianix is in position.

We start again.

Ianix is more cautious now as we clash several times, probing, testing each other's defences. I don't hold back anymore, don't pretend to any lack of skill. Ianix's face is frozen in surprised concentration. The crowd has stopped their mocking calls and are almost silent aside from the occasional shout of encouragement. Bemused, I suspect, that the fight is still going.

I'm only holding on, though, not winning. With a sword actually in hand, there's a good chance I'd be better than Ianix. This Amotus device, though—even with the hours of practice I got in last night and this morning—is too unfamiliar. My strikes are clean and fast, but not accurate enough; I'm still guessing at where I'm hitting, too often sliding off armour even when I get past Ianix's defences. My own defence, always my best skill, has kept me in the match, but it's inevitable that I'll make a mistake eventually.

Which is why it's so infuriating when I finally get in a clean hit to Ianix's shoulder, and nothing happens.

I hiss, baring my teeth in pure frustration as I back off, glancing around and praying for someone to shout out in protest. Nobody does. Maybe they don't notice, or more likely they're like me—they know how it will look if they stop the fight again, and there's nothing apparently wrong. I suspect there are plenty of people in the latter camp; Taedia's peering at Ianix as if trying to figure out some sort of puzzle, and even Veridius is leaning forward with an intent frown.

Dultatis isn't looking like he's enjoying himself anymore, either. He must have arranged this with Ianix as a fail-safe against luck, not with the expectation that I'd get in more than one good hit. He has to know that too many more times, and someone's going to be doing some thorough testing on these accursed armour sets afterward.

That's not going to be good enough for me, though. Even if there's an investigation, even if there's *proof*, it won't come in time. I know how these things work. Ianix will be ensconced in Class Five and will claim he had no knowledge of any wrongdoing. Dultatis will argue the same. There will be no one to categorically blame, and eventually things will just be left as they are.

So I have to win this, here and now.

I press down the riled fury that's building inside me. Not yet. *Not yet.* I need to think. Ianix isn't especially large; I definitely have the size advantage over him. If my sword isn't of any use for triggering the Will reaction in his armour, then I need to win some other way. I can't attack Ianix himself directly, either, tempting though it is. It's very strictly against the rules and even if I succeeded, I wouldn't be awarded the victory.

I back up several feet and then, before Ianix can follow, let my rage fill me.

Charge.

Ianix is ready, calm and in position, but about six feet away I throw my sword at him. Hard. He never expects it; he reacts instinctively by ducking and batting away the spinning blade, putting himself out of position. A second later I'm crashing into him, my Amotus tackling his to the ground and wrestling manically for his sword. He shouts in panic; I almost lose my grip from a wild laugh as I catch a glimpse of him from the corner of my eye, rolling around like a madman, desperately fending me off while trying to keep track of what I'm doing in the contest. There's a gasp from around the quadrum, then yells, but I can't understand what any of them are saying.

I'm in my element here; fighting in Letens has made this a far more comfortable environment than having a blade in my hand. I bare my teeth in a rictus grin and roll so that Ianix's sword arm is trapped between my body and arm, twisting and yanking hard. He shrieks in pain as something gives way, and his blade clatters to the ground.

I don't give him a chance to recover. I'm too angry for anything else. Angry that I'm having to do this. Angry that I've been put in this position. People like Ianix and Dultatis are the epitome of the Hierarchy. They've taken everything from me, and yet they want more. They always try to take *more*.

I roll again so that Ianix is pinned underneath me, grab his helmet with both hands, and smash it as hard as I can against the stone.

A horrified gasp echoes around me as Ianix's head thirty feet away rises and then slams into the ground in concert with his Amotus's, metal ringing clear across the quadrum. Protection or not, the shock of this is going to disorient him. Hurt him. And these helmets, steel though they are, aren't impregnable. I don't let go, do it again.

Again. I let the rage take me. *Again.* The steel beneath my gauntleted hands starts to buckle. Ianix is screaming. Wailing.

I drive the helmet into the ground one last time, and his screaming stops. No sound replaces it. It's like everyone watching has stopped breathing.

I don't look up at them. Ianix is unconscious, but I need to win. I'm not strong enough to tear off his armour but his helmet's not secured; I pull and across from me, the corresponding one on Ianix's head drags itself off, the imbued portion of it apparently still unscathed. It's dripping blood. The back has been bashed in, the wood splintered and crumpled inward. I think it's scored a gash along the back of his head. I hope that's all it is.

I'm tired now. Drained. I crawl across to Ianix's sword, pick it up, and carefully place his helmet on the tip. Nothing happens; Ianix remains unconscious and his armour remains clad to him. I stand, walk across to my own sword, add it to the first so that the helmet is balancing on both points. Still nothing happens.

My Amotus collapses where its stands as I detach the stone activation tile from my breastplate, then toss both swords and helmet on top of it. They clatter in the shocked hush.

I strip the wooden armour from my body as I stalk toward the Praeceptors, only pausing to fetch Ianix's bloodied wooden helmet, which has rolled into my path. Otherwise I keep my eyes up and forward, focused on Dultatis. The man's drained of colour. The others have stepped back from him.

I stop about ten feet short of Dultatis, breathing heavily, then toss the helmet disdainfully at his feet, never letting my gaze leave his. Blood spatters on the hem of his toga.

I want to attack him. To call him out. To denounce him a cheat, a liar, and the small, bitter man that he is. My blood is pumping so hard that I almost do all of it at once.

Then beyond, I see Callidus. Everyone else is watching in stunned horror. He's just beaming, a fist raised high in silent, jubilant victory. Celebrating for me. Celebrating *with* me.

"It seems you need to check the equipment again." I say it calmly, but somehow Dultatis looks even more taken aback. Oddly fearful for a man who could summon the strength of a dozen men and snap me without a moment's thought.

I sigh, and push past them.

"Where are you going, Vis?" It's Taedia.

I stop. "To eat. But I will see you tomorrow, Praeceptor. I look forward to your classes." I don't let any hint of question enter my voice. I've earned my place.

She glances back at Ianix, still motionless on the ground. A couple of the other Praeceptors have recovered themselves enough to rush over to him, but he seems to be groggily waking up. For all the fury that still boils in my chest, I'm relieved.

Then she nods, still not looking at me. "Of course. You can move your things in the dormitory up a level tonight."

I half expect another one of the Praeceptors to speak up, to block my departure, to condemn me for what I've just done. They don't, though. I suspect they're still in shock—and the fact that Dultatis was clearly complicit in the cheating is probably muddying the waters for them. I don't care anymore, regardless. Taedia has publicly confirmed that I won the bout. That's all I need.

My anger's fading, and with it the last of my energy. I'm bruised and battered. The rest of the students part before me, giving me a wider path than necessary to walk through. None of them speak. They just watch as I trudge away.

I want to talk to Callidus, but he's disappeared, so I head for the mess. I've made a lasting impression, this evening. As tired as I am, it's best to reinforce it by acting as if it were nothing, rather than collapsing somewhere out of sight.

My head spins, and I find my hands shaking as I walk. There's no joy in this success, no sense of accomplishment. I just did what I had to.

That will have to be enough, for now.

XLVI

"Y OU," SAYS CALLIDUS QUIETLY AS I SIT OPPOSITE HIM, NOT looking up from his reading, "have an anger problem."

It's still dark, the morning after my victory over Ianix. My move to the Class Five floor of the dormitory last night was easy enough, even if I felt oddly reluctant about it—with Eidhin as my roommate, my room in Class Six was as comfortable a place as I've been since my arrival. But the lodgings are an improvement. More personal space. Three to a room, everyone getting their own private dresser to use, and a desk twice the size of those down a floor.

My two roommates were still up and studying when I arrived. Weary and sore though I was from the bout, neither offered to help, and I didn't ask.

The sound of distant waves washes over us. "You're just figuring this out?"

"No, no, I knew. Everyone *else*, on the other hand . . ." Callidus finally shuts his book, flicking an amused glance toward the quadrum. "Rotting gods, they're *terrified* of you now."

"I imagine it wasn't quite the controlled fight they were expecting."

"It. Was. Not," agrees Callidus with facetious emphasis. His speech is a little stiff though. Distracted.

There's another few seconds, the both of us looking for words.

"Say you were right, yesterday morning." I lean forward and keep my voice low. Tap the stone bench nervously, focusing on the movement of my finger. I've rehearsed this. I want to see his reaction, but the appearance of being unable to make eye contact is important here. Makes it seem more genuine. "And say that I felt . . . a little bad, for not admitting it. Or telling you sooner. Would that be enough?"

There's silence, and then, "A little?"

I chuckle ruefully, raising my gaze to meet his. "A *little*," I repeat firmly. It's worked—I can see that much already. He's taking it in good humour. Glad I'm addressing the tension between us.

"I understand. I do. Really." The rigidity has gone from Callidus's posture as he leans back. "You know I *am* going to figure out the specifics eventually, though." He raises an eyebrow at my wince. "That bad?"

"You tell me. What's the penalty for misleading the Census?"

"Oh. *Oh.* True." Callidus is thoughtful. An affair resulting in an illegitimate son is one thing, but the resources needed to omit me from the Census altogether would be staggering. It would be a scandalous abuse of power. The sort of thing that could potentially bring down even a highly ranked senator.

And if it ever came to light, I'd most likely disappear along with my mysterious parent into a Sapper.

Hopefully that's enough to stay Callidus's hand from using his father's resources to check into my past. I'm banking on his valuing our friendship over any advantage the information might bring him—which, given everything, I think is as safe a bet as I can make.

"Alright," says Callidus eventually. "It's a start."

I smile my relief.

He grins back, then jerks his head toward the dormitory. "At least now I understand why you hate the rest of them so much."

"I wouldn't say I *hate* them."

"Ianix would. And I've seen the way you look at them." He nods sagely at my glower. "Yes. Perfect. Exactly like that."

I break into a laugh, not pursuing the matter further, though I do make note of Callidus's observation. I haven't exactly made an effort to connect with people here, I suppose. But I thought I'd done better than coming across as *disliking* them.

"I was glad you came to watch, yesterday. It helped."

Callidus grunts. "Don't get too weepy. I was just there to make some money off you."

"What?"

"If there's one thing that just about everyone here loves, it's gambling. I'd already heard people talking about how embarrassing that fight was going to be for you. Catenicus, stuck in Six. Nobody thought you could beat Ianix. *Nobody.*"

"Except for you."

"Except for me. Who thought it was going to be close," he clarifies.

"Get many takers?"

"Yes." Callidus leans back jauntily. "Oh yes."

I sigh. Another boost to my unpopularity, probably. "Only fair, I suppose. Compensation for your helping me practice. Not that you need the money."

"Not at all," he agrees enthusiastically. "But I do love taking it from them."

"Glad I could help."

We rise at an unspoken agreement, moving over to where we usually conduct our daily sparring. "So I imagine this explains why you're so bent on making Class Three," Callidus says quietly. "Makes a lot more sense now."

I concur, letting him think the lie. If I really was the illegitimate son of a senator, I'd be an invaluable asset if my connection to them was unknown—so long as I reached a high enough position. Anything less, on the other hand, would make me nothing but a liability.

We start to spar. Callidus has been improving; he'd still be no match for me if we ever fought in earnest, but he's quick on his feet, decisive, knows how to land his punches and where. There's no sound for a while except our breathing and the occasional grunt of pain or muttered curse. Still, the other boy seems off this morning. A step slow. Distracted.

I frown, stepping back. "Is something wrong?"

Callidus steps back too, wiping a bead of sweat from his brow. Dawn's breaking, clear and clean today. Steam drifts from him. He pauses, looking as indecisive as I've ever seen him.

Then he slowly nods.

"I didn't think I was going to need to tell you this," he admits, a little wryly. "But the fact is, Taedia's a half-reasonable Praeceptor. You're probably going to be in Class Four by the Festival of Pletuna. So it's better if you know sooner rather than later."

I feel my brow furrow. "Out with it."

He lowers his voice. "It's . . . dangerous, being in Three or Four."

"What do you mean?"

"I mean that for the past four Academy cycles, at least a couple of Thirds and Fourths have died. *Every cycle.*" Callidus glances around as he says it, though we're completely alone. "Not like Feriun, but here. At Solivagus."

I study him. "That can't be right. People would know. There would be outrage. Investigations."

"You would think so." Callidus is grimly certain. "You would be surprised at how far a combination of coin and favour can go toward silencing whole families."

"What about the other students who were here? Surely they'd say something."

"The deaths happened during the Iudicium, away from most of them. Some of those who probably know seem to have gotten preferential placement within Religion. And everyone has a writ of Silencium attached to them anyway. Breaking that would mean risking a Sapper."

"Silencium?" I squint, trying to remember the term. "I thought those were for legal proceedings."

"It's part of the paperwork to attend the Academy—your father would have signed it on your behalf before you started here. It's meant to maintain the integrity of the school. Make sure that those who come from a heritage of attending don't get an unfair advantage." The disdain in his voice indicates just how ineffective he thinks that is. "It's never enforced like that, which is why he obviously didn't bother mentioning it to you. But for covering something up, the threat would be more than enough."

I shake my head. Unsettled at the thought of Ulciscor binding me to something like that without telling me, even if it's the standard. "So students have died. How?"

"Accidents, supposedly." He takes a breath. "And there's more. From those same four cycles, another ten graduates from Class Three have since vanished from their pyramids. Presumed dead. They were all in positions of power, but nobody seems to have done more than give their disappearances a cursory glance." He sees my dubious expression, rolls his shoulders uncomfortably. "I know how it sounds. I *know*. But there's something going on here, and putting yourself in the higher classes . . . it's a risk."

My mind races. I think of the Labyrinth in the ruins. The copy of it here. This has to be connected.

"So this is why you're in Seven?" I ask eventually.

"What I told you before is true. But this helped make the decision easier."

I signal my acceptance of the explanation, even if it still doesn't sound quite right to me. Callidus is practical, certainly. Pragmatic. But more the type I would expect to investigate, rather than avoid the risk in silence.

"So how do you know all this, when nobody else does?" The answer occurs to me as the words come out of my mouth, and Callidus nods as he sees the dawning on my face.

"My father. The Census." He fidgets. He's not comfortable admitting this. "He told me. Warned me, before I came." He impresses the importance of what he's revealing to me with his look.

I feel the weight of it. If anyone found out Callidus's father had revealed Census information, even to his son, then it would be *disastrous* for their family. The Hierarchy protects that information above almost everything else. Tertius Ericius would be removed from office, maybe even put in a Sapper for violating his covenant so blatantly.

I'd have no actual proof if I tried to claim it, of course, but Callidus confiding this to me is . . . it's beyond trusting. He's placing a faith in me that I don't deserve. "I won't breathe a word of this to anyone."

"I know." Callidus studies me. "Still want to move up?"

"I have to." No lie there. If Callidus is right—and I have no reason to believe he isn't—then the added risk is something to keep in mind, but it doesn't change what I need to do. "Thanks for the warning, though."

He gives me a half smile, understanding that I'm acknowledging the belief he's showing in me, and then we resume our sparring. Callidus has a renewed energy, a lightness to his movements that wasn't there before. The knowledge has been weighing on him.

Soon enough we're done; breakfast is spent in pleasant conversation, the tension of the past day acknowledged and put behind us. I find myself relaxing, laughing, able to ignore the sidelong stares of the other students as they walk by. I've passed the hurdle of Class Six. I've investigated the ruins on the other side of the island, well ahead of schedule. I have friends here, allies who will help me. People who trust me.

At least in this one, bright moment, the rest of the year feels like it will be positively easy by comparison.

%% %% %%

THE NEXT FEW WEEKS ARE A PLEASANT HAZE OF WORK.

I start each morning with Callidus, sparring, then sitting down to study both before and during breakfast. It's the other boy who suggests the addition to our routine; now he's warned me of what may lie ahead, he seems happy, even excited, to engage in academic work with me.

I soon realise why: his boredom in Class Seven must be profound. He's smarter than I am. *Much* smarter. Soon enough, we're tackling theory far advanced from what I'm learning in Class Five. Distributed Conditionals. Will interplay with mechanics. Methodology of secondary fail-safes. Limitations on locking, calculations of upper and lower bounds of strength based on position and ceding ratio and imbuing. My understanding of the Hierarchy and how it works, how it perpetuates, how it's built what it has built, increases dramatically.

Emissa joins us some mornings, too, in the glimmering pre-dawn light before we head to the mess. Rarely for long and only occasionally, but enough for me to look forward to the possibility. She and Callidus seem comfortable around each other, clearly having gotten along during their brief time in the same class. And her contributions show that the subjects we're studying don't faze her in the slightest. A good sign that I have plenty of improving to do, if I want to compete in Three.

Callidus is never short of a sly remark after she leaves. I continue to ignore him.

Classes themselves, for so long the bane of my day under Dultatis, become—if not *interesting*, then at least not a waste of time. Taedia runs a tight daily schedule, pushing each of her twenty-four students without overburdening them. Her lessons are informative and clear. Though I'm still usually either familiar with the subject matter or can pick it up easily, I learn more under her tutelage in three weeks than in the two months I spent with Dultatis.

The students themselves are easier company, too: not friendly, but civil enough and willing to interact when necessary. It's the most I can hope for. I'm too focused on distinguishing myself to Taedia to make an effort to endear myself, and after my fight with Ianix, my reputation is such that—according to Callidus and Emissa, at least—I'm viewed with some hesitancy by the wider body of students. Combined with the Catenicus nomenclature, and Iro's lingering influence, I'm considered a . . . *somewhat less than approachable figure,* as Emissa delicately puts it.

My evenings are for the most part spent tutoring Eidhin. Though he remains reserved, I enjoy these sessions, too. The large boy is a quick and willing student; his foundation in Common is already relatively strong, but he advances with astonishing rapidity once he has someone who speaks his own language to guide him. I'd had my suspicions, but after a couple of weeks, I'm convinced that he should be in a higher class than he is, too. He's not at Callidus's wide-ranging level of intellect, perhaps, but he's smarter than anyone in Six. Anyone else in Five, too, I think. It's only his inability to effectively communicate—and Dultatis's unearned dislike, of course—that has held him back.

Dultatis himself, much to my disgust, appears to escape censure over his attempt at cheating. Ianix, too; he was out of the infirmary the day following the fight and straight back into Class Six. He avoids me now.

None of the Praeceptors have spoken to me about the fight. They all seem to want to act as if it was won fairly. I can't see an advantage to pressing the point.

It's hard, keeping what I saw in the ruins to myself, but I have little choice in the matter. I can't freely communicate with Ulciscor before the trimester break, and I can't bring myself to involve any of my friends—even Eidhin, who already knows about some of it. So instead I lie awake each night and ponder the Labyrinth. Puzzle again and again over its purpose. Its twin in the Academy feels increasingly like a proving ground. Veridius and Religion's attempt to find someone who can run against the nightmares in the original.

Which in turn, leads me to again wonder if the missing students Callidus told me about saw their end in there.

Despite the heavy discomfort of those thoughts, time passes quickly. My mood improves. I work hard. Do everything I can to be a model student.

And then Callidus is right about something else. Two days into my fourth week under Praeceptor Taedia, I'm raised to Class Four.

XLVII

"YOU'RE A GOOD STUDENT. SMART. DULTATIS HELD YOU BACK for far too long."

Praeceptor Scitus absently rakes back his shaggy black hair. It's just before dinner, and we're in his private office. It's not as spacious as Veridius's, and certainly doesn't have as good a view, but it's neat. Shelves line the wall and books are arranged by what looks like topic, dividers between sections. The desk, large though it is, has only a perfectly stacked sheaf of papers in the top-left corner, a pen, and a lamp. There's not a speck of dust anywhere.

I hear it coming, so I ask. "But?"

"But if you're going to join Class Four, you need to start connecting with your classmates. And I'm not talking about you being friends with Sevenths and Sixths, either. 'Stronger together'—you remember that, right? I need to know you're going to keep that in mind."

I look at him, nonplussed. I don't know what I was expecting, but this wasn't it. "What if my classmates aren't interested?" I wasn't exactly a popular figure, even before the Ianix fight.

"Make them be. Charm them. Bribe them if you have to—I don't care."

"That . . . won't be easy. Half of them seem afraid of me."

"They are afraid, and it's more than half." Scitus scratches his scruffy beard. "And I don't blame them. You have a reputation as a killer, Vis. One who was in the right, but—someone who has taken another human life. And then everyone watched you bash in Ianix's head. Which, again, was justified," he agrees as I open my mouth to protest, "but it doesn't exactly say 'welcoming.'"

"Maybe I like it that way."

"Nobody likes it that way—and even if you do, I don't care. I'm telling you what you need to do in my class, as a baseline. Otherwise I'll send you right back to Five, no matter your other attributes."

"Why?"

"Fourths and Thirds end up in the Senate. Every single one of them. Yes, I want my senators to be intelligent. Strong. Capable of wielding an immense amount of Will. But none of that matters if they can't convince others. If they have no charm. If they can't build networks and actually make a *difference* in the Republic." He says it all with calm conviction. "This is a skill too, Vis. An important one, no matter how much you wish it were otherwise. So show me that you're willing to work at it."

There's not much I can do but nod. There are only six months until the end of the year, and a month of that is the trimester break. Plenty of time to advance and take my shot in the Iudicium, but not if I get on Scitus's wrong side. Especially as, at least from Emissa's and Callidus's accounts, Class Four is a significant step up in competitiveness.

"Good." Scitus examines me. "The first thing you need to do is sit with your classmates at meals. Ericius will need to find a mealtime partner from Seven, if he wants one."

"Fine." I'll miss the comfortable routine of eating with Callidus, but he'll understand. He's even suggested previously that I might be forced into just this situation.

"And you'll have to spend your time after dinner studying in the dormitory with them, too."

"No."

"No?"

I shake my head. "I've been tutoring Eidhin."

"He's in *Six*. I don't care if you're friends. Focus on your peers."

"I'll make friends—that's fine. But don't expect me to abandon my old ones, or break an oath I've already given." I hold his gaze. "Or is that what you want from your senators too? A complete lack of loyalty?"

Scitus considers, then allows a small, reluctant smile. "Point taken. Continue with your evenings, then. But I won't accept it as a reason for falling behind."

"Understood."

He rises, indicating that I should follow suit. "Then welcome to Class Four, Vis."

※ ※ ※

I HEAD TO DINNER IN THE MESS, WHICH IS WELL UNDERWAY. I pause by Callidus's table.

His usual cheer dies away a little as he looks up and sees my expression. "Ah. It's time?"

"Just had the conversation with Scitus," I confirm apologetically. "'Spend every meal with the class.' I'm supposed to make friends with them."

He almost chokes on what he's eating. "Right up your alley."

"Shut up." I grin to show I'm joking. "You watch. They'll be eating out of my hand in no time."

He sighs. Gestures. "Well. Tomorrow morning before breakfast, then?"

"Always." I clap him on the shoulder, then start up toward Class Four's level of the mess.

The eleven other students around the table are laughing about something, but quiet as they spot my approach. I adopt a friendly, relaxed posture. Force myself to act as if I'm looking forward to this.

While friendships have never come easy to me, I *do* know a little about getting people on my side. I was going to be a diplomat, once. I have a fair idea of how to ingratiate myself with others.

I just, on the whole, never cared for it. Having to feign interest in those you don't like, or at least don't know well enough to have an opinion on. Pretending to have their interests at heart when in reality, you're just figuring out how to make the best use of them. It's all so . . . disingenuous.

I arrive at the table, standing awkwardly at its head. Normally I'd try to look confident, but my reputation's such that showing a small amount of uncertainty might actually help. Make me relatable. "I'm Vis." I glance over at Aequa, hoping she'll take the lead here. She's the only one I've spoken to before.

There's silence—surprised, I think, more than standoffish—and then Aequa leans back. "Took you long enough."

"We had bets on when you would make it through Five," explains the girl sitting next to her, studying me intently. She has emerald-green eyes in a pinched face that accentuates her cheekbones.

I smile at her. "Who won?"

"That would be me." The boy closest to me stands. He's confident, with curly black hair that frames a chiselled visage. "Axien." He extends his hand.

I shake it, the warmth of my reaction not entirely faked. I didn't expect to be rebuffed, exactly, but there was certainly no guarantee of a gracious reception here.

There's another hint of hesitation, and then I'm offered a seat and the others begin introducing themselves. It's unnecessary; everyone in the Academy knows who's in Three and Four. But I let it happen anyway, part of the social contract. Aside from Axien, there are six boys—Lucius, Felix, Marcellus, Atticus, Tem, and Titus. The girls are Cassia, Ava, Valentina, and of course, Aequa. All of them from powerful families, with either high-ranking senators or regional proconsuls as parents. None of them are enthused by my presence, but nor are they inclined to brusqueness, either. It's a start.

"You got promoted faster than most of us thought," observes Valentina, the green-eyed girl sitting across from me. Her accent, not to mention her blond hair and pale skin, indicates southern blood. "Only Aequa thought you'd be faster. How did you do it?"

"Well I didn't have to punch anyone this time. So that was nice."

There's a moment, and then some chuckles around the table. The tension eases a little. I wait until there's quiet again, then shrug. "I put in the work. Plus I already knew a lot of what we were learning. Praeceptor Taedia thought I'd acquit myself adequately in Four, and it seems Praeceptor Scitus feels the same."

"Tell us," says Tem, brown eyes curious as he leans forward. His teeth are white against dark skin. "Where in the gods' graves did you learn to use the Amotus? We've been debating about it since you beat Ianix. There are rumours, of course, but . . ." He motions, indicating his dissatisfaction at not hearing it from the source. "It was very impressive."

"I fought in the Victorum in Letens, when I was an orphan." Fighting in the games isn't something that's going to impress the children of patricians, but everyone knows my background anyway. It's what I've been telling anyone who will listen; only Callidus, as far as I know, suspects there's anything more to it. Better this half-truth than uncomfortable questions later.

"Ah." His gaze flicks to Aequa before returning to me, as if checking for her reaction.

The conversation proceeds fairly well from there, as I'm peppered with questions that range from my upbringing to, of course, the naumachia. Aequa, I'm pleased to see, remains friendly. Hopefully it means her enquiries about when I left the Necropolis came to naught.

While everyone's willing enough to talk, Axien, Titus, Atticus, Tem, and Cassia are the most immediately friendly. All from Military families, I realise soon enough. It's a divide that quickly becomes obvious: Lucius and Marcellus are from Religion, and they seem content to have their own private conversation for most of the meal, while Aequa, Ava, Valentina, and Felix—while participating in the wider discussion—seem more inclined to have quiet asides among themselves, too.

It's a dynamic I noticed becoming prevalent in Class Five, and Callidus has remarked on it happening in Seven as well. He thinks it's a natural outworking of increasing tensions in the Senate. I'm beginning to agree. It was probably a popular topic at the Festival of the Ancestors, which is when these divisions seemed to start.

"Is it true you actually won the Labyrinth in Six?" asks Ava, a short girl who wears her black hair in a tight braid. Her father's a Tertius in Governance, from memory.

"Well. We got disqualified, but it was because Dultatis said that communicating in another language was cheating."

"How is that any different from using pre-arranged signals?"

"Good question," I agree wryly.

"You'll have a better running partner than Tiberius, then, Aequa." Felix chuckles. At the mention of the boy, a few of the group glance down to the level below us. I follow their gaze, spotting the glum figure among the other Fifths.

"Not a high bar," notes Axien.

I glance askance in Aequa's direction.

"We'll be paired for the Labyrinth. Best and worst ranked," she says, a little apologetically. "Tiberius was . . . not the best. Don't worry. Our next run isn't for a few days yet. We have time to work out a code."

I accept her observation, though the mere thought of the Labyrinth makes me mildly uneasy; despite Veridius's implying that I could practice it early in the mornings, my discoveries since mean that I haven't been back by choice. We only ran it once during my time in Class Five, too. An abject failure: my partner was both awful at manipulating the control bracer, and then thoroughly misremembered our agreed-upon signals when he ran.

But the Fourths practice it every few days, and the Thirds even more often. I'm going to have to get used to it.

Dinner comes to an end, and I judge it as successful an introduction to my new classmates as I could have hoped for: I'm unlikely to enjoy meals the same way I did sitting with Callidus, but no one in the class is actively combative. It's a good sign.

I pass Praeceptor Scitus on the way out. He glances up, and I acknowledge him with a nod. He gives an almost imperceptible one back. Approving.

I find myself smiling as I head for the Academy Bibliotheca.

※ ※ ※

"I HEAR CONGRATULATIONS ARE IN ORDER."

I give a sweeping bow to Eidhin as I join him at the table in the near-empty Bibliotheca, tossing down the text I've chosen for tonight's study in front of him. "Just moved my things."

"How are the new quarters?"

"Acceptable," I say airily, grinning as the other boy scowls at me. I slip into the seat opposite. "Nice. They're nice," I amend, more sincerely this time.

My new lodgings on the second-to-top floor of the dormitory are, in fact, very nice. Emerging onto the landing was like stepping into another world: the floor was richly carpeted, the hallways wide and inviting, and the same floor-to-ceiling archways that Veridius has in his office lined the left of the entrance corridor, providing an incredible view out over the Sea of Quus. There were mosaics on the wall opposite that, while I don't have an eye for what passes for fine art in Caten, looked expensive, too.

More importantly, with just the eight boys in Class Four and an entire floor to ourselves, I now have my own room. Which means that if I do need to embark on any more late-night trips, they won't carry anywhere near the risks of last time.

"I'm glad they meet with your approval." Eidhin grumbles it in Common. He enunciates carefully, but the flow of his words is considerably more natural than it once was. Our recent emphasis on grammar is paying dividends.

"Dultatis say anything?"

Eidhin's lips twitch into something dangerously close to a smile. "No. But I suspect he knew. He was in a fouler mood than usual." He preens slightly. "Though that may also have been thanks to my embarrassing him in front of Praeceptor Taedia and the entire class, this morning."

"How so?"

"I corrected his Common. Twice."

I laugh aloud. "Then our lessons have truly paid off." I raise my mug of water, and he clinks his to mine solemnly.

We sink into the routine of our studies after that, a combination of text work and practicing speech in Common. It's a hard grind, this late in the day, but our integration of texts from Class Four helps. I don't learn anywhere near as much as I do with Callidus in the mornings, but it's enough to make the process rewarding for me, too.

"None of the Sixths would even know this, let alone be able to express it so clearly," I say admiringly, sitting back as Eidhin finishes our session by explaining a complex, high-theory imbuing concept to me entirely in Common. "You really should at least be in Five."

"Four, if you've managed it."

"Bah." I make a dismissive gesture, smiling, recognising the jest despite Eidhin's words being delivered with absolute sincerity. I'm more accustomed to his humour now, able to spot when he's making a joke. Most of the time, anyway.

We begin clearing up. "You sat with the Fourths, this evening." Eidhin's switched back to Cymrian, indicating he's done practicing for the evening.

"Scitus told me I needed to try harder with other people. He basically forbade me from sitting with Callidus."

"Hm."

I've come to recognise the meanings behind Eidhin's noncommittal grunts, too. "You don't think I should have?"

"It is your decision to make."

I give him a mildly annoyed glare. "I want to move up to Three. If I'm going to do that, I need to have the Praeceptor on my side."

Eidhin shrugs. "As you say."

It's delivered with indifference, a complete lack of judgment. I still feel it, though. "You wouldn't do the same?"

He shrugs again. "It is the way of the Hierarchy." A no, from the manner in which he says it.

I'm stung by that, probably far worse than by anything else he could have said. "What do you mean?"

Eidhin looks reluctant. Knits his brow. "They ask something small of you. A thing you would prefer not to do, but is not so terrible. You think you are working your way up, but in fact they are changing you. Moulding you into what they think you should be, one compromise at a time." He says it simply, but there's rock-hard belief beneath the words. "I am not suggesting you should have ignored what Scitus said. I am just saying that in this place . . . each man has to find his line. Has to find it *ahead* of time, and be resolved never to cross it."

I don't say anything for a few long seconds. I think it's the most Eidhin has ever said to me at once.

"I know," I say eventually. The old scars pull on my back. "You don't need to worry about me on that count, Eidhin. I have my line."

The muscular boy looks surprised, as if expecting disagreement. He hesitates.

"It was the Principalis," he says abruptly.

"What?" I have no idea what he's talking about.

"That first day you were here. When you punched me." Gruff, but something mortified in the deliberate, succinct way he says it. It's a painful revelation for him to make. "The morning you arrived, the Principalis pulled me aside. He said that several people would be aiming to send Callidus's father a message. Implied that perhaps if I were to knock him down in front of everyone, it may satisfy their need to hurt him without him being seriously injured." He sneers. At himself, I think. "And he implied that if I did this, he might find a way to . . . help me with something. A problem from before the Academy."

"Oh." I grimly process the information. Veridius really did plan the whole thing, then. Perhaps not with the intent of getting me expelled—he *did* have the opportunity to step in and stop me when I gave Eidhin his Threefold Apology—but at least in order to make me look bad. To put me on the back foot and ensure my barely born reputation as Catenicus wasn't allowed too much air within these walls.

Not a surprise, I suppose. It's still troubling.

"I am sorry."

"I stopped worrying about it long ago. Callidus did, too." I see where his outburst about the Hierarchy came from now. "Thank you for telling me, though. I'm glad to know."

He nods, eyes fixed on the floor.

"You . . . don't talk much about your life before the Academy," I press on cautiously.

"It was not my favourite time."

I chuckle. "All of it?"

"All of it."

My amusement wanes. I don't think he's joking.

The conversation seems to have ended; we finish packing up and start the journey back to the dormitory, walking in silence. The night's warm and still, an echo of a summer long since fled. There's an animated conversation between two students on the other side of the quadrum, but we're to all intents and purposes alone.

"I was in a Sapper."

It takes me a long moment to process the words, to turn them over in my head and make sure I haven't misheard. "What are you talking about?"

"Before the Academy. That's where I was." Eidhin's gaze is fixed straight ahead. His voice is flat. "For almost a year."

I gape into the darkness in front of us, flustered. "In a *Sapper*? I . . . *why*?"

"Because I killed people. Three Praetorians."

"Three Praetorians," I repeat, a little faintly. Highly trained men and women of at least Sextus status, wielding Razors.

We've reached the dormitory. Eidhin's huge form is silhouetted against the orange flames of the torches on the walls. "I understand that this could . . . change your opinion of me. If you wish to be released from your obligation, I will bear you no ill will. On my honour."

I shake my head. "No. I'll see you tomorrow night."

"Even if I wish to say no more on the matter?"

"We're friends. You don't have to tell me."

He studies me, then gives a short acknowledgment. "Tomorrow night, then."

He turns and walks off. But I swear I see him smile as he does so.

XLVIII

Lesson for Class Four are, immediately, markedly more intense than anything that has come before.

Scitus is by far the most engaging and energetic teacher I've had. He practically bounces up and down the classroom, enthusiastically pinging questions between us, encouraging conversation on any number of topics and then forcefully dragging anyone who stays silent into the debate. In my first two days, I have an hour-long discussion over how Conditional imbuing might be better utilised in agriculture, end up in a heated debate over the historical accuracy of the invasion of Sytrece—backing down only because I'm aware of how genuinely annoyed I am at Felix's dogmatically Catenan views—and then talk myself into a corner while trying to explain Namina's philosophy of Will Maximisation.

It's not just Scitus, either. The eleven other students in Class Four are sharp, hard-working, and aggressive if they sense a weakness in someone else's argument. Oratory skills which were merely taught in previous classes—and which, to be fair, I have ample training in from my younger years—come into play more and more. Verbal jousts are a common occurrence.

Interestingly, once again, I notice factional themes emerging in these debates. If Axien makes a statement, most often Atticus or Cassia will jump in to defend it. If Aequa attacks an argument, it's always Ava or Felix lending their support to her objection. It's not quite enough to say that it happens every time. But it's enough to stand out.

For my part, I maintain neutrality, choosing to side with whomever I actually think is right. It earns me some glares from Axien, in particular, and some surprised looks from everyone else. But Eidhin's observation has stayed with me. I won't let myself be changed by them. Become one of them.

Even so, for the next few days, I sit with Class Four. I eat meals with them. Aside from mornings with Callidus and evenings with Eidhin, I study with them and train with them. I'm welcomed with surprising ease into their small group, quickly made a member of an exclusive club. I still sometimes catch a sideways glance—the spectre of my reputation won't vanish that easily—and there are plenty of conversations and jokes about long-previous classes that I simply can't contribute to. But for the most part, the Fourths act as if I've been with them for as long as anyone else.

Two things become evident as the days pass: Aequa is considered to have the top rank in the class—both by Scitus and the other students—and of the entire group, she's the least liked. Atticus in particular enjoys making soft asides about her to Cassia, who tends to encourage him with a girlish giggle that I find inexplicably annoying.

Jealousy of her position aside, though, I can't see any reason for the antipathy. My own interactions with Aequa are nothing but friendly as we work out our signals for running the maze. I feel like things are going well.

Then, at the beginning of my fifth day in Class Four, we head to the Labyrinth.

%% %% %%

"THE THIRDS ARE HERE TOO?" I VOICE MY SURPRISE TO AEQUA as we descend onto the raised platform above the Labyrinth. Emissa, Indol, Iro, and the others are hanging over the balcony a little way over.

Aequa's mouth twists as she spots them. "Nequias likes to have them watch sometimes."

"Why?"

"Motivation, apparently. To keep them looking over their shoulders. Remind them that the rest of us are improving." She shakes her head, showing she doesn't believe the narrative. "It's really just so Nequias can spend a few hours doing nothing, and the Thirds can feel good about how much better they are at this." Unmistakeable bitterness creeps into her tone.

"Are they? Better, I mean."

"They practice every day. We get one session per week. It's inevitable."

Praeceptor Nequias is with his class, standing a little apart with a book in hand, openly bored. He barely looks up as the Fourths enter, acknowledging Scitus and then scanning the rest of us disdainfully before going back to his reading. I feel a flash of Aequa's irritation.

The Thirds pay more attention to our entrance. Iro's eyes meet mine and his lips slide into a sneer, as they tend to do when he spots me. I've done everything I can to stay out of his way—an easy enough task, thus far, given our respective classes—but it's no secret that he despises my presence at the school. That I've made it this far likely isn't sitting well with him.

I issue a cheerful smile, despite knowing I should just ignore him. Iro's expression darkens.

"Everyone here?" Scitus scans our group and then, content that all dozen of his students are present, points to Aequa. "Let's start at the top. Aequa, you have the first run. Vis, you're her partner."

Good. No time to be nervous. Labyrinth runs are regular enough in Class Four to count heavily toward our ranking. I've acquitted myself well enough over the past few days, but this is my first real opportunity to impress.

I strap the control bracer to my arm and settle myself above the starting point, a little self-conscious in front of the Thirds. In their class, the runner wears the bracer as well, with partners there only to call out information. Another indication that this is some sort of proving ground for the maze on the other side of the island.

Aequa descends, and Felix, Marcellus, and Valentina do the same on the far side of the Labyrinth. Tem, Atticus, and Lucius set themselves at the appropriate points on the balcony, one on each side and one at the end. Everyone in Class Four will be experienced at this, far more competent than anyone else I've come up against so far. I compose myself.

Scitus signals the start, and Aequa is away.

I'm immediately impressed by her speed, by the way she lithely darts around the corridors, taking cues from how I'm opening passageways without a moment's hesitation. I move steadily around the edge of the platform, watching, occasionally calling coded instructions, but doing my best to indicate a path using the bracer alone. It's a tactic we've discussed, and Aequa seems to have no problem reading what I'm trying to do. My shifting of the control stones on the bracer is smooth, quick, in rhythm. I start to feel confident.

I don't even realise I've moved in front of the Thirds until I hear Iro's voice behind me.

"Left," he murmurs, making me flinch at how close he is. "Back. Left. Right. Open. Right. Forward. Shut."

It's not much, but the half second of distraction ruins my cadence; I hesitate and suddenly Aequa's skidding to a stop below, waiting for a door that should already be open. I lurch for the stone on the bracer as Iro's voice continues to tickle my ear. My motion's jerky and the door opens, but with a rough, squealing grind that makes everyone on the balconies cringe. Aequa darts through, but not before shooting me a glare. Valuable time lost.

"Iro." It's Emissa, her voice sharp. "Don't be a child."

There's a delay, and then Iro's voice returns. Even quieter than before, so that only I can hear. Calm and dark. "She's a bit of a whore, isn't she."

My breath catches. Red tints my vision. He's goading me. I want nothing more than to turn and punch him, and we both know that if I do that, there won't be any escape for me this time. Iro's a Third. Veridius will have no choice but to expel me.

I try to open another passage for Aequa, but my hand's shaking from anger. The grinding's worse this time. The stone comes away in my hand. Aequa curses, immediately changes direction.

"Iro. I'm sorry about what happened to your sister." I'm not, in that moment. Not at all. But I have to try and defuse this situation. "You have to know it wasn't my fault, though."

"How long did you take to save your little friend down there? How many thousands died while you chaperoned her through the sewers?" Pain. Fury. "Own up to your blame, *Catenicus.*" There's so much venom in the name that my shoulders twitch, anticipating an attack.

I manage to keep my eyes on the Labyrinth. Any sense of cohesion has gone from mine and Aequa's run. The hunters are closing in. I can already see she's lost. There's a heated discussion in the background, Emissa's voice raised. Nequias replying. Someone else—Indol, maybe?—supporting her. It doesn't matter. The damage is done.

I turn to Iro as Aequa's cornered below, keeping everything loose and calm, refusing to let him see how furious I truly am. He's standing too close. I let him. "I stand by what I did."

The red fades. I breathe. Brush past him. Risk a glance over at Emissa and Indol, hoping to see them making some headway with Nequias. Instead, the old man is looking on with undisguised amusement, shaking his head at whatever argument Emissa is making.

I hand the bracer back to Scitus. He looks at me, then over at Iro.

"Men and women don't wield Will in silence, or without distractions. It doesn't matter what he said to you. He didn't physically interfere. That was a poor showing."

"It was, Praeceptor. I'm sorry." There's no point in making excuses. "I'll do better next time."

"See that you do."

I move to walk away, but Scitus reaches out. Grabs me and leans close.

"It was also a commendable display of character. An improvement on the last couple of months, if I am not mistaken," he adds softly. "We all know Iro's quarrel with you, and it is unwarranted. Your restraint was admirable. Well done."

My back straightens. I walk over to the entrance, facing Aequa as she climbs the stairs.

She starts glaring at me well before reaching the top, and doesn't stop. "Well, that was embarrassing."

"Iro was being . . . well. He may try to distract you, too." I feel the need to warn her, at least. "I'll go left, so you don't have to walk past them."

She glances over at the Thirds, who have stopped their debate, though Iro's still smirking and Emissa is still staring daggers at him. "Go whichever way I tell you to go. If he tries something, I'll punch him in the face."

She stalks off.

My run through the Labyrinth is significantly more successful than Aequa's. True to her word, she walks around to the right, and if Iro says anything to her then she ignores it far more capably than I did. Doors swing open and closed without a sound, guiding me deeper into the maze. I never have to pause. She only calls out instructions a few times for the entire run. I'm ascending the exit, dripping sweat but victorious, after ten minutes.

Aequa is marginally more pleased with me this time, though the sting of defeat from her own run clearly still smarts. Even so, she joins me on the balcony to watch the subsequent runs, not talking much, but indicating by her presence that she's no longer holding it against me.

It's about a half hour later when Indol splits off from the Thirds and wanders over to us, pulling me aside with an easygoing smile.

"Vis." He has his hands behind his back, as if he's standing at attention. Comfortable, but not casual. "Tell me. What are your plans for the trimester break?"

"The break? Return to Villa Telimus, I suppose. Train." I'm not sure where Indol's going with this. The break isn't for more than a month yet; I've barely thought about it. The Festival of Pletuna is before that, only a week away.

He nods as if he's not really listening and doesn't care about the answer. "What if you were to train with us?" He signals to where the others in Class Three—minus Iro, who's talking with Nequias—are watching our conversation with unashamed interest, though we're well out of earshot.

I blink, genuinely taken aback by the offer. Ulciscor and Lanistia doubtless had plans to continue my education, especially now I'm in a higher class. But the chance to study with the Thirds seems just as good an opportunity to learn, if not better.

It's also surprising. I'm a level below Indol, barely know the boy. I was aware that some of the Thirds were intending to remain together over the break—Emissa offhandedly mentioned it a while back—but there's no reason for Indol to invite me.

"My father suggested it," Indol says by way of explanation, no doubt seeing my puzzlement. "He heard you were promoted to Class Four. He's been taking an interest in your progress, apparently, and has been looking for some way to express his gratitude for what you did at the naumachia." He says the words calmly enough, but I can sense an undercurrent of resentment to them. Directed more at his father than me, though, I suspect.

"Iro may not be—"

"This would only be for Military families," Indol adds quietly. "Emissa, Belli, and I would be there."

I pretend to think it over, but I already know the answer. It's what Ulciscor would want me to do. What Relucia would want me to do. What would be best for my chances of advancement.

I can't really refuse.

"That sounds wonderful. I'd be honoured." I extend my hand; after a second's hesitation, Indol grips it.

"Good." He sounds relieved, as if he wasn't sure whether I'd actually accept. "We will be travelling straight from here. I'll confirm with my father, and he can let yours know the details."

"We're not staying here?"

"Oh, gods no." Indol chuckles. "Solivagus in the middle of winter is quite unpleasant, I assure you. No. My family have an estate in the north, where it'll be warm. Beautiful beaches. I've only been once before, but it should be a perfect place to both train and relax."

"It's by the sea?"

"It's *on* the sea." Indol beams. "A little island called Suus. Don't worry. You'll love it."

He claps my shoulder and wanders back to the Thirds, not noticing the blood draining from my face.

XLIX

FROM THE DAY I HAULED MYSELF FROM THE ELDARGO STRAIT, blind with exhaustion and pain, I've assumed that I would never see my childhood home again.

The following week passes in a haze as I wrestle with the challenging of that notion, try to imagine ways I can get out of going. Partly because I'm terrified at the prospect; though I doubt we'll be mingling with the locals, there's still a far higher chance that someone there might recognise me.

Beyond that, though, I'm simply not ready to face those ghosts. I'm not sure I ever will be. The very idea twists something inside my chest, tightens it so that it's difficult to breathe. I try not to let it, but it haunts my days, distracts me from both study and training. I see flashes of my home that I haven't remembered in years. I see people that may or may not still be alive. I see the last moments I had with my family, again and again. My father's bloodied visage, eyes straining after me as I fall. My little sister, washing out to sea. I never even heard whether they found her body.

My work suffers. Not markedly, not so much that I fall behind or make a fool of myself. But I'm not as sharp as I should be. Scitus reprimands me a couple of times, though I think it's because he knows I'm capable of more, not because I've performed inadequately.

My friends notice I'm distracted, too, but I deflect by telling them a half truth: that I'm surprised and worried about my invitation from Indol. They laugh and assure me that it's a good thing, a sign that I'm expected to make Class Three myself eventually. I just nod and continue fretting.

The only way I'm able to soothe my anxiety is knowing that the Festival of Pletuna is fast approaching. My hope rests, as loathe as I am to admit it, on my meeting there with Relucia. She'll understand the danger. See the risk of exposure. She might be able to convince Ulciscor to excuse me from this.

It's two days before, Scitus dismissing us after the chime for dinner, when Aequa approaches me.

"Vis. Are you coming to Caten with us?" There's immediate interest from Axien and Cassia nearby, and encouraging looks from Atticus and Felix. It seems most of the class will be at the festival.

I keep my expression neutral. We were always going to be taking the same Transvect, so going as a group implies staying together as a group. Relucia's supposed to be meeting with me in secret. Joining the Fourths seems . . . unwise.

Scitus is standing off to the side; when I glance over at him, he raises an eyebrow meaningfully. He's overheard, wants me to accept. Of course he'd be here right now. Of *course* he'd think that this was a way for me to show him I'm making an effort.

"I'd love to." There's no other option, really. I'll just have to figure out how to slip away without attracting attention.

"Good." Aequa seems pleased with the response. We start walking to dinner.

"Did you hear about Feriun?" When I shake my head, Aequa looks bleak. "His family have officially damned his memory."

My heart drops. "I'm sorry to hear that." Inevitable, for a suicide. I still worry that it wasn't.

Aequa's watching my reaction. "Did you see him at all before it happened? At the Festival of the Ancestors, I mean?"

"No."

"I thought you might have seen him while you were out walking."

I squint at her. "No," I repeat, mystified.

"It's just that the Magnus Quintus said you were out exploring the valley, both times I stopped by the Telimus crypt. He said he'd pass on that I'd been there."

"Oh." I do a reasonable job of not betraying my alarm. "He never mentioned you'd been by. He's like that," I explain apologetically.

"Forgetful?"

"Rude." I give her what I hope is a charming, relaxed smile, and after a second she returns it. Good. Ulciscor must have done all he could to cover for me, but the Festival of the Ancestors is hardly an event which allows for unexplained absences. Concerning that it's taken Aequa so long to bring it up. It's evidently stuck in her mind.

Conversation turns to our strategy for the Labyrinth, which we're due to run again in three days' time. Aequa seems to have dropped the matter of the Necropolis, but I'm still uneasy. The more I see of her, the more I'm realising that she deserves her spot at the top of the rankings. She's intelligent, focused, and fiercely hardworking.

Smart enough to keep harbouring suspicions about me, I'd wager. To keep pushing for answers.

Which means that Class Four is going to be even more difficult than I'd thought.

※ ※ ※

"I CANNOT BELIEVE YOU GET TO GO TO THE FESTIVAL."

Callidus fiddles with the control bracer; I cringe as there's a screeching groan below, a punctuation on Callidus's obvious disappointment. We're the only two in the Labyrinth this morning, luckily.

"It can't be *that* much better in Caten."

"You're joking. The Festival of Pletuna is . . ." He sighs wistfully. "Did you know that gambling is legal for the day? There are dice games on every corner of the city. *Every corner*, Vis. And the women . . ." He sighs again.

"It sounds like maybe it's a good thing you can't go?" I show my amusement as he shoots me a glare, holding up my hands defensively.

Callidus growls, then returns to his inspection of the Labyrinth. "Have you ever wondered how this works?"

"Will-locking, obviously. But then there must be some serious Conditionals in there, too. For the bracer to move entire panels so easily . . ." I gesture, indicating it's beyond me.

Callidus nods, clearly having come to the same conclusion. He moves a few more stones—unsuccessfully in most cases, the others with more awful scraping sounds— and then stops, frowning down at the maze. "It's a waste of Will, keeping this powered."

"I thought that too." I join him at the edge of the balcony.

"And it's complex. *Weirdly* complex. I mean, I can see the benefit. It fits all the categories for being good at wielding Will, and tests them without anyone needing to actually *wield* Will. But surely there are simpler ways to do mostly the same thing. To make this just for training doesn't seem very efficient."

I'm quietly impressed. The conclusion seems obvious to me now, but before my trip to the ruins, I was like everyone else. Didn't think to question it. "Why else make it, though?"

Callidus, not to his detriment, shakes his head. "Who knows." He unsuccessfully tries one last movement, then indicates I should take his place. "When's the next run?"

"Day after the festival."

Callidus sighs again. I give him a sympathetic look. "Your parents are still un-happy, I take it?"

"My father is." The topic is still of some discomfort to him. "I won't be alone, at least. Almost none of the Sixths and Sevenths are allowed to go. And only a few of the Fifths."

"Even Emissa's parents said no to this one," I agree consolingly.

Callidus immediately perks up. "Disappointed?"

I ignore him. "It makes sense. I'm actually surprised the Academy is letting us go at all."

"Religion runs the Academy. It's a religious event." Callidus spreads his hands to indicate the inevitability. "They don't mind when families say no, but they'll never stop anyone from going." He hesitates. "Speaking of which. Are you sure *you* should be going?"

I don't answer straight away. The Festival of Pletuna has a reputation for being wild, beatings and muggings and worse a common occurrence. It was like that even in the provincial towns, which I know because I risked attending once, before I was at the orphanage.

But that's not what Callidus is getting at. This won't be like the Festival of the Ancestors where I was accompanied by a Magnus Quintus, with the Necropolis under Military control and one of the most secure places in the world. The threat of the Anguis—and, judging from what Relucia told me, they *are* a threat—makes a raucous Caten hardly the safest destination.

"I'll be fine. I can't worry about it forever."

"I mean, you *can*. If you want to. Not that *I'm* worried, of course. Obviously. But I can imagine how upset Emissa would be if something happened to you."

I grin. "You just want to deprive me of the fun you're so sure you're missing out on."

He laughs at that. "Maybe."

The chime for breakfast soon sounds, finishing our half-hearted morning practice. "I expect tales when you return. Lots of tales," he calls sternly as we part. "Don't let those Fourths keep you from doing the fun stuff."

I chuckle and wave my acceptance, though my mind's already back on my meeting with Relucia. Wondering how she's going to be able to contact me in secret. Trying to fathom how to excuse my slipping away from the Fourths for any period of time at all.

I head to breakfast, paste on a chirpy demeanour, and prepare to board the Transvect for Caten.

L

THE CATENAN PENCHANT FOR RELIGIOUS HOLIDAYS HAS AL-
ways irked me. In part, I think it stems from there being so *many* gods. Mira for war,
Arventis for luck, Sere for fertility. Ocaria for rivers, Vorcian for metalworking, Ferias
for keys and doors. Each has its own domains, its own sacrifices, its own specific forms
to follow. Without all these celebrations, I doubt anyone but the priests would be able
to remember who they had to pray to for what.

The Festival of Pletuna, though . . . the Festival of Pletuna has always been the
exception, for me.

That first year after Suus meant starving more often than not. Stealing food and
trying to resist the urge to sell myself into indentured servitude, doing all I could to
avoid becoming an Octavii from sheer, petty hunger. Religious holidays like the one
for Jovan often provided the lure of handouts, but those were never enough to fill a
famished fourteen-year-old boy.

During the celebration of Pletuna, goddess of the harvest, though, that wasn't
an issue. Even in the provinces, the enormous public feasts meant that no one had to
go wanting; the Princeps supplied ample food for even the most ravenous of crowds,
and I, proud though I was, had no compunction about taking their charity. There was
drinking, and dancing in the street, and brightly coloured decorations wherever you
went. Gambling was legal for the entire day, and you couldn't pass a street corner without a game of dice being played. Of course, there was never any way to tell whether
the dice were Will-imbued, so I was never stupid enough to participate. But it was still
fun to watch.

I finished the night warm, with a full stomach. Smiling. It's the only day I can
remember when I felt like I might actually be able to make it on my own.

"This is the first time you've been back?" Scitus has joined me at the glass as our
Transvect descends toward Caten. He's here along with Praeceptor Ferrea to escort all
the students attending, not just Class Four, but I'm uneasy at his presence. Yet another
pair of eyes to evade.

"It is." The clouded sky means it's already dark, but the city below looks little
different than it did during the Festival of Jovan. No tinted lanterns painting the
buildings this time, but the streets heave with light and motion. I feel a tinge of

queasiness at the size of the crowd. Glance over at Aequa, who's seated at a window farther along. She catches my look and nods an unsettled acknowledgment. She feels it too.

"Take this." Scitus produces a stone tile. He hasn't noticed the exchange with Aequa. "Keep it on you."

"That's not necessary."

"Everyone is getting one."

"Alright." Refusal will just make him suspicious. "But you don't need to worry. The Anguis have no way of identifying me."

"That you know of. I know you can take care of yourself, but be careful out there tonight, Vis. And make sure you're back by midnight." He indicates the grey, twisting pillar below that stands a hundred feet tall, looming over everything else nearby. Lordan's Column. The agreed-upon meeting point before we return.

I disembark with the rest of the Fourths into the festive maelstrom of activity that is Caten. Nobody's wearing their mark of office or uniforms, tonight; beyond the intimation of the quality of their clothing, there's no way to tell whether someone is closer to Octavii or senator. Unrestrained roars of delight come from the crowds watching street performers and shows, many of them lewd. There are fights, music, Victorum matches. Colour everywhere.

I get a friendly elbow from Marcellus. "It's you." He's grinning as he points to a nearby building.

I take in the crudely drawn depiction on the wall with grim dismay. Ships burning, two men in their midst. One stabbing the other in the head. Just in case it wasn't obvious, **CATENICUS** is scrawled below it.

"Come on!" Aequa's call distracts me from the unpleasant reminder. She's positively glowing with excitement as she spots something down the crowded street. "There are Foundation games!"

"Of course she'd choose Foundation over . . . you know, *anything else*," Atticus grumbles next to me as we hurry after her down the stairs.

"Lucky Belli didn't come," mutters Felix. "Otherwise we'd be here for hours, watching her win money."

"We can always find something better," I point out, seeing the opportunity.

"Safer if we stick together," says Marcellus. "Plenty of cutpurses looking for easy targets at these things."

I lower my voice, glancing across at Aequa. "As long as you're happy doing whatever she wants to do all night."

There's a rumbling of agreement among the boys within earshot. Atticus, much to my delight, immediately takes it a step further. "Aequa! We're going this way."

The raven-haired girl looks put out. "You want to split up already?"

"We'll stay in the area."

Aequa sighs, evidently expecting this would happen at some point. "Don't go far."

Aequa, Valentina, and Lucius eagerly seat themselves at the Foundation tables as soon as the space opens, laying down money and unmistakeably enthused about their chances. I snort as I watch Aequa offer to flip a coin to determine who starts. She was showing off for us just a few days ago, must have landed fifteen heads in a row, at least. Never once looked like she was cheating.

Elsewhere, Axien and Felix wander off, looking for different forms of entertainment, and then Cassia disappears with Atticus trailing after her. None of the other students from the Academy are in sight, nor the Praeceptors. That's encouraging. It may not be as difficult to get away as I first expected.

I watch the Foundation matches for a while with Marcellus, curious. None of the players—not the students, and not their opponents—are anything more than skilled; even Hrolf back at Letens would have beaten any of them. I feel a wave of nostalgia as I think of the craggy-faced jailor, tinged with sadness. It's been more than half a year. Whoever replaced me has probably reported his lapses to the higher-ups. He's likely already an Octavii in a retirement pyramid.

I'm intent enough on the games that I almost don't notice the gentle tugging on my cloak.

I turn, but there's nobody near me. Strange. I go to resume my observation of the matches, but the tugging comes again. Stronger than the wind, but not by much. There's definitely no one around.

Someone's imbued my cloak.

I ignore it for almost a minute, gritting my teeth. Finally, though, when an especially impatient-feeling tug almost makes me stumble backward, I sigh and catch Marcellus's attention. "I'm going to wander around. If I'm not back soon, I'll meet you all at Lordan's Column."

"Looking for a dice game?" He sounds hopeful.

"I was thinking of watching some of these shows." I'm aware of exactly what Marcellus thinks of the shows, and actors in general.

"Ew." He waves me on my way.

I can see Aequa glance up as I start to leave, and she looks about to call out, but I disappear into the crowd before she can say anything. She's by far the most suspicious of the students; if I can get away while she's busy, all the better.

As best I can, I head in the direction the cloak is pulling me; whenever it's toward a collection of buildings, I weave my way around them until I'm on roughly the right track again. Reluctance keeps my pace slow. I occasionally glance over my shoulder to check that no one's decided to follow me, but there are no familiar faces. I've moved away from the brighter, more open areas now into a region that seems more run-down, albeit no less full of people celebrating.

I pause by a distinctive red-framed door to conceal Scitus's tracker. It's not valuable or even recognisable if found by a stranger, and I can easily fetch it on the way back. I doubt Scitus will use it to try and locate me before midnight. Even if he does, I can always say I dropped it.

After another twenty minutes—and three more walls showing colourful depictions of me at the naumachia—the insistent tugging leads me first past, then back to a house. Two stories tall and wooden, ramshackle, and dirty. The same as a hundred others clustered around it.

I grimace at the entrance, then knock.

It opens a crack, then just enough for a hand to snake out and pull me roughly through. I shrug the grip off as I stumble into the dimly lit space, footsteps echoing. The door is swiftly shut behind me, sealing me in.

I turn and scowl at the sole occupant of the room.

"Good to see you again, Son," says Relucia.

※ ※ ※

I'M NOT SURE WHETHER THE YOUNG WOMAN STANDING BE-tween me and the doorway thinks she's being charming, but I let my sour expression state just how little I'm amused.

"Let's make this quick. The others will notice if I'm gone for long." I scan the room. It's small without being crowded, a table and chairs in one corner. Through a beaded curtain I can see a bed in the room beyond, and a small shrine. This is someone's home. Probably unrelated to Relucia, just some citizen whose house she was able to discreetly break into. Who could probably also be back at any moment.

"I've no intention of doing otherwise." Relucia bolts the door and throws herself into the nearest chair. She's still smiling, but her eyes are hard. "Sit, Diago."

I do as she says.

"You've progressed since we last spoke?"

"I'm in Class Four." Frustration and anxiety bubble in my chest, even as I'm hesitant to ask. "When I got promoted from Six, it was because a student in Four died. He was at the Necropolis when it happened."

"Yes." It's an affirmation of both my statement, and the implication.

I close my eyes. My breath comes shorter and sharper than I'd like it to. It's my fault, then. "You didn't have to kill him."

"We didn't have time for anything nicer."

"I don't care. You won't do it again."

"That's not your decision."

"It is. You kill someone else because of me, and we're done. Consequences be damned." I hold her gaze, showing her exactly how serious I am.

Relucia sighs, waves a hand tiredly. "I make you no promises, Diago. This isn't a game. But if there is an equally effective alternative, I'll choose that next time." The way she says it indicates that she doesn't think there will be an alternative, and she definitely thinks there will be a next time.

I don't acknowledge the statement, but nor do I waste time belabouring the point. "There's another problem—one you might actually be able to help with. I've been asked to accompany the Thirds during the break next month. They're holidaying in Suus. Ulciscor will insist that I go, but maybe if you—"

"Oh, I know. It was my idea."

"What?" I'm confused.

"My idea," she repeats, looking unconscionably pleased with herself. "Military are holding a summit there—not their first choice, but after a few reports of the Anguis targeting their other locations, they came around." She smiles sunnily. "Ulciscor's going, and half the other senators have been dying to meet you. All it took was me hinting at the idea of you coming along in the trimester break, and he was suggesting it to the Dimidius the next day."

I'm too stunned to respond for a few seconds. "*Why?*"

"Because every senator worth anything from Military will be there, and I'm interested in what they're going to be talking about."

"But it's *Suus*. It's the one gods-damned place I'm going to be recognised!" I hear the note of panic in my voice, but don't care. Relucia was my last hope for getting out of this. "*Vek!* Every single person on that island knows who I am!"

"They knew who you were." Relucia's calm in the face of my trepidation. "It's been three and a half years, Diago—you were a child. And in their minds, you're dead.

Even if someone spots a passing resemblance, they're not going to start shouting that their prince has come to visit posing as a student from one of Caten's most . . . *Catenan* institutions." She shrugs. "Besides. Suus was overthrown: most of your former country-men won't be in positions of power, particularly if they used to be. I'd be surprised if you saw anyone you once knew."

I study the dirty floor, teeth clenched. It does nothing to ease my fears, but she's not wrong.

"So this Military summit. You want me to somehow . . . listen in? Uncover why they're having it?"

"Oh, I know why they're having it. They're getting worried about Governance and Religion," says Relucia. "That's what they'll be discussing for most of the three days, and I don't need you for that. But on the last night, Ulciscor and the other lower-level senators will go home, and there will be a council solely between Military's Quartii, Tertii, and Dimidii. I need to know if Dimidius Quiscil requisitions anything in that meeting. *Anything.* Along with any other information that may be of interest, of course."

My chest is tight. Not just returning to Suus, then. I have to spy while I'm there. "That's vague."

"Yes." The way she says it indicates it's deliberate, and not going to change.

I try anyway. "If I knew more about—"

"I'm not telling you any more in case you get caught."

My lip curls. "Your plans for me won't get far if that happens."

"True." Unworried. "But I assume you're not so arrogant as to think that you're our only project, Diago. Or even that you're vital. You are an *option*. A cog. One we haven't even seen prove its usefulness, yet."

I glower. Probably not a lie, though, given how apparently willing Relucia is to risk me. "Fine. Then how exactly do you propose I make myself privy to this secret meeting?"

"You're a resourceful boy, Diago, and the summit will be in your ancestral home—where you will no doubt be quartered. If anyone can find a way to listen in, it's you."

I pause at that. Think of the network of secret tunnels via which I escaped, the ones that run for miles through the palace and nearby cliffs. The myriad back ways through the corridors that only I and my siblings really knew.

As much as I hate to admit it, she may have a point.

There's a long silence as I grapple with the news. Wanting to back out but knowing I can't, the struggle pinning my chest until it feels like it's being crushed.

"Why are you doing this to me?" I know how it sounds, but my frustration is too much and it slips out. "Rotting gods, why are you even in the Anguis? The Hierarchy *benefits* people like you. Why do you want to destroy it so badly?"

"Isn't it being unfair enough of a reason?"

Ulciscor. The Transvect. The naumachia. Feriun. "No."

There's a spark in Relucia's eyes as she turns away. "Your father would say differently."

"You didn't know my father." It's a growl. A warning.

"I know he didn't want his son to turn a blind eye to all of this."

"He didn't approve of the killing of innocent people, either, believe it or not."

"Innocent? Those people out there? You already had this conversation with Melior." Relucia's suddenly, openly angry. "You think an Octavus who gives his Will is somehow less responsible than the Sextus who kills with it? The weak and poor endure in the Hierarchy because the alternatives are harder, not because there are none. They know the system is wrong, but they choose not to think or speak up or act because they ultimately hope that in their silence, they will gain. Or at the very least not have to give more than they have already given. They are driven by myopic self-interest and greed just as much as the senators and knights, and it's as Melior said—you of all people should hate them for that. The decision may have been made by the few, Diago, but it's the Will of the many that killed your family."

I stare at her. Breath short from the verbal violence.

"I know." I say the words softly, let them escape from between gritted teeth. "But that's the world. You can't punish them all. Even if you want to." I waver, almost swallow the words, but her anger has stoked some of my own. "And I don't want to."

"That's the problem, Diago. If you do not hold them accountable, nothing will change. Don't mistake inaction for neutrality." She studies me. "You shouldn't grow so attached to your classmates," she adds eventually. "They are the enemy. If you told any one of them who you are—"

"I *know*."

Relucia observes me for a few more seconds, then nods her satisfaction. "Then we're done here. I'll send a gift to Suus with Ulciscor. A stylus. Will-locked to one on my end, Conditionally activated by wax. You will write everything you learn, and then break it." She reaches over, makes a show of touching my cloak to take back her Will. Her eyes cloud. "And you *will* learn whatever there is to learn, Diago."

"And if I don't? You won't give me up over something like this." Despite what she said before, she's gone to too much effort to put me in this position. There are certain things that we both know aren't important enough for her to undo all of that.

Her eyes stay dark. "No. But I will kill one of your friends."

It's said with such breathtaking matter-of-factness that I almost don't understand. Then the blood drains from my face, my hands tightening to fists.

"As I said. Our business here is done." She motions to the street. "Don't keep those friends of yours waiting."

I stand stiffly and march to the door. Unbolt it.

"You hurt any of them," I say softly, voice shaking, "and on my oath, I will burn you and the Anguis to the ground. No matter the cost."

I leave, slipping out into the boisterous night before she can respond.

LI

THE CROWDS SEEM MORE AGGRESSIVE THAN BEFORE, WRITH-
ing around me, shrieking discordantly with drunken laughter and off-key music as I
orient myself and start making my way back to the others. I'm not sure whether the
night's simply progressed, or whether I'm noticing it more after my discussion with
Relucia. I do my best to avoid being buffeted and try to really look at the faces around
me. To see them as people, not a mass of Will draining away to the Hierarchy. Not just
a crowd of accomplices to my family's deaths.

It's harder than it should be.

After a minute I stop, pull my cloak from my shoulders and carefully make a small
tear. Not enough to ruin it, but enough that Relucia's Will would be lost. I don't believe
for a second that she actually took it back.

Then I turn and hurry back to a shadowy doorway, within sight of the one I just
exited.

Of all the obstacles in my path, Relucia is currently by far the most problematic. I
have a real chance to reach Class Three and win the Iudicium this year. To graduate the
Academy, choose a position at the embassy in Jatiere, and potentially gain years without
having to touch an Aurora Columnae.

But she'll never let me do that, no matter what she told me at the Necropolis—I
can see that now. I need to force her hand, starting with forestalling this trip to Suus. I
need to find something I can use against her.

And she was in a hurry, back there, just as much as I was.

Relucia emerges a couple of minutes later, face hidden beneath a hood; she glances
around, but the crowd's thick enough that she has no chance of spotting me. She hurries off in the opposite direction. I allow some distance, then follow.

The revelry provides easy cover, and though Relucia does occasionally delay to
check behind her, I'm always too far back and too well concealed to be in danger of
discovery. I shadow her for almost ten minutes before she reaches a bustling market
square, gaudily lit and full of shouting merchants and cacophonous music. She stops.
Looks around—not suspiciously this time, but searching.

Another minute passes, and then a tall, slim figure appears behind her and places a
hand on her arm. She turns and peers up under the man's hood. Follows him.

I trail after, this time down narrow, less populated streets. Several times I have to allow the two of them to vanish from view and then hurry to catch up, rather than get too close. They don't look around, though.

The pair finally arrive at a wooden two-storey structure, one of the many in this part of the city. They pass into a courtyard overlooked by balconies on every side; as I watch through the entrance, they head upstairs and disappear through a far door.

I examine the people milling around. There's nobody watching, no guards. I hold my breath and slip inside, darting up the stairs and placing myself below the nearest window, concealed from the doorway by a scattered pile of crates. Words filter from inside. Quiet, but the buffer of the courtyard allows me to make them out over the more distant noise of the festival.

". . . think they will accept?" A male voice. Smooth and calm.

"They have to." Relucia. "A ship is a small price for a Cataclysm weapon." The last part sounds mocking.

Sure enough, there's a sharp laugh, followed by another question that's lost in a swell of clamour from out on the street.

"They say they've figured out how to use it as an anchoring point. It should be stable enough."

"Should be?"

"Will be."

"Can we trust them?"

"We'll see soon enough."

There's another question, something about how many, and Relucia's reply—I think—indicates that there will be "enough." I close my eyes, ears straining, mentally untangling words from the surrounding racket. The two inside are only barely audible, but this is as close as I dare get.

"I assume we will need to keep them from coming back, too?" I hear that question from the stranger easily enough.

"Of course. Our man should be the only one they can question."

I hold my breath. Risk a look through the window.

It's dim inside. Two figures sitting at the table: Relucia and the man with her. Between them lie three shapes that, for an instant, I think are some sort of large, furry fruit.

Then my eyes adjust, and I make out the strands of hair. The staring eyes. The blackish fluid smeared around them.

I flinch back down, clamping my teeth together to keep from crying out.

"Nobody saw you tonight?" Relucia again, the calmness in her voice chilling now.

"Nobody. It still hurts, but it's getting easier to use. I can go farther."

"Show me."

A pause. "It's dangerous. The other side are looking—"

"I need to see how effective you are."

After a few seconds a barely audible, growling *thrum* vibrates the air. The hairs on the back of my neck stand on end.

Silence from inside, then from my right, footsteps coming up the stairs. I shrink back into the shadows behind the crates. The door creaks as it opens. "Satisfied?"

I stiffen, confused. The newcomer sounds like Relucia's companion.

"You're a lot faster than you were."

I chance another look inside. Relucia's still sitting at the table, grisly trophies in front of her. The other man is taking a seat opposite her.

No one else is in the room.

"I have to be." The man's pulled back his hood, revealing close-cropped brown hair. He's younger than I would have thought, not much older than Relucia, and has a wicked scar splitting his face diagonally from forehead to chin. "It helps to know the terrain, though. Do you have maps?"

"This way."

I sink back down again; there's a scraping of chairs, and for a heartbeat I think they're coming outside. But the footsteps fade into the house. Disappear.

I hesitate, then retreat. Whatever they're talking about, those severed heads are a perturbing reminder that Relucia isn't to be trifled with.

It doesn't take me long to retrace my steps and retrieve Scitus's tracking stone. From there, I wind my way back to where I left Aequa and the others, but they've left the Foundation games, no doubt in search of other entertainment.

That's fine by me. I wander for a while, not really paying attention to anything or anyone in particular. Just thinking. Whatever I just overheard, it's not anything I can use to make Relucia change her mind about Suus.

Eventually I realise I've strayed farther than I meant to. There's still at least an hour before midnight but I have no real interest in the festivities around me; my father often used to say that the Hierarchy's true power was not in Will, but in their ability to distract those who gave it up. The drunken laughter and merrymaking echoing down every street grinds at me.

I swivel to head back to Lordan's Column, and spot the two men following me.

It's not hard, with neither being particularly subtle about it as they stutter to a stop fifty feet away. No way to tell how long they've been tailing me, but when they see I've marked them, one of them mutters something to his companion. They both have ugly looks on their faces.

Anguis.

My heart starts to thump. I walk in the opposite direction, throwing a glance over my shoulder. They're coming for me. I increase my pace. It's possible that staying in a crowded area might help if it comes to a fight, but it might equally mean nothing if the intent is to stick a knife in my stomach. I have to get away.

I run.

The buildings are tightly packed here, many of the alleyways narrow and dark, despite the raucous, brightly lit main streets. I twist through several quick turns, ducking around people, breath short.

I'm still darting glances behind, beginning to think I may have gotten away, when the hands grab me and wrestle me into the shadows.

I try to shout out but there's a sweat-salty palm enveloping my mouth; I'm hauled a good twenty feet into the darkness before finally being shoved forward, hard and unexpectedly enough that I sprawl clumsily to the dirt. I growl and roll to my feet, palms stinging from grit, half blinded by the dim.

The alley's a dead end, that much I can tell immediately. I turn to face my attackers. There's just the two of them, silhouettes at first against the distant light of the street. One thin, one burly. As my eyes adjust, I start to make out their features. The big one has a crooked nose and scarred lip. The other is a rat-faced man with a weak chin. They're both completely, grimly focused on me.

"What do you want?" I take a cautious step back, hands outstretched, palms facing toward them. "I only have a little money, but you're welcome to it." I fish my coin pouch out and toss it to the ground at the weedy man's feet.

"We're not interested in your coin. We're here to kill you, Catenicus." His voice is reedy and filled with promise. It's almost imperceptible in the light, but his eyes begin to flood with black. A moment later, his companion's do the same.

Vek.

"You know who I am?" My mind races. The use of Will means nothing; the Anguis have shown they're not above it. Regardless, these men are surely at best Sextii. Maybe only Septimii. Of course, there are two of them. And we're in a confined space. "At least tell me who wants me dead before we get started." I'm speaking too quickly, nerves giving me away. Perhaps it will help. Perhaps these two will be overconfident, give me an opening.

"I don't think so." My attackers advance as one. I glance desperately past them. People are walking by at the end of the alley, but no one's looking in here, and the shadows are too deep for them to see anything anyway. I could yell but I can also tell that the noise from the street will easily cover my cries. There's no point wasting breath.

These men probably have blades on them, but they haven't drawn them yet. That's a mistake.

I charge.

Their reactions are quick; even taken by surprise, the one I'm aiming for—the smaller one—braces himself enough to avoid getting knocked down. Still, I know where to aim, where to apply pressure. I deliver a sharp punch to his neck before dancing back again, just out of reach of the big man's swinging fist. I have to stay clear. With Will behind it, one hit could be all they need.

The rat-faced man reels, eyes wide, gurgling as he clutches his throat. His partner twists to look so I abruptly change momentum, darting forward again, ducking my shoulder and barrelling viciously into his torso. He's heavy but he's taken by surprise. I slam him into the wooden wall behind, hear the wheeze of air being ejected from his lungs.

I twist, using my impetus to snake between the two. For the briefest of moments, there's clear air between me and the street.

Then there's a hand around my ankle, painfully tight. I trip, fall, barely preventing my head from slamming against the cobblestone. I'm being dragged violently backward.

"Rotting little bastard." It's the thinner man rasping the words as he pulls me back. The man I slammed against the wall is straightening, too. Surly. They weren't expecting resistance.

I'm tossed the rest of the way toward the dead end, sliding up against the far wall. Before I can recover there's a short, swift kick to my ribs, eliciting a moan of pain.

Then I'm being hauled to my feet. I struggle, slapping away hands as best I can but unable to match their strength. There's a grip on my throat—not squeezing, not yet, but tight enough to make me fearful—and spots behind my eyes, made worse by the sudden unshuttering of a lantern. The crooked-nosed man holds the light close; I squint and shy away, but he forces my face back with a hand clamped on my jaw, and then pries my eyes open. The stinging illumination elicits tears.

"Nothing." The word's called out, directed back down the alley.

"Then that's quite enough. Let him go."

I slide to the ground, gasping my breath back, as the two men abruptly, inexplicably retreat. I blink furiously as two more figures come into view. I'm still blinded from the lantern. I know that voice, but I'm having difficulty placing it.

"Vis. Are you alright?" The man speaks again, crouching beside me. I shy away, but he makes a calming motion. My eyes adjust.

It's Praeceptor Scitus.

"Praeceptor?" I stare up at him, eyes still watering. "What . . . what's going on? Why are you here? Who were those men?"

My gaze travels past him. Aequa's standing a few feet back, leaning up against the wall. She's not looking at me. Pale, even for her, even in the dim light.

"They weren't meant to seriously hurt you. I . . . apologise for the ruse. I apologise wholeheartedly." The Praeceptor sounds genuine; in fact, he sounds horrified. "That was far more physical than it should have been."

"The *ruse*?" The word comes out as a hoarse growl, feral enough that Scitus flinches.

"It's my fault. I didn't tell him the details." Aequa uses her back to launch herself upright, looking resolved, if somewhat sickly. "All he knew was that I was going to trick you into using Will."

"What?" I'm still dazed. "You thought . . . but we're not allowed . . ."

Things slide into place. I almost laugh at the notion. Almost.

Aequa thinks—or thought, now, I assume—that I was cheating. Using Will to improve my performance, climb the ranks at the Academy. It makes sense, I suppose. She's never been able to properly resolve my account of the naumachia with what happened. The more she watched, the more obvious it must have seemed. My win against Ianix. My unexplained absence at the Necropolis. My comfort with the Labyrinth despite, supposedly, no practice.

It would have all looked frustratingly suspicious. *Was* suspicious, I suppose. She just guessed at the wrong reasons why.

"I owe you an apology." Aequa still can't bring herself to look at me.

"You're gods-damned right you do." I croak the words but put bite into them. Partly because I need to look angry at such a serious accusation, and partly because I genuinely feel the anger.

"That's not all you owe, I'm afraid." Scitus looks bitterly disappointed as he turns to Aequa, and she shrinks from his gaze. "I let this go ahead because you were certain, Aequa. You *swore*."

"I made a mistake—"

"Yes." Scitus's voice is iron. "You did. And you staked your ranking on it." He gestures tiredly to us both. "Come on. Let's get back to the Column. You're both done for the night."

We trail after him, me keeping ahead of Aequa, not interested in being anywhere near her.

"I'm sorry. Truly sorry. Please . . . please don't tell the others." Her voice is small. Barely cuts through the noise of the crowd.

We walk the rest of the way in silence.

%%   %%   %%

THE RIDE BACK ON THE TRANSVECT IS AWKWARD; THOUGH NO one else knows what happened, the other Fourths can plainly sense the tension between myself, Aequa, and Scitus. They're mostly quiet, occasionally murmuring to each other, but otherwise keep to themselves for the entire trip.

Everyone else retires straight to their quarters when we get back, but I need to talk to someone, so I head for the ground floor of the dormitory. Callidus is usually still up at this hour.

I slip inside, making my way through the rows of sleeping students, marvelling a little at how I thought the small, hard-looking cots here were a luxury only a few months ago. Shuttered lanterns burn low but provide enough light to navigate.

When I reach Callidus's bed, though, he's not there. Not sleeping and not at his desk, lantern extinguished.

"Looking for Ericius?"

I start, turning to see a dim figure sitting up in one of the cots across the way. I walk closer, the face of a blond-haired boy I recognise resolving in the dim. Drusus. "Yes."

"He left five minutes ago. Outside, not to the lavatory. Not sure where he was going."

"Thanks." I suppose I shouldn't be surprised at the help, no matter our previous interactions. A lot has changed since I was a Seventh.

I consider waiting, but I've nothing to do but sit with my thoughts in the dark. I could use a stroll, even if I don't find Callidus. Give the muscles still tender from my beating a stretch. With the festival on today, and given the hour we got back, I can't imagine I'll find any trouble for being out late.

Outside, the Academy is quiet. Decorations are still up from the celebrations here—flower wreaths draping doorways, colourful banners hanging everywhere—though aside from that, everything remains spotless. I doubt the festivities were anything akin to those in Caten. Petals rustle underfoot and skitter in the breeze across the quadrum as I walk the empty expanse, searching for any hint that Callidus might be nearby. There's nothing, though. The gymnasium and other buildings are dark.

I frown, curious now. There aren't that many other areas on campus that Callidus would be headed at this time of night. I doubt he'd risk a trip to the girls' dormitory; it's strictly off-limits even during the day, and I'm fairly sure he would have told me if he was interested in anyone there. Still. There, and the parkland in between, is about the only other place I can think to look. I'm not going to get in trouble if I stroll by at a distance.

The crisp night air prickles at every inch of exposed skin as I walk. The Academy's tree-lined paths are sparsely lit here.

It's a couple of minutes later that I spot movement.

There are two figures walking at an oblique angle to me, away from my position, heads bowed and clearly deep in conversation. One of them is Callidus. He's with a girl.

I falter, suddenly worried I might be intruding. They pass beneath one of the lanterns and I recognise the flash of vibrant red, the mass of curls stretching down to her waist. It's Belli.

I smirk. "Good for him," I murmur to myself, retreating a few steps to conceal myself behind the trunk of a tree. I can't begrudge him the secret. Belli's probably insisted that he not say anything to anyone, given their respective classes.

I'm about to turn away when something catches my eye. A flick of the wrist from Callidus. I can't hear anything that's being said—I'm too distant from the pair for that—but it's an irritated gesticulation. An angry one, in fact.

I hesitate a moment longer, then leave. Perhaps I'm seeing the end of a relationship, not an ongoing one. Or perhaps I'm completely misreading the situation. Either way, it's not my business.

I put it from my mind. In a few minutes I'm back in my quarters, and asleep.

※ ※ ※

THE REST OF THE FOURTHS NEVER FIND OUT THE CAUSE OF the tension between Aequa, myself, and Scitus—I never tell them, anyway—but over the next few weeks, it becomes apparent to everyone that something has irrevocably shifted.

It starts the morning after the festival. We're in class, learning about the potential decaying of Conditionals relationships. It's a review class more than anything else, an easing into things before tackling more difficult fare. Scitus has asked a question about mental versus physical degradation in the imbuer themselves, and the potential consequences.

I raise my hand. More out of habit than anything else; it's to indicate I know the answer, not because I expect to be called upon. Aequa's hand is up, too, and she always gets preferenced.

"Vis."

There's a breath of surprised silence. Across the room, Aequa shuts a mouth already open to answer, nonplussed, and lowers her hand.

I take a heartbeat longer than usual to respond, as taken aback as the others. "Um. Physical degradation of the imbuer doesn't matter for Conditionals; as long as they're alive, the Conditional will operate. But the trigger could easily change with mental degradation, depending on the specificity. And even with very specific ones, significant mental lapses can result in a Conditional completely misfiring. That's why retirement pyramids aren't allowed to support them."

"Very good." Scitus acknowledges the answer as satisfactory and moves on, but I can sense the others are staring. Half of them shooting curious, sideways glances at Aequa, the others at me.

The class continues in much the same vein for that day, and the following, and the ones after until it's clear that it's not a temporary pattern. I suddenly find myself being challenged by the questions being asked, pushed by Scitus in ways I wasn't before. I can no longer drift in class, half pay attention at any point, even if I'm comfortable with the material—because Scitus will always call on me, always probe the edges of my knowledge, trying to determine whether I've learned something by rote or can actually apply it to unique situations. Just as he used to do with Aequa.

In the mornings, I start to run the maze with Callidus, despite the unease it brings me. Again, and again, and again. He calls down questions as I run, forcing me to answer at the same time as navigating the twisting passageways. I'm getting faster, more and more adept with the bracer.

I gently probe, from time to time, about Belli. Nothing direct—just leading questions. He never alludes that there's anything going on, that he has any connection to her beyond knowing who she is. Sometimes I feel a little offended that he doesn't trust me. Then I remember what I'm keeping from him, and decide not to judge.

My evenings continue with Eidhin, though his Common is good enough now that it's barely necessary, and I benefit from the study almost as much as he does. He never says more about his past, and I don't press.

Aequa, for her part, retreats into herself. She avoids me where possible, no longer going out of her way to sit by me, or to make small talk. I don't make the effort either.

Over all of that, though, the trimester break looms. I'm advancing, improving, getting closer and closer to my goal every day—but I'm nauseous whenever I think about what's coming. The days pass faster and faster.

And then, three weeks later, I'm bidding Callidus and Eidhin farewell, and joining the Thirds on a Transvect bound for Suus.

IN CAUDA VENENUM

PART III

LII

I DREAMED OF GOING HOME SO OFTEN, THAT FIRST YEAR after the Hierarchy came. Sometimes I even thought I *was* home. I stayed near the ocean because I couldn't sleep without the lapping of the waves. I kept southward. Sometimes going for weeks without seeing anyone. But I would slumber on the beach, or in a forest nearby, and I would wake to the smell of salt and the hissing slither of water on sand and I would, just for a moment, think I was there again. Camping with my family, maybe. Or simply napping in the afternoon sun.

Then one day, after I remembered where I was, what had happened, I broke. Wept for hours. There was this ache in me that I'd been pressing down over and over, but even after I'd shed my tears it was still there. A chasm I could never fill. So I struck inland. I had to get away. Even though it was riskier. Even though I could no longer fish for food, was taking myself increasingly out of my comfort zone. Staying so connected to home, to what I'd lost, was more than I could bear.

It's been more than three years since then but as our Will-powered ship scythes through the vibrant, brilliant blue toward Suus, my ghosts return. It's everything—not just the sight but the smells, the sounds, the gentle warmth of the sun against my face. The very idea that in ten minutes or so, I'll be stepping back onto the land I fled so long ago, again be among the people my family once led. Already there are places I'm envisaging, faces I'm remembering that I'd pushed to the corners of my mind long ago. Will it feel the same, or will it just be another part of the Republic now?

"Vis. Are you alright?"

I ignore my aching chest and paste on a smile, glad that the moisture in my eyes is covered by the sea spray off the bow. Emissa, Indol, and Belli are standing a little off to the side; Emissa's the one who asked the question. "I don't do well on the water," I lie.

Indol chuckles. "Better than Belli, at least." Emissa wrinkles her nose at the reminder, while Belli glowers queasily. She didn't make it to the railing before her bout of retching.

"You've been on a boat before?" Emissa stares out toward the island, though it's clear she's talking to me.

"Once or twice. My family lived near the Edaro River, just north of Cartiz. I went with my father downriver sometimes to the capital for supplies." I make a face, selling the hurriedly crafted lie. "It was nothing like this, though."

"The Edaro? I thought that was largely rapids. No good for trade until we dredged it," Belli observes absently.

Vek. Was it? "The stretch we used was calm enough for a small vessel, as long as you knew what you were doing." I allow a small pause, as if melancholic. "I didn't know they'd changed the river."

The others seem to accept the statement. Why wouldn't they? It's not something that can be proven. Still, I'm already uneasy. Off-balance, thanks to the steadily growing shape of Suus off the prow.

The conversation drifts away from difficult topics again. Friendly enough. I've gotten to know Indol and Belli a little better after the eleven-hour Transvect journey which deposited us a few miles from the strait. Indol is a perfect Catenan: handsome, confident, the son of Dimidius Quiscil. He's got a quick wit when it suits him, but he's often content to sit back and watch the conversation unfold, only chiming in when he has something valuable to contribute. There's no doubting his intelligence, though. He's Nequias's current favourite, the one considered most likely to win the Iudicium.

I should hate him—he's the closest thing the Hierarchy has to a prince—but I don't. In fact, somewhat annoyingly, I find myself rather liking him.

Belli is a strange one. Daughter of Quintus Volenis, the Sytrecian governor. Lineage from the south, though, judging from her pale skin and long red hair. She's not unfriendly, exactly, but . . . absentmindedly condescending, at times. The other two have offhandedly implied that she's the smartest among them, the best strategist. The best at running the Labyrinth, too. She hasn't tried to correct them.

And then there's Emissa.

It still feels strange to be so openly companionable with her around others, but she makes no effort to hide the fact that we've been friends for a while. The other two don't seem surprised, either. Her presence, our familiar banter, has been the one thing that has helped take my mind off our destination. Kept me sane.

Our boat draws steadily closer to the shore. I try to focus on the conversation, but my heart can't help but wrench. Cliffs I used to climb, beaches I used to play on with my sisters. The way the warm, salty wind caresses my face. The crashing and hissing rhythm of the waves.

This was home.

The pier has changed, I notice as soon as it resolves in the distance. It was once a small, wooden thing, sturdy but unremarkable. Now it's a stone monstrosity, wider and jutting a hundred feet deeper into the ocean, waves railing against its smooth, Will-cut edge. Not just for small boats like this anymore. There's a whole array of new buildings a little farther away, up the path, where once there was the lighthouse and nothing more. Shops, from the looks of it, set up to trade with the mainland. A few people wander between them. Despite the new scar on the landscape, everything looks peaceful.

I should probably be pleased about that. I'm not sure if I am.

A hard-looking woman with a pockmarked face and tinted glasses greets us on the dock. Indol introduces her as Sextus Auctia, apparently the Dispensator of the Quiscil household. She's pleased to see Indol, polite to the rest of us as he introduces us over the raucous shouting of fishermen and the lapping of waves.

"The Magnus Dimidius is waiting for you," Auctia says soon enough, indicating that we should follow. We trail after her. The others looking around curiously. Me, trying not to be overwhelmed.

"It really is beautiful here, isn't it," murmurs Emissa to me as we walk.

"It is," I say softly. Commanding bluffs. Vibrant green forests. Glittering ocean. Growing up, I took it all for granted. Even my memory never quite did these vistas justice.

"I'm so glad my father decided to have the summit here," enthuses Indol, overhearing us. "I've only been once before, and that was a couple of years ago. It wasn't as nice back then. We needed more security, and a lot of the infrastructure wasn't as advanced."

I bite my tongue. Taste blood in my mouth.

"I can only imagine," chimes in Belli, looking around. Not disdainful, exactly, but she doesn't strike me as one to appreciate natural beauty. "Wasn't this one of the last places to be civilised?"

"They didn't use Will at all. It was basically tribal." Indol grins. "My father was lucky. Several senators wanted the palace, but he was part of the mission to take it. Put in his claim to it a few days after. The Sextus in charge of the island lives there too, but he's more of a caretaker while we're away."

My fingernails are digging painfully into my palms. I gaze around under the guise of fascination, unable to look at Indol or any of the others. It's a little easier to deal with this time, at least; I've already been part of a few such conversations since we left the Academy. Casually discussing Suus's conquering, as if it were a footnote. Belli even described it as "bloodless." I wasn't able to talk for near ten minutes after that.

Still. I hate it. I hate the idea that my home is now a holiday destination for senators, I hate that they think of it as ever having been anything less than civilised, and

I *hate* that they're so nonchalant about what was done to me and my family. Perhaps this was part of why Relucia arranged all this. Maybe she thought it would stoke my passion for the fight again.

At the moment, it's working. Not even the excited sparkle in Emissa's eyes can stir anything but ugly feelings.

We walk up the cliffside path—another change; rather than a simple track, there are elegant stairs carved into the stone—and come within sight of the palace.

I stumble.

If only small things have changed below, the building we're approaching is almost unrecognisable. Gone are the beautiful etchings over the entrances, the ones that re-layed the history of my people, the ones my ancestors spent years carving. Gone is the character-filled hewn look of the sandstone.

In its place is a monstrosity. Walls smoothed, polished, and painted garishly in the colours of Caten: orange and white and purple. New friezes decorate the palace's outside and though they're just as impressive as any I've seen elsewhere in the Hierarchy, they're nothing to do with Suus. They show Catenan heroes. Catenan ideals. Catenan victories.

It's such a slap in the face that I can't contain my visceral reaction. My breath short-ens and I can feel blood rushing to my face, unable to stop noting every gory detail. The palace's bones remain; the doorways are all in place, the structure is the same size and shape as it once was. Simpler, probably. More expedient to change only the façade.

"Impressive," murmurs Belli from behind me.

I clasp my hands behind my back to keep them from shaking. I don't know why I expected otherwise, but the *palace* . . . it was Suus's jewel. More than five generations of my family had lived there. Some part of me thought of it as sacrosanct. Too beautiful to touch, even for Caten.

Aside from the stomach-turning despoilment of my former home, the walk to the palace goes well. I see people off on the horizon, but they never get within hailing dis-tance let alone close enough to recognise me. I hang toward the rear of the group, silent as the others prattle on about what they're seeing. I'm glad no one asks me anything. If I have to talk, there is no guarantee I can be civil.

We're ushered inside, and part of me is relieved to find that the interior, at least, remains familiar. The marbled floors are the same. The layout is just as it was, with a grand, winding staircase off the main foyer, multiple doors branching off into separate wings. I'm so caught up in my study that I almost miss the group standing off to the side, waiting to greet us.

"Magnus Dimidius," says Auctia, bowing slightly in deference. "Your guests have arrived."

There are several men in the party by the stairs, but no mistaking to whom she's talking: the one stepping forward takes all my attention, and I can tell from the collective intake of breath that I'm not alone. He's a little over six feet tall, broad-shouldered and handsome, but it's not just his presence. He *exudes* power. Radiates it. Like some kind of instinctive survival mechanism, I can't take my eyes from him.

"Indol!" Dimidius Quiscil beams as he spots his son, wrapping him in an embrace that feels like it should crack Indol's bones. The boy's unfazed, though, laughing and slapping his father on the back as they part again. They seem close.

I keep my breathing steady. This is one of the men responsible for the invasion here, for killing my family. And now he's sharing a happy reunion with his son. In my old home. My hands twitch as I think about all the different ways I might be able to take him by surprise, right here. It's probably lucky how quickly I realise none of them will work.

Indol's introducing us all; the Dimidius is doing the rounds, asking quick questions and generally indicating that yes, Indol's talked about us, and yes, he's very impressed by what he's heard. A senator through and through. I mask my disdain with a force of will I wasn't sure I had in me. Calm, push the emotions to the side. I'm not a prince of Suus, not anymore. I'm Vis Telimus Catenicus, and Vis Telimus Catenicus is honoured to have been asked here.

"And this is Vis," says Indol as the two of them reach me.

"Of course! Ulciscor's boy. Catenicus. I've been looking forward to meeting you for some time." He sticks out his hand, offering me the greeting of an equal. I can see Indol's eyebrows quirk a little off to the side. It's a move meant to honour what I did at the naumachia. One he doesn't have to make.

I hesitate, almost as much from surprise as anything else. Then, chest close to bursting from reluctance, I clasp his arm and wear a flattered, grateful smile. "An honour, sir. Truly."

It feels like something dies inside me at the words.

"Your father should be here in the next few hours, but I would like very much to carve out some time to talk more with you, too. Perhaps at dinner?" The Dimidius looks around, including everyone in the statement. "Beginning tomorrow, I will sadly be inundated with matters of state, but I'd be very pleased if you would all join us for a meal tonight."

I don't say anything, but don't do anything to signal disagreement with the others' enthusiastic responses, either.

"Of course, there will be certain rules to follow once tomorrow comes," continues the Dimidius. "The eastern wing of the palace will be off-limits to any of you for the next three days. Including you," he adds with mock-sternness to Indol, who chuckles good-naturedly. "We cannot be lenient, either, I'm afraid. Anyone breaking that rule won't be returning to the Academy. No exceptions."

Quiscil speaks jovially, but there's something in his voice that changes at that last part, and I can hear the seriousness of it. The others can, too. We all nod.

It's not until the Dimidius instructs Auctia to show us to our rooms and moves off that I notice the man in his entourage trailing after him. He's perhaps in his forties. Short, stockily built, with rapidly thinning black hair and the darker skin of a Suus native. In his Catenan uniform and tinted glasses, I almost don't recognise him.

It's Fadrique, one of my father's old advisers. In charge of . . . trade, I think? An important man.

And one who tutored me, for a time. Who most definitely knew me.

I don't move, do everything I can not to shrink back. He's not looking at me. He saw us come in, though. He must have at least glanced at my face.

I fade to the back of the group, heart constricting, then watch as he leaves with Dimidius Quiscil. He doesn't look around, doesn't give any indication that he's curious about me. Perhaps he didn't see me—or perhaps, as Relucia predicted, I'm simply unrecognisable. I didn't place him immediately, after all, and I've been on the lookout for familiar faces.

The relief of his leaving is quickly supplanted by icy anger. The man was supposed to be a loyal subject, a friend to my father and my family. And now he's working for the Hierarchy? He's a Sextus, too, judging from the glasses. Surely the highest-ranking position on the island. To be awarded that, he likely would have had to make a deal before my family's bodies were cold.

"You look a bit dazed."

I jump at the voice by my shoulder. It's Emissa, amused at my distractedness.

"My first time meeting a Dimidius." We start after Auctia, who's showing us to our quarters. I know the way. We're not heading toward my old rooms—those would surely be reserved for the senators—but the palace has an extensive guest wing. The passages through the cliffs have some access points there, too, though they're fewer.

"Impressed?"

"He's certainly hard to miss."

She laughs. "That's one way to put it."

She seems like she expects me to keep the conversation going, but I'm in no mood. We lapse into silence.

I make sure not to lag behind as we walk. Every corner we turn is a reminder of what I've lost, but I'm rapidly becoming numb to it, and I can't afford to get distracted. If I've guessed our destination correctly, there's only one room there with access to the tunnels.

"You can take your pick of these rooms." Auctia indicates the entirety of the guest hallway as we arrive. It's adorned in Catenan colours, Catenan tapestries. "They're all the same."

I'm slipping past Indol and heading for the third room along before she finishes; it will seem a strange impatience to the others, but nothing more than that. They're still standing with Auctia when I push the door open.

From the moment I enter, I hate everything about the room. Massive though it feels to me now, I can't help but remember how much bigger my own quarters were. How much nicer. I can hear the comforting sound of waves through the window, but it's tainted by the decor: banners and Will-carved furniture, Hierarchy colours everywhere. As if Caten is a plague that has infected everything I love.

I shut the door behind me, not caring if the others will think it rude. Slump against the wall. Slide to the ground. I hold my hands out in front of myself, watching them tremble. Just focusing on them. Trying, trying to get myself back under control.

I don't think I can do this. I can't keep up the façade, not here.

My breath comes in gasps, then sobs. I bury my head between my knees, hands clasped over the back of my head, and close my eyes. Let the tears come. Softly though, in case someone's just outside. Even my grief has to be stifled.

Minutes pass. The wash of sorrow fades, abates enough for me to grit my teeth and find my resolve again. I just have to get through this. The Iudicium is only four months away. Reach it. Win it. Maybe find a way out from under Relucia's thumb in the meantime.

Hard, but not impossible. And if I can do it, I can get away from all of this.

I stand, locking the door and finally assessing the room tactically rather than emotionally. There's a plush-looking bed up against the far wall, a couch and a desk in the corner. Like most outlooks from the palace, the stunning view is from right on the cliff's edge. No danger of someone walking past and seeing in.

And then there's the fireplace. Every room along this hall is laid out identically, so there's nothing unusual about it, nothing to make it visually distinct. But—to my immense relief—it hasn't been altered, blocked over, or remade. Why would it?

I kneel in front of it. Fireplaces don't get used often on Suus; even our winters are mild, and it's only during rare cold snaps that we ever feel the need for heating. I lean in, making sure not to get old soot on my clothing, and fumble around up the chimney.

The hidden lever, small though it is, clicks to the side without too much effort.

The back of the fireplace swings away from me, revealing a yawning black space beyond.

I crouch there, staring, for several seconds. It still works. A piece of my memory the Catenans haven't touched. I do my best to place where this particular entrance connects to the tunnel system, but I almost never used this one.

Careful again to avoid getting soot on me, I snag the hidden door and pull it shut. No time to explore now, and I still have three days until the majority of the senators leave and the highest ranks hold their final meeting. I'm going to need an excuse to be in here and undisturbed throughout that evening. An illness will probably work best, but it will have to be convincing. I should be seen to be coming down with something for at least a day in advance.

I examine the fireplace to make sure there are no telltale signs of my activity, then unlock my door again. Someone will be coming to fetch us to dinner soon.

For the moment, best to just brace myself for more defiling of my memories, I suppose.

LIII

I'M LYING ON MY BED, STARING AT THE CEILING, WHEN THE knock finally breaks the morose hush.

"Vis. Son." Ulciscor's enthusiasm seems genuine as I open the door, all the more so for Lanistia being the only other person around. He offers his hand. "I'm so glad to see you."

"You too, Father." The nomenclature feels more bitter on my tongue than usual, but I clasp his forearm in familiar greeting, summoning an understanding nod. We can't talk about anything important, not here. I'm expected to put on a show until whenever we do get a chance to speak in private.

I embrace Lanistia next, kissing her lightly on both cheeks.

"You're well?" Lanistia asks as I step away again, her dark glasses flashing.

"Well enough. And lots to tell you both."

Ulciscor's eyes gleam, but otherwise the man hides his excitement well. "Excellent. But for now, we've been told in no uncertain terms that we are not to come to dinner without your company."

"Of course." I smile wanly and move to pull the door shut.

"Wait! Before we go." Ulciscor rummages in a pocket, then produces a small, thin box. "A gift from your mother. To let you know how proud she is of your advancement."

I take the slim wooden case, opening it. A beautifully crafted gold-plated stylus lies on velvet within. *Stronger Together* is delicately inscribed on the stem.

"It's beautiful. You'll have to thank her for me." I duck back into my room and tuck the box into a desk drawer before rejoining the other two. We start walking.

The day's bright outside the wide archways, blue sky broken only by wisps of white far above. I breathe in as I look out over the view, letting it wash over me, focusing on it rather than the corpse of my home. There are more boats docked on the massive pier below. The senators have started to arrive in number.

We make small talk for the few minutes it takes to walk the near-empty passageways to the dining hall. Ulciscor is excited at my elevation to Class Four—a note of what seems to be genuine pride in his congratulations—and then unabashedly pleased when I briefly tell him about the Festival of Pletuna and Aequa's attempt to "unmask" my cheating. I'm not sure whether his delight is more at my rapid advancement in the class, or that it's come at Aequa's, and therefore Advenius's, expense.

I try to match his enthusiasm, but my heart's not in it. Hard to blame Aequa for thinking as she did, regardless of her actions.

We reach the dining hall. Gone is the long table in the centre, replaced by several smaller ones, each surrounded by three broad couches in the Catenan style. The floor has been overlaid with gold and obsidian in an intricate Catenan mosaic. The walls are decked in Catenan art. Catenan sculptures skulk in each corner.

None of the Thirds are here yet. The room's filled, though, at least two dozen mostly older men split off into groups of two or three as they laugh or murmur together. I recognise only Dimidius Quiscil and his wife, who are reclining on couches around the unmistakeably preeminent table at the far end of the room.

Before I can properly take it in, a senator is introducing himself. He's Magnus Quintus Omus. I remember the name from Lanistia's lessons. I politely ask after his holdings in the east. He's pleased I know who he is.

We speak for a spare few minutes, and then Omus is replaced by the next senator. And the next. And the next. It goes like that for at least the next half hour as Ulciscor shows me to each in turn like a proud father. I do my part. Smile, shake hands, offer the occasional compliment or other pleasantry. Every single one commends me on my bravery at the naumachia, and most go on to say that they expect to see me doing great things once I reach the Senate. I try to sound enthusiastic in response.

Finally, though, I feel a gentle tap on my shoulder, and turn to find Indol behind me.

"My father has asked that you join us, Vis." He motions politely with his head toward the far table. Not a slight, but it's clear the invitation is for me alone.

Ulciscor's not fazed, urging me away in assent. "We'll speak later."

"Thanks for the rescue," I murmur as we head across the room. Finally having a chance to look around again without coming across as bored, I spot Emissa and Belli at a table in the centre of the room. Like everything else in the Hierarchy, the seating arrangements indicate rank, and I'm interested to see that the Thirds are placed between the Quartii and Quintii. Emissa gives me a small wave as she notices my inspection, which I discreetly return.

"Don't thank me yet," says Indol cheerfully as he guides me over to his parents.

"Catenicus. Welcome. Please, join us." The Dimidius's easy demeanour seems at odds with the power emanating from him; genial though the words are, they still come out an irresistible command.

"It's an honour, sir." I perch on the couch indicated, trying to look appropriately flattered. The words are ash in my mouth, but I can't risk showing him even a hint of my anger. The Dimidius isn't someone to be trifled with.

"So what do you think of our little island here?" Quiscil asks as Indol moves off to join the other two Thirds, leaving us alone.

"It's beautiful, sir."

"It is, isn't it?" The Dimidius looks around, as if admiring the additions he's made. "It's come a long way in three years." Thankfully I'm spared from responding by the arrival of the first course: pheasant, lobster, and raw oysters among the dishes, nothing new to me, but exotic for most Catenans. Even the dinnerware is gaudy, silver encrusted with semi-precious stones. I keep my eyes on the food, worried that if I look up, Quiscil will see my simmering fury.

"I've been looking forward to speaking with you, ever since the naumachia." Somehow both casual and intense. "I've heard the stories, of course. Read the reports. But *you*. You were *there*. You saw it up close." He leans back, downing an oyster in one smooth motion. "Tell me *everything*."

He means it. He's not just asking from form. Not going to take what I say at face value, either, I can tell.

The next hour is one of the most tense I've spent. Quiscil's not shy about asking direct, probing questions, which come constant and hard and focused. It doesn't help that I'm still off-balance, thrown by my surroundings. My answers feel neither quick nor smooth enough, despite the many hours of rehearsal I've done to satisfy exactly this sort of grilling. Hopefully the Dimidius just marks it down to my being intimidated.

Though he's cautious, clever in his approach, it doesn't take long for me to spot the angle to Quiscil's interrogation. Of course. He's not suspicious of me—he simply wants to know as much as he can about the weapon the Anguis used. Undoubtedly interested in both finding a defence against it, and acquiring the power for his own means. It's probably why I got the invitation here in the first place.

Once I realise what he's after, my answers become easier, even if the nervousness remains. To make matters worse, Fadrique makes several appearances during our conversation, quietly relaying information into the Dimidius's ear before disappearing again. At least I haven't spotted anything unusual in his behaviour.

That doesn't stop my muscles from tightening every time he walks in the room. I've been sure not to talk too much in his presence, either. I've worked for more than three years on smoothing away my accent, but I'm terrified that hearing my voice might prompt a memory which sight alone hasn't.

After a while we're joined by two other senators—both Magnus Tertii, it turns out—but even when the Dimidius's attention is elsewhere, the dinner's interminable. The food is all wrong: there's fish, but it's broiled in the Catenan manner; fresh clams, but clearly prepared by someone other than a cook from Suus. The Dimidius proudly proclaims the authenticity of the dishes to us, describing some as local delicacies. Tells wildly inaccurate, exaggerated versions of Suus's history. Regales everyone with stories of the conquest from three and a half years ago, about how bloodless it was, about how eagerly the populace welcomed the advancement of the Hierarchy. Of civilisation.

It takes all I have not to spring out of my seat and leave. To feign enjoyment and play along. *Ignore it. Get Relucia's information. Leave all of this behind.* I don't know how many times I repeat it to myself.

"Vis." The female voice finally sounds softly in my ear during a break in conversation, accompanied by a light touch on my shoulder. I turn to see Emissa standing behind me. She smiles at me, then addresses Quiscil. "I apologise for interrupting, sir, but I need Vis here to settle a debate between myself and your son. Do you terribly mind . . ."

Quiscil glances between me and her. "Never keep a lady waiting." He holds out his hand as I stand, concealing my utter relief. "A pleasure, Catenicus. I trust we will speak more, once the summit is over."

I clutch it firmly. "I look forward to it, sir."

Emissa steers me away. Her eyes dance as she looks across at me. "You know, I think that might be the first time I've seen you so utterly uncomfortable."

I wince. "That obvious?"

"No, no. You're quite good at hiding it. But I could tell."

I glance over at the table where Indol and Belli are sitting. We're not heading there. "I take it there was no dispute?"

"No dispute. Just boredom."

I grin at that, despite myself, despite the surroundings. "So you're saying I'm an improvement on those two?"

She makes a vague, indecisive gesture with her hand. "I'm saying you're different, at least."

I bump her reprovingly with my shoulder, and she grins back.

We wander to a dimly lit corner and stop at an unspoken signal, turning to face the room and observe in a small pocket of privacy. The conversation between us remains light, idle but comfortable. There's entertainment: a poetry recital which we mock quietly but mercilessly, followed by acrobatics which are surprisingly impressive. At one point Emissa points out a senator whose face looks exactly like the whole roasted turtle being brought out on a platter, and I almost choke on my wine with laughter.

Despite everything, the horror of my surroundings starts to fade, just a little. My chest doesn't feel as constricted. Even when we're not joking about something, my smiles feel . . . genuine.

The next two courses go by before there's movement from the corner of my eye, and I turn to find Ulciscor wandering over to us. "A friend of yours, Vis?"

"Emissa Corenius." She offers her hand.

Ulciscor clasps it and bows over it politely. "Ah, of course! I know your father. A shame he could not be here. We have had many *robust* discussions in the Senate." He beams to show he doesn't mean it in a negative way. "How are you finding the Academy?"

"Challenging, of course. I'm looking forward to the end of the year and moving into public service."

"No plans for family?"

"I'd prefer to improve my position first. I still have five years before there are tax implications."

"Of course. Of course. My wife was the same." He nods to her. "A pleasure, Emissa, but I do have to steal Vis away, I'm afraid. There are a lot of senators still anxious to meet him, and they're only here for a few days." The last is more for me than her. A slight reproval.

Emissa takes the cue with good grace. "Nice to meet you, Magnus Quintus." She gives me a final, half-pitying smile farewell, then drifts away back toward where Indol and Belli are sitting, deep in conversation.

Ulciscor watches her go, not moving. "You need to be careful of that one, Vis."

"I know. I am."

"It didn't look that way." He finally glances at me. "She was the one who gave you the drink after the Transvect attack."

"She was." I meet his gaze. Some of the relief I've felt while talking to Emissa starts to fade. "I'm being careful."

He studies me for a few long moments. "Alright."

I trail after him back into the fray of senatorial inquisition. Somehow, though the next hour or two lasts an eternity, the evening draws to a close and people begin to retire. I make my excuses as soon as I think is polite. I'm almost blind with weariness— much of it an emotional toll, I know—as I finally get back to my room, shutting and locking the door behind me. I want nothing more than to collapse onto the bed and shut my eyes. Leave this day behind.

Instead I force back a yawn, light the lamp from my desk and shutter it, and then stumble over to the fireplace.

※ ※ ※

THE TUNNELS ARE PITCH-BLACK ASIDE FROM THE DIM LIGHT of my lamp. Smaller than I remember, the sides brushing my shoulders at points. I hurry to the east, wracking my memory at every juncture. I'm not intending to be long in here, but it's been years, and the Hierarchy knows about these passageways. I need to check there are no guards, no Will-based alarms, no ways blocked off between my rooms and the halls where I expect the senators will hold their summit.

There's nothing, though, as far as I can tell. Perhaps, with my family dead, the Catenans simply decided these secret ways weren't worth worrying about. Few others on Suus knew of them, and their one external access is all but impossible to traverse. Hardly a security risk in what is now little more than a holiday home.

The silence weighs on me as I shuffle carefully along, marking the way I've come at intersections by scoring small marks on the stone with my dagger. The scratching echoes into the darkness whenever I do so, but it's a necessary precaution. As much time as I once spent in here, it's easy to get turned around in the dark.

There are three halls I think would be large enough to accommodate all the senators. Each, thankfully, still have their listening slots: head-height doors that slide soundlessly to the side, blending perfectly with the surrounding stone when closed. Even knowing about these tunnels, the Catenans may never have spotted them. None emit any sound tonight, as expected.

I'm on my way back when I pass the entrance to the Great Hall.

I pause. It makes for a fourth possibility, I suppose. It's where my father used to sit and accept submissions from our people. Even with all the changes here, I'd be surprised if it was being used for the summit, though. It's too large, too overwhelmingly grand. There are better spaces for the purpose.

Still, I linger, ear pressed up against its listening slot. Like the others, there's flat silence.

I should move on, but morbid curiosity drags me over to the door. I crack it. Peer through. It's empty, though the lanterns are lit.

I used to spend hours watching my father give verdicts on cases in here. He heard them all himself. Never delegated. When I was younger, he would explain his decision to me after each one. Then the last year before the attack, he started asking me what I thought the verdict should be. Making me explain my reasoning before telling me how he was going to rule. I wasn't always right—sometimes I would miss a legal technicality, or misunderstand an aspect of an argument. Sometimes, rarely, we simply disagreed on who was in the right. Most of the time, it was depressingly dull.

The ache in my chest as I miss it is a deep, hollow pain.

As with everything else in the palace, the hall is different now. The familiar furnishings are gone. Like the dining room, Catenan tapestries and statues are everywhere. But the memories remain.

I stand there for a minute. Two. Just being there. Feeling the pain of it, but not wanting to stop.

Eventually, though, there's some distant sound that snaps me from the moment, sends me fleeing back into the passageways and hurriedly, quietly clicking the hidden door shut behind me.

I go back to my room after that. Melancholy. Drained.

After meticulously cleaning myself and the floor of any sign I've been scrambling through the fireplace, I collapse onto the bed. Close my eyes. Today has been a nightmare. Maybe the hardest day I've had to endure since the last time I was here.

Still, at least there was one reprieve. I think back on my time with Emissa this evening. Find myself half smiling again at some of her witticisms, a glad warmth in my stomach as I lie there. I don't know if I could have finished the day sane, if not for her.

Eventually, I sleep.

LIV

"VIS! BELLI! AREN'T YOU GOING TO JOIN US?"

I sit on the dune, arms around my legs, watching the clear blue waves as they glitter in the early morning sun. It's before breakfast; as little as I wanted to come down here, I know I can't be seen as disinterested or overly standoffish. Emissa's waving at us. She and Indol are in light clothing, swimming and splashing in the shallows. Behind me, the palace is hidden just over the high, jagged cliff to the east. I refuse to look toward it.

"I don't really swim," I say apologetically as Emissa jogs up.

"Neither do I. It's shallow enough not to matter. I promise."

I'm not able to be convincingly cheerful. "Thanks, but I'm happy just to sit."

Emissa narrows her eyes at me but then sighs, turning to the girl reclining a few paces away. "Belli? What about—"

"No." Belli pushes back a long strand of curly red hair, giving Emissa a firm look. Emissa rolls her eyes. "You two are no fun." She runs back to Indol.

I lean back, closing my eyes and letting the warmth of the sun caress my face. There's no pleasure in the act, though. No pleasure to being here, at the beach where I used to play with my siblings. It was once one of my favourite spots. I can almost see Ysabel doing cartwheels along the sand, or Cari building the elaborate sandcastles that I took far too much pleasure in knocking down.

Instead, a little way along, I see the place where I dragged Cari's lifeless body to shore. Where I spent too long and not enough time trying to revive her. And then the inlet where I released her body to the sea. Watched it tumble and roll as it was taken by the rip. The last of my world borne away with her.

"Not much of a swimmer?"

I'm shaken from my thoughts, twist to see Belli looking at me with some amusement. She must have seen my expression as I stared out over the water.

I force a chuckle. "Not my favourite thing."

"We have that in common." She makes a disdainful motion. "It's fine while you're actually in the water, but the sand afterward . . . ugh."

"Exactly." Not something that's ever bothered me, but Belli's so aloof, I'll take any chance I can get to connect with her. "You'd prefer to be inside at a game of Foundation, I take it?"

"Something like that." She looks over at me curiously. "Do you know how to play?"

I almost laugh aloud at the presumption, though I suppose it does make a small amount of sense: most orphans would have neither time nor inclination to learn the game. "The basics." I've seen her in action on several occasions now: she's technically proficient but has none of the inventiveness of a great player, makes no moves that I couldn't see old Hrolf having made.

"Do you want a game?"

I wave my hand to indicate hurried refusal. "I've seen you play. I've got no interest in being humiliated, thanks." I smile to show it's meant as a compliment. Skill at Foundation is valued almost as highly as being able to run the Labyrinth, in the Academy. There's no point revealing I can play until I can take full advantage of it.

Belli shrugs and resumes her observation of the others.

"Did you ever play Callidus, when he was in Three?" It's not planned, but I've been wondering about their relationship since seeing them together after the Festival of Pletuna. A gentle prod won't hurt. "He's mentioned that he enjoys the game."

It's subtle, almost imperceptible, but Belli tenses. "Ericius? Rotting gods, no. What a waste of time that would have been. There's a reason he's a Seventh."

"He's smarter than that."

"He never showed it when he was with us. And why else would he be in Seven?" She glances over.

"You're wrong about him." There's something off about Belli's words. I don't think she's faking her dislike of Callidus—my presumption of romantic involvement was, I'm rapidly realising, wildly inaccurate—but she's watching my reactions too closely.

I lose whatever I was going to say next as I spot movement at the far end of the beach, a single figure trudging toward us across the sand from the palace path. It's Fadrique, the man's balding head and broad shoulders distinctive even from a distance.

"Looks like we're being summoned," I observe to Belli, trying to tamp down my uneasiness.

The red-headed girl turns to lazily observe Fadrique's approach, then gives a grunt of what I suspect is relief. "Time to go!" she shouts at the two in the shallows.

Emissa runs up, long hair dripping and shining in the sun. Her clothes cling to her.

"Have fun?" I keep my eyes firmly on her face.

She flicks water at me playfully. "I did. I haven't been swimming in . . . I don't know how long." She leans close, lowering her voice so that only I can hear. "I was thinking of maybe sneaking out after dinner and coming back, actually. If last night is anything to go by, it will certainly be warm enough."

I glance at her. There's the hint of an invitation there. It's undeniably tempting, but I need the evening to try the tunnels again, to make sure the summit is actually being held where I expect it to be. "More swimming. Enjoy that."

She grins back, though I don't think I'm imagining the glimmer of disappointment in her eyes.

Everyone's gathered by the time Fadrique arrives, allowing me to keep myself positioned at the back of the small group. I can see my father's former adviser mentally checking off that we're all present once he reaches us. He doesn't pause when he looks at me.

"Your father thought it would be instructive to break fast in town today," he says eventually, addressing Indol. "You won't have many opportunities to see the island once your training starts." Despite this being a month away from the Academy, I've been left under no illusions as to what we'll be spending most of our time here doing. As Belli bluntly noted when I questioned it, "We don't want to let you Fourths catch up."

Indol looks around at the rest of us and, seeing no objections, gestures. "Lead the way, Sextus."

I try not to let my concern show as we start along the beach toward the main township. Risking Fadrique's presence is one thing, but mingling with the people of Suus is quite another. I often travelled into town with my father, who always insisted that a king was useless if he did not spend time among his people. Too many of them knew me by sight.

But I can't think of a way out, either. It's too early to fake illness; if I play that card now, its efficacy tomorrow night will be greatly reduced. And multiple days of being bed-ridden will raise questions, draw more attention than I would like. A single day and evening, and I may not even have to fake symptoms to the local physician.

So instead I fix on Fadrique's back as he prattles cheerfully to us about the wonderful changes that have been made in town since the Hierarchy came. It's all I can do to prevent my hands balling into fists. My father trusted this man. My *family* trusted him.

"A bit disturbing, isn't it," murmurs Emissa from beside me.

I blink, then follow her gaze ahead, where I suspect she thinks I was staring. Belli is talking to Indol, walking close to him. *Very* close. The Dimidius's son looks distinctly uncomfortable.

"Oh, I . . . oh. When did this happen?"

"Last night. I think we may have accidentally done Indol a disservice, leaving him alone with her for so long." She shakes her head solemnly.

I choke back a laugh. "We'll have to apologise later. How did we not notice?"

"Well. I did, after I went back to them. You had admirers of your own to fend off, I suppose," Emissa says cheerfully.

"Hm." I watch the two of them. "You don't think Indol might be a little bit interested?"

Emissa hides a smirk. "No. Trust me."

We're entering the township. It's grown since the expansion of the port, main streets paved, a hundred similar-looking stone houses dotted around its outskirts. The streets are busy, horse-drawn wagons moving alongside Will-powered ones, many of them taking timber down to the docks for transport. Trade was always Suus's primary source of wealth, and it seems the Hierarchy has worked hard to increase it over the past few years.

Fadrique continues to tell us pointless facts about Suus, though at least these ones are accurate. The streets here are eerily familiar, but the weary faces are not. There's a mechanical torpor to the bustle. My people were a people of verve, of passion, of cheer and laughter as they toiled. Now they're Octavii. Enough energy to work. Not enough to find the joy in it.

Finally we stop in front of a tavern I recognise: an institution in Suus that overlooks the harbour. I've been here before. It once wore the royal insignia over the entrance. Only empty wood remains in the space it used to be.

"The finest food in Suus," Fadrique assures us as we're urged through the doors. There are a few people reclining on benches outside, and though Fadrique doesn't seem to notice, the glares they give him are anything but friendly.

The interior of the tavern is spotless, bright and cheerful, with large windows to the water letting in plenty of morning light. Several customers lounge at tables. At the sound of the door opening a huge man emerges from the back, broom in hand and a broad smile on his face, despite the telltale dark bags of an Octavii under his eyes. He's Suusian through and through: sun-browned skin, broad shoulders, and gleaming white teeth. The last disappear as soon as he sees Fadrique. "You're not welcome here."

Fadrique laughs awkwardly at the blunt, and clearly honest, statement. "Now, now, Menendo. I was just telling the *Dimidius's son* and his friends about how things have changed since our transition to the Republic."

Menendo's eyes rake over us, and I swear there's a flicker of hesitation when he looks at me. My heart stops, but he moves on, his scowl progressively deepening. "You mean since the invasion? The one where they hanged our king and his family like common criminals in the square? Is that what you're talking about, Fadrique?" The broom in his hands is looking more and more like a weapon.

Thankfully, everyone's so focused on the innkeeper that they don't see the way my face drains of blood at his words. Don't see how I'm light-headed with emotion, just for a second, before I can recover myself.

Indol steps forward smoothly. "Sir, please. We don't want to cause trouble. We've been told that you serve the finest—"

"Get out."

Indol's lip twitches. He draws himself up, affronted. "I am the son of Dimidius—"

"I said get out." The calmness in Menendo's voice is more menacing than a shout could ever have been.

I can't help but drink it in. This is what I've been waiting to see, have been *desperate* to see, since I arrived. Menendo will get in trouble for this, but he doesn't care. He hasn't forgotten my family. He hasn't forgotten Suus. There's a lump in my throat at the realisation.

"Come on." Fadrique is flushed, glaring but retreating. I notice for the first time that almost to a man, the other patrons' expressions are stony as they watch Fadrique. It seems the man's far from popular.

Indol looks like he wants to argue the point, but Emissa tugs on his arm, and then we're leaving.

"That was unacceptable!" Indol fumes once we're outside. I can see the others looking varieties of outraged and shocked, too. "When my father hears of this—"

"Let me speak to him about it. Please." Fadrique says it quickly. "This is my fault. My mistake in bringing you here. Menendo's a stubborn man. I should have known he would react that way."

Indol's mouth twists, but he relents.

We find our meal elsewhere, after that—a small shop run by a Catenan citizen suits our needs—and though our shoddy treatment is the topic of much offended discussion for a while, eventually everyone seems to forget about it. Soon enough the conversation turns to our plans for training, the areas to be focused upon hotly debated. My opinions, when I bother to voice them, are largely disregarded. For all their friendliness over the past couple of days, it's clear they all still very much see me as a Fourth.

I'm not bothered by the discovery at all.

For the first time since we got here, I feel just a little bit like I'm home.

LV

T HE SUN'S GOLDEN GLOW HAS LONG SINCE DISAPPEARED BY the time I get the opportunity to head back to my quarters again. I walk the open palace hallways alone. It's a clear night and the moon is already rising, its reflection a silver smudge on the swells far below. I glance across at it and shiver, memories sharp.

I'm weary tonight. Training with the Thirds began not long after our morning meal, and barely let up throughout the day, reminding me more of Lanistia's brutal schedule than anything I've experienced at the Academy thus far. A constant mixture of physical and mental exertion, sparring moving on to an economics debate followed by a run that had my lungs burning by the end. After which, the other three—who barely seemed to be breathing hard—proceeded to quiz one another on imbuing mathematics that I could follow, but not meaningfully discuss.

As well as I'm doing in Class Four, there's still more than a small gap between me and the Thirds.

Exhausted though I am, I know I'm hours away from sleep. The senators will be talking well into the night, so this will be a good opportunity to find out which hall is being used, test how well I can overhear them, and then listen in for a while. Relucia may not care what's being discussed over these first few days, but that's because she can find out from Ulciscor. And she won't tell me anything she doesn't think I need to know.

I'm lost in thought as I round the final corner to the guest wing, starting a little at movement up ahead. It's Indol, looking as fresh as if he'd just woken, strolling in the opposite direction.

"You kept up well today," he says as we come closer, his genial demeanour indicating he means no offense.

I chuckle. "It was a little harder than I'm used to."

"You'll adapt. Everyone does. Gods, even Sianus managed it." He claps me on the back. I've always wondered whether his effortless charm is something he cultivates for the sake of the others, but it's no less prevalent because we're alone. He goes to move on, then hesitates. "I wanted to apologise. About this morning."

I frown. "For what?"

"The way we were treated." A shadow passes over his face. "As soon as the summit's over, I'll be having a word to my father about that innkeeper."

"That's not necessary." When he looks at me quizzically, I shrug. "Send too many of them to the Sappers, and the whole island will be in an uproar. Your father has to walk a line between respect and control. We all understand that."

Indol nods slowly. "I suppose. Yes. Thank you for reacting so well." He's feeling some of the burden of hospitality here, evidently. He glances out the window, toward the ocean. Smiles slightly. "You're not taking Emissa up on her offer of an evening swim, I see?"

I shrug again, this time uncomfortably, though I cover it with a sheepish smile of my own. "I'm not sure it was exactly an *invitation*. But I'm exhausted, anyway."

Indol chuckles. "Wouldn't stop most people. And that lagoon is *very* private."

I start to respond, but the words stick in my throat. "Lagoon?"

"You know—the one along the beach where we were today. She said she was going to sneak out and—"

I'm running before he finishes, leaving whatever else he was going to say behind.

I do the calculations as I sprint to the palace entrance; the hallways are mostly empty, but I have to skid around a few Octavii here and there, who give me surprised looks but make no attempt to stop me. The tide's going out. The riptide will be strongest right now. And as far as I know, no one's warned Emissa. I certainly haven't heard anyone mention it—though this morning when the tide was coming in, the danger wasn't there, and so perhaps no one thought of it.

The strongest swimmers I've known were never a match for that current. And Emissa, by her own admission, hasn't swum properly in years.

Only moonlight illuminates the clifftop, but I run it at full speed, relying on memory as much as sight to guide my feet. I slip a couple of times on loose shale, treacherously risky given the steep drop on the left. When I finally reach the path leading downward, I skid to a halt, scan below. I'm a long way away, but this is the best vantage point.

For a long few seconds, there's just smooth water, oily in the night.

Then I see her. A dark shape struggling, floundering pointlessly against the current. If she wanted any chance at all, she'd be trying to swim along the coastline, out of the rip. It won't drag her under; if she simply floats and waits for help, I'll be able to reach her. But she doesn't know that.

I can't make it down to the beach, then out to her—that will take minutes she doesn't have.

Fear energising me, I sprint for Aznaro's Bluff. The rip will drag her past there, and we used to dive from it as children. Occasionally. It's a fifty-foot drop to the water. We'd do it in daylight, with someone else present. And we never told our parents.

I track Emissa's shape as I run, willing her to keep her head above water. She's still thrashing. Splashing wildly. She's fit and healthy, but with the energy she's expending, I don't have long.

I reach the bluff and jump without breaking stride.

Prepared though I am, the drop lurches my stomach into my chest. Everything crystalizes. I stiffen and point my feet at the water, noting Emissa's struggling form, almost absently calculating where she's heading. I'm still going to have to swim for her. And I can only see her head now. She's fading.

The impact is sharp, but I can see clearly and I'm prepared for it, embracing the chill of the water and orienting myself quickly. As soon as my descent slows, I push upward. My tunic's dragging me down. I keep calm, strip it off and propel myself again. Eager for air by the time I break the surface, but not desperate.

I immediately strike out at an angle, toward where I know Emissa's being swept. The swells are thankfully light tonight, but I can't see her; I'm almost at the point of panicking when I register a weak splash about fifty feet ahead, followed by gurgling gasps.

I reach her in less than a minute. She's flailing, half sobbing and half choking; when she realises I'm there she has a renewed rush of energy, clinging onto me. Her nails score my shoulder.

"Emissa! Stay calm!" She's dragging me down. I sputter as I inhale water, trying to keep my voice stern and gentle at the same time. More panic will only make things worse. I grip her tightly, force her to make eye contact. "We're fine, but you need to stay calm."

"Vis?" She coughs the name, as if not believing what she's seeing, and for a moment I think she's not going to listen. But then something in her takes control. She adjusts her grip on me so that I can hold her up.

"Just keep your head above water." I've been caught in the riptide, too; the shore's already significantly farther away. "We need to swim along the shoreline, get out of this current first. Don't swim against it."

We eke our way out of the rip; it's hard to tell when we're free but at some point, I realise Suus isn't getting any more distant. That's good. As much as I'm trying to project composure, I was already more than a little concerned at just how far back we were going to have to swim.

The next hour is a nightmare of straining through dark swells, stopping constantly to tread water or float in an effort to conserve strength, supporting Emissa as much as I can, fearful that if I let go she'll simply sink. Her panic's well past, now, and she's doing everything she can to help, but she's exhausted. Barely hanging on.

I try to place where we are as the cliffs of Suus finally grow larger. We've drifted east, to where the wind-blown bluffs meet the sea. There's no beach here, but I don't think I have the strength to get us to one. There are caves nearby, ones my siblings and I used to explore by boat. They will have to do.

Eventually we get close enough for me to spot a deeper darkness in the towering stone: only a few feet wide, little more than a crack, but I remember it. It opens up inside. Will be dry and out of any wind that might start up. The night's warm enough and the water isn't anywhere near freezing, but there will be no way to dry ourselves.

"In there?" Emissa baulks as she realises where I'm pulling her toward, but either from trust or simply exhaustion, she doesn't resist. We paddle through into the darkness. Almost immediately there's stone in front of me and I'm hauling myself up, bare stomach scraping against the jagged edge, then using the last of my strength to pull Emissa after me. We both collapse onto our backs, gasping relief. Water splashes only inches from our feet, echoing through the chamber. This place is smaller than I remember. But the tide's still going out. We're safe enough.

Our rasping breathing rattles around the space for a while, that and the waves the only sound. Eventually we both quieten. My eyes have adjusted to the dim; the moon's reflecting off the water at the mouth of the cave, providing enough light to see. I glance across at Emissa. She's awake. Just staring up into the darkness. She flinches as she senses my movement.

"Are you alright?" I ask it as gently as I can.

She nods. Barely more than a spent lifting of her head. "I'm sorry," she whispers.

I can't help but cough a laugh. "For what?" I prop myself up on one side, facing her. "It's not your fault."

She bursts into tears.

I stare, frozen, unsure how to react. Then I lever myself into a sitting position and shift over to her, taking her hand awkwardly in mine. She responds by sitting, too, and throwing her arms around me. She's shaking, her face buried in my shoulder.

We just sit like that. After a while her trembling stops, her breathing eases. I realise, with a soft chuckle, she's fallen asleep.

I lay carefully back on the stone, keeping her head on my shoulder. She doesn't stir.

Uncomfortable a bed though it is, I'm asleep within moments too.

※　※　※

SUNLIGHT'S BOUNCING OFF WATER AND RIPPLING ONTO THE cave roof when I open my eyes again.

It takes me a bleary instant to remember where I am, what happened last night. Emissa's gone from her position beside me. I groan as I stir, every muscle reminding me of why people don't have stone beds.

There's movement from just behind, and then Emissa is settling beside me, look-ing out through the cave mouth over the glittering water. She doesn't say anything for a time, then turns to me. Smiles. "I thought you said you didn't swim."

I smile back. "I said didn't, not couldn't."

She holds my gaze. "Well I'm glad you *can*, then. Thank you."

I'm suddenly aware of how close we are. Only a foot between our faces. I flush, looking at the water. "Are you alright?"

"Hungry. A bit tired. Nothing to complain about." She's still looking at me, still close. "Where are we?"

"I'm not sure." I indicate the sun. "East side of the island? We might have to swim again to get to a beach. I couldn't see one last night. If we wait for low tide, though, there might be enough shallows to just wade around."

"Either way, at least we can stay right by the shore. Take it slowly. It doesn't look too rough out there." Emissa doesn't sound as confident as her words, but I'm glad she's already come to the same conclusion. "Lucky you saw this cave. It just looked like a crack in the cliff, to me."

"Lucky Indol mentioned you were going to the lagoon." I hate lying to her right now, but I have to cover myself. I made decisions last night that are going to look awfully suspicious. "I heard one of the locals talking about the rip there yesterday, how dangerous it was. I used to swim with my father when we went down to the coast— there were rips there too, and he was always worried about them. I should have said something." I hunch forward. Frown through the opening in front of us as I consider what else I did. Knowing it was safe to leap from Aznaro's Bluff is hard to explain, but I can pass it off as simple recklessness. What I've just said should cover most of the rest.

"You couldn't have known." Emissa lays a hand lightly on my arm. My skin tingles at her touch. I know I should pull away; I can hear Ulciscor's warnings ringing in my ears. But I don't.

There's an abrupt intake of breath from Emissa; when I turn to see what's wrong, she's just staring at me. At my shoulder. Carefully, she puts pressure on my arm, com-pelling me to twist away. I resist as I understand what's caught her attention, then realise there's no point. Reluctantly turn my back to her.

"How?" she whispers, aghast.

I don't reply for a long moment. "The orphanage."

"*They* did this to you? That's . . . that's *barbaric*." Real anger creeps into her voice as she processes.

"It's just the way things were." I keep my tone neutral. Give her another second to examine the scars, then deliberately point them away from her again. "It's in the past."

Emissa watches me. Sad, but not pitying. "Alright." She looks like she wants to say more, but she sees something in my expression. "Alright."

Something loosens in my chest. I go back to sit beside her. Neither of us talk for a while.

"You think they'll be worried about us?" I finally ask. The sun's already indicating mid-morning, and the four of us were supposed to start training at first light.

"Not for a while. They'll probably just make assumptions."

"Ah." We exchange half-rueful grins. "Well. Indol might wonder, at least, after the way I rushed off on him last night. If he's worried enough to go to his father—"

"He won't. Indol hates his father."

"What?"

"They put on a good show, but that's all it is."

"I don't believe you."

"You will once this year's done."

I glance at her curiously and she flushes, looking angry at herself. A pause, then, "Indol's not going to serve in Military when he graduates." It's a reluctant admission.

"*What?*" I'm sure I've misheard. It would be strange for any graduate of the Academy not to join their family's faction. For the first son of the Dimidius of Military not to do so is unthinkable.

She gives a brief chuckle at my reaction. "That's what I said when he told me. He's moving across to Religion, apparently. Wouldn't say why. I have some guesses, but . . ." She looks at me warningly. "You can't say anything. And if you do, he'll just deny it."

"Of course." I rub my forehead. "Rotting gods. That's a big thing to tell."

"I guess he must like me."

"I meant, to tell me."

The corners of Emissa's lips curl upward as she shrugs. "I guess I must like you," she says softly.

She leans in, cautious. Head bowed so that her forehead almost touches mine. Her breath's warm on my face.

I know, somewhere in the back of my mind, that I should pull away.

I kiss her.

There's sea salt on her lips as we stay like that for a few heartbeats, awkward and sweet and soft. Despite the past few days, despite everything, I feel giddy. Light-headed, short of breath, and delighted. We eventually part, drawing back only a little, gazes meeting. Her eyes are lit by the reflecting water, bright and vibrant green.

"Finally," she murmurs, and leans in again.

%% %% %%

LOW TIDE, IN A LOT OF WAYS, COMES TOO SOON.

It's a clumsy journey around the edge of the cliff; the stone's rough and slip-pery, and we're constantly buffeted by breaking waves. But it's not dangerous. There's a newfound lightness to everything; falls that would have been frustrating are cause for laughter and teasing, excuses to be caught or hauled up close by the other. We're tired and progress is slow as the sun burns high overhead, but neither of us mind. The terror of last night seems a distant memory.

By the time the sloping sands of Solencio Beach come into view, though, I've had some time to think. What I've already said to Emissa should account for most of my apparent local knowledge, but I need to ensure Indol hears the same sooner rather than later. Suspicion is easy to prevent, far harder to dispel. I cannot risk allowing it to take root.

The fishing village off Solencio Beach is small, all locals but no one I recognise; soon enough we're being given a hot meal and dry clothes, both Emissa and I promising repayment once we reach the palace. The Octavii here aren't thrilled to find Catenan citizens washing up on their shore, but nor are they unkind. Exactly the response I'd hope for from my people. My good mood is brightened by their generosity of spirit.

I'm saved having to explain how I know my way back to the palace by a fisher-man who offers us transport to the main harbour. He's a cheerful fellow, sun-burned, bare-chested, and rugged, his constant stream of chatter on the hour-long journey an indication that he's more than pleased at the company. I think he spots the way we look at each other, stand together, though neither of us is trying to make it obvious. His smiles are too knowing to be directed at anything else.

My lightness of spirit—only buoyed by the trip, the sun on my back, sea spray wafting as our small vessel scythes through the waves—inevitably dampens as we come in sight of the rebuilt jetty of the harbour, along with the anchored mass of slick Will-powered ships that brought the senators. I've found a moment of joy here with Emissa, but it doesn't change anything. I still have a job to do.

So by the time we're stepping off the boat, I've noticeably coughed a few times.

When we're ushered into the palace to the at first amused, then horrified expressions of Indol and Belli as we explain what happened—minus some details—I make sure to let my throat go hoarse. Sway on my feet, look grateful for the opportunity to sit.

I bravely wave off the concerns of the others, including Emissa. Smile wanly and assure them it's just weariness. But once dinner is complete, I don't object to being directed to get an early night. Which, to be fair, is not part of the act.

I'm sorely tempted to scout the tunnels again once I'm back in my room—I've already lost one night, and if I discover the meetings aren't being held where I expect, I won't have time to come up with a solution—but Ulciscor and the other senators will hear about our exploits once the meetings end today. The risk of getting a visit is too high.

My caution proves wise when a gentle knock pierces my consciousness sometime later in the evening.

I don't have to feign lethargy as I stumble over to the door. The moon has risen outside the window. It's late.

"You're awake. Good." Ulciscor assesses me as I open the door wider once I see who it is. "Are you well?"

"Could be worse," I say noncommittally, giving my voice a slight rasp.

Ulciscor enters. Lanistia's close behind, impassive, dark glasses reflecting the silvery light. Once they're inside I shut and lock the door again. Ulciscor is using the excuse of checking on me, but he'll no doubt take the opportunity to talk about more sensitive things.

"Well. Congratulations. You've managed to get all the senators here talking. Again." Ulciscor sounds as though he doesn't know whether to be impressed or exasperated as he slumps onto my bed. "Risking your life to pluck a drowning girl from the ocean. One who, if she had died, would have let you straight into Class Three. A hero straight from a gods-damned saga."

I stare blearily at him. "I . . . apologise?"

He glares, then sighs and waves his hand wearily. "I thought I told you to stay away from her."

"I didn't think that extended to letting her die."

"It didn't," interjects Lanistia, with a reproving look in Ulciscor's direction.

Ulciscor nods, and I wonder if I'm imagining the motion's reluctance. "I wouldn't ask that of you. But word is already getting around that the two of you seem more friendly than ever, since you got back. And I know how friendly you already seemed two nights ago."

I flush. "I'm being careful."

Ulciscor sighs again. "Make sure you are, Vis." He glances around, as though checking the room for some hidden listener. "Now. After the Festival of the Ancestors. Did you make it to the ruins?"

The extra tension in Ulciscor's voice betrays his anxiousness. He's been wanting this conversation since I left the Necropolis.

"I did. It didn't go *quite* as planned, but . . . I saw it. Saw what I think Caeror was trying to tell you about, what Veridius and Religion have been hiding."

I relate my journey and experience at the red dome in as much detail as I can, making sure to appear weak and tired, preparing for my apparent onset of illness tomorrow. Ulciscor just listens with head bowed, occasionally glancing up at me, otherwise moving only to take off his cloak as the room heats up with three bodies in it. His arms bulge as they jut from his tunic. His deep brown eyes return to studying the stone floor once he's done, but I can tell he's devouring every word.

Lanistia, true to form, barely reacts to anything I say. Not even when I explain about Artemius and Elia, about how their eyes were like hers.

When I finish, Ulciscor exhales, brow furrowed into the silence. Thinking.

"You'll have to run it. At the Iudicium, I suppose, would be easiest."

The words hang in the air, punctuated by the distant, echoing waves below. I don't react for several seconds, certain I've misheard, or misunderstood, or that he's joking. But he continues to look dourly at the floor, silhouetted against the glistening swells out the window beyond.

"You heard what I just said, right? About Artemius being torn apart by whatever it is down there?"

"I did."

My confusion turns to anger. "No. I've held up my end of the bargain, and—"

"You have done no. Such. Thing." Ulciscor stands abruptly, his voice low. Harsh. "I asked you to find out what happened to Caeror. What you've done is describe to me places Caeror might have been. Now, if you find *proof* of how he died—something you can bring to me, something I can then take to the Senate—before the Iudicium, then I absolve you of this. But if you do not, then it's what you need to do. This is what will fulfil your obligation to me. Do it, and you can truly be of House Telimus. Or not. You will be free to go wherever you wish upon graduation, with no interference from me." He looks at me, all cold determination. "It can't save you, you know. This reputation you've been cultivating. Fail, and I *will* put you in a Sapper. No one will stand in the way of my rights as your father, and I'll still have that right for weeks after the Iudicium is over. Have no doubt that I will exercise it."

I gape. Stunned. So that's why he's been short with me tonight, why he wasn't pleased about me saving Emissa. He still feels like he's losing control of me.

"I . . . I'm not good enough at the Labyrinth. I'll die," I stutter eventually.

"Then improve. You still have four months."

"Lanistia. Say something." I turn to her, pleading for her to talk some sanity into the Magnus Quintus.

Lanistia sighs. "He's right."

"You see, Vis? You just—"

"Not you. Him. *Vis* is right." Lanistia's voice is steady as she turns to Ulciscor. "He's done what you asked of him. We have information we can work with now."

Ulciscor glares at her. "We won't get this opportunity again." He turns back to me. "I *am* sorry, Vis. I understand that this is dangerous. But I asked you early on whether you were willing to risk your life. You said yes."

I'm lost. Speechless. For perhaps the first time, I'm seeing the depth of Ulciscor's obsession—or at least, that his determination to find out what happened to his brother far outweighs any concern he may have for me.

"I suppose I don't have a choice, then." Bitter and dazed, the illusion of having achieved enough with that brutal journey to the ruins dashed. The heaviness of this place and my position here, briefly forgotten, returns to smother me.

"No. You don't." Ulciscor rubs his face tiredly. "We've already spent too much time in here with you. I doubt we'll have the chance to talk again like this before I leave the island. Maybe not before the Iudicium, in fact. So is there anything else you need to tell me?"

I shake my head numbly.

He clasps me briefly by the shoulder. Grim. "Then gods guide you for the next four months, Vis."

He leaves, not looking back.

Lanistia moves to follow him, but pauses at the door.

"You picked up the Labyrinth faster than most I've seen. Train hard. You can make it through." She lowers her voice even further. A whisper of emotion in it. "Don't die."

She follows Ulciscor, leaving me alone once again.

LVI

I T'S NOT HARD TO CONVINCE EVERYONE OF MY SUPPOSED ILL-
ness the following day.

I've been wide awake for much of the night, fretting; my red-rimmed eyes and sluggishness during our morning sparring on the beach help sell my story, even before I start coughing. Spending time with Emissa—who, happily, seems to have recovered well after a good night's sleep—is a brief balm, but even that can't dispel the spectre of Ulciscor's demands.

When I struggle to rise and then feign a stagger after the meal, Emissa tells me in no uncertain terms that I need to go and rest. The others smirk and make loudly whispered comments about our relationship, but we ignore them and I reluctantly accept her advice.

Back in my rooms, I draw the curtains and lock the door. It's tempting to actually get some sleep—I'm genuinely still very tired—but if there's an unforeseen issue, I need to give myself as much time as possible to get around it. And no one is going to disturb me. The senators are still ensconced, and the Thirds will be training all day.

I'm pleased to discover the senators in the Lesser Hall, one of the locations I'd guessed at for the summit. I make three trips there throughout the day. Their discussions filter through to the tunnels clearly, and I sit by the hidden slot for an hour at a time, just listening. It's largely dull. A combination of arguing over how to outmanoeuvre the other senatorial pyramids, and arguing over internal politics. Occasionally I hear Ulciscor lending his voice to one side or another, though it's always with a crowd and he's never afforded the chance to speak alone.

None of it is useful. But I'm at least confident I'll be able to overhear the meeting tonight.

I emerge from my quarters just before dinner, making sure to look as dishevelled and drained as possible. Not hard, given I've still barely slept. Better to present myself now, show I'm still unwell, rather than risk an unexpected visit later tonight by anyone who's wondering. I speak briefly with the Thirds—mostly to Emissa, who I reluctantly refuse when she asks if I'd like company for the evening, insisting that I'll almost certainly be asleep—and then go down to the docks to see Ulciscor and Lanistia off. Ulciscor embraces me in front of everyone, as if I am truly his son. Lanistia looks on impassively.

I watch them sail away against the setting sun, and wonder if they expect to see me again.

Back in my rooms, I lock the door and shutter my lantern. Grab a couple of wax tablets and a stylus from the desk, though I leave Relucia's "gift" in its box.

It's time to find out what, exactly, she's so willing to risk my life for.

%%   %%   %%

VOICES TRICKLE INTO THE TUNNEL AS SOON AS I INCH THE Lesser Hall's listening slot open. I exhale when one of them is Dimidius Quiscil's. It seemed a safe assumption that the remaining senators would continue to use this room tonight, but there was no guarantee of it.

I settle down by the opening, and wait.

It's a jumble of voices for the first two hours. Some idle rumblings about a proposal for land reform being pushed by some minor Military patrician, but otherwise just polite small talk. People asking after other people's families. Remarking on how beautiful the weather is here. Exchanging stories about their trips up, bemoaning the lack of a direct Transvect, and generally commenting on the need for proper civilisation in this part of the world. I ignore the latter. I've heard it from the Thirds more than enough since we arrived.

Finally, though, there's a door shutting. Chairs scraping. The chatter dies away as Dimidius Quiscil's power-laden voice cuts through it all, apologising for Dimidius Werex's absence—he's apparently needed in Caten, at present—and then moving on to what appears to be official business. "Reports, Ciserius?"

A cough into a brief hush, the Tertius sounding like he's shuffling some papers. "The updated list has seventeen known conspirators and another twenty-three potentially weak to coercion. The most pressing concerns are House Remus, who we have documented proof have been bought by the Council of Four, and House Juvalis, who reliable sources tell us are strongly considering a move to Governance."

Muttering. Some cursing. Apparently either the numbers or the names aren't ones the gathered senators like.

"We'll review them all, Ciserius. Let's start with the known quantities," says Quiscil, quietly enough that I can only barely hear him.

The following two hours is devoted to discussing anyone of note within Military who is suspected of working against them. I carefully scratch name after name onto my tablet, the lettering as small as I can manage. The details of each, though—

documented or suspected acts, theorised reasons for turning, projected consequences of them being removed from the political equation—I have to commit to memory, along with each individual's inevitable list of weak points. Vices. Illegal businesses. Illicit romances, current and past, some with members of the same sex and thus prohibited under Birthright. Progeny other dalliances may or may not have produced. It shouldn't shock me that so many in the Senate are corrupt, but the litany is disturbing.

And valuable, valuable information for the Anguis. Some on the list have simply been marked as concerns: not necessarily traitors, but with damaging enough secrets that they could easily be coerced by outside forces. Others have been bought by knights, flagrantly circumventing the senatorial ban on engaging in any form of business. Still others have been documented supporting either Religion or Governance interests. There's even one Quintus who, according to some reports, is outright working for the Anguis. I make a note against him.

There's heated discussion after each report. Opinions inevitably ranging from wanting to try and entice the suspected traitors back, to consigning them to Sappers. Most often, the committee decides to simply have them watched. But not always.

My muscles are cramped from fear of moving by the time the list comes to an end. Quiscil announces a short break. I noiselessly stretch out my limbs and then sit on the stone floor, staring at the names on my tablet contemplatively.

After a minute, I carefully memorise and erase three. Quintus Elevus. Magnus Sextus Doria. Magnus Sextus Tirus. Ones who the committee in there have decided not to interfere with, for the time being. I hope it never comes to it, but if I *do* ever need to coerce a senator, this information will be useful. And Relucia shouldn't have any way to notice their absence from what I send to her.

When I hear the proceedings inside restarting, I lever myself into position again. It's Quiscil talking.

". . . the things we will need again. Let me know who can supply what, and then these lists are to be burned."

There's the scratching of paper being handed around. My fists clench. This has to be what Relucia wanted me here for, but there's not much chance I'm going to be able to see what's written.

"A *ship*, this time? I have concerns, Dimidius." Ciserius's voice is sharp.

Indol's father sighs. "Very well. Speak your mind. I know many of you have been eager to discuss the Anguis incident at the Festival of Jovan."

"'Incident'?" It's Magnus Tertius Nasmius. "That is a very kind way of putting it,

Dimidius. And yes. We have been eager." There's a muttered agreement from a number of senators. "A disaster I would not see repeated."

"Disaster?" Quiscil's tone is mild. "How so, Nasmius?"

"How else would you describe it?" Nasmius is irritated, even if the hint of deference never quite leaves his voice.

"I lost ninety-seven in my pyramid," agrees Ciserius.

"I lost a hundred and thirty-five. I blacked out when it happened," chimes in someone else. Magnus Tertius Olicus, I think, though he's been quiet for the most part. "We gave them too much leash. Overfunded and underestimated them."

I frown. Bow my head and lean closer, sure I've misheard.

"And I lost almost four hundred," observes Quiscil. Chiding. "Which is exactly why not even the possibility of our involvement has been considered. Personal loss is a necessary screen, my friends. Yes, I know the timing took you by surprise. Yes, their attack was more destructive than we could possibly have anticipated. But that was all to the *better*. We all have to make sacrifices. I would hope that the inconvenience of rebuilding your pyramids is not your measure of success or failure."

"I disagree," says Nasmius after a few moments. "Perhaps if Melior were still alive, the Senate would be more pliable—but with him gone, they almost see us as *less* important, not more. Have we at least found something more about the Anguis's weapon?"

"No. But I am told its secret died with Melior." Quiscil's still calm, though this is the first time I've heard anything resembling actual opposition to him. "And changing the hearts of the Senate was always a possible by-product, never the aim. The *people* believe we are more vital than ever. And most importantly, the Anguis believe they have contacts who can be trusted. They won't hesitate to do what we need them to do now."

"Do they know we are involved?"

"Of course not."

I lick my lips, trying to come to terms with what I'm hearing. There doesn't seem to be much doubt.

Military helped the Anguis attack the naumachia.

"Are you sure? The way they've been preventing us from using the Necropolis hasn't sat well with you, Dimidius—you cannot tell me otherwise."

"That was Melior's doing. There has been nothing since his death."

"Still. At least the Festival of Jovan required only information and some uniforms, but this time you want to give them weapons? Will designs? A whole *trireme*? What happens when one of them gets caught? Someone will figure it out."

"They won't, because interrogation remains our jurisdiction."

"We should at least know where the attack will happen." Quartus Redivius speaking up.

"*No.*" Quiscil's voice, peaceable up until this point, is hard. Not loud, but the latent power behind it feels like it's pulsed through the wall, and I briefly lean my head away from the listening slot at the single word. Silence, then much more placidly, "Ciserius, with your fleet, I assume a ship going missing would not be too unusual?"

"Ships often get lost at sea, Dimidius," agrees Ciserius. He sounds shaken. "The *Navisalus* is due for a voyage to Tensia. The crossing can be quite dangerous."

"Take care not to crew her with anyone you would like to see come back."

Another silence, then, "As you say."

I feel a chill. The Dimidius is making plans that countermand Birthright entirely, and no one is saying a word. A few minutes ago, I knew I'd be in trouble if I was caught listening to this meeting. Now, I doubt I'd be left alive.

"Why is this so important?" It's Nasmius again. "If we just understood—"

"The Princeps says it is. That's all you need to know."

The Dimidius's pronouncement effectively ends the discussion, and soon the conversation is moving on to other matters.

None as significant as what I've just heard, though.

Eventually, the meeting fades to a close with a scrape of chairs and murmuring voices. I wait in case there's anything further, some idle final scrap of discussion, but after a few minutes, I'm convinced everyone's left. I slide the listening slot shut, gather up my tablets and lantern, and start back toward my room.

The damp passageways echo as I walk. The *Navisalus*. Relucia mentioned something about a ship while I was eavesdropping on her at the Festival of Pletuna. That it was being used as an anchoring point. But the other man wasn't sure if their partners could be trusted.

This has to be why I'm really here, why Relucia wanted to know what the Dimidius was requisitioning in secret. I'm making sure that Military are holding up their end of the bargain.

I grit my teeth. Whatever's planned, it must be something big. Vital to the Anguis. But even if it's another attack—what do I do, what *can* I do about it? Anything? Sending the wrong information to Relucia seems more likely to put myself in danger, than sabotage a scheme I know almost nothing about. I don't owe it to the Hierarchy to expose myself by trying to tell someone else. And there's not even much to tell. Not enough for anyone to take me seriously, let alone actually prevent whatever is coming.

I'm still deep in thought when I round the final twist in the tunnel. I don't notice that I'm not alone until I see movement. By then it's too late.

I take a couple of stumbling, panicked steps back, scrambling for a good course of action but failing to find one. The man clambers to his feet from where he was slouched opposite the entrance to my room. He steps forward into the lamplight.

It's Fadrique.

LVII

"PLEASE." FADRIQUE WHISPERS THE WORD. HOLDS OUT A hand, as if worried he'll scare me away. "You have nothing to fear from me."

I waver, confused.

"It's truly you, isn't it?" He looks at me as if seeing a ghost. Which, in many ways, I suppose he is.

I fix on him, frozen. He's already caught me in here—in the tunnels only my family and a few scant others knew about—on the same night as Military's meeting. So even if this is some ruse to trick me into admitting my identity, it's close to moot.

Fadrique, apparently, takes my lack of response as affirmation, because he's suddenly striding forward. I flinch away, but he wraps me in a fierce embrace, clutching me close as if I was a long-lost child. Then he takes my head between his hands and forcefully kisses me on each cheek. His eyes, to my shock, are glistening.

"Master Diago. My prince. Master *Diago*." There's no denying the sheer delight in his voice, the release the words are bringing him. There's joy but also disbelief, sadness, regret.

I push him away, not unkindly but firmly. "If I *were* who you think I am, I would probably ask why a former citizen of Suus is now a Sextus. I would probably ask how much the Hierarchy paid him to betray his people. I would probably ask why he was allowed to live and thrive, after the entire royal family he served were murdered." It's an accusation, I know, as well as close to an admission as I can manage. It's hard—almost impossible—to say the truth aloud, after so many years of practice.

Fadrique is still overcome with emotion. There's pain as he looks at me, so much that I can barely stand to meet his gaze. "Your father told me to look after his people."

"So you became one of *them*?" I'm more vehement than I mean to be.

"I and my family survived. And we stayed."

There's no heat to it, but the indictment is one I physically flinch from. My mind spins, a surreal mix of relief and anger.

"Forgive me, Highness." Fadrique is moving again. Dropping to his knees, bowing his head. His voice shakes. "I didn't know what else to do. I asked for no benefits to my position, but they said it was required. That if I wished to act on behalf of Suus, then I had to accept everything that came with the job." There's so much shame in the words. "Please, my prince. I beg you to believe me. I did not want this."

I still want to rail at him, but some part of me already suspected, I think. I knew Fadrique. Or rather, my father knew him, and well enough to trust him. He wouldn't have taken on this role if he didn't think it was the best thing for Suus.

It doesn't dispel my anger, but it diminishes it enough.

"I . . . believe you." The words are a release of tension, a letting go. "The Hierarchy would have needed one of us to help them manage our people, but they couldn't let you be popular. Even if the benefits didn't buy you, they knew being a Sextus would set you apart. Make everyone else think you were bought, regardless." I hesitate, then step forward and gently lift the man to his feet again. "No kneeling, Fadrique. There's no royal family in Suus anymore."

It hurts to say it. It might be the first time I've admitted it out loud, in fact.

The man accepts my help, his relief and gratitude almost too much to bear. "As far as I am concerned, there is for as long as you live. Your Highness."

I swallow at that. Nod. "How did you know I would be in here?"

"There are Imbued alarms on most of the hidden doors. Set by me," he adds reassuringly as he sees my burgeoning panic.

"Is there any chance someone else will come by?"

"No. They sealed off the underwater entrance. There's no way in or out through these tunnels otherwise, so they just forgot about them." He smiles fondly. "Not much different to your day, Highness. It was really only you and your sisters who ever made use of them."

I smile at that, too, through the ache in my chest.

Eventually I sigh, moving next to Fadrique and sliding wearily down the wall until I'm seated. Fadrique sits too, our backs against the cold stone. Silence settles.

"When did you recognise me?"

"I saw the resemblance as soon as you walked in, but . . ." Fadrique shakes his head. "I only thought it might not be coincidence when the entrance to the Great Hall got opened the other night. Then I saw which room you'd chosen, and . . . I knew." He stares at the opposite wall. "Are you here to kill him?"

"What?" I look over at him blankly. "Who?"

It's Fadrique's turn to be surprised. "Quartus Latani." He frowns at my confused expression. "The man they call Suusicus? The one who led the assault here, ordered the deaths of your family?"

I don't fully understand at first. Then I'm cold. Dizzy. "Latani?" I met him.

"Yes. First time he's been here since . . ." He trails off. "I don't think anyone in town knows."

I breathe, more heavily than normal. "I didn't either."

"Well. Violence is no answer to grief, Your Highness, but if you give the word, I'll find a way to show him justice." Fadrique was always a soft-spoken, placid man, but there's steel in his offer.

I consider it. I consider it for a long, long few seconds.

"There's being brave, and then there's throwing your life away." I say it even as fury blisters my chest. "You do anything like that, you end up in a Sapper. You end up in a Sapper, and maybe whoever they choose to replace you here doesn't have our people's interests at heart. And they suffer as a result." I feel the last of my wrath toward Fadrique drain away with the words. I turn to him. "I am sorry, Fadrique. I shouldn't have been angry. My father would be proud of what you've done—what you've sacrificed. I *am* proud of it."

Fadrique bows his head. It takes him a few moments to recover his voice. "Thank you, my prince."

Silence again. I shift, not wanting to ask the question, but having to know. I've been wondering these past few years. Torturing myself with the different scenarios so much that the reality, surely, could not be any worse than what my imagination has conjured. "How did they die, Fadrique?"

"Your family?" Fadrique turns quietly sorrowful. "Hanged."

Just like Menendo from the tavern said. "Ysa too?" My voice is small.

"Her too, Highness."

Something in me wrenches, though every logical part of me knew that would be the answer. Information about their deaths has been so scant, near impossible to find. I *knew* they were dead. *Every single account* said they were dead. But then . . . every single account said I was dead, too. Some small part of me, I think, had still hoped.

Then I'm suddenly, unexpectedly weeping. Huge, gasping sobs, arms wrapped around my knees, forehead resting against them. I don't know why the grief hits me so hard, then and there, but it does.

I feel Fadrique grip my shoulder. A gesture of solidarity and comfort. Somehow that only makes me sob harder.

"Did you see it?" I manage to whisper the question.

"I did," says Fadrique gently. "It wasn't public, but I was asked to bear witness, to confirm their deaths. Myself, Gelmiro, and Polo." A consoling squeeze. "It was quick. They were brave. Especially your sister."

I try not to imagine it, but I do anyway. My family with nooses around their necks, dropping from the gallows. Another sob wracks my body and then I force some deep breaths until I'm settling, emotions back under some semblance of control. "Was it all at once?" I ache at the thought, but I want to know that none of them had to watch the others die.

"Yes, Highness. They showed them that mercy." He exhales. "And it wasn't until two days later that Princess Carinza's body was found. So for all your parents knew, she had escaped along with you."

The sadness hits me all over again. "Good," I choke. "That's good." I wipe my face with my sleeve.

Neither of us talk as Fadrique lets me recover myself. Eventually, I shake my head. "I have so many questions, Fadrique. About what happened that night. About what's happened since."

Fadrique stands. "Before you ask—there's something I would like to show you. But we shouldn't risk speaking until we get there. We need to pass by several occupied rooms."

I frown, but stand too. "Alright."

Fadrique picks up my lantern and leads the way, deeper into the tunnels. He seems comfortable navigating, not hesitating at intersections. I have only vague memories of this area. Enough to find my way back out, probably, but that's about all.

Finally, Fadrique turns into a small chamber. He picks a candle from the wall and holds it to the lantern, then lights several more around the room.

I watch, puzzled. There's a jumble of things in here. Piles of objects stacked in the corners.

As light starts to reveal the closest ones, my heart stops.

"Is that . . . my mother's bow?" I already know the answer. I crouch beside it, pick it up reverently. The wood's intricately carved with scenes from Suus's history. A gift from my father, wrought by Suus's finest craftsmen. It was one of her proudest possessions.

I'm transfixed, running my fingers over the wood, for long enough that when I look up again, the room is properly lit.

For a surreal moment, I've been transported into my past.

Everywhere I look is a memory of childhood. Trinkets that belonged to my parents, some truly valuable, others I know they kept for sentimental reasons alone. Toys from my room, my sisters' rooms. Things that we made for one another. Instruments I learned how to play. Even my old Foundation board is here, the small leather pouch beside it bulging with stones.

"They were going to sack your rooms, sooner or later. I know I shouldn't have taken it upon myself to hide it, but—"

I stride over and fling my arms around the startled man.

"This means everything, Fadrique." I break off the embrace and step back again, looking around in disbelief. A crack in my voice. "Everything. I know it shouldn't, but it does."

I spend the next few minutes just . . . browsing. Touching things I never thought I'd see again. I flip through pages of books rescued from my rooms: some educational texts, some stories I'd forgotten even existed. I laugh as I find a set of crude wooden ships among my father's things. I carved them when I was ten. Two large ones, three smaller ones, our names etched under hidden slots on their decks. I didn't even know my father still had them. The one with my name is missing. I ache again when I realise it. It seems appropriate.

There are coins here, too. A pile of circular silver. I finger one, gazing at my father's regal silhouette on the back. It's not legal currency anymore. I slip it and a couple more into my pocket. Easy enough to say I found them, or got them from a local, if asked.

Finally, I turn back to the older man, who's been watching me with a beaming smile.

"Thank you, Fadrique." I put all the gratitude I have in me into the words. "I never thought I'd see any of this again."

He bows his head in happy acknowledgment. "I did have some help."

"Who?"

"Friends." His pleasure slips to melancholy as he says it, and I can tell the people he's talking about are gone. Then he straightens. "You are not alone here, my prince. That's why I took you to Menendo's tavern, the other morning. I knew he would recognise you. I wanted you to know that you still have allies here. People who aren't afraid to stand up to the Hierarchy, given the right motivation."

"Thank you. It helped to see that. Truly." I make sure he sees my appreciation.

Fadrique ruminates, then motions to the floor and sits there himself. "Sadly, I couldn't save the furniture. But I know you have a lot of questions. So ask. I'll tell you everything I can."

The next few hours—maybe more—is spent on that uncomfortable stone floor, just talking. I learn about life on the island since I escaped. The chaos and fear of the first few days, when the Hierarchy soldiers began pouring in, but all most people knew was that they'd been told by their king not to resist. The fury and outrage after they discovered that my family had been executed, the riots that followed.

I am selfishly glad of the last, even if they were soon quelled by the Hierarchy's liberal use of Sappers as punishments. It helps to know my family's murders did not go unchallenged.

Fadrique gradually fills in the gaps after that. The Catenans, after the riots, began proscribing those accused of resisting. Some of my countrymen, I am ashamed to hear, took advantage. Fear of the Sappers took hold. Within three months, most of the population had visited the nearest Aurora Columnae, leaving only the occasional outburst against the Hierarchy's presence. Within six, that had faded to nothing more than grumbling.

Which, at least as far as Fadrique is concerned, is largely how things have stayed. The lingering resentment toward the Hierarchy remains, but fades a little more with each passing day. Where once people hated the idea of Will-powered devices, now they're clamouring for a Transvect to ferry them to and from the mainland. Where once they used to threaten violence at the alterations to their land, their history, their way of life—now they just murmur. Accept it as progress.

Eventually, Fadrique falls silent. I glance across at the older man, and I can see the questions in his eyes.

"I don't want to know all the details, Highness," he says quietly. "But I have to ask. The naumachia. They say you stopped the Anguis. Is that . . . ?"

"It's true enough." I see his face cloud. "People were dying by the thousands, Fadrique. People who were defenceless. Some of them children." I decide not to mention Estevan. They knew each other, but the addendum here would only be a cruelty.

Fadrique chews his lip, then gives a soft, rueful laugh. "Your parents' son," he says, and the touch of approval in his words makes me swell a little. Not with pride for myself, but for the gentle admiration with which he speaks of my mother and father. "I should not have been surprised that you're not here for revenge. They would never have wanted that."

I swallow a lump in my throat. Nod.

"I was sent here to find out what Military were meeting about." I look at him meaningfully. I have to trust him—there's no real alternative—but I won't give away more information than I need to.

He seems to understand. Acknowledges me thoughtfully.

"Fortunate," he murmurs.

"Why do you say that?"

He shrugs. "You—probably the only man alive who knows these tunnels well— happen to be sent here, just as Military also hold their meeting here? It's *fortunate*."

"It was arranged."

"By someone who knew you could get around like this?" Fadrique sounds dubious, and looks even more so when he sees my hesitation. "I won't ask if you have an ally from Suus, Highness—better that I don't know—but I cannot imagine how you were expected to succeed, if they didn't know you had that advantage."

I say nothing. He's right. Relucia said she sent me here because I was familiar with the place, that I was the best person to eavesdrop. But there's no way she could have known about these passageways. And without them, listening in to that meeting tonight would have been . . . well. Not impossible, maybe, but close enough to be touching it.

Estevan wasn't supposed to know about them—few in the palace were—but in his role as Melior, he must have told her.

"I hear rumour you have found companionship at the Academy, too, my prince?"

I blink, misunderstanding for a second, then flush. "You mean Emissa?"

"You seem to like each other very much."

There's no judgment in Fadrique's tone, but I worry about it anyway. "We do." A moment, and then I ask. "Do you think . . . do you think it's a betrayal?"

"If all were still as it should be, Highness, I would wonder at her potential to be a princess of Suus. But now . . ." Fadrique sighs. "They are the world, my prince. Pride and self-respect may mean we never give in, but if they are all our enemies, we will never be happy."

I give him a grateful nod. Neither of us speaks for a while.

"Do you want to know where I've been?"

"Better you don't tell me." He's rueful, this time. "I've learned two things tonight. One, that you are no longer the carefree boy I knew. And two, that you are still your father's son." He reaches over. Puts his hand on my shoulder. "That is enough for me."

I swallow down another hard lump at the words.

That should be it, but neither of us move. To me, at least, it feels as if doing so will be letting go of this place. Leaving behind the final remnant of what we've both lost.

Then Fadrique starts talking. Remembering to me a time—five years ago, perhaps?—when he realised my sisters and I had been lying to both him and Iniguez about our schedules and were instead sneaking off to the beach while both tutors thought the other was taking our lesson. We laugh about it, about the boldness of the plan, and the ridiculousness of our ever thinking it would work. All it took was for Fadrique and Iniguez to run into each other in the palace, and the whole thing came crashing down. We were still reaping the consequences for weeks after.

And so we just . . . speak into the silence. Take it in turns to share memories of my family, of the days before the Hierarchy. I hear stories of my father that make me genuinely guffaw, stories I've never heard before, stories he honestly probably never wanted me to hear. It's strange to say, but I learn more of him as the night goes on, seeing him through different eyes in a way that would never have been possible while he was still king.

And I think Fadrique does, too. As a child, I would never have thought to sit with him like this. With any of our tutors, no matter how much we liked or trusted them.

We reminisce, and laugh, and occasionally weep. It's hard sometimes, but there's a release in it all that I didn't realise I needed. I'm not tired, not the way I should be. It's not as if the weight has lifted from my shoulders—that, I suspect, is something I will never experience—but I feel lighter.

Finally, though, there's the barest brightening of the passageway outside as light begins filtering down through the crevices. "It's getting close to dawn."

"You're right." Fadrique says it with sadness, rising stiffly to his feet.

I do the same, muscles groaning from the abuse of the awkward, cold seat. Then I hold out my hand.

"I am very glad to have talked tonight, Fadrique." I hold his gaze. "I cannot begin to tell you what it's meant to me."

Fadrique clasps my arm as he understands my meaning. We won't be able to speak again, even in secret like this. "As am I, Highness." He lingers. "What will you do about Latani?"

I don't answer for a long few breaths. My stomach is still a knot of rage when I remember that I have someone to blame now, that he's walking around Suus as if he's done nothing wrong. But tonight has freed something in me, too.

"Violence is no answer to grief," I say eventually.

Fadrique wraps me in an embrace. I return it.

"If you ever need safe harbour, my prince, you know where to find it." He smiles at me, then takes a deep breath and starts to walk away.

"Fadrique!" The man pauses. Glances back. "I am proud, and thankful, and grateful for what you've sacrificed for our people. And I know my father would be too."

Fadrique stares at me, not saying anything. His eyes glisten. He nods.

He disappears down the passageway and into the darkness.

LVIII

I WAS TWELVE, THE DAY MY FATHER ASKED ME WHAT GAVE US the right to rule.

I lie there in bed after my night talking to Fadrique—still not sleeping, despite the dawn creeping through the window—and for some reason, it's all I can think about. It was summer, and he had brought me to the top of the East Tower, the one that provides a vantage over the entire island. I knew he wanted to talk to me about something important. He was quiet as we climbed the stairs. Thoughtful. It made me nervous, sure I was about to be castigated for something.

We watched the horizon for a while once we reached the top, not saying anything. Then he finally turned to me. Handsome, tall, powerful. Black hair and sun-dark skin and brown eyes that spoke of strength and consideration and kindness. A king in every sense of the word.

"Do you believe you would make a good ruler, Diago?" His deep, calming voice was almost wistful, but I could hear the intent.

"Of course," I replied without thinking, indignant.

"Why?"

The question threw me, and I knew immediately I'd been caught out. I floundered. "Because I care about our people." Undoubtedly the wrong answer, but I was stubborn. Preferred to pretend to know something than admit I didn't.

"You *care* about them." My father said the words deliberately, drew them out and tasted them. "That is one aspect of being a good ruler, certainly. But many people care about Suus, and they are not leading it. So let me rephrase. What do you believe makes a good ruler?"

I thought for a while. "Education. Knowing how to govern."

"Many could be taught. And most would attempt to learn more diligently than you," he added, a gentle stab that came with a smile.

I rolled my eyes. "Fine. I don't know. Enlighten me on the qualities of a good ruler. What do I need to be?"

My father sighed. "Smart."

"I'm smart," I protested.

"And strong."

"I can be that."

"And brave. And kind. And cunning. And frugal. And generous. And disciplined. And moral. And cutthroat." He paused for a breath. "You need to be caring, and judgmental. You need to pre-empt but never unfairly. You need to be completely honest with your people, but be mindful of what information could harm them. You need to—"

"It's impossible," I said, somewhat impatiently. "You're saying there's no such thing as a good ruler."

"There isn't." He sounded surprised that I got the answer so quickly, though he didn't compliment me on it. "And this is the risk of our world, Diago. The flaw of our system is in its head. In us. The qualities of a king change the kingdom. And not one of us is perfect enough to have a *right* to lead."

I stayed silent, trying to understand what he was getting at. "You don't think we should rule?"

"I didn't say that." My father stretched, the muscles in his arms cording as he offered them to the sun. "I want you to understand that no country's governance is perfect. Anyone who looks at a system of people and thinks the system is the problem, is a fool. But I also want you to understand that the Hierarchy's is far more insidious. Because it's not imperilled by a flaw. It is built on one."

"The Hierarchy?" I was puzzled. The Hierarchy were a wall, smooth and strong and impossibly tall. They were an insurmountable obstacle, a force beyond my comprehension. "What flaw?"

"Greed." My father turned to me then, and his dark eyes held mine. The wind whipped us, a chill to it that far up. "Greed is by definition the moral ruler of the Hierarchy, Diago. All decisions are based upon it. It is not the strong who benefit in their system, no matter what they say—it is the weak. It is the ones willing to do anything, sacrifice anything, to rise. It rewards avarice and is so steeped in a wrong way of thinking that those within it cannot even *see* it." He shook his head sadly. "There is no form of government that is immune from mistakes or from corruption—but it is the Hierarchy's foundation, Son. Never forget that."

Those words have stuck with me through the years. Not just because they revealed, for the first time, the depth of my father's disdain for the Catenan Republic—though that is one reason. But because they were like scales falling from my eyes, even then.

The sun is rising outside my window. I haven't slept. There's joy from my conversation with Fadrique, a release at having been able to talk to him. But there's new pain, too. Knowing how Suus has suffered, exactly as my father thought it would. Knowing that people like Fadrique have been punished for doing the right thing. Tiredness will come later, I know, but for the moment I let my emotions carry me.

I rise, dress, and wash in the basin provided. The mirror shows dark circles under my eyes, but given my supposed illness, it's not damning. I could easily remain in my rooms for the rest of today, but the sooner I rid myself of the information I gathered last night, the better. And it would be best to show myself in this state, anyway. Give the appearance of a gradual but steady recovery.

I take Relucia's stylus from its box in my desk, then slip back into the tunnels. It only takes a few minutes to trace over the details from my wax tablets. Then I add what I overheard. The dissatisfaction from the other senators about the naumachia. The *Navisalus*. The request for weapons and Will designs. I don't leave anything out.

Once I'm done, I break the stylus in two and wipe the wax slates clean. No trace of what I've done.

It's not ten minutes later that there's a cautious knock on my door, and I open it to find Emissa standing outside.

She crosses her arms when she sees me, appraising. "You still look terrible."

"Saving you was harder work than I thought."

She laughs and punches me gently. "Are you joining us on the beach this morning? I promise to stay away from the lagoon." She keeps smiling, earnestly hopeful.

I grin back at her. "I think I can manage that."

She glances around discretely, then leans in and gives me a soft, quick kiss. "Good." She's looping her arm through mine and marching me down the hallway before I can react.

I happily allow her to pull me along. Everything seems different this morning. Same people, same beach, same clear sky and warm sun and blue, shining ocean. But I don't feel like a stranger intruding in my own home anymore. I'm not comfortable, exactly. I know it will never feel like it did. But speaking to Fadrique has changed something in me. Sanded the jagged edges off my pain. This isn't just the beach where Cari died. This is where I spent years before that, playing with her. Tormenting her. Teaching her. Growing up with her.

It's why I can smile now, when Emissa makes a joke. Can participate in conversations without feeling like I'm forcing myself to. And why I don't feel so alone when I beg off exercising with everyone else, citing my ongoing recovery.

To my surprise, after a while, Indol comes and sits next to me as the others continue their sprints. We watch, reclining on the golden sands, soaking in the sunshine.

"How long has it been since you were here?"

He asks the question idly, still gazing out over the glittering waters; it's abrupt, but casual enough that I'm briefly confused.

Then I understand what he's getting at, and my heart constricts.

"A couple of days." I give him a quizzical glance, refusing to let him see my panic. "I haven't been down here since two mornings ago."

He rolls to the side, fixing me with a stare. "Not what I meant, Vis. But I think you know that."

I don't respond, continuing to plaster a bemused look on my face. No matter what Belli thinks—or anyone else, for that matter—Indol is the smartest student in Three. He simply doesn't flaunt it in the same way Belli does. And he's so *genial*, handsome and athletic and easygoing. So naturally popular that no one seems to want to think of him as brilliant, too.

"I saw the way you looked, when we first got here," Indol continues lazily, returning to his back and closing his eyes, drinking in the morning sun. "It doesn't matter how good an actor you are. There's something about coming home that you can't hide."

"Home?" I force a chuckle. "I told you where I grew up. It wasn't far from here," I allow, "but I've never been here."

"You've done well, not showing it. But aside from your panic when you heard where Emissa was, the other night? You might want to stop walking the clifftop paths without looking. Haven't you noticed how cautious everyone else is up there? Rotting gods, a fall could kill you. But you act as if it's nothing. And then there's the palace. You pretend not to know where you're going, but I can tell. Something about the way you move through doorways. You know every inch of that place." He stretches. "Tell me that I'm wrong."

"You're wrong."

Indol cranes his neck, checking that the two girls haven't come any closer. They're talking, not paying us any attention. "Look, I don't know what you were. Friend of the royal family, maybe? The son of one of their advisers? But it's clear to anyone with a brain that you've had training. No orphan makes it this far." He shakes his head, then looks at me again. Gaze intense. "I don't care, exactly. What I want to know is, why lie about it?"

My mind races. He's too sure of himself: if I deny it, I'll only make things worse. And he doesn't have an inkling of who I really am.

"You heard what everyone was saying when we got here. You heard the jokes they were making." My face reddens, though luckily the difference between embarrassment and anger isn't always obvious. "Who's going to take me seriously if they know I'm from a place like this? I'd be a barbarian to them for the rest of my days." I put all the disdain I can muster into my tone.

I'm not sure I could have done this yesterday. It hurts, pretending to scorn my own home, my own people. But I'm playing a role. Like Fadrique said at one point last night, it's what my parents would have wanted. They would have wished things were different, but they still would have chosen a life for me over a noble death.

Indol looks immensely pleased that he's been proven correct. That's good. If he thinks he knows all there is to know, he won't ask questions elsewhere.

"Don't worry. I'm quite good at keeping secrets," he says eventually. "Under the right circumstances."

"So am I," I say meaningfully.

Indol doesn't understand for a moment. Then he glances from me to Emissa, then back again.

He groans softly, and nods.

We don't talk again until the others join us.

⁒ ⁒ ⁒

AFTER THE INSANITY OF MY FIRST DAYS BACK AT SUUS, THE next three weeks pass in relative peace.

Training with Emissa, Indol, and Belli continues to be challenging; particularly academically, the subject matter is more advanced than anything I've been exposed to thus far. Usually related to the technicalities of wielding Will, often referencing concepts I've never even heard of. The first few days I feel out of my depth. It's only because Emissa spends her evenings with me, and sometimes helps me catch up, that I start to feel like I can hold my own.

And for all my making peace with the past, Emissa is the reason I don't go insane. She's the reason I can walk the palace hallways and smile. It's not that we're inseparable—sometimes I like to study alone, and sometimes she prefers to train with Belli or Indol rather than me—but when we're together, we're *together*. Gravitate toward each other naturally, unconsciously. Talk all day, and still want nothing more than one another's company in the evening. It's more than a distraction. Here of all places, she makes me feel like I'm still moving forward.

The others' jokes soon die down as they see we're making no real attempt to hide our relationship. Belli, at some point, realises that Indol isn't reciprocating her interest and gracefully slides back into aloof friendship. I casually ask Emissa if she ever noticed anything between Belli and Callidus; she says there may have been something, early on, but nothing so obvious that anyone took note. The conversation makes me wonder how my friends are faring over the break. As much fun as I have with Emissa, I do miss spending the days with Callidus and Eidhin as well.

Part of me starts to feel uneasy at the sensation. Once this year's done, the plan is supposed to be to never see any of them again.

I avoid town for the most part: easy enough, as after our first experience, the others do the same. But on our last day, as afternoon fades, I decide to go for a stroll. And before I really know my own intentions, my feet are leading me toward the harbour. The sun's low in a cloudless sky, more orange than gold. Bright across the water.

And then I'm walking into the tavern.

It's quiet inside. About how it was when I came here with the others a month ago. I catch a few looks from patrons at the far tables, but I pay them no heed. Take a seat by the window. Stare out over the harbour. A Will-powered vessel is pulling away from the extended dock, cutting through the swells. I ignore it. Focus on the smaller fishing boats farther out, their sails furled. Not everything has changed.

After about twenty minutes there's motion at my shoulder, startling me from my reverie. It's Menendo, the hulking barkeep who threw us out on the first day. I look up at him. Despite what Fadrique said, I still half expect to be told to leave.

The big man doesn't meet my gaze. He just sets a plate and drink down in front of me. Oysters, crab, lobster. I can smell the sweetness of wine in my mug. As fine a meal as I would have seen at the palace when my father was king. A traditional king's feast on Suus.

Menendo leaves without a word. I resume my introspective gaze over the ocean, and eat. It's better food than the Dimidius could ever have provided. Prepared to perfection. Exactly as I might have had years ago. I feel more comfortable, more at home in that moment than at any other point over the past month.

I take my time. Savour the meal, the view. The feeling of being among my people again. The sun sets, spraying purple and gold across the sky.

When I leave, I walk over to the bar. Take the coins I grabbed from Fadrique's hoard from my pocket and press them firmly against the counter. They click as I set them down. My father's shadow in the silver.

I leave without saying a word, without looking back.

The clean air and smell of salt fills my lungs as I wander the cliffside path back to the palace. I needed this. Needed this month, needed to come back here and see my home one last time. But it's over now. I'm feeling more comfortable in my ability to compete with the Thirds, yet increasingly realising that my advancement is what's going to be the sticking point. Not because I'm not good enough—I am—but because, at least according to the others, there's no one obviously unable to keep up in Three. No one with deficiencies that would let me usurp their position.

I'm going to have to do more than simply continue to top Class Four. I'm going to need to do something to get everyone's attention.

And I'm going to need to figure out how to do that soon, because we'll be back at the Academy tomorrow.

And now there's less than three months until the Iudicium.

LIX

HOURS AFTER THE LAST OF SUUS DISAPPEARS INTO THE HORI-zon, leaving for the second—and probably last—time still leaves me hollow.

It's a different kind of sadness than three and a half years ago. Back then, all I could see across the water was the loss of my family, my sister's death, the people who were surely preparing to pursue me. All terror and heartache and failure. This time, it's so much more than that. It's not running from my home. It's saying goodbye to it.

This time, it feels like Suus is truly lost to me.

I'm quiet, contemplative, on the Transvect back to the Academy. Emissa naps on my shoulder. I occasionally catch Indol watching me from the corner of his eye, but I ignore him. Our interactions have been perfectly amicable over the past month. We've come to an unspoken understanding, I think.

Most students are already back at the Academy when we arrive. The grounds are bustling. There's a sense of familiarity as I walk back through the Will cage at the entrance, but after Suus, there's no mistaking it for coming home.

After tossing my meagre possessions back into my room, I find Callidus sequestered away in a corner of the library.

"Vis!" Callidus spots me, jauntily waving me over. "I hear we have reason to celebrate?" I look at him blankly, and his grin widens. "You and Emissa? A romantically heroic rescue from the depths? Marooned together for the night, only one another to keep each other warm, your clothes sodden—"

"Alright. Alright. That's enough." I laugh, even as I flush, despite it not being a secret. "How did you hear about that?"

"Quintus Dolivus was there for the summit. Anax in Five is his son. It's been public knowledge for the past week, here."

"Gods' graves." I shake my head, taking the chair opposite.

"So." Callidus leans back, still beaming as he steeples his fingers together. "Tell me *everything*."

I catch him up on my last month, though of course I glaze over a lot of the details. Partly because the most interesting stories are ones I can't tell, but partly because it still hurts too much to talk about it. Despite my reticence, Callidus drinks it in. I get the strong impression he's been starved for entertainment.

"What about you?" I ask eventually, coming to the end of my narrative.

"It's been a delightful month of . . . *this*." He gestures expansively around the empty library.

"So your family didn't change their minds?"

"No." I can see the flicker of pain at that, even now. He quickly moves on. "But at least that let me get to know our mutual friend Eidhin a little better. He's meant to be meeting me here quite soon, actually. His Common is coming along rather well. I daresay because I'm a much better teacher than you," he adds modestly.

I chuckle. Both Eidhin and Callidus were intending to stay at the Academy over the break—Eidhin for reasons he refused to go into, and Callidus because his family asked him not to come—so I suggested they spend some time in each other's company. Neither seemed terribly enthusiastic about it, when I mentioned it before leaving. I'm glad to hear they didn't simply avoid each other.

"In that case," I say suddenly, "would you be against Eidhin joining us in the mornings?"

"Not at all." Callidus's expression is sly. "Why? Other plans for your evenings?"

"I want to run the Labyrinth." He raises an eyebrow, and I sigh in defeat. "With Emissa." I'd prefer to spend time with her in a more relaxed setting, but Ulciscor's ultimatum has been weighing on me. And I'm going to have to use every second at my disposal to improve, because as hard as I've tried, I still cannot see a way to satisfy him without returning to the dome.

"Run the Labyrinth. Of course," says Callidus merrily. He shakes his head in amusement. "No other news? No other casually heroic acts, no other tales of daring romance I should know about while you were away?"

I snort. "Unless you count Belli cuddling up to Indol for an awkward day or two."

I'm watching for his reaction, otherwise I might have missed it. A moment of sadness as he processes, before the expression's gone and he's looking at me nonchalantly. "Awkward?"

"For Indol. Belli got the message eventually."

"Oh." His gaze strays. He nods for a touch too long, the silence stretching as he gathers himself. "He didn't save her life too, I take it?"

"Not that I know of." I watch him intently. Openly.

"What?" He frowns as he spots my gaze, and there's red in his cheeks.

"You're not going to tell me?"

"Tell you what?" When I just keep looking at him steadily, his brow furrows. "Nothing to tell."

I hold up my hands in acquiescence and let the conversation move on.

Eventually Eidhin arrives, grunting as he sees me sitting with Callidus in what could almost be interpreted as a greeting. He pulls up a chair. "You are back."

"I am."

"I hear you are with Emissa."

"I am." I eye him. He's speaking Common, the words a little halting but smooth enough. Perhaps Callidus wasn't exaggerating.

"About time." He looks at Callidus. "Well?"

"All true. Saved her from certain death," Callidus assures him cheerfully.

Eidhin checks my expression to see whether Callidus is lying, then scowls. "Fine. I will pay later." He thumps a thick tome down on the table between us. "Shall we begin?"

"You bet on whether it really happened?" I don't know whether to be amused or offended.

"Eidhin simply doesn't have as much faith in you as I do."

Eidhin glares at Callidus, who stares back glibly before turning to me. "Is he always this sour around you, too?"

"Always."

"Must be exhausting, being him."

"I can understand you," Eidhin growls.

"I know," replies Callidus chirpily. "The question is, can you explain why being you is *not* exhausting? In Common?"

"I can explain how injured you are likely to be in a moment."

"This is nice," I interject with a grin.

Once the friendly bickering is done, we spend another while just talking, and it's quickly apparent that Eidhin and Callidus have a comfortable rapport. Eidhin's Common really has improved dramatically too, I'm pleased to see.

"Before I forget—Eidhin, would it be alright if we worked on your Common in the mornings, with Callidus?" I say suddenly, remembering.

"That would be fine." His eyes narrow. "Why?"

"He's planning to *run the Labyrinth* with Emissa," supplies Callidus helpfully.

"Ah. Run the Labyrinth. I see," says Eidhin, nodding slowly, saying the phrase as if trying out a new euphemism. Callidus half chokes a laugh as I roll my eyes.

I endure a few more jabs from the two of them, but soon enough the dinner bell is chiming. We walk to the mess together. There's curious, occasionally awed looks from many of the students as I enter. It seems Callidus wasn't overstating about my exploits on Suus being widely circulated. Probably exaggerated, too, knowing how these things tend to go.

I ignore the gawking, sitting with the Fourths and spending the next hour being crowded around and giving much-abbreviated versions of my time away. My efforts to deflect and politely ask what everyone else's break was like are unsuccessful. At the table on the level above, I see Emissa watching. I shrug, and she shrugs back with sympathetic ruefulness.

Only Aequa is quiet during the meal, all but snubbed by the others. The month away has cooled my anger toward her, and I try to include her in the conversation, but it rarely works.

I endure the questioning until the bell chimes again, content in knowing that everyone's curiosity will quickly fade once classes resume tomorrow. Pleased that I've already been able to talk with Callidus and Eidhin, too.

It's not good to be back at the Academy, exactly, but it *is* good to see my friends again.

%% %% %%

I STILL HAVE A LIGHT SWEAT, FOREHEAD COOL AGAINST THE night's ocean breeze, as I walk back from the Labyrinth to the dormitory.

My mood is upbeat. Partly because I find it almost always is after seeing Emissa; if I was worried that the surrounds of the Academy might change things between us—aside from the minor irritation of not being able to sit with each other at meals—then I can rest assured now that it hasn't.

But it's mostly because I'm more confident than ever that practicing with her will force me to get better. Callidus and Eidhin have done everything they can to help in the past, but they haven't had her months of near-daily experience with the Labyrinth. She's better than me by a significant margin. Even after one evening, she's shown me plenty of ways I can improve.

I'm so lost in thought that I don't see Callidus's shape detaching itself from the shadows of the dormitory until he's almost in my path.

He smirks at me as I stop short in surprise, though there's a touch of nervousness to the expression. An uncertainty that looks foreign on his face. He jerks his head back down toward the nearby parkland. "Hail, Vis. Can we talk?"

"Of course."

We start walking away from the dormitory. There's no one around, late as it is, but Callidus doesn't say anything more until we're well away from the building and surrounded by trees. I'm burning with curiosity but wait for him to speak.

Finally he sighs, gesturing to a bench beneath one of the pole-mounted lanterns. We sit.

"Look. Vis. There's something I want to tell you." He slouches forward, elbows on his knees, staring out into the darkness before looking at the ground in front of him. "It's about Belli."

I resist the urge to make a joke. There's a weight to his words.

Callidus's lip curls in frustration; there's another silence while he gathers his thoughts, glances around as if desperate for an excuse to put off his explanation. We're alone, though. No chance of anyone overhearing.

"It was three months before first trimester." Back to staring at the ground. "A few of us who were coming here began training together. Belli, Iro, Axien, Sianus, and me. My father organised it, invited them to our villa. He thought it would be beneficial. A way for us to get ahead, but also to form some bonds across Senate lines."

"Makes sense." Sianus is from a Governance family, like Callidus, and Iro is from Religion. With Axien and Belli from Military, it's a reasonable mix.

"It does." Callidus shakes his head. "It was good. Fun, for the first couple of months. We all seemed to get along. Even my sisters were enjoying having them around. And Belli . . ." He reddens, grits his teeth. Struggling to admit the next part. "I thought Belli and I were getting along better than everyone else. I thought we were at least friends, and . . ." He barks an abrupt, rueful laugh.

"You liked her."

"Rotting gods, yes. I thought I was in love." Clearly still hard words for him to say, though he delivers them matter-of-factly. "Stupid, I know. Looking back, I still can't believe I . . ." He sighs. "Anyway. I found out about the deaths in the Academy—the ones I told you about, a while back—and I was trying to warn Belli, but she wouldn't believe me. So a couple of weeks before the Academy started, I took some proof."

I close my eyes, half a wince. The pieces fall into place. "You stole official, Will-sealed documents from your father. From Governance. That's . . ." I rub my forehead in disbelief. "You could end up in a *Sapper* for that."

"Oh. Really? Thanks for the warning."

I wave my hand apologetically. "So what happened?"

"Exactly what you're imagining. I gave her the documents. I still don't know if I was trying to impress her, or was actually worried she might get herself killed. But I trusted her. Told her to read them over and give them back to me the next day so that

I could replace them. It wasn't as if anyone would be looking for them, *ever*, but a few days wasn't going to hurt."

"And she kept them?"

"And she kept them." Callidus's face is pale at merely the memory. "Told me that if I didn't drop down to Seven after the first few weeks, she'd hand them over to her father. That wouldn't have just been a nightmare for me," he adds, almost pleading for me to understand. "It would have destroyed my father's standing in the Senate. My family's name. They might even have ended up in Sappers, too. Governance doesn't look kindly on that sort of information going astray."

"I can't imagine they do." Information, *particularly* regarding the Census, is Governance's source of power. Callidus isn't exaggerating the potential consequences of being discovered. "So she's been holding it over you this entire time? Because . . . she thinks you're a threat to her?"

"Partly. She would have been at the bottom of Three, if I'd stayed there. But that wasn't all." Callidus's voice is low. "She's been pressing me for information. More and more, these past few months. I'm not going to give it to her," he assures me, "but she's getting bolder. More threatening. It doesn't make sense for her to actually show anyone those papers, yet—I'm better off under her thumb than in a Sapper somewhere—but if something happens, if my father does something she doesn't like . . ." He trails off.

I watch him, anger and sadness for him twisting in my stomach. He's terrified. He's hidden it well—better than I would have believed, actually—but he's in a situation that he can't see a way out of. Or a way to control.

"Does your father know?"

"Gods' graves, no."

I nod. His tone says it all: telling his father won't help. "Alright. Well. At least we've established once and for all that I'm smarter than you."

There's a pause, and then Callidus gives a soft laugh. He finally looks up at me. "Don't equate having less heart with more intelligence."

"I'm not sure it was your heart making the decisions, to be honest." I give him a half grin. "The question now is, how do we fix this?"

"There's no fixing it." He's doleful, his moment of humour vanished. "I've thought about it every day since it happened, and I just . . . I don't think there's a solution."

"She'd have the documents here. She wouldn't risk keeping them at her home."

"I assume so. Otherwise, if I did ever admit it to my father, he might figure out a way to get them back before she can do anything about it."

"So somewhere close by. Secure, though."

"The girls' dormitory, presumably. On the top floor." Callidus makes a face. "Even if I knew where to look, there's no sneaking in there. Someone would see me. And then it's expulsion, which is worse than being in Seven. And *then* Belli would release the papers anyway, because I'd be worth nothing to her."

"Hmm." I lean back, thinking about my time with Belli. What I know of her. Callidus is right: there'd be no sneaking in and stealing the documents back, even if we knew exactly where they were. And I can't ask Emissa to risk the consequences of being caught rummaging through Belli's private possessions. Still. Everyone has weaknesses, and Belli's no exception. "We'll figure something out."

"Thanks, but don't get upset if we don't. It's not your burden." Callidus forces a smile. "I'm glad I found the stones to tell you, at least. I'm sorry I lied to you. I hated doing it. I wanted to tell you a few times, but it just seemed pointless."

I press down the wriggling unease of my own secrets. "Nothing to apologise for."

We talk for a while longer after that. Not about Belli—the subject's plainly still raw for Callidus, and he seems more relieved than anything else when I let the matter drop—but just casually. A way for my friend to unwind after his taut admissions.

Soon enough, though, we're standing. Classes begin again tomorrow, and I need to sleep—need every ounce of energy I can find for this final push. Theoretically, I can be raised to Class Three at any time up until the Iudicium. But the closer it draws, the less likely it is that the Praeceptors will decide to make a change. If I'm going to advance, it needs to be soon.

Even so, I find myself ruminating on Callidus's situation as I climb the stairs to my rooms. Rueful that he could be so careless—I only didn't castigate him because I know he's punished himself more than enough already—but far more furious at Belli for putting him in such an untenable situation.

As I lie down to sleep, something occurs to me. An idea I've had for a while, but one that was too high-risk to consider. There's more at stake now, though.

Advance to Three, and help Callidus. There may be a way I can do both.

LX

I SPEND THE NEXT TWO WEEKS MULLING THE VARIOUS ASpects of my plan, trying to smooth over its roughest edges, weighing up exactly what I need to risk to make it work. By the end, though, I'm as confident in it as I can be.

But I can't do it alone.

"I have a favour to ask." I'm walking with Emissa to the Labyrinth. Wandering, really. Her arm's looped through mine.

Her eyes sparkle as she looks up at me. "Oh?"

"I think I may have a way into Class Three."

"What makes you think I'd want to help you with *that*?"

I give her a gentle bump with my hip. "Please. The lure of seeing me all day is too strong, and you know it."

She sighs dramatically. "Fine. Let's pretend I'm interested." She's still smiling, but sincerity enters her voice. "You're going to have to do some serious convincing for Scitus to get Sianus dropped down. He's been working twice as hard since hearing about you at Suus."

"Not Sianus. Belli."

Emissa slows, just for a second, clearly thrown. "I'm listening."

I outline my plan to her, keeping my voice low despite our isolation; we're almost to the Labyrinth but no one's in sight at this time of night. Emissa listens with a frown, at no point looking particularly convinced.

"That's not a good plan," she confirms once I'm done.

"It will work."

"It *might* work. *Maybe.* With some luck. And if you're actually as good as you think you are."

"It's worth the risk."

"If you say so." She stops, leans in, and kisses me gently. "But, yes. Of course I'll help."

I beam stupidly at her. "Thanks."

"When do you want to do it?"

"Tomorrow. Dinner." There's no point delaying.

"I'll be ready."

We keep walking. "There's one other thing. Belli . . ." I sigh. "Belli has something of Callidus's. I can't tell you what," I add as she opens her mouth to ask, "but I'm going to try and use this to get it back."

She studies me. "This is why you're gambling, rather than just working your way past Sianus." She says it with such a mixture of frustration and affection that I have no idea whether it's an insult or a compliment. "I hope he knows how lucky he is to have you as a friend."

I shrug awkwardly. "He'd do the same for me."

"He would," she agrees reluctantly. Definitely more affectionate than not, this time.

I grin at her, and we head down into the Labyrinth.

% % %

EMISSA AND I ARRIVE EARLY TO THE MESS THE FOLLOWING evening. There's no one else around; dinner won't be served for a good half hour yet. We take the Foundation board that usually sits on Class Three's table and bring it down one level to mine, then sit opposite each other.

"Are you sure about this?" I say quietly as we set the pieces. "She's going to know you helped."

"If you knock her out of Three, she's going to assume I had something to do with it anyway," Emissa observes cheerfully. "And Belli has always been clear on the fact that this is a competition to her. She can hardly complain when someone tries to compete."

We start to play, not with any haste or intensity, and me purposely making a few mistakes to provide Emissa with a distinct, though not overwhelming, advantage. Soon enough other students start to trickle in. The other Fourths eye Emissa in surprise, but when they see what we're doing, give polite greetings and talk among themselves. I can see them checking on the progress of the game occasionally, though—Aequa, especially. Curious to see if I can beat a Third.

It's another five minutes before Belli arrives, Iro trailing after her. Emissa and I pretend not to see them. It takes only another minute before there's movement and a small stir as Belli wanders down a level again.

She stands behind Emissa. "You took our board." Mildly irritated.

"Vis and I thought we could get in a game before everyone came. Sorry." Emissa smiles brightly across at me. "I won't be long."

I make a face at her, then move one of my red stones deliberately to the right. A reasonably smart move. Unorthodox.

There's a heartbeat when Belli balances on her toes, looking like she's going to retreat once more to the Class Three table.

Then she settles again. Studies the board.

Emissa examines my move, then responds in fairly predictable fashion. I've seen Emissa play Belli before, and she's like most of the other Thirds: she's smart, can think a few moves ahead and has a good understanding of the fundamentals of the game, but she doesn't stand a chance against anyone with real training.

I push at a red piece, lining it up with two others. I don't look at Belli but I hear her breath released through clenched teeth, as if having to physically restrain herself from castigating me over such a bad move. Which it is, I have to admit. Three moves along and Emissa will be able to break apart my pyramid entirely, cutting through my lines and weakening my force catastrophically.

I let a flash of irritation cross my face. Show her I've heard, but don't say anything. I've seen Belli watching other matches. She inevitably comments. Usually snidely. I have to wait for that.

I don't have to wait long.

Two moves later, I make another poor play. Not an obvious one, but one which will effectively finish the game in a half dozen turns if Emissa is alert to the possibility. Belli scoffs as my finger leaves the stone, shaking her head disdainfully. "I thought you said you'd played before."

Inwardly breathing a sigh of relief—if the match had ended without her provoking me, this wouldn't have worked—I glower at her. "Must be nice, thinking that beating the same five people all the time makes you an expert."

Belli flushes, more visibly stung than I would have expected. It probably doesn't help that almost all the Fourths are watching with unabashed interest, and I've slighted one of the few things she truly prides herself on. "You had your chance to play me. You said you were too scared," she says dismissively.

I let my back stiffen. Gesture to the board, trying to look offended. "Care to show everyone how good you are, then?"

"Vis." Emissa shakes her head. Visibly warning me off.

We've drawn a small crowd by this point. In the corner, Nequias and Scitus are peering over, too, though they're too far away to hear what's being said.

Belli hesitates. Her reputation in Three is built on her intelligence, and rightly or wrongly, much of that is tied to her ability in Foundation. It's a trap she's built for herself, an idea she's pushed too hard. Her constant victories are seen as incontrovertible proof that she has a superior tactical mind, that she's a stronger strategist than any of the others in the class. A loss to me would be embarrassing. Maybe even affect her standing.

"No thanks. Not worth my time," she says airily, recovering quickly. "Besides. You're already playing Emissa." She doesn't think she'll lose to me, but she's too smart to risk it.

"That's alright. I concede. She's going to win anyway." I irritably start setting the pieces back to their starting positions.

"Still not worth my time."

"You're afraid I can beat you." This baiting is something that I've been considering for a long time. The problem—the reason I haven't attempted to act on this idea much sooner—is that Belli really *is* very good. I've played since a young age, taught by some of the greatest to ever have played the game, and I *should* be able to beat her. But it's no certainty.

Belli looks like she wants to walk away, but there's a crowd now. Even if she backs out, there's enough interest to ensure that this is a competition that will happen sooner or later. "Fine." She rolls her eyes and sits huffily in the chair Emissa's just vacated. "Let's make this quick."

"Praeceptors!" Iro is beckoning over Scitus and Nequias, who have been watching but keeping their distance. "You might be interested in this. Vis and Belli are going to play Foundation."

It takes all I have not to laugh. I needed at least one of the Praeceptors to take an active interest—Emissa was going to call them over if they didn't investigate themselves—but Iro thinks I'm going to be embarrassed here.

"This will be interesting," agrees Scitus, arms crossed as he comes up to the table. "Vis, I didn't know you played."

"A little, Praeceptor."

Nequias glowers at me. "This is a waste of Belli's talent." I rarely interact with the severe, hazel-eyed man, but he's never hidden his dislike of me.

"I suppose we'll see," replies Scitus, motioning that we should continue.

Soon enough the stones are laid out in their starting pyramids, my red arrayed squarely against her white.

"You know what? We need to make this fair," says Belli, loudly enough for everyone to hear. "You can take a piece off the board. For free. I wouldn't feel right, otherwise."

There's a smattering of laughter, and I feel a flash of panic. She's taking a precaution, pre-empting any real competition by allowing herself to start at a disadvantage. It's a clever move.

I recover. Shrug, reach down, and remove one of my own pieces.

There's more laughter from the crowd, though this time a little disbelieving, as if shocked at my disregard for Belli's abilities. Nequias snorts, and even Scitus just sighs and shakes his head.

"This is *not* worth my time." Belli's face is as red as her curls. She looks as if she's about to get up and leave, despite all the attention.

"Why don't we put stakes on it, then?" I ask, flipping the red stone I've just picked up from one hand to another.

"Like what?" She sneers at me, increasingly annoyed at being forced into this contest. "What could you possibly have that would interest me?"

"I'll pledge to Governance if you win."

The chattering and laughter fades. The Praeceptors look a combination of shocked and outraged at my casual offer. Belli's eyes are wide. Even just as a Fourth, switching loyalties like this wouldn't go unnoticed by the outside world—and I'm Catenicus on top of that. It's a coup that would raise Belli's stock considerably, within Governance as well as in here.

She licks her lips. "And if you win?"

"I get your spot in Class Three. Which"—I glance over at the Praeceptors—"I feel should happen anyway, if we reach that point."

Emissa steps forward, puts her hand lightly on my shoulder. I look up to see her eyes so full of concern, I almost laugh at how well she's playing her role. Or maybe it's not feigned. I didn't mention what I was going to bet. "Don't," she says. Softly, but the gist is undoubtedly obvious to anyone who's paying attention. "She's too good."

I wave her away, maintaining my façade of irritation. Emissa gives me a frustrated look.

Belli says nothing for a long time. The crowd has swelled well beyond the Fourths, word of the contest spreading. I spot Eidhin in the back, expression unreadable. Several people call out for her to accept. She ignores them, but I can see her calculating. Weighing risk against reward. Trying to decide whether backing down now, in front of all these people and the Praeceptors, is going to hurt her chances in Class Three. I think it would, and I think she believes the same. I can see the realisation in her eyes, and then— looking at me again—the hunger. Above all, she believes she'll beat me. She thinks she can bag a prize here, strike a blow against Military that her father will be proud of.

"Alright."

There's so much in that word. It's eager and pensive and confident and confused, all at once.

I don't display anything except for vexed acceptance. That, unfortunately, was the easy part.

Now all I have to do is win.

※   ※   ※

STARTING A GAME OF FOUNDATION WITHOUT ONE OF YOUR stones isn't a death sentence, but it does rely on your opponent making at least one mistake.

Belli, from what I've seen, doesn't make *many*. The question is really whether she's truly adaptable: favourable position though it is, beginning from a stone up is unusual, and an unforeseen advantage still requires adjustment. Many of the strategies she'd try are suddenly rendered pointless. And while I'm theoretically suffering the same disadvantage, I *have* had a deal of experience at playing from a stone down. Whenever I'd play against Cari, I'd always let her take stones off the board. And she had the same tutors as me. She got quite good, toward the end.

There's a swell of emotion at the thought of my sister, and I take a moment. The Praeceptors have stepped away to argue: Nequias is vehement, Scitus calm but firm. I can imagine what Nequias is saying, and I'm glad to see that Scitus is having none of it. If I do beat Belli here, it will be nothing but infuriating if the Praeceptors don't recognise the bet.

Callidus has appeared alongside Eidhin at the back of the crowd. I make eye contact with him, see his questioning look. Shrug. He glances from Belli to me thoughtfully.

Dinner's been underway for a while, but few people are eating. That doesn't bother me. Belli, on the other hand, is clearly unsettled. She scowls constantly, her face is flushed, and she keeps glancing up at the crowd as if waiting for them to exhort her. She rubs her thumb across the nub of her missing finger between turns, as if it's cold.

It's a good sign, but Belli's not stupid, either: she knows she's distracted, and she knows I'm not. The first few moves, she takes her time, refusing to let the pressure of the onlookers get to her. I've set the stakes high, and she's not going to let anything rush her. That's fine. Distraction is still distraction. It will show itself not in the immediate moves, but in the missing of strategies later on.

Still, I struggle to keep her at bay for the first ten minutes, particularly as she becomes more confident, more aggressive. It's absolutely the right way to play from her position—attacking from all sides, trying to find the opening that inevitably comes from my inferior number of pieces. But she's predictable, too. Can be led. I've had the advantage of watching plenty of Belli's matches. I can pick her favourite moves, favourite stratagems. I give her glimpses of holes in my line, tempting her to position for an attack that will overextend her.

She doesn't take the bait the first few times, but eventually impatience—or perhaps the pressure of everyone's expectations—gets the better of her. She thinks she sees an opening. She moves in.

I've heard Foundation described as a beautiful game. That usually comes from people who don't play it, or don't play it well. It's not a dance, not a show. It's as blunt and bloody as war; you win through positioning, which allows you to maximise attrition. You don't mind losing a piece if you can take two. You don't mind losing five if you can take six.

At the end of that first exchange, I'm down eight pieces, and so is she. She missed the way the first bloodbath—where I lost one more piece than she did—would set me up to initiate the second, where I took four of hers with only two lost. When I complete the final move of the sequence, there's a low murmuring. The weight of eyes is on me rather than just the game, now.

I risk a glance up. Belli's staring at the board, but something's changed in her gaze. There's not just concentration anymore. There's fear.

She's realised she has a fight on her hands.

In the background, I can see the two Praeceptors standing together, looking on with a curiosity which is as intense as the students'. Nequias is openly dismayed, while Scitus, seeing my glance, gives me a nod. I quickly return my focus to the game, not letting anyone see my relief. Scitus wouldn't have made the gesture if Nequias hadn't conceded that they had to honour the terms of the bet.

Belli's wounded by the exchange, retreating to resupply her pieces; I do the same, ensuring that we essentially reset to equal status. The positioning's different, but we're back to the start of the match—this time, without my disadvantage.

I attack.

I'm not shy about what I'm doing, going about it like a blunt instrument, smashing my pieces against hers in ferocious equal exchanges. It's a common ploy for players who think they're outmatched, who can't handle or process the breadth of options a full board gives them. Belli knows it, too, and though there's nothing visible, she starts to make her moves with more certainty. She was thrown by the fact I managed to claw back to even, but I can almost see her deciding that there had to have been luck involved, or perhaps inattentiveness on her behalf. That I'm not capable of outplaying her consistently, not if I need to resort to this.

But again, I'm positioning myself. This was one of my tutor's favourite tactics: using seemingly random carnage to carefully organise, not allowing any respite, not allowing your opponent to do anything but react. Small skirmishes that form a master plan.

It works—works perfectly, to my surprise. Belli's playing as if from a textbook, responding to every single move in the smartest way—except for the fact that she's gradually, gradually, leaving her pieces where they will expose the heart of her pyramid. I look around again. Everyone's fascinated, but nobody's seen what's happening, as far as I can tell. Emissa looks worried. Callidus looks worried. Even Scitus has gone from approving to a thoughtful frown.

Belli's the first to spot what I'm doing, but she sees it too late. I hear her caught breath, see the way her hand hesitates and then falls as she realises what I'm about to do. There's thirty seconds of silence as she studies the board. A minute. Her face becomes more and more pale as she sees there's no way out, no sequence of events that can save her except if there's a mistake by me. Her hand starts to tremble.

I glance around and then stand and lean over, mouth to her ear, voice low. "We can still draw. If you want to renegotiate."

She doesn't look up from the board, and for a few seconds I wonder whether she's heard me. "What do you want?"

"What you took from Callidus. All of it. Right now."

She stiffens. "After."

"No. You're in no position to haggle. We take a break, you fetch it, and if he confirms it's all there, I'll settle for the draw."

Her jaw twitches beneath clenched teeth. "What's to stop you from winning anyway?"

"Nothing. But I'm one, maybe two moves from everyone realising my position. So if you don't want it to look suspicious, now's the time."

She sucks in a deep breath. "Alright."

My heart unclenches and I stand up straight, addressing the crowd. "I'm afraid my bladder's going to burst. Sorry, everyone. Back soon."

A mock groan goes around the room, the babble of voices starting as it's clear there will be a few minutes before the game resumes. Belli rises too and makes her excuses, moving swiftly to leave. I pause as I pass Callidus.

"Go with Belli. Check it's all there. Come back and let me know, either way. Then if it is, you go and secure it somewhere no one will look, then pretend you've burned it. Straight away."

Callidus's eyes go wide as he gets my meaning, but before he can respond, I'm climbing the stairs.

It's ten minutes later that Belli returns, looking composed. Callidus trails behind her. He meets my eyes. Gives me the slightest of confirmations, then disappears up the stairs again.

Good.

"It's done," Belli mutters as she sits.

I take my time after that, grabbing a plate of food, making sure Callidus has plenty of opportunity to hide the evidence. It's another few minutes before we're back at the game, and Belli's making her next move. The only one open to her. The one that splits her forces, gives me an oblique path into the heartland of her territory.

There's a shuffling from across the room and I see Scitus whispering smugly to Nequias, who's looking increasingly dismayed. The Praeceptors have spotted the opening, even if no one else has. Belli looks up at me expectantly.

I calmly move my piece, then meet her horrified gaze.

There's a murmur, soft at first, then rising, as some of the students see what's about to happen.

"What are you doing?" Belli mumbles, maintaining a façade of calm. She moves again, giving me an out.

I don't take it. "Showing you what consequences look like." I'm past her defences now. Her pyramid's broken, and I'm going to be capturing pieces for the next several turns. "Not pleasant seeing your trust betrayed, is it?"

The crowd's getting louder, exclamations of disbelief at Belli's position distinctly audible. "I can still tell them what Callidus gave me. Get them to search his belongings if I need to."

"Not anymore." Callidus has been standing at the back for the last minute, almost as if on cue. I surreptitiously indicate him; the blood drains completely from Belli's face as he waves some charred remnants of paper at her.

"They'll notice the papers are gone. If I tell Governance what's missing, they'll believe me."

"Maybe, but they sure as all hells won't let the other factions know it was true. And they won't do a gods-damned thing without evidence. Except maybe expel you from the Academy for making unfounded accusations." It was tempting to get Callidus to actually destroy the papers—it would have been simpler—but I'm not sure he would have, even if I'd asked. This way, he has a chance to put them back without anyone ever noticing they were gone.

The girl opposite me says nothing for a good long while. Then suddenly she's shaking, and then to my shock, sobbing. She reaches a trembling hand for a piece and moves it; I follow by decimating her support base on the board, steeling myself against her increasingly loud sniffs. Even if it wasn't from necessity, I wasn't lying about considering this a hard lesson.

Two moves later and Belli's standing, her choked sobs and glistening cheeks evident to everyone. "I concede." She's shoving her way through the crowd, almost sprinting for the stairs. People step out of her way, watching with undisguised shock until she's out of sight.

I don't feel particularly good about it, no matter the outcome, but I did what had to be done. I look up at Scitus and Nequias. "You heard that?"

"She resigned. You win." Scitus confirms the result before Nequias has a chance to speak. The older man scowls, but jerks his head in acknowledgment.

I meet Nequias's gaze. "Then I'll see you tomorrow morning, Praeceptor." I give a nod of thanks to Scitus, and walk off before either man can say anything further.

The crowd parts for me too as I leave, though this is less a scuttling out of the way and more a . . . reverent stepping aside. Callidus is waiting for me by the stairs, and easily falls into step as we leave.

As soon as we're up in the Curia Doctrina, he laughs out loud. A true laugh, a release, long and deep and joyful. "Gods' graves, Vis. Rotting gods. Rotting *gods.*" He curses a few more times, then slaps me dazedly on the back. "Remind me to never get on your bad side. I have no idea how I'm going to repay this."

I laugh too, his joy infectious.

"I'm sure I'll think of something," I say, returning his grin.

LXI

MY FIRST FEW WEEKS IN CLASS THREE ARE HARDER THAN I could possibly have imagined.

Given Nequias's attitude toward me since I first arrived at the Academy—and knowing about his friendship with Dultatis—I've been braced for a repeat of my time in Class Six. And from the minute I enter the class, it's clear Nequias has no small dislike for me.

Unlike Dultatis, though, Nequias doesn't focus on me. Doesn't exclude me. He treats me as he treats everyone else: with cold, unrelenting pressure, disdain when I make mistakes, anger when I'm too slow, threats when there's even a hint of me not paying attention. Gaunt old man though he is, he's a terrifying force in class. A storm, ready to thunder at any small slip.

I've had tutors like him before, but never fused with the difficulty of the subject matter. My first day, we're calculating how Causal and sub-Harmonic imbuing can be combined to reduce the amount of Will needed to operate complex machinery. Then we're moving straight on to the socio-economic ramifications of applying those potential improvements to Harvesters, theorising how it will affect the Octavii, the provinces, the stability of the Republic as a whole. Then we're running the Labyrinth for three hours, where I'm soundly beaten again and again in a dispiriting lesson of just how much I need to improve. Then we're examining reports on the pre-Cataclysm ruins of Altaris Machia, arguing over whether the Aurora Columnae found there were confirmation of whether that lost society wielded Will exactly as the Hierarchy does, or whether they had some more powerful means of doing so. And whether or not that power destroyed them, or if there was some external event that precipitated their extinction.

My eyelids are heavy by dinner, my head aching. I still run the Labyrinth with Emissa afterward, doing all I can to absorb her suggestions, hone my abilities. Knowing just how much further I need to go keeps my exhaustion at bay for an extra two hours, but after that, I have to admit defeat. My respect for Emissa—who's still, somehow, moving as though she has energy to burn—increases.

And the day after, and the day after that, are the same. On and on. A haze of concentration and effort. This is what Lanistia was preparing me for, I realise by the end of the first week. This, not any of the classes before, was why she drove me so hard, was so worried about my capacity to compete. Without those months of preparation, I would never have been able to keep up.

But I do.

Toward the end of my first month, something changes. The days start to feel more like a routine. An immensely challenging routine, still, but one I can manage. I continue to improve at the Labyrinth, the extra exercise making me even leaner, my body harder. I have enough energy to enjoy my time with Callidus and Eidhin in the mornings, with Emissa in the evenings.

In the weeks that follow, I begin to challenge the others at the Labyrinth. Feel confident that I can improve my positioning in Three in short order. There's no chance I'll overtake Indol or Emissa—those two are so far ahead of the rest of the class that it's almost comical—and Iro, loathe though I am to admit it, is probably impossible for me to eclipse before the Iudicium. But Prav and especially Sianus are within striking range, and they've been operating at this level for months now. They plateaued long ago. I'm the only one out of the six of us who's prospering.

Nequias begins to notice it, too. And though I cannot claim he has discriminated against me thus far, I still think that's why he decides to bring up the Iudicium earlier than any of us expect.

%% %% %%

SPRING'S EARLY BLUSTER IS IN FULL EFFECT OUTSIDE CLASS Three's full-length windows this morning. No rain, but wind rattles the massive shutters, and before they were closed the sea was whipped white, waves smashing against the Seawall pillars far below. The air has a bite to it that even after almost four years I still despise. This would be the sort of day we might get once every year at Suus. In the miserable south, it's been a regular occurrence for months.

The Thirds' regular room is, unsurprisingly, by far the best-situated of the classes: a view over the ocean similar to the one from the mess, comfortably large, with couches and plenty of other trappings. Emissa and I are last to arrive today. We slide into our usual seats, and I murmur a greeting to Iro and Indol nearby. They nod back, though as usual, Iro's is curt. He's tolerated me since my promotion, but makes no pretence at friendliness.

"Before we begin today." Nequias has been waiting for us to get here; he's talking before we're settled. "The Principalis and I have decided to start proceedings for the Iudicium."

My cheerful smile wilts. I look around, seeing as much surprise on the others' faces as there must be on mine. Based both on what Ulciscor told me and what the other Thirds expected, I wasn't anticipating this for another few weeks, maybe more.

"Already?" It's Indol speaking up. Calm and measured as always, but it's clearly a question.

"Yes." Nequias doesn't care to elaborate. "As of this morning, your positions in Class Three are secure, and your rankings for the Iudicium are set."

Emissa glances sympathetically in my direction. Catching up though I have been, there's no denying I'm still last within this group. From the corner of my eye, I see Sianus's burly, long-haired form relaxing, the twisting snake tattoos running down his arms flexing as he stretches.

Nequias pauses, as if waiting for protests. His gaze wanders over the class, and I feel as though it lingers on me. If he expects me to complain, though, I don't give him the satisfaction. I'm smart enough to know that nothing I say can change this decision.

"The specifics of the Iudicium will, of course, be kept secret until it begins," the Praeceptor continues eventually. "But over the next three days, you will need to choose two students from among the other classes to follow your command during it. The official current rankings of Class Four in particular are available to you, and your rankings will be made available to them. If a student receives multiple offers, they are allowed to choose whom to join. And they are also allowed to refuse entirely, if they so wish." Nequias's tone indicates he's saying the last for form, rather than because he thinks it's a real possibility. "Once you have two students who have agreed to work with you, go to the Principalis with their names. He'll instruct you from there."

Nobody talks as we process the information. The Iudicium changes from cycle to cycle; while the basics are always the same—it's held on Solivagus, necessarily unfamiliar territory to everyone, and it's a competition to complete a specific task—the details can vary wildly. Ulciscor told me that Caeror's Class Three were left by themselves in the middle of the forest, had to spend an entire week evading capture by all of Class Four and Class Five. And he said the one after that involved the Thirds each commanding a dozen students in some sort of mock wargame.

"What criteria do we use, if we don't know what we'll be doing?" It's Prav, voicing what all of us are thinking. He's an almost remarkably plain-looking boy: neither handsome nor ugly, tall nor short, imposing nor invisible. Just . . . there.

Smart, though. Quick on his feet. Not to be underestimated.

"That will be up to you. But decide quickly. We need two names from each of you by the end of three days, or you will be assigned ones. Any other questions?" Nequias waits and, taking the silence to mean there are none, moves briskly on. "Now. This morning we're going to cover refined Reactive relationships in engineering. We know from the pre-Cataclysm ruins of Serica that . . ."

I half listen for a while—reaping a tongue-lashing when Nequias catches my inattentiveness—and calculate furiously, knowing each of the others will be doing the same. The rankings are fairly clear: Indol first, Emissa second, then Iro, Prav, Sianus, and myself. There will doubtless be rewards for all members of the winning team, so the Fourths will want to join the highest-ranking Third they can. The three obvious candidates, then—Axien, Cassia, and Marcellus—are inevitably going to go to Indol or Emissa. After that, Iro might take Felix and Valentina as a pair—they're strong and capable Fourths who work well together—and Prav and Sianus will probably just pick whoever's next in the rankings.

The unknown, really, is whether anyone will consider asking Belli or Aequa.

Belli is by far the most capable student in Class Four, but the Iudicium is almost certainly going to be a physically demanding contest: while she's fit, her skills in sparring and weaponry leave a lot to be desired. Worse, since her demotion she's looked drained. Hollow. A ghost, drifting through the days. And even if the rankings say her drive has remained the same, we all know her too well to believe she'll be a good subordinate.

Whenever I see her, I tell myself that she's reaping consequences. It does little to assuage my guilt.

And then there's Aequa. Her position's suffered thanks to her mistake with me, but whether Scitus has kept his promise to keep her as the lowest-ranked student in Four, I have no idea. Luckily, I don't think the other Thirds have any clue how good she is.

"Figured out who everyone's going to ask yet?" Emissa takes advantage of Nequias's turned back to murmur the words in my ear.

"I've got some guesses."

"Are you going to take Callidus and Eidhin?"

I give her a haughty look. "Perhaps. Who can say?"

She grins. "You're so mysterious and unpredictable."

She's assumed correctly, of course; there was never a question in my mind who I'd be asking. Callidus is one of the smartest students in the Academy, while Eidhin is one of the most physically gifted—and neither is a slouch in the other's area. I cannot imagine a better combination.

But more importantly, I know them. I trust them. The idea of choosing anyone else is almost unfathomable.

Of course, there's no guarantee either of them will say yes. Callidus, despite the real reason he's in Class Seven, has maintained his concern about the Iudicium and its deadly history—expressing several times how glad he is not to be participating. Part of me thinks it's bravado, a way of making himself feel better about missing it when he's so obviously qualified. But I suspect he's truly relieved, too. The papers he took from his father are evidently conclusive enough for him to worry.

And Eidhin . . . well. Eidhin is Eidhin. Even after several months of spending hours a day with him, I still barely know him. Enough to trust him, to trust his character, but not enough to gauge his decisions.

Beside me, Emissa hesitates. Leans in close.

"Promise me something." Her tone's serious; when I look at her, she locks her gaze to mine. "Swear that this won't change anything. We compete against each other, and whatever happens, happens. But afterward, there's still *us*."

My chest tightens. Aches. The Iudicium's felt so distant, even as the pressure of its approach has been building. But once it's over, I'm gone. Either to some distant part of the Hierarchy where I don't have to cede, or fleeing, or in a Sapper.

And no matter which way it goes, Emissa can't come with me. Won't. The same way I can't stay just for her.

"Of course," I say softly. I smile at her. "Of *course*."

I hate myself, in that moment.

The rest of the day ostensibly passes as usual, but there's an edge to everything now. Any interaction between Thirds and Fourths during meals, any stray glance, seems suddenly meaningful. Not that it's hard to guess who will pick who—after reviewing the Class Four rankings and seeing Belli and Aequa toward the bottom, I'm fairly sure I already know most of the eventual participants—but the reality of the Iudicium has arrived. We're rivals who have been forced to work together for a time. That time is coming to an end.

I don't ask Emissa who her choices will be, that night, and she doesn't offer them. We don't talk about the Iudicium at all, actually.

I sleep uneasily.

※ ※ ※

THE FOLLOWING MORNING, CALLIDUS IS WAITING FOR ME when I arrive at the Labyrinth.

"I need you to help me in the Iudicium," I say without preamble as I sit next to him.

Callidus freezes. Then he slowly finishes rubbing his hands together against the cold, not lifting his gaze. "What?"

"You had to know I was going to ask."

"Oh. Of course. After everything I mentioned about all the mysterious covered-up death, I should have assumed you'd want me along."

"Right. Because of how much you love danger." I nod straight-faced at him, then slip to a rueful smile. "Look, I know it's something you'd rather avoid. But I need people I can trust."

"You need to find a way to stay out of it. Or lose quickly." He sees my face and leans forward, intense. "I mean it, Vis. It's not worth it."

I study him. He's earnest. He'd be saying the same thing, acting the same way, even if he was in my position. My heart sinks.

I'm about to respond when there's movement at the entrance, and Eidhin emerges from the stairwell. He signals a greeting to us, oblivious to his interruption.

"I'm going to ask Eidhin, too. But I have to warn him of the risks. I won't tell him where I got the information from." I say it low and fast.

Callidus makes a face, but concedes. "Of course."

I acknowledge him gratefully, then turn to our burly friend as he approaches. "Eidhin! I have something to ask you."

Eidhin stops at the pronouncement. Peers at me warily.

"I have to choose two people to join me for the Iudicium. I want you to be one of them."

"What will I have to do?"

"I don't know."

"Will there be fighting?"

"Probably? They haven't exactly been forthcoming on the details yet." I cough. "Before you give me your answer, though, you should know something. There have been . . . incidents, in the past, that Religion have covered up. Students dying. And then other students who were in the Iudicium disappearing after graduation, too. Don't ask me how I know, but it might be dangerous. Probably *will* be dangerous."

Eidhin considers me. "But you will be competing against the other Thirds."

"Yes."

"And if we win, it will improve my standing."

"Yes."

"Very well. I agree." He moves past me, sits by Callidus, and starts adjusting his boots in preparation for running the Labyrinth.

"You're sure?"

He pauses. Glares up at me. "I said I agree."

I hold up my hands in amused self-defence. "Alright. Thank you."

Eidhin looks across at Callidus. "You, too?"

"He only just asked me. I'm still thinking about it."

Eidhin gazes at him. Nods thoughtfully, and resumes what he was doing. There's no judgment, and I can see how grateful Callidus is for that.

We run the maze for a while, me with the bracer and loudly announcing each turn I make, simulating having spotters. Even with only two opponents rather than the usual three, it's hard: Eidhin and Callidus are both frustratingly quick, and judging their movements based off only sound and guesswork is beyond difficult. Theoretically they're disadvantaged, too: if they want to coordinate, they need to call out to do it. But the two of them have run so many times against me now, they've developed an unspoken understanding. An almost prescient knowledge of where each other will be, depending on how I approach the run on any given day.

I slip through twice on nine attempts this morning, sweat pouring off my body by the time the bell chimes for morning meal. I'm still breathing hard as we climb the stairs.

Eidhin, as always, disappears off to the parkland stream to bathe. Callidus and I head for the mess, but after a minute, Callidus suddenly stops. Jerks his head toward the dormitory. "Come with me. I want to show you something."

He starts walking, not waiting for a response.

Class Seven's floor is deserted at this time of day. Callidus does a quick circuit to make sure no one else is around anyway, then unscrews one of the posts of the unused bed two spaces down from his. Reaches in and extracts several rolled-up pieces of paper.

"That's where you're keeping them?" I ask worriedly, guessing immediately what they are.

"As opposed to all my other options?" He fixes me with a look. "Would you have thought to look there?"

"I suppose not." If anyone even knew the posts were hollow—and I certainly didn't—they'd be checking Callidus's bed, not the ones nearby.

"Here." Callidus hands me the documents. "Read for yourself."

I take the papers and scan through what's written. Each one is an accounting of a death that has occurred at the Academy over the past two decades. Prior to six years ago—before Veridius's year—there were only two: an accident involving an Octavii worker, and a student's suicide.

Since then, there have been eight. All of them Thirds or Fourths taking part in the Iudicium, each except for Caeror listed as accidents. Falls. Animal attacks. Drownings.

"So many?" I feel my brow furrow as I scan the list. "Rotting gods. How have they kept this quiet?"

"I told you. Silencium for the students. Bribery and self-interest for everyone else. Even for the families, I think." He folds his arms. "It's been one or two people every year. One or two out of six. Or eighteen, I suppose, if you count all the Fourths. Still. Are you really going to risk those odds?"

I don't respond for a while, studying the papers further. "And Military and Governance really know nothing of this?"

"They must know something. Promising students of theirs have gone missing, too, not just Religion's." Callidus shakes his head. "But as far as I can tell, your father is the only one who's ever stirred up trouble over it."

I hand him back the sheaf silently, letting him roll it up and slot it back into its hiding spot. I can see why he showed me. Seeing it documented like this—supposed accidents, but all so clearly linked—is different from simply being told.

"I still have to do it," I say quietly. "I still have to try. But I would never blame you if you decide not to—"

"Bah. Don't be a fool. If you're going, of course I'm coming with you." Callidus doesn't look at me as he screws the bedpost back on, sealing the papers in again. "Just had to make sure you appreciate the risk I'm taking for you." He shoots me a sideways glance. Grins.

I grin back. "Well now I know." Callidus is putting on a brave face, but he's uneasy. I don't blame him. "You're sure?"

"I'm sure."

"Thank you." I clap him on the back. "I'll let Veridius know before lunch."

The matter settled, we head back to the mess.

LXII

I T'S BEEN MONTHS SINCE I'VE BEEN IN VERIDIUS'S OFFICE. Months since I've interacted with the man, in fact. As wrong as that feels—a large part of why I'm here is to figure out what he's doing, after all—it's not as if he'd leave evidence lying around, waiting for an enterprising student to find. Not to mention that there would be Imbued alarms protecting anything valuable, impossible for me to detect until it was too late. Simply sneaking in and looking through his things was never an option.

I knock, then step through the doorway and face the blue-eyed man behind the desk as he calls me in. The view over the island on one side and the school grounds on the other is as impressive as ever. Veridius finishes writing something and then looks up, brightening as he sees who it is.

"Vis!" He gestures me to the seat opposite. "Wonderful. I've been meaning to congratulate you on your advancement to Three. As impressive a rise as any of us could have hoped for."

"Thank you, Principalis." I accept the compliment with the requisite amount of respect.

"I take it you've chosen your team for the Iudicium? Everyone else has already submitted their names."

I hide my surprise. Inevitable though the choices seemed, that was faster than I expected. "I have. Callidus Ericius and Eidhin Breac."

Veridius leans back, hands steepled. Considering. "Interesting choices. Why them? Everyone else picked from Class Four."

"Eidhin would be in Class Four if he'd been more fluent in Common when he started. And Callidus could easily be in Class Three."

"But he's not," points out Veridius. "A teammate unwilling to live up to his potential could be far worse than one who will give his all."

"I trust him." I'm firm. "I trust both of them."

Veridius watches me, then to my surprise, beams. "Good! That is good, Vis. Excellent, in fact. If there was one criteria I would suggest basing your decision on, it would be just that. *Trust*. Ericius. Breac. Excellent." He's enthusiastic as he writes down the names. "I'll be having a discussion with both of them over the next few days. If they tell you the details, it will result in their expulsion and your disqualification from the Iudicium. So don't ask them about it."

My eyebrows rise. "As you say, Principalis." I hesitate. "Sir. Am I able to ask something about the others' choices?"

"Depends on what you want to ask."

"Did anyone pick Belli?"

"Ah." He studies me. Sympathetic and not, all at once. "Yes. She'll be participating in the Iudicium. Though I would stay clear of her, during," he adds mildly.

I give a small smile. "Good advice, Principalis. Don't worry. I'll take it."

Veridius starts recording something on the paper in front of him. I take it as a dismissal. Stand to leave.

Veridius, still scribbling, raises a finger without looking up. "One more moment, if you please, Vis."

I sink back into my chair.

Veridius finishes his task. "How is your training in the Labyrinth progressing?"

"Well enough, Principalis. I'm competitive now."

"Of course. Of course. I hear you run it mornings and evenings?"

"The rest of Class Three have all had tens of hours more experience than me. I'm just trying to catch up."

"Why?"

The question throws me. "I . . ." I give a half laugh of confusion. "Because I'm behind?"

"But you're not, from what I hear. You're as good as any of them. Maybe the best of the lot, except Belli." Veridius issues the ghost of a smile. "And perhaps more saliently, you don't need to be. Your position in Class Three is set. You cannot advance and you cannot be replaced. Yet you keep practicing." It's a question.

I shrug. "It's become a habit, I suppose."

Veridius looks on the verge of pressing, but sighs instead. Shakes his head ruefully.

"Trust," he murmurs. "It's a funny thing. I don't know what your father has asked of you, but don't push yourself too hard. You're a student of the Academy. You'll have my protection, regardless of what happens over the next month."

He's fishing. And suspects, correctly, why I'm training so hard at the Labyrinth. There's a heartbeat where I'm tempted to believe his oblique offer. Desperately want to think that, just maybe, I don't have to sneak off to the dome again after all. I still have nightmares of Artemius's grisly demise at the hands of the Remnants.

But Veridius, just like everyone else, is playing his own game here. He wants whatever it is that's past the maze. And if I'm right, he's designed the entire Academy around finding students to get to it.

"Thank you, Principalis." I give him a grateful nod as I stand. "I appreciate that."

Veridius studies me, then gives me another smile. This one is vaguely sad.

"Stronger together, Vis. I'll see you in a few weeks at the Iudicium."

⁂ ⁂ ⁂

IT'S TWO DAYS LATER WHEN I FIND EIDHIN WAITING FOR ME AT the midday meal.

"Come," he says, jerking his head in the opposite direction to the mess.

I make a face. I'm starving. "Can I just—"

"No."

"Alright." Even for Eidhin, he seems brusque. Uncomfortable. Whatever he has to say must be important.

We find a secluded spot on the steps of the Curia Doctrina. The sky's grey today, as it has been for the past several. The wind's biting but there's no rain. Once we're settled, I look expectantly at Eidhin. The large boy examines the quadrum for a few seconds.

"Have you heard of *ddram cyfraith*?" he asks in Cymrian. He rarely talks in his native language now.

"The . . . Right to Death?" My brow furrows. "No."

"It is a code that honours death as a sacrifice. That sees living past one's time as a disgrace. It is the code by which my tribe lives. Lived." He pauses at the correction. Exhales. "It is not as opposed to Birthright as it sounds, but it is certainly not in harmony with it. The Hierarchy value life, but they do not respect it. *Ddram cyfraith* does. I was raised to know how to kill, and taught when it was necessary. We avoided the attention of the Hierarchy because we lived in the mountains, our villages inaccessible for most of the year. We were self-sufficient. Even though the Catenans had conquered Cymr, they didn't pay us much attention. We thought we were safe. Ignored." His words, native though they are, are halting. This isn't easy for him to relay. "Almost three years ago, that changed. The Hierarchy attacked. No warning, no attempt to negotiate."

I don't say anything. That part is achingly familiar.

"They took us by surprise, but we fought. Killed enough of them that they were forced to retreat, regroup. But they caught some of us. Myself included." The weight to those last two words is immense. "Most of my people accepted that they were in a fight they could not win. Rather than submit, they chose the honourable path and committed themselves to dust."

I open my mouth to ask him what that means, then close it again. It's fairly obvious.

"But my father didn't." Bitterness, thick and angry. "He and a number of others betrayed our orders. And then he struck a deal. In exchange for being made a Quintus—and our new leader—everyone else would live. And I would spend a year in a Sapper."

I look at him, horrified. "Your father negotiated to put you in a Sapper?"

"He negotiated to lessen my sentence. They put me in a Sapper because I killed three Praetorians before they took me."

"Oh. Of course. Well, that's . . . hm."

"When they woke me, my father told me what he'd done. Told me of his cowardice." Eidhin's lip curls. "He said that if I did not attend the Academy, and then serve under him after I graduated, we would all be placed in Sappers. Me, him, and the remainder of our people."

There's silence.

"That's . . . a heavy burden." I'm not sure I can understand, not fully—in his father's position, I would have done the same—but there's no denying the pain in Eidhin's words. The betrayal and self-loathing. He's trapped here. More like me than I realised.

Still, these revelations aren't on a whim. "Why are you telling me this?"

"Because I want you to understand that I hate them just as much as you do." Eidhin speaks quietly as he looks at me, daring me to protest. I don't. "I want you to know that you are my friend. That you have my full trust."

"Of course," I say carefully. "And you have mine."

"No, I don't." Eidhin is reproving. Not angry, not hurt. Just knowing. "But that is alright." He takes a deep breath. "I cannot join you in the Iudicium."

I stiffen. Taken aback. "Why not?"

"I cannot say. If I do, I risk both of us being expelled." He meets my gaze firmly. "You *are* my friend, Vis. But there are more important things in life. If I were to go with you, you would not be able to trust me. And so I cannot go with you."

There's a sick, sinking feeling in the pit of my stomach. I'm bursting to probe, to understand, but Eidhin is being as open with me as he has ever been. He wants me to know it's not because of anything I've done, nothing to do with our relationship. But he's not going to budge.

"Alright." I exhale, clearing my head. "I'm disappointed, of course, but I'm sure you have a good reason."

Eidhin relaxes, just a touch. Nods appreciatively. "Who will you ask to replace me?"

I consider for a long few seconds before replying, though I already know the answer.

"That," I admit, "is going to be a very interesting conversation."

%, %, %,

AEQUA STARES AT ME AS WE STAND OUTSIDE THE GIRLS' DORMI-tory, well-lit beneath the three lanterns that guard its entrance. "You want me to *what?*"

"Be part of my team for the Iudicium," I repeat patiently.

She continues to look at me as if I've gone mad. Which, admittedly, perhaps I have. "Me," she says flatly.

"You're the best in Class Four by a long way."

"Clearly not."

"You made a mistake, thinking I was cheating. But I understand why you did. And if you went about trying to prove it too . . . vigorously . . . then, well, you wanted to win. It's a quality I can use. And I *know* you want the chance to improve your standing."

Aequa finally looks away, forehead crinkled. She shakes her head. "But why risk it? What makes you think I won't go out of my way to sabotage you instead of help you? Why would you give me a chance like that?"

"Honestly? Because you apologised."

She gives me a blank look, then guffaws. "Because I said I was *sorry?*"

"Because I think you meant it. You didn't get anything out of saying it, couldn't have possibly thought it was to your advantage. I believed you." I squint at her. "Was I wrong?"

"No," she says slowly, laughter fading to vaguely amused puzzlement. "It was arrogant to think you were cheating, and even if you had been, I should never have tried to expose you that way. It was dangerous and petty. I'm still horrified, when I think about it."

"Perfect." I grin at her sour expression. "You see? It's a chance at redemption. Help me win, and we're even. *And* you get to benefit."

She chews her lip. "Hard to argue with that."

"Then it's settled. Let's go and tell Veridius."

"Now?"

"If that's alright." I'm not going to wait another few nervous days only to find out that Aequa's changed her mind, too.

We start walking toward Veridius's office.

"So. How many people did you ask before me?"

"Just one."

"Huh." She clearly thought it would be more. "Who?"

"Eidhin, from Six."

"Why did he say no?"

"If you ever find out the answer, let me know."

We reach the quadrum and head up to Veridius's office. He's there, thankfully. I explain the situation.

"Ah." Veridius nods to himself. "Disappointing, that young Breac turned you down. But I understand. Don't blame him," he adds quietly to me. Then he motions to Aequa. "Take a seat, then. We need to have a talk. Vis, you can wait downstairs if you wish. This won't take long."

I retreat; sure enough, Aequa is coming back down the stairs less than ten minutes later. She looks shaken.

"Are you alright?" I join her as she heads for the exit.

"Yes. Yes, fine." She manages a wan smile.

"And you're still coming with me?"

She confirms it slowly. "I can't tell you anything about what Veridius just said, though."

"I know." Relief floods through me. If Aequa had turned me down, I'm not sure who my next choice would have been. "Eidhin, Callidus, and I have been practicing in the Labyrinth every morning, about an hour before eating. Perhaps . . ."

"I'll be there." She seems to have recovered herself a bit now. "And thank you. For giving me another chance."

We part ways, and I return to my room. Tired though I am, it's a long time before I can sleep. It's only three weeks until the Iudicium, but I've finally got everything in place.

Now all I can do is run the Labyrinth as often as I can, and wait.

LXIII

THE MORNING OF THE IUDICIUM, I'M AWAKE HOURS BEFORE dawn. The cold void of night still waits outside; I can faintly hear the sounds of crashing waves on the distant shore, intermixed with the soft sigh of the breeze that brings it. My mind is full of plans and worries. I'm constantly revisiting ideas for how to approach the next few days, trying to decide whether they're good. Adequate. Flawed.

Eventually, though, the lightening of the sky outside is noticeable enough that I stretch and emerge from the warmth of my bed, dressing with overly careful motions. Dreading what's to come, if I'm being honest. Even if the dome didn't await, the stakes would be painfully high. As it is, when I allow myself to stop and think about the consequences of failure, I can barely breathe.

Indol, Sianus, and Prav emerge from their rooms at the same time as me; unlike most days, we do little more than exchange polite, slightly stiff greetings before heading to the quadrum. There's no small talk, no excited chatter.

We're among the first to arrive, giving muted salutations to Praeceptor Nequias and Praeceptor Scitus before standing patiently, a little apart from one another. There's about ten minutes of waiting in the chill as people drift in. Teams gather; soon there's a low murmuring as hushed discussions begin. Aequa and Callidus appear at almost the same time, a few minutes after me.

"It's cold," Callidus grumbles softly as he sidles up to me, rubbing his arms vigorously and glancing sideways over at the other groups.

"So manly," says Aequa as she casually bumps my shoulder with hers in greeting, hands carefully bundled beneath her cloak. The weeks of training with Callidus, Eidhin, and I have made her comfortable with us to the point of, to my vague surprise, friendliness. "Did you sleep?"

"Like a lamb."

"Liar," they both murmur in unison. All three of us smile. Nervousness falling away just a little.

Soon enough all eighteen of us are present, Prav rolling his eyes at Tem as the boy stumbles blearily into the quadrum last. The teams are mostly as I expected: Indol stands alongside Axien and Cassia, Emissa with Marcellus and Titus, Prav next to Valentina and Tem. Iro is the one who selected Belli, it turns out. The red-headed girl is talking quietly to Felix, her other teammate. She's seemed more alive over the past few weeks. This morning especially, she looks as sharp as she ever did. Focused.

Finally there's Sianus, who's taken Ava and Lucius. Somewhat unpredictable choices, given their families are all from different senatorial pyramids, but the two Fourths have always been friendly. They'll work well together.

"We're all here?" It's Veridius. He's at the top of the stairs to Jovan's temple, his voice echoing across the icy stillness of the quadrum and cutting through any vestiges of conversation. "Firstly—congratulations to all of you. Simply by being here, you've proven yourselves to be among the elite of Caten. You will be leaders in the Republic. I expect I'll be reporting to some of you before long." He smiles, and there's a murmur of polite laughter.

"But before any of that, we need to determine your final rankings." He gazes out over us. "The Academy isn't just about telling you how to use Will; it is meant to prepare you for the experience of wielding it. And that means leadership. Will is ceded, but that does not always mean it is cheerfully given. Pyramids are not built on friendships. We are stronger together, but every block in a pyramid is still an individual. One with its own opinions. Its own goals and desires. Loyalty is only given to those who can convince the ones lifting them up that they will succeed."

I can see a few faces frowning. Emissa and I exchange glances. Veridius continues, "There is a single Will-imbued object being guarded by two Sextii somewhere on the island. The Heart of Jovan." He draws our attention to the life-sized statue that adorns the entrance to the temple. After a moment, I see what he's referring to. A triangular-shaped hole where the golden symbol of the Hierarchy used to be, on the left side of Jovan's chest.

Some shuffling of feet. None of the others had noticed it was missing, either.

"The victor of the Iudicium this year will obtain the Heart, get back here, and return it to Jovan. If that student is from Class Three, they will become Domitor. And those on their team will be ranked at the top of Class Four, and rewarded accordingly."

There's a pause, a breath, as I and the rest of Class Three process the statement. Callidus and Aequa are looking at the ground. None of the other Fourths seem surprised, either.

"And if one of our team replaces the Heart instead?" Indol asks the question we're all wondering.

"Then they are the victor of the Iudicium. They receive a reward which they have been privately offered. And the Class Three rankings are determined by other means, which I will explain when we arrive."

There's another silence, this one longer. My stomach twists as I try to reason against my sudden nerves, my urge to start second-guessing Callidus and, in particular, Aequa. I can see the other Thirds doing the same. Unconsciously leaning away from their teammates. Eyeing them. Assessing them.

"Rotting gods," I hear Iro mutter under his breath. I glance across at him, and our gazes meet. A wryness to his glare. A shared frustration. Maybe the strongest connection I've had with him.

"A boat is waiting to take us to the other side of Solivagus. All of you, follow me," finishes Veridius.

We start walking, trailing after the Principalis. Callidus and Aequa fall into step beside me.

"You don't have to worry about me," says Callidus quietly.

"Or me," adds Aequa, giving the boy a glare for not including her.

"We couldn't say anything." Callidus is apologetic.

"I know." I give each of them a long, searching look, then exhale. "I know."

Inwardly, I'm still uneasy. Callidus, I trust as much as I trust anyone. Aequa, though . . . I wonder now if I made the right choice. Even her newfound friendliness of the past few weeks suddenly seems suspicious. But showing any of that won't help.

We trail mutely after Veridius.

%% %% %%

THE NEXT TWO HOURS PASS IN HUSHED DISCOMFORT.

Veridius takes us down to a sheltered cove via a Will elevator in the Praeceptor's quarters; once there, we board the waiting boat and begin the journey around the island. It's unbearably tense, too crowded for any private conversation. Dawn shimmers on the horizon, though its first rays are hidden behind a thick bank of clouds. The wind whips violently, cutting through my cloak. Several of the others shift uneasily at the choppy motion of the waves. Belli's confidence is temporarily lost to nausea.

As the northern tip of Solivagus comes into view, Veridius starts moving among us, silently handing out satchels. I open mine and peer inside. There's spare clothes. Rope. Rations enough for several days.

Scitus hugs the shoreline, the boat's hull scraping sand as the sun finally creeps from behind the clouds. Another Will elevator carries us up the sheer northern cliff face, onto a small, open plateau before the trees begin. I shuffle as I spot a dozen men and women grouped together at the forest's edge. They look lean, hard. Each one wears a deep green cloak.

Once we're assembled, Veridius signals to Nequias, who tosses him a small sack.

"Each of you in Class Three will receive one of these." He pours out its contents. There's a white stone triangle framed in gold, with a cord attached to it. Alongside it in Veridius's palm are six stone spheres, all different colours, as well as a much smaller black bead about the size of a pea. He holds up the medallion first. "Don't lose this, and don't break it. While the Iudicium is underway, this is your life. You won't be allowed to replace the Heart of Jovan without it."

Nobody says anything as we process the implications. Veridius hasn't said it outright, but it's immediately clear that if we're able to take another Third's medallion, or smash it, we'll eliminate them from the contest.

Veridius waits to make sure we all understand, then holds up one of the coloured stones next. "These track either one of the other medallions, or the Heart of Jovan. Indol, as our top-ranked student, gets all six. Emissa, as second, will get five— everyone's except Indol's. Iro will get four, and so on."

"Rotting gods," mutters Callidus, and I have to agree with him. Everyone's going to be able to track us, and we will be able to track nothing except the Heart itself.

Then Veridius displays the last, significantly smaller black bead.

"These are for your safety. You'll need to swallow them." He holds up his hand as a discomforted murmur goes around from the Thirds. "They will pass through your bodies after a few days without harm. But in the meantime, we need to ensure we've taken every precaution. There are alupi in these forests. Venomous snakes. Deep ravines. So we have decided that each of you will have two Sextii assigned to tracking you. You won't see them unless they're needed, but they'll never be more than a quarter hour away." He indicates the group standing at the forest's edge.

"How will they know if we need them?" asks Sianus.

"Smash your medallion. Or leave it behind." Veridius says it matter-of-factly. "It's paired with this internal tracker; if the one in your stomach gets too far from its sister medallion, it will alert every single safety team. One of them will come to collect you."

Emissa shifts. "So we'd be out of the contest, in that situation?"

"Yes. If a safety team has to come and get you, then you go back to the Academy with them. No exceptions."

"Will we know when that happens to someone else?" It's Prav.

"Only if the medallion's broken. The safety teams will go after the internal trackers, nothing else."

Silence as we all calculate. So if a Third is eliminated by having their medallion taken, there won't be any indication for the rest of us. Those stolen medallions could easily be used as decoys. Snares.

"What about us?" asks Axien, indicating everyone not in Class Three with a vague wave.

"You'll have medallions that the safety teams can track, too." Veridius produces another stone triangle with cord attached, this one black and framed in silver. "If you place it against a Class Three medallion"—he demonstrates; there's a strange warping in the air around the two pieces of stone as they touch—"then they become linked, to the exclusion of all other connections. If a Third wins, any Fourth who is linked to them shares in the victory. And if a Fourth wants to replace the Heart of Jovan themselves, their medallion still needs to be linked to the medallion of a Third. Otherwise it won't count."

Another silence, this one strained. So the Fourths can switch teams. Or they can steal their Third's medallion to win on their own.

My mind races as I process the rules. We're disadvantaged—something I expected—but it's not impossible. These rules are going to sow a lot of doubt among the others. No wonder Veridius recommended picking people I trust.

"If one of our teammates returns the Heart," I say suddenly, "how are the final positions in Class Three determined?"

"If you're eliminated, you'll move below anyone not already eliminated in Three. Otherwise, the order remains as it is presently."

I can see a flicker of worry cross Indol's face at that news. Good. As long as he survives to the end, his position won't change if one of his Fourths is the winner. That's surely going to create some extra tension between Axien and Cassia.

"As far as boundaries for the contest go," continues Veridius, seeing no one has a follow-up, "there are two major rivers that divide the centre of the island from its east and west. None of you are to cross them. If you do, you'll be immediately eliminated."

Expected though it is, that still hurts. The dome is on the west side of the island.

Veridius points to the south. "Also, anyone within three miles of the Academy's grounds is considered to have finished the Iudicium. So don't think you can simply head back to the entrance and wait for one of the other teams to bring you the Heart." He glances at the sun. "You all have until sunset on the third day. If the Heart of Jovan isn't returned by then, then there's no winner, and only eliminations affect rankings."

I swallow. That's not much time to do what I need to do out here.

Veridius looks across at Scitus and Nequias. "Anything else I'm forgetting?"

"They shouldn't kill one another?" suggests Scitus cheerfully.

"Ah." Veridius chuckles. "What the Praeceptor means, is that you need to be mindful of your actions out here. Show restraint. We'll know when two teams run into one another." He sighs, as if regretful the reminder's even necessary. "Any other questions? If you have them, now is the time."

Nobody speaks.

Nequias begins handing out medallions, starting with Indol's team. Veridius joins him, giving Indol one of the small black beads and watching intently as he swallows it. The Principalis makes him open his mouth afterward, going so far as to look under his tongue. Then he hangs the paired white medallion around Indol's neck, murmurs a few words in his ear, and signals for him to leave.

Indol starts moving, trailed by Cassia and Axien. They reach the edge of the forest, but then Indol stops. Turns.

"Fourths!" The Praeceptors and Veridius pause, and we all turn our attention to the tall, dark Catenan. "You all know I have the advantage here. Anyone who wants to join the winning team, can. One of us will be waiting a mile or so to the north of the Heart of Jovan until dawn tomorrow. All you have to do is turn up with your Third's medallion." His gaze sweeps over us. "I'm the only one who doesn't benefit from replacing the Heart myself. Don't forget that."

He delays to ensure his words have registered, then vanishes into the trees. Two of the Sextii at the edge of the forest stir; I can see them peering at what looks like a thin stone circle, almost a foot across. They don't move, though.

Emissa gives me an uneasy look. I grimace back. Smart, on Indol's part. Frustrating for the rest of us. I can see Scitus glancing over at Veridius; the Principalis just shrugs. Not against the rules, clearly.

Nequias and Veridius keep moving in order of rank, handing out medallions and trackers, Veridius fastidiously checking the small ones are swallowed by the Thirds before letting them break off into the forest. Emissa gives me a final smile before she disappears. I take note of her direction, and the directions of the others, though I doubt any of them will maintain them for long. I can also see that the Principalis is deliberately taking his time. I open my knapsack and chew a little bread while we wait.

"You think we need to worry about an ambush?" It's Aequa, voice low despite no one being close.

Callidus shakes his head before I can answer. "We're not worth the risk. Not this early."

"I doubt it too," I agree between mouthfuls, "but it might still be tempting. Not being able to track anyone makes us not much of a threat, but also the most vulnerable. And I'm the only one guaranteed to displace everyone if I win." I see his dubious expression and grin. "You're right. It's a bad move. But you have to remember to account for other people's stupidity."

Callidus snorts, but accedes the point. "So how do we go about this?"

"We can't expect to eliminate everyone, so we obviously have to go after the Heart. But we *will* get ambushed if we head for it directly." I chew. "We go around. Try and stay out of it for the first day, day and a half. Hope that some of the others get knocked out. Play it by ear." It's not much of a plan as far as the Iudicium goes, I acknowledge to myself. But my first goal is to get to the dome.

Sianus, Ava, and Lucius finally disappear into the thick undergrowth, and Nequias and Veridius walk over to us. It's been about twenty minutes since Indol first left. Several of the Sextii pairs have disappeared into the forest now, too, examining those circular plates as they go. It must be how they're tracking us.

"How are you feeling?" asks Veridius quietly as he hands me the small black bead, along with a water skin.

"Nervous." I put it in my mouth without hesitation and swallow, allowing Veridius to examine beneath my tongue afterward.

"Well. At least you're honest." He hesitates. "Be very careful out there."

I look at him blankly.

He sighs. "You know your family history here. And your uncle wasn't the only one. Students have died in the Iudicium. Taking it too seriously, risking their lives to win. You need to keep perspective. No matter what happens, you're going to graduate in Class Three. You're going to be given incredible opportunities in the Republic. Compete hard, Vis, but remember that there's nothing out here worth dying for."

I almost laugh. Ulciscor will see me in a Sapper if I don't run the Labyrinth. I'll either be ceding in Caten or on the run if I don't win the Iudicium.

Taking it less seriously doesn't feel like sound advice, at present.

"Thank you, Principalis." I let him hang the paired white medallion around my neck. "I'll remember that."

He hands me a gold-painted spherical stone, no wider than my thumbnail. It pulls almost directly to the south as I cup it in my palm. "Don't lose it," says Veridius dryly. He grips me briefly on the shoulder. "Luck, Vis."

Nequias has finished giving Aequa and Callidus their medallions. I nod to the Praeceptors, and then gesture to my teammates.

We head into the forest.

"You're taking us very *west*," observes Aequa, a little uneasily, about two minutes after the Praeceptors and the remaining Sextii are replaced by underbrush behind us.

The forest is thick, branches clawing across the narrow trail—more of an animal track—that we're following. It's a chilly spring morning and the leaves are damp when we push them from our path, frost only now fading from the grass, most clearings we come across still dusted in slippery white. There's a stillness to everything, no wind, only faint birdcalls snatching at the edges of the hush.

"If anyone's planning on ambushing us, we need to make them chase us—we're best to get close to the western boundary, well out of anyone's way. It will take a little longer, but none of the others will try to get the Heart without scouting where it's being kept. We have time."

"It's a risk. Puts us behind," observes Callidus.

"We're starting at a disadvantage. We need to take risks."

I forge ahead, not waiting for a response, trying not to show how desperate I am for Aequa and Callidus to just accept our direction.

We walk for about ten minutes, and then I hold up a hand, bringing us to a stop by a stream.

"What is it?" Callidus frowns at me. "We can't delay if we're going this way."

"I have to get this tracker out of me."

Their expressions turn from confusion to distaste as they realise what I'm saying. "Why?" asks Callidus. "It's just for safety. The others can't use it to see where we are."

"It means we can keep the medallion and the tracker together, even if I'm not there. We can misdirect the other teams."

Aequa and Callidus look at each other. "We'll wait over here."

I spend the next five minutes awkwardly jamming a finger down my throat and retching. The bread I ate earlier helps; I'm not sure the small stone would have come out, but the half-masticated chunks of white force it up. I give a racking cough, wiping acidic spittle from my mouth, as I pluck the black bead from the ground and wash it, and myself, in the clear running water. Then I spit for a minute before taking a long drink.

"Done?" asks Callidus wryly as I rejoin him and Aequa.

I hold up the bead in weary triumph, then tuck it into the pocket of my cloak.

We walk on for another hour before pausing to rest, quietly arguing our best course of action for much of the time. Without a way to know what the other groups are doing, we're all but blind. Callidus is of the opinion that we should be staking out the Heart, risking an ambush in the hopes that we can make use of the chaos that's

sure to erupt once someone tries to take it. Aequa maintains that we're better off circling completely around, positioning ourselves on high ground somewhere between the
Heart and the Academy. That way we can move when it moves, pick our terrain, lay
our own ambush.

I listen to both arguments, but neither of them feel like good options. I occasionally check the golden tracker for the Heart, but it continues to point solidly toward
the middle of Solivagus. It's not terribly accurate, though: it only shows direction, not
distance. And as long as we're moving, it will be difficult to assess whether the Heart is
moving as well. Especially if it's a long way away.

"We can't win like this," I say suddenly, interrupting Callidus.

"Inspiring," observes Aequa.

"I'm not saying we can't win. I'm saying we need to improve our situation before
we try anything else." I rub my forehead. "Did either of you see those stone circles the
Sextii had?"

They both nod. Then pause. Then frown.

"Vis . . ." Callidus says slowly. "No."

Aequa opens her mouth to agree, but instead her eyes go wide. There's a crashing
of foliage from my left. Callidus yells something incomprehensible. I flinch, on instinct
twisting and raising my arm; something hard and heavy crunches into it, sending a
shiver of agony ricocheting through to my shoulder. I howl in shock and pain and
wrench away, only able to glimpse the threatening dark shape bearing down at me from
the trees before I'm being tackled to the ground, the air knocked out of me. I gasp but
to no avail, too dazed to fend off the next blow as it connects squarely with the side
of my head. Or the next.

There's more shouting, vague and panicked and furious. It soon fades, along with
everything else.

LXIV

WAKING ISN'T A PLEASANT EXPERIENCE. THE FIRST THING I'm aware of is the throbbing of my head, followed swiftly by the duller but no less painful ache in my arm. I'm propped up against something hard and coarse. There are bindings both holding my wrists behind my back, and pulled painfully tight around my stomach. I assume I'm trussed to a tree.

I don't open my eyes, but the change in my breathing must give me away, because there's a rustling as someone nearby stirs. "Belli. He's awake."

A crunching of footsteps, getting louder. No point pretending; I open my eyes, squinting against the sting of what looks like noon filtering into the clearing. A dark shape looms over me. "Welcome back."

"Thanks." I surreptitiously test the knots that secure me. Too much to hope that they weren't tight, unfortunately. "Where are the others?"

"We're here." It's Callidus, off to the right somewhere behind me. Close.

Belli is smug as my vision finally clears. Iro's off to the side, arms crossed. I'm not sure where Felix is.

The red-headed girl sighs, looking disappointed. "I thought this would be harder, to be honest, Vis. Everyone's been going on and *on* about how good you are. Catenicus. Seven to Three in less than a year." She shakes her head disdainfully. "And now you've been eliminated less than six hours into the Iudicium."

My heart skips a beat and I glance down at my medallion. Still there. Still in one piece. "How did you get ahead of us?" My voice is steady, thankfully, and ignoring her gloating seems best. I should have known Iro and Belli would come after me. But they haven't eliminated me yet—not properly. There must be a reason. Something they want from me.

"Does it matter?" Belli crouches, bringing herself to my eye level. "All you really need to know is that you were outplayed." Behind her there's a low, ugly chuckle from Iro.

"You hit me in the back of the head. Outplayed indeed," I say dryly. "Still sore about losing at Foundation, I take it?"

I regret the words as soon as they're out of my mouth. Belli's expression darkens. She straightens, draws back her boot, and kicks me square in the face.

Pain explodes across my cheek and everything briefly goes dim; I can hear outraged yelling from Callidus and a couple of other urgent voices, but I can't focus on what any of them are saying. My head lolls, and then I suck in a breath and pull myself upright again. Spit blood. It was vicious, but not full force. No worse than taking a hit in the Theatre. I don't think anything's broken.

I take a few more breaths, both to steady myself and to cool my fury. Then I look up at the two of them again. Iro's yanked Belli away, holding her back as she glares at me, but she's not struggling, and she definitely pulled her kick. Despise me or not, they've remembered Veridius's warning. They still want to win.

"So. You haven't taken my medallion yet, which means you think I might be of some use. How can I help?"

Iro sneers. "Don't get the wrong idea. We've only just finished tying you up. I just needed to make sure we were ready to leave before bringing the Sextii here."

I'm still trying to fully extract myself from the torpor of multiple hits to the head. "I know you want to win. I'm more valuable to you as an ally. Together we can cover more ground, take out the other teams. You may not trust me but if you go it alone, you have to know that Indol or Emissa will win anyway."

"He's right," calls Callidus.

"He's half right," counters Iro. "We need more people. But we don't need *him*."

There's silence as Iro looks behind me. I twist to see Callidus and Aequa. Felix is standing a small distance away from them, watching. Callidus is smirking and shaking his head. "I don't think so. Not without Vis."

Belli ignores him, gaze fixed on Aequa. "That's fine."

Callidus frowns and turns to the girl across from him. I watch her too. She's locked gazes with Belli, and I can see the wheels in her head turning.

"She's not going to let you go, Vis, no matter what." Her voice is soft. She doesn't look at me. "And I don't want to lose. I *can't* lose."

"Aequa." Callidus's expression is growing indignant.

"Smart choice." Iro walks over, crouching down. Apparently whatever anger he has toward me over the naumachia, doesn't extend to Aequa. I'm fuming, but say nothing. She's right. I'm in no position to win.

A small part of me still hopes that this is part of some plan of Aequa's, but that's dashed as she leans forward, exposing the back of her neck. "Take it."

Callidus bucks futilely against his restraints, looking at Aequa darkly. I hang my head, feeling more melancholy than anything else. I've misestimated. I thought she would feel some obligation to me, thought she had more loyalty in her than this. But I can't bring myself to blame her. In her position, I may very well have done the same thing.

Felix unloops her medallion and gives it to Iro, who presses it against his own. There's that strange warping in the air, a bubble of distortion, gone in an instant. "Done." He hangs the medallion back around Aequa's neck, then considers her. "I'll untie you once we destroy Vis's medallion."

"Don't do that." Aequa gives him a reproving frown. "We can eliminate him just by taking the medallion with us, and then the others won't know he's out of the Iudicium. They'll have to at least consider the possibility that we've temporarily teamed up."

Iro reflects, then glances at Belli, who signals her agreement.

"We'll have to keep you tied up for the next hour or so. Until we can be sure the Sextii have come to collect him."

"Of course."

Belli helps Aequa to her feet, retying her hands in front of her. "We should get moving."

"Let's take their cloaks, too," says Aequa. "The nights will get cold, and they won't be needing them."

More cursing, even more vulgar than before, from Callidus, and this time I join him in the vitriol as Felix strips our cloaks. But it's mostly to hide a glimmer of hope.

"And their supplies?" asks Felix.

"No point," says Iro. "We have more than enough, and Aequa won't be able to carry much while she's tied up like this."

Belli walks across to me. I resist the instinct to shy away as she leans down, instead letting my gaze bore into her. She meets it, snagging the cord around my neck and yanking sharply. The skin on my neck burns. There's a snap, and then the cool white stone is being pulled from beneath my tunic.

"You lose," she says softly.

She pockets the medallion and the four of them walk off, ignoring the furious railing that Callidus aims at their backs.

% % %

IT'S HUSHED IN THE DARK AS WE WAIT. THERE'S THE CONSTANT, gentle rustling of branches in the wind, which is too cold for my tunic alone to fight. The occasional scrabbling of nocturnal animals nearby as they catch our scent and bolt in the other direction. The flapping of wings overhead, though rarely any birdcalls. Callidus's steady breathing from the tree six feet away. And nothing else.

"Still awake?" My voice splits the air, rough from lack of water and overuse.

"I doubt I'll sleep until she gets back."

I've been working at my bonds constantly since Iro, Belli, Felix, and Aequa left. My wrists are chafed raw, painful to move now, and I'm pretty sure the sticky slickness covering my palms isn't sweat. I still occasionally let frustration get to me, strain vainly against the thick rope, try and yank my hands apart or through the loop. It never results in anything except a dull ache.

"She's not coming back, Callidus."

We talked for hours after the others left. Debated Aequa's plan, mostly. There's no doubt she took my cloak to ensure the Sextii wouldn't come for us; she knew the tracker I'd swallowed was secreted away in there. At the start, I shared Callidus's optimism. Even came up with a plan. I didn't believe she would just leave us here—it's hardly a death sentence, as someone will eventually wonder why Callidus's medallion isn't moving, but it seemed unnecessarily cruel.

After a few hours, though, I knew the truth. She's intending to use my tracker as a weapon, a means of sabotage, drawing our safety team to someone else instead of us. Executed at the right moment, it could be the advantage that leads to her winning the Iudicium.

Callidus didn't want to entertain the possibility. Still doesn't. But as our conversation has petered out, leaving us with nothing but encroaching night, I think he's more and more come around to my point of view.

"What do you think Veridius offered her?" Callidus asks the question idly.

"Must have been something big."

He grunts. "It shouldn't have mattered."

I smile affectionately into the darkness. "You could have gone with her, you know. I would have understood."

"And put up with Belli for three days?" Callidus forces some humour into his tone, deflecting the suggestion. "Gods' graves, no."

I chuckle, glad of the brief levity. Glad of Callidus's company, too, even if I'm responsible for his plight.

There's quiet again, and then I have to ask. "What did they offer you?"

Callidus takes his time replying. "Domitor."

"What?" I shake my head, sure I've misheard. "*What?*"

Callidus chuckles. "My reaction too when the Principalis told me, word for word. He said that if I was on the winning team, I'd graduate as part of Class Four. And if I brought the Heart back myself . . ." I can almost hear his shrug. He's embarrassed.

"Rotting *gods*. High stakes." I'm struck by the enormity of Callidus's decision. "You're a better friend than I deserve."

"Not really. I just figured not causing any trouble was the fastest way back to the Academy."

There's a pause, and then I cough a genuine laugh. I can hear Callidus joining in. I lean back, resting my head against the coarse bark, and peer upward through the leafy canopy at the diffuse starlight that occasionally peeks through. "You really don't care about where you end up after all this, do you?"

"I care. I just think there are more important things."

I keep smiling at the sky. I'm terrified of what's coming, but there's a simplicity to the answer that's somehow comforting. "You really still think she's coming back?"

"An hour tied up. A decent while before they let their guard down. She might even be waiting until they're asleep." There's a sort of desperate resolve in his voice. He hates the thought of Aequa betraying us. "She's our friend, Vis. These past few weeks have meant something."

"I envy you, you know. Your capacity to do that. To trust like that."

There's a silence, then he snorts. "For a second, I thought that was going to be a compliment."

"I mean it." I'm reflective. I know we've lost, have known for hours now. It's left me introspective. "I'm not just talking about Aequa. I mean things like telling me about Belli, about why you're really in Seven. I mean how you chose to warn me about the Iudicium, even after it burned you so badly last time." I lick cracked lips. "Gods' graves, Callidus. You showed me where you hid the documents. You did it like it was *nothing*."

He chuckles, a little uncomfortably. "Well, I trust *you*."

"I'm not sure I'm worthy of it."

Another silence. "I know you won't tell anyone." He's bemused. "Are you alright?"

I squeeze my eyes closed in frustration, the act barely making a difference against the near pitch-black.

I want to tell him. I don't think he would turn me in. I think Callidus would take my secret to his grave.

"I'm tired," I eventually say softly, cursing myself for my cowardice. At least it's true. I'm tired of lying. Tired of fighting. Tired of being afraid. "And thanks. You're right, of course. I'd never tell anyone."

Nothing for a while, only the wind whispering through the trees touching my ears.

"Why do you think they do this?" Callidus asks suddenly.

"Do what?"

"This. The Iudicium. Pit us against one another while no one's looking. Bring us down to this level." There's a note of bitterness. "It's not exactly the culmination of all we've learned at the Academy."

"I don't think it's supposed to be. I think it's meant to be the final lesson." I say it with cynical certainty. "This is the real world. They're looking for people to lead, and in Caten . . . it's like Thavius says. Caten rewards greed above all. So this, out here, is about seeing who will do whatever it takes. Who will do whatever they can get away with to win."

There's a hush for a while, and I can tell Callidus is processing the words. "That's a grim way of looking at it."

"Tell me I'm wrong."

"No. No, I don't think you're wrong." There's a shuffling, Callidus repositioning himself against his tree trunk. "So if it's not us, are you hoping Emissa's going to win?"

"Yes." I mean it. "She has a good chance, too. Indol's going to be hard to beat though. Especially if he gets more Fourths over to his team." I sigh. "Honestly, at the moment? I don't mind, as long as it's not Iro and Belli."

"Absolutely. I cannot believe she actually kicked you in the face. I knew she wasn't a graceful loser, but that was . . ." Callidus raises his voice to a fairly decent approximation of Belli's. "'*All you really need to know is that you were outplayed.*'"

"'*You lose,*'" I copy him.

It's not that funny, but it's enough to send us into a coughing fit of giggles, loud enough that neither of us notices the cracking of twigs until a voice cuts through our laughter, sharp in the pitch-black. "Do you idiots really not care whether you get eaten by alupi, or do you not know how loud you are?" Torchlight creeps over the ground around me.

"Aequa?" I twist, heart leaping even as the rope grinds against my raw wrists.

"Who else would it be?" she says impatiently, slender form emerging from the shifting shadows. She crouches down by me, torch in one hand, steel in the other. "Hold still."

"Rotting gods, Aequa. What took you so long?" calls Callidus.

"*Quiet.*" She shoves me forward to get to my hands. There's a pressure on the rope, a frenzied sawing motion for about ten seconds, and then the cords that have been holding me in place for the last several hours fall away. I almost topple with them, unbearably stiff, but manage to clumsily catch myself. Before I can stand, she's moving over to Callidus and repeating the process.

"How did you get away?"

"We hit a dead end a few hours ago, had to double back for almost an hour.

They're terrible at woodcraft. I offered to scout ahead for a while tonight, make sure the new path was clear. They didn't even consider I might be double-crossing them."

"Hah. How foolish of them. Hah," I say weakly as I lever myself to my feet, gingerly stretching out. "Do you have my trackers?"

"No. But I'm going back to get your medallion." She finishes what she's doing. "The other one's in Iro's stomach."

"*What?*"

"I slipped it into his broth at dinner."

"That's . . . amazing." Callidus is awed. "And *disgusting.*"

Aequa's calm, short of breath though she is. "It was spur of the moment, but I think it will work. I'll suggest branching off with Vis's medallion to act as a decoy in the morning. No reason they'll see it as suspicious—they think you're out of the Iudicium, and it would be insane for me to try and win by myself this early, with no way of knowing where anyone else is. Once the tracker in Iro's stomach activates, the safety team will make contact, and they'll all be eliminated. I'll meet you after that."

I breathe out, as impressed as Callidus. "And Veridius only said we needed the medallion to win." I work the blood back into my fingers. "How long did it take you to get back here?"

"Only about an hour. We got blocked by a cliff, had to come back east before we made camp." She shakes her head, locks swinging in the dim light. "It was lucky. I was getting ready to grab your medallion and just run for it when they realised there was no way forward."

I frown. "East?"

"They had the same idea as you: go west, skirt the boundary, keep clear of Indol and Emissa until the Heart starts moving. That's how they got ahead of us. Just bad luck."

I grunt. It's not an *awful* plan from Iro, but . . . certainly a coincidence.

"How is your face, by the way?" She falters. "You know I would have stopped her, if she'd gone near you again."

"I know." I rub my bruised jaw. "It's no worse than the rest of me."

"Good. We should move, then." She holds up her torch and starts jogging back into the forest, not waiting for a response.

Callidus elbows me. "Told you," he says softly.

I give him a superior look. "Never had a doubt."

We both grin, and chase after Aequa's retreating torchlight.

LXV

I TELL THEM MY PLAN ON THE WAY. NEITHER OF THEM SEEM to like it.

"That is a terrible plan," says Aequa.

"It is," agrees Callidus between gulping lungfuls of air as we jog. "And if anyone is going to do something that stupid, it should be me. You'd be risking yourself for no reason."

"He's right," huffs Aequa. She's leading us, setting a remarkable pace given that she's both navigating by torchlight, and has already made this journey at a run once tonight. "Though I also think it's just unnecessary."

"We're blind out here. What happened with Iro and Belli proves it." My own breath comes in short gasps, but I'm feeling surprisingly good. A benefit of having drowsed, however uncomfortably, for a few hours this afternoon. "From what Veridius said, those stone circles the Sextii have can track all of us. Every single one of the Thirds and Fourths. So we need one. And this might be our only chance to get one." There's no judgment in the statement; Aequa's plan was smart, the right move under the circumstances. But it means that now—knowing both Iro's location, and the direction he's just come from—is our only opportunity to act.

"Then we should go together," says Callidus.

"Agreed."

There's a pause, and then Callidus grunts. "Good." He clearly expected more resistance. "So . . . we're going to take on two Sextii. Or maybe four, if our safety team has come across Iro's. By ourselves."

"We're going to steal their tracker," I correct him. "I'm not insane."

Callidus exchanges a dubious look with Aequa in the flickering torchlight.

"One of them will be watching it the whole time," warns Aequa. "Even with Iro camped, they'll want to know as soon as he moves. And they'll have to monitor for any emergencies, too."

"That's why Callidus here will distract them," I explain brightly to her. Callidus shifts, suddenly looking less enthused about coming along.

"If either of us is caught, we'll be disqualified." Callidus isn't protesting so much this time as making an observation. He knows me well enough to know I've made up my mind. "Even if we're not, if anyone finds out later . . ."

"We're not breaking the rules as they were laid out."

"We'd be breaking the spirit of them."

"Whatever it takes," I remind him.

There are a few other arguments after that, but they're weaker. Callidus and Aequa both know we need an advantage; no matter how good we are in a fight—and between us, we *are* reasonably good—it won't help if we're taken by surprise again.

By the time we slow and Aequa motions for us to quiet, it's been decided. Aequa will rejoin Iro and Belli, while Callidus and I locate one of the two safety teams now following them, and steal their tracking plate. Aequa will find a way to break away from Iro's team with my medallion in the morning. We'll regroup tomorrow before noon at the base of a towering cliff, about an hour north-east of where we are currently.

There's a lot that could go wrong. But given the risks of stealing from the Sextii, it will be easy enough to separate myself from Callidus.

That gives me an entire night and morning by myself, untracked, to cross the western river. Find the dome. Run the Labyrinth.

"This is it," Aequa whispers as she catches her breath. "Iro's a few minutes farther up. We came from that way." She orients herself against the nearby looming mountain and points. "There's a deep ravine. Walk along the left-hand edge. It's the only passable section for miles, so if they're really only fifteen minutes behind, at least one safety team should be along there somewhere."

"Thanks."

She nods. "What happens if you're not there by noon tomorrow?"

"Start toward the Heart of Jovan. I should have a tracking plate by then. I'll find a way to catch up to you." Aequa opens her mouth to protest, but I shake my head firmly. "If something happens to us, that's my fault. If we never turn up, you try for the win yourself." Aequa looks displeased at the prospect, so much so that I laugh. "It's not my ideal scenario, either."

Callidus snorts, while Aequa just half smiles. "Fine."

I watch as Callidus unhooks his medallion from around his neck: he can't wear it tonight, not if we want to take the Sextii by surprise. He doesn't hesitate as he hands it to Aequa.

I move to depart, then delay.

"I owe you an apology." I'd considered not saying anything, but it had to have been obvious. "I actually thought you were switching sides, back there."

Aequa, to my surprise, smirks at me. "I know. It was kind of hard not to laugh at your expression." She waves her hand dismissively. "Wouldn't have worked if you didn't believe it."

"I still should have trusted you."

"No, you shouldn't have. You had every reason not to. And I counted on the fact you wouldn't." She looks at me. "You should *now*, though."

"I do." I mean it. She's proven herself, as far as I'm concerned. "Luck, Aequa."

"You too," she returns quietly to us both.

Callidus and I split off from the path, foliage quickly taking Aequa from view.

We press forward in the direction Aequa indicated for the better part of an hour, mostly without words, progress slowed both by the tangled underbrush and the need for silence. Everything's hushed. My muscles ache from tension. Walking in the dark like this is deliberate, dangerous going, but we can't risk a torch.

I'm just beginning to wonder whether we've somehow missed the safety teams altogether, when a bright flicker of orange pokes through the trees up ahead.

"Vis," breathes Callidus from behind me.

We drop low. I ignore the way the brush scratches my arms and digs into my tunic, and worm forward. Faint voices drift to us, and then a burst of raucous laughter. The Sextii sound in good cheer. Relaxed.

". . . Latrius is a better rider."

"Bah. Maybe, but Red's a better team."

There's immediate, boisterous disagreement from the other one. Both men. They're huddled close to the fire, talking about chariots; Latrius is one of the more famous participants from Blue.

"Just the two of them." Relief in Callidus's whisper.

"Can you see the tracking plate?"

"No. It can't be far, though."

The friendly argument in the camp continues for several minutes—longer than it should, really, given the subject matter—and I continue to creep forward, refusing to surrender to impatience. The two of them are broad-shouldered, grey tunics sharp against the muted colours of their surroundings. Despite the cold, neither is cloaked.

There's some brief talk about something I don't quite catch, and then the conversation moves on to grumbling about restrictions in Caten for the upcoming Festival of Ocaria. Idle talk, but the constant flow of chatter gives us an easy way to creep around the camp's perimeter without being heard.

Time passes in a tense haze of slowly, slowly worming along, constantly pausing to see if the tracking plate is discernible. The Sextii's names, from what I gather, are Borius and Darin. After about twenty minutes, Darin grunts as he's fetching some wood for the fire. "Damned arm," he mutters, rubbing at his shoulder. He glances at Borius. "They take your blood too?"

Borius nods. "Makes a man uneasy, that stuff."

Darin finishes adding fuel to the flames, then peers at something on the ground. "The stray's been back with them for an hour now. I don't think they're moving again tonight."

"Lucky us." Borius rubs his forehead. "I wish he'd just get out of the way."

"It's not like it matters until tomorrow night, anyway." Darin shifts, and I feel a thrill of elation as he picks up the circular tracking plate and offers it to Borius. "You want to take first watch?"

Borius accepts it, passing a disinterested gaze over its surface before putting it on the log beside him. "Six hours?"

"Wake me then."

I signal with my head to Callidus as Darin prepares his sleeping roll a short distance from the merrily crackling fire. We retreat, gradually enough that it takes five minutes before I feel safe dragging myself up again, taut muscles groaning. "Aequa was right. They're not going to let that thing out of their sight."

"They have to relieve themselves eventually. Or one of them might fall asleep on watch."

"I doubt they'll go farther than the edge of the camp. And they're Sextii. They're not going to nap on duty, even if they think there's nothing to worry about out here." I give him an apologetic look. "We need that distraction."

Callidus scowls. "Why do I have to be the bait?"

"Do you want to try and fight them if this doesn't work?"

Callidus huffs. "What do you want me to do?"

"Nothing big. Don't go setting the forest ablaze or anything. Something that's just enough to pull them to the other edge of the camp. I can get close. All I need is a minute to sneak over, take the tracking plate, and get back into the trees." I think. "Try and make it something unthreatening. Best case, Borius doesn't even wake Darin before going and having a look."

Callidus raises an eyebrow. "So something distracting but unthreatening. And quiet enough not to wake the sleeping guy."

"Easy." I grin at him. "Circle around and start in about . . . a half hour? That should be enough time for Darin to get to sleep, and Borius to settle. Once you've done it, though, just run. Don't wait for me. Don't risk getting caught."

Callidus doesn't argue. He understands the difficulty of trying to escape a Sextus. "After that?"

"Head back to where we're meeting Aequa. I'll have the tracking plate. I'll find you on the way."

"What if you don't?"

"Then I've been delayed. Just get back to that cliff and wait for me there." I have no intention of finding Callidus tonight; I'll be heading west, straight for the dome. But a story about evading capture by two Sextii should explain the lost time well enough.

Callidus confirms with a nod and turns to go, then pauses. "What do you think they meant about tomorrow night, back there?"

I shake my head. I caught that too. "No idea."

Callidus wryly indicates the same, then takes a deep breath. "Luck, Vis."

"You too. See you soon."

He vanishes into the shadows.

※ ※ ※

BEFORE TOO LONG THERE'S STEADY BREATHING FROM DARIN'S direction, a hush falling over the woods. Borius whittles down a stick with a short blade, mostly staring into the fire. He's awake to watch the tracking plate, then, not ward against intruders. That's good. He won't be paying as much attention to his surroundings, and his night vision will be impaired.

It's hard to assess the passing of time, frozen in place as I am like this, every breath feeling like it lasts an hour. I'm just beginning to wonder if something has happened to Callidus when I see Borius stiffen. Frown toward the opposite line of trees.

A second later a strong male voice floats along the breeze, faint but audible.

". . . to answer her pleading request, to tell her the part he thought best, he told her she wouldn't have guessed . . ."

I almost have to stifle a laugh as I recognise the tune. One of the Fourths was teaching it to everyone a few weeks ago—not much more than a dirty rhyme set to music, but catchy. Callidus is hardly the most impressive singer, but I suppose in context, his off-key wailing is effective.

"What in the gods' names?" Borius checks the stone circle beside him and then stands, glancing over at his sleeping companion. My heart stops as he wavers, then takes a step in the opposite direction. Two. His head's cocked to the side, as if still not quite believing his ears. The tracking plate remains on the log where he left it. Between me and him.

"*. . . he liked her so much, he went into the brush, and now he's . . .*"

I will Borius forward. His hand's resting on the blade at his side. Steel, not a Razor. A few more steps. He's almost at the far end of the small clearing. I hold my breath. Resist the urge to move straight away. It's wise; Borius glances back around at the still-sleeping Darin, looking torn. His eyes are black.

With a confused shake of his head, he makes his decision. Vanishes into the trees.

I don't delay, scrambling to my feet and darting the thirty or so feet to the plate. A quick glance tells me it's what I'm looking for: small coloured stones litter its surface, and don't move when I snatch it up. I'll have to figure out how to read it later.

I turn to go, then spot a cloak lying in shadow on the ground nearby. I take a few extra steps and snag it. It's cold tonight, and while I can probably survive in my tunic, I don't want to have to. Especially as I'm going to have to swim soon enough.

"Stop."

Ice ripples down my spine as Borius's command comes while I'm still ten paces from the safety of the trees. I do as he says. Close my eyes. Only the sound of dying embers disturbs the hush. Once he sees my face, it's over.

"Wha—?" It's a sleepy half question from Darin.

I'm a hundred feet from Borius. He'll be able to smash through the forest far more easily than me, but being a Sextus lends him no extra speed.

I run.

"STOP!" Borius roars it, loud enough that birds sleeping in the surrounding bushes burst into flustered flight. I'm already into the trees, but there's suddenly a horrendous creaking behind me. Something scythes through the air, not ten feet from where I am. Spinning and smashing through branches with a roaring crash.

It's a tree. Borius just threw a *tree* at me.

Birthright does not seem to be his primary concern, right now.

I dive away to the left, into the deep brush. Then I force myself to crouch and move methodically, shuffling rather than pressing on blindly. A twisted ankle will be almost as bad as getting caught, here, and worse—if I'm too noisy, Borius will be able to pinpoint the direction I've gone. There are plenty more trees for him to uproot and hurl after me.

There are confused shouts from Darin, answered by a furious and unsettlingly close Borius. The crashing of another massive object thundering through the woods, though farther away this time. Before the deafening noise fades I lie prone in the midst of a thick clump of bushes, ignoring the prickles raking my skin, doing all I can to still my ragged, panicked breathing. I think I had enough of a head start that Borius could believe I got away. Rather than waste time searching for me, he and Darin will surely head for somewhere they can report what's happened.

Borius rails at me, and the still-groggy Darin, and the gods. After a minute his raging eases to incensed shouting as he starts ordering Darin to pack up camp, and then there's an unsettling silence. I don't move, all but holding my breath, eyes straining in the direction the two men lie.

There's nothing for a minute. Two.

Then a crackling of twigs and a flicker, light against darkness. Borius is holding a torch high, stomping through the woods, orange flame showing grim fury. He glowers into the forest, and though he's fifty feet away, I still have to restrain a sliver of panic as his gaze sweeps over my position.

"I know you're still here," he calls, more of a snarl than anything else.

He's fishing, of course. Desperate.

My confidence wanes as he bends down, examining something on the ground, and then starts walking in my direction.

Vek. He's probably a capable hunter, and I was hardly able to cover my tracks during my initial, desperate dash. Once I slowed, I think it will be harder to spot where I went—and I *did* change course a couple of times—but he's going to find me.

I force my breathing to a quiet rhythm. Judging from the trees he was hurling earlier, there's no chance I can take him in a fight. I'm going to have to run; the question is when, how long to hold off, how long to risk hoping that he'll just give up. The closer he gets, the less likely it is that I get away.

Borius picks his way forward, focusing on the ground, though his head twitches to the side at any hint of movement in his peripheral vision. He's thirty feet away. Twenty. On a different trajectory to where I am, but he'll end up close enough that I don't think I can avoid being seen, even hidden here beneath the shrubbery.

"Borius!" It's Darin. "Ready!"

Borius doesn't respond, scanning the nearby area, eyes narrowed.

"*Borius!*"

"*Coming!*" His head snaps back around in the direction of his comrade, shout filled with frustration. He puts his hand against the thick trunk of a nearby tree. The entire thing seems to shiver; suddenly it's ripping from the ground, crashing against the surrounding foliage, hovering in mid-air. Darin's facing me. He snarls and hurls.

It takes everything I have not to do more than flinch, not to break from cover and dive away from the destructive force that smashes past less than ten feet away. Branches snap and fly off, some raining down into the bushes where I'm hiding.

The forest swallows the final echoes of the destruction and Borius whirls, stalking away back in the direction of his camp.

I wait until he's out of sight before I close my eyes and lay my forehead against the rough ground, exhaling shakily. That didn't go according to plan, and the "safety" team was very definitely less inclined toward safety than I expected. I can still hear Borius barking orders, Darin sounding a mixture of defensive and exasperated. Receiving a small portion of what Borius wants to heap on my head, no doubt.

I give it twenty minutes after the last of their voices fade into the night, unwilling to chance their having decided to double back. There's nothing, though. No indication that anyone is nearby. Hopefully Callidus is already well away from here.

Finally I crawl out of the bushes, stumbling to my feet and making my way over to a newly fallen log. I toss the cloak I stole around my shoulders and sit. Enough moonlight filters through the trees for me to see now, and I bring the tracking plate up close to my face.

It's about a foot across, thin but still with some weight to it. On its surface, dozens of stones protrude, firmly attached, and some—I think, though it's hard to tell in the dim, silvery light—a different colour from the majority. I frown, poking at them. None move. I twist the plate, flip it, turn in a circle. None move.

"Vek," I mutter. Did it rely on Borius having possession of it, somehow? That seems unlikely; he was checking it without touching it this evening. Could I have broken it, somehow, in the mad dash to get away? Nothing appears cracked or even chipped.

I slip it in my satchel, push to my feet again and orient myself against the waning moon, leaving a more detailed inspection for later. I don't have time to waste.

I strike out westward, toward the river. Toward the dome.

LXVI

I'VE LEARNED TO MANAGE FEAR, OVER THE PAST FEW YEARS. Accept its lurking presence. Sleep despite its slinking touch. Strangle it down deep when I need to.

It's different, tonight, forging my way through the forest in the thin moonlight. There's a nervousness that grinds in my chest, sharpening every time I remember where I'm headed. The more I try not to think of the Remnants and the way they tore Artemius apart, the more the images slip into my consciousness. My steps grow leaden. I think of a thousand tales I might tell Ulciscor in place of actually going.

But I know that none but the truth will satisfy him. It's the only way I'm able to force one foot in front of the other.

I'm confident in my navigation skills, but it's still more than an hour before I reach the river that demarcates the boundary of the Iudicium. I pause on its eastern shore, staring across. It's not terribly wide, perhaps a hundred feet, but it's fast-moving and the current strong. Swimming an unknown like this, alone and at night, is not something I'd normally attempt.

And once I'm across, if something happens to me, I won't be found. No one will think to look for me in Solivagus's western quarter.

There are no options, though. No better choices. I strip off, carefully tucking everything into my satchel. Then I head down to the water.

It's icy, probably flowing down from one of the taller peaks on the island; I brace myself against the sharp cold, teeth clenching as I sink past the reeds, soft riverside mud squelching between my toes. I press on, submersing my body as quickly as possible while holding my satchel above the waterline. I don't anticipate I can make it to the other side with it completely dry, but nor can I afford to have sodden clothes for the rest of the evening.

I wasn't wrong about the current, but I make the other side with few issues, my bag dripping but its contents largely unscathed. I'm probably five hundred feet farther downriver than where I started, but that doesn't overly matter. I pull myself up onto shore and then, shivering violently, start drying myself with my cloak.

My brow furrows after a moment. My skin's being smeared with something dark. I rub at it with a numb finger. Some of it flakes away.

Blood.

I search for a cut for almost a minute before I realise there is none. It's the cloak. A darker patch against the green cloth. Soaked in it.

I scrub it from my body as quickly as I can, trying to decide its significance. There's a lot of it. It could be from an injury I didn't spot; Darin in particular barely moved the entire time I was watching, and being a Sextus, he could easily have been compensating for a wound. Or the blood's from an animal. Something they hunted, perhaps using the cloak as a sling to drag it back to camp.

Both are possible. Neither seems likely.

Borius reacting to losing the tracking plate with such violence was bothering me already, and this does nothing to ease my disquiet. But it's a puzzle I'm going to have to worry about when I get back. Tonight's task won't allow for distractions or delays.

I wash the affected part of the cloak in the river as best I can—the smell of blood isn't something I want on me, alone in the forest—before dressing again. I'm still juddering from cold even after my clothing's on, but exertion should fix that soon enough.

It's past midnight now, I think. Twelve hours to get to the dome, run the maze, and then return to Callidus and Aequa.

I jog westward.

※ ※ ※

AN HOUR LATER I'M SWEATING, THE CHILL OF THE EVENING and my swim no longer an issue. The woods are unsettlingly quiet here. Through the tops of the trees, I catch occasional glimpses of the mountain which conceals the crimson dome. That's useful; several times I find myself turned around, the paths jagged and steep, most of my concentration taken up in making sure I don't trip down one of several sharp inclines as I progress.

I finally decide to rest, sitting on a rocky rise in the ground and unslinging my satchel. There's no birdsong, no buzzing of insects. The moon is high, providing light here in this small stony area with no trees to block it. I take a quick draw from my waterskin, then pull out the tracking plate I took from Borius again.

"Rotting *gods*," I mutter to myself as it comes out of the bag smooth, no stones on it. I dig around in the bottom of the satchel, finding some and placing them hopefully on its surface. Nothing happens.

I stare in morose disbelief, then slot it irritably back and pour the stones after it. "What a waste."

There's a rustling behind me at the words, one that would be inaudible if I was still moving, and my shoulder blades twitch. I don't react, don't do anything to indicate I've heard or sensed anything unusual, continuing to sort through my satchel. I locate and draw out my hunting knife, the only weapon I have. Tuck it in my belt before standing again.

The hair on the back of my neck stands on end as I press on, straining for any hint of pursuit. There's nothing for what seems like an age, though it can't be more than ten minutes. Then snapping twigs behind me. Distinct between my breaths and the silence.

I can't take the tension anymore. I'm in another clearing, the light good enough to see by for tens of feet. I take the knife from my belt.

A low, rumbling growl fills the air.

I freeze, eyes combing the undergrowth. I'm not sure what I can do here. Turning my back and running is a terrible idea; whatever it is, I have no doubt it will be faster than me. But I'm not likely to stand a chance against it with my knife alone, either.

The growl deepens. My knuckles are white on the knife's hilt. Just the one animal, I think, but it sounds *big*.

There's motion in the shadows. Bushes rustle as a darker shape emerges. Dappled moonlight glints off two slitted eyes and bared teeth.

An alupi.

The creature takes another step forward, then another, gaze fixed on my knife as I hold it out defensively. I back away at the same pace, mouth dry. It's huge. More than half my height. Drops of saliva glisten, highlighting the thinnest, keenest points of its teeth.

I'm still furiously trying to calculate a solution to the situation when the alupi attacks.

I'm not even aware it's coming until it's in the air, all shadows and teeth and grace as it arrows for me. I try to twitch the knife into position but I'm too late; the full weight of the animal slams into my chest and right arm, knocking the blade free and sending me sprawling backward. Air flees my lungs at the impact.

My dizziness clears to slavering jaws filling my vision. I wrench around but the creature's on top of me, and I barely budge. Its breath stinks of rotten meat and blood.

The creature's eyes, inches away, bore into mine. Its lips are curled back, revealing what I've been told too many times are razor-sharp teeth. It growls again. I lie back, trying to show that I'm surrendering. There's not really much else I can do.

The monstrous ball of fur and muscle continues its ominous rumbling.

Then, to my astonishment, it leaps off me again. Stands a few feet away.

I glance over to where my knife fell, but immediately hear the change in timbre of the alupi's warning. I look away again, making it clear I'm not going to dive for it. The wolf stands almost four foot tall at the shoulder. Its black fur accentuates the wet silver of its teeth in the moonlight.

I squint. There's a line in the hair on its back, a missing streak which is scarred over.

"Diago?" I whisper the name. Still how I think of the cub I saved six months ago, though this monster can't be him. Surely. And yet I can't take my eyes off the scar. It's in the same place. "Is that you?"

I sit up and slowly, carefully, start to stretch out my hand.

The wolf's snarl increases until it leaps forward, snapping viciously at my fingers; I snatch them back just in time to avoid having them bitten clean off.

"Right. Right," I mutter shakily to myself. "Don't do that."

I stay sitting as the alupi begins stalking to the side, circling me. Its gaze never leaves me.

It completes two whole circuits and then, as abruptly as it appeared, turns and pads back into the forest. Within seconds and before I can react, the shadows hide it from view once more.

I hold my breath, then exhale, barely daring to believe I'm uneaten. *Could* that have been Diago? Bizarre, but the coincidence seems too much to ignore. Either way, I'm not fool enough to think I'm safe, nor that the wolf has really gone. The smell of blood on my cloak must have drawn it.

There's not much more I can do than press on, ears sharp for any indication of the alupi's return. If I was uneasy before, now I'm almost light-headed with anxiety. My nerves are an incline against which I'm walking, each breath harder than it should be. But there's nothing from the forest around me. No sign that the creature is tracking me.

It's about a half hour later, through the treetops, that I catch my first glimpse of the dome.

It's with both relief and dread that I pause and greet the sight, the menacing red drinking in the subdued silver from the sky. The trees are thinning, and that strange, heavy muteness here presses down harder than ever. I trudge on.

When I finally break through the last of the shrubbery to the dome's base, the alupi is waiting for me.

I stop dead. It's motionless, on its haunches. It doesn't react to my appearance.

I take a step forward. It bares its teeth and emits that terrifying, low growl, muscles bunching.

My blade is at my side, but I don't reach for it this time. Visibility is better here without the cover of the trees, and I was right about the creature's scar: it matches the one from the cub I saved. It *must* be him. His growth is close to unbelievable.

"Diago." I know he's not going to recognise the name, know the word's not going to have any meaning at all to the wolf, but I say it anyway. More for my own comfort than anything else. "Diago. Do you remember me?" I take another step.

Diago's rumble becomes more threatening. I retreat. The growling stops, the snarl lessening to bared teeth.

"Gods' graves," I mutter to myself. I'm glad the creature's not attacking me on sight, but I still need to get past it. I can't kill it—even if I tried and somehow succeeded, there's no chance I could come out of that fight without a serious injury. And given that it must have been following me all this time, I doubt I can simply walk away and then slip back later once it's wandered off.

I don't move for almost a minute, gaze locked with the wolf's bright grey eyes. Neither of us waver as I calculate desperately, all too aware of the time slipping away.

Reluctantly, I come to a decision. The alupi has been tracking me for at least a half hour, probably longer, but hasn't attacked. And I can see the massive Hierarchy symbol that marks the entrance. If I can just get through there, I can shut the door behind me.

I take a step to the right of Diago; immediately the wolf's lips curl back and that rumbling growl returns. I swallow, breath short, and take another step. Then another. Diago doesn't move, but he's snarling now. Saliva drips from his mouth.

"Scintres Exunus," I say firmly.

The mountain groans and the pyramid splits, red glass folding back. The alupi doesn't turn or budge. I'm not far—twenty feet, give or take. Still too far to make a dash for it; Diago would catch me before I made the first step down. So I take another sidling step, heart in mouth, hands outstretched to show that I mean no harm. It doesn't seem to make a difference. Diago keeps growling and then takes a stalking, threatening pace toward me.

I grimace. Carefully unsling my satchel and place it on the ground. It will be a hindrance if I'm attacked, and it's not as if I'll need it inside the dome.

Then I confidently begin walking toward the entrance.

I almost falter as Diago's warning thunders off the mountain, but there's no time to waste, and doing this in such small stages is too much for my nerves. The first five steps are agony as I wait for the inevitable attack.

Then, to my surprise, the growling stops. Fades to a whine as Diago sits, still watching me.

"Sorry," I murmur to him, not stopping and doing everything in my power not to break into a sprint. "I don't have a choice."

Then I'm stepping into the darkness, twisting to look back at the wolf. It's stopped whining. On its feet again, just staring at me mutely.

I shiver. "Scintres Exunus." I hate losing the sliver of light from outside, but an unsettling few minutes in the dark trumps being mauled to death from behind.

The doorway begins to close. I risk a quick glance down the stairs, watching regretfully as the faint silver that would have lit my way dwindles.

When I look back through the shrinking opening, the alupi has vanished.

LXVII

THE CAVERNOUS HALL IN THE HEART OF THE DOME IS EX-
actly as I remember it.

Torches flare to life one by one, illuminating rows of columns as the stone platform bears me to the ground. At the far end, hundreds of feet away, warm light reflects
off those three diverging lines of bronze set into the wall. The glittering pyramid symbol they form towers over the vast, empty space between.

I step off the platform as soon as it touches the floor, no time for hesitancy. Stride
to the centre of the room.

"I want to take the test!" I yell it to the walls. My words are engulfed by the enormity of the space.

Waiting for it though I am, I flinch at the voice behind me.

"I was known as Elia Veranius. I was a traitor to the commandment of isolation.
I attempted to gain synchronism and remove the seal to Obiteum during the eleventh
era after the Rending. I have thus been lawfully condemned to servitude, guiding those
who come after." The hollow-eyed woman with the snarled black hair and torn clothes
is standing behind me. As with last time, I'm unsure how she got there.

"Elia. Good. Good." I cross my arms, mostly to hide my discomfort. "Do you
remember me?" I ask the question expecting no answer, and receive none. That's alright.
I don't have time to waste anyway. "I would like to take the test."

Expression never changing, she brings her hands from behind her back. Unstraps
the control bracer from her left arm and offers it to me.

I stare at it for a grim few seconds, then take it.

There's that same sickly, slithering sensation as I put it on; the hall between us and
the far symbol explodes into activity, black walls grinding upward into place. I watch
bleakly, attention fixed on the archway at the entrance. I've practiced ceaselessly for this.
Day after day after day. But I still don't feel ready. Don't know enough about the rules
here, or the Remnants, or what lies beyond.

"Elia. Is there any way to see the Labyrinth—the test—from higher up?"

There's no answer.

I'm unsurprised, but it was worth a try. "What about a way to practice the test? Is
there something like that?"

"An overview can be activated."

"Oh." I wasn't expecting a response. "Let's . . . do that?"

Elia moves to one of the columns and presses her hand against it.

The floor grinds and shifts again, this time almost at my feet. I leap back in alarm, but it stops as abruptly as it started, a mass of perpendicular lines about ten feet long and five wide jutting an inch from the ground.

I peer down. It's easy to recognise the patterns.

"This is the maze?" No response from Elia. I bring the control bracer up and twist a stone. There's a faint grinding from the Labyrinth as a panel moves within.

And a corresponding movement in the version in front of me. Stone swinging across, exactly where I would expect it.

I frown down at the miniature version of the Labyrinth. "This is good," I say slowly, "but I want to see how the Remnants move, not just the walls. Is there any way to track them?"

"Motion will be displayed when present."

"Ah." I uneasily examine the small version of the Labyrinth, then the towering black one ahead.

Then Elia.

"Elia," I say quietly. "Are you alive?"

No response.

"I . . . I don't want to condemn you to die. But . . ." I take a deep breath. "I'm not convinced you are alive. Not really. And if I'm wrong and you're stuck in this . . . *state*, surely that's just as bad." I'm saying the words mostly to myself, as reassurance. I steel myself. "So *if* you are not alive, Elia, I would like you to demonstrate the test."

Elia turns and heads for the entrance.

I shiver. Assuming her compliance is an indication that she's actually dead, it means I'm not responsible for Artemius's demise. It means I have a chance to assess how these Remnants hunt before I go in there.

On the other hand, her being dead raises a *lot* more questions.

Elia reaches the archway; as she passes beneath it the air around her ripples, the passageways beyond seeming to waver before solidifying again. Immediately there's a change on the ground in front of me. A bright, sickly green dot of light at the representation of the maze's entrance. It doesn't hover above the stone, though. It's as if the illumination is etched into it. Exactly like the scrawled writing and diagrams in the ruins near the Academy.

A heartbeat passes and then there are three more dots of green light. All at the far end of the Labyrinth. Unlike the one denoting Elia, these stutter and wane, pulse uneasily.

They burst into motion.

Elia's pace hasn't changed; the black Labyrinth walls have hidden her from view now, only the near green light allowing me to track her progress. It's glacial compared to what I assume is the Remnants. Their dots in the miniature maze flicker through passageways and around corners with terrifying speed as they converge on their prey. As each one moves, it leaves an etching of pulsing green in its wake, showing its route thus far.

"Vek." I bring the bracer up, start twisting and flicking stones to block the Remnants' way. The lights don't hesitate when I do, altering course immediately and smoothly. Heading straight for the next most efficient route to their target.

I swallow. Work the control bracer furiously. I delay them for a minute. Two. Elia keeps steadily, deliberately forward. Never increasing her pace.

She's not even a quarter of the way through before one of the fast-moving lights smashes into hers. There's a fuzzing, a sputter.

The other two Remnants stop. When the one that reached Elia begins moving again, her light is gone.

I stand there, cold, not knowing how to feel. Remembering what happened to Artemius, knowing I just consigned Elia to the same fate. Telling myself that she was already dead. She was already dead, and this is necessary.

My gaze drifts to the glowing green lines that traced the Remnants' paths. I focus. Examine them. Replay my choices. After a minute, the representations of the Remnants begin to fade. Soon they've disappeared completely, along with the routes they took.

"I was known as Dorail Numinus. I was a traitor to the commandment of isolation. I attempted to remove the seal to Obiteum during the second era after the Rending. I have thus been lawfully condemned to servitude, guiding those who come after."

I don't turn at the unfamiliar woman's voice. Continue to fix on the miniature maze. On the point at which Elia and the Remnant met.

"If you are not alive, Dorail, I would like you to demonstrate the test," I say hollowly.

※ ※ ※

I GET THROUGH FOUR MORE DEMONSTRATIONS BEFORE I CAN take it no longer.

In each one, I learn something new about the Remnants. The monstrosities start from the same position every time, at the far end of the Labyrinth, close to the exit— that's good. When I use the bracer to switch paths, delay them, they immediately choose the next most efficient route. That's good, too, I decide after a while. Perfect predictability makes this a puzzle of logic and timing, not one of bluffing and out-thinking an unknown opponent. The Remnants appear to be relatively mindless, entirely aware of where their prey is and the state of the Labyrinth, but not inclined to block off ways forward or simply wait by the far door.

Most importantly, though, they never vary.

During the third test, I see a potential way through. Assuming they always take the shortest paths to their target, and move at the same speeds, I can predict where each of them will go. And on the fourth run, I prove to myself that if I can time certain alterations to the maze precisely, I should be able to make it to the other side.

Maybe. *Maybe.*

I should keep experimenting. Keep practicing. But time isn't on my side, and when a young girl—she can't be more than twelve, vaguely reminiscent of Cari—appears behind me, long brown hair almost concealing her eerie eyeless gaze, I know I'm done.

"Alright." I face her squarely. Blood pounding in my ears. She's told me her name, but I've already learned to stop listening. "I'm ready. I want to take the test."

"Are you certain? Once through the entrance, retreat is impossible."

"Of course it is." I gesture gloomily. "I'm certain."

"Then proceed."

My breath's short, hands shaking as I clench them by my sides. I walk toward the black archway, calculating and recalculating. The Remnants move at a constant speed; I'm going to have to count out the seconds as I run, switch passageways at just the right time to redirect them. One mistake, and it will be over.

Before I can change my mind, I step into the Labyrinth.

There's that strange warping in the air, a vibration that makes everything briefly shimmer, as if I've just walked through the surface of a massive bubble. The hair prickles on the back of my neck and I'm immediately reminded of the aura around Melior at the naumachia. No strange visions here, at least.

The walls tower around me. Black and smooth, ten feet taller than the ones at the Academy. Their height makes everything feel closer, suffocating.

I shake off the chill that shudders through my body, start the count, and run.

One. Two. Three.

As scared as I am, as strange as my surroundings are, my hours upon hours of practice make movement something I barely have to think about. I turn right after five seconds. Sprint forward for another ten. Make my first adjustment on the bracer, one that should redirect the Remnant on the right into a circuitous reversal. Three quick turns, open the way ahead. That will cause the left-most Remnant to change course, take the easier path toward me. I shut it again after another five seconds. Creating just enough of a delay for me to slip past before altering its path once again.

I fall into an almost meditative state for the first five minutes, every turn a familiar one, every adjustment of the bracer practiced, flawless. I don't even see a Remnant, though I hear one a couple of times, scraping menacingly along the floor in some nearby hallway. But my confidence rises.

Then I turn the corner, and see Belli's torn body.

She's pinned to the wall about five feet off the ground. Blood spatters the stone below her, pooling in a thick, dark crimson from where it's flowed down her body and dribbled off her feet. Her face is untouched, though. That long, curly red hair framing a pale expression of pain and horror and disbelief. Half her torso is missing.

Shock. Confusion. Revulsion. Sadness. They all war for my attention, obliterating whatever focus I'd had. I stumble to a stop, half step toward her as if to see whether there's anything I can do before realising just how foolish that thought is. How is she *here*? I flinch as she seems to flicker, translucent for a heartbeat. Blood still drips. This is recent. Maybe from not long before I arrived.

With a jolt I realise I've stopped. Am just staring. I've lost my count. Lost track of where the Remnants should be.

I gasp. Fear and shock threatening to overcome me as I register I'm about to end up the same way. That even Belli, the best of us at the Labyrinth, didn't make it through.

Somehow, I force my legs to move. Will myself to sprint on.

I lost . . . five seconds, maybe, staring at Belli? Ten? That's bad, and even worse that I'm not sure.

I pour desperate speed into my legs. Five seconds, I might be able to make the next junction. Ten and I'm dead.

I skid around the corner, and see the Remnant at the end of the long hallway. Rushing toward me. Maybe fifty feet away.

If the Remnants were intimidating from a distance, they're terrifying up close. A mass of edged obsidian that hurtles forward like a twenty-foot-high wave, chattering hungrily against stone, eager and formless.

I sprint toward it.

It's faster than me but not by much, and the passageway I need is closer to me. I barely stop to turn the corner, letting my right shoulder slam hard against the wall and allowing myself to bounce off as I desperately twist the corresponding stone on the bracer. There's a faint grinding sound. I've been too hasty. Failed to close the door, sealed my fate.

A quick glance behind me shows me I'm wrong. Nothing but smooth stone, a newly formed dead end.

I don't stop to celebrate.

I still have a path, but this isn't the way I wanted to take. I try to refactor as I run, calculate the trajectories of the three different Remnants based on their speed, my current position, the current state of the Labyrinth. It's something I've become well accustomed to doing during practice, but that doesn't mean it's easy. It certainly doesn't mean I'll get it right.

I run for another two minutes, lungs starting to burn, sweat trickling into my eyes. I can hear the chill, rattling scrape of pursuit at almost every turn now. I adjust the Labyrinth once every thirty seconds. Still no mistakes. I'm focused again. Trying not to let my success distract me.

And then, finally, I round a corner and see the shadowed exit that has appeared beneath the massive bronze pyramid.

The archway is open. Unguarded. I was flagging, but the sight lends a burst to my legs. It feels like I'm barely touching the ground.

With thirty feet to go, I hear a Remnant behind me. I don't turn. I'm almost to the arch when another Remnant appears. About ten feet past the exit. Barely farther from it than I am.

I am going to die.

I keep charging at the towering wall of glinting, cracked shadow, refusing to falter. Whirling black death flows toward me.

I scream as I fling myself through the exit, into the darkness beyond, arm in front of my face as I slide along the ground and wait for the biting obsidian to tear me apart.

Nothing happens.

I lie there for a terrified, frozen second. Two. Just trembling. Gradually, I force myself to twist around and look back.

The Remnants fill the archway like jagged shades, only three feet away. Gyrating shards of dark glass flail angrily at the very edge of the Labyrinth. There's a screeching, scratching thunder as they rattle at the opening. I fumble urgently with the bracer. Unstrap it and toss it away, as if the act could somehow remove the memory of my last ten minutes.

The exit begins to slide into the ground, taking the dim light with it. Within moments, it's gone, maze and Remnants alike hidden from view.

Then there's silence.

LXVIII

FINALLY, I STOP SHAKING.

The utter darkness left by the sealing of the Labyrinth's exit has been broken: this new, unsettling illumination is a virulent red, the colour of a dying flame, coating the walls and yet with no discernible source. A tunnel stretches out ahead. Five-foot-wide symbols are cut at regular intervals into the floor. Some of them are familiar—it's the same language as from the ruins near the Academy, I think. Bloodshot light casts deep blacks where the symbols are furrowed, providing an unnerving path forward.

I don't move for a few long minutes. Still trying to ease my breathing. I keep picturing Belli. The Remnants didn't consume her like they did Artemius and the others. How she was still pinned there, after the Labyrinth walls had presumably retracted after her run and then emerged again for mine, I have no idea. And she surely can't have been the first casualty of this place, yet I saw no other remains.

No telling if Iro knew her plan or not, but this was probably why they were heading west. Veridius must have sent her.

And now she's dead. All in pursuit of whatever is back here.

Carefully, stiffly, I haul myself to my feet. Start down the passageway.

I must be underneath the massive Hierarchy symbol at this point, though there's no indication of it down here. The red light fuzzes around me. Quivers. Walls start to warp from the corner of my eye, and echoes touch my ears, the dying breath of shouts that sound as if they have travelled miles to reach me.

I walk for . . . a minute, perhaps? Hard to tell. The symbols underfoot continue the entire way; some of them repeat, but not in any pattern. I keep my focus on them, mostly to avoid nausea from the visual twisting around me. Are they a story of some kind? A warning? Instructions for whoever passes through here? I hope not the latter. The air grows heavier.

The passage ends in stairs that disappear downward. I press on.

Before long I'm stumbling to a reluctant, nervous halt as the stairs end in a red-drenched chamber: not much more than a large room, albeit one with a ceiling too high for me to see. In its centre, several razor-thin protrusions of what appear to be bronze emerge from the floor, arranged in a circle. They're tapered, pointed at the tips. Like enormous blades. The crimson light in the room is emanating from somewhere behind the arrangement, casting it in a near-silhouette.

I hesitate, but there's nothing else to focus on. No exit that I can see.

The warping in the corners of my vision eases as I approach. The bronze blades are about my height; they all curve inward as they rise, metallic claws grasping from the earth. There's nothing inside their ring, nothing to indicate why it's there. The air within seems to quiver.

Surrounding the circle is writing. A long inscription etched on the floor around the blades, spiralling outward. I crouch. More of that ancient Vetusian dialect.

I start pacing the edge.

"Herein lies the way to Luceum and Obiteum, offered to all those who would contest our . . . extinction?" I mutter to myself, translating. "Know that none who accept this task may . . . remain? The burden of . . ." My brow furrows and I pause at a word. "Togetherness? Harmony?" I choose the latter. "Is reserved for the one who seals the . . . authors? The authors of the war from this world. Only he may . . . exceed? Exceed the hobbled capabilities of this . . . duplication? He and he alone may risk . . . *harmony* . . . to make the great . . . sacrifice? *Vek.*"

I shake my head, trailing off. For simple phrases, context can usually make up for the strange dialect and gaps in my knowledge. But this is beyond me. Far too specific. Maybe with time, though—with other Vetusian texts to help—I might be able to figure it out. I complete several more circuits, mouthing the foreign words to myself as I try to memorise the phrases. The more I have to give Ulciscor, the better my chances that he doesn't consign me to a Sapper.

Once I'm satisfied, I make a quick tour of the rest of the room. There's more writing on the far wall, several sentences, though this time it's in the same language I found in the other ruins. Not something I can even begin to translate.

There's nothing else. No other points of interest and, more worryingly, no way out except back.

I return to the ring of bronze blades, studying it uneasily. *The way to Obiteum and Luceum.*

The inscription around it is a warning, but its unknown danger still feels far preferable to the alternative. Even if navigating the Labyrinth from this direction should be simplicity itself—given I'd be running away from the Remnants, rather than toward them—I can't escape the image of Belli's eviscerated body. Can't countenance going back that way, right now.

And Ulciscor . . . part of me knows that what I've found thus far won't be enough for him.

The air shivers and trembles as I stand at the circle's edge. Cautiously extend an arm inside. It feels a little warmer, pressure on my skin. It doesn't hurt.

I take a breath. I've come this far.

I step between the massive, curved talons of metal.

Nothing happens, to begin with, giving me just enough confidence to take another step, into the centre of the ring. I glance around. Nothing in the room has changed.

I try to exhale, and fail.

I can't breathe.

My eyes widen and I try to shuffle back but I can't do that, either. It's as if the air around me has congealed, clotted into something that's completely encasing me. Writhing panic begins crawling through my veins.

The blades forming the surrounding circle start to move. Grow. Curl inward. They stop before they touch at an apex, but only just, no gaps at the base of the ring now. The bronze claws glow with white light, until suddenly there's a blink of darkness and then everything's coated in that dying-ember red again.

Except this time, it emanates not from a single source, but from hundreds of fine designs inscribed on the insides of the blades. Lines upon lines upon lines lit up in crimson, rippling, as if blood were pulsing through the metal itself.

The pressure on my body increases. Becomes unbearable. A relentless, crushing compression. Then, abruptly, it releases, but rather than bringing relief it becomes the opposite, a force tearing me in every conceivable direction. Pulling as if trying to rip flesh from bones. I'm lifted upward, hovering in mid-air, completely helpless. I try to scream but there's no sound, no air for me to inhale or exhale. My vision's blurring. I'm fading.

And then it's over.

I'm sprawled on the ground, sobbing, choking in great lungfuls of air. Everything burns, as if I've been stung across every inch of my body, as if something has crawled inside my lungs and stomach and head and stung there, too. The encircling metal, I vaguely recognise, is retracting again. There's a gap I can escape through. I drag myself desperately toward it.

I don't make it before everything fades.

※ ※ ※

THE BURNING SENSATION WANES, TOO SLOWLY, SO MUCH SO that I'm not sure when it actually ends and becomes simply a memory that makes me twitch in place.

I don't know how long passes after that. Shadowed bronze blades glower around me. I just lie there on the cold stone, shivering, staring up at the darkness, my mind doing all it can to cover over the pain and fear.

Finally I sit. Take note of my surroundings. The eerie red light has returned to the room, though it's muted this time by what appears to be a cloud of wicked obsidian shards that cloaks the ring I'm in. Hovering. Quivering.

Within that black fog, I discern with a jolt, are figures.

"Who's out there?" My voice is hoarse, words escaping in a whisper. None of the dark silhouettes move. There must be a dozen of them. They all have weapons, too, I realise grimly. Long blades, held at the ready.

There is a path through the cloud, though. An open corridor that leads to the stairs.

Uneasy though it makes me, there's nowhere else to go, and right now I want nothing more than to be out of whatever this place is. I'm about to stand when I notice my tunic is dark over my left arm. Sodden and sticky. I gingerly roll up the sleeve, using it to clear away the worst of the blood so that I can see the source of the wound.

There are lines, etched into my skin. I feel a chill as I wipe away more blood.

The red, puffy cuts form a single word.

WAIT

"Complete the journey, Warrior." The lifeless command in Vetusian comes from the darkness. I can't tell from which direction.

"Doesn't seem like much of a journey." I groan as I pry myself off the floor. "I thought this was meant to take me to Luceum or Obiteum."

"Complete the journey, Warrior." Another voice.

"That's the way I came in. This is the same gods-damned place."

"Complete the journey, Warrior." A woman, this time.

I shiver. I don't think I'm going to get a different response from whomever, or whatever, is out there.

I stand there apprehensively for a minute. Two. Nothing outside the circle moves.

I'm just beginning to second-guess myself when there's a twitch in the obsidian shards. A ripple in them that glimmers in the red light.

Then they start to move.

I watch in horror as they swirl, circling the claw of bronze blades, flying faster and faster until I can hear the air being cut as they buzz like hundreds of black wasps. The figures standing in their midst don't move at first, but it's not long before they start to stagger. Twist. Weapons dropped, arms raised to protect themselves.

They soon vanish, the blurring black slivers a concealing hurricane.

Then there's a sudden, stinging burn on my left arm again. I rip back my sleeve as new lines of blood begin to well, slithering cuts opening unnervingly in the skin.

R

Out past the bronze circle, the obsidian trembles. Falters. Shards begin launching off wildly to the side, shattering against the stone walls.

Within seconds, none are left. Where the silhouettes had been, only mangled, bloody piles of flesh remain.

U

I run.

Back the way I came, everything bathed in dark red light that fuzzes and twitches in the corners of my eyes. There's a minute where there's nothing but my gasping breath and the vibrating air around me. I feel nauseous, dizzy from whatever happened to me back there. Too terrified to do anything but keep my legs moving.

I ease to a jog only when the dead end of the Labyrinth greets me. Trembling, I check my left arm. Still only R U scored into the skin. Blood drips onto the floor.

The bracer is still where I left it, discarded in the corner. I stoop.

Reluctantly pick it up.

The arched doorway grinds from the ground as soon as I put the bracer on. Once the boom of the rising walls echoes away, there's no sound out there. Just like before. The Remnants won't appear until they're able to reach me.

I make some quick adjustments to the maze, allowing for an almost straight run.

Then I sprint.

It's mere moments before the chilling clatter of the Remnants scratches to life behind me, but I'm already past, already into the main passageway down the centre of the Labyrinth. It's easy, from this direction, running away from them. A couple of quick twists to block off the most direct avenues of pursuit and, fast though they are, they never have a chance of reaching me. I'm bursting through the archway on the other side and tearing the bracer from my bloodied arm, lungs burning, within a couple of minutes.

Everything's quiet out here. No hollow-eyed advisors announce themselves. I head for the platform, step on. Sigh in relief as the red balustrade pulses to life.

The journey upward finally gives me a chance to breathe. My hands tremble, gripping tight to the railing though they are. My left arm burns. I don't understand what just happened.

The platform reaches its destination and I step off it gladly, allowing the dull red glow from the balustrade to provide me a few steps of safety. "Scintres Exunus," I yell into the darkness.

Somewhere up ahead, hazy light ripples and filters downward, unveiling the silhouettes standing between me and the stairs.

I skid to a stop. There's just enough illumination to see the empty recesses lining the corridor.

Behind me, the red light dies.

"Complete the journey, Warrior."

There are a dozen of them crowding the way in front of me. More. Not advancing, but no doubt as to their intent. I battle a wave of nausea. Back away, until I'm stepping onto the narrow platform again.

Nothing happens.

"Vek." I frantically grasp the railing a few times. "Vek, vek, *vek*." Spin back. Nothing's changed.

"Complete the journey, Warrior."

The words resound off stone. I glance in desperation at my arm. Willing that burning pain to start again, to signal that someone, or something, out there still wants me to survive. There's nothing but seeping wound.

I take one tremulous step forward. Another. I have no weapons, nowhere to run. I'm going to have to try and break past them. Make a hole, somehow, and flee.

They don't move. I suppose they don't have to. I can come to them, or wait for death.

I'm twenty paces away, muscles bunching for a final, vain sprint, when the furious ball of black fur and flashing teeth hurtles down the stairs and smashes into the group.

I'm frozen only for a second; then I'm running headlong into the gap Diago has created, leaping over thrashing bodies and rolling before scrambling to my feet and sprinting up the stairs. Snarls echo in the tight hall, choked by what I can only assume is teeth ripping into flesh, but there are no replies of pain or alarm. Feet slap the stairs behind me, a patter of pursuit. Diago yelps. I don't look back.

"Scintres Exunus!" I scream as the triangular opening nears.

Dawn's first blush slams into me, along with blessed, chilly air. I don't stop. Risk a glance over my shoulder. I took too long to command the door to shut; two men are already through the sluggishly closing entrance, eyeless gazes focused on me. More pour from the dwindling hole behind them.

I snatch up my satchel as I pass, fumbling my knife from it. There's no panting of breath, no howling or yelling for me to stop from behind. Just dogged, fleet-footed determination. I don't know how many made it out.

I run for the forest. Maybe I can lose them in the trees. Though I have no idea how their sight works.

I crash through the brush for about thirty seconds, the snapping of twigs and branches behind me indicating my pursuers are getting closer and closer, before I reach a clearing and realise I have no other choice. I stop. Turn. Hold my knife at the ready.

A half dozen men and women burst from the trees and slow, recognising that I've decided to fight them. They quickly spread out, though no communication appears to pass between them. My gaze flits to the trees behind them, but there's no more movement. There were surely others. My skin crawls at the thought of more circling around through the undergrowth.

The six advance and I take my stance, breath short, muscles tensed. I'm going to have to attack first, and attack hard, if I want any hope of coming out of this alive. Not that I think there's much chance of that.

There's a blur of shadow from the corner of my vision, and then one of the men is down as Diago leaps onto his back.

The other attackers don't waver, continuing toward me. There's the terrible wet sound of tearing flesh, followed by a red-black spray as Diago jerks his head to the side, the man's throat opened. The wolf doesn't bother to check whether its victim is dead, snarling as it leaps onto the back of the next and wrestling him to the ground, massive jaws clamping over his skull and twisting. There's an audible *snap* as the man's face is twisted and ripped away, neck at an unnatural angle.

Four left, and they've turned now, clearly deciding Diago is a threat that needs to be dealt with. The three men and a woman leap with horrific, animalistic abandon at the wolf, grappling it, ignoring the shredding inch-long claws and gnashing teeth that bite down on them over and over and over again. A maelstrom of limbs and snarling and blood.

I'm tempted to run again but I know there's no point; if they could track me before then there's no reason to believe that getting any farther away will help. I have to take advantage of my ally—assuming Diago is one and isn't simply crazed—while I can.

I charge.

My knife finds the first of the men in the back, sliding between his ribs with sickening ease, right to where his heart should be. He jerks around with a powerful backhand, catching me off guard and spinning me, pain arcing through my shoulder. It's not the blow of a normal man—not as powerful as a Septimus, maybe, but stronger than an Octavus.

Certainly a harder hit than I'd expect from someone who's just been stabbed in the heart, anyway.

Diago's growls are interspersed with shrieking whines as the empty-eyed human husks bite and claw at him; my stomach turns as I see the woman rip her head to the side, just like Diago did moments earlier, blood spraying and her teeth stained red.

My attack hasn't gone unnoticed, and two of the men have broken off, including the one I stabbed. They come at me, no subtlety to the assault. It helps. I weave, slipping by one and tripping the other, riding him to the ground and gripping his head. With all my might, I twist.

There's a sharp crack, and the man lies still.

There's no time to celebrate; I cry out as the other man's teeth find my left arm, biting deep at the back near the bicep. I slam him away but not before there's blood pumping from the wound. I growl and summon the last of my energy to punch him in the head; though it doesn't down him it does seem to disorient him, and I do it again, and again, and again through a haze of sweat and shadows and tears. Finally, when he stops moving for long enough, I break his neck too. It's the only thing that seems to truly stop them.

I vainly cover the wound in my arm with my opposite hand, wincing at the sticky, warm fluid leaking between my fingers. Bodies litter the grass, tinted by the gradually brightening dawn. Diago is crawling away from the last of them toward me, whining interspersed with soft yelps. It's a piteous sound, high-pitched and heartbreaking.

"It's alright," I say softly to him as I drag myself over. He gives a half-hearted snarl as I reach out to him, but he's either too weak to act or in too much pain to keep up the façade. I brush his head gently. He stiffens at the touch and then leans into the stroke, closing his eyes with a rattling breath.

I sit there with him, sprawled, the massive creature's head in my lap. He occasionally whimpers, struggling to breathe, and I keep petting him, trying to calm myself as much as him.

"Thank you," I whisper, bowing my head over his. "Thank you." I know he's just a wild animal, a predator that's apparently remembered a chance act of kindness from months ago. If he gets hungry enough, I have no doubt he'll still eat me. Yet I feel a bond with him.

Diago's straining pant is getting slower and slower, and I don't think he's conscious anymore. He doesn't have long. I want to wait with him, see it out with him until the end. But though my wound's not fatal, I've lost plenty of blood. I'm spent.

I fade to the rasping sound of the wolf's laboured breathing.

LXIX

To MY CONFUSION, DISGUST, AND DELIGHT, I WAKE TO A LUNG-
ful of Diago's snuffling breath.

The alupi is still sprawled on the ground beside me, but his eyes are open, his
breathing regular and unhindered. He twitches away warily when he sees me stirring,
stumbles to his feet, and backs away. Considers me. No growling, no teeth bared, just
impassive.

Then he turns and limps into the forest.

I watch him go, worried the creature's wounds will still overcome him, but
knowing there's not much I can do about it. Diago might be injured, but I am
too—not critically, I think, but enough to make contending with an uncooperative
alupi too daunting a prospect. The bite on my arm has mostly stopped bleeding,
but I'm unwilling to peel back the blackening strip of cloth that's sealing it. The
whole limb aches, burns, and tingles. I just have to hope that it's not infected, and
that the exertion I'm about to undergo over the next two days won't break the
wound open again.

The cuts from the instructions on my forearm have stopped seeping, at least; the
sleeve of my tunic is a congealing mess, but I can wash it off in the river. I've no desire
to try and explain those injuries to the others.

I gaze at the words etched into my skin for longer than I should. One more mystery to add to the list. Someone helped me get out of there. Somehow stopped the way
to Obiteum, or Luceum, or wherever it was supposed to go, from opening—if what
I read about it was even true—and then cleared that room so that I could escape. But
after all of it, I'm not even sure I know more than before the night began.

I can only hope that what I do know, will be enough for Ulciscor.

I shuffle to my knees and then my feet, vaguely surprised to find myself less sore
than expected, less exhausted. After the battering I took from fleeing the dome, I
should be barely able to move. But I feel . . . fine, as I flex and stretch my legs. Not
energetic, exactly, but strong enough to push on.

The sun's doing more than peering over the horizon now, helping me orient myself. I trudge back toward the river. Twice, I think I hear something following me and
whirl. I never see anything. I don't know for sure that Diago and I killed all the human-

shaped husks that escaped the dome. It could equally be Diago himself, I suppose, trailing along behind me. Or some other wild animal.

I strip off and swim the river, though I stop on the other side to build a fire and scrub my tunic. The smoke will be visible, but it's hard for me to care. Nobody will be close enough to come for me in the next hour or so. And the Iudicium seems . . . not irrelevant, but a laughably small concern compared to what I just went through.

I sit on a log, near naked as my clothing dries. Dig through my satchel for some damp food, my stomach not allowing me to go any farther before satiating it. My hand brushes the bottom of the bag and I pause. I can only feel a couple of the stones that should be in there.

I open it properly this time, drawing out the stolen tracking device. Almost all the stones have reattached themselves; when I try to move them or pull them off, they refuse to budge. Nor do they shift when I rotate the circular plate, still don't seem to react to different orientations at all—but it's something.

I eat the last of my sodden bread, dress, and start the journey back east to rejoin Callidus and Aequa.

%% %% %%

"WHAT IN ALL THE ROTTING HELLS HAPPENED TO YOU?"

Callidus is staring pointedly at the tattered, still somewhat bloodied wreckage of my tunic, while Aequa examines me with what I suspect is a hint of worry, too. I smile and shrug, doing my best to convey that I'm alright.

"Alupi." It's the best explanation I could come up with, given the obvious wound in my upper arm. "Did enough to scare it off." If I'd killed it, they would have expected me to bring back some meat.

"Ah." Callidus sounds vaguely disappointed. "Need us to take a look at that arm?"

"It'll be fine." I don't want him looking too closely at the toothmarks.

"No it won't." Aequa speaks for the first time, sharp and authoritative. I open my mouth to protest but she muzzles me with a glare. "No. *No.* I'm not going to let us lose because you're too heroic to accept some help. That needs cleaning and bandaging, or it will get infected." She's already digging through her pack, looking for something to do exactly that.

I sigh. She's right, of course; I did my best with the wound after I swam the river, but it's still oozing blood and in an awkward position. I'm surprised it hasn't affected me more, in fact.

I sit while Aequa carefully peels away my tunic, hear her sharp intake of breath as she takes in the full extent of the injury. "Rotting gods, Vis. You idiot," she mutters, the curse a surprise coming from her mouth. "When did this happen?"

"This morning." I only allow her to take the tunic half-off, still managing to cover the writing lower down on my arm.

Callidus peeks over her shoulder, then immediately pales and backs away. "Right. Well," he says, looking a little sickly.

I frown and then twist awkwardly, trying to see past my shoulder and down, but it's an impossibility. From the feel of it, I know the skin's torn up and raw down there, and the reflection I could make out in the water indicated it was a large gash. "Is it really that bad?"

The fact that Aequa's not answering, instead concentrating on cleaning the area— which doesn't sting as much as I think it should, oddly enough—is concerning, but I choose to let it go and just wait patiently for her to finish. Callidus sits opposite me, still looking green. "So. I assume other than the gaping hole in your arm, everything went as expected? The Sextii certainly seemed . . . miffed, from what little I heard before I decided it was time to leave."

"They were." I force some joviality against Aequa's touch. "By the way, your little ballad was quite something."

Callidus gives a tiny bow. "So we have a tracker?"

"Yes and no." I lean forward to get the tracking plate from my satchel, drawing a reproving growl from Aequa. I pass it to Callidus while trying not to move my arm. "The stones are Will-bound to the plate. But they don't seem to react to anything."

Callidus rotates the thin, circular stone experimentally. "They're not anchored around the plate itself, then. That makes sense."

"It does?"

"It's more efficient, at least. You only need the medallions to be Will-locked to a central point, rather than to each and every plate. That central point holds the state of everyone's positions, and broadcasts it back."

"Hm." He's right; I'm mildly annoyed I didn't think of that earlier. "So what's the central point?"

"It doesn't matter," says Aequa absently from behind me, most of her attention still taken with her task. "All you need is the alignment."

"Exactly," concurs Callidus. "The plate just needs to be pointed in the correct direction—probably using this mark up here." He indicates a thin line scored onto one edge of the circle. "North is most likely, I'd imagine."

I nod slowly. "And the stones aren't moving—or don't appear to be moving—because it's covering such a wide area. An inch is probably an hour's travel."

"Agreed." Callidus is squinting up at the sun, then turning himself so he's facing north. "We're not far from the western boundary, so you'd have to imagine that this is us here. The little square one probably represents the tracking plate itself. And your stone's missing a half, because you don't have the tracker in your stomach anymore." He nudges the leftmost group of small stones on the slate, one a distinct black semi-circle with marbled white streaks. "Which would mean the closest team to us is . . . miles away."

"If you're right," I add, more to remind him it's not confirmed than to suggest he isn't.

"I'm right."

We continue to study the plate, but the longer I look at it, the more I'm convinced of Callidus's theory. Most of the other groups are clustered around the centre of the island. Around the golden stone, which surely represents the Heart of Jovan. A quick test—aligning the slate, then using the tracking marble we were originally given—backs up the idea, with both of them indicating the same direction.

"This has to be Indol," says Aequa, pointing to a grouping of four stones around a unique white one, which itself is made of two tightly connected halves. All the distinctively coloured ones are the same in that respect. "He's the only one who could have convinced another two Fourths to switch sides this early."

"Iro's gone," notes Callidus thoughtfully.

"Belli and Felix, too." Aequa frowns as she makes the observation, pointing to the clear area near us. "Belli must have got back not long after I left, then—I was worried the safety team might get there before her. She went to scout ahead sometime last night, but she still wasn't there when I left this morning."

My stomach twists, but I push past the memory. "Looks like another Third's been eliminated, too." Aside from the Heart, there are only four unique stones left on the board.

"Speaking of which. You should have this back," says Aequa suddenly, briefly stopping her ministrations to unhook the white medallion from around her neck and loop it around mine.

"Anything else we need to know about last night?" asks Callidus.

I think, then between gritted teeth from Aequa's continued attention, tell them how Borius tried to stop me when I took the tracking plate. And then about the blood on the cloak I found. I'd almost forgotten about the latter, amid everything else.

"Surely he was just trying to scare you out of hiding," says Aequa. "The blood could be from hunting, or from an injury one of them got hiking around after us."

"It could have been," I admit.

"I'd probably have thrown some trees around, too, if I'd just been humiliated by one of the students I was supposed to be protecting." Callidus is grinning.

I let it go and the discussion moves on to Aequa's and Callidus's time since we were last together, but their reports are brief and dull. Callidus never came close to being caught and made it here without incident. Aequa left Iro's team under the guise of acting as a decoy with my medallion. For them, everything went very much according to plan.

We spend a while after that deciding what to do next: the tracking plate gives us not just a new breadth of viable options, but ones the other teams won't know we have. In the end, though, we agree on caution. I'm injured, and while I can move fast enough, I'm probably not going to be as useful in a fight. And it's smarter if we let one of the others try to take the Heart from the Sextii guarding it, anyway. Hopefully more teams will be eliminated before we're forced to act.

Aequa shifts behind me. "Done." It's taken longer than I'd expected—ten minutes, I think, from beginning to end. Mostly painless, though, which I'm not sure whether to be concerned about. I roll my shoulder experimentally, feeling a renewed pull, and she slaps me lightly on the side of the head. "Don't do that, idiot. Give it as much rest as you can."

I growl, rubbing my ear. "How bad is it?" She and Callidus exchange a glance. "I need to know."

"I think it's infected," Aequa admits. "The whole arm's looking bad. I've cleaned and bound it as best I can, but you'll need to see someone as soon as we finish."

I nod reluctantly, wondering how I'm going to explain away the bite marks to anyone who knows what they're looking at. Not to mention the writing on my skin.

After a light meal we start moving again; Aequa and Callidus both suggest I rest at various points, but eventually my disdainful glares stop their prodding. My arm *does* hurt, and under normal circumstances I'd want nothing more than to stop for a few hours and close my eyes. But I've already done the hardest part, exactly as Ulciscor wanted—I don't think he'll throw me to the wolves now, even if his questions about Caeror remain unanswered. All I need to do from here is provide myself a path to that embassy position in Jatiere.

I'm so close, I don't think I'll be able to make myself rest until it's over.

We angle directly for the nearest team, though Aequa estimates they're the better part of a few hours away. Callidus keeps a close eye on the stone plate, after a while announcing in somewhat smug fashion that he was right: pointing the tablet north, our progress tracks perfectly with the black and white half-stone, small square stone, and accompanying two grey ones.

We push on through thick forest, over streams, and across ravines, at one point having to skirt a bog of some kind for almost a mile. It's tiring, dreary work, requiring enough focus that conversation is all but impossible. There are a few times I think I hear rustling leaves or cracking twigs behind us, and part of me wonders whether Diago has somehow swum the river and continued to trail after me. I don't mention it to the others. I'm not sure how I'd even explain the possibility to them without sounding insane.

The sun's beginning to sink when Callidus swats away another tree branch, peers at the tracking plate, and holds up a hand. "We're getting close. Maybe an hour away."

"Already?" He's been giving us updates throughout the day, but I'm still surprised. We've been moving as fast as we can, but given that we're rarely following established trails, I didn't think we would get here so quickly.

"They're not moving. Everyone's watching the Heart, waiting for someone else to take it." He shakes his head, frowning. "That tracker is still spinning, too. I'd have thought one of the safety teams would be there by now." One half of the blue stone fell off the plate not long after we set out, and its corresponding semi-circle began gradually revolving. Callidus's hypothesis is that it indicates a Third's elimination, but that a safety team hasn't collected them yet.

"*Assuming* your theory about how the plate works is right," says Aequa.

"Of course it's—" Callidus starts to snap an answer back at her but then looks up, seeing our matching smirks. We've been wheedling him for a while about this. He narrows his eyes at us. "Yes."

We come to a halt, Callidus showing us the plate.

"Indol won't know we're coming for him," I say, pointing to the white stone with the four grey ones clustered around it. There are another four clustered around the other remaining Third now, too—at least one a defection from blue's elimination, we think. "We've been heading in a straight line for him, and he only knows our direction, not how close we are. He probably thinks we've stopped somewhere. But whoever else is left will realise we're getting closer. We need to split up."

We've been talking about this—arguing about it—for a while, and Callidus and Aequa's nods are still more reluctant than I'd like. One of us needs to take our trackers ahead, not too far from the Academy itself, as if we were positioning ourselves to wait for the Heart to be taken. It's what we would have done without the tracking plate. And it means that we can both maintain the element of surprise here and now, and force any team that does get away with the Heart into a slower, more oblique course as they skirt our supposed ambush.

"So who's going?" I trust them both. I don't want to lose either of them.

They look at one another. They've each spoken at length about why they should be the one to stay.

"We'll flip for it." Aequa produces a bronze triangle from her pocket. Balances it on her thumb, then points it at Callidus. "Call."

"Heads."

Aequa flicks the coin into the sky, then catches neatly and displays it. "Pyramid. I choose to stay with Vis."

I hold my tongue. She's the better fighter.

Callidus scowls but accepts the result, reluctantly taking my medallion and then Aequa's. I hand him the golden marble to track the Heart, too. "Keep an eye on this, and give yourself a good view," I remind him. "I doubt anyone will go out of their way to try and eliminate me if the Heart's already on its way to the Academy, but you can't be too careful."

"I know." Callidus pockets them, then sighs. "Look after yourselves. If something happens, no one will be able to find you."

Aequa snorts dismissively. I force a grin. He's thinking about the deaths from the past few Iudicia—deaths I'm almost certain were caused because Veridius, for some reason, has been sending students into that accursed dome. There's nothing to worry about on that account, at least. "We'll be fine. I'll find you once we have the Heart."

Callidus pauses again, as if he wants to say more, then returns the grin.

He slaps me on the back, and disappears into the forest.

LXX

AN OCCASIONAL BLAST OF WIND RIPS UP THE HILLSIDE AS Aequa and I crouch, examining the maze of crumbling walls in the distance where the Heart of Jovan seems to be hidden.

"There," says Aequa, stabbing her finger toward dual towers overlooking the deep, fast-moving river that flows through the valley. The ruins appear to be of an ancient fortified town. Not pre-Cataclysm, like those around the dome or near the Academy, but at least a century old judging from their disrepair. Aequa indicates the way the golden stone on the tracking slate is lined up with the barbican. "It's probably in one of those towers."

"Difficult to get to without being seen." Aside from the river protecting the western edge of the fortress, the forest is cleared for a good few hundred feet around the broken walls. We're north-west of the Heart. Indol is camped across the valley almost directly south of it, if our assumptions are correct, and the only other remaining coloured stone—which I'm quietly hoping is Emissa—is off to the east. All within a few miles of one another now. "We should move south a little more. Confirm it with a different angle."

"Alright."

We start off again, keeping low. Nobody's able to track us, but we're exposed up here.

I check the tracking plate from time to time over the next fifteen minutes. As the ground begins to level out again, and the trees become thicker, I frown at it. Then again, a few seconds later.

"What is it?" Aequa's noticed my hesitancy.

"We're going to pass fairly close to whoever got eliminated."

Aequa frowns. "No." She sees my expression. "No. That's what the safety teams are here for."

I think back to the blood on the cloak I took. As easily as Callidus and Aequa dismissed my concern, it hasn't been sitting well with me. "We don't have to make contact. Just scout." I rub the back of my neck when she glares at me. "It's been hours since it started spinning, and the other two eliminations had both halves fall off the plate. I've spent a lot of time with these people, Aequa. We may not all be friends, but I don't want any of them to die." *Any more of them.*

"You're in charge," Aequa says, in a way that indicates she thinks perhaps I shouldn't be.

We adjust our course slightly to the west, increasingly careful. The small square stone representing the plate's position gets closer and closer to the gradually rotating semi-circle, until they're almost touching.

Eventually, I stop. "It says we just passed them," I mutter, showing Aequa.

Aequa peers at the plate, then back into the clearing we've just traversed. "You want to look?"

"We're here now."

We retrace our steps. It's late afternoon, plenty of light. I stand in the centre of the open patch of grass and study the tree line, frowning. There's a buzzing coming from some shrubs. Flies, I think. I walk over.

It's the smell I notice first. Sickly-sweet. I grab a branch from the ground and apprehensively push aside the nearest bushes. I half suspect what I'm going to see before I do it, but the sight still makes me reel backward.

"What? What is . . ." Aequa's behind me; she's smelled it too, but I'm blocking her view. My stomach churns but I steady myself with the branch as a crutch, then use it to properly sweep aside the covering of leaves, other hand over my mouth.

Behind me, there's a gasp, and then Aequa retches. I don't even think to take my eyes off what's in front of me to help her.

I don't know how many bodies are in the open grave. A dozen? More? All lying in a terrible, tangled pile of limbs and torsos and torn clothing. It's their heads that arrest my attention, though. Each one of them is split open, bashed and shattered, flaking black-red blood infused with chunks of grey across blobs that are unrecognisable as faces. Flies swarm, feasting.

"Ahhh." Aequa lets out a great, shaky breath, wiping her mouth and reluctantly coming to stand beside me.

I nod absently, still in shock as I try to dissociate myself sufficiently from the sight to make sense of it. I recover enough to turn in a slow circle, examining the surrounding hillside. There's nothing. As far as I can tell, whoever or whatever did this is long gone.

"It's the safety teams," whispers Aequa.

She's right; impossible to recognise the faces, but some are still wearing the distinctive dark green cloaks. The one I'm wearing, thoroughly washed though it is, suddenly feels foul against my back.

"And Sianus," I add softly. I point. An arm protrudes from the bottom of the pile. It's bloodied, but the serpentine tattoos are unmistakeable.

This time, I retch.

"This . . . this was done using Will." Aequa's repossessed herself more quickly than me; she's still shaky but her tone has turned analytical. She points to holes in the ground past the mass grave. "There were trees here. It wouldn't have been hard to hit them before they knew what was happening."

I take a breath through the cloth of my tunic. Light-headed, but after last night, also somewhat inoculated to horror. She's right. "This was a trap." I look around again, even though I know that if the killers were still here, we'd already be dead. "They knew the safety teams would come. They wanted to exterminate them."

"Why?"

"It's an attack." I feel a chill as pieces fall into place. "The safety team we stole the tracker from were talking about something happening tonight. We have to warn the others."

"They won't believe us."

"They'll have to." I run a hand through my hair. "One of us should go for Callidus—"

"No." Aequa lays a hand on my good arm. At first I think she's going to object—I can see the fear in her expression—but instead she just takes a breath. "We'll warn him, but there's a chance nobody's even following him. He might be the safest out of all of us at the moment." She motions to the plate in my hand.

I reluctantly take her meaning. "Right." I check the stone circle again. "Indol's closest, then whoever else is left." *Emissa. Let it be Emissa.* I feel sick as I wonder what we actually brought down on Iro. Then I glance at the sky. The sun's already dipping below the tree line. "Should we split up?"

"Not yet. We'll pass right by Indol on our way to the second team, anyway. Once we reach him, one of us stays to convince him. The other can take the plate and head for the last team. After they've both been warned, we join Callidus, he throws away the trackers, and we all get back to the Academy."

I concur, grateful for her clearheadedness. We start to move, then I delay. Glance back at the crawling mess of bodies. My stomach roils as I play out what's about to happen.

"We have to do one more thing," I say grimly.

※ ※ ※

WE START TOWARD INDOL, WHO IS LESS THAN A HALF HOUR away, judging from the tracking plate. For the first few minutes we keep silent, scanning the woods around us, flinching at every imagined motion or misinterpreted sound.

"Why is this happening?" Aequa's voice is small as it reaches my ears.

I don't answer straight away. Through the shock and revulsion of our discovery, I've been trying to decide the same thing. It didn't take long for me to wonder whether this could be Relucia's Military-sponsored Anguis undertaking, that one I overheard discussed at Suus. I dismissed the idea out of hand, at first. But the more I consider it, the more it makes sense.

"Who benefits from the consequences?" I can't just tell her what I know.

"The Anguis. It has to be the Anguis again."

I can see it now. Can see why the Dimidius thought the naumachia was such a triumph. The Anguis being able to infiltrate Solivagus, kill Sextii and some of the Hierarchy's most prized students, would have been unthinkable a year ago. Now the question doesn't even cross Aequa's mind.

"Maybe." I push a branch from my path, wincing as it snaps. "But why would they attack the Academy?"

"We're an easy target. None of us wield Will, but we're the sons and daughters of the most important people in the country. And they may not be aiming to kill us all," she realises bleakly. "Ransom would be easy."

"And how would they know *exactly* how the Iudicium works?"

She opens her mouth, then changes her mind about whatever she was going to say. "They must have informants." She frowns. "You don't think it's them?"

"I don't know. It probably is. But it seems so obvious, I just wonder . . ." I hesitate. "Who else benefits? What actually happens in the Senate if we all die out here?"

Aequa glares at me for reminding her of the possibility, but I can see her considering the question. "I don't know. Everybody loses. All three pyramids are represented out here, so they all lose potentially strong leaders."

I say nothing. Wait.

"But I suppose . . . Religion would be blamed," she adds slowly. "They're the ones who are supposed to be keeping us safe."

"They'd lose their hold over the Academy," I agree. "Military would be asked to step in."

"That's not reason enough to do something like this, though." Aequa's voice is low but vehement. "Gods' graves, we're about to warn Indol. He's the Military Dimidius's *son*."

We all have to make sacrifices, Quiscil said.

"What if I told you he was going to defect to Religion, once the Iudicium was finished?"

Aequa stops. "You're sure?"

"As sure as I can be."

She doesn't ask how I know. "That would be embarrassing. A big blow for Military. But it proves nothing." Still confident, but the absolute certainty is gone.

It will have to do. I can't risk telling her more. "I know. But if you get out of this and not me, don't just assume. Whoever's doing this, we can't let them get away with it."

We lapse into tense silence again as we near Indol's position, the woods thinning, progress becoming easier.

"If we assume this is Indol"—I share the tracking plate with Aequa, pointing to the white stone our square marker is approaching—"then he must be on the high ground up there." I indicate a rise up ahead.

"He's set up to watch the Heart. And sitting between it and the Academy," Aequa says with a nod.

"We should circle around and come from behind him. From a direction his team aren't watching." I point to the grey stones clustered around the white one. "It looks like he's only got one Fourth actually with him, and the rest are spread out. Keeping guard, I imagine. Makes sense for him, seeing as no one's supposed to be able to track him. But there's a chance he'll move if he's alerted we're coming."

We adjust our course, walking for almost twenty minutes as we slip behind Indol's position. He's taken some of the highest ground available: a small distance from the Heart, but with enough of a view to track anyone who approaches it. It's the smart strategy for him. Patient and effective.

Finally we hear the mutter of voices, and I signal to Aequa. We crouch low, creeping forward until there's a splash of colour through the trees. Indol has made his camp well, high up but hidden from below, no easy approach.

"So. Options? He's going to think we're attacking him," I whisper.

"We could still just leave him to fend for himself." I fix her with a stare. "I said *could*, not *should*."

"Hm." I grunt, then shake my head at the angle of the sun. It's getting low, and the need to press on is burning in me. "Nothing for it. We can't waste time." I press the tracking plate into Aequa's hand. "Indol's not going to believe just you, and I don't know how long it will take me to convince him. Get to the other team. Show them what we took. And if that doesn't work . . . if it's Emissa, tell her what I told you about Indol. She's the one who told me. She'll know I would never have said anything unless this was about more than just the Iudicium." I take a breath. "I'll join you as soon as I can. Then we'll go and find Callidus."

Before she can protest, I stand. Walk forward, not bothering to conceal myself or stay quiet. "Indol!" I yell, raising my arms. "It's Vis! We need to talk! I swear on my ancestors I'm not here to fight!"

There's scrambling ahead of me, followed by a heavy silence.

Then Indol's voice cuts through the trees. "Talk, Vis." He sounds angry. I imagine I would be too, if moments ago I'd been comfortable with the locations of everyone else in the contest. "Try anything, though, and—"

"There are Anguis out here, Indol." My voice is lower this time; I keep walking, into the clearing where Indol has made camp. I can't see him, but I'm guessing he's close enough to see me. "They've replaced our safety teams and can track us. I overheard one of them say that they're going to make their move tonight." I stop in the middle of the clearing, arms still raised. "I think they're here to kill us, Indol. All of us. We need to run."

"This is a ploy." Indol's voice comes from a different direction this time. Muffled by thick foliage, impossible to pinpoint. "Not even a very good one."

I unsling my satchel. Take out the bloodied green cloak—the cleanest one I could find in that pile of bodies—and lay it on the ground. Unwrap it.

I pick up the hand by a finger and hold it up, stomach clenching at both sight and smell. I turn slowly, making sure that wherever he is, he'll be able to see it. "This is from one of the safety teams. I don't know whose, because they were all in a pile." I falter. "Along with Sianus."

"Rotting gods." There's a delay, then rustling ahead of me. Indol steps into the clearing, horror pasted across his face in the waning light. Beside him, Axien emerges wearing a similar expression. "Toss it on the ground over here."

I do as he asks. Indol crouches beside it, looking up and around, still expecting some sort of trap. Once his gaze fixes on the hand, though, it doesn't move.

"You don't have your tracker?"

"Threw it up as soon as we started."

Indol grunts. "Thought about that. Didn't seem like it was worth it." His regret is thick. "How did you find me?"

"Stole a tracking plate."

His eyebrows raise, though his eyes still don't leave the bloodied hand. "Clever." The compliment's hollow, though. Quiet. He's as shocked as I was. "Still got it?"

"Aequa does. She's gone to warn the one team that's left. Callidus doesn't know yet; he went ahead with our trackers before we found out. We'll find him next. I don't know where the others are."

"I eliminated Sianus. He and Ava wandered too close to the camp." Indol's voice is soft. "Gods' graves. I left them there for the safety team to find this morning."

I wince. Ava's probably dead, too, but saying it aloud won't help. "Let the rest of your team know, then split up. These Anguis are Sextii, maybe higher. There's no safety in numbers. We need to just scatter and run."

"Alright." Indol sucks in a deep breath. He's calm, taking this with more poise than I could have hoped for. "I'll get the others to attach their medallions to logs and float them down the river, when they can. Or tie them to wild animals. Or leave them in place after a few hours, if they can't do any of those."

"Good idea." We both know Indol's going to be the target, but this will give the others the best chance of getting away. "You should head west. Get over the river. I don't think the tracking extends that far."

Indol acknowledges the statement. "Go and get the others," he instructs Axien quietly. "Tell them what to do, then go yourself. No point in any of you coming back here."

Axien gives us a worried glance, but ducks his head and vanishes into the trees.

Indol waits until he's gone, then turns back to me. There's a heaviness to his bearing. He knows his odds. "What happened to your arm?"

I glance down. Grimace. There's a black bruise travelling along it, visible through the tears in my tunic. Almost touching my wrist. "Alupi bite."

"It looks bad. Make sure Ulnius sees it as soon as you get back." He turns to leave.

"Wait." I have to let him know. It may be my only chance. "Once all this is over, be careful of your father, Indol."

"What?" Indol's expression hardens, but he catches sight of the hand on the ground again. Swallows whatever angry retort he was planning. "Why would you say that?"

"I overheard something. At Suus." I keep my gaze locked with his. "It sounded like he was assisting the Anguis with something. And if he's heard that you're planning to defect to Religion . . ."

Indol blanches. "How did you know about that?"

"Emissa told me." I thought he'd already figured that out.

"How did *she* know?"

My heart skips a beat as I process the question. "She said you told her."

"She lied." He watches my expression, then sighs. "You're going to find her, aren't you." He shakes his head, then digs into his pocket and tosses me something. A sack that clinks. "She's the green one. Last one left, other than us. Luck, Vis. If I don't make it out of this . . . thank you for trying."

He gives me a tight, weary smile, then slings his satchel over his shoulder and disappears into the underbrush.

LXXI

I CUP EMISSA'S TRACKER IN MY PALM. CHECK I'M STILL HEAD-
ing in the right direction. Push forward again as fast as I dare. I left only a couple of
minutes behind Aequa.

My thoughts continue to race as I force my way through scratching bramble and
damp leaves, the shocked haze of finding the corpses gradually lifting. If this really is
the Anguis's Military-sponsored attack, then Relucia knows they're here. And if she
knows they're here, they surely have orders not to kill me.

But on the other hand, she did say that only one other person in the Anguis knew
about me. That I was a cog.

And if the Anguis here don't know who I am, then I'm still a target.

Maybe, for many of them, *the* target.

It's not fifteen minutes later that I'm bursting into a clearing to find Aequa and
Marcellus facing each other. Marcellus looks ill. Aequa flinches at my arrival, giving me
a reflexive glare before relaxing again.

"He knows," she says, gesturing to the severed hand on the ground between them.

"Where's Emissa?" I check the tracking marble. It's pulling directly at Marcellus.

"She did what you did. Vomited it back up and used it as a decoy." Aequa's grim.
"She convinced Valentina and Tem to join her, too, after she eliminated Prav. Those
three and Titus are going for the Heart right now."

"It's at the top of the eastern tower," supplies Marcellus, his voice weak. "She's
using the other three to draw out the Sextii on watch. Then she'll go up there and get
it herself."

My blood turns cold. "How long?" When Marcellus doesn't answer immediately I
snarl, take a threatening step toward him. "*How long since she left, Marcellus?*"

"A quarter hour. Not more."

I glance at the sky, mind whirling. She'll move just as dusk turns to night. I turn
to Aequa. "Show me the tracking plate."

It doesn't take long to see what Emissa's planning, given how Titus, Valentina, and
Tem are arranged. Emissa guessed that Indol would be watching, so she's letting them
be seen. Using them as a distraction for both Indol and the Sextii who are supposed
to be guarding the Heart, while she slips around and approaches the tower from the

other side. The fading light, the muddying of other team's members being involved . . . it would have been difficult once she had possession of the Heart, but still the best possible start. Confusing to everyone except her.

I frown around at the forest. There's something tickling at my mind. Like a sound I can't quite hear, a movement I can sense but not quite see. Distant.

"Are you alright?" Aequa looks at me worriedly.

"I'm fine. You get to Callidus. Marcellus, you're with me. We need to warn the others."

Marcellus unhooks the two medallions that were sitting around his neck and drops them to the ground. Then he digs in his pocket and tosses a small black bead alongside them. "No."

Aequa and I look at him. "What?"

"I'm leaving." There's shame on Marcellus's face, but also resolve. "I'm not dying for this."

"You rotting, fetid coward." Aequa spits the words and looks about to follow up with something worse, but I put a hand on her arm.

"Ignore him. No time."

Aequa's expression is still black, but she turns her back on Marcellus. The boy hurries away into the forest. I let him go.

"Warn Callidus. Get him to smash my medallion." I channel my father as I give the command. Calm and stern. "We've delayed long enough; these people are going to realise something is wrong very soon. And if this is the Anguis, they may want me dead more than anyone else." I press Indol's bag of tracking stones into her hand as she opens her mouth to protest. "If you get spotted, don't risk your life. Just run and get the rotting hells away. If my stone's still on the tracking plate, I'll know something went wrong and find a way to warn him myself."

Aequa looks at the bag. "I still think—"

"Wait." I hold up a finger, cutting her off. There's something from the direction of the deep forest. The same feeling as I had before, but more insistent. A pulse of sensation, but not audible or visible. It's growing stronger. "Hide."

"What are you—"

"*Hide.*" I hurriedly kick the hand on the ground into the brush, then forcibly drag her into the thickest undergrowth nearby. She has the composure not to protest, though she shakes my grip and glares with confused irritability afterward.

Ten seconds pass. Twenty. Aequa shifts, looking like she's about to reprimand me.

There's a rustling, and two men walk into the clearing. One of them is carrying a tracking plate.

"Should be here," the one with the plate mutters, head bowed over it. The other scans their surroundings, eyes narrowed against the rapidly fading light. His gaze passes over us. There's no sign he sees anything out of the ordinary.

That strange sensation is emanating from them. It's impossible to describe. A pulsing beacon that I know is entirely in my head, but that I can pinpoint in physical space.

The second man suddenly steps forward, snatches something up off the ground. Marcellus's and Emissa's medallions. "Another two."

"Little bastards know."

"How?"

"Doesn't matter how." The bigger man tosses the medallions to the ground again. Stomps on them emphatically, stone crunching as it breaks. "We just have to get as many of them as we can. Come on."

They vanish the way they came. The pulsing sensation fades.

Aequa and I crouch for a good twenty seconds longer before she turns to me. "You heard them coming?"

I nod.

"Good ears." I can see she wants to probe further—she doesn't believe me; it's the naumachia all over again—but instead she yields. "Alright. You're right. I'll go and warn Callidus. Just . . . be careful down there."

We exchange tight smiles. Without anything further, she disappears southward.

※　※　※

THE DUAL TOWERS LOOM AGAINST THE FADING HORIZON AS I run at a crouch, chest constricted, then scramble over a collapsed moss-covered wall and duck out of sight.

The guard's footsteps pad along the other side of the stone a breath later. I feel his passing in my head, risk a peek out once he's past. I can't see his face, just dirty-blond hair hanging past his shoulders. He's wrapped in a grey cloak. I have no idea what the men guarding the Heart would have been wearing, but it doesn't matter. Whoever's behind this attack knew enough to take out all the safety teams. They wouldn't have risked leaving the last two opposing Sextii alive.

The man clomps around the corner, and I lever myself back up. I haven't had time to question this strange new ability, but it's proving useful: this is the third time I've felt the presence of someone before I've seen or heard them. Without it, there's no way I could have made it this deep into the fortress without being spotted.

I school myself to patience, waiting before moving. As tempting as it's been to simply rush in and scream a warning, I know it would be pointless; aside from the obvious danger to myself, Emissa and her team would just assume it's a trap. All I'd be doing is alerting our attackers.

I consult my tracking plate. Marcellus seems to have been right about the Heart being in the tower ahead, and thankfully—or perhaps worryingly—it hasn't moved. The three students acting as Emissa's diversions are nearby, most likely hiding in a cluster of largely intact buildings just to the north. Hopefully she's still with them.

As the pulse of danger dwindles from my senses I emerge again, keeping low, creeping toward the overgrown buildings. Dusk is fully upon me now, pink-tinged wisps of cloud fading to grey above. Dead leaves crunch underfoot. Everything else is silent.

It takes me two minutes to scurry from shadow to shadow, as fast as I dare, before I reach a large, walled courtyard. The remains of a fountain lie in its centre, arches surrounding it. I frown at my tracking plate. Scan the area.

Shrink back in horror as I spot the darker shapes high against the wall to my left.

The bodies are untouched, except for two areas. Where jagged stone spikes have nailed them, spread-eagled. And where their heads have been beaten to grisly, unrecognisable pulps.

Just like the safety teams. Just like Sianus.

My hands shake as I tear my gaze from the ruins of their skulls, looking for any other identifying features. There are just the three of them. One girl with long blond hair—Valentina. One with dark skin—Tem. And the other boy must be Titus.

I'm ashamed at my relief that Emissa's not among them, even as my hands ball into fists.

"Do not mourn them."

The words are accompanied by an abrupt presence behind me. Too close. Burning bright inside my head. I whirl, knife out and at the ready.

The man is tall and slender, narrow features cut by a pink-white line stretching from forehead to chin. It takes only a moment to place him.

The Festival of Pletuna. Relucia's mysterious meeting.

"You know me," the man says, cocking his head to the side. "From where?"

"I don't know you." I don't lower my knife. "Stay back."

"Now, now." The man's gaze flits from me to the corpses draped on the wall behind, then back again. "We have time, young man. Let us talk."

"We have nothing to talk about."

"I disagree." The stranger begins circling. Slowly. Not coming toward me, but more as if he wants to get a better look at me. "Interesting. Oh, *interesting*. Of all the people in this world, we two have at least one thing to discuss." He makes an odd sign, tapping his heart three times with three fingers.

I ignore him. My knife firmly between him and me. "Why are you doing this?" I jerk my head at the Fourths' bodies, never taking my eyes from him.

The man looks disappointed. "That is not *the question*, young man. That is not an exchange worth having." He produces a knife of his own. Smaller than mine. He flicks it idly in one hand. Lets it roll across his fingers, the wicked-looking short blade in and out between them, smooth as water. "But I shall indulge you, just this once. We are doing this at Military's behest, though they think we don't know. They expect that like the naumachia, we will be eager to claim responsibility. They expect that this will solidify us as a threat to all the Republic, allowing them to push through new laws and shore up their crumbling power in the Senate. And they expect the Senate to demand that they take over the Academy, to ensure such a massacre of promising young leaders never happens again. Because they do not know why this island is special—but they *do* know that it is."

He continues circling, toying with the knife. "Of course, this will end with only one of our number being captured. And his interrogation will reveal that it was an attack sponsored from within the Hierarchy, a play to strip Religion of their control of the Academy. Though not who, exactly, was behind it." He smiles. Shadowed and dark. "And even should others gain access to Solivagus because of this little incident, they will never find the gate. Because Veridius will bury it before he ever allows someone else near it."

My heart pounds. "I don't know what you're talking about."

The stranger sighs.

The air *warps*, and he vanishes from view.

A second passes. Two. I stare around wildly. Not sure what to make of it.

"Yes you do," the whisper comes from behind, a cold blade resting against my neck.

I drop my knife and splay my fingers in surrender, otherwise staying perfectly still. The pressure on my throat eases, but doesn't disappear.

"Now," murmurs the man. "Your safety team knew not to attack you, but these others . . . well. I *could* tell them. But then they would wonder why the boy who killed their leader was being spared. And we can't have that. So go. Claim your prize." A note of pleased amusement to the stranger's voice. "Now that I know we are kin, young man, I am *so very eager* to see what you can do."

I don't speak immediately, fear and fury clotting my tongue.

"No. Relucia should have known better." I get it out eventually. My voice shakes. It's the wrong move, the wrong thing to say, but something's breaking in me. The Anguis are responsible. The Anguis are responsible and at least in part, they're doing all of this to make me Domitor. "I thought we'd come to an understanding. I was willing to cooperate, before this."

"Relucia?" The man pauses, then laughs delightedly. "Oh, come now. She just does as she's told. Our little revolutionary dreams too small for the likes of us, I fear."

My brow furrows. At the Festival of Pletuna, I thought Relucia was giving this man orders. But the way he's speaking about her here is fondly condescending.

"Why in the rotting hells would I do what you want me to do, then?"

"Because she is up there, too."

My breath catches. The way he says *she*, there's no doubting who he means.

"She's alive?"

"For the moment."

"Touch her, and I will find a way to kill you."

He chortles, as if I've just made a grand joke. "Win, and you have my word. She shall remain unharmed."

I think. Scrunch my eyes closed in frustration. "Agreed."

The pressure on my throat vanishes. I turn carefully. The man has stepped back.

"One last piece of advice, young man," he says quietly. "You should prepare yourself to lose that arm. None of us get out without scars." He touches his disfigurement lightly.

There's another warping in the air, and then he's gone.

I release a shuddering breath once I'm sure I'm alone, scrambling over to my knife and snatching it up again. My sense of the stranger has vanished; there are only two fainter pulses from nearby, both from atop the left-most tower.

I peer up. It's close, only a few buildings away. The square façade stretches perhaps a hundred feet into the air, though it shows plenty of gaps where time has worn the stone away. It's in better condition than its twin, though, and its peak looks intact. No motion from up there, but there's light. And no mistaking those unsettling beats in my head.

I slip through the deepening shadows to its base, and begin to climb.

The stairs creeping around the tower's core are old and crumbling. A short waterfall in the river below hisses into the night. I ascend as swiftly as I can while still being quiet. If the stranger was telling the truth and Emissa's up here, she probably has no idea what's happened down below. Probably has no idea of the danger she's in. That leaves me with few options. She still thinks we're in opposition to each other; as long as she's still trying to get the Heart, yelling a warning will do nothing except draw every Anguis in the area.

Which means I'm going to have to face whoever's up here, and hope that Emissa helps take them down before they alert the others or kill me.

The pulsing above increases in intensity as I climb. Definitely two sources. I'm still profoundly unsettled by the idea that I can sense people like this, but for now, its utility outstrips my trepidations.

I reach the top, stealing a look over the stone parapet. Torches are lit around the tower's edges. A single man lounges in the centre of the battlement. He's enormous. A half-foot taller than me, lean and muscular. Bigger than many of the Octavii I used to fight in Letens.

There's no sign of Emissa or anyone else, but the other pulse is coming from a jumble of wooden crates and rubble on the opposite side of the tower. Emissa must be hiding in there, waiting for her team to cause a distraction below. She probably scaled the far wall to avoid the guard's notice.

"Come for this?" The man rolls lazily to his feet, holding up the golden Heart of Jovan between two fingers, though he never looks at me. He must have heard me coming, despite my best efforts.

There's no point in hiding. I climb the last few stairs and step onto the battlement. "Yes."

The guard finally turns to me. His face lights up in recognition.

"Catenicus." A low and harsh delight to the name.

His eyes flood to black.

LXXII

THE WILL-IMBUED ANGUIS SOLDIER SNARLS AS HE LEAPS AT ME.

There's no subtlety, no cat-and-mouse here. He covers the twenty feet between us in a single, powerful lunge, fist drawn back. No mistaking his intent.

I'm prepared for the attack and still only barely dive away in time. Climbing up here, some part of me wondered if I had a chance in a straight fight, my victory over the Sextus in Letens in the back of my mind. Now it's too late, I can see how ridiculous a thought that was. My opponent in the Theatre was barely a fighter, weak for his rank, and even then I only beat him because he decided to ignore me. There's no crowd here. No distractions.

And this man . . . this man seems neither weak nor inexperienced.

The realisations come in a wave as the guard's fist crashes down on the spot I was standing. The tower shakes as stone shatters, chunks the size of my fist spraying away off the side and vanishing into the steadily darkening void. I roll back to my feet, breath coming heavy. He's a Sextus, then; no Septimus could do that. A cloud of dust drifts across the nearest torch as he turns. Brushes debris off his knuckles with a wide smile. "Melior will be watching this with great joy."

"Melior's dead. Remember?" I give him a self-satisfied smile of my own. Probably a bad idea, but I can't think of anything else to do. I don't have a chance if he's in control of himself.

The Sextus's smirk withers. His body stiffens.

He charges forward. No snarl this time, no leaping. Just midnight eyes and hatred and utter silence.

My experience against Septimii in the Theatre serves me well here; this was a common enough tactic of theirs, even if they weren't actually trying to kill me. I dance to the side, unbalancing the Sextus as he adjusts, then at the last second dive in the opposite direction, barely under a swing that would have removed my head. I twist as he stumbles past, punching him with all my strength in the kidney. It's like punching stone.

He feels it; I can tell from the way he gasps, falters. That lasts for less than a moment.

He growls. Still facing away from me. Aims a punch at the wall in front of him.

It explodes outward, showering debris downward.

Then he's spinning. Moving like I didn't touch him, like he didn't just slam his fist through stone that's three-foot thick. Coming at me again, this time more deliberately. Trying to pin me against one of the edges of the tower. I can hear the rushing of the river far below.

The Sextus isn't imbuing anything, despite there being plenty of rubble lying around: he's either not skilled enough, or it will take too long. That's my one advantage at the moment. Given how easily Ulciscor killed Sacro after the attack on the Transvect, it's beyond fortunate.

We circle, me focusing on quick movements, not allowing myself to get cornered. The Sextus's lip curls in frustration—he thought this would be over by now—and then he stops. Bends down and picks up a block of stone maybe twice the size of my fist.

Stupidly, I think he's going to imbue it. He doesn't.

He just throws it at me.

I dodge but I'm too caught by surprise by the simplicity of it, too accustomed to fighting by a set of rules. The stone catches me on my injured arm, tearing through my tunic. There's searing pain, a crunching sound. I'm spun by the sheer force of it.

My left foot slips backward, searching for a foothold. Nothing's there. I sway precariously, lurch to the side. Fall with half my body dangling from the tower, scrabble madly to haul myself back up, barely able to see from the agony.

My vision clears to find the Sextus standing over me. He raises a foot to kick me off the edge.

A strange expression comes over his face. Puzzlement, more than anything else. He takes a stumbling step. Then another. His fist opens, the Heart of Jovan clattering to the ground next to me. The darkness fades from his eyes. The pulsing in my head from his presence dies.

He keels forward.

I snatch the Heart up before he lands on it and then wrench myself away, just enough that he slumps past me and over the side. I catch a glimpse of something dark detaching from the base of his skull and flitting back behind me. Blood spurts as his body tumbles through the air, a strangely slow shadow in the murk, until there's an echoing splash when it hits the river far below. He's face-down as the water carries him off.

I turn to see Emissa standing there, a short, dripping obsidian blade in her trembling hand.

Her eyes are black.

"He was trying to kill you," she says softly. Disbelievingly. "Not just stop you from taking the Heart. Actually *kill* you." She rushes over to me. Gentle. Concerned. Her eyes have faded back to their normal, beautiful green.

"Pretty much." I groan as I lie there, letting her examine my injuries. My arm's thundering with pain.

"Why?" She hisses a breath as she takes in the blackened limb. "Rotting gods, Vis. What's going on?"

"That was an alupi." Breathing is coming hard, the wind still knocked from me. "But the safety teams, everyone here who's not a student—they're Anguis. They're trying to kill us all, Emissa. We need to go and find Callidus. The others are either already dead or running for the Academy."

Her face is pale in the rising moonlight. "My team?"

I shake my head.

Emissa draws a shuddering breath. I can almost see her compartmentalising, separating the horror of what I've told her from what needs to be done. She believes me, though. It's hard to explain how grateful I am for that. "We have to get out of here, then. But not before I look at that arm."

"Aequa already bandaged it up." I try to rise.

"That was before you got a wall thrown at it." She forces me back down with very little effort. Smiles wanly, her eyes meeting mine as she cups my face in her hand. There's so much in her gaze. Concern. Relief. Affection. Guilt.

"You used Will," I observe weakly.

"We can talk about that later." Emissa's brisk as she takes her obsidian blade and deftly cuts away some of my tunic, hissing again as she sees the extent of the damage to my flesh. "We need to get you to . . ."

She freezes.

"What?" I crane my neck down at where she's staring, but can't see anything. "What is it?"

"Nothing." Her voice is odd. She doesn't look at me. She carefully replaces the folds of my tunic and then stands. Backs away a few steps.

"Emissa?" I drag myself to my feet. "What's wrong?"

"You need to give me the Heart."

I snort a weak laugh, though my humour wilts when I see she's serious. "We have more important things—"

"I need it. I need to win the Iudicium." She looks up, and to my disbelief, her eyes are black again. The obsidian dagger's resting in her hand. "I can't risk us getting separated. Please."

I stare at her in utter confusion, the sense of betrayal shockingly painful. "You didn't need to threaten me," I say softly. I stagger to right myself. Toss the golden triangle at her feet. It clatters against the tower.

She gazes at it without speaking, hair hanging over her face. Her chest heaves, and I realise that she's sobbing.

I take a step forward, concerned as well as confused now. "Emissa—"

The dagger flies toward me. I flinch, but not enough.

It buries itself in my stomach.

There's a moment of disbelief, where I almost don't register the terrible burning in my gut. I let out a little gasp. Too stunned and hurt to do anything else as the dagger keeps pushing in. I pull at its hilt but it's too strong. Drives me backward.

Off the edge.

I flail. Topple. Emissa's still looking at the ground, still shaking. I let go of the dagger and reach out to grasp at the air. Frantic. Searching for anything at all to hold on to. Knowing I'm going to die and not understanding why.

The Heart, still lying at Emissa's feet, snaps back into my hand.

I have just enough time to see Emissa's tear-stained face jerk up in confusion before she vanishes from sight.

I fall.

There's no control, no thought of righting myself. Just pain and weariness and confusion and deep, deep hurt.

I sense the water rushing up more than see it. I was too high, this time. Too unprepared. Too injured. The impact isn't going to be much better than hitting the ground.

I close my eyes, and finally give in.

LXXIII

IMPOSSIBLY, I WAKE.

The world feels like it's on fire; the first thing I do is vomit up water, twisting and coughing and hacking my lungs onto the pebbles around me. My vision clears. It's night. Moonlight gleams silver off the river, which flows all around me, numbing. I drag myself higher onto the stony beach using my good arm; the other one moves when I command it to, but with significant accompanying pain. There's blood dribbling off my forearm from small puncture wounds. Blood still leaking from my stomach, red wafting away from my tunic and mingling with the clear water until it dissipates.

My fist is clenched, locked painfully tight. I force my fingers to unfurl.

The Heart of Jovan glitters in my palm. Cold comfort.

There's movement up the bank. A mass of matted fur, eyes glinting as they watch me.

"Diago?" I croak the name. The massive alupi shifts, continues to stare.

I crawl a little farther, wheezing. Dizzy. Some part of me recognises that the marks on my arm are from Diago's teeth. He dragged me from the river. Saved my life. I reach out toward him. He growls.

"Same to you," I mutter wearily, letting my hand fall.

There's no part of my body that doesn't ache. No part that doesn't feel like it's been broken. That seems only right, though. I should be dead. Perhaps someone imbuing themselves could have survived that fall—a Sextus, maybe even a Septimus. But not me. Especially not in the physical state I was already in.

I lie on my back. The stars are bright tonight. My fingers reluctantly make their way to my stomach. Probe gently, waiting for the accompanying rush of pain, the feel of torn flesh, the gushing of sticky blood.

There's tenderness—but not as much as I expect. I lever myself up on an elbow, gently pull back my shredded tunic.

The puncture in my stomach is there, washed clean by the flowing water. It's still seeping blood, but it's a trickle. No worse than my arm. And the wound looks smaller than it should be. Shallower.

I gain enough courage to press a little harder; immediately a pulse of blood slips out and I stop quickly, grimacing. Not miraculously healed, then. Just not as bad as I thought. It was, admittedly, a very small dagger.

It just felt a lot worse, buried in me and pushing me off the tower.

Emissa tried to kill me.

The nauseating memory worms its way through everything else. I can't understand it. The thought robs me of energy, of any desire I might have to get up off the ground. She was upset about it, but she did it. All for . . . what? To win the Iudicium? Surely not. I'd already given her the Heart. And I know her better than that.

Or, I thought I did. A wave of bitterness threatens to overcome me.

My satchel's still tied to my back; with an effort I unsling it and paw through its sodden contents until I find the tracking plate. Most of the stones are gone. The ones from Emissa's team remain, though, which allows me to estimate how far east I've been washed. Several miles, I think. That's good. Useful.

I realise the marker for the Heart is missing as well. Another examination of the Heart itself reveals no damage, nothing that might have deformed it enough to cause the imbuing to fail. Strange. I shiver as I remember the way it flew into my hand. I was flailing, reaching for anything that might stop me from falling, and it just . . . came.

My ability to sense other people without seeing them, and now this. My skin crawls. Something's wrong with me. A result of whatever that place past the Labyrinth did to me last night, I assume. It's the only explanation.

Sick though the thought makes me, at least whatever imbuing was on the Heart seems to have been lost, so I can hold on to it without being tracked. I push my other concerns to the side, touching the black half-stone that shows my medallion. It hasn't moved from where it was when I last checked. Hasn't fallen off. And judging from the moon, much of the night has passed.

Urgency lends sudden energy to my limbs.

The aches persist but once I'm on my feet, I'm surprised by my body's ability to resist collapsing again. My left arm goes numb with pain if I do more than let it dangle limply by my side, but everything else seems simply sore. Tender, but not incapacitated. The more I move, tentatively stretching out, the more I'm convinced that everything is badly bruised rather than broken.

I wring out the worst of the water from my clothes, head clearing enough to assess. Callidus is probably a half-day away, maybe more; even a small delay for Aequa would mean she hasn't been able to get to him yet. But it's equally possible that she did what I told her to do. Value her life. Run in a different direction, if the need arose.

I fish some sodden meat from my satchel and chew grimly for a few minutes, aware that starting off without gathering at least some strength would be foolish. I toss a small piece to Diago, who's still lying by the river. He ignores it. I glare at him. He ignores me.

Finally, just as dawn is colouring the sky, I reach the point where I know I have to move. Far from rested, but beginning to stiffen up. Too in danger of falling asleep.

So I start toward Callidus.

The day passes, my movements sluggish, progress far slower than I'd like despite my determination to press forward. Diago disappears into the undergrowth; occasionally I see him flitting through the trees, but otherwise he keeps to himself. I don't mind. Partly because the creature still makes me uneasy, and partly because I think he might be scouting ahead. Making sure my path is safe.

My half-stone on the tracking plate never moves.

The sun's burning near its zenith by the time I get close enough to start the awkward climb to Callidus's elevated position. It's a smart spot, with a view for miles to the north. My disquiet grows. He should already have spotted my approach. And Callidus would be quick to show himself, to come and help, once he saw my sorry state.

But there's nothing. Just birdcalls and snapping twigs and the rustle of the breeze through leaves.

My legs ache, my eyes strain, and my left, blackened arm is worryingly unresponsive as I haul myself higher.

Up ahead, there's a scream.

I break into as much of a sprint as my body can manage, tearing through branches and bursting into a clearing. My heart stops. Two men lie at the far end, and even from this distance I can see red glistening on their tunics.

Both lie motionless. One of them is Callidus.

"Vek!" The word rips from my throat. I dart over, skidding to my knees beside my friend.

Callidus is on his side; the other man is staring sightlessly at the sky, throat torn clean out. I gently roll Callidus over, groaning as I see the wicked cuts across his chest and stomach and arms. He's lost a lot of blood.

I start as he suddenly gives a rasping, sputtering cough.

"Callidus." I tear a strip from my tunic, begin binding the wounds as best I can while cushioning his head with a hand. "*Callidus*. Wake up."

Callidus stirs. Moans. His eyes flutter open. "Vis?"

"Stay still. You're injured."

"Really?" Callidus gives another cough, then a strange, uneasy wheeze. "But I feel so good."

"Maybe I'll just leave you here, then." I smile, though I doubt it's doing anything to hide my concern. There's blood *everywhere*. "Don't worry. I can get you back."

Callidus eyes me. "Are you sure you don't need me to get *you* back?" He coughs again. There's a fleck of blood at the corner of his mouth. "Gods' graves, man. You look terrible."

I bark a laugh that's half choked with fear. "I'll manage. Just need to tie up these gashes a bit better." I tear another strip. "What happened?" I don't really need to know, but it's the only thing I can think of to keep him talking. To keep him with me.

"Not sure. Minding my own business, and then . . . this." He turns his head weakly to look across at the dead man. "He was angry. Kept saying he'd been left behind. Was talking about how he was going to take his time with me. Charming fellow. Must have had me for an hour, at least, before that alupi came and ripped out his throat." He wheezes. "Good times."

"He was Anguis. They assassinated the safety teams, got their tracking plates. Tried to kill all of us."

"I . . . wondered. Aequa?"

"I don't know." She must have been forced away from here. I shouldn't have told her not to risk it. "A lot of the Fourths didn't make it. And Sianus."

"Rotting gods."

"See? Things aren't so bad for us."

"I feel so lucky."

"Exactly. Now hold on. I'm going to pick you up. This . . . will probably hurt."

I try to lift him as carefully as I can, but my left arm's excruciating and all but useless; I'm hardly able to carry him at all, let alone smoothly. Callidus lets out an agonised moan as I awkwardly cradle him.

"Didn't . . . hurt . . . at all," he gasps.

I start walking.

"You . . . should take this."

I seriously consider throwing away the white medallion he's offering me, but it sounds like the attacker Diago killed was the last one. If it wasn't so important—if it didn't, perhaps, mean all the difference for me—I'd do it without a second's thought, and to rot with the Iudicium. But I need it. I still, after all this blood and pain, need to win. So I take it awkwardly and drop it in my pocket.

"Vis?" Callidus sounds sleepy.

"Stay awake, Callidus."

"You'll tell my father?"

"Tell him what?"

"Why I was in Seven." He gives a little sigh. "You don't have to mention Belli. Better to say you don't know who it was. But I . . . I really want him to know."

I don't tell him that Belli's dead. I'm not even sure how much it would register.

"I'll tell him." The lump in my throat hurts. I don't know what else to say.

We stumble on for a while. I do my best to talk, though I need every breath to keep going. I make jokes. Complain about how heavy he is. Tell him how jealous he's going to be when we're both in the Senate, and I'm explaining to everyone how I single-handedly saved him. Callidus is silent for the most part, just speaking enough to indicate he's still with me.

At one point, I'm babbling about the time of year, and something occurs to me. "What's the date today?"

"I . . . don't know. Seventh . . . day . . . of Jovanius?"

I give a single, helpless laugh. That's what I thought.

"What . . . is it?"

I plod on. "Nothing. Just funny how quickly time goes."

I remembered it once or twice, in the lead-up to the Iudicium, but this is the first time it's struck me since then.

Today is my eighteenth birthday.

% % %

I DON'T KNOW WHAT TIME CALLIDUS DIES.

He slips first into a rasping unconsciousness, perhaps an hour after we start out. I try to wake him, but it's to no avail. I know that if I stop, I won't be able to go on again. So I keep moving. Keep carrying him. Still talk, now and then, even though I know he can't hear me. Encourage him. Exhort him. Demand he stay alive.

It's only when I'm excitedly relaying the fact that I can see the Academy up ahead that I realise there's no rise and fall to his chest. I push on, even as my vision starts blurring. I don't know what else to do.

The guards at the entrance see me coming up the path from a distance away, rush to help. I snarl at them. Shrug off their hands. Keep walking. They look at each other, then follow without a word.

I don't see anyone else until I reach the quadrum. The sun is beginning to dip in the west. This is the last hour of the Iudicium, I realise vaguely. A half hour later, and all of this would have been even more pointless than it already is.

Veridius is at the top of the stairs to the Temple of Jovan. He's addressing the school. Talking about the attack. The tragedy of it. The losses. Emissa's up there next to him, face drawn, eyes red. So is Indol. Iro. Aequa. A few other Fourths. Not as many as I would have hoped.

Veridius stutters to a halt as he spots me staggering into view.

There's a hushed murmur, a rippling of movement as faces turn toward me. I stumble forward. The crowd parts. Silent. Their faces are white. Horrified. I don't know whether they're looking at me or the body in my arms. I don't care.

I lay Callidus gently on the stone at Veridius's feet. Meet his gaze, then Emissa's stunned, horrified one. Put all my venom into my voice, keeping it low so that only they two can hear. Blood coats every part of my skin. I must look a nightmare made flesh.

"I'm going to make sure you burn for this."

As the last light of afternoon fades from the quadrum, with the last of my strength, I slam the golden pyramid into place on Jovan's chest.

And then, my task complete, I collapse to the stone and embrace the escape of oblivion.

LXXIV

I FADE IN AND OUT OF REALITY.

I am in the infirmary. In that same bed I was in the first time I came to the Academy. Emissa and Indol and Belli curious about me, curious about the destroyed Transvect. One of them dead now. One of them broke my heart. I see their afterimages, like ghosts. Belli at the door. Emissa peering down at me. Smiling. Beautiful.

Then sleep, then a parade of faces. Callidus joking about his death. Aequa promising to warn him. Eidhin refusing his place in the Iudicium.

Tear-stained Emissa stabbing me over, and over, and over.

Then, finally, my father. Sitting beside my bed, face drawn. As real as I could imagine him to be, but unchanged by the years. Another figment. Blurred by exhaustion and pain.

He sees my eyes open. Sees me looking at him. Smiles gently, with such tenderness and grief that my heart can take it no longer, and I feel tears welling. I try to move to wipe them away but I can't; I'm bound to the bed. Immobilised.

There are tears in my father's eyes, too. I have only ever seen him cry once before. It only makes me sadder.

"My boy." Heartache in the words. He reaches over and clasps my shoulder. Resting his hand there. No different to any other human's embrace, and yet it means everything.

I close my eyes against the pain remembering his loss brings. Hate that this spectre can give me more comfort with a touch than anyone living. My breath's short, emotion threatening to choke me.

"You're dead."

His look of sorrow deepens. "Yes," he says softly.

I nod. Grit my teeth as his admission settles in the pit of my stomach. I wanted him to be alive. To be real. I wanted it more badly than anything I have ever wanted. The realisation breaks something in me. I shake with sobs. Tears and snot trickling down my face. Near four years of scars, opened in an instant.

"I'm so alone," I whisper to him. I feel the words with all my hopeless heart.

Then he's there. Kneeling by the bed. Cradling me, head pressed against mine, and we weep together.

Finally my choking subsides and he leans back, wiping my face tenderly with the edge of the sheet. "I never wanted this for you," he tells me. "But I am *proud*, Diago. Proud of the decisions you have made, of the strength you have shown, of the man you have become. Proud beyond measure." He strokes my forehead. Pushes back strands of hair. "I know it will be painful, but you cannot give up now. Remember who you are." He pauses, moves as if doing something just out of sight. "You have to *fight*."

"Why?" I croak the word, looking up at him. Heavy-hearted, but I don't know what else to say. "I've tried. I've tried so hard to live in this world and still be me. Still be your son. But what's the point? Suus is still gone, and the Hierarchy still takes everything from me, one way or another." I think of Callidus, lifeless and cold in my arms. I'm hollow, though. Have no more tears to shed. "I can't do this anymore. I can't lose anyone else, Father. I just . . . can't."

"You mourn your friend." He cups my cheek in his hand. "But death is a doorway, Son. You will see him again. No one is ever truly lost." He leans down and presses his lips gently to my forehead. "I am so glad I got to see you again. Even if it is too short. Even if it ends up being the last time." His voice cracks a little. Aching. "I love you, Diago. I love you, Son. Never forget that."

He turns as if ripping himself away. Starts walking from my vision.

"Don't go." I know he's not real, but I can't help myself. Pleading. My voice weak and breaking. "Please, Father. Don't leave me."

He doesn't stop.

"Courage," I hear him whisper as he vanishes into the darkness of the dream.

※ ※ ※

WHEN I WAKE, VERIDIUS IS WHERE I IMAGINED MY FATHER WAS.

I rasp, and the man stirs from where he was dozing in the chair. He's wearing his white physician's cloak. I force my eyes to stay open, take another uneasy breath. Even that hurts. My lungs burn. My body aches all over.

When I try to move, I can't. A quick, panicked jerk confirms it. I wasn't imagining being bound to the bed.

"Easy, Vis." Veridius sounds weary. He turns to someone behind him. "Go and fetch the committee. They'll want to know he's awake."

Out of sight, I hear someone shuffling away.

"Am I a prisoner?" The croaking words scald my throat, and I give a half-retching cough afterward. Talking is going to be difficult.

"No." Veridius pauses, as if considering the question again. "No."

"Why—"

"We needed to keep you still." He's talking gently. My expression must give away my confusion because he leans forward and loosens the bindings around my chest. Carefully draws back the sheet on my left side. "I'm sorry."

I look down. There's a disconnect, a moment where my mind refuses to accept what I'm seeing. My left shoulder is swathed in white bandages, clean and tightly wrapped.

There's nothing attached to it.

I stare. Hands trembling. *Hand* trembling. It feels like the arm's still there. I can see it's gone, but throbbing discomfort shoots down it nonetheless.

"It was some kind of rot. There was no saving it."

I still don't say anything. There's newfound anger and frustration and hopelessness, but I'm weary of the emotions. They've lost all meaning to me.

Veridius glances around the otherwise empty room. Lowers his voice.

"Your blood's been tainted, Vis. If the wrong people see it, they'll kill you. So when I say I need you to be honest with me about what happened, I am not understating the situation." He waits, checks that I understand. "You ran the Labyrinth in the ruins, didn't you?"

I just nod. Too disoriented and in pain to come up with a good story, if there even is one to be had.

"The writing on your arm. Was that help getting back out?"

Another weak nod.

To my surprise a small, irrepressible smile flickers on Veridius's face. "How did you know the Labyrinth was there?"

"Ulciscor." My voice grinds; Veridius quickly holds a mug to my lips and I slurp greedily, water trickling down my chin. "He was convinced . . . it had something to do with you . . . murdering Caeror."

"Gods' graves, I wish that man would just listen." Veridius sounds drained. "Did you see anyone else in there?"

"Belli's dead." I grate it flatly. Let him know I know it's his fault.

Veridius hangs his head, and doesn't respond.

"Emissa will want to see you," he says eventually. "She's been distraught."

"She tried to kill me."

"She didn't."

"I was there."

"No, she . . ." He grimaces. "It was your blood. She thought you were past saving. She wants to see you. Just . . . it might be easier to let her explain."

"I don't want to see her."

There are faint sounds outside in the hall. Voices. Veridius hisses in frustration. "We're out of time. You're going to need to trust me, Vis. Things are about to get very complicated. Tell the committee you want to join Religion. That you want to be an Imperator under Magnus Tertius Pileus. This isn't anything to do with politics." The words rush from his mouth. He pours all he has into them. "Please. We need your help avoiding the next Cataclysm."

Behind him, the door swings open, and whatever else Veridius was going to say is lost.

Eidhin enters.

I barely register who it is; Veridius's last claim is so grand, so outlandish, that I'm having trouble processing it. With an effort I push it to the side, focusing again. The hulking boy coming toward us has dark circles beneath his eyes. He's looking at Veridius. "They are outside."

Veridius sighs. "Let me talk to them." He leaves, shutting the door behind him.

Eidhin walks over to my bed and sits next to it. We study each other, and then he gives me a single, meaningful nod. He's relieved to see me awake. He's pained by everything that's happened.

I shift my gaze to the far wall.

"He didn't want to come." I admit the miserable words to the silence.

"Yes, he did." Quiet and calm. Sure.

"I tried to save him." My voice cracks. "I *tried*, Eidhin."

"I know." No judgment. No blame.

"They weren't even looking for him. They were looking for me. It was just so . . ." I curse. Bitter and low. "It was so *meaningless*."

Eidhin glances around at the sound of an argument out in the hallway. Stands again and leans over. Grips me by my good shoulder and waits there until I reluctantly meet his gaze.

"No." His eyes are sad. "Death is only meaningless if it does not change us, Vis."

The door to the infirmary opens again and Eidhin lets go. Steps back.

"When you are well, we will celebrate him together," he promises softly.

He turns away and politely skirts Veridius and the other men entering. Leaving before he's ordered to go.

Three strangers approach my bed now, none of them familiar, but all looking infinitely relieved to see me awake. "Thank the gods," says the short, bearded one on the right, smiling broadly. He claps Veridius on the back. "Marvellous work, Principalis." He's an older man, in his fifties, more than a few streaks of grey at his temples. The other two are of a similar age. All senators, judging from the purple on their togas.

"He's still weak, not out of danger yet. Don't make him talk too much." Veridius doesn't hide his displeasure at the men's presence. "But it appears you'll still have your hero, Magnus Quartus. Still have your Domitor."

Of course. The Iudicium has already been a disaster of unimaginable magnitude for Religion. But my death at the hands of the Anguis, given my reputation after the naumachia, would have been a blow from which they may never have recovered.

"Domitor Vis Telimus. I extend the congratulations of the Senate on your victory, especially under these trying circumstances. I am Magnus Quartus Vaesar. I have been asked to convey to the Senate whether you have a desired assignment upon graduation." The pronouncement from Vaesar is all pomp and ceremony. I remember his name from Lanistia's lessons, but other than his being from Religion, the details are vague.

"Can't that wait?" I need time to think.

"It cannot. The Censor's office is . . . hostile to the Academy as it is, at present. If you don't make your intentions known soon, they will be within their rights to assign you to military service."

I glance in confusion at Veridius, who nods. "It's been five days."

I'm silent, processing the news. Thinking desperately. It's right there. All I have to do is say I want to take up a post with the embassy to Jatiere. I'll be far away from Caten, far away from the threat of having to cede. I'll have years to figure out my next move. It won't even seem terribly strange, given . . . everything.

But if I do that, nothing will change.

The slow, tumbling realisation is nearly too heavy to bear. I'll still be running. Hiding. And this time, I'll be fleeing a fight I might actually be able to impact. I'll be leaving the people responsible for the death of my friend to keep doing what they're doing. Making the Hierarchy what it is. Keeping it as it always has been.

I wasn't a coward, that night at Suus. I was fourteen, and alone, and scared.

I wasn't wrong, to refuse to cede all these years. I needed to keep that part of myself sacred. I needed it to stay *me*.

But that doesn't mean they are excuses now.

Somewhere, deep down, the decision's made. That part of me that has held on for so long breaks.

I look up. All four men are watching me intently. Veridius especially.

"Alright," I say quietly.

I still have no idea what to think of Veridius's claim about avoiding another Cataclysm. But even if he's somehow telling the truth—and given the surreal events of the Iudicium, I'm almost inclined to believe him—Belli's mangled corpse is still fresh in my mind. I refuse to leave myself anywhere near the man's influence. At least not until I fully understand what's going on.

And I can't join Military. I just can't. Not knowing their involvement in the massacre. Ulciscor might see it as a betrayal, but even if he isn't satisfied with what I have to tell him about the Labyrinth, he won't send me to a Sapper. Not after all this. I'm Catenicus. Domitor. An important witness to a Iudicium that's surely already infamous. Even if he tries to invoke his rights, the Senate will stop him.

"I want to work for the Censor."

There's dead silence.

"Vis," says Veridius delicately. "Think about what you're—"

"I've thought about it." Despite everything, Callidus always spoke highly of his father. And if I'm to do anything, make a difference, then the Censor's office is where I need to be. The place through which all information in the Hierarchy flows.

Vaesar is reluctant, but also relieved to have an answer. He bends over a nearby table to write the details on a piece of paper, then uses a candle to melt three blobs of red sealing wax onto the bottom. Each of the three senators take turns impressing their signet rings. Their eyes flash black as they imbue the embossed wax.

"Done and witnessed." The Quartus takes the sheet carefully. "I will submit this to the Senate today, Vis. Thank you. And congratulations again." He turns to Veridius. "Principalis, if we could arrange for the Transvect to return as soon as possible . . ."

"Of course." Veridius is calm, his expression smooth. "I'll be right with you." He waits until the door is shut before facing me. His façade of composure has vanished. "Vis, you can't—"

"You were supposed to be protecting us." I interrupt, voice low and hard. Let him hear my anger. "But you've been using us. You've been sending students to their *deaths*. So I'll listen to what you have to say at some point, Principalis—you have my word. But we are a long, long way from working together."

Veridius's face is stony. I think it's the first time I've seen him without even a hint of the easygoing charm he usually exudes.

"Then for now, that will have to be enough," he says. "I need to see to the senators. Rest. We'll talk soon."

He leaves.

I don't move for a long time. Just lie there. Hollow.

Eventually, I force myself to sit up. Just that is a painful, clumsy movement. I almost topple, muscles screaming, as my brain throws my left arm back to no effect. The effort of staying upright leaves me light-headed.

When I'm finally sitting securely on the edge of the bed, my gaze roves the room. No way to tell whether the empty beds are because everyone else injured during the Iudicium has recovered, or I've been placed in isolation. The symbol of the Hierarchy, STRONGER TOGETHER inscribed below it, leers from the wall at the far end. I shudder. I can't see it without seeing the Labyrinth, now.

The table next to my bed holds a lamp, a jug of water and mug, and what looks like a toy ship. I frown at the latter, registering its incongruity. It's wooden. Roughly carved. Familiar.

With a jolt, my confusion fades to something else entirely.

I shuffle along the bed until the table is within easy reach. Lean over with a trembling hand and pick up the ship. The carving's not unskilled, but far from the work of an artist.

Just about right for a ten-year-old boy trying to impress his father.

I turn it over. Clumsily feel along its prow one-handed until I find the hidden catch, unlatch it, and let the deck slide off. The name of the ship is scratched along the inside of the wood. Diminished by time, but legible.

Diago.

EX UNO PLURES

SYNCHRONISM

THE BURNING SENSATION WANES, TOO SLOWLY, SO MUCH SO
that I'm not sure when it actually ends and becomes simply a memory that makes me
twitch in place.

I don't know how long passes after that. Shadowed bronze blades glower around
me. I just lie there on the cold stone, shivering, staring up at the darkness, my mind
doing all it can to cover over the pain and fear.

Finally I sit. The eerie red light has returned to the room. Everything's as it was.
The stairs down which I entered are still the only way to leave.

Uneasy though it makes me, there's nowhere else to go, and right now I want nothing more than to be out of . . . whatever this place is. I'm about to stand when I register
the persisting ache in my left arm, notice that my tunic's dark there. Sodden and sticky.
I gingerly roll up the sleeve, using it to dab away the worst of the blood so that I can
see the source of the wound.

There are lines, etched into my skin. I feel a chill as I wipe away more crimson.

The red, puffy incisions form a single word.

WAIT

I stagger to my feet, staring in apprehensive horror at the message carved into
my flesh. Stand there, frozen by indecision, for a full minute. Two. The air blurs and
shimmers out beyond the encircling metal talons. Nothing happens. I shift from foot
to foot. No idea whether I can trust the grisly warning.

Then there's a sudden, stinging burn on the same arm. I rip back my sleeve as new
lines of blood begin to well, slithering cuts opening unnervingly in the skin.

R
U

I run.

Back the way I came, everything bathed in dark red light that fuzzes and twitches
in the corners of my eyes. There's a minute where there's nothing but my gasping
breath and the vibrating air around me. I'm nauseous, dizzy from whatever just happened to me.

I ease to a jog only when the dead end of the Labyrinth greets me. Trembling, I
check my left arm. Still only RU scored into the skin. Blood drips onto the floor.

I look for the bracer. It should be where I dropped it in the corner.

It's gone.

Another thirty seconds of fruitless searching does nothing to quell my rising panic. My hands ball into fists as I pace back and forth. The red, hazing light burns my vision.

I'm distressed enough that I almost don't notice the writing on the stone.

I stumble to a stop. Squint at the inscription on the wall that blocks the way to the Labyrinth. It wasn't there before, I'm certain of it. Written in old Vetusian, just like the message around the bronze blades. I slow my rattled breathing and focus.

SEALED AGAINST THE TOOLS OF THE ENEMY AFTER THE RENDING. THE PASSAGE TO LUCEUM REQUIRES A TOLL TO ENSURE VALIDITY.

There are two circles etched below it, each less than a foot across. Positioned at about my chest height and shoulder width apart. Both contain the symbol of the Hierarchy.

I read the words again. And again. *The passage to Luceum.*

I'm too tired and confused and afraid to second-guess myself. I need to get out of this place, and it seems clear what I'm supposed to do.

I place my hands in the two circles, palms against cool stone. The pyramid symbols pulse to life beneath my touch.

There's a flash. Encompassing. White and blinding.

Then searing, unimaginable pain in my left shoulder.

I'm suddenly on the floor. Screaming, writhing. I clutch across with my right hand, but it slides away sticky and wet and warm. My vision clears just enough to take in the pulsing red stump where my arm used to be.

Through the shock and agony, I register I'm not in the passageway anymore. I'm lying in the middle of a vast rotunda, surrounded by columns. White stone everywhere, except where I'm staining it crimson. Icy wind whips my face. There's white beyond the columns too. Snow. We're high up. Cloud-topped mountains in the distance.

Everything flickers. For a heartbeat I'm back in the darkness. Like an afterimage. The way in front of me is open, exposing the vast hall beyond that contains both the Labyrinth and the platform out.

Then it's gone again. Snow and ashen stone reasserting itself.

There are people rushing toward me. Two men and a woman. Yelling at one another in a language I don't know. Their tone is panicked. Vaguely, I'm aware that two of them are skidding to their knees next to me, while the other hurries off out of sight.

"Traveller. Traveller, stay with us." The man with the red beard is cradling my head. He's talking in rough Vetusian. "The other from your world will be coming."

He turns to the woman, says something I don't understand. She argues.

Their voices mix and mutter and fade, and pass from my consciousness.

☥

THE BURNING SENSATION WANES, TOO SLOWLY, SO MUCH SO
that I'm not sure when it actually ends and becomes simply a memory that makes me
twitch in place.

I don't know how long passes after that. Shadowed bronze blades glower around
me. I just lie there on the cold stone, shivering, staring up at the darkness, my mind
doing all it can to cover over the pain and fear.

"Get up."

The voice penetrates my consciousness. Soft and urgent. I prop myself up with a
groan. The eerie red light has returned to the room. There's someone crouching a few
feet away, just beyond the surrounding talons.

"We don't have much time." The man peers in at me. He's five, maybe ten years
older than me. Dark and slim, with a thick, unkempt beard and mop of curly black
hair. There's a mass of scar tissue across his cheek, stretching back to replace his left
ear. Serious brown eyes bore into mine. "What's your name?"

"Vis."

"Welcome to Obiteum, Vis. Did Veridius send you?"

"What? Not really. I . . , no." I look past him. Head still spinning. "This . . . is
Obiteum? It looks the same."

"You'll change your mind once we get outside." He says it dryly. "You *do* know
Veridius, though?"

"Yes. He's the Principalis at the Academy." I stagger to my feet. Anxious to leave
this ring of metal, but wary of the man beyond it. He doesn't seem inclined to enter
the circle. "Who are you?"

"Principalis. Of course he is," the stranger murmurs to himself, a small smile on
his lips. He focuses back on me. "My name is Caeror. I don't know how much you
know, but we have about two minutes to save you back in Res. So you need to trust me,
and come out of there *now*."

I struggle to comprehend it. Look at him again, really *look* this time. The similarities are so obvious that I feel foolish for not noticing it before.

"Rotting hells. It's you. Your brother thinks you're dead."

Caeror freezes. "You know *Ulciscor*? Is he well? Is he . . ." He trails off, shaking himself back into motion. "Later." He beckons urgently.

Uncertainty still arrests my feet. "What do you mean, 'save me back in Res'?"

Caeror grits his teeth. Breathlessly fretful. "You've been . . . copied, I suppose. The same way the world was thousands of years ago in the war against the Concurrence. It's how you got here." He grunts as he sees my look. "Came as a surprise to me, too. But it's not important right now. You're still strongly connected back to Res and Luceum, but that's going to fade fast. I can explain more later, but only if you're *not dead*." He's speaking so quickly that it's hard to follow. There's no mistaking his desperation, though. He's pleading with me to believe him.

I close my eyes. I'm in over my head. Don't understand what's going on.

I could do worse than trust someone who apparently does.

"Alright." I'm still shaky. The red light fuzzes and flickers. I take a step toward him. Another, then another, until I'm stumbling between the gap in the bronze.

Caeror steadies me as I reach him. Grips me tight and nods reassuringly. "Good. The first thing we need to do is get a message to you in Res, so you don't move out of the gate just yet."

He draws a short blade from his belt. Apologetic as he presses the hilt firmly into my hand.

"Pull back your sleeve, Vis."

ACKNOWLEDGMENTS

THIS BOOK IS THE SUM OF THE TIME, SUPPORT, EFFORT, AND talent of a team of people putting in work over the course of several years (and in this case, also during a global pandemic). My sincere thanks are owed to each and every one of the following:

Paul Lucas, my phenomenal agent. I'm getting to do this nonsense as a job and not just a hobby because of your efforts. To say that I appreciate what you do would be an understatement.

Joe, my overworked-but-fantastic editor, who has made this book the tightest and best version of itself. It's a genuine pleasure to go through this process with someone who's both enthusiastic and reliably on the same page as me. Even, I will reluctantly add, when it means making cuts.

The rest of the team at Saga. I couldn't be happier with how everything has turned out with this book, from copyediting to design. Brilliant work. I'm genuinely looking forward to continuing this journey with you all.

My beta readers, including but not limited to Sonja, Elisabeth, Nicki, Chiara, and Jordan. You cheerfully put in hours and hours of your time to read something that, let's face it, was probably a coin flip as to whether it was any good at that point. Your feedback and encouragement have been invaluable.

My assistant, Elisabeth, without whom I'd probably still be writing this thing. Em dashes remain the devil's work and I refuse to make a Word shortcut for them, though (copyeditors past and present, I am so sorry).

Those at Audible, for your excitement at a new world from me, and your patience in waiting for it to be delivered.

My kids, for mostly not deliberately disturbing me when I'm working and sometimes also not being too loud. I love you.

And finally, but most importantly, my wife, Sonja, who remarkably continues to put up with my head being in made-up worlds more often than the real one. So much has changed over these past few years, but your love and support—and how vital they are for me—have not. I love you. Neither this book, nor the ones previous, would exist without you.

MAJOR CHARACTERS

Advenius Claudius (*ahd-VEN-ee-us CLAW-dee-us*) – Father of Aequa. Governance senator who visits Vis at Villa Telimus.

Aequa Claudius (*EE-kwah CLAW-dee-us*) – Class Four student at the Academy. Daughter of Advenius. Attended the naumachia with Vis.

Ascenia (*ash-EN-ee-a*) – Septimus in charge of the stables at the Academy.

Atrox (*AH-troks*), **Matron** – Woman in charge of the orphanage at Letens.

Atticus (*AHT-ik-us*) – Class Four student at the Academy.

Auctia (*AWK-sha*) – Sextus and Dispensator of the Quiscil household.

Ava (*AH-vah*) – Class Four student at the Academy.

Axien (*AHK-see-en*) – Class Four student at the Academy.

Belli Volenis (*BEH-lee voh-LEN-iss*) – Class Three student at the Academy. Known for her prowess at Foundation and running the Labyrinth.

Brixia (*BRIK-sha*) – A child from the orphanage in Letens.

Caeror Telimus (*SEE-roar TELL-ee-muss*) – Brother to Ulciscor. Killed during the Iudicium at the Academy several years ago.

Callidus Ericius (*CAHL-id-us er-EE-see-us*) – Class Seven student at the Academy.

Carinza (*cah-RIN-zah*) / **Cari** (*CAH-ree*) – Vis's younger sister, princess of Suus.

Cassia (*CAH-see-ah*) – Class Four student at the Academy.

Cristoval (*KRIS-toh-vahl*), **King** – Vis's father, king of Suus.

Diago (*dee-AH-go*) – Vis's birth name, and also the name he gives to the alupi he saves as a pup on Solivagus.

Drusus Corani (*DROO-sus cawr-AHN-ee*) – Class Seven student at the Academy.

Dultatis (*dool-TAH-tis*), **Praeceptor** – Teacher in charge of Class Six at the Academy.

Eidhin Breac (*EYE-din BRAK*) – Class Six student at the Academy.

Ellanher (*EL-an-her*) – Woman in charge of the fights at the Letens Theatre.

Emissa Corenius (*em-EE-sah kor-EN-ee-us*) – Class Three student at the Academy.

Estevan (*ESS-teh-vahn*) – Also known as Melior, leader of the Anguis. Former advisor to King Cristoval, and former tutor to Vis.

Exesius (*eks-EE-see-us*), **Princeps** – Princeps of Military.

Fadrique (*fah-DREE-kay*) – Former advisor to King Cristoval, and former tutor to Vis. Current steward of Suus under the Hierarchy.

Felix (*FELL-iks*) – Class Four student at the Academy.

Feriun (*FEHR-ee-un*) – Class Four student at the Academy.

Ferrea (*FEHR-ee-ah*), **Praeceptor** – Teacher in charge of Class Seven at the Academy.

Gaius Valerius (*GUY-us vah-LEER-ee-us*) – Physician who tests Vis's blood after the naumachia.

Gaufrid (*GAW-frid*) – Bookkeeper for bets on fights at the Letens Theatre.

Hospius (*HOSS-pee-us*) – The fake name Ulciscor uses at Letens Prison.

Hrolf (*ROLF*) – The Septimus in charge of Letens Prison, under whom Vis is employed.

Ianix (*YAN-iks*) – Class Six student at the Academy.

Idonia (*id-OHN-ya*) – Ellanher's "cousin" at the Letens Theatre.

Indol Quiscil (*IN-dole KEY-skil*) – Class Three student at the Academy. Son of Dimidius Quiscil of Military.

Iro Decimus (*EYE-roe DEK-ee-mus*) – Class Three student at the Academy. Younger sister killed during the attack on the naumachia.

Kadmos (*KAHD-moss*) – Dispensator in charge of running Villa Telimus. Former head of the Azriat in Sytrece.

Lanistia Scipio (*lah-nis-TEE-ah SKIP-ee-oh*) – Tutor to Vis during his time at Villa Telimus. Assisting Ulciscor in his search to find the truth about Caeror's death.

Lerius Telimus (*LEHR-ee-us TELL-ee-muss*) – Ulciscor and Caeror's father.

Lucius (*loo-CHEE-us*) – Class Four student at the Academy.

Manius (*MAH-nee-us*), **Proconsul** – Catenan in charge of the Tensian province.

Marcellus (*mar-KEL-us*) – Class Four student at the Academy.

Marcus Carcius (*MAR-koos KAR-see-us*) – Assistant to Veridius at the Academy.

Menendo (*men-EN-doe*) – The owner of the harbourside tavern in Suus.

Nateo (*NAH-tee-oh*) – A Sapper-bound prisoner in Letens Prison.

Nequias (*neh-KEY-us*), **Praeceptor** – Teacher in charge of Class Three at the Academy.

Prav (*PRAHV*) – Class Three student at the Academy.

Quiscil (*KEY-skil*), **Magnus Dimidius** – Indol's father.

Relucia Telimus (*reh-loo-KEY-ah TELL-ee-muss*) – Ulciscor's wife.

Scitus (*SKEE-tus*), **Praeceptor** – Teacher in charge of Class Four at the Academy.

Sedotia (*seh-DOH-chee-ah*) – The name given by the Anguis agent who arranges the attack on Vis's Transvect.

Sianus (*see-AHN-us*) – Class Three student at the Academy.

Solum (*SO-lum*) – The name given to all orphans in the Hierarchy.

Taedia (*TAH-dee-ah*), **Praeceptor** – Teacher in charge of Class Five at the Academy.

Tem (*TEM*) – Class Four student at the Academy.

Titus (*TYE-tuss*) – Class Four student at the Academy.

Ulciscor Telimus (*ull-KEY-scor TELL-ee-muss*) – Senator who meets Vis at Letens Prison and ultimately offers him the chance to attend the Catenan Academy.

Ulnias Filo (*ull-NIGH-us FEEL-oh*) – Physician at the Academy.

Valentina (*vahl-en-TEE-nah*) – Class Four student at the Academy.

Veridius Julii (*ver-id-EE-us YOOL-ee-eye*) – The Principalis, in charge of the Academy.

Vermes (*VER-mez*) – A child from the orphanage in Letens.

Vis (*VISS*) – The name adopted by Diago after he fled Suus.

Ysabel (*EE-sah-bel*) – Vis's older sister, princess of Suus.

GLOSSARY

Alupi (*AH-loo-pie*) – Massive, intelligent wolf-like creatures indigenous to Solivagus.

Anchoring point – Stone monoliths used as infrastructure for Transvects.

Anguis (*AN-gwiss*) – The group continuing to rebel against the Hierarchy.

Arventis (*are-VEN-tiss*) – God of childbirth, prophecy, and luck.

Aurora Columnae (*ow-ROAR-ah COLE-um-nigh*) – The pre-Cataclysm devices which enable people to cede Will.

Azriat (*AHS-ree-at*) – The most prestigious learning institute in Sytrece.

Bibliotheca (*bib-lee-oh-THEE-kah*) – Library.

Bireme – A military ship with two decks of oars.

Birthright – The set of Catenan laws designed to "honour life."

Cede – The act, in the Hierarchy, of giving half your Will to someone ranked directly above you.

Censor – The Governance senator in charge of determining who can be nominated for the Senate.

Curia Doctrina (*COO-ree-ah DOC-treen-ah*) – The main hall of the Academy.

Ferias (*FAIR-ee-us*) – God of keys, doors, livestock, and ports.

Foundation – A popular strategic game in the Hierarchy, played with red and white triangular stones.

Iudicium (*you-dih-KEY-um*) – The final test at the Academy for Class Three students, used to determine their rankings.

Jovan (*YO-vahn*) – God of sky and thunder, the king of the gods.

Mira (*MEER-ah*) – God of war and fighters, agricultural guardian.

Naumachia (*now-MAH-key-ah*) – Gladiatorial battle taking place on ships, on an artificial lake. Participants are called Naumachiarii.

Ocaria (*oh-KAH-ree-ah*) – Goddess of rivers.

Pletuna (*pleh-TOON-ah*) – Goddess of autumn and the harvest.

Praeceptor (*PRAY-kep-tor*) – Teacher status in the Academy.

Praetorium (*pray-TOR-ee-um*) – Building housing the teachers' offices at the Academy.

Quadrum (*KWAD-rum*) – The large, central courtyard of the Academy.

Razor – The name for an obsidian blade forged by a Catenan officer.

Sere (*SEH-ray*) – Goddess of spring, flowers, and fertility.

Silencium (*sigh-LEN-key-um*) – Binding legal agreement in the Hierarchy to not speak of something.

Transvect (*TRANS-vekt*) – Massive Will-powered transport devices.

Trireme – A large military ship with three decks of oars.

Vitaerium (*vit-EYE-ree-um*) – Devices that can force-feed Will into any body or substance capable of decay.

Vorcian (*VOR-key-an*) – God of volcanoes, deserts, the forge, and hard work.

LOCATIONS

Acharnae (*ah-KAR-nigh*) – Small Sytrecian village.

Agerus (*ah-GAIR-us*) – The region near Caten where the Necropolis is located.

Alta Semita (*AHL-tah sem-EE-tah*) – A district of Caten.

Aquiria (*ah-KEER-ee-ah*) – Small country bordering Suus. The country in which Vis officially claims he was born.

Aznaro's (*az-NAH-roe*) **Bluff** – A cliff overlooking the ocean in Suus.

Butaria (*boo-TAH-ree-ah*) – A sea-bound region to the west of Caten.

Cartiz (*kar-TEEZ*) – The Aquirian capital, near which Vis claims he grew up.

Caten (*cah-TEN*) – The capital of Deditia and of the Catenan Republic, considered to be the centre of the known world.

Catenan (*cah-TEN-an*) **Academy** – The Academy which Vis attends, located on the island of Solivagus.

Catenan (*cah-TEN-an*) **Arena** – The great stadium in Caten which can house up to one hundred thousand people.

Catenan (*cah-TEN-an*) **Republic** – The name used to describe any region governed by Caten's laws.

Cymr (*KYE-meer*) – Country to the south-west of Caten.

Deditia (*deh-DEE-chee-ah*) – The region immediately surrounding Caten.

Deopolis (*dee-OP-oh-liss*) – The capital of Sytrece.

Edaro (*ed-AH-roe*) **River** – A river in Aquiria.

Eldargo (*el-DAR-go*) **Strait** – The stretch of water separating Suus from Aquiria.

Esquilae (*ESS-kil-igh*) – A district of Caten.

Ganice (*GAH-niss*) – A Catenan territory.

Guridad (*GOO-ree-dad*), **Port** – An Aquirian trading town, located opposite Suus on the Eldargo Strait.

Jatiere (*YAH-tee-air*) – Country whose treaty restricts Catenan ambassadors there from using Will.

Letens (*leh-TENS*) – Capital of Tensia.

Letens (*leh-TENS*) **Prison** – The prison in which Vis works.

Lordan's (*lor-DAHN*) **Column** – A famous landmark in Caten.

Luceum (*loo-KEY-um*) – A mysterious place, usually referenced alongside Res and Obiteum.

Lyceria (*ligh-KEER-ee-ah*) – A Catenan territory.

Masen (*MAH-sen*) – A Catenan territory.

Necropolis (*neh-KROP-oh-lis*) – A large area dedicated to the Catenan dead, located in the Agerus region.

Nyripk (*NEER-ik*) – Desert-locked country far to the north-east.

Obiteum (*oh-bit-EE-um*) – A mysterious place, usually referenced alongside Res and Luceum.

Praedium (*PRIGH-dee-um*) – District of Caten.

Quus (*COOS*), **Sea of** – The sea on which both Solivagus and Caten are located.

Res (*REZ*) – A mysterious place, usually referenced alongside Obiteum and Luceum.

Sarcinia (*sar-KIN-ee-ah*) – District of Caten.

Solencio (*sol-EN-see-oh*) **Beach** – A beach in Suus.

Solivagus (*soh-liv-AH-gus*) – Island on which the Academy is located.

Suus (*SOOS*) – Vis's island homeland.

Sytrece (*sit-REES*) – Country to the east of Deditia.

Tensia (*TEN-see-ah*) – Southernmost populated country in the known world.